Madelaina

Michaela Morgan

Madelaina

VOLUME 2

CORGI BOOKS
A DIVISION OF TRANSWORLD PUBLISHERS LTD

MADELAINA
A CORGI BOOK 0 552 10812 X

First publication in Great Britain

PRINTING HISTORY
Corgi edition published 1978

Copyright © 1977 by Gloria Vitanza Basile

This book is set in 10/11 pt. Times

Corgi Books are published by Transworld Publishers Ltd.,
Century House, 61–63 Uxbridge Road,
Ealing, London, W.5.
Made and printed in Great Britain by
Hunt Barnard Printing Ltd., Aylesbury, Bucks.

For
Jim and Roz Schiros
With Love and Devotion

Book Five

Lago Diablo de Los Muertos

Chapter 17

"*Señora! Señora!* You must awaken now. It's important!"

Madelaina awakened with a start at the anxious sound of Lola's voice. She bolted upright to a sitting position. Blinking in the darkness, she looked for her husband. In the distance came the sounds of the mariachas, muted trumpets, and guitars.

"Come downstairs. It's Paco. He's raving, out of his head."

"Yes, yes, I'm coming." She sprang from her bed and reached for the sheer cotton batiste wraparound Peter had bought for her. She quickly brushed her midnight black hair off her face and let it fall behind her shoulders.

Catching sight of her pale reflection in the mirror as she passed, Madelaina paused at the unfamiliar image bouncing back at her. Her eyes, haunted, with dark sunken hollows around them, had an unnatural glow. Yet no more unnatural than the peculiar aura about her head. Her hands moved up quickly as if to brush it aside, but the faint mistlike emanation remained. Something other than her own will propelled her to leave the room. Moving as a sleepwalker might, she glided across the length of the upper hallway and descended the staircase which tunneled below her. Something outside herself pulled her, pushed her ahead in the direction of Paco's room.

Vaguely she heard cries in the night, somewhat muffled, not clear in her mind. She cocked her head hesitantly from side to side, angling it sharply to the right, then to the left. Following the sounds, she walked through the large salon along the lower corridor until she came to the door of Paco's room. Her hand grasped the large metal ring and turned it. She pushed on the door. The room was dim and shadowy. Her eyes came to rest upon the tormented body of the corporal who'd saved her life so many times.

Lola, frightened and distraught, stood close to him, bending over his feverish body, wiping the sweat from his face and neck with a cool, damp cloth.

"No!" he screamed in Spanish, "You can't do this! Leave me, *bruja*! I am stronger than you! You've wreaked enough havoc in my life. I'll outlive you. Out with you! Out! Out! Out! I cast you out" He ranted and raved and thrashed about the bed, the sweat-soaked sheets which Lola had already changed twice.

"*Señora*, we must send for the doctor. He's in terrible fever. I've never seen such fever—such madness. He talks out of head—" She stopped, arrested by the glazed, almost opalescent lights in Madelaina's eyes. What she saw in Madelaina's eyes, on her face, frightened her. Recalling instantly the things Paco said in his delirium, she felt her stomach knot tightly. "*Bruja—witch!*" Did Paco mean the *señora*? "*Madre de Dios!*" she exclaimed, clutching the ornate silver crucifix around her neck. "*God protect me!*"

"What is it, Lola?" she asked in a controlled voice.

The girl in all her uncertainty stood there trembling, afraid to speak. If ever she'd seen a woman possessed with evil spirits, it was this woman, right here and now. Her voice, dried and cracked, could hardly speak. Never once did Lola take her startled blue eyes off her new mistress.

"We must send for the doctor," Lola managed to say at last with affected bravado.

"Where is my husband?"

"He's been gone all day, *señora*. On business with Pancho Villa."

"All day?" Madelaina blinked her eyes and shook herself. "All day? What day is this?"

"Wednesday, *señora*."

"Wednesday?" Had she slept two whole days?

454

"Turn up the oil lamps, girl." Madelaina touched her forehead. Two whole days lost. How? Where?

The young mestizo obliged, but she remained cautious, keeping one eye on this strange woman who sleeps day and night while her husband, *un mucho macho hombre*, a gringo at that, walks around with swollen loins, just aching to assert his manhood. She had little respect for a woman who couldn't satisfy a man. Especially a man such as Señor Tom Mix.

Madelaina placed a cool, slender hand on Paco's forehead. What a fever! He continued to emit low growling sounds as he tossed and turned on the bed. She lifted the thick, cumbersome bandage and inspected the wound.

Madelaina recoiled in horror! The stench from the gangrenous wound was unbearable. "Give me a lamp! Hurry, girl!" Whatever it was that controlled Madelaina earlier had evaporated. She was once again in full command of her faculties.

She held the lamp over him and stared aghast at the condition of the pus-filled, infected wound. "Lola. Go! Find the doctor! It is very bad!" She turned away from the horrifying sight, recoiling noticeably. "And for God's sake, try to find the *señor*. Understand? You must find my husband!"

No sooner had Lola straddled her horse and ridden out of the courtyard toward Parral, when several riders descended upon her.

Peter Duprez, Captain Tracy Richards, Rosalia Quintera, and Lucia reined their horses with force to prevent colliding into Lola. She recognized Peter instantly and called to him loudly.

"*Señor! Por favor, señor.* I must go to fetch the doctor. Paco is delirious. *La bruja! La bruja! Aye, Dios mios!*" She rattled off in her Indian dialect which Peter didn't understand. "I go now for the doctor."

She kicked her heels into the horse's flanks and took off like a whirlwind.

The gringos and the women spurred their horses into the courtyard and tethered them to the hitching posts.

Bruja! Bruja! Peter rolled the words over in his mind. Those were the words Paco muttered. He turned to Lucia who had surprised him by arriving with Rosalia Quintera. He'd gathered his friends and brought them to the hacienda to meet Madelaina.

"Lucia," he said, holding her back. "Tell me, what does *bruja* mean?"

Lucia crossed herself. "You mean what that crazy girl was raving about out there?" She gave a little quick jerk to her head.

"Precisely that."

Rosalia Quintera overhead Peter and holding Tracy's hand she moved in closer. "What she said, gringo, is that the man is possessed by an evil spirit. Paco is his name?"

Peter nodded.

"Then, this Paco is possessed. Also that the *señora* is a *bruja*—a witch!"

"That's plumb crazy," said Peter with irritation.

"Hey, gringo, don't get mad on me," said Rosalia, laughing in her usual gay spirit. "Ees not me who say such theengs."

"Yeah," said Peter. "You're right. We better get inside ta meet the missus."

Lucia couldn't help but feel more than a pang of jealousy at the possessive way he said "meet the missus." She had loved Peter Duprez for so long, the ache in her heart had become a part of her. She wrapped herself in a lace shawl she had bought in the *tienda* just before she met Peter. For an instant, when she saw Lola, with those sky blue eyes and that auburn hair, she filled with remorse. Peter always surrounded himself with beautiful women. She sighed and followed the others inside.

"Madelaina!" he called. "Madelaina!" He turned toward the corridor and headed for Paco's room. "Make yourselves ta home," he told the others. "Trace —there's plenty o' booze, buddy. Jus' help yerself, heah?"

He found Madelaina staring at Paco, unable to do

anything to help him. She lifted her eyes at the sound of footsteps entering the room, her features lax and lifeless, her expression masked with a harshness he'd never seen before.

He whispered quietly as he approached her. "How's he doing, little one? He any bettah?" Peter moved in closer, reaching out to her.

For an answer she lifted the bandage from Paco's shoulder and held the oil lamp for him to see it in all its putrefaction. Her eyes met his.

"Mah God, darlin'." He looked away, trying hard not to show his innermost feelings. "How's it possible that in three days it could've turned out like that? Good thing ya sent for the doctor." He watched his wife wipe the perspiration from Paco's face.

"He's out of his mind," she told her husband. "Delirious with fever."

"Ya wanna come out and meet Tracy's *vieja* and her friend, Lucia? Lucia is cousin to the Sandoval girls."

"You must be mad to bring company at a time like this—with Paco close to death. Peter, how could you?" she exclaimed with a stinging edge to her words.

Peter's nature didn't allow him to be talked down to by anyone; not a man or a woman—especially a woman he loved. He turned stern and irritable, a deep frown creasing his brow. "There's no need ta shake youah rattles at me." Then recalling all she'd suffered and been through, his manner grew softer.

"Ah didn't know we'd have company. Ah tell ya it was unexpected. But the least thing mah missus can do is ta greet mah guests," he said. "Then ya can get back ta yore—" He stopped in time.

"My what? My what?" she demanded. "My lover— is that it? Is that the word you've tried not to think? Well, why don't you say it, Peter? You're thinking it, aren't you?" She'd never spoken so harshly to him. She threw her hands up in the air in a gesture of helplessness. "Is that why we couldn't consummate our love earlier?"

He was about to slap her, to shake her out of this

457

mood—anything to end this stupid, ridiculous confrontation. He thought he had explained about the doctor, about his understanding of what she'd endured. He turned to leave, exercising as much self-discipline as he could muster. *Patience, patience, patience,* he told himself.

"Peter!" she cried in alarm. "Peter!" She ran into his arms. "Darling, I don't know what's come over me. I don't recognize myself. I am so confused, so frightened by the changes in me." She clung to him, wrapped her arms about his waist, and inclined her head against his shoulder, tears slashing down her cheeks.

"Theah, theah, Little Fox. Theah's nothing ta be frightened about. Ya just expect too much too soon. Jus' relax. Paco's in God's hands. The doctor will be heah in no time—youah'll see, little darlin'."

"I've been a real bitch! A screaming *puta!* Why do you put up with me?"

"Ya ever heard of a thing called love?" He raised her face to meet his. "It's gonna be all right, youah'll see," he said soothingly.

All of a sudden Paco let out a screeching wail that echoed through the villa and brought Tracy Richards and the girls on the run. Startled, Madelaina and Peter rushed to the side of the bed. Paco had bolted upright, his eyes like burning black balls. He was on fire. Sweat rolled off him like raindrops in a cloudburst. He was like nothing they'd ever encountered—a gargoyle—a demon.

He recoiled, staring at some unseen object. In another fast movement he was on his knees, pivoting from one knee to the other, trying to follow some object in his mind. The others stared in utter fascination. He screamed again, this time, his voice, hoarse and dry, cracked and the words came out garbled. Madelaina, in a strong effort to control herself, clenched her fists and screamed, "Golden Dawn! Golden Dawn! You godforsaken whore of Satan! Begone! Vile, contemptible bitch! Leave him alone! You've done enough damage!"

Madelaina had a clear sensation of panic; her breathing accelerated, her stomach twisted into knots. The others, unable to comprehend, stared at one another. Rosalia Quintera and Lucia became aware of what was transpiring and withdrew in alarm, both girls huddling and cowering against a far wall.

"We go!" cried Lucia in terror. "We go!" She tugged frantically at Rosalia.

The next few moments were moments of acute indecision and terror in the hearts of those observers.

"*Diableros*!" uttered Rosalia Quintera. "*Diableros*! Jesus, Mary, and Joseph! They are possessed!" she cried. The girls crossed themselves over and again. They spoke between themselves in a language incomprehensible to either Peter or Tracy Richards. Rooted to the spot, they focused on Madelaina, who in only seconds appeared to have changed. Her features hardened, her eyes turned to steel points, the expression on her face was unlike anything any of them had ever seen. She contorted, bent over in the manifestation of an old crone. With a voice unlike her own, she let out a howl.

"Die!" she cackled. "Die, Paco! You cannot escape me! You will die. You and Dolores, the both of you— and Madelaina, too. You will all die, because I possess all of you!" The language was Yaqui.

Paco stared at her with violent hatred in his eyes. Suddenly he lunged at her, grabbing her by the neck and before their very eyes trying to squeeze the life from her. It took a moment before either Peter or Tracy had the presence of mind to spring forward and pry Paco from her. He had the strength of ten men and the gringos had all they could do to break his hold on Madelaina.

"Ah hate ta do this, Paco," said Peter, letting out with a strong jut to the jaw. Paco's head snapped back, he wheeled away with a look of lunacy in his eyes. Peter let out another punch and caught him on the side of his head. Paco fell back onto the bed, unconscious.

Madelaina gasped and choked and cackled hoarsely.

459

The wind had been knocked out of her. Her head fell back and she was Madelaina again. A tired, spent, weary, but normal Madelaina who had no recollection of what had happened. She glanced at Peter, then at Paco sprawled out on the bed.

"Peter, darling, what happened? Why is Paco like that? Please help me put him back in bed, under the covers." Madelaina was once again herself.

The Americans were confounded. Peter Duprez stared at his wife as if she had sprouted ten horns. The *campesinas* withdrew in terror, huddling together.

"Darling, please take our guests into the salon. I'll prepare refreshments until Lola returns with the doctor. As long as he's sleeping, he'll be all right." Madelaina fussed over Paco. "I do believe his fever's broken— look, he no longer perspires."

Rosalia Quintera herded the gringos into the other room against their protests. "Is nothing you can do, gringos. For now is over—until he returns again."

"Who returns?" asked Peter in alarm.

"*Diableros*—the devils," she replied softly. "Your wife and this Paco are under the influence of a sorcerer."

"Now look, Rosalia," began Tracy, "don'cha try to spoonfeed that kind o' garbage on ole Peter and me, heah?"

Once she composed herself, Rosalia acted exasperated. "*Hombre*, you are some crazy man. What does Rosalia have to do with such things, eh? With jur eyes ju saw what we saw. Leesten, for her sake—jur *mujer*—ju better find out who put hex on her or else—" She drew an imaginary line across her throat. "Ju don' have her for too long. *Es veridad.* Ees truth what I say to ju, *comprender*?"

When Madelaina entered the salon, the only hint of what had happened only moments before was an unnatural pale hue to her skin. Dark circles under her eyes gave her a slightly mysterious appearance. She moved gracefully, pouring wines and whiskey for her guests as if nothing had happened.

She wore a pleasant smile and adopted a gracious manner as she served them. She moved toward her husband with love brimming in her eyes and, encircling her arm with his, led him toward the leather sofa. If she noticed the strange and unusual pallor in his face, the bewildered expression in his dull blue eyes, she gave no hint. She was the hostess, the *hacendada* of a manor, who was simply entertaining in the manner of a loving wife. She hardly noticed Lucia's dark eyes critically studying her or the quizzical look of assessment in Rosalia's eyes.

"How does the fighting go? Rather the celebration? There was no fighting, was there? Well, at least Pancho Villa is back in business again." She smiled reassuringly at her husband. "You think it will end soon, dearest?"

Peter Duprez sat in total absorption watching his wife. The obvious change in her comportment made it difficult for him to reconcile the things he saw, much less understand them. Earlier Rosalia had insisted someone had put a hex on Madelaina, a spell which must be removed before drastic and irrevocable damage was done her—even death. The shrill ringing of a telephone interrupted Peter's thoughts.

Tracy Richards, on the other hand, took it quite lightly. He was making light talk when Peter moved across the room to pick up the receiver on the wall phone. "Ah'm listening," he spoke into the mouthpiece, his eyes on his wife.

"Is this you, gringo?" came the voice of Pancho Villa at the other end.

Peter hesitated.

"Look, I can't see you, gringo, so you'd better tell me if it's you. I am Pancho Villa at his end. Who is it there?"

"It's Tom Mix all right. Ya wanna talk ta Captain Richards, *Jefe*?"

"Hey Trace, it's the *jefe* foah ya." He held the receiver in his hands until Richards swaggered across the room to his side.

Peter glanced up in the direction of the door as Lola rushed inside. Frantic, drenched to the skin in perspiration, she ran to Peter's side.

"I cannot find the doctor, *señor*! He is no place to be found. What will we do?" She grew hysterical.

Rosalia spoke sternly to her in their Yaqui dialect, words Peter couldn't make out. Lola glowered angrily. Snarling like a cat, she glanced at Madelaina and hissed the word, "*Bruja.*"

Madelaina turned to her, her dark eyes flaring with fierce, volatile lights. It happened so fast that none of the spectators were prepared for what happened. Madelaina lept upon the young Lola, and drawing a knife from some mysterious hiding place, she plunged it into her enemy's shoulder.

Peter dove into the melee along with Rosalia who tried desperately to pin Madelaina down. The daughter of General Obregon had suddenly developed the strength of ten men. Lucia dragged the bleeding Lola away from them and attempted to stop the flow of blood with her lace shawl. She had to struggle desperately to hold back the young tigress. "Move!" she commanded Lola. "Go into the kitchen! Move, I tell you!" Finally subdued and breathless, Lola still refused to budge. In a trancelike state she was compelled to watch the sudden madness possessing Madelaina, giving no thought to the wound she had sustained.

They all watched husband and wife scuffle as Peter tried to release the viselike grip Madelaina had on the knife. His shirt had been slashed, blood trickled from the cuts on his face and hands. Finally, in a desperate move, he shouted aloud, "Sorry, little one. Ya gotta understand what ah'm doing." He swung his arm back and with a powerful fist connected to Madelaina's jaw, knocking her unconscious.

She sagged back and fell limply into Rosalia's arms, totally disheveled, her long, raven tresses matted with blood, portions of her cotton shirt torn and blood stained. She was a mess. Peter picked her up out of

Rosalia's arms and dutifully took her upstairs to the bedroom, with Rosalia Quintera following at his heels.

"Gringo! Gringo! Leesten to me. Something must be done for her—ju understand me? If the spell ees not broken, che will die."

"Now, look heah, Rosalia," said Peter patiently as he headed for the bedroom. "Ya gotta get all that crap right outta yore mind. There ain't no such thing as witches and goblins and evil spirits. Madelaina has been through terrors no human being evah should experience. She jus' needs time ta shape up. Rest, good food, medical supervision. Ah aim to do that foah her as soon as we get to El Paso."

"Listen, *amigo*. You *saw* what Rosalia *saw*. This Lola is Yaqui Indian, more than Lucia. We all know the special tricks of our ancestors." She crossed herself and pleaded. "Ju, I love like a brother—don't do these to her or to ju. We must remove the spirits of evil, the *diablero* from her." She paused, knowing he wasn't listening. "Ju *gringos* all alike! Bah!"

"Whaddya 'espect me ta do, fiahcrackah? Ah don't know the first thin' about what yer ranting about." Frustrated, Peter turned to her after he placed Madelaina's still form on the bed.

"Gringo, ju know what it is to lose one's soul?"

"That's just a figure of speech."

"Ees no fig—fig— ees no what you say. Jur *mujer* is suffering from the loss of her soul. Soon they come and take it all and she die. Jus' like dat!" She snapped her fingers and tossed her head to one side. "I tell ju, Madelaina is bewitched like Paco. He, too, is bewitched. Ju know sometimes the noise of a bird can trap people who are bewitched and are losing their souls and lead them to their deaths?" She spoke in a whisper, a faraway look to her eyes.

Peter's hands flew to his forehead. "Ah don't believe all this! Ah jus' can't believe what's happenin'. Ever since me an' Little Fox arrived at this here hacienda, crazy things have been happenin'. It wasn't bad enough back at the Lomas *rancho*, when dangers lurked all around us. No, heah we hafta deal with hobgoblins!"

"While ju talk, her life is slipping away, gringo," said Rosalia with such solemnity Peter was forced to take her seriously. A physical change came over the young woman who'd given birth to Tracy Richards' child. Her face grew haggard, her eyes extended into large orbs as she fixed her attention on Madelaina's inert form on the bed. "Rosalia don't know who has trapped jur *mujer*'s soul. Who it ees, ees going to kill her or make her *muy mal*, very sick, gringo. Are ju willing to take a chance weeth Madelaina—or do ju want to lose her? Eef ju weesh to take a chance, Tom Meex, I beg of ju to be *cuidado*—careful—and ju must listen to me. Is possible Rosalia can help. Is not for sure. I try, no? If I get lucky, I can arrest this evil until a true *bruja* can do the job, *comprender*?"

Peter shrugged helplessly. "Whatevah ya say. Ah guess ah've gotta trust ya, Rosalia." He ran his fingers nervously through his curly hair.

"Good! Ju must bring Paco upstairs. Bring another bed in here or place him on the sofa, tied down firmly. *Ondolay, pronto, amigo*. Hurry, quickly."

"Paco?"

"*Si*, Paco. He too is possessed! We shall learn who. Trust me. *Ondolay, pronto! Ala chingada*! Bring Lucia to me. And the girl Lola—if she is strong enough. They will both help me." She glanced about the room. "Candles, gringo—I need candles. Ah, here." Rosalia moved like a fleet-footed fawn. "Gringo!" she called, running to the door after him. "Bring rope. Plenty of it!"

In the room she moved even faster. She dragged, pulled and pushed, trying to get the four-poster bed to the center of the floor. It was difficult to budge. She whipped the blanket off the bed, folded it, and pushed it to the center of the room.

Lucia came rushing into the room. "Rosalia, what you want?" She watched the girl in action and listened as Rosalia spoke rapidly in their Indian dialect.

464

"I need an ally, maybe two. Will you help? Little Fox is about to lose her soul." She couldn't lie to Lucia. The girl had to know the dangers ahead.

"No! You don't intend—" Lucia shook her head and looked at her friend as if she'd lost all her senses. "You crazy woman! Not me! No! Never!"

"She will die if we don't help."

For an instant Lucia's dark eyes flickered with dangerous lights. Glancing at Madelaina's inert figure on the bed, she asked herself why she should care. If the girl died, why should she give a fig? Her way to Peter would be without obstacles. Her eyes lit up with anticipation, an almost victorious look.

"I know what you are thinking," snapped Rosalia in their mestizo dialect. "But if you are thinking—and I pray you are not—you know the consequences, Lucia. The condition of this woman at this moment should prove to you what can happen if you fool around with things you don't understand. You want a hex put on you?" Rosalia became an authoritative figure in those few seconds, imposing and firm.

Instantly Lucia cowered. She shook nervously. "N—no. I will be your ally. My journey into this life has been painfully unbearable up to now. If it became worse, I wouldn't be able to live. I'll help," she said resolutely.

"*Muy bueno.* Those are the most intelligent words to pass your lips, *chica. Ondolay*! Go to the butter room and bring back oil and water. If you can, lift up the rocks in the garden and try, Lucia, in God's name, try to find a lizard or two. If you can't, then bring me a chicken from the hen house. Move! *Pronto.*"

Peter entered the room with Paco in his arms.

"Here, on the sofa, gringo. Where is Tracy?"

"He returned to Parral. The *jefe* wanted to confer with him. The Redflaggers of Orozco intend to return to do battle with us sometime tonight," he said tightly.

As Rosalia took in the full import of his words, she ordered him to tie Paco down to the sofa. "And do a good job," she cautioned. "Ees important ees not possible for Paco to break through the restraints. Do the same with Little Fox. And, gringo, again I caution ju. Be sure ju tie them both with such firmness that God himself bestowing upon them the strength of ten tigers cannot break through the bindings. And don't argue!"

Peter did as he was told. Then he and Rosalia pushed the bed into the center of the room.

"Why?" he started to ask.

"Don' ask. Ees no time for to explain. Ju trust me. *Madre de Dios*! Ju pray for us, gringo. Ju pray my allies give me needed powers. Now, go. Bring firewood—dry as possible. Outside in courtyard are copper and clay pots. Bring one thees size." She held her fingers before her in a circular gesture, indicating the size needed. Peter nodded and left instantly to do her bidding.

Rosalia double-checked the ties on both Paco and Madelaina. By the time Lucia reappeared with Lola, who fortunately only suffered a superficial wound which had been dressed, she cornered them and spoke to them in their curious Indian dialect.

"I will need you both as allies. Shortly, I will need great power. I will need your strength to help me, advise me, and give me the strength necessary to perform acts required of me in the next few hours—or however long it takes to finish the job."

Peter came in and stood very still while she talked.

"Gringo, light a fire in the pot and place it facing the north at their feet."

"Rosalia," said Lucia shivering. "I am afraid."

"M—me, too," said the frightened, blue-eyed mestiza, Lola.

"There is nothing to fear. You have known me a long time, Lucia. Have you known me to do anything bad or evil?" she asked in their native tongue.

"No, *es veridad*."

"Will you trust me, Lola? Even though we never met before this night?"

She somberly fixed her attention on the girl's eyes. She took Lola's hands in her own firm, strong hands.

"Trust me, *chiquita*. You both must give me the added strength I need. The danger is in *my* life—not *yours*. When I speak out, you must follow my instructions to the letter. No matter how you are distracted. No matter how much you want to disobey my orders. You must stand within the circle I draw for you and under no circumstances are you to step from this spot. Do I make myself clear?"

The girls nodded. Rosalia took the oil and poured a thin stream of the viscous oil in a circle to the east of the large center circle containing the bed, sofa, and two victims. She poured another stream of the fluid in a larger circle around Madelaina and Paco.

She set the can down, and from a small leather pouch around her neck, she removed a small bottle and another sack containing a powdery substance. Her eyes darted around the room. She found a bottle of wine and two glasses. She picked up one, poured some red wine into it, and with a dropper allowed eight drops of the liquid to spill into the wine. She picked up the glass, swished the contents around, and poured half in one glass. She gave one to Lucia and the other to Lola.

"Drink," she commanded authoritatively, allowing for no refusal.

Finished, the girls gave her the glasses. Rosalia flung them into the fire Peter had started. Instantly a bright flame spurted into a myriad of colors. Peter watched the ritual in utter fascination.

Rosalia took the girls' arms and led them into the smaller circle. She began to chant some Indian song of their ancestors. "You who must have enormous vigor, who must seek to endure fatigue and hunger, will soon experience a strength of *herculeo*. It is this strength you will transfer to me when it begins to appear that I have none. Understand this clearly. Do not give it to me before I need it—or when it might be too late. You must keep your eyes only on me. Not on Paco or Madelaina or any other disturbance that might interfere with your concentration. Understand? You, Lucia, know me well. Let no other image fool you or attempt

467

to deceive you. If you do, my life will be taken in forfeit."

The girl, frightened and shaking, nodded, recognizing the enormous responsibility placed upon her.

She cautioned again. "Only when it appears that I need it and not until then! Soon you will feel a lightness and a strength that will make you feel you can grow wings and fly. But you must not let your mind soar. Be aware every second of what we're doing. It is dangerous only because the *diableros* will take any form. You *must not* pay any attention to them. You are safe within the circle I have prepared. Do not give in to any temptations—be it fear or promises of ecstasy—nothing!"

The girls nodded. In moments the fear-ridden faces changed into faces that demonstrated strength and fearlessness. Their shoulders pulled back defiantly. They stood firm, feet spread apart, hands on their hips.

It is simply remarkable, thought Peter, *how unreal it all seems. And I stand here allowing this insanity to continue.*

"*Muy bueno*," said Rosalia, observing the changes in the girls. "You will maintain these positions when things get very bad. If something should happen when I'm away, if at any time you should feel vulnerable and think you can't endure it any longer, you are to hop twice on one foot and twice on the other without raising your foot off the floor." She demonstrated an ancient tribal Indian dance movement the girls knew well. They understood. They nodded mutely.

Rosalia walked to Peter's side. "Is time ju go, gringo. Listen carefully. I will lock the door, bolt it with the bar, and place before it a heavy chair. Ju must not enter the room, *comprender*? Is *muy* important, *amigo*. If ju hear screams, crying, braying—even the howling of coyotes—*do not enter*. If ju hear Madelaina scream and call to ju, cover jur ears. Do not let anyone enter this room until I, Rosalia Quintera *as ju have known her to be*, open the door and ask ju to enter. "Is most *importante* what I say. Do not enter or jur

468

mujer, me, Lucia, Lola, and you will die. Is no joke, *amigo*."

"But where will you go? I heard you tell the girls you were leaving."

"Aye, is so. I must go to find who has taken Madelaina's and Paco's souls, and if possible, try to get them back." She placed two pinches of the powdered substance into her mouth, under her tongue. "I go inside now. Oh, jes, *amigo*, may I have one of jur guns— loaded. Make sure it is ready to fire."

"Mah God, girl. Ya'll expecting to shoot someone?"

"Only if I am in danger of losing my life."

Peter leaned over and kissed Rosalia tenderly and gratefully. He held her close to him. "Ah'm not good at thankin' ya, m'am. Ah jus' wanna tell ya how much I respect ya and love ya for what yer doing for Madelaina. Ah don't begin ta understand, *chiquita*, what yer up ta. But God bless ya, honey."

Rosalia raised her hand and touched his face tenderly. Once again she cautioned, "Be aware of everything, gringo. No matter *who* comes to ju—for whatever reason—do not permit jurself to be bedeviled or bewitched."

She disappeared inside the door. He heard the lock click shut, the bar bolt slip into place. He could hear her drag heavy furniture into place. Peter's tongue wet his parched lips and a burning sensation flared in his mouth. He recalled her taking the powder, and he quickly wiped his lips with the back of his hand. Instantly his mouth went numb. He wanted to run downstairs to drink some wine, to wash away any powdery particles, but he chose to remain outside the door. He dragged a chair from one end of the corridor, placed it next to the door, and sat down, worrying about his lips from time to time until the numbness left.

What he wouldn't give to be inside that room. He'd like to witness this battle Rosalia alluded to among the devils, demons, and spirits of whatever it was she was going to contact. For some strange reason, Peter Duprez, who hadn't experienced fear since he was a child, began to sense a disturbing fear. Her words had produced a state of anguish in him, a feeling of premonition coupled with foreboding. Something dreadful was about to happen—of this he was certain. He heard a loud, piercing scream rip through the room, one filled with such torment that the hairs on his neck and arms stood up. He sprang to his feet and lit a cigarette. He glanced at the pocket watch in his vest. It was 7:30 P.M. His hands were trembling visibly as he paced to and fro like a nervous cat. A quiet lull hung over the hacienda. There were no noises, only the whistling of winds on the desert. Tension mounted in him, and the strain of waiting grew nerve-wracking.

An hour later, the wind had risen noticeably. He heard horses pull up into the courtyard. He glanced at his watch. It was 8:30 P.M. He heard Tracy Richards call to him. "Hey there, *amigo*. Where the hell are ya?"

Under normal circumstances Peter would have sprung from his chair and hailed Captain Richards in his usual hearty voice. However, with the sting of Rosalia's words still burning his eardrums, he cocked his head, fully alert, and listened again. It was Tracy's voice all right, he conceded, but not the usual tone of voice he was accustomed to hearing. And the words used were slightly different. Trace had rarely called Peter *amigo*. Good buddy, yes, fella, even Tom Mix. Rosalia's words cautioned him further, and he stood his guard at the door as a chill passed through him and he broke out into a cold sweat.

Damned if she ain't got me thinking about devils and spooks, he told himself angrily. He continued to hear footsteps outside the house. He became aware of every sound. Snuffing out his cigarette, he sat in the chair, listening for noises inside the bedroom.

Inside, Rosalia had lit seven candles and placed them outside the greater circle: one at the north, south, east, and west positions, the remaining three in the position of an inverted pyramid around the burning fire. Seated cross-legged before the fire, she closed her eyes. The hallucinogenic mixture she'd ingested had begun to take effect. A series of dreamlike images came to her, in no sequential order, surrounded by vibrant colors swirling through the images in a serpentine manner. A sensation of vagueness began to clear as Rosalia departed her body. She had the sensation of being outside herself, observing the entire scene from some distant point. Her eyes, focused on both Paco and Madelaina, blinked from side to side and she perceived them as if through the eyes of a bird.

A series of changes manifested themselves upon the countenance of Madelaina, beginning with a glow of dull lights and continuing in a mist until it cleared. Rosalia had the clearest recollection of another face superimposed upon that of Madelaina; a white-skinned Indian with black hair and holes for eyes. The vision grew clearer and clearer until she saw the body thrashing about the bed in the sexual embrace of a dignified, dark-haired man in his forties.

Rosalia observed the scene stoically as voices came to her loud and clear. The voice of a man, a stranger, said, "*Querida*, you make me happy, contented. With you I could wish for none other." The eyeless woman lying next to her lover caressed him with passion until the fires in her sensuous body ignited his. "You will never want anyone but Golden Dawn," said the writhing body that had possessed Madelaina. "Only Golden Dawn shall be the desire of your heart, *mi Generale*."

The scene shifted and changed as vibrant splashes of translucent colors thundered into a motionless sea of sharp, painful lights, where the jagged edges of stalagmites and stalagtites, illuminated by an infinite variety of flickering lights, changed their luminosity. In another instant, small blobs, shadows which took human form, came at Rosalia like a battalion of warriors with pointed spears and blazing shields reflecting a blinding sun in her eyes. Recoiling, protecting herself by crisscrossing her arms before her eyes, she tried to fend them off as they swarmed upon her. She brushed them off, swept them aside, slapped her body in an effort to rid herself of these verminlike tempters and tormenters.

471

Now, Tracy Richards entered the room, calling to Rosalia, sternly at first, then loudly demanding she come to him at that moment. Angry at her apparent indifference, he called her vile names, threatened her with hated anger and scorching contempt. "If ya don' come heah this instant, *puta*, ah'll find me ten moah whores ta sleep with, ya lowly side-windin' greaser!"

Before Rosalia's eyes, the captain began to clap his hands and dance an obscene dance before the two girls, Lucia and Lola, tempting them, luring them. His voice became gutteral, lascivious, and suggestive. "C'mon' ya gorgeous hunk o' women," he said to them. "Let's y'all an' me show Rosalia what lovin's all about, heah?" He singled out Lola. "What say ya, little kitten? Come find out what a real man's like."

Lola, shaking like a leaf in a tempest, began to wind up in ritual dance. She hopped twice on one foot, then on the other. She began to chant an Indian song, avoiding as she did the outstretched arms of Tracy Richards. He removed all his clothing and, holding his sexual organs, continued to make obscene gestures as he danced a short jig around her. He leered at Lucia, grabbed for her breasts. "Let's youah an' me fuck, baby," he called seductively. "Youah, too, Lola, baby. Weah'll all three fuck. Weah'll show the ole sow what it's really like, heah?" Hidden in his eyes and visible only to Rosalia were malicious, mocking lights shaded with lust.

Lucia, trembling with fright, began to dance as Lola danced, sang along with her partner, their voices growing louder and firmer until suddenly the apparition of Tracy Richards dissolved and another form manifested itself.

"Come with me, girls," said the voice of a seductress, a woman dressed in diaphanous flowing robes of gold. "I'm Golden Dawn. Come with me and you'll have the desires of your heart. Don't stay with this old whore's whore. This gringo tart can give you nothing but the hard life of a *puta*! Who is she to command you? Listen—" She began to sing a sweet plaintive song that tore at their heart strings. Nothing they had ever heard could match the exquisite sound of that golden voice of promise.

Golden Dawn moved as if on a cloud. She tried to break through the outer circle of protection to reach Paco. His eyes had fluttered open earlier. Madelaina also became aware of the strange happenings. She grew frightened by the things she saw and heard. She tried to move and couldn't.

"Paco," purred Golden Dawn. "I want you to be my lover, Paco. Don't you want to be with me? Say you do and I'll help you free yourself."

Paco strained against his ties. "*Si*, Golden Dawn. I will come whenever you say. Come and get me." He strained at his bonds. "I'll come. I'm ready."

Lucia and Lola stepped up the momentum, their voices grew louder and louder as they chanted and sang their songs. Their dance became livelier

Golden Dawn moved toward the body of Rosalia Quintera. She reached in closer to the fires to touch her, but instantly withdrew her hands.

"Whore! I know you aren't inside." She cocked her head and glanced about the room. "Where can you be, you little whore? You peasant scum of a mestiza! I'll find you if it takes all our lives. You meddling *puta*! You'll be next to taste my wrath!" Her head whirled around and her eyes landed on an overhead beam where she caught sight of a gray lizard. "I see you, Rosalia Quintera. I know what disguise you've assumed. Heed my words or you'll live to regret the evil of Golden Dawn. Give up, whore. You can't win. Don't you know who I am? You! You dare contest me? You, Rosalia Quintera, the illegitimate misbegotten daughter of a whore's whore. What right have you? How do you dare? I'll see your flesh burn in hell, the same place I've put the bastard son conceived by you and the gringo, Tracy Richards. You know what he thinks of you? A greaser, a Mexican whore not fit to be his wife. You see how he craves the delights of woman? Any woman! But I have something more important than

Tracy Richards. I have your *niño*, your little son—your gringo son!" she cackled.

Outside the door, Peter Duprez' face had turned the color of sickly vomit. He had heard every voice, every word, the screams, the chants, the sound of feet stomping to the rhythm of the chanting. To him it sounded like horses' hoofs thundering over a wooden bridge. He heard Tracy Richards shout obscenities. At one point he shoved his shoulder against the door and was about to break it open, when he remembered Rosalia's warning. *God! Ah can't be that strong,* he told himself. Sweat rippled off his brow. There were times he wanted to run away, get as far from Parral and Mexico as he could.

The sound of Madelaina's voice calling him tore at his heart.

"Peter, Peter," she whimpered. "Come and get me, darling. I'm afraid. Oh Peter, it's terrible. Awful. Tell Rosalia to stop all this. I want to come into your arms and make love with you. Please, darling, tell them all to go away. Don't you remember how it was aboard the *Mozambique*? We can relive all those memorable nights, if only you stop this stupid game these girls are playing. We're fine. Paco and I are going to be fine—just as soon as you tell them to leave us alone. Darling, come and untie me so we can make love. Don't you want me any more? Don't you want to feel my warm passionate body next to yours?"

Peter Duprez clasped his hands over his ears. *Stop! Stop*! he screamed inwardly. He whirled about like a dervish and reached for his gun. He was about to shoot the lock off when once again he recalled Rosalia's words. Suddenly he feared for Tracy's mistress, for the girls, and especially for Madelaina and Paco, but his hands were tied. He could do nothing. It took the strength of ten devils to keep him from busting through that door. If someone had told him this would happen, he wouldn't have believed it. *God have mercy on all o' us!* He repeated this time and again.

Inside the bedroom, shadows and mist formed into

474

swirls of darkness. Golden Dawn had disappeared. In her place came the sultry, impassioned Dolores. "So, Paco, look at the predicament you've gotten yourself into, all because of this whore of Obregon's and his shameless daughter, this nothing. For this woman, you brought the wrath of Lucifer upon you. Have you had enough? Eh? Tell me you've had enough and I'll save you."

Paco strained at his ties. His wild-eyed expression as he banged his head from side to side and screamed was indescribable. "Dolores! It's you! Yes. Yes, all is forgiven. You were right. The daughter of Obregon is a whore! She has turned my world into crumbling ashes. Come and untie me. And we'll go. I promise never to look upon another woman again. Only take me. Take me now." He thrashed wildly on the sofa, moving the furniture with him. It bounced off the floor, rattling and banging loudly. "Lucia! Lola, come and untie me. Free me so I can take my woman home. See? She loves me. She has come for me. Lola, for the love of God, woman, release me."

Lucia and Lola increased their tempo. They were dancing their little hearts out. Their voices increased in volume. The chants grew frantic.

There came the sound of gunfire, a steady barrage of guns firing at a fast clip.

Captain Tracy Richards came through the door, bleeding, full of bullet wounds. "Rosalia—where's mah woman?" He stumbled, fell, picked himself up, gasping and holding the wounds. He paused before the image of Rosalia. "Help me, woman. Help me. I'm dying, can't you see?" He gasped for breath, choked, and made gurgling sounds inside his throat.

As Rosalia observed all this, she felt herself weakening. The feeling came over her of being sucked into a vortex, swirling black waters against which she couldn't fight. Down, down, down she went, swallowed up by an unfamiliar darkness. Her energies waned. Her body ached, every muscle stiff and painfully contracted. She had returned to her body now, unsure of what was happening. She blinked her eyes open and saw her lover bleeding to death inches away from her. She only had to reach out to hold him and protect him. Here was the father of her child, the one she wanted to raise in America, like his gringo father. What was she doing here? Helping two people she hardly knew, endangering her own life—and for what? Not even a thank you would she receive for her troubles. Hah! A mestiza, no, three mestizas helping a *gachupín* and her gringo friends! Are you some crazy woman, Rosalia, she asked herself.

She was in her own circle of protection, just as Lucia and Lola were. Neither could penetrate the others. "Come, Lucia. Come, Lola!" she sneered with an ugly look on her face. "Enough of this. Let us finish this farce. Let that whorish daughter of our enemy do as she wishes. We have done enough. Why should we mix in any of this? She got into this mess—she and that Corporal Jimenez. Let them get themselves out!"

Lucia and Lola stopped for a second. The look on Rosalia's face was not the Rosalia Lucia had grown to know and love. Lola, her resolve weakening, was about to pierce the outer circle of protection. "No!" screamed Lucia. "It is not Rosalia! Sing! Dance! Hop!" she commanded. "Faster! She needs our strength! Now!" She took Lola's hands in hers and held them firmly. Both girls continued their incantations and movements as prescribed earlier.

"Peter? Hey, gringo. It's me, Rosalia. It's over, gringo. Your *mujer* is going to be A-O.K. You hear what I tell you? Come in now. Come and get her." The voice pierced the door and reached Peter's ears.

Peter was bewildered. It was Rosalia all right. He recognized her voice. How could he break into the room? It was locked, bolted, and reenforced with furniture abutting it. He continued to pace as he chainsmoked. It was nearly 11:30 P.M. Goddamn! Four hours of excruciating drama. He felt a profound despair clutching at his heart.

"Peter?"

He spun around. Not three feet from him was Rosalia Quintera.

"What's wrong, gringo? Did ju not hear my voice?" She purred ever so nicely. "Imagine what a dumbbell is Rosalia Quintera? I 'ave lost the key. So, gringo, shoot off the lock, eh? We go and finish this thing. Madelaina is fine. In time she will be most well again. A-O.K. Is good?"

"Thank God," he exclaimed, suddenly relieved. "Ya know what it was like out here, listening ta all that garbage?" He pulled the gun from his holster, but just before he shot at the lock, he caught sight of her face. "You ain't Rosalia," he said sharply. He turned the gun and pointed it at her. "Jus' who the hell are ya?" He took a step toward her, and Rosalia receded far into a tunnel, whirling and spinning into a black abyss.

"Hey theah, Tom Mix," called Tracy Richards scaling the stairwell two at a time. "Who the blazes are ya talkin' ta?" He stopped short at the sight of Peter's distraught appearance, at his menacing posture, gun in hand.

"Stay wheah ya are, partnah. Don'cha move a muscle if'n ya want ta live," ordered Peter, uncertain of who the interloper was at this point.

"Hey, boy, what in tarnation's happening? Wheah's mah woman? The others?" Tracy had never seen him acting so peculiar.

"Just toss yer gun belt down, ole buddy, and if ya make one move—one suspicious move—ah'll cut ya in two. Heah?" Peter's voice had never been deadlier.

Tracy's hands shot up into the air. "All right. All right. Jus' ya take it easy, ya heah? Ah'm gonna lower mah hands, Pete, to the buckle and unclasp it. Ah promise, man, ah won't do nothing wrong." He did as he said he would. The gun belt off, he kicked it forward along the tiles.

Peter kicked the gun belt behind him. "Now, you an' me's gonna sit right heah and wait. Y'all make one move—whoever the hell ya are—and ah'll keep mah promise." Perhaps he was melodramatic, but after what he'd seen. . . .

"Don'cha even wanna hear what ah gotta say? Parral's gonna be attacked in jus' about two hours. You an' me gotta get cracking. Ole Pancho wants ta fight this one. He's got one o' 'em brilliant plans as usual, buddy. We jus' gotta get back to 'im to get ouah ordahs straight. The Gringo Brigade is gonna mow 'em down." Smart enough to know something was wrong, he tried to keep calm.

"Ya don't think ah'm gonna fall for that crap. Now keep yer trap shut, before I shut it for ya." Peter was straining to listen to what was happening inside.

Lucia and Lola had grown frantic in their demonstration. Madelaina seemingly arose from the bed, shedding her restraints as if they were tufts of cotton. She walked toward Rosalia. "How can I thank you, my dear, for all your help. I would have been dead if it hadn't been for you and these nice girls."

Behind her, Paco grew delirious. He gasped for breath. "Untie me also, Madelaina. We'll thank her and the others together."

Madelaina ignored him, with a look of disdain. She continued to walk toward Rosalia. Behind her, the lizards Lucia had brought into the house scurried close to her feet. Rosalia felt numb with fear, her hands slid down alongside her until they gripped the gun. A sudden surge of strength filled her, and in a matter of seconds she felt a rolling, rocking sensation course through her as a scream, beginning at her toes, crept up through her body and out her mouth, like the wailing raging of a demon. It was loud and shrill, a chilling outcry that seemed to rock the villa's rafters. Rosalia, shuddering inwardly, raised her shaking, gun-filled hands unsteadily and fired point blank into Madelaina's face. The apparition continued to move toward the mestiza unhesitantly. With all her might Rosalia hurled the gun into the face of her pursuer. A scream, prolonged and piercing, directed her aim and suddenly the figure of Madelaina staggered backward, clutching at a

478

face filled with holes like running ink blots. It disappeared with a wailing sound of defeat tunneling after it, into a well racing toward infinity.

Outside the door, Peter Duprez angled his head at the sounds of the screams accompanied by gun shots. Tracy Richards heard it, too: the chilling silence, the sudden cessation of all activity; what the hell was going on? What had happened to Peter? His questions were compounded by the urgency he felt at what was happening in Parral, what would happen if he and Pete didn't get back to Villa's camp? He glanced at his watch and murmured in apology, "Look, Pete—"

Pete's gun was aimed at his heart instantly. "Ah said, don't move! Ah mean it!" he growled sternly. "Do ah have ta tie ya up?"

Tracy raised his hands, shook his head reluctantly, and said nothing, but his eyes acquiesced to Peter's command. Sounds inside the room drew his attention as they had Peter's. They both strained to listen.

It was past midnight when Rosalia, drained of all energy, mentally and physically exhausted, stirred slightly. She rose to her feet, picked up two lit candles, and moving into the circle, she inspected the pale, sweating features of Madelaina Obregon and Paco Jimenez. Madelaina's dark, tortured eyes flickered and blinked several times until they opened wide.

"Rosalia," she said weakly. "Where are we? Where's Peter?

Rosalia placed a cool hand on the girl's forehead. It felt clammy and cold to the touch. She brushed aside a few strands of the girl's hair and spoke softly to her. "Don't be worried, *chiquita*. Is fine. Is going to be fine, everything."

The oppressive, stifling air seemed to lift and thin, and Rosalia breathed in deeply as she moved toward the two allies. She smiled as they continued to critically assess her features and behavior. "It's me," she said softly. "It's over." She extended her arms toward the girls. For several brief seconds, Lucia held Lola's arm as she scanned Rosalia's face. When the woman of

Tracy Richards stepped over the circle, she knew it was the real Rosalia Quintera. Instantly the girls fell into her outstretched arms and she hugged them dearly to her bosom. With barely the strength to talk, she thanked them in a subdued voice. "Bless you both. Without you it couldn't have been done."

Both girls were drenched in perspiration; Lola's auburn hair a mass of ringlets, her eyes grateful and relieved at the end of the ordeal. Lucia cried like a baby. All three women were exhausted. "If it hadn't ended when it did," Lucia babbled on incoherently, "I couldn't have endured it much longer."

Together they moved the bureau drawers and chairs barricading the door. Outside, Peter, alert and tense, heard the scuffling of the furniture and tightened his grip on the gun. With one eye on Tracy Richards, the other on the door, he backed away at an angle, poised for any new and bizarre occurrence. On this night he'd seen more than his eyes would see in a lifetime. He didn't dare speculate on what else could happen. Filled with disquiet, he heard the key turned in the lock and the bolt snapped back. As the door began to open, Peter could feel the sweat rolling off his face; his stomach was tied in knots.

Rosalia's face appeared first, followed by the girls behind her. They looked at Peter, then at Captain Richards and his menacing posture with little reaction.

"You can go and untie them, *amigo*," said the spell-breaker with considerable effort. "Ah, you're back, gringo." She smiled wanly at her man.

Peter stood hesitant and uncertain, still unsure of anything on this night. For a moment he looked blank, uncomprehending. Suddenly he knew. He didn't know how he knew, but it was clear to him. He rushed into the room as Rosalia fell into the arms of her lover.

Lola followed Peter into the room to help untie Paco Jimenez. She smoothed his hair back off his face and stroked his cheeks gently, murmuring endearing words to him. His fever had broken.

With Captain Richards' help, they got Paco downstairs into his own bed.

Peter untied the ropes binding Madelaina. He sat down by the bed, rubbing her bruised wrists and ankles where welts had formed from the pressure against the confining ropes, deep concern scrawled over his face.

She sat upright and encircled his neck. "Dearest Peter, I can't tell you what horrible nightmares I had. They were terrible." She snuggled close to him. It was as if nothing had happened at all.

"Tomorrow, Rosalia Quintera will tell ya all about what happened in heah, little one," he said softly. "Ah for one will be most anxious ta learn all about it." He stroked her face gently.

She yawned and stretched and lay back against his chest, curled up like a small, vulnerable child. "You were *apasionado* this evening," she told him suggestively.

"Don't ya think ya better get some sleep, little one? Ah can't say as ah'd be so chipper if ah'd gone through what ya'll went through tonight."

"Peter?"

"Yes, *chiquita*."

Her hand felt the hardness in his crotch, and she lay back against him, rolling her eyes at him, daring him, enticing him. It was like old times. He sighed in relief. "Tracy's waitin' fer me. We've gotta get back to Parral. Looks like those *Orozquistas* are bearing down on the *jefe*." He cocked a deliberating eye at her. Her hair was so dark he could barely see it in the flickering candlelight. Her dark eyes, heavy-lidded from lack of sleep, could have fooled him. Beneath the lids they were eager, bright, and filled with the promise of love.

Within moments they had shed their clothing. "Ah never like ta make love with an army waitin' fer me, darlin'. Ah've never been one for quickies—ah like a full production an' ah know y'all do, too."

Her legs, wide open, were as inviting as her lips. He kissed her while his hands moved over her stomach, fingers pulling lightly at the tangle of black curls. His hot passionate lips transferring to her all the pent-up emotion, the frustration he felt this evening and for the past two days. It was over now, thanks to Rosalia. He kissed her and kissed her with passionate urgency.

"I had almost forgotten what it was like with you, Peter," she whispered in his ears, sending a thrilling sensation shooting through him.

Peter was at the point of no return. He couldn't hold back the flood of love, the contents of his heart. He drove deeper and deeper inside her as her body met his in undulating desire. His hands grasped her hips, raised them up to meet his thrusts. He was unable to hold back. He came inside her with a wild, outlandish, animal-like shriek that seemed as if his soul had been ripped out of his body. Peter hadn't rested but a moment or two when he withdrew from her. He pried her thighs apart and lifted her legs over his shoulders as a low moan escaped his throat. His hands held her breasts, playing with her nipples as his mouth found her. Madelaina's body writhed and undulated, and she jerked convulsively when his tongue touched the key to her excitement. Her hands played with his curly hair until she grasped him firmly, pulling him in and out in a circular motion, directing his every move.

Madelaina's head thrashed from side to side. "Ohhhhh," she moaned. "Ohhhhh! Yes—yes—yesssssss!" She wailed aloud in animal sounds and her body bounced into the air and continued to bounce and twist and writhe until the two of them were nearly off the bed. When she was spent, Peter moved up and entered her and began to go through the motions again until it was over for him.

What the hell made him do such a thing, he wondered. He'd never done that to her before, never gave it a thought. He smoked a cigarette, knowing he should have been dressed and out of there with Tracy Richards. Madelaina lay back against the pillows, a sweet look of contentment on her face.

She let me do it without a sense of shame—not even a complaint, he thought.

482

He heard his name being called with urgency. "Yeah, yeah, Trace, ah'm coming," he shouted. He got up and dressed. Damn, he felt like he needed a bath. Well, as soon as the fightin' was over, he could take all the baths he wanted.

Dressed, he leaned over his wife to kiss her. Her eyes flared open with a wicked grin on her face. She whispered, "Peter-dearest, you are the *Golden Dawn of all my desires*." Seduction spilled from her amorous eyes.

He nodded contentedly and moved to the door. Glancing back over his shoulder, he gave a start. His eyes caught sight of a lizard clinging to the pillow sham next to his wife on the bed. By the time he moved back to the bed to scatter it, it was gone.

Chapter 18

The skirmish at Parral staged by Pancho Villa lasted until noon of the next day. The general in charge of the Redflagger *Orozquistas* had misjudged Pancho Villa, as many had done before him and would continue to do. Aware of the *guerrillo*'s reputation on horseback with his mounted cavalry, General Campa's plan was to pelt the town with light artillery fire, then crush the weak defense by overpowering it with infantry.

Villa's uncanny grasp of organization enabled him to place the right men in the right places at the proper time. It was the first time he actually had federally trained soldiers at his disposal and he used them all well. As the Redflaggers' pyramid-shaped attack progressed, the Gringo Brigade opened fire and contained them. Withdrawing, General Campa shelled again and resumed the attack. Again he was sent into retreat. The last attack took place at dawn, when the eerie lights played tricks on a man's eyes. Pancho Villa counterattacked, smashed through the Redflaggers' center, then, as Urbina destroyed one wing, the gringos destroyed the other, bringing victory to Villa and a stinging defeat to the enemy.

Peter Duprez had been shot. He took a bullet in the left shoulder and one tore a hole through his left wrist. The pain wasn't bad and binding his wrist as best he could, he had continued through the three attacks. Before noon, word arrived that three trains were en route to Parral with over 5,000 *Orozquistas*, supported by cavalry and heavy cannon. Villa, no fool, considered the odds carefully. Outnumbered and outgunned, he had little hope of holding the city against such force.

Still, Pancho Villa wasn't about to cede Parral without a fight.

By then, Peter's arm had begun to swell and throb painfully. He was in fever. At one point, his eyes, like seas of blue glass, fairly popped from his head as he flagged Captain Tracy Richards a few feet from him. He sank to the ground just as Richards caught him and laid him under the shade of a tree along one side of the garrisoned fort. Tracy assembled all the necessary equipment to help him get the bullet out of the infected shoulder. A canteen filled with tequila was forced through Peter's lips. He gagged and sputtered but managed to swallow.

"Damnit, why didn't tell me yer arm had begun to swell?" cussed the captain over and over.

While Tracy probed for the bullet, Pancho Villa, close by to aid the gringo, outlined his plans, his facial features wincing with every shove and twist of the metal prong directed by the friend of Tom Mix. At last, when the bullet casing was expunged, Villa sighed in relief, as if he personally had undergone the painful ordeal.

"If I was a drinking man, gringo, I'd have consumed more than what your friend drank," he told Tracy. "Such a bad wound—and he said nothing all night?"

"Nothing. Stupid bastard! If he'da told me when the swelling began, ah could've saved him most o' this pain! He'll sleep for a while, all right."

"What you think, gringo? We'll be outnumbered, so we can't remain in Parral. I'll send the women ahead to Durango with the necessary escorts. Meanwhile, we will give this General Campa and Salazar something to remember us, eh? Is no question Orozco controls the trains from Juarez to Torreon. But not the hills or the desert sands. We can move through both and join Madero's Division of the North at Torreon."

"As usual, *Jefe*," said Tracy Richards with profound respect for Villa's uncanny strategy, "mah hat's off ta ya. As it is, ah jus' can't see how ya managed to multiply the sixty of us into nearly 500 strong. But ya did."

485

"Only because men such as you and Tom Mix are loyal to me, Captain," said Villa, watching the gringo roll a few cigarettes and place them neatly into his jacket pocket, lighting one with a match struck against a rock.

"Ya wanna a smoke, *Jefe*?" he asked, watching Villa's eyes fill with curiosity.

Villa shook his head. "Imagine a tough, pistol-packing *bandido* like me has never taken time to learn to smoke—or drink. Hah, if it was known by my enemies, they'd laugh me into submission." He laughed as he imagined such a thing happening.

Two days later, the *Orozquistas*, led by Generals Campa and Salazar, and reenforced battalions bombarded Parral. For hours the attack prevailed unceasingly, and the Redflaggers marched into Parral only to find Pancho Villa had long since vanished into the hills. What they had been attacking so relentlessly was a tiny handful of volunteers. So scandalized and angered by this carefully executed plan of Villa's were the Redflaggers, they rounded up this scrawny bunch of scarecrows and executed them on the spot—without mercy.

When news of this abominable act reached Pancho Villa, this pigeon-livered demonstration of chicken shit behavior, he vowed openly that when caught, the Redflaggers of Orozco would never receive any mercy from him. It would be death on the spot for all of them. And Villa was growing more well known as a man who kept his promises.

Unable to determine how Villa had eluded them, the two generals who had co-commanded the counterattack upon Parral concluded it was either luck or a stroke of genius.

News arrived at the hacienda where Madelaina and the other *campesinas* were housed that they'd been ordered south to Durango. Madelaina demonstrated considerable reluctance to travel with Rosalia Quintera and the other camp followers, because the unstable condition of Paco Jimenez necessitated slower travel, with more frequent rests. Madelaina therefore ordered the others to progress without them. Lola flatly refused. She insisted upon remaining by Paco's side and challenged Madelaina openly.

"You'll not get me to leave him. Understand me well," she said defiantly, her pale blue icy eyes staring imperiously at the legendary Little Fox.

Madelaina shrugged indifferently. "Do as you please. Only know you'll not be traveling under the protection of Pancho Villa's *guerrillos*. We'll be forced to take back roads, through mountains and deserts. You'd best make sure you can handle a gun."

"And a knife also," added Lola. There was no mistaking her meaning—the mestizo knew the consequences.

Rosalia Quintera embraced Lola, and as she turned to Madelaina to express her farewell, a vast shadow appeared in her dark eyes. She scrutinized the regal posture of Peter's *mujer*, her eyes narrowing in thought. "Take care, *querida*," she said with polite reserve. "You've been through much hell." The women had spoken of that nightmarish night with reservation, only to explain pointedly to Madelaina that she had endured no nightmares, only reality in its most precarious form.

"Tell my husband I shall join him as swiftly as possible," she told Rosalia upon their departure. She watched the *campesinas* ride out of the courtyard on their horses. "*Buenos suerte*," she called. "*Adios, muchachas!*" She waved to them until they rode out of sight.

In preparation for their trip, both Madelaina and Lola, dressed somewhat shabbily as peasant women, rubbed dirt on their faces and arms and scratched their fingers in the earth to lodge dirt under their fingernails. Paco lay back in the rear of the wagon dressed in his peasant pantaloons and shirt with a serape over him and a wide sombrero shoved forward on his pale face, partially covering him. Alongside him, concealed by blankets, were three rifles and a few hand pistols, all

487

loaded. His arm bothered him considerably despite the doctor's assurance that in time it would heal. He kept his complaints to a minimum and seemed annoyed that Madelaina watched over him like a mother hen. He insisted he could manage for himself, that he was a man, not a child, but she would hear none of it.

"If it were not for you, Paco, I wouldn't be alive today. I won't rest until I see you returned safely to your home in Zacatecas."

It was Madelaina's idea, and the others concurred, to take the back road out of Parral. Rather than travel at night, they chose to rest and arise at two in the morning, then take the roads back along the desert toward the Sierra Madre mountains in the direction of the Lomas hacienda. If needed they could pause there to rest and pick up supplies.

Madelaina and Lola sat forward on the uncomfortable hard seat of the creaking wagon, their *rebozos* wrapped tightly about them in the early morning air. The trio said very little in those first hours. Their concentration was directed at spotting possible *bandidos* or worse, Pasquel Orozco's Redflaggers, now the enemy of Pancho Villa and the state.

When Paco first saw both girls dressed so shabbily, he shook his head in wonderment at the difference clothing and cleanliness make in a woman. He watched this redheaded girl, Lola, and the fondness he felt for her grew into desire, despite the constant pain caused by his injuries. *A man will never lose his manliness*, he chuckled to himself, *not when there's a wench such as this around to possess*. Besides, the girl liked him— perhaps more than liked him—no?

He thought about the gringo, Peter Duprez. He liked the man. There was something very masculine about him, a fierceness, a hardness, yet there had been something he'd seen in the man's love for Madelaina—quite unlike that which a Mexican displays in a relationship. They made a good pair these two. It would be interesting what would happen when General Obregon met the gringo. Ayeiii!

488

Paco had learned what Rosalia Quintera had done for both Madelaina and him the night they were possessed. Knowing the ways of his ancestors, Paco felt the worst was over and he hoped it would all end soon. However, Lola, skeptical about his love affair with Dolores Chavez, even hating the sound of her name, wondered about this woman who could possess Paco as she herself had done one night when he was feeling chipper and needed to satisfy his *machismo*. Lola had frolicked with Paco enough to know he was her man. That night she laid claim to him and had no intentions of giving him back to Dolores—especially not Dolores.

At the Lomas *rancho*, they found no one, not even a caretaker. Unsure of what this meant, Madelaina moved rapidly. She shot the lock off the door leading to a hidden cellar stocked with foodstuffs. She and Lola took what provisions they needed, hopefully enough to last two weeks, cast a last look at the place, and took off as quickly as possible, taking the road behind them that led into the mountains. They were high into the hills when they saw the Redflaggers below them, winding their way toward the Lomas *rancho*. The red flag fluttered in the breeze, its bold white lettering reading "Reform—Liberty—Country."

Madelaina had pulled up alongside a few trees and turned back to stare at the activity. Using a pair of field glasses she picked up at the Lomas *rancho*, she focused them on the activity.

"They make themselves at home, no?" she asked Paco, handing him the glasses. Her hidden meaning was sufficient. Lomas was an *Orozquista*!

"As if they knew in advance they must camp there. It doesn't seem possible that Lomas could be a man of such insincerity, but then, *chiquita*, he had fooled us, no?"

Lola's eyes were caught by some activity not far from them, where a scouting party had paused for several moments to inspect the area. "Is best we go," she told her companions. "And go with God's speed. It would do us no good to be caught by either side. Advance, *chica*. We have no other way to go."

Madelaina saw the scouting party in a second. She picked up the reins and moved! They moved as fast as the donkeys would move. She purred to the animals and lashed the whip overhead—making certain it never touched them. How they moved for her. The route was growing thickly wooded and the cool air chilled them despite the hot noon sun they'd just driven through. Paco grabbed a blanket and wrapped himself as best he could. The girls clutched their *rebozos* more firmly about their heads and shoulders. Still the mountain air chilled them. They had ridden for more than four hours, when it dawned on Madelaina that the atmosphere had changed drastically as they followed the winding path leading into the interior. Madelaina's forehead furrowed with deep thought as she glanced about the terrain. Where in Mexico, she wondered, would there be such a climate. The thick undergrowth was the most verdant and luxurious she'd ever seen. It was a primitive jungle, overflowing with exotic tropical flora of all species. Before they were aware of the shadowy, mistlike cloud up ahead of them, they had ridden into its center, into a devastating pocket of bugs, flying insects that attacked them in a violent onslaught.

The women screamed. Lola began swatting at them with her shawl. Madelaina, fighting off the attacking insects that were ravaging them without mercy, was unable to combat the pervasive hordes. There was only one avenue open to her—step up the mules, gather more speed, and ride out the marauding bombardment. The mules, as much victims as the humans, sensed the untenable predicament, broke into a stiff-legged gallop, and managed, after several of the longest moments the girls had ever endured, to outride the holocaust.

Only when they reached a clearing where Madelaina felt it was safe to stop, did she managed to reign back the asses. The girls were in a terrible state. Bitten, eaten alive by the rampaging swarm of flesh-loving

490

bugs, their arms, faces, and necks were bloodied and distended. Paco had escaped most of the assault by covering himself with a blanket.

Lola and Madelaina exchanged pain-filled glances. They knew that something had to be done immediately to relieve the unendurable discomfort, but they felt helpless. It was Lola, the mestizo, who spotted a thick bed of succulents along the wooded path beyond the rocks. She wasted no time in jumping from the wagon. Running toward the boulders, knife in hand, she hacked off the verdant, sizable pods and split them into pieces. Hastily, she rubbed the juices onto her arms, neck, and face, seeking instant relief. The juices turned her skin a dark brown, but in seconds she felt the soothing penetration and refreshing absence of pain.

She called to Madelaina and proceeded to rub the juices on her, sniffing the succulents as she did from time to time with native curiosity. "Perhaps, if we spread this on our bodies," she suggested, "we shall be immune to any further such encounters, *señorita. Dios mios!* What an ambush we ran into!"

Without a moment's hesitation, both girls disrobed and rubbed their bodies with the liquid, staining their skins a dark, berry brown.

"Pray it isn't poisonous," cautioned Paco when they insisted he do the same. As he descended from the wagon, his eyes took in their surroundings with a curious, faraway expression. "*Señorita?*" he addressed himself to Madelaina. "You do not think we may be approaching the land that Francesco Lomas spoke to us about?"

For an instant their eyes met. Then Madelaina, pausing in her work, stood up and gazed around with a similar look of apprehension and expectation in her own dark eyes. "You mean Lago Diablo de Los Muertos?" Half-scoffing, half-believing, she shook her head. "Who could believe anything that seven-tongued viper had to tell us!" She dropped the subject instantly.

Finished with their body staining, the trio commenced their journey into the interior. After two more hours of travel, the terrain began to look suspiciously like the land described by General Lomas to Paco, and Madelaina felt an inner trembling that wouldn't abate. Seeing something which corresponded to Lomas' story, Madelaina would often turn to Paco. Their eyes would meet in silence, neither daring to express their thoughts. Growing more annoyed by these secret looks without knowing their meaning, Lola began to show her disapproval. She was just about to air her indignation when she felt the wagon come to a halt.

Up ahead, several hundred feet beyond a clearing, a scattering of unusual natives, primitive in appearance, caught Madelaina's eyes. She felt for the security of her weapons and alerted the others.

"Perhaps, Paco, the legend might come to life," she said slowly, as her eyes glanced about the scene before them. "Tell me what you make of it."

For some time, Paco had been silently eyeing this wonderland of flora and fauna through the eyes of a skeptic. They had pierced the rugged mountains at dawn of the first morning. By noon they had passed canyons and rested in the shade of a hanging cliff. He noticed the mountains in certain areas were solidified lava, weathered over milleniums into dark brown porous rock. Here and there a few weeds struggled for life. But immediately after the beastly attack of the insects—as if they were some armed guard to protect the entrance to another world—the terrain had changed into one of unbelievable beauty. The farther inland they traveled, the more breathtaking grew the panorama. Perpendicular canyon walls contained fiery colors of every conceivable hue. The bright, dazzling sunlight produced an exquisite jewel-like reflection. The setting was embued with such vibrations, as if it were alive and pulsing with life, that the trio had ridden on in a trancelike state.

Madelaina's question shook Paco from his reverie. He hoisted himself up from the back of the wagon. Stretched out before him he saw a scattering of natives unlike any he'd ever seen in all of Mexico. Their scant attire was unique. The men wore loincloths, and their upper torsos were adorned with silver and jeweled amulets and feathers of rare and exotic birds. The women, in sleeveless, calf-length, buckskin sheaths, and fringed with beading, were reminiscent of northern Indians of Montezuma's day. They wore their hip-length hair straight, banded with beads at their foreheads.

"What can I say, *señorita*?" asked Paco in open-mouthed bewilderment. "I have never seen such a place or a people like them." He studied them quietly. "Look upon their faces, such calming countenances," he observed. "And upon the men, I see no weapons. At least they aren't visible," he added as they drew closer to the village.

Unlike any Mexican village they'd seen, it resembled an ancient Indian village with mud huts and straw roofs where teepees and tents might have once been used. A few women made exquisite pottery at a wheel, turning it by foot and shaping the vessels by hand. Some made leather moccasins. A few wove fabrics on handcrafted looms that were unique and cleverly designed. There were a few women seated in a circle, listening to a white-haired elder instruct them in the craft of lapidary, gem cutting.

To Madelaina it was as if the pages of history had been turned back centuries, a scene from the Incan civilization, combining Aztec, Poltec, Mayan, Yucatan, even Yaqui, into one. But there was more, much more, to stoke their curiosity. Hardly any of the natives looked up from their work to give the newcomers a second glance. Moreover, what Paco observed earlier was apparently true. The men carried no weapons; they all appeared quite pacific in nature.

Madelaina, possessed of an insatiable curiosity, pulled the wagon onto the sands. "We must find out where we are," she told her companions. Lola, filled with apprehension at the sight of such beauty and calm, had been struck silent. She gazed about the area as one in a dream, as if she had been suddenly thrust into a utopian wonderland that her mind, having witnessed no previous blueprint, was incapable of conceiving.

Madelaina stepped boldly off the wagon, gathered her skirts about her, and swept across the path of polished stones where some women were grinding meal on an ancient *metate*. She addressed them in Spanish. The women glanced up at her, smiled shyly, and shook their heads. Lola, moving in behind Madelaina, spoke to them in her mestiza dialect. She also employed a unique sign language of her people, an ancient, seldom used manner of communicating.

One young woman, who looked no older than fourteen, smiled and nodded her head. She spoke in an ancient tongue the trio hadn't heard before, bowed her head, and absented herself from them.

"I think she went to find someone," suggested Lola, fully enchanted with the unusual people and the immaculate cleanliness of the place. She was standing alongside Madelaina, not far from where Paco stood, when suddenly she felt pressure on her arm. Paco had grasped both their arms and whispered in warning. "Don't move. Both of you remain motionless," he added as two sleek jaguars padded silently into the compound.

The animals, at least six feet long, were a golden tan spotted with black, the texture of velvet, with massive heads and bodies and short, thick, muscular legs. With complete command of the area, they didn't appear threatened or challenged. In fact, they seemed at home among humans as were the natives with them.

One of the sleek cats sniffed at Madelaina from a distance of four feet. She looked into his opalescent black eyes. The cat only hesitated a moment, then languidly slithered over to her. Lola and Paco held their breath, not daring to move, yet wanting to warn her to be careful.

"Don't concern yourself," Madelaina quietly told her companions. "A jaguar rarely attacks man." She allowed her hand to move behind the animal's ears to stroke him affectionately.

The young native girl returned, accompanied by what Madelaina felt was the most magnificent man she'd ever seen. He was a tall, muscular man whose body was formed perfectly. His flowing white mane falling below his sun-bronzed shoulders was an incongruity which struck the trio simultaneously. The body and face were far too young for the snowy white hair. He wore a loincloth of soft chamois leather, girded at each side with jewels in the shape of amulets.

Suddenly, without provocation, the second jaguar hissed at Lola. He bared his wet, glistening fangs and stretched his jaws, revealing ugly yellowed teeth. Lola withdrew, sinking against Paco's outstretched arm; the other, still bound tightly, remained immobile in a sling. "Be still," whispered Paco, eyeing the irritated cat.

"I am Tolomeo," said the strapping man whose indescribably beautiful body resembled that of the mythical gods, with rippling muscles and bulging biceps of incredible dimensions. He uttered a few remarks in a language his guests didn't understand. Instantly both jaguars withdrew and moved soundlessly across a small area at the center of the village.

Madelaina became spokesman for her friends. "Tolomeo, I am Madelaina. These are my friends, Paco and Lola. It appears we are lost. We were hoping to reach Sinaloa and travel southward along the coast to Tepic to the land of our people. Where do we find ourselves?"

"You are in the land of Realidad, close to Lago Diablo de Los Muertos, much off the path to your destination. However, since you are incomplete, it is no wonder you've come to us." He spoke gently, in the most wonderful and soothing voice Madelaina had ever heard, using enigmatic words and phrasing.

"Forgive me, *señor*, you speak in riddles. You say we are in the Land of Reality? That we are incomplete?" She looked deeply into Tolomeo's spectacular eyes and felt a stirring in her loins, a rapid beating in her heart.

"When you've cast your eyes upon Lago Diablo de

Los Muertos, the riddles will not confound you." He bowed politely. "You need rest and nourishment. You have traveled far." It was a statement, not a question. He glanced at Paco, at the bound arm, and at the pained expression on the Mexican's face. He moved toward him. "You're in pain. What has happened?" he asked quietly.

"An accident. A gunshot wound. One of those freak accidents that occur from time to time, Señor Tolomeo," interjected Madelaina. *"Es muy mal."*

Tolomeo stood tall, slightly over six feet. The muscles in his forearms and legs looked as if they could crush ten men. His unlined coppery skin was beardless, smooth as a baby's buttocks. On his wrist he wore identical solid silver bands, approximately three inches wide, carved with some ancient hieroglyphics. Around his neck he wore an amulet, shaped much like an Aztec calendar, on a narrow strip of leather. The amulet, slightly larger than a silver dollar, was two-sided and convex. Later they learned the hollowed disc contained ground, dried golden mushrooms at least three years old. His loincloth, woven in the shade of natural beige, was held together by thongs over each hip spaced an inch apart. From these thongs dangled a variety of leather pouches and flacons containing special herbs.

Spectacular as he was in appearance, it was his eyes that held the newcomers spellbound, hypnotizing them, holding them seemingly powerless. His eyes, the color of clear amethysts, a pale lavender with green flecks, alternately changed from a light orchid to a deep purple, the shaded hues of an amethyst twilight.

It appeared that only Lola was in rapport with Tolomeo and this obviously bothered Madelaina. She found him most unusual, someone she wished to explore and pursue. But Tolomeo ignored her, choosing instead to make ovations to Lola and Paco upon whom his interest was focused. Pangs of jealousy shot through the daughter of General Obregon in a way she couldn't understand.

496

Tolomeo extended one arm, indicating he wished them to follow him into a nearby hut. They entered the cool, neatly kept interior which was totally unadorned. "Please be comfortable. If you need anything from your vehicle, our young men will assist you. While that's attended to, may I please see your arm, Paco? Your injury?"

"The wound is serious," spoke up Madelaina in an imperious tone. "Are you a healer—a *curandero*? He needs the professional, expert opinion of a physican."

Tolomeo said nothing. He helped Paco remove his serape and shirt. Slowly, with painstaking effort, he began to unwrap the bindings, layer by layer, until the wound lay bare. Madelaina had moved in close, took one look, sniffed the pungent stench, and averted her head noticeably. Watching her, Paco paled excessively at her reaction. He knew her to be brave of heart and this indication wasn't comforting. Even the look in Lola's eyes, try as she did to conceal it, was revealing of the wound's severity. And if their expressions weren't enough, Paco himself could attest to the excruciating pain and hell he'd endured since the injuries were inflicted.

"Tula," called Tolomeo quietly, summoning the young woman they'd met earlier. She moved soundlessly to his side. Her dark, smoky eyes glanced at the pus-filled, swollen, angry infection that had spread its poison past Paco's elbow clear to his wrist and into his fingers. The arm was nearly twice its usual size. "Bring me the necessary preparations," he instructed gently.

Tula, prepared to do his bidding, hesitated. "It's Navojolla. The cat is restless. His spirit is thinning, Tolomeo," she spoke quietly, looking into his eyes.

Tolomeo turned to Madelaina. "You will not be safe in the same hut with Paco. Go with Tula. She will keep you safe. You must abide carefully by my directives, *señorita*. Do not, I repeat, do not go near the cats. Understand?"

Madelaina's eyes bore into his for several seconds.

"No," she replied. "Since this is your domain, I shall follow your wishes."

Tolomeo nodded curtly. "I can ask for nothing more until I can explain further. I repeat again, *señorita*. Under no circumstances are you to go near the cats—not even an ocelot, if it should appear."

Lola's blue eyes filled with confusion. Deep down inside her, she seemed to know Tolomeo—even though they had never met or known of each other. From the moment they arrived in this strange village, she had the feeling of some mystical experience, something quite rare. Watching Tolomeo as he stroked Paco's arm and muttered incoherent incantations, she was mesmerized. Madelaina had left with Tula. They were alone.

Two young men brought in a table. Paco was ordered to climb upon it and lie down. Overhead was a mobile of three spirals moving in alternate paths.

"Focus your eyes upon the spirals, Paco. Soon your eye will pick out one over the others. Allow your eyes to remain fixed to that particular one and do not take your attention from it. You understand? I will be transmitting my energy to you and soon you will feel no pain. The pain will be gone and all that you felt will flow into my body. Do you believe me?"

Paco nodded almost against his will. His eyes fixed on the others.

"Very well. Take a deep breath." Tolomeo took a small vial from among the items Tula had brought in. He anointed his fingertips and drew an imaginary circle around the wound on Paco's shoulder. "Now, repeat after me: *There is no pain in my body. There is no pain in my body.*"

Paco did as Tolomeo instructed, repeating the statement as many times as requested of him. His eyes stared overhead in the direction of the mobile. First one spiral, then a second and a third shifted into position. Before his eyes, like an optical illusion, the three spirals fused into one.

"Take another deep breath, then push hard in the area of your solar plexus," instructed Tolomeo, touching the area in the upper abdomen. "At the same time, using your powers of imagery, you are to believe that you are pushing the infection and the pain out from your body. Do you understand?"

Lola watched the goings on in utter fascination as Tolomeo massaged the angry and swollen arm, while the incantations progressed. She was startled to see physical changes actually taking place in Tolomeo. She saw them with her own eyes, there could be no doubt. His skin darkened, his left arm began to gradually swell with an apparent infection. She was stunned. Earlier Tula had returned with several bowls containing various potions and herbs on a tray. Several knives of varying shapes and sizes were spread out on a snow white cloth. She had lit a brazier, and when bright orange-red flames shot up into brilliant lights, Tolomeo held a sharp knife over the flame with one hand, while the other, which was swelling rapidly now, firmly held the wrist of Paco's infected arm.

Faster than the eye could see, Tolomeo ran the razor-sharp knife tip expertly around the area of the outer shoulder where pus had turned the skin a gangrenous greenish-yellow. A geyser of pus exploded and overran the sides of Paco's arm, like rivers of molten lava spilling from a fiery volcano. With precise movements, he allowed the pus to drain, then poured the liquid contents of one bowl over the fresh incision. Paco, tempted to remove his eyes from the moving spiral, was softly and encouragingly told to continue the fine job he was doing.

"In a matter of moments it will be over," said Tolomeo. "Do you feel any pain?"

"No, nothing," replied Paco wondrously.

Tolomeo selected a second knife from the collection, held it over the flame, and muttering his incantations, allowed it to turn molten white. This time he worked so swiftly not even Lola realized what he'd done until it was over. He'd cut out a hole approximately a half-inch larger in diameter than the original bullet wound. A cone-shaped, pus-filled corklike piece of tissue popped out and landed on the table. It resembled the root ball of a plant with countless threadlike appendages forming a ganglia of nerve endings. Tolomeo covered it with a cloth.

Instantly he poured the contents of a second bowl over the open wound. Lola would later swear she saw the wound bubble and boil over for several moments. When the aerating properties subsided, Tolomeo applied a thick, yellowish, gooey substance to the open wound and lower incision. He then packed the area with clean green leaves from a plant Lola could neither recognize nor identify, and finally Tula moved in to swathe the arm in clean white strips of material as sheer as onion skin. She worked swiftly, gazing periodically at the swelling on Tolomeo's arm.

All this was done without whiskey, or anesthesia, or drugs, or potions to dull the pain, thought Lola. No one would believe the miracles she'd seen on this day, she told herself. No one, not even Paco. Not even Madelaina! She wondered why Tolomeo hadn't permitted the *señorita* to witness this miracle.

Tolomeo had moved in toward Paco as Tula finished the dressing.

"Paco," he began. "In a few moments, the pain, however slight, will return. It will not be as it was. You will feel only a dullness. I must transfer the pain to its rightful owner since the infection has departed your body." He raised his powerful arm and turned the spiral mobile in the opposite direction. "Now then, Paco, slowly, you'll return to your previous consciousness and awareness. When I count to three, you'll sit up and feel only a slight discomfort. One . . . Two . . . Three."

Oh, the things Lola had seen this day. Miracles on miracles. At the count of three, Paco sat up, completely rid of fever, his arm reduced almost to its original size, and traces of infection totally absent. Paco, with no recollection of what had transpired, knew only that he felt intensely better. He could almost move his arm.

"Paco!" Lola gushed excitedly. "You won't believe

500

what happened!" She turned to Tolomeo. "Oh, *señor, gracias. Gracias!*" She kissed the mystic's hand. Instantly he withdrew it from her lips.

"There's no need for that," he scolded gently. "The things I've done here could be done by any man if he but had the faith to believe in himself."

Lola was woman enough to detect a certain sadness in his voice, but she possessed neither the sophistication nor the knowledge to comprehend the things of which Tolomeo spoke. She grew more baffled when she gazed at his arm and noted the redness, swelling, and momentary discomfort were gone.

As she turned to explain what she'd seen to Paco, a young native boy rushed into the hut to speak to Tolomeo and Tula in words neither she nor Paco understood. One thing they were certain of—it had to do with Madelaina.

When Tolomeo and Tula left the couple, with apologies, Lola lost little time in trying to describe what Tolomeo had done. But if Paco had entertained any doubts about Tolomeo's ability earlier, he'd become a full and devout believer. The excruciating pain which had consumed him the past week was gone. He felt only a dull sensation, as if an army of healers were at work mending his body properly. He was ecstatic. As they spoke of their concern over Madelaina, however, a loud scream pierced the air, shaking the walls of the hut. It was followed by a loud, roaring, animalistic growl.

Alarmed, they left the hut and went in search of Madelaina Obregon.

Outside the hut where Madelaina had been housed, activity ensued. Two young natives, looking more warriorlike than any others, stood guarding either side of the entrance. They were cautioned not to enter the premises by Tula, who employed sign language to convey the directives to Lola. The young corporal and his Lola stood huddled close together, seeing or hearing nothing except the frightening sounds emanating from the hut.

Inside the small enclosure, Navojolla, hissing, baring fangs, and moving with impatient strides from one end of the hut to the other with marked ferocity, stood locked in silent combat with Tolomeo. His slanted cat's eyes, large, black, and glazed, looked upon Tolomeo as his fiercest, deadliest enemy. His huge jaws would open intermittently, and he'd snap viciously at the powerful man who held him at bay through sheer will. A powerful claw with razor-sharp nails reached out savagely and came within inches of Tolomeo's eyes. The cat spit, snarled, and growled angrily at his obstructor who kept him from a delectable feast—the prone figure of Madelaina, lying unconscious on a cot between them.

Tolomeo's smoky purple eyes leveled on the cat as he artfully moved the amulet around his neck to his lips. He tipped it and sprinkled the dried pulverized mass of mushrooms on his tongue. He did all this without disengaging his eyes from the cat.

In a few moments he began to talk with the cat as if it were human.

"I know it is not you, Navojolla. Neither you or Teleco would consider such diabolical depravity. Listen to me, Navojolla. Allow your personality to subside so I can see who is behind the evil who tries to possess the soul of this young woman. Sleep, Navojolla. Listen to Tolomeo. Sleep."

The cat grew languid and its vigor abated. It yawned and lay down. In moments it fell into complete repose. Out of the jaguar came a filmy apparition of mistlike clouds that separated and shifted and kneaded until the figure of Golden Dawn appeared. She faced Tolomeo. Between them Madelaina moved, stirring restlessly, finally sitting up on the cot. She blinked several times, then glancing from one to the other, oblivious that this was a contest to the bitter end over who would possess her soul, she was arrested by the strange powerful emanation that seemed to extend from Tolomeo's luminous eyes. At one point, when Madelaina felt she could no longer breathe, things began to fall away in shifting confusion. Tolomeo's eyes grew more vivid, as if no light in the world could be brighter than that reflected in his eyes. His face and form, lost in shadow, became almost nonexistent as the face and form of Golden Dawn became more prominent. At this point, Madelaina felt as if she were sinking into a black abyss of blood-sucking fluid, as if the very life was draining from her. She felt helpless and became transfixed. Her soul seemed to soar right out of her body like ethereal wisps of transparent silk and hesitate in a fluttering motion before the presence of the powerful sorceress, Golden Dawn, whose outstretched arms with long pointed fingertips awaited greedily like suction cups to draw unto herself these silky wisps emanating from Madelaina.

Renewed mystically by a saturation of fresh energy, Tolomeo obstructed Golden Dawn's progress. The Indian sorceress grew enraged, frustrated, and apparently failed to draw up more energy with which to combat Tolomeo's power. She began to show signs of weakness, a sapping of energy, a fact which enraged her.

Madelaina, fully aware of the inner turmoil and powerful struggle for supremacy between these two sorcerers, was powerless to intervene. Golden Dawn, having met her match, refused to be cowed. Despite her strong determination to emerge victorious, Madelaina could see changes manifesting themselves in the Indian mushroom eater. Golden Dawn withdrew slightly, hands falling limply to her sides, her head drooping slightly like a wilted flower, until she no longer radiated lights from her eyes or energy from her presence. Her vision grew dimmer and retreated, growing smaller and smaller until she evaporated into infinity. The silky wisps of mist, no longer fluttering beyond Madelaina's body, were sucked up in a whooshing sound, returning inside her. Only she and Tolomeo remained in the hut.

Tolomeo, standing rigid and tall with rippling muscles, pulsing and bulging periodically, permitted his supernatural eyes to dim by degrees as he wheeled and cavorted about the interior hut, pausing now and then to cock his head to listen as he suspiciously sniffed the air in the hut.

Watching him, Madelaina's eyes saw all that happened and heard the sounds and felt the enormous power radiated by the two contestants. Yet, more was happening to her. A sense of normality, such as she hadn't felt in many months, was returning to her, an indescribable feeling of contentment and comfort which permeated her being. Now, as if seeing Tolomeo for the first time, her dark lustrous eyes admired his majesty, his posture and body, and his unaffected composure. Something within stirred as it never had in her young life, and she found herself committing to memory all she saw of him.

He had the nose of a bird of prey to give him the expression of primitive fierceness, yet, in his eyes was buried a love such as she'd never experienced or seen in another man. She'd never been taken by the beauty of such a man, and when he moved soundlessly over the earthen-floored hut and lay a lean, hard hand on the head of the reposing jaguar, Navojolla, she was unable to take her eyes from him.

The caressing touch of his hand upon the jaguar awakened the inert cat. Navojolla yawned, his large jaws opened wide, and a deep throaty sound emanated from his throat. He shook himself, stretched his long body, and assumed his former docile manner. He rubbed up against his master, paused a moment to study Madelaina, then turned and indolently sauntered outside.

Tolomeo seated himself on straw mat close to Madelaina and studied her for a time.

Chapter 19

Outside, the frightful heat of the afternoon sun shimmering over the village of adobe and straw huts reflected the beginning of an early fiery-orange and golden sunset. The odors of food cooking over campfires filled the air and Madelaina sniffed hungrily, her appetite stimulated into a ravenous hunger.

She was unable to articulate the many things she wanted to ask this man, for she suddenly felt as young and naïve as a schoolgirl. Thoughts came to her and left as suddenly, leaving her confused and uncertain of everything, including herself. She felt magnetized by the man and was unable to take her eyes from him.

From a small brazier near the mat upon which he sat cross-legged, Tolomeo lit a taper and drew it toward him to light a small hand-carved pipe he'd removed from his loincloth. He finished packing the curious-looking pipe with a powdery substance removed from a pouch and sat back puffing until it was evenly lit. For a time he smoked in silence, inhaling long even breaths from it. His breathing wasn't the normal kind; he gulped at the air as if the very act of intake invigorated him and replenished a diminishing supply of energy. It wasn't until Tolomeo concluded the ritual that he spoke.

He handed her the pipe, suggesting that she inhale the substance. Hesitant at first, she threw caution to the winds. Hadn't he proven himself no enemy?

The taste of peyote wasn't new to her, yet the smoke contained something more, something like the taste of a heavy cigar. It left a more than usual bitter taste in her mouth and she made an appropriate facial grimace. Tolomeo smiled.

"The taste will pass. The first is always the worst. It is necessary, however, that you inhale the essence, since you've been through a terrible ordeal. It was an ordeal which you must guard against as long as you live," he spoke soberly with a deep resonant voice which commanded her to listen.

"Your soul, Madelaina, is impressionable, too trusting and without guile. It is necessary that you protect it at all costs. You must never permit another steeped in the knowledge of soul taking to entice it again. Awareness—constant awareness—shall be your only ally, your only defense against such possible invasion."

She shook her head. "I don't understand a word you're saying, Tolomeo," she told him, watching the amber-colored lights slant through the hut's opening. The flaps usually covering the opening had been folded back and the lights permeating the interior were almost hypnotic—or else she was beginning to feel the essence of the pipe she smoke, she told herself. The spectre of her earlier hunger vanished, replaced by the feeling of contentment flowing through her body.

"Are you aware you've been the victim of spiritual possession? You and this man, Paco, were subjected to the wrath of an evil *bruja*. Fortunately for both of you, her work was greatly hampered by what the mestiza, Rosalia, did for you."

"How do you know about Rosalia?" asked Madelaina in total bewilderment.

"Simple. I saw it."

Madelaina stared at him, incredible amazement in her eyes. Still, she wasn't too taken aback. "Then, it's true. Such things can happen? Raised by the holy fathers and sainted sisters to frown on all this primitive mumbo jumbo, you can see it isn't easy for me to put credence into such mysterious ways of your people."

"You saw what happened here moments ago. You know such a person—Golden Dawn?"

She nodded. "Yes." Madelaina once again accepted the pipe, inhaled twice more, and returned it. "No more, thank you. I am experiencing strange things

506

within my body and mind." She held up a restraining hand.

"Because you are still vulnerable to Golden Dawn's sorcery. Only when you fully experience Lago Diablo de Los Muertos will the spell be broken. By then, you'll have learned not to make yourself vulnerable. You'll sense an inner power that will protect you from ever falling slave to any man. A fearlessness will manifest itself in you to take you through this earthly journey unscathed."

As Madelaina studied this magnificent man, a thousand questions formed on her lips. Who was Tolomeo? From where did he come? Why did he content himself to live in the wilderness? He wasn't the usual tribal Indian. His vocabulary, his command of so many languages, and more important, his command of himself intrigued her. He was an enigma to her. Oh, there was so much she wanted to know. Why had he troubled himself with her? The questions wouldn't articulate themselves into words. She seemed powerless to speak out as a self-consciousness gripped her.

"Madelaina." He addressed her sternly as if he read her mind. "You look upon me as a man. Because you do, you'll not learn what I must teach you."

Madelaina lowered her eyes, a flush moved like a wave to bring color to her cheeks. "But you are a man. And I'm a woman. Can you deny this?"

"There is nothing to deny. You are interested only in externals. I gaze upon the internal spirit, the power that allows you to look upon things as they really are—not as they may appear."

"Tolomeo. You speak in riddles. Truly, I understand none of this."

"The answer to a riddle is always obvious. You are not trained to perceive them as readily as I am. You will, soon enough. And when you do, there will be no deception your eyes can't perceive. When you can truly perceive truth—not the illusion with which man deludes himself—only then will you attain the strength needed to protect you in this lifetime. There'll come upon you an inner awareness that you'll perceive as truth—a truth you'll not be able to deny. Once you've seen the light, falsity, like darkness, will weigh like an anchor. You'll know the difference."

"And this truth will protect me? It will make me strong and not subject to the whims and caprices of another? Surely you aren't speaking of will power?"

He smiled indulgently. "Will power is the opposite of won't power. Both are controlled by the vain imaginings of man—not truth. Can you see the difference?"

"I—I think so. No. I don't know." Madelaina grew ambivalent. "I'm overwhelmed by what's happened to me on this day. It's extraordinary to say the least. Yet, I ask myself, why you, with the powers you have, aren't in a place closer to civilization where you could help humanity?

"Whoever needs me will find me, just as you and Paco have done. You could have traveled no farther in your condition without dire consequences. You came to me out of tremendous need. You found me because you had to find me."

Madelaina concurred, even though she was still confused. "But aren't there others with such needs at opposite ends of the world?"

"Those in dire need will find their Tolomeos, just as you did. And that reminds me, child, I must caution you not to reveal my whereabouts, you understand?"

Madelaina nodded. The serious expression on his face touched her to make a solemn oath never to speak of him in the outside world. But there was more.

She began to feel an enormous physical attraction to this man who sat before her like a rajah, and she filled with embarrassment and a peculiar humility that she gazed upon him with carnal desires. She felt a tinge of jealousy toward Tula and the way the young girl moved in and out of the hut as if she belonged to Tolomeo. She saw none of the usual telltale glances pass between them, yet something about the intimacy of their relationship ruffled her feathers.

Tolomeo smiled at her with tolerant understanding.

"Perhaps when you are fully complete, we shall couple, if it stirs you to such impatience," he said with such overt politeness it fairly offended the wife of Peter Duprez.

About to protest, she realized the futility of any such expostulation, for this sorcerer could read her inner thoughts as if they were scrawled out before him on tablets. She blushed, and although she felt perturbed that he had such powers, she was exquisitely pleased at the promise he made so easily.

They spoke for some time. Tolomeo told her he'd left the outer world because he'd observed the needless pain, suffering, privation, and uncertainty, the hardship and struggle with which men needlessly burdened themselves. Unable to assist his fellowman in the achievement of a more perfect life, he and a small band of followers traveled for months, years, until they happened upon this isolated land where few men have traveled. "Here in this marvelous land of beauty and enchantment we've found the way of life to which we are dedicated."

He explained to Madelaina that he was like a watchful eagle. That people like Golden Dawn could easily turn into birds, night owls, and often employed mountain lions and jaguars in which to materialize to lure their prey, so that at the very moment they weren't guarding their souls, it could easily pass on to them. "Most people would be too frightened to contest a jaguar like Navojolla," said Tolomeo thoughtfully. He rose to his feet, extended his hand to her. "I want you to come with me now."

Outside, the dazzling sunset was settling into vibrant amethysts. Two fine and magnificent horses, the color of smoky pearl, readied by Tula, stood patiently nearby. Tolomeo sprang to his stallion and Madelaina expertly mounted the other, barebacked. Tolomeo nosed the stallion out past the village and motioned her to follow.

They rode like the wind for several moments, swift and silent through the canyon until they reached the

5

desert, where the bloodred lights of a dying sun transformed the desert into a wonderland. Huge boulders, black as ebony, crusted with prophyritic sparks, scattered at either side of them as they climbed the steep ravine, created the most spectacular panorama Madelaina had ever seen. They stopped the horses at the edge of the ledge overlooking what to the young Spanish woman seemed like another world, unlike anything she'd seen in her travels. Her eyes gazed slowly around her.

Angled pillars of stone jutted skyward like the ruined gateways to an ancient temple. They had encountered no living person or creature in this blazing universe of red fire and black boulders, sparkling deep purple and crimson earth, and frightful loneliness. She became appalled at the limitless fiery sky and limitless ruined earth imbued with the supernatural lights of hell and unshaking silence of death. Once past the Inca, Aztec, and Poltemic styled ruins, past the slight rise of a shallow terrace, Tolomeo pointed to an unearthly scene below them.

A great misty lake, shadowy blue and violet, lay in a sunken valley, floating cool and lost, catching no flaming lights from heaven. Its waters were as fixed as shadow-filled glass, its shores outlined nebulously. Madelaina felt something terrible in the aspect of remote, motionless water seemingly untouched by man, like a dream in a fiery twilight. Immobile, yet drifting, it seemed within her grasp, then, many miles away, deepening and paling in its hues of murky purple and dulled jade.

Madelaina gazed in awed silence at this magnificent creation of nature, feeling as she did a terrible compulsion to ride down into the valley and fling herself into its cool, calming waters. Sensing her disquiet, an impatient need to satisfy her insatiable thirst for beauty, Tolomeo laid a hand on her horse's bridle, staying her. "It is useless for you to go down there, Madelaina. The lake is not real. The entire scene is but a mirage, like a dream. It appears shortly after sunset transforms itself into twilight, each day, in this very place, unchanging. Men call it Lago Diablo de Los Muertos, a lake cursed by Lucifer. Many men have lost their lives seeking to approach it. During the day, when the sun basks at its zenith, there is nothing but gray, sun-bleached dust, strewn with gray, lifeless stones amd the sun-bleached skeletons of an era passed."

"No," cried Madelaina, uttering a strangled cry of disbelief. "With my own eyes I see it. Can I no longer trust my eyes? I don't believe you. It's real, I tell you—real!"

Tolomeo, a black silhouette against a luminous sky of purple fire, shook his head. "It is merely an illusion. Legend claims once a lake did exist, nestled in a valley of the ancient civilizations, the many forerunners of Montezuma. This is but a ghost of that lake, a lingering evil illusion painted into the landscape by Mephistophles, luring men who pursue the visions to their death."

Stunned, outraged, and impassioned beyond her normal limitations, Madelaina slid off the pearl white mare, and moving closer to the ledge, she felt an irresistible compulsion to descend upon the lake, regardless of Tolomeo's warnings. The mare, with its pink velvet nostrils and candy-glazed eyes, bobbed its head from side to side and whinnied as it moved in closer to the stallion.

Tolomeo slipped off the stallion's back and moved silently behind the girl, unnoticed. Madelaina was so overwhelmed at the deception of the lake that she wept.

Darkness fell upon the earth like the vast lowering of a midnight curtain. Peering over the next ridge, a colossal moon crept boldly into view, illuminating the earth. Stars blinked awake until one by one the entire ceiling of sky was ablaze with crystals of light. Tolomeo's manly smell wafted to her nostrils, and she sensed his presence until the fine hairs on her neck and arms stood up.

Strange, thought Madelaina. In all the time she'd

511

been here in Tolomeo's land, she hadn't thought of Peter Duprez until this very moment. It was only a fleeting thought, so swift it came like a whisper on the wind and lasted less than a second.

Tolomeo took her small hand in his and led her along the ridge, as their horses sauntered along behind them. They descended a slight embankment along the ravine, making their way to another spectacular sight of nature. Some fifty yards ahead of them was a waterfall. Incredible. A waterfall in a mountainous, desert region in the bowels of a land she never knew existed? Was it to be believed?

"Is this also a mirage?" she asked with abated sadness.

"This is no mirage," he replied. "At times I'm given to such thoughts."

The moonlight filtering through the wooded area reflecting upon the waters resembled liquid silver as it cascaded from the upper regions and fell into a frothy pool of midnight blue water. Tolomeo pulled her gently onto the mossy bank that smelled as sweet as clover.

The excitement and thrills coursing through Madelaina's body were indescribable. She felt high on peyote, with the scintillating relaxation brought on by marijuana, combined with the vigorous feeling of an overwhelming love such as she'd never experienced. For a time they looked into each other's eyes as Tolomeo held her hand, stroking it lightly with a feathery touch.

His eyes made the kind of love to her she'd dreamed of experiencing. What next, she wondered. How much more electrifying would their physical contact be? Just seated next to him, his magnetic orchid eyes looking into hers, she must have experienced a half-dozen orgasms—or something resembling such phenomenon. The urgency of burning physical desire set her on fire.

Was this love at its most sublime stage? Was this the love as provided by the Lord in the rapturous Garden of Eden? She attempted to think, but was unable to accomplish anything. She only knew she was his at this

512

moment, at this place in time. She could belong to none other.

Madelaina was in love as she'd never before experienced it. Tolomeo slowly removed her clothing, which she permitted without protest, without shame. When she was completely naked, he picked up her sun-kissed body in his powerful arms and walked with her into the crystal pool, where he kissed her, gently at first, then with increasing fervor. Somewhere, somehow, at some time, he'd shed himself of his loincloth. Now, in the tepid water which soothed and comforted them, he entered her body and Madelaina moaned in ecstasy.

Her head fell back; her dark hair fanned on the water's surface like wisps of black lace; her neck, a graceful curve of ivory satin, reflected in the moonlight. Her body grew electric, sparking at every pulse point and she clung to him breathlessly, growing more passionate with each thrust of his body.

"I love you," she said almost against her will. "I love you. Sweet, sweet Jesus!" she exclaimed. "Never have I experienced such emotion, such love! Speak the word, Tolomeo, and I shall remain with you until my last dying breath." Madelaina's body quivered and trembled with sensations.

Tolomeo heaved her up out of the water and carried her to the mossy embankment, where he lay her clinging body on a slightly rounded knoll. He kissed her lightly with open, wet, inviting lips. His hands artfully caressed her body until it quivered like a field of heather in a light wind. Her body involuntarily jerked from one erotic sensation to the next in a ripple of perpetual spasms that refused to cease. When he touched her, the stimulation was almost unendurable. If he breathed on her neck or ears or lay his cool wet face on her bosoms, she writhed in exquisite pain and sublime pleasure. To Madelaina, Tolomeo was agony and ecstasy all in one. Time had no meaning. She couldn't begin to estimate how long they'd been together, making love, fulfilling the other's needs until she saw a rosy hue in the eastern sky marking predawn lights.

She had awakened in his arms, feeling neither the cool morning air or the need to cover herself. She was in paradise. She never wanted to leave. No other thoughts wafted into her consciousness except for their togetherness. Nothing existed beyond this moment. She wanted nothing else. Her eyes devoured his strong, godlike body. Slowly, she reached out to touch him, feel his warm exciting skin, and she felt a warmth of honey spill between her legs. Her dark eyes, fluttering in ecstasy, opened wider until she noticed Tolomeo's compellingly majestic eyes, which seemed to contain the wisdom of the universe, were fixed smilingly on hers.

She smiled secretly like a child caught doing something rather scandalous. Then she raised her head and pressed a wet kiss on his full lips. He kissed her back until Madelaina moaned and surrendered herself in total submission. She wanted to savor each moment, make them continue for all eternity. Orgasm after orgasm shook her body. She experienced the completeness of woman as Aphrodite might have felt it—as Venus and all the goddesses of love. No one could be as complete as she.

From nowhere, it seemed, Tolomeo produced a slender knife with a two-sided blade. He held it firmly in his hand, inches from her face, to make certain she wouldn't miss seeing it. An inscrutable shadow fell across his face as he contemplated her. Startled, Madelaina escaped his arms and sat up, her long hair spilling over her shoulders, her exotic eyes filled with alarm and uncertainty.

"What will you say, Madelaina, if I severed my phallus?" he asked quietly.

"Y—you wouldn't!" she stammered. "You can't! Oh, Tolomeo, what on earth for?" Her hands flew to her mouth, a look of utter horror frozen on her face.

"Would you still love me as you professed to love me last night? Would you still remain with me until death as you insisted?"

514

"I'm not sure I understand. Why are you confounding me? I'm bewildered."

"Answer me, woman. Will you love me if I can no longer couple with you?"

"What you ask is unfair. I don't know." She grew nervous and edgy, never thinking for a moment he wouldn't plunge a knife in his life-giving loins.

"Ah, then you don't love me. You love my sexual organs. Good, then I shall cut them off and give them to you so you can take them with you—to love evermore."

"No!" she screamed. "That's not true. I love you—all of you! Oh my God, I don't know what you expect of me!" she wailed, wringing her hands, glancing about the wooded area for some means of escape.

Tolomeo tossed the blade onto the ground next to him. His gentle eyes filled with infinitesimal lights. "You are living in a world where man is unpredictable. Animals are predictable. Birds, also predictable. Man, unfortunately, hasn't evolved to the plane of predictability, therefore you must be on your guard and learn to evaluate the real from the imaginary, the important from the unimportant. You must perceive everything and look at very little. Last night I made love to you. Before I even entered your body, you experienced countless orgasms; therefore, you don't need my body to achieve this. For many hours we were one, on a mental plane where all is perfection. Now, I ask you again, explicitly: If you were never again to experience physical expression, the coupling of two bodies in sexual embrace, could you exist and not make it your god? Could you live without the feel and touch of a man's penis?" He pressed.

"No, I couldn't live like that."

"There's a man in your life, your husband."

"But how did you know?" Her eyes widened in astonishment.

Ignoring her question, Tolomeo continued. "If this man were to cease loving you sexually, would this fact diminish your love for him?"

Thoroughly confused, Madelaina faltered. "I tell you I don't know. I've never given it thought. It's too much a part of life—of everything. I'd want to love him with my entire body and soul. Oh, Tolomeo, why do you torture me so? What has all this to do with the development of my strength against an onslaught of unsuspected *brujas*—witches?"

"Simply this. You must conquer all physical urges before you can conquer the mind. If you do not control your body and your mind and your passions, there is no hope against someone like Golden Dawn—or your father—or your enemies."

Madelaina glanced at him sharply as things in her mind fell into chaos and more confusion. She shivered noticeably as a chill coursed through her naked body.

"Put on your clothing, child," he said softly. "Soon you'll be thrust back into the earthly reality for which you must prepare." His voice, so beautiful and strong, so unbearably sweet, clutched at her heartstrings.

Madelaina did his bidding, but she wanted to fling herself back into his arms to recreate the previous night of bliss. Why couldn't she live suspended in time as she had the previous night? She stepped into her peasant skirt, pulled the *camisa* over her head, and tucked it inside the skirt. She sat down again, close to him, as countless changes occurred in her. Something stirred in her.

She drew her legs up to her chin, hunched over, and glanced into Tolomeo's face. Oddly enough, her eyes focused on nothing external; they focused inward on something she felt instinctively was more important than anything she'd ever encountered. Afflicted by a sharp clarity of perception, she closed her eyes, dropped her forehead on her knees, and concentrated on the inner scenes forming in her mind.

The feeling of belonging to part of the universe prevailed. She wasn't a separate entity; she was a part of the whole scheme of things. She'd never given such matters any thought and wasn't certain why it should be in her mind at this time. Yet she was overcome with an immense feeling of detachment, as if she were on the outside of the world looking in, seeing those things which made up Madelaina Obregon. As she viewed herself from this new perspective, she heard Tolomeo speaking softly, in a hypnotic, suggestive voice, which she heard with every one of her senses.

"Knowledge to most men is frightening. Few like changes in their lives. They feel confident and content in an old rut, in the role they've played their entire life. With this special knowledge, Madelaina, the ordinary world will appear mundane. You might feel more special than anyone else. You must guard against this vanity as you guard against letting anyone possess your soul. Know fully that you'll be contested every inch of the way by well-wishers, those who desire for selfish reasons to detain you, and by those who wish to harm you. You must be keenly aware of all obstacles thrown in your path and never allow fear in any shape, manner, or configuration to enter your consciousness."

Tolomeo paused a moment and studied her posture. His hand reached out to touch her but he forced himself not to. "You must remained detached from the world if you wish to understand its riddles. To be detached doesn't mean you must give up living, or go into retreat, or fear the shadow of your own soul.

"On the contrary, you must acquire a natural lust for life—which you have to a great degree—and an awareness of man's natural powers. You must be master at decisiveness, master of your choices. Choice, your sole responsibility, is the only freedom man can express. Once your choice or decision is made, there's no time left for regret or recrimination. They must be final or death will stalk you in countless ways, leaving you no time for attachment to anything. And so, it is with an awareness of death, a needed detachment, and an inner power of self-determination, you can begin life with strategy—with a certain cleverness needed to guide you.

"Let me repeat, Madelaina, so there's no confusion in your mind. The inevitability of your death guides you into necessary detachment and a silent lust for life. The power of making final decisions allows you to choose without regrets, for what you choose is always best for you at your level of consciousness, therefore you'll live with gusto and a lusty efficiency. Above all, you must be patient. When you've learned to see within yourself, the secret to all life and knowledge will reveal itself to you. And if your life is beset with complications, you must take every precaution to rid yourself of those tentacles which rob your peace of mind. So, you must rearrange your life, knowing your first obligation is to yourself—none other."

Madelaina stirred at these words. The guilt she felt over the estrangement with her father had stifled her, preventing her from drawing a free breath for too long. She hadn't been aware that her relationship to him had actually motivated her entire life—until this moment. Having been coerced into living his way of life, the Spanish life of a young, highborn woman, she had every reason to feel incomplete, she told Tolomeo. "How can I think one way, feel another, and expect to be a whole person when my actions negate all three?"

He explained. "You've cut your father loose physically but not mentally. You can never hope for the ideal of self-expression, for you are tearing yourself apart."

His words brought on a terrible melancholy, and Madelaina began to sob. Tears streamed down her face and loneliness engulfed her. Watching her, Tolomeo said nothing to comfort her. In moments the tears were gone. She sat up, arched her back for a second, then fell once again into the attitude of repose she'd assumed earlier.

"Tell me the colors you see in your mind," commanded Tolomeo.

"Green, dark green. No, it grows lighter and lighter, nearly a lime green. No, it's a pale green. Now there's purple—orchids and pale greens and bright yellows. Yes, a golden yellow—lighter, brighter than the shade of a pale gold."

Madelaina rambled. "It's growing lighter, almost white now." She averted her head, eyes closed, as if she focused on a light of super-bright intensity. "It's too bright—I can't focus on it."

"You must—you will. Stay with it and when it shifts, tell me what you see."

"Clouds—like cotton. Bouncing along the sky." She stopped. "I see—I see—" Madelaina gasped. "I see Peter. He's lying in a pool of blood. He's dying, I think. I can't stand it! I want to open my eyes. I don't want to look upon any of this."

"Now tell me what you see," said Tolomeo calmly.

"Men fighting. War! War!" Her voice cracked and grew harsh and filled with venom. "I see General Huerta and Major Salomon!" She grimaced with hatred and vengeance.

"What else do you see?"

"I see a murky red, a dull crimson, deep brown, and black surrounding the bodies of these men, my enemies," she said with a hate-contorted face.

"Now concentrate on them until they dissolve of themselves, and in so doing, admit to yourself they are no longer your enemies. They have no control over you. You must view them with detachment. Your hatred is the fuel they use to control you and bring havoc into your life. Only enemies have power to destroy you. Do you understand?"

An internal struggle commenced within the girl. She wanted to understand, but didn't. There was no way she could remove the hatred she felt for either of these men, her mortal enemies. The struggle grew to sizable proportions, causing her to break into a cold sweat and shake as if afflicted with epilepsy.

"Remove the hatred from your heart. Say to yourself, 'They have no power over me. I am unaffected by their deeds. They have no power over me.' Set them free, Madelaina, in your mind. Only then will you be free of their influence. Set them free—set them free. Absolve them of all their crimes and sins against you," commanded Tolomeo firmly.

Madelaina's body shook and trembled with visible spasms. The internal battle raged for several moments, fighting Tolomeo's suggestions every inch of the way. From the loincloth's belt, Tolomeo removed a small silver flask, the size of perfume flacon. He tipped it to the tip of his tongue, then leaned in toward the resisting figure of the girl. He forced a drop onto her tongue and lay her sagging head back against his inner arm, keeping it there for a moment. Then he allowed it to sag forward into the original position.

Madelaina fought a valiant battle against his suggestion for as long as she could until her resolve dissolved. Consciously, she told herself, she could never forgive Huerta or Salomon. She could never erase all the hatred she felt for those despicable devils. At some time in this mind-bending experience, she suddenly realized that for as long as she was affected by their deeds, she'd forever be in their power. It was hard for her to understand Tolomeo's instructions to free them from her mind. The key words for her became: "The chains that bind you are the chains that will free you. Understand that and detachment will follow in a natural course."

The chains that bind you are the chains that will free you. Over and over and over again she repeated those words. She almost came to life thinking she understood totally what Tolomeo meant. Then he dropped the next bombshell.

"Forgive them. Forgive both Huerta and Salomon and any enemy who may have wronged you. Forgive them in your heart, and you'll never see in them an enemy."

Once again her face contorted with hatred and violent emotion. "No!" she screamed, trying to reject his words. "No! I can't forgive them. I won't. If you knew what they did to me, you wouldn't ask such a thing of me. No, I say!" She protested loudly with uncoordinated movements and the facial gestures of one possessed by fiends.

"And I say yes. A thousand times yes. You must

forgive your enemies—or you'll never know a moment's peace. You must also forgive Golden Dawn. You hear? Believing in their evil gives them power. You must release their power from your mind!" commanded Tolomeo authoritatively.

She fought him with trembling lips and twitching facial muscles, wringing her hands together as if she intended to clutch the skin from them. "F—forgive? For—give?" She resisted his commands formidably. "Never!"

"And your father! You must forgive him above all!"

Madelaina's face paled. She jerked and twisted convulsively. "Nooooo!"

"Picture them in your mind, all four of them: Huerta, Salomon, your father, Golden Dawn," commanded Tolomeo gently, then he repeated himself in a firmer tone, more paternalistic. "Do as I say! If you wish to be rid of them forever, forgive them, Madelaina—or you'll never see Peter Duprez again."

Tolomeo removed another pouch from the chamois bag on his loincloth. He spread some powder over Madelaina's navel and rubbed it in a semicircular motion, extending for two inches beyond its diameter. It left a slight ashy residue.

For several moments longer, Madelaina resisted, then she succumbed as if against her will. She began to nod her head, bobbing it up and down slowly.

"I forgive them. I forgive them for all their savagery, their unendurable torture, and the torments inflicted upon me. You, Vitoriano Huerta. You, Simon Salomon. And you, Golden Dawn. All who have seen fit to torture me and use me as a means to your own evil ends, I forgive you with all my heart. You have no power over me . . . no power over me . . . none whatsoever . . ." She repeated after Tolomeo's voice again and again. Finally, she added, "You, too, Papa, I forgive."

Watching her face and body inscrutably, Tolomeo, for the first time in this full day's work with Madelaina, began to relax. A remarkable change came over her face. The strain and worry lines melted away, and she

521

relaxed. She had been through enough for now, Tolomeo told her.

"At any time you wish to open your eyes to join me, you may do so. You've made remarkable progress."

Her thoughts were clear now. She no longer experienced fatigue, drowsiness, or the uneasy sensation in her stomach which promoted an anxious state. She was ravenous and told him so. "After all, Tolomeo, we haven't eaten in a full day and night, have we?"

"It would be impossible to experience miracles so soon," he said, smiling tolerantly as he watched her rise to her feet and walk to the water's edge.

"May we jump into the pool again?" she asked rapturously. "It was such a magnificent experience, I never wish to forget it."

"Of course."

She skipped into the water and fell in with the gaiety of a child. "Come in, Tolomeo," she called. "It's even better than last night."

Tolomeo carefully removed his loincloth and lay it on the bank next to her clothing. Before he entered the sparkling crystal pool of blue water, he touched his amulet to his lips, allowing the dried mushroom powder to spill on his tongue. He recapped the amulet and joined Madelaina in the pool.

For a time they laughed and played and splashed, filled with the playfulness of children. They swam the length of the lagoon and back several times. At one point, Madelaina paused to ask, "What lies beyond the waterfall, Tolomeo?" She swam away from him before he could reply. Catching sight of her direction, Tolomeo dove beneath the waters and, with sure, swift strokes, caught up to her just before she caught sight of the underwater grotto.

He grasped her feet and for a time they both submerged; she, thinking it was a game, and he, fearful she'd see the intriguing world beneath the water and demand to explore it. At this stage, Tolomeo was afraid to rush the truth, sure she couldn't handle it.

His powerful arms reached out to encircle her body

until she lay against his chest as they surfaced, kissing passionately. They tread water a little longer as he steered her into the shallows, where he kissed her with more fervor until she became vulnerable to his love. Tolomeo returned her kisses with increased passion, when suddenly he stopped, his will somewhat shattered.

"You didn't answer me," she purred softly, snuggling in his arms as they lay on the moss embankment. "What's beyond the waterfall?"

"The waters of absolute truth," he replied cryptically.

"Oh, Tolomeo, don't you ever relax? I don't want to think of anything but absolute love, like this," she teased.

For the next several hours or more—Madelaina couldn't tell how long they were there since time seemed to stop for them—they engaged in lovemaking more exciting and fulfilling than their previous encounter. They lay side by side, the warmth of their bodies generating an excitement that dulled any outside cares. They hardly moved, his face next to hers, his body wrapped around her, his hot breath on her neck, her lips, her breasts until she could no longer endure the exquisite and rapturous pain.

"Look into my eyes, beloved," he whispered. "I will stand long where you leave me, the countless days and nights passing with the tedium of a turtle returning to his burial grounds. You've been total in my eyes, indelible in my soul, and will remain with me in each passing face I see. My world has become more magnified. The stars, moon, and skies have never been as beautiful, more alive, and all of nature has become a blanket of jewels in which we wrapped ourselves so greedily." Tolomeo turned her face toward him and silenced her lips with his fingers. "No, listen. How easy it would be for me to say, stay here with me. Stay with me and be my love and we will love forever—"

"Tolomeo—" She wanted to protest, to assure him she'd stay.

He shushed her tenderly and continued. "Soon you will leave my world. And I, who will never be the same since we've touched, must exercise my will, beloved, and thrust you from me. All the things you will be one day, you will be because my love is like the magic touch of heaven, if you will but let me whisper to you and you hear my voice. You will wear my love and my strength, and all those who gaze upon you will know you've been touched by something special—something quite magic. Allow me to work through you, Madelaina, my beloved, and you shall never be alone." He smoothed her wet hair off her face and pressed his moist lips lightly on her forehead, nose, cheeks, and lips, until her body shivered involuntarily.

Tolomeo continued. "And I, beloved, shall be forever a part of you. Although I must forget you to preserve my sanity, visions of your naked body, bronzed by the sun's kisses, lying next to mine as we both soared into eternity, shall fade as all things fade in time. The excitement I've felt with you has been unique—unlike any earthly experience. It is for this I must help you depart. It would be wrong to entice you to stay here. Your destiny lies out in the world beyond Lago Diablo de Los Muertos, where a life awaits you, one which must be lived as only you can live it. While you are here, you will remember me and my teachings vividly. When you venture forth into the outer world, visions of me will fade, but my teachings will remain, deeply implanted in your sub-conscious mind.

"I will make love to you once again—for the final time. Shortly, the time of separation will form an invisible barrier between us. You will remember me only whenever you need my help—not too often, for then you'll not have learned to depend upon your own reserves. When the first star falls, you will depart."

Madelaina heard him and understood every word he spoke with extraordinary clarity. However, something deep inside her, try as it did to resist his words, was unable to do her bidding. She fell into a golden fog of euphoria, into the rapture of a sexual love of such pleasure and erotica that nothing else mattered except what she felt and experienced in these next few moments. She had been looking with torrid intensity into his jeweled eyes. For a time she felt as if she had entered his body through his eyes and now lay curled inside him, forever and through all eternity a part of him. Every touch of his fingers upon her passionate flesh was like an electric impulse of scintillating pleasure to her brain, like the ripples that move outward from a central point when a stone has been hurled into a pool of water. Her entire body became effervescent with bubbles which moved only upon his touch and from time to time burst into tiny explosions of ecstasy in her brain.

She tried to talk, to tell him how breathless and love-filled he made her, but Tolomeo whispered, "Hush, my love, please don't speak. Words are superfluous. Just feel and let your senses do the rest. The time is short."

She could only nod. Tiny bubbles came into her field of inner vision, bubbles that looked like golden teardrops, and she watched them mushroom and multiply and disintegrate and shift in and out of her mind. She saw a series of pictures now, a hacienda in a strange land, unfamiliar to her, except for a brand, an insignia of sorts, that hung over an entrance leading to the property. Madelaina tried to erase these pictures; she wanted nothing to interfere in her interlude with Tolomeo.

Once or twice she shook her head in an effort to rid herself of the unusual pictures. But the pictures persisted. A face out of her past appeared, the face of Manuelito Perez. He stood in an arena, a plaza de toros, strutting and prancing before the *aficionados*, completely oblivious of the dangers that stalked him. He had just finished performing a superb *verónica*, and he turned to the crowds for their cheers. He failed to see the bull turn and charge. The next thing Madelaina saw was Manuelito's body hurled into the air, gored through the left thigh with the bull's horn. He was impaled against the animal's horn for several moments before he was dislodged and his seconds rushed in to attract the beast. The picture faded. Madelaina broke into a cold sweat. She cried out, "No!"

Tolomeo loomed over her, ready to penetrate her body. Her eyes snapped open and in them he saw the truth. "Shall I stop now, *señorita*?"

"No. Please. Let me experience the joy of our final journey into ecstasy," she begged deliriously. "Please, Tolomeo."

"It will make no difference," he said somewhat sadly. "You will not recall the joy for long. A star is about to fall. Soon your dreams will be different."

"Please, my sweet, sweet love," she silenced him. "Don't remind me that I must soon walk alone again. Already I feel you slipping from my embrace, and I'm frightened." She clutched at him as if she were taking her dying breath. "Oh, Tolomeo, you're the essence of life, beauty, the pleasure of all joys. Before distance widens beyond our reach and sight, hold me close, that the gods in heaven may see us and allow us more time. You are what every woman needs to make them complete. If only I could have been more meaningful to you." She sighed sadly. "I see now it could never be." Their strength was waning.

"The pity of it is, I exist in every man and woman, if they'd only look for me."

She stroked his silver white hair as if it were precious. "Will we see each other again, Tolomeo? Perhaps one day, I can return—?" Madelaina shuddered. She reached to him and clinging passionately to him, rained kisses all over his face, arousal once again seeking release in her loins. "Tolomeo, Tolomeo," she purred.

They kissed and walked naked into the clear crystal lagoon, leaving their bodies like old clothes on the shore.

"Madelaina! Madelaina! Oh, *señorita*, please awaken." It was the mestiza, Lola, shaking her shoulders, hoping to arouse her. "You've been asleep for four days! *Dios mios*! Is that all you know to do—sleep?" she asked, recalling vividly the incident in Parral when Madelaina slept for so long.

She sat up on the straw bedding stretched out on the floor of the hut and yawned lazily. Glancing at Lola, she smiled. "Four days?" She yawned again and stretched her arms and arched her back. "*Muy bueno*, it's time we return to our original destination, no?"

Lola sat down on the floor next to her. "*Señorita*, many things have happened to Paco and me since we've spent some time in this crazy place. To begin with, we are in love. We wish to get married, find us a small house to live in, and raise babies. You think your father, the general, would permit such a thing? Must Paco stay in the army and run the risks of getting killed or shot up again?"

"How is Paco?" asked Madelaina. "His arm—is it any better?"

"Like new, *señorita*." She nodded insistently and crossed herself at the sharp look she received from Madelaina. "I swear on the Blessed Virgin de Guadelupe, he is feeling like new! There is something magic about these people," she exclaimed in an almost frightened manner. "This Tolomeo is *muy magnifico*."

"Then Paco will have to return to Zacatecas, to the camp of General Obregon. I will write to my father and explain the valiant bravery Paco has shown in the face of inestimable danger. He should then receive an honorable discharge from the army, Lola. Perhaps with enough of an endowment for you to realize your desires."

Lola's smile was like a ray of sunshine. She was truly a beautiful young woman, thought Madelaina. The azure blue eyes fringed with dark lashes made her think of Peter and she filled with a deep longing.

"What of you, *señorita*? What will you do?"

"Return to Zacatecas with you. What else?" she said with a newborn firmness. "Now that Madero and my father are allies with Pancho Villa, there is no point to the life I once lived."

Perhaps it was because Lola had only seen Madelaina while under the influence of Golden Dawn's possession and she had no yardstick by which to measure the strong-willed determination in the girl. Whatever it was, she couldn't remove her eyes from Madelaina, as if seeing her for the first time in this new role of determination and courage. "When shall we be ready to leave?" she asked finally.

"At the first falling of a star," she replied.

"At the first falling of a star? *Que va*, at the first falling of a star? It makes no sense, *señorita*. Who knows how long it takes to see a falling star?" Lola faltered.

"You heard my orders. Not until then." She watched as Lola, staring at her as if she was some crazy woman, backed away from her and left the hut.

Etched vividly in the deep recesses of Madelaina's mind were pictures which brought a blush to her cheek. She hurriedly stepped into her clothing, unable to understand why her imagination had taken such fanciful flight into erotic vignettes, and of all people, why with this tribal leader, Tolomeo?

She could feel her heart beating rapidly and a peculiar breathlessness coming over her. *It's good we're leaving,* she told herself. *I musn't stay here so close to him. If I do, I'll love him too much. I'll never be able to turn back. To think I've dreamed of him in this fashion. I mean—a total stranger! Could I miss Peter so much that I fantasize over other men?* She felt a hot blush surge through her body as the pictures in her mind continued to form and dissolve. *God forbid that Tolomeo should read my mind!* Dios mios! *I wouldn't be able to look him in the eyes.*

She brushed out her long hair. There was no mirror in which she could study the facial changes which had occurred the two weeks of their stay in the interior. In fact, when she learned two weeks had passed since their arrival, she found it too incredible to believe. It seemed only yesterday.

Consciously, she remembered very little of her encounters with Tolomeo, subconsciously however, she kept getting flashes of pictures. Anyone who knew her before and saw her now could detect a change in her, but, what it was, they were not able to tell and wouldn't for some time to come.

The morning of their departure, Madelaina ran breathlessly about looking for Tolomeo. He was nowhere to be found. Dismayed, she felt saddened, thinking he refused to be present for some foolish thing she may have said or done. She asked Tula and all the others she encountered where Tolomeo had gone. They could give her no answer. Paco, well on the road to full recovery, was anxious to depart. He had many things to consummate, and the sexy and lovely Lola was ready and willing to consummate them with him.

"We will wait, Paco. I cannot leave without thanking Tolomeo for your life and my own. You have your whole life ahead of you," she reprimanded sternly, still marveling over the rapid healing of his arm and splendid health.

Paco angled his head at her. "Unless it is stopped by a *Rurale* bullet or a *bandido*'s *riata,*" he said scornfully.

"If you take that attitude," she said coolly with an air of detachment, "you deserve what you get." She moved away from him as if he didn't exist.

"*Si, querida*, it ees true," wailed Paco to Lola. "She has changed. She grows more like her father each day. I give thanks she is not my *mujer*—wife." He gathered Lola into his arms with love and affection. But, like most Mexican men, he did not display his affection for other men to see. So, in the usual custom, he pretended to be brusque and rough with her. "Take notice, woman. You will never be such a macho woman—or it is finished between us, *comprender*?"

Lola reached up and pinched his cheek affectionately. "*Si*, Corporal Jimenez. I see how tough an *hombre* you can be and I tremble before you, respectfully, of course."

"*Muy bueno*, woman." Blushing, Paco gazed about

529

the shaded area of the compound to see if they'd been observed or overheard. If the natives, moving about in their duties, had noticed them, they gave no outward show. "Now, go and prepare the wagon for our journey home. We must be ready—whenever this star decides to fall, eh?" He laughed mockingly and shook his head with growing irritation.

Earlier, Paco had been gloomy and annoyed by what Lola announced were Madelaina's orders. But gazing upon Lola's beauty and adoration erased all his hostility. Paco Jimenez was truly in love—really in love—and it felt wonderful. The miraculous healing of his arm and feeling of love permeating this unusual village had inspired him to the point that he entertained thoughts of defecting entirely—of not returning to the outside world. Who was there to miss him back in Zacatecas? No one. He had everything right here, with Lola and these wonderful people who had fed him, nurtured him, and inspired him to higher thoughts. Perhaps Señorita Obregon may decide to remain here, too, he thought hopefully.

It was twilight by the time Madelaina found Tolomeo standing by the shimmering waterfall, his back to her, staring into the silent pool of liquid silver several feet from the embankment upon which they'd made such scintillating love.

"Tolomeo!" she called out suddenly. "Look—a falling star!" Her eyes followed the blinding streak in the sky as it whirled in an arc and sputtered lifeless. She felt a sinking feeling in her stomach. "It is time to say good-bye," she said quietly.

"*Adios, querida. Vaya con Dios.* Live fully and in peace." His voice seemed deeper, more constrained. Still it excited her as before. He didn't look her way.

"Is that all you'll say? I wanted to speak to you of many dreams I've had, for which I need explanations. Now it's time for our departure. Won't you see us off?"

His manner, calm and dignified, was so remote as to give the impression he moved mechanically as in a dream. Still he didn't turn to look at her.

The sweet smell of earth and clover permeated the air like a heavenly intoxicant, and she inhaled deeply to stir her senses and remember this setting. She heaved a forlorn sigh of sadness. "Tolomeo," she called softly. "Won't you look at me? Say good-bye? I can't believe that you wouldn't grant me that, at least. Is it something I've said or done? I've been known to be headstrong and foolish and independent and nasty in the past. Somehow, I can't seem to recall it. It all must have happened a very long time ago."

Madelaina's soul retreated in confusion to its inner fortress of new and sudden detachment, much to her amazement.

"I came to say farewell, to thank you for your kindness, generosity, and the miracles performed on Paco and myself. I came also to offer you my allegiance. Should you ever want me, I will come from wherever I am."

These extraordinary words, spoken in a firm voice without arrogance but with limitless strength, aroused Tolomeo. Still he did not turn toward her. He spoke quietly. "It was necessary for you to learn to place things in the proper perspective. To know one thing is no more important than another, that pure love transcends all and reduces all else to its own worthless state—nothing. As death can be nothing, so are the stresses of life. The philosophy is so simple. It is overlooked by mankind because the brain desires such things to be complex. Where pure love is, there can be nothing else, and all dangers fall away of their own accord and dissolve into nothingness." Tolomeo paused a few moments. He seemed to be staring straight ahead at the waterfall. His voice softened, became more endearing.

"You will never have to be concerned that a sorcerer can possess you ever again. You have learned how to be a warrior against such threats. Golden Dawn will never harm you again. Now that you've shown your claws to her, she'll never try tricking you. As powerful and relentless as she can be, she will not

531

again trifle with your life, for we've met in the arena. The rattler has no effect on the eagle. Remember, before you can be trapped, you must be willing. You must never abandon yourself. To do so is the crux of all trouble.

"You have acquired much knowledge in the past two weeks, knowledge for which you shall be held to account. You have no choice but to learn more, if only to defend yourself and put your life into better order."

There was something about the way Tolomeo kept his back to her that was truly maddening. She moved a few inches to the right to see him—if only in profile— but Tolomeo would turn to the left. When she moved to the left, he turned to the right. Why did she feel such a palpitation of the heart, she wondered. Knowing she was leaving, knowing she'd probably never see him again, she had wanted the parting to be memorable. She inclined her head sadly and stared at the verdant, velvety knoll on which she stood, then gazed into the aquamarine pool that glistened iridescently in the bright twilight.

"If you won't look at me, Tolomeo, I can only express my deep sorrow and profound disturbance. I thank you for the enlightening and knowledgeable teachings. Truly, I'll never forget them and shall practice them to the end."

"It is one thing to mouth those words, another to put them into practice," he spoke up again. "It is too easy to forget what you've learned if outer things become more important. Outer things: opposing someone, avoiding things, preparing for certain things and not others; something is always more important to us than the self. The world is full of frightening things, and for the most part, people become helpless creatures, surrounded by inexplicable, unbending forces, which they assume cannot be explained or changed. It's like a belief in destiny, the belief that one is powerless against such forces, a fatalistic approach. Knowledge of these forces will enable you to use them by redirecting yourself and adapting to their direction."

"It will make me more powerful than the rest of mankind," said Madelaina, suddenly on the same wave length as Tolomeo.

"It will make you more vulnerable. Make no mistake about this. Your life may become more precarious and cumbersome—"

"Any more than it's been? *Dios mios*," she exclaimed. "Truly, I do not understand. Only a moment ago I was certain that I had been endowed with infinite wisdom—"

"And that would make you swell with vanity, place yourself in a loftier place than your fellowmen. No, Madelaina, knowledge is not for that purpose. The more you come to know, the more you are responsible for. You will perceive things much more readily than others, and because you know the consequences, you will avoid these forces. Knowledge forces you to live your life as a warrior and do battle each and every day of your life. You spoke of your father as an enemy. He is not your enemy except for making you indulgent, soft, and given to custom. The warrior in you combated him, attempted to assert itself, for the spirit of your being isn't geared to complaining or indulging— nor is it geared to victory or defeat. A warrior is geared to struggle, meeting every encounter head on. The outcome is of little importance. Only the necessity to permit the spirit full freedom and complete expression is imperative. And knowing this, striving for this, he can laugh and laugh and laugh at the fraudulent lives lived by others."

Madelaina strained to see his face. She grew dismayed. Her voice had grown husky and thick with emotion. "I'm confused, Tolomeo, by things I don't understand. Please, can't we remain longer? I've no desire to return to what I left before our arrival." She elevated her spirit. "May we go for another swim? It's endurable, this paradise of yours."

"No," he replied firmly. "You're on the threshold of a new life—a new world—and will no longer feel safe in your old ways. You must choose your ways in this new life with premeditated caution. If ever there is doubt in your mind, go into the silence. Your spirit will reveal to you the necessary path to follow." He removed a small silver flacon from his loincloth girdle, reached behind, and held it out to her in his lean, outstretched palm. "Here, take this. If you should find yourself unable to go into the silence, rub this powder in the area of your umbilical cord, speak to your abdominal brain, demanding courage and strength to overcome your dilemma. Command all internal dialogue to cease so that you may hear the voice of the spirit."

Madelaina's hand reached hesitantly for the flacon, then, with her free hand, she grasped his wrist, pulling him toward her. "Please, Tolomeo," she pleaded sadly with a catch in her throat. "Won't you turn to look at me? I want to remember the sparkle of amethyst in your eyes, the sun-kissed glow of bronze of your body. And when the wind whispers and the woods are motionless, I'll remember how an evening star fell and set aglow for all eternity the knowledge of how two bodies like burning candles melted into each other, and where they fused into one, we saw God lit brightly beneath an eternal torch of heaven." Madelaina paused, waiting for Tolomeo to turn to her and express his love. "My lips move, calling to you, Tolomeo. But it is so quiet, so very quiet. Can you not hear me?"

Then, like a whirlwind in slow motion, he turned to her. There was no sun in the sky, yet its dazzling rays caught prisms on the silver amulet around his neck, causing it to sparkle with such brilliance that Madelaina for an instant was blinded by its glare. She blinked several times, averting her eyes. When she could, her eyes fixed themselves on Tolomeo's eyes. All at once the dawn of light broke, as a flaming star shot overhead like burning wick, and in its wake she saw him fully.

They gazed at each other in pregnant silence. An expression, startled and frightened, yet fascinated, moved across her face as one awakened from a terrifying dream by an appalling stranger. Her heart swelled and pressed against her lungs. She couldn't breathe. She grew pale, frightened, and terribly confused, and she stared at him unable to articulate.

"What did you expect from a sorcerer?" he asked. "I did what was necessary. I had to save your life, and I succeeded. Now, you are complete, your soul is yours for eternity if you abide by the precepts you've learned. And my dear, if you don't, I will be helpless to aide you."

Madelaina, unable to speak her thoughts or put into words her feelings in the next few moments, felt her mind growing hazy and cluttered with a montage of pictures of the world and people she knew intimately before entering Tolomeo's world. What seemed to cause more anguish than she could handle was the swiftness with which Tolomeo's world began to fade from her consciousness.

She clutched her breasts as if this movement might help to abate the pounding heartbeats which took her breath away. Her dark eyes blinked hard and rapidly as she tried to wall up an avalanche of tears threatening to break through.

"Noooo," she whimpered softly. "I don't believe it. I'll remember all of it. All, do you hear? I will for all eternity—no matter what you do or how you try to deceive me! I shall never forget our love, regardless of your sorcery!" She was sobbing now, incredibly shaken.

Tolomeo stood before her in all his majesty, the same godlike warrior with a magnificently firm and muscular body; the same she'd loved and had been loved by. Staring at her, *muy dolor*—much sadness—was on the countenance of a leathery, wrinkled old man, skin the color of smoked walnut. Ageless perhaps, but obviously the face of a man in his eighties. Certainly he wasn't the man with whom she imagined herself helplessly in love—or was he?

She bent her head in abject humiliation and, turning from him, ran from this Edenic garden of her most sublimated dreams with the fleet-footedness of a gazelle. Even as she ran, she began to assimilate a comprehension of things that moments before seemed insoluble.

At the village she searched for Tula. Locating her at the well, Madelaina, in a gesture of love, removed the golden locket from around her neck, a gift from Peter Duprez, and placed it around the young girl's neck. The girl shrank away from her in fright. She shook her head, removed the obscenity from her person. Only then did Madelaina recall the Indian superstition that gold brought ill and misfortune to Indians who had the misfortune to adorn themselves in it. "Forgive me, Tula. I only wanted you to have something of mine to remember me. It was just a gesture of our appreciation for your courtesy, your hospitality, and all you and Tolomeo have done for Paco and me. Take care of your master, Tula, there is none like him in the world."

Tula managed with sign language to assure Madelaina that it wasn't necessary to thank them, that she appreciated the gesture of the locket. She removed a leather tine from her buckskin shift and removed the silver flacon gripped tightly in Madelaina's hand, the gift from Tolomeo. Moving expertly, Tula made a slipknot for the flask and tied it around Madelaina's neck. She tucked the silver container between the girl's breasts.

Madelaina kissed the girl on the cheek and joined Paco and Lola, who'd seen the falling star earlier and awaited anxiously for Madelaina's arrival, so they could be on their way, with the overhead stars to guide them.

Paco spurred on the mules, and Madelaina, seated on one side of him, with Lola on the other, never looked back as they left the interior village.

Book Six

Hacienda de Sietas Lunas

Chapter 20

They traveled by day and they traveled by night, taking turns driving the cumbersome, creaking wagon along the back roads to Zacatecas. Their journey was painfully slow, unbearably hard on them. Two weeks of constant stop and go travel, avoiding the *Federales* and hiding to stay clear of marauding *bandido's,* whom they heard stood in readiness to pounce upon, rape, and rob any unsuspecting travelers, kept them from making as much time as they predicted they'd make traveling to the fort.

Madelaina had avoided thinking about the reunion she expected with her father; she dreaded it because her father wasn't a forgiving man. As they drew closer to the fort, however, she recalled what Tolomeo had taught her, and she began to draw on a reserve of energy and concentration to put her in the proper frame of detachment. She could feel a strength surge through her as she drew herself up in a reserved manner which would preclude apology for her past behavior to her father. For a time she was sustained.

Observing the trundling wagon with its three occupants approaching the fort, the soldiers on duty flung open the gates and they were permitted entrance. Odd, thought Madelaina, the atmosphere was as usual, as if they'd never been missed—as if they'd never been away. *Campesinas* milled in and about the main compound as usual, going about their business with sullen resignation and typical boredom.

Paco Jimenez recognized both the uniformed men at the gates who stood now with rifles at the ready, demanding to see their papers. He saluted them briskly, tossed the reins to Madelaina and jumped off the

539

wagon, against her protestation. She continued forward, glancing back over her shoulders to see the men slapping each other on the shoulders as thick dust particles exploded from Paco's jacket. The astonishment was apparent on their faces. Long ago they had assumed Corporal Jimenez to be dead. It was like seeing his ghost.

Madelaina pointed out the barracks to Lola. "This is where Paco will stay. The last building is where my father is housed. If you wish, you may stay in my *casa* with Concepción."

"Whatever is your wish, *señorita*," replied the wide-eyed mestiza who was still trying to handle what Paco had told her about Madelaina. Imagine, she was the daughter of the illustrious General Alvaro Obregon.

"It would go to know the status of the revolution," she said, gazing about. "*Dios mios*, it is strange for Lola to be walking among the *Federales* without fearing for her life," she admitted, glancing apprehensively here and there at the soldiers moving about in their duties.

"You need have no fear as long as you're with me," said Madelaina, reining the burros a few feet before the general's quarters.

Before the wagon came to a full stop, Paco had caught up with them. He was out of breath and filled with a peculiar ebullience. His dark eyes darted about the compound as if he might be looking for someone special. Catching the expression on his face, and knowing that look well, Madelaina spoke up sternly. "It's best you prepare yourself for the ordeal ahead, Corporal, and not go looking for trouble. You've had enough to last a lifetime, no?"

Lola's blue eyes gazed from one to the other, unable to fathom what they were silently sparring over. Both Paco and Madelaina knew he was looking for Dolores Chavez. The guilt of this knowledge brought a flush to Paco's face. He stood up straight, braced himself, and nodded affirmatively. "It's best I prepare myself, wash,

540

and put on a clean uniform before I meet General Obregon."

"*Si*, Paco. It's best. And let no one or anything deter you."

"*Si, señorita.* No one. Nothing." He saluted her and turned to Lola. "Woman, come with me to my quarters." He paused a moment. "What if there are no quarters for Paco? They think me to be dead?" He frowned noticeably.

"Then, find Concepción. She'll attend to you."

"And if Concepción is no longer in Zacatecas? You know how long we've been absent from the fort?"

"I know. Now, stop this. Find someone who can instruct you. If you are unsuccessful, come to my quarters. *Ondolay, pronto.*"

"Habit, *señorita.* I am here not five minutes and already I am a soldier again." He smiled sheepishly and helped Lola down from the wagon.

Madelaina watched them walking hand in hand along the dirt path. Here and there, faces turned toward them with expressions of interest as they beheld the stunning beauty of the blue-eyed Lola. Both men and women appreciated such beauty.

She took in a deep breath and all the old familiar odors of spicy foods and tacos and animal excrement and the raw smells of the wilderness brought back instant recall of this place. No more stalling, she told herself. Get yourself inside and face the general. She turned and walked the few steps to her old cottage. She knocked on the door. There was no sound. She opened the door and entered the shadowy room. The blinds had been drawn, admitting no sunlight.

For an instant, she waited for her eyes to grow accustomed to the dimness. She gave a start and stopped in her tracks when she saw the sprawled figure of a woman lying on the bed in which she'd slept most her life. Sensing the presence of another person, the woman in bed sat up abruptly.

Madelaina's dark eyes narrowed to slits, her hand

fingered the knife in a sheath at her waist as fires of vengeance stoked her memory.

"What are you doing here?" demanded Madelaina in a cold, hard voice.

The woman blinked her eyes and gave her an amazed look that turned into one of icy contempt. Even as she stood there, the Indian was stunning, so sure of herself. Her vivid Yaqui coloring in that nude lace negligee gave her the look of sun-kissed goddess, thought Madelaina, fighting for control.

"What are *you* doing here?" asked Golden Dawn arrogantly. Her face grew pale, and she drew up the covers close to her.

A strange thing happened to Madelaina. The voice of Tolomeo came at her as clearly and distinctly as if he had been in the room with her. *Forgive her. Forgive her and radiate divine love to Golden Dawn, and she'll no longer possess power over you!* Madelaina struggled against the voice of Tolomeo as if she did mortal combat in an arena with a gladiator of inestimable strength. In those split seconds the formidable feat of strength was tried as forces combated each other.

"How dare you return to the camp of your father?" screeched Golden Dawn. "You traitor! Whore! You'd better leave before the general himself takes measures to liquidate you. It appears you've escaped my clutches, whore, but I assure you what the general has in store for you will not promote your freedom to further humiliate him." As she spoke, Golden Dawn tried to call upon her sorcery to seduce Madelaina's mind.

It was a peculiar sensation for Madelaina to experience. She heard the soft rustle of leaves and a fragrance, one she wasn't familiar with, engulfed her. The wind created a pressure in her ears. It seemed as though the sun had burst into a million fragments behind Golden Dawn. Then, as it slowly rolled around the room, it gathered up all the fragments and formed a fiery ball which remained in the corner of the room like a round spotlight casting its rays on a spot before her.

Forgive her. Forgive her. Remove the hatred from your heart. Say to yourself, she has no power over me. I am unaffected by their deeds. Set her free. Set her free. Absolve her of all sins and crimes against you. The chains that bind you are the chains that will free you. Cut them loose! Madeliana, Golden Dawn is powerless over you when you are filled with divine love! Forgive your enemies in your heart and you'll never see in them an enemy!

Before her eyes, Navojolla, the jaguar, materialized. As quickly as it appeared, it vanished. The sound of dry twigs snapping repeated itself. The sound of rifles cracking in rapid-fire shots sounded. All the unusual sounds came and left like a distant echo. Madelaina stood her ground as the internal strength of Tolomeo manifested itself in her body and mind. Her hand fell from the sheath. When her normal vision returned, she saw Golden Dawn standing before her, a pitiful figure, drenched to the skin with perspiration, fatigue lines etched into her face. Confusion at her lack of power left her disoriented and frightened.

For Madelaina, the incongruity of that moment was her reaction to the phenomenon: Instead of being terrified or moved to violence, she was laughing as if a ten-ton weight had been removed from her shoulders, and she found the entire thing hilarious. The feeling of elation that struck her was like nothing she'd experienced.

Golden Dawn's reaction was an instantaneous loss of her usual aloofness and objectivity. She had unquestionably lost her confidence. Her dark eyes, filled with fright and indecision, darted about the room, looking for something in which she could trust. She appeared to have been seized with stomach cramps. Doubling over, she rolled onto the bed, her knees drawn up tight to her chest. Her face was contorted with the most indescribable expression of half-animal, half-human grotesqueness, as the sounds of flapping wings sounded dangerously close in the room. They weren't loud or intense, but soft and insidious, producing spasms of

543

alarm in Golden Dawn. They stopped as quickly as they had begun, slowly and gradually diminishing until they could no longer be heard.

Madelaina heard something like the swift flight of an eagle outside on the roof of the building. She ran to the window and glanced up into the fiery blue skies. Overhead a flock of giant birds soared and wheeled arcs, then took off to the south.

She quickly flung open the door and went outside to gaze into the distance. Shading her eyes from the hot sun, she peered into empty skies. Madelaina felt a tightness in the muscles of her stomach. She remembered the silver flacon Tolomeo had given her and the instructions he'd given her as to its use. She removed it from around her neck, pulled up her peasant blouse, tilted the flask, and in a second rubbed the powder onto the area of her navel.

She took several deep breaths, and soon she felt a warmth pervade her body with an energy somewhat strange to her, yet familiar enough to be a part of her. Almost as if in a daze, she returned inside.

Golden Dawn lay sprawled out on the bed, arms outstretched, legs dangling over the side, her pale face covered with moisture, quite dead.

Madelaina was unmoved by what she saw—as if it were an everyday occurrence. She walked slowly to the office of her father, General Obregon, only to be told he was on maneuvers. Concepción, it seemed, hadn't been in Zacatecas for many months. Dolores Chavez was no place to be found. Word among the *campesinas* had it she simply disappeared one day, never to be seen again. No doubt the skullduggery of Golden Dawn, she thought.

She spoke with Lieutenant Guiterrez, who was acting C.O. in her father's absence. She explained about Paco. Left a letter with him to give to the general, suggesting Paco be given a commendation for his bravery. She posted a letter to President Madero, suggesting the same thing, just in case her father remained too bitter to be forgiving. One thing was certain: Alvaro Obregon was a true military man. He would always act upon orders. He wasn't as canny and unpredictable as was General Huerta or Major Salomon. At least he had this much in his favor.

Madelaina said her farewells to Paco and to Lola, explaining what she'd done on their behalf, and took her leave, without mentioning Golden Dawn to them.

When at last she arrived in Cuernavaca, she was almost grateful to be in familiar surroundings. She rested for nearly two weeks, babied and fawned over by her old servants, who fed her well and made certain she put a "few pounds of flesh on those scarecrow bones." Her father, it seemed, hadn't been home in nearly five months. He was on active army duty in Sonora, she was told.

It was while she was in Cuernavaca that she learned the status of the revolution. And it was there that she first heard the stunning news that Pancho Villa had been ordered to face a firing squad by General Huerta. That he was subjected to such an atrocity was simply incredible to her. When she and Raoul Madero interceded on Pancho's behalf, directly to President Madero, he stopped the execution just as the soldiers leveled their rifles at the man who had commanded thousands of guerrilla bands. But then she was further appalled that the *presidente* immediately transferred Pancho Villa to the Federal Penitentiary in Mexico City for disobedience, insubordination, and robbery! Why Francesco Madero didn't dismiss the absurd charges against Pancho and censure that vile General Huerta for attempting to execute Villa on his own was too much for her politically inept mind to grasp.

The confusion of alternating facts and opposing loyalties and a leader who was too blinded by his office to see the true loyalties kept her confounded and withdrawn. She hadn't bothered to call upon any of her old friends.

It was on this day in early May that Madelaina sat hunched over in the floral courtyard at her father's hacienda. She contemplated the deplorable state of affairs, over which she had no control, and her own recent experiences, wondering what it all meant and where it would lead her. The sound of voices coming from inside the villa and the clicking of leather heels on the floor tiles attracted her attention and she turned toward the door.

Instantly her face lit up with radiant smiles. "Felipe!" she cried out in genuine affection. She sprang to her feet, denouncing custom and protocol, and dashed madly across the courtyard, dressed in a bright blue batiste dress drawn in tight at the waist and worn over full floor-length crinolines, which didn't encumber her movements.

They hugged and kissed, and he whirled her about in a circle. Finally he held her at arm's length and searched her face. "Madelaina. Oh, my dear Madelaina, how I've worried about you."

"Oh, my dearest Felipe," she said huskily as tears fell freely on her rosy cheeks. "Truly, I never believed we'd see each other again."

"Where, Madelaina? Where in God's name have you been this time?" he asked with open concern. "Are you still in some kind of trouble? What has happened? If you only knew how out of my mind I've been over your disappearance. I—I thought. Well, when we didn't hear, we thought the worst. That you were dead." He sat down on the sofa with her and watched the servants bring him refreshments. Iced tea and small cakes.

"How did you know I was here?" she asked wondrously.

"I didn't. I stopped only for word of your father. And Doña Louisa with tears in her eyes told me you have been here for a few weeks. Why didn't you let me know?" he asked grimly. "You could have let me know, Madelaina." Now he was stern.

She took his hands in hers. "Don't be angry with me. Perhaps when I tell you where I was, you won't want to hear. I half-hoped my father would be here so that I could tell you both. I missed him in Zacatecas,

546

and here, also. But I'll tell you, Felipe. Pray that one day, if I'm not here to narrate the story, you'll do it for me." With this, after she poured their tea, she took him back over the rocky, perilous, frightening road her life had traversed since they last saw each other.

At first, Felipe listened attentively, politely, and with reserve to the story. Soon he showed marked agitation and incredible disbelief as she recounted her experiences at Madrigal de Los Altos. The knuckles on his tightly clenched fists rose like white mounds on his tanned, veined hands.

"Salomon! That devil!" he hissed with venom. "And Huerta! That vile animal ordered such treatment to the daughter of General Obregon?"

She quieted him and continued the story. She told him of their escape, of the boy Lazaro, of the records she'd stolen, and how her father had been cheated over the years. She mentioned she'd met Zapata and once again described her encounter with Major Salomon. How she owed her life to Paco Jimenez, the man her father sent to Madrigal for having coupled with her.

Felipe winced once or twice at the mention of the sexual atrocities, but to learn she'd been a willing partner for Jimenez ruffled his feathers somewhat.

She ignored his reaction and continued with her story. She mentioned how General Lomas had completely fooled her in his role of a small landowner. And how grateful she was to have been reunited with her husband, Peter Duprez.

When she explained she was still in love with her husband, Felipe's hurt and sorrowful eyes struck her like a stab wound to her heart.

"I must be honest with you, Felipe. I love Peter. I'd be deceitful to deny it." She saw the worry lines across his handsome face deepen as she admitted to this love, and reaching up to his face, she stroked it gently. "I'd give anything, if it could have been you, Felipe. But since I am not at the rudder to steer my life in the way I decree—" She paused, forming the words in her mind. "I am at the mercy of destiny—" Once again she

547

paused, trying to stimulate her memory. "I'm sorry, Felipe, I can't seem to think. I seem confused."

"After what you've been through, is it any wonder? Word reached me that you interceded for Pancho Villa, that you approached President Madero on the *guerrillo*'s behalf. Haven't you learned yet?"

With full composure, Madelaina took time to explain. "Mind you, I'm not defending my actions or attempting to justify them. I went to Madero for several reasons. First, the thought that Pancho Villa was to be executed by that contemptible Huerta galled me. Moreover, that the *presidente* permitted Huerta such license was something I wished to speak of to his face. Mark my words, Felipe, Madero gives Huerta too much power. I couldn't believe that Madero would permit the man who handed him the presidency to be executed by a firing squad! Madero is blind—blind—blind! Can't he see that Huerta is afraid of Villa? That he plans to slay Villa because the *guerrillo* stands between him and the presidency?"

"Huerta aims for the presidency—the throne in the palace?" Felipe seemed amazed. "I've heard no such rumors, *querida*."

"You think such a man announces his plans openly while the man he intends to slay sits on the throne? Hah! He's much more clever than that!" she exploded angrily.

Felipe poured himself a cognac from the sideboard and gulped it down. "Didn't I warn you Madero would be no better than Diaz and probably far worse? Francesco Madero abandoned Villa. Isn't that proof enough of the treacheries in high office? Do you still pursue dreams of being a revolutionist, *querida*? Now Madero is in office and another revolution has begun—not the real revolution, mind you, but one between those political snakes who threaten to topple Madero. Won't you give up your rebellious thoughts?"

"I'm no longer a rebel, Felipe. Haven't you noticed? Do you not detect a change in me? I want only to find my husband, make peace with my father, and be left to a life of my choosing. Many things I desire to do are not possible to accomplish here in Mexico. I plan to reside in America where the morals of the past aren't carried over into the future. When moralities imposed upon a nation prevent their progress then something is wrong. The lack of progress breeds stagnation. It is this stagnation that defeats us and permits our oppressors to enslave us. And, *querido,* the stink of it all rises like a nauseous poison that slays us a little at a time, even as we continue to hold our noses and inquire, 'What is it that smells so fetid?' We, none of us, can breathe with such a stench of rotten politics, but nothing is done to eliminate the corruption or the men who prostitute our lives."

"Marry me," said Felipe passionately and compulsively. "Marry me and we'll both go north to make our home. I'll do what you desire, Madelaina. Anything you want. If you don't let me take care of you, I fear for what will happen to you."

His quiet presence, although welcome and calming, wasn't the consolation her soul yearned for. She couldn't help that she loved Peter. Over the last few days, thoughts of him hung heavy about her. She hadn't heard of him or from him since they left Parral. She vaguely recalled the strange dreams she had of him and all that had happened when she'd been under the influence of Golden Dawn, and once or twice she had the frightening feeling that he was in trouble. Where could she begin to find him? Even in their quiet moments he'd told her very little about himself. Something about owning a parcel of land near San Antonio, that he was often in El Paso—but never anything definite.

"Madelaina?"

She turned to Felipe. "I'm sorry. My mind wandered a bit," she apologized. She wanted to tell Felipe more, but her lips wouldn't articulate the words forming in her mind. "Perhaps another time you'll ride to Cuernavaca and I'll tell you more," she told him. She brushed her forehead with a gesture of forgetfulness. "I guess I'm more fatigued than I permit myself to think. Will you forgive me, sweet Felipe?"

"Don't think for a moment that I'll rest until I've brought General Huerta up on charges, *querida*. And that Salomon! He'll get his just desserts, believe me."

She nodded quietly and stood up to walk him to the door. They embraced as friends, and she watched him mount his stallion and ride off with an escort of six soldiers dressed in the uniforms of the Constitutionalist Army. At last Mexico had uniforms of her own design. But, the diehards, the army regulars still clung to their German- and French-influenced uniforms.

Felipe hadn't been gone two hours, when Madelaina arose from her meditation, went to her room, and packed a few belongings. Without preamble or much forethought, she had decided to go to El Paso. Madelaina hadn't really consciously willed herself to go north. In her meditation, she saw herself in a city in Texas which she presumed to be El Paso. Continuous flashes in her consciousness kept coming at her, similar to the psychic awareness she had experienced in the land of Tolomeo, in which Peter had been depicted in some sort of distress. Moreover, she kept seeing Manuelito Perez as she had in a disastrous encounter with the bulls in the Plaza de Toros. These visions prompted her to pack and prepare to travel north. She didn't recall making a decision to leave. She was following some deep silent voice within her that guided her.

From Mexico City she took the train to Chihuahua. In the capital city of that county, she suddenly decided to travel the rest of the distance to Juarez by coach. The uneventful trip grew wearisome, and she questioned her sanity for changing her mode of travel. It was insanely hot, the desert unbearably stifling. Her clothing, warm enough for Mexico City at this time of year, was all wrong for the desert. Her only consolation was having the coach to herself. Most sane people rode the train. What an idiotic sense of timing, she thought. Too ridiculous, she told herself as she bounced unceremoniously in the creaking, swaying coach that never failed to make her nauseous.

She felt the momentum of the coach pick up speed, heard the crackling sounds of the whips whistling over the six team horses as the driver poured forth his energy to yell out a warning. *"Bandidos! Bandidos!"*

The words were loud and clear and perfectly understandable. *Bandidos!* As her body pitched and tossed and jostled about the carriage, Madelaina attempted to move forward in her seat to see out the window. In the distance she saw clouds of dust. Damn their impatience! More delays now. She wasn't frightened, only annoyed and a bit curious. Why would bandits choose to stop a mere stage carrying only a lone passenger? How did they dare maneuver so close to the gringo border? Madelaina was about to learn why the stagecoach carried no other passengers; it carried a large gold shipment which someone intended to intercept. Of course, she knew nothing of this for the moment.

Her thoughts were interrupted as she was flung bodily to the opposite side of the coach when the driver braked the coach. The sudden stop caused the vehicle to shake and shudder and come to a skidding halt against the snorting protests of the six team horses. Outside, Madelaina could hear the loud "Yahoos" and "Yippies" and the triumphant cries of savage barbarians. The coach door was flung open before she could pull herself up from the floor boards, and she was rudely hustled outside by two of the dirtiest, fiercest ruffians she'd ever seen.

"Ah, such a desirable gringa wench!" these hillsmen told each other in their native tongue. They touched their sombreros with a mocking salute and eyed her with sheer animal lust. They were both covered with soot and desert dust, wearing the remains of what she identified as piecemeal khaki uniforms of the revolutionaries. Each man wore no less than four—even five—ammo belts strapped to his person wherever room could be made for them. Low-slung gun holsters over each hip toted six-shooters.

Madelaina pulled herself up from where she'd fallen in the dirt. In an imperious manner, she dusted off her travel costume and deliberately avoided eye contact with either brute. Her eyes skirted past them to the six men who unloaded a heavy metal chest and to those who stood with rifles at the ready, watching the operation and for the approach of any obstructors. Twelve men in all.

Before she knew what happened, sudden movement near the driver's seat brought forth a blast of rifle shots, and both the driver and his assistant, who made the stupid blunder of trying for their shotguns, fell back with a loud scream to the ground, their bodies bleeding from the volley of rifle fire that tore them up. Their fate evoked a round of laughter from the diabolical and terrifying hillsmen.

"Consider yourself *muy tardes*—very lucky," said the man called Ruiz. "One false move and you join your friends, woman," said the largest and dirtiest of the two as he sipped tequila from a canteen and wiped his drooling lips on the back of his shirt sleeve. "You gonna come quietly with me, woman?"

"Move!" called a man on horseback to the six men struggling under the weight of the metal boxes. "Hurry with that gold. *Vamenos! Ondolay! Ondolay!* You hear me? *Vamenos pronto!*" He called out loudly, shooting his pistol in the air overhead. The sweating men moved a beat faster as they loaded the containers of gold into the flat buckboard waiting a few feet from them.

"Hey, *muchacho*?" called Madelaina's captor. "What we do with thees gringa, eh? Ees little time for me to fuck her, no?"

Madelaina decided to use a ploy she once used to save her from such a fate. "Ees plenty time, *muchacho*, especially if you want wan beeg surprise to grow in your projectile," she said with obvious innuendo, alluding to the dreaded disease gonorrhea. "Now tell me *hombre*, who is your leader?"

Ruiz stared at her with open-mouthed astonishment at first, then, with narrowed eyes, he sluffed off her first remark. "Hey, *muchachos*, the gringa speaks with the accent of a Sonoran!" He laughed raucously and sipped more tequila to clear the dust from his throat. As he did, he moved slowly away from her. He'd let the others find out for themselves as was the usual custom, then later he could laugh about it and unmercifully tease the man who became diseased. Madelaina knew their habits and idiosyncrasies well.

The predatory lights she saw flickering brightly in the eyes of these hill bandits intimidated her for a moment or two. Finally, when no one responded to her inquiry, she spoke with an Indian dialect as she'd learned to do as a *campesina*. With her hands on her hips, she demanded to be taken to their leader. She didn't doubt for one minute that all twelve of the men, some of the fiercest, vilest, and most scurrilous dogs she'd ever seen, were about to rape her and rob her of all her possessions, diseased or not.

She let loose a string of expletives and phrases she'd learned and demanded to be heard as one of them. She mentioned Pancho Villa, but not the fact that she was Little Fox, because she didn't know these men. For all she knew they could have been counterrevolutionaries. If so, she'd certainly be killed in a most undesirable manner, but only after they tortured her bestially.

It was obvious from the expressions on the faces of the men they'd been startled by Madelaina's command of the vernacular. Her attitude of fearlessness stayed them off. They weren't used to being sparred with—not by a woman.

A few of the men conferred in excited tones as the men on detail moved the gold from under the floor boards of the coach onto a buckboard, sturdy enough to transport the precious commodity. When they had finished, the men were ordered to return to their camp.

Standing in the dust, averting her head to keep it from smarting her eyes, Madelaina stood in a field of uncertainty. Suddenly, a rider galloping toward her swept her up in his arms onto the rear of his saddle and followed the other bandits into the hills. The

553

stench of the rider nearly knocked her out, but Madelaina had no recourse but to hold on to his waist for dear life as he spurred the horse into an open gallop. In the distance she recognized the Rio Bravo. They were close to Juarez, all right. But where, she wondered. Just when she felt she could no longer endure the hard ride, she caught sight of a scattering of camp followers through a wooded clearing near the river. She heaved a relieved sigh. Her body ached from the abuse given it these past twenty hours, first from the calamitous coach ride and now on this horse's rump behind the saddle. *Dios mios!*

She was unceremoniously hurled from the saddle and dumped with the other *campesinas* near the fires where the evening meals were being prepared. She shuddered as she gazed upon these women. Filthy, unkempt animals, all of them. The ways of a *campesina* were too well known to her. Still she wondered, had she allowed herself to fall into such disrepute when she was one of them? Had she looked as they looked to her now, when her father had her abducted and returned to Zacatecas? She forced the thoughts from her mind because she found herself suddenly sympathizing with General Obregon.

Despite the garments she wore, which destroyed the illusion she wanted to employ as being one of them, she assumed the swaggering walk and stance of the most outgoing. A hard-lined expression formed on her face as she picked herself up from the dust and stared back at the women as they stared at her.

If any of these savage women entertained thoughts of overtaking her and robbing her of her personal effects, the posture she assumed and the look in her dark eyes were enough to deter them. She found a place to sit down and did so, glancing about with ever-watchful vigilance. Curiously enough, she thought she recognized some of the women. Closer examination of their dirty faces convinced her some of these were followers of Pancho Villa.

An older woman, one with soul lacking in the

554

younger ones, approached her with a mug of black coffee in her dark brown hands. Madelaina gratefully accepted it, although she would have preferred ice cold water. Something of an alarming nature in the older woman's red-veined eyes was enough to cause a shiver to run down her spine. The woman's eyes seemed to spring from their sockets, but it was too late. Madelaina had been attacked from the rear.

Only pure instinct caused her to move in time to avoid the deep thrust of a narrow blade held menacingly in the hands of a shrewish-looking Indian half-breed. Madelaina immediately pulled up the side of her skirt and grabbed for the knife inside her boot. Since her very first indoctrination to the life of a *campesina,* she had never stopped carrying a knife in this fashion. Now, the contest was one to one.

The dark-skinned half-breed, with jet hair braided at each side of a center part, backed away to pace her moves. The other women backed off away from the action, huddling in a circle and watching with blood thirsty eyes. It soon became obvious to all concerned that this woman in gringa clothing knew how to handle herself. She heard the warnings shouted to the girl called Isabel—her opponent.

"Ayeiii, *cuidado*—be careful, Isabel—this is no usual gringa!"

"*Ala chingada!*" cursed Madelaina in Indian dialect. "Come and get me, you unspeakable obscenity! Daughter of a whore's whore!"

The women circled each other. Isabel, the *puta* of the man who had ridden her into camp, mistook her for keen competition. She meant to cut out Madelaina's heart. Spurred on by the cries of her companions, Isabel was moved to demonstrate her agility with a knife. She wouldn't be shamed by this tramp masquerading as a fine lady. She lunged forward in an unexpected move and pierced Madelaina's arm, drawing blood. Madelaina glanced from the warm blood oozing down her arm to the girl's hate-filled eyes and she blinked hard. Inside, she heard a faint voice stirring her into what she

555

consciously might label an act of stupidity. Nevertheless, as the girl readied herself for another attack, Madelaina, against her will and letting go her earlier resolve to teach the half-breed some respect as well as manners, pulled herself up out of a crouch position and dropped her hands to her side. The knife relaxed limply in her palm in what appeared a gesture of submission.

"They call me Zorrita," she said loud enough for all to hear.

Unfortunately, her timing was off by a hair. Isabel, filled with the venom of jealousy and hatred, didn't hear what the others heard. As a hush swept over the crowd of women, Isabel moved quickly and plunged the knife into Madelaina's left shoulder.

In that instant the name Zorrita registered in the half-breed's mind. She fell back against the others, a look of alarm on her dark face, coupled with fright over the consequences of her enraged act.

Little Fox staggered backward, and caught by several women, she was laid gently on a stack of blankets as Isabel fled through the crowd like a frightened hare running from the hounds.

The women sat in awe-filled silence as they watched Madelaina grasp the the knife buried in her shoulder with the hand of her right, injured arm. Bracing herself for an instant, she paused to gather her strength and then swiftly extracted the knife from her body. She tore the ruffling from her petticoat, and gathering it in her free hand, she lay the thickness against the blood oozing from the wound. One by one, the woman offered to help her. They insisted she lay back quietly and allow them to dress her wounds. They were experts at such duties after all the wars their men had fought, they told her. She, above all, should know of their expertise.

Madelaina reluctantly gave in. She knew of their expertise, all right, but she also knew more men died from the infections that developed as a result of unsterile conditions than from the bullet and knife wounds themselves.

The women insisted they recognized Little Fox, although she didn't look as robust and fiesty as the gutsy *campesina* they remembered. She was some scarecrow now, twenty pounds lighter. The courage she demonstrated by dropping her knife against one of their kind was whispered about the camp.

Luz Lopez, the old woman who had tried to warn of Isabel's treachery, watched over Madelaina for the next three days as a raging fever engulfed her body. The application of countless green leaves and herbs to the infection was to no avail. On the night of the third day, during a moment of clarity, Madelaina recalled the silver flacon given to her by Tolomeo.

She felt between her breasts and, with all the effort she could muster, she lifted the silver flask and weakly signaled to Luz Lopez. "Please, *por favor, señora.* Be kind enough to rub this powder in the area of my umbilical cord."

Nodding, the woman called Luz reached for the flask and stared suspiciously at the unusual carvings on the outside. Her eyes moved from the girl's face to the horrible infection on her body. She'd seen knife wounds before, but, *Madre de Dios*, that Isabel must have dipped her blade into a pot of poison before sticking Little Fox. This was one terrible infection. Her experienced eyes told her the girl wouldn't last the night.

What would it hurt to grant Little Fox a last dying wish, eh? Later, she'd keep the silver flask and the fine clothing as mementoes for the others to grow jealous over. The silver flask was that beautiful!

Behind Luz, several other women, respectful in the presence of death's avenging angels, crossed themselves and muttered silent prayers. They came to gaze upon the face of the legendary Little Fox, who had aided and befriended Pancho Villa. She was one of them, this pale-faced *gachupín*, and they knew it. *Pues*, that stupid, blundering Isabel would surely reap the fruits of that day's bitter labor. When their *jefe* returned to camp and learned of this monstrous attack upon Little Fox, she was as good as dead.

The black angels of death were hovering over Little

Fox, fighting for her soul, insisted the old woman, Luz Lopez, who was herself a *curandera*—a healer. If anyone could save her, it was Luz Lopez. But the old woman shook her head sadly, signaling the others that Little Fox was lost to them.

Their *jefe,* Tomàs Urbina, who had led the clan of *Villistas* since their beloved puma was hustled from the swift injustice of a firing squad to the Federal prison in Mexico City, had been out raising hell some place since they successfully intercepted the gold shipment. It would be up to Urbina to get word to Pancho, who sat rotting in the Federal prison. Poor Panchito, to hear such news while he is so helpless would be too much to bear, no?

The old crones gathered around the campfire to watch Madelaina's life flow from her body. They saw the old *curandera,* Luz Lopez, loosen the girl's skirt and pull up her blouse. What is that old fool up to now, they wondered. The woman must be soft in the head. Little Fox's wound is in the shoulder—not her stomach. Blind fool! Toothless old hag! Blind as a scarecrow at that. The sun must have fried her brains— or else she's on the last legs of her journey also.

Luz leaned in close to Madelaina's parched, pale lips, listening carefully to the words she whispered. Luz Lopez, with whiskers of age on her yellow-skinned chin, smacked her lips together, nodding in understanding. *Que va*—understand? She understood none of this, but she would comply with the dying woman's request. She proceeded to rub the area of Madelaina's navel with the powder from the flask. As expected, the area turned black from the ashy residue. Earlier, when Luz inspected the feet and ankles of Little Fox, she noticed a purple hue creeping up from the toes; now at midcalf, Luz calculated her death would take place at a little after sundown.

The women watched in total absorption.

"What are you doing, Luz Lopez?" they asked in mocking tones, careful lest the angels of death hear them and take vengeance upon them.

558

Luz, short for Luzmilla, grew annoyed at their constant harassment.

"Be silent, you hags of the desert. Your cackling voices sound as drums for the soldiers of Lucifer. If you don't remain silent, they'll descend upon you and scatter you into the fiery furnaces of hell!"

"But, pray, tell us what you are doing," they insisted. "We've never seen you perform this ritual. Is it something new? Where did you learn such black magic, eh?"

"Shut up!" she snapped. "Don't make fools of yourselves and I'll not make a fool of myself by talking with people who have no understanding. I am performing the last wishes of a dying woman. Are you blind?" She capped the silver flask and was about to slip it into her skirt, but too many were watching her. There'd be time later to remove it from the girl. She replaced it around the girl's neck, lifting her head as she draped the fine chain around it, then laying it carefully upon the blanket. She rubbed her hairy mole-dotted hands together.

Not five minutes passed before Madelaina began to stir. For three days she'd lapsed from consciousness into unconsciousness, recalling little of what happened. There were moments of lucidity in which the face of Tolomeo came to her as if in reprimand, telling her she hadn't abided by the precepts she'd learned. *The more knowledge you amass, the more you're responsible for*, he kept repeating. *Draw on your strength. Command your inner resources to do your bidding. The outer picture is unreal—like Lago Diablo was unreal. Only the mind is power—real power that can command life or death.*

Madelaina's face broke into pools of perspiration. Her eyes snapped open, and blinking hard for several seconds, she attempted to orient herself. Her pale skin flushed with sudden color as circulation was restored to her body. She moved noticeably, and the old woman, Luz, moved in to help her sit up. She reached for a gourd filled with water and lifted the vessel to the girl's lips for her to sip. When she finished, Luz set the gourd aside and continued to rub her hands as if she could feel the residue left by the substance she had rubbed onto Madelaina's navel. She rubbed them on the folds of her skirt with much annoyance, then casually glanced at them. Holding her hands out before her palms down, she stared at them. She turned them over and over in total absorption.

Noticing her interest in her hands, the other women leaned in and stared in astonishment, which changed rapidly into superstitious awe, as the hairs and moles seemed to disappear from Luz's hands. It was not to be believed!

They were so caught up in Luz's hands that very few, including Luz, herself, noticed that Madelaina sat up unassisted, seemingly awakening from a lengthy sleep. She yawned and stretched and scrambled to her feet, favoring her wounded shoulder. The women gasped and drew back, huddling together like frightened sheep. *Dios mios*! This woman had defied the black angels of death!

"Luzmilla! See this! What has happened? A miracle for sure. Ahhhh—and why not?" They murmured amongst themselves. Wasn't this Little Fox? The woman who assisted their benefactor and leader, Pancho Villa? It's true—the stories they tell, she must be enchanted. But see what has happened to Luz's ugly old hands! What miracle is this? Touching Little Fox, medicating her, has passed on the magic to Luzmilla Lopez.

"*Ridiculous,*" said some.

"No," said the others. "*Incredible!*"

Some feet away from this bustling activity, turning slowly as he listened to his men, the wicked, perennially grinning Tomàs Urbina tried to pierce the crowd of woman hovering around Madelaina. He wore his usual *charro* pants with leggings, shirt with kerchief around his neck, double bandoliers, and double-holstered guns with a floppy sombrero flung to the back of his head.

"Little Fox, eh? Who gave you this manure to swallow?" he asked his men, when they reported the events of the previous days.

"She did. Besides, she's been raving in fever. Luz Lopez declares for sure it is Little Fox. The women who saw her before are mixed up. She's skinny—no meat on her bones like before. Now you're here, *Jefe*. You will tell us for sure. Oh boy! That Isabel is so scared, she's hiding from her man."

"*Si*, eh?" Urbina flung down his cigar. "We shall see," he said, certain the stranger must be a fraud. He had seen Little Fox in Parral. She'd been sent south with the others. By now, she must be with her gringo husband, Tom Mix, he reminded himself.

In Villa's absence, Urbina was next in command. He moved where he could, but he didn't live and breathe the revolution as Pancho did. Urbina enjoyed life—took as much as he could, exploited every rebel, and provided for a future day when the pickings would be lean. The sound of his thickly rawled spurs drew instant attention, and the women parted to make room for him as he passed among them. It was evident they thought little of this larcenous man and his petty thievery, but still in Villa's absence he was acting *jefe* and was accorded respect.

One look at Madelaina and Urbina not only recognized her, but he filled with wrath and violent anger, knowing full well what would have happened to him if harm had befallen the girl while in his camp. He raged and ranted like a madman, making profuse apologies to the girl in one breath, demanding the life of Isabel in retribution the next.

"Ayeiii, *señorita*," he moaned, lowering his shame-filled eyes to the ground. "If Panchito hears about this disgraceful act, I shall be banned forever from his sight." He couldn't apologize enough. Despite Madelaina's protestations that since she was fine, she desired no harm to befall the girl Isabel, *Jefe* Urbina shook his head. "No. I cannot grant your request. The girl must be punished. And to make it just, it shall be her man who does the whipping."

"And I say no!" shouted Madelaina defiantly. "No. There is enough animalistic behavior among the people. It must cease before there is any hope for the *peón*—you understand?"

Urbina, given to explosions of laughter, especially when he lacked understanding of a subject, grinned obsequiously, nodding his head in assent.

"At your command, Zorrita," he said helplessly.

"Then give me escort to Juarez at once."

"Si, señorita," he replied in complete accord.

While they waited for horses to be saddled up, she told Urbina that Pancho Villa was presently doing time in the Federal Penitentiary at Mexico City. News of such importance traveled fast and Urbina had already heard.

"With *Maderistas* defecting to the right and left of us, Zorrita, there is only one man who can save Madero—and he lets him cool his *culjiones* in prison! All the work Panchito did is gone—it has turned into manure, *señorita*. Pure manure! What good does it do to tell Pancho Madero was a weak man? He will be squashed like the *cucarachas*—you'll see. And you know who'll be the next *presidente,* Little Fox? Huerta! That's who! Huerta! And you know who stands behind *him, señorita*?" Urbina grinned his diabolical, leering grin. "That sleek, well-fed cat in the fancy uniform, that panther who wears medals and gold braids—that General Alvaro Obregon! Already he's responded with his Fourth Sonora Battalion."

If Tomàs Urbina noticed the sudden paleness of the woman, the slight slump of her shoulders as Madelaina digested this piece of information, he gave no indication. The fact was he didn't know she was the daughter of that "sleek, well-fed cat" of whom he spoke.

A horse had been saddled for her, and Madelaina mounted it and fell in behind Urbina and the other escorts who were committed to seeing her safely to Juarez. On the ride back along the desert bed of the Rio Bravo, Madelaina considered this new and stunning information. News that her father had joined forces with General Huerta had shattered her resolve. She wondered how Felipe would take this news. Now, *Dios mios,* there'll be no returning to Mexico as the daughter of General Alvaro Obregon. This one act, this unification with Vitoriano Huerta, had spoken so clearly what she felt all along in her heart. Her father was more ambitious than she credited him with being. They opposed Presidente Madero. Joining forces meant one thing—Madero would soon lose the strength of the *Federales.* With the army against the president, who would he have?

Apart from the obvious political coup intended by these plotting leopards, Madelaina knew in her heart that her father had disowned her. She no longer existed for him. Could she blame him, she asked herself. She had heaped his life with shame and humiliation, and even placed his own life in jeopardy for a time. The one man she really loved with all her being was now her bitterest enemy. Forever and for all time there could be no reconciliation. General Obregon must have known what General Huerta and Major Salomon had caused to happen to her and to Paco Jimenez at Madrigal. Yet, they'd joined forces.

Very well, Little Fox, she told herself. There was one avenue open to her. She would expel all thoughts of him from her mind, just as she'd have to do with her past. She'd break with the past and go forward, carve a new life for herself, a new future which would bring her security and comfort and provide what she desperately craved—the love and affection of a man who loved her desperately. If need be, she'd even forget Peter Duprez, she told herself with an air of secret detachment.

Her escorts left her a short distance from the city's gates, waving their sombreros into the air over their heads. Before their horses reared on their hind legs to gallop off to their refuge, Urbina told her to get in touch with him should she ever need his service. "Urbina is always close by, Little Fox."

563

Chapter 21

Two Months Later January, 1913

It was Sunday afternoon in El Paso, Texas. Madelaina Obregon strolled along the streets, admiring the fashions worn by the gringas. To her it seemed the entire city was in festival. She saw tourists with box cameras crowding the streets, pausing at intervals to photograph the colorful Mexicans who sold their wares in the vending stands in the old Chihuahua section of the city. Men on flat wagons cranked the wheels of motion picture cameras as they shot the various sights in and around the city.

El Paso, a curious city to her, was a mixture of contrasting architecture: newly constructed buildings standing side by side with rundown, old buildings humiliated in abject poverty. There were fine hotels, private homes, bawdy houses, and gaudy gambling palaces and saloons sprawled throughout the city, and a central depot for cattlemen eager to sell their herds to more anxious northern packing plant buyers. It was a rich town filled with excitement and danger, a carry-over from the gay nineties atmosphere of New York and Chicago, much larger than life, but an unmistakable imitation of the eastern cities. The streets filled with Indians, Mexicans, half-breeds, foreigners, so-called American frontiersmen, plotters and planners, intriguing politicians, swashbuckling soldiers of fortune, and not least of all, cowboys toting six-guns and firing them whenever they chose. It was a melting pot—a typical border town despite the whitewashing and face scrubbing given it by the city fathers.

In some sections, the streets were still unpaved. The closer to Juarez one walked, the shabbier became the area. Still, the sun shined brightly in this thriving cattle town, which had already begun to display its carefully structured social levels. El Pasoans had erected a social barrier, an unwritten taboo against Mexicans which obstructed any integration of the two nationalities. Most of the wealth had been acquired by the early pioneers, who, without education or refinement, suddenly emerged as a loud, boisterous ruling class. They were rowdy, uncouth, ostentatious, and crude, conspicuously consuming all things material. Their manners offended Madelaina as she walked among them. Even a lowly *campesina* demonstrated better manners, she observed.

Madelaina had taken lodgings in a small boardinghouse run by a quiet widow who, with excellent business acumen, rented to five boarders in all. Uncertain of what she would do with herself, Madelaina lived frugally. She had had enough money to take her through these last two months, but only that morning she discovered her funds were running low. She would have to find work. Uncertain of what kind of work a woman of her calibre could obtain, she had set out on this day to try and puzzle out this new development.

Madelaina had walked through the city streets before. Thrust suddenly among so many gringos, it was only natural she'd search the faces of every man for the one for whom she longed, Peter Duprez. Each time she'd see a man resembling Peter in stature, her step would quicken and she'd catch up to him, only to be disappointed at an unfamiliar face glancing at her in surprise.

She had to tell herself to stop playing such games or one day she'd find herself in trouble with one of those men who wanted to show more than affection for what they assumed was a mere pickup.

She entered deeper into Old Chihuahua. There weren't as many gringos here as there were closer to the main artery of El Paso. This section of town wasn't considered safe by the upper classes, and they kept their distance, unless they decided to come slumming, in which case they brought plenty of protection. Here, the night clubs, saloons, and gambling palaces were jammed together, with barkers standing before each establishment, hawking their specialties and trying to entice customers inside. Mexicans themselves crowded the narrow streets, making it difficult for Madelaina to pass. Mistaking her for a gringa, they harassed her to buy their wares. Little children begged coins from her. She had sewn her costume herself—a pale blue muslin, nipped at the waist over a corset, was caught with sprigs of matching flowers and fell with a panier drape to ankle length. Her high-buttoned shoes and straw hat piled high on her head were quite fashionable and American.

From time to time Madelaina would pause long enough to explain in Spanish that she was one of them and not to disturb her. Most would back off instantly, but others stared sullenly at her, disbelieving her appearance. She didn't have enough money left to be giving it away. Not now. She needed employment. What could she do? She had no skills, no training. Women could hardly find what was considered decent employment except as modistes, dressmaker's helpers, or flower venders begging on the streets.

With these thoughts, she skirted the crowds, picking up her skirts to avoid the dusty debris collecting on the paved areas, and hoping the unpaved paths wouldn't soil her costume. Shopkeepers selling baskets and countless straw items, artificial flowers, and pottery of all shapes and sizes, bargained with the gringo tourists in loud voices. It struck Madelaina as hilarious. The shopkeepers wished to sell and the buyers wished to buy, but they haggled over prices for so long, it seemed such a waste to her. The sellers could have made ten times more sales in that length of time if they'd kept their prices reasonable at the outset.

She continued on her way, her attention suddenly caught by the loud, commanding sounds of an elegant open carriage drawn by four matched bays and driven by a liveried servant, as it came bowling down the dirt street. A fleeting picture of a well-dressed woman with bright, flame-colored hair, brighter than a summer sunset, sped by her. The driver handled both horses and cabriolet with such well-practiced skill that Madelaina couldn't help but stare as the carriage came to a stop before a gambling palace called the Diamond Slipper.

When Madelaina reached the entrance of the spectacularly well-lit club, where elegantly dressed pages hawked the club's specialties, her eyes were drawn to a large billboard at one side of the doorway. Her eyes scanned the billing: *Un Guapa Apasionate*—An Exciting Woman of Great Beauty. *Danzanta Profesional*—A Professional Dancer of Extraordinary Skill. Madelaina couldn't take her eyes from the familiar face and scantily attired body pictured on the billboard. *La Gatitta!* The Sex Kitten!

Madelaina grinned noticeably, her eyes twinkling in amusement. She could feel the inner excitement of old returning to her. Taking a deep breath, she smoothed her skirt and pulled down her jacket. She patted a few wispy curls into place and tipped her hat jauntily. She glanced at her reflection in the window glass covering an array of glossy photographs of other entertainers, squared her shoulders, and entered the bawdy place where music rang loud and raspy over a tinny P.A. system. She plugged her ears defensively.

"Little Fox, is it really you? Are my eyes deceiving me. I cannot believe it! *Dios mios!* Such a rare pleasure!" Antonetta stared at her as if she were seeing an apparition. Finally she grabbed Madelaina and hugged her affectionately until she couldn't breathe. Then she held the general's daughter at arm's length, scanning the smart suit, the updo hairstyle, and broad-brimmed straw hat with nodding approval. "It's you! Chihuahua! Little Fox in the flesh!"

"Antonetta," cautioned Madelaina, drawing her friend into the shadows away from the crowd. "It's not wise to use that name. I am no longer Zorrita."

"What is wrong, child? You look pale. Have you eaten?" asked the former *campesina* of Pancho Villa, her red hair like pink fire. "Look, come into the office

567

where we can talk like old friends, away from so many noisy people."

"The office? Will anyone mind if we are so bold?" asked Madelaina.

"Who is there to mind if Antonetta is the proprietor, eh, Zorrita?"

"Please," she repeated. "Don't call me Zorrita."

"What then?"

"Madelaina."

"*Muy bueno,* Madelaina," she muttered, ushering the girl to a room beyond the bustling barroom filled with laughing, talking men, shouting to be heard over the loud ethnic music.

They were followed by an enormous, brawny, red-necked bouncer named Ed, to whom Antonetta shouted, "Have a waiter bring in refreshments—food also."

She closed the door behind them and seated herself in the charming room done in early El Paso—whore-house red with velvet sofas, gold tassles, and brassy appointments designed to look "classy."

The room contained two love seats facing each other over a mahogany table before a real fireplace. Marble-topped tables at the ends of the sofas held vases of bloodred roses. At the far end of the room, a large mahogany desk graced the corner with an overstuffed chair of red velvet behind it. A beautiful silk screen partition concealed a wardrobe of numerous exotic dancing costumes.

"Antonetta not only owns the Diamond Slipper, *querida,* she also stars in the shows and personally manages the business from this office," she told her amazed guest.

"I'm so happy for you to be so affluent, Antonetta," she told her friend with genuine pleasure. "It is some lifestyle, especially after seeing you with Pancho, as a *campesina.*"

"I thought I told you about myself," she began, frowning in thought.

"You did, but in truth, I am ashamed to say, I didn't believe you."

Antonetta laughed. "I can see why you wouldn't—not in those surroundings and those circumstances. But, what of you, *querida*? What happened to you? You disappeared from Pancho's camp so suddenly I was certain you had met with foul play."

"Ah, *si*," replied Madelaina, recalling what happened after her father's men had abducted her from the desert of Mapimi. "You might say that is exactly what happened," she began, giving Antonetta a play-by-play description of those harrowing weeks. She explained about her subsequent encounter with Concepción Montoya, who turned out to be the sister of Pancho Villa. She elaborated on the story of President Diaz' ball and how with the aid of Concepción a message had been sent to Villa to attack Juarez.

"Aha! So that's how Pancho became such a hero, eh?" Antonetta laughed with good humor and patted her dazzling red hair into place. She lit up a cigarette, and puffing inordinate amounts of smoke, she waved her arms about the room.

"All this is mine, *chiquita*. I thank the sweet, sainted Jesus that I didn't give up all I had for that sweet-talking honey bee, Villa. The revolution was over before it began," she chattered on brightly. "And all because you convinced him to attack Juarez instead of Chihuahua!" She shook her head in amusement. "You see, it pays to put enough away for a rainy day. When Pancho returned to his home and family, Antonetta had no place to go, so she came to El Paso to her own home." She waved her hands about the room. "And family, meaning the customers in the outer rooms." She laughed again and poured the ice cold beer which the waiter had brought in moments before. "Drink, *chiquita*. Now, Panchito, lured from the hills, gives 'em hell once more, eh?" She sipped the beer, draining half of it in one tilt of the glass. "You see, Little Fox, how nothing changes."

"Please, Antonetta," urged Madelaina, "try to

569

remember Little Fox is no more. Forget about Zorrita. She is a thing of the past. Already that snake Huerta has made my life unbearable. I don't intend to give him a second opportunity. To make matters worse, Francesco Madero made him a general in the Constitutionalist Army!" she scoffed ironically.

"So then what is your concern? You make no sense, *chiquita*. If this snake Huerta is on the side of Madero, you are no longer enemies."

"No longer enemies, eh?" Madelaina hesitated. An inner urging tried to caution her. *Bless your enemies and they have no further power over you*. This new thinking was precisely that—new. Madelaina hadn't been fully converted to the teachings of Tolomeo despite all she'd seen and heard. The old role of hatred and vengeance was difficult to rid herself of, so, by the time Madelaina took Antonetta through the terrors of Madrigal de Los Altos and what she'd suffered at the hands of Huerta and Major Salomon, the former *soldadera* had turned chalk white and the fires of vengeance had again begun to smolder.

Antonetta remained silent during the terrifying tales her friend recounted. Only her lips twitched from time to time as she nervously flicked the tips of her long, red-lacquered nails. What depravity the poor child had endured. No wonder Little Fox's hatred of General Huerta twisted her mind.

"You see, Antonetta," continued Madelaina as she nervously tugged the linen handkerchief in her lap. "I don't trust Huerta, not then, now, or ever. It wasn't for the love of Francesco Madero that he joined the Constitutionalists. He's a *Porfirista* through and through. He's always been loyal to Diaz. That *bastardo* even tried to execute Villa before a firing squad." She told Pancho's mistress of the ordeal she'd endured with Madero. "Imagine, Huerta received orders just when the *Federales* cocked their rifles, ready to end Pancho's life."

Madelaina paused to delicately sip her beer. She noticed that Tonetta's fragile face had already changed hues several times. The redhead leaned forward.

"And then?" she asked, almost afraid to pursue the topic.

"And then, what do you suppose that spineless cur did, the one who sits on the throne handed to him by the Centaur of the North, eh? He ordered Pancho jailed. Don't look so surprised, It's true. Imagine? Madero ordered Pancho jailed for insubordination and disobeying orders!" Madelaina had risen to her feet. Pacing back and forth in marked agitation, she exclaimed, "Is this to be believed, Tonetta? The thanks Pancho gets for giving Madero all of Mexico is jail. I tell you, Francesco Madero was not the revolution. He is a fraud, no matter how loudly he protests the fact. Only Villa was the revolution. No one but Pancho Villa. Our old *jefe,* who sits rotting in jail, should be made aware of the plottings against him. He didn't believe me, Tonetta."

"What do you wish from me, *chiquita*?" asked the proprietress of the Diamond Slipper. "How can I help ease your pain? It grieves me to see you pressured by so many complications. Sit quietly, *querida.* Rearrange yourself. It doesn't help to concern yourself over matters you cannot control."

"Yes, I suppose you are right. I keep telling myself not to involve myself in such affairs. That's why I insist that Little Fox is no more. The past is over. I try to keep it from my mind—all this injustice and double-dealing. *Querida,* it isn't easy. It makes my blood boil to think they've cornered the only man who ever helped Mexico. Goddamn them all!" Madelaina made a disorganized gesture when she saw the solemn and fixed expression of worry in Tonetta's eyes. "Not to worry, *chiquita*," she told the buxom, leggy dancer. "I'm all right. I need a job to support myself for a while. I came to El Paso in hopes of locating my husband whom I've not seen since the Parral encounter. I tell myself, with more reasoning, that if I do not locate him, it will not matter. I will find a life for me and do what I must."

She glanced at her friend with a feeling of awkwardness for not being totally honest with her. "There is something else, something you do not know." She sat alongside Antonetta, picked up her hand, hoping for understanding. "Tonetta, I am Madelaina Obregon, daughter of General Obregon."

Tonetta's sea blue eyes widened. "The daughter of Villa's enemy?" She withdrew her hand.

"Perhaps once they were enemies. The war has ended. Now Obregon works for Madero against the *Orozquistas*. *Si, chiquita*—with Huerta, too. It's too crazy a world even for me to comprehend. Much too confusing." She studied the exotic dancer, fascinated by the shimmering fire in her hair.

"The daughter of General Obregon? Ayeiii! It's a crazy world, as you say—much too complicated for Antonetta's head." She guzzled the remains of her *cerveza*—beer. "*Pues*, you have a job here with me. Can you still dance as you danced once for me in Villa's camp?" she asked, her eyes lighting up with dollar signs. "If you can, *querida*, the Diamond Slipper has just struck oil! *La Gatitta* is going into a quick, much-needed retirement."

"I'll do my best."

"Listen, you mentioned this man—your husband—"

"Duprez. Peter Duprez."

"*Si*, Duprez. All the time gringos come to Antonetta's Diamond Slipper, *chiquita*. Is possible one night he will come. Every now and then, that handsome, virile gringo Captain Richards comes here. We drink. We sing. We dance. We do things people usually do to pleasure themselves. But I have not seen this gringo Duprez. If I have, he has not made himself known to me."

Antonetta arose and, catching her image in the oval floor mirror, she patted her curls into place. "Now, *chiquita*, we go to my house. I have also a boarding-house, like a small hotel, where I rent rooms to respectable people. You will stay there with me. First, you must get well. I never see you so skinny. You must

572

fill out a little, no? The customers here like women with meat on their bones—not the way you are now." She shook her head. "Imagine what they did to Little Fox—forgive me, Madelaina," she said, realizing her error.

An hour later they both entered the modest boardinghouse Antonetta had bought on her arrival in the Texas city after leaving San Francisco. In her cheerful room, connected to Antonetta's by an adjoining bath, Madelaina sank wearily into a large wing chair covered in a bright calico print. A double window gave her a view of the park across the street. After a moment, she crossed to the window and flung it open, inhaling the floral-scented breeze fluttering in through the opening, causing the lace curtains to billow in and out. There was a large, brass double bed and a bureau topped with a marble slab, upon which stood a white milk glass bowl and pitcher. Next to it stood an oval mirror on a hickory base.

Antonetta had stopped at Madelaina's old quarters to pick up her belongings, and now she lay them across the bed, ready to put away.

"It is not the Obregon hacienda, *querida*, but it will be comfortable, you'll see," said the redhead, mistaking the sad expression in Madelaina's eyes for disappointment. She seemed to relax more in the confines of Antonetta's home, whereas earlier at the Diamond Slipper, she seemed anxious that someone might overhear their conversation.

"This is a palace compared to some places I've lived. Not like Madrigal." As Madelaina spoke, her feelings of bitterness dissolved, adding confusion to her mind.

"*Querida*, you mustn't let memories of that hell on earth embitter you forever. You will forget. You must. Leave it behind where all things of the past must remain."

"Forget? You honestly believe I can forget what that animal Huerta did to me?" she blurted out irrationally.

"Huerta again. The same Huerta who sent Pancho

9   573

Villa to prison. The same Huerta who stands falsely alongside Madero. The same Huerta who plots for the throne. He was the one, eh? The one who did those things to Little Fox." She let loose a string of curses that would have put Tomàs Urbino and Solis to shame. "What is wrong with Francesco Madero?" Her eyes widened to pools of fire. "Has he lost all senses? Has the crazy disease contaminated his brain? Ayeiii! *Desgraciados!* Sons of the sons of black Satan. Before, at the club, Tonetta couldn't express herself. Now I can explode. I swear if Pancho Villa hears of this, he will cut off their balls!"

"If Pancho Villa hears what?" asked a deep voice from behind them. He pushed open the door and stood in the doorway.

Both women, alarm on their faces, turned, holding their breaths as the door opened to reveal the figure of a man standing, observing them both.

There he was, dressed in conservative Norfolk tweeds and a Stetson hat on his head, without a moustache or the long hair he formerly wore. Francesco Pancho Villa, a bit self-conscious, a bit awkward, perhaps, stood there in the flesh, wondering why they didn't know him.

It took only moments for Tonetta to regain her composure, and when she recognized the former *guerrillo,* she sprang forward, leaping in long strides, all ladylike pretentions totally dissolved. She fell into his arms, laughing and crying. A look of insane bewilderment on her face, she twirled about the room in his arms, in sheer ecstasy. "Pancho! You son of a grizzly bear! It's you? It's really you? I knew it! I knew it! There is no prison in the world to keep the likes of Pancho Villa inside its walls." She had straddled him like a horse, and together they whirled about the room, frolicking as they'd done so many times in the past. Finally, Villa dropped her gently from his back and he grew silent. He placed his finger upon his lips in a gesture of silence. He moved back to the door, closed and bolted it shut. He glanced at Madelaina in recognition. Again

574

he held his finger to his lips. He crossed the room and peered from behind the curtain, out the window to the street below. Satisfied, he returned to the women.

"Little Fox, it's you," he said not trusting his eyes. Her pallor and recent loss of weight had disguised her well. "I am enchanted to meet with you once more. To say I am grateful doesn't truly describe my feelings. I learned what you did. But what brings you here?"

"Later, Panchito," interrupted Antonetta, happy to see her former lover safe and sound. "First, tell us how you managed to escape prison? What you are doing here in El Paso?"

"Listen, my little kitten. First, you must forget I am Pancho Villa. I am Doroteo Arango. If anyone should guess my identity, it could prove most dangerous for all of us."

His little kitten understood. *"Muy bueno.* First, we celebrate. A feast, plenty of wine. Then we shall exchange stories. Ayeiii, Pancho—I mean Señor Arango—some stories will prove most enlightening to you." She winked at Madelaina.

"No, my *gatitta.* No celebration. Merely a reunion of old friends. We remain here. Bring in food and we talk. I intend to bring no attention to myself. I have much important business to do here in El Paso."

Tonetta continued to scrutinize him. "There is something very different about you, my big bear. Not your clothing or your moustache—although I must say I like you better with than without," she laughed. "Very well, Doroteo, forgive me if I mention it, but you are not the Panchito I used to know."

Villa's eyes twinkled in merriment. "Of course not. The man you knew, little cat, was illiterate. He could not read or write. The man who stands before has been transformed into a human thinking machine. I read. I write. Imagine? Pancho Villa writing and reading? He understands things now. No wonder Madero had no use for that dirty ignorant peasant—"

"No! That isn't true!" countered Madelaina. "You were loyal! The only true friend and patriot Madero ever had—and look what he did to you! Look what Huerta had power to do to you without even a reprimand from *El Presidente!*" She spoke those last two words with biting sarcasm, as if the words themselves were heinous. "I myself ran to the palace when word arrived you were about to face Huerta's firing squad. *Demonio!* What it took for Raoul Madero and myself before *El Presidente* would send the wire! And to sentence you to prison was the worst infamy. And you, Doroteo Arango, to be so loyal to an undeserving man is beyond my comprehension!" Madelaina was shaking. Tears sprang from her eyes at the bad memories, all the pain and anguish she had suffered for a lost cause. "And now, you stand before me, the man for whose cause I defied my father, my best friend, and the only life I knew, and tell me in so many words that you condone Madero's shabby treatment of you. Are you so blind you can't recognize that you sacrificed your life for the wrong man? A weakling? A man so afraid of his own shadow he hasn't the guts to fight for what he believes in? *You* put Madero into the presidential palace—*not* Vitoriano Huerta! *You* won Juarez for the revolution—not Orozco or Huerta! And even after Madero placed Huerta in charge of the Northern Division of the Regulars, it was Pancho Villa who won victory after victory against Orozco and his Redflaggers. It was *you* who won victory at Torreon!" She stopped, out of breath.

Struck by Madelaina's emotional outburst, Pancho Villa stood transfixed, his eyes staring at her as if she were some apparition. Was he so thick-headed he couldn't understand such dialogue? In prison he'd learned plenty about the rotten politics and intrigues that ate away at the nation's capital. Was he to learn more from this mere slip of a woman? "You think Huerta is a threat to Madero?"

"You amaze me, Panchito," said Tonetta. "Ask yourself why Huerta lined you up against a wall with a firing squad ready to shoot you."

"You're so smart, *gatitta,* you tell me," he replied in

576

annoyance. A woman trying to tell Pancho Villa his business! Hah!

Madelaina rose to the occasion, not wishing to cause ill will between the old lovers. "Because you were a threat to him. Like I was a threat to him. You, *Jefe,* were fast becoming a legend. You became the power of the revolution. You are strong like iron. Like Zapata you are a stubborn Indian, incorruptible, unpredictable, with a heart that beats for Mexico. Huerta wouldn't be Madero's right arm if he permitted you to exist. It should be the puma, Pancho Villa the conqueror, seated at Madero's right arm—not Huerta!"

"Even without reading or writing?" It was incredible the things she said.

"Even then," said Madelaina flatly. "I, too, stood in Huerta's way, *Jefe.* Shall I tell you what Huerta did to me, *mi Generale,* in detail?" And so once again she gathered up the memories of those bad days at Madrigal and laid them out before him in all their grotesqueness.

Pancho Villa didn't move. At one point he lit a cigarette, took a puff, and quickly snuffed it out, remembering he didn't smoke. Before she finished, Villa shook with rage. His black eyes smoldered and he clenched his fists until his knuckles threatened to break through the skin. At one time he wouldn't have understood such intrigues, such complications. True, he was an Indian. A stupid, stubborn land-tilling *peón.* Once he held fast to a premise, he wouldn't let go.

"I should have told you all these things, *Jefe,* when we met in Parral. You knew I'd been imprisoned against my will, but you knew nothing of the vile treatment which I was forced to endure. Now, you know. I tell you only to acquaint you with the despotic, satanic personalities of both General Huerta and Major Salomon. I will never trust them—allies or enemies."

He stared at her for several long moments as he recalled the countless rumors he'd heard in prison that General Huerta was bent on crucifying Madero. He himself had been asked to participate in a plot, along with the old army irregulars who had fought against Diaz and now plotted against Madero because they found him unfit for the responsibilities of the presidency. Damn them all! Damn the stinking politicians, the *Porfiristas*, Huerta, Salomon, even Pasquel Orozco and his bastard Redflaggers! All those ambitious, corrupt politicians who wanted power—power—POWER had nearly taken his life, not once, but many times. If he lived to be a hundred, he'd never forget the feeling of being marched into the dusty courtyard and backed up against the adobe wall. Someone had offered him a blindfold. Even then he didn't believe what was happening. He refused a last request, offered by a young *capitán*, whom he was certain would at any instant break into a smile and admit it was all a joke.

He had heard the words. *"Atención! . . . Listo . . . Apuntar . . ."*

Still Villa didn't believe it. It was when he caught sight of the flashing steel sword upraised before the *capitán's* face that Villa convinced himself the scene was indeed real. Before the final order was given, in that last breathless moment, Villa raised his arms and cried aloud, demanding to be told why he was going to be shot. He insisted he'd been given no trial. He saw the six rifles leveled against him, when suddenly he heard the sounds of hard riding and the loud, outraged voice of Raoul Madero ordering that the execution be halted. In his hand was authorization from President Madero.

Never, never, never would Villa forget that incident or forgive the man who brought it about—General Huerta. Even after he was imprisoned in Mexico City, he was unable to shut the scene from his mind. He made a silent vow never to trust another man against his instincts. But instinct told him he should still trust Madero—because Madero had no one he could trust.

Madelaina's words had stoked his own memories of Huerta's attempted treachery. Pancho temporized, aware that his stubborn loyalty to Madero, whom he venerated illogically, frustrated both women. He convinced himself women could never hope to understand the logic that came to a new thinking man. This he told himself with newborn, fierce pride. To Madelaina he was more direct.

"In this world, comes time for everything. We cannot settle here and now what will be settled in time, Little Fox," he told her patiently. "I make a solemn oath to you, that I, Pancho Villa, will straighten out this government of Mexico in the near future. I make also this vow. Huerta will pay for the infamy done to you. And that vulture, Salomon, will feel the spur of fear in his ribs before I finish with him. Villa has never forgotten your friendship and what you suffered for him."

Villa paused. He glanced at Madelaina sitting in the stuffed wing chair by the window like a lost soul. She seemed to be in another world. He glanced at Tonetta and nodded when the redhead suggested in a whisper that they leave her to rest. Antonetta led the way to her suite of rooms, through the adjoining bathroom, with Pancho following at her heels. She had gone on ahead. Pancho Villa paused at the door to glance back at Madelaina. He disliked what he was about to say, but his Indian instinct forced the words.

"It is simply *maravilloso* what a man learns by reading, *señorita*. Only this morning I read that General Alvaro Obregon, a new friend and associate to Huerta, Salomon, and Carranza, has reenforced the battalion at Sonora to help defeat that sidewinder Orozco. Even after Orozco's recent departure, the battalion continues to exist. All this against President Madero, it said in the paper. Imagine that, Little Fox?"

Madelaina gave a start, her face as pale as lifeless cloud. "Huerta and my father united against Madero?" she exclaimed softly. "Truly, *señor*, I am doomed." Then Urbina's rumor was true.

Villa stepped back into the room. He squatted on one knee and looked deeply into her gravely concerned eyes. He patted her hand reassuringly.

"No, Little Fox. You are not doomed. Pancho never forgets a friend. It took much courage to break out of jail. One night my way was made clear through much travail. I found my way here—to begin anew what was started before my time. As long as Villa lives, you are not doomed." He kissed her damp hand, blinked his eyes, and placed a cool hand on her feverish forehead.

"The poor child has fever. Is there no doctor you can summon, *gatitta?*

"You can thank that stupid bastard Urbina for this!" snapped Antonetta, listening from the doorway.

"Urbina? Tomàs Urbina?" Pancho's eyes lit up with enormous excitement. "Where is that little devil?" he grinned openly. Just as quickly his eyes clouded over. "What you mean, woman, I can thank him for this? Speak up."

"Come, *mi Generale*. I'll tell you while I summon a doctor."

The next few weeks sped by rapidly for Madelaina. She had fully recuperated from the periods of profound weakness she experienced at Antonetta's boarding-house. The doctor attributed the condition to acute depression and the wounds she'd suffered at Isabel's hand. But Madelaina knew better. She wasn't adhering to the teachings of Tolomeo. How long would it take for her to remain on the track and stop derailing because of her emotional immaturity?

She began to concentrate on her career as a dancer. She rehearsed daily, and with Tonetta's constant encouragement, her faith was restored in both her dancing ability and her womanly charms. "You're a gorgeous woman, talented and young. Ju can capture the heart of many men," Antonetta would tell her. "Ees better ju choose a reech man than a poor man. And here in El Paso, *chiquita*," she'd say in her pigeon yankee, "ees many reech men looking for such a beautiful meesus. So be smart. Ju, weeth jur face of a gringa, attract for jurself such a reech man."

On the day Antonetta spoke these words, they had

visited the new shop where Madama Fifi of Paris sold Paris- and New York-inspired apparel for women. Under the firm persuasion of Tonetta's excellent taste, Madelaina had ordered many gowns, "far too many for what I really need," she protested.

She'd complained of a severe headache during the fittings and cut the buying spree short. Truth was, she was getting flashes of those same pictures she'd seen in the land of Tolomeo, and they all had to do with her old and sorely missed friend, Manuelito Perez. Vivid impressions of him in the arena came at her with more frequency. They all ended the same way, with Manuelito being gored and trampled by the bull before the picadors and other cape men could divert the attention of *el toro*. She saw him in death, at a funeral held for him in which he was greatly mourned by his people.

Then, because Madelaina forced the pictures from her mind, they'd cease. Such images were not the kind Madelaina relished, and she grew as puzzled as she was annoyed that she should see them with such frequency.

She and Tonetta left Madama Fifi's and crossed the busy thoroughfare, prepared to step into Tonetta's handsome carriage. Suddenly, Madelaina gave a start. A blast of horns and the loud beating of drums announced the coming *corrida* in the Plaza de Toros, as a small procession of dazzling matadors waved to the crowds from the top of a gaily decorated wagon. On an enormous double-sided placard was the image of a man whose face she'd never forgotten. A few years older perhaps, more mature, but still that handsome, dark-skinned gypsy face she knew so well.

"Matador Manuelito Perez!" came the voice over the loudspeakers. *"Señoras y señores, atención, por favor.* Ladies and Gentlemen. Jur attention, if ju please. Direct from Spain, the world's greatest and bravest matador of all time makes hees American debut. Saturday afternoon at four o'clock in the Plaza de Toros, will be Matador Manuelito Perez! King of all matadors!"

Madelaina heard no more. She had fainted in Tonetta's arms.

Two hours later, in the privacy of her home, Madelaina awakened on her bed with Tonetta standing over her, concern on her face for her friend.

"Manuelito," said Madelaina frantically. "Where is he? I must see him!"

"Who? What are ju talking about?" The redhead was concerned by these strange headaches and by the unusual comportment of her friend these past few months. "Manuelito—who?"

"Perez—the matador. Who else?" replied Madelaina, sitting up on the bed. She swung her legs over the side and stood up. "I must see him, *chiquita*. I must."

Antonetta understood. "Ju mean thees matador whose name is on the lips of all El Paso? Ju know heem, *chiquita*?"

"*Si*. I do. He is a dear friend from Las Marismas."

Antonetta's eyes lit up once more with dollar signs. "Ju theenk ju can influence these matador to come to the Diamond Slipper, *chiquita*? Ees much good for business," she insisted, rubbing her fingertips together in a gesture of money.

Madelaina smiled lightly. "Perhaps. For now, with the loan of your driver and bays, I will try to go and see him."

"No, *chiquita*, wait. Ees no good dat way. Leesten to Tonetta. I will send my driver with a note, inviting him to see the *Magnifica La Bomba*. Eef ju go, so many managers weel theenk ju are jus' another *aficionada* and will not let ju see him. Leesten to me, I know how eet ees."

"But Manuelito will see *me, querida*. We were very close."

"Dat close?" asked Tonetta with a suggestive smile.

"Not that close, you wicked woman. Like brother and sister."

Antonetta shrugged. "Whatever ju say. Ees no my

582

business. My business ees Pancho. And for days I 'ave no seen him. I go to find him. Ju sure jur O.K.?"

Madelaina nodded. "I'm sure. And Tonetta— remember, not Pancho. Doroteo Arango."

"How I forget all de time, eh? For so long ees Pancho to me, not dis Doroteo Arango." She tapped her forehead in mock annoyance. "I go now, *querida*. I see you much later, eh. At de club." She moved with a swish of her taffeta dress, leaving behind the fragrant smell of delicate musk. "Madelaina, eef all change their names, why not call me Toni? No? Ees more better?"

Chapter 22

"What exactly did you expect from me, Señorita Obregon, after the shabby way you and my cousin Armando treated me?" Manuelito Perez said coldly as he gazed down at her.

They sat in the drawing room of the hacienda rented by him during his stay in El Paso. She, demure and prim in a pale gray moire suit with her black hair cascading down her shoulders; he, swaggering back and forth in his trim matador's dress suit with a white ruffled shirt open at the neck. He had turned into an exceedingly handsome man, the pox marks on his face hardly noticeable.

Dismayed by his unexpected aloofness, Madelaina's crestfallen expression and her inability to understand such estrangement was like manna from the gods to the formidable matador. For years he had prayed for the day when he could repay the hurt she'd inflicted upon him during that sensitive and tender time in his life. And now, this was his day. He'd let her know exactly how he'd felt all these years, how he'd learned to hate her.

"How can I begin to tell you how sorry I am? I tried to find you that day, Manuelito, but you had left. No one knew where you'd gone. Why? Why did you disappear, *querido*." She paused. "*Your* cousin Armando? Why do you call him your cousin?" she asked with mild astonishment.

"Does it surprise you that I should be of *gachupín* blood? I am the son of Armando's uncle. That makes me his cousin."

"But that is wonderful, Manuelito. Simply wonderful. At least you know your roots. It wasn't so before."

"Stop trying to be so agreeable, Señorita Obregon," he countered rudely. "For so long I have remembered you and Armando's treatment of me with hatred in my heart—"

Madelaina interrupted. "Why is that? The letter I received from a most repentant man, which I have memorized in my heart, led me to believe that I was the victim." She quoted by rote. "*Querida*: I am writing to tell you of my wickedness. My conscience tears at me because I permitted a *bruja* to bewitch you. Forgive me. My heart bled with the pain of loving you because I could do nothing to convey my love. When I saw you leaving the bordello of Madama Tarragona—"

"*Basta!* Enough!" he interrupted. "I changed my mind since then. I was emotional and filled with guilt at the moment. But when I took time to reflect, I realized I had always been the wronged person. And this in itself consumed me with hatred."

"Manuelito," said Madelaina softly, rising to go to him and comfort him. "Please, don't let your heart spill over with hatred."

The nearness of her, this wench whom he'd always loved and couldn't stop thinking about, stirred his senses and created in the matador a burning desire for her. He wheeled around and, grasping her firmly and savagely, kissed her with a pent-up ardor that had fermented since his childhood.

"No, Manuelito," she protested, pounding his strong muscular shoulders. "No! Don't do this to either of us!"

"No, eh? Not to Manuelito will you say such a thing again, woman." He bent over and swooped her up into his arms. "I intend to do what I should have done long ago!" He moved to the circular staircase despite her loud protests and climbed the stairs. Holding her squirming, protesting body in his arms, he kicked open a bedroom door. "Now, *querida,* I will show you what it is to be loved by a real man—not a tea drinker like Armando."

"Oh, Manuelito, not like this." She stopped fighting

585

and ceased to protest when he dumped her unceremoniously on the large four-poster bed. "Much has happened since we last knew each other—"

"Silence, bitch! You think I don't know you were deflowered by Armando long ago—and God knows how many men after that. *Dios mios!* I find you dancing like a common whore in a place like the Diamond Slipper, displaying your body like—like—oh, don't pretend to me with your virginlike ways. Why do you blush? Why did you not blush last evening when hundreds of lust-filled men eyed you with desire in their eyes and hearts. To think I have loved an illusion all these years. That I permitted my life to be wrecked by the innocence of my youth. You, Madelaina Obregon, a cheap *puta*—a whore."

She winced under the cruel blow of his caustic tongue. "Don't judge me, Manuelito. You don't know the half of it—"

"Half? You mean your life has been far more sordid than it appears?"

He was irrationally incensed, thought Madelaina. Why, after all these years, he acts as if he owns me. "Listen, my dear friend," she began temporately.

"*Listen, my dear friend,*" he taunted. "*Que va,* my dear friend? Stop with this unnecessary talk!" He pulled off his shirt and stood before her in the dim bedroom lights, his powerful torso exposed. His trousers went next and in moments he stood naked, his body surprisingly muscular. "Now, *querida,* dear friend," he taunted, "remove your clothing or I shall tear them from your body!"

After all Madelaina had endured in her young life, she could still feel the pang of fear. Oddly enough, fear wasn't what motivated her in these moments. She rationalized that Manuelito, for all his loud ranting and raving and injured pride, was perhaps the last person she should fear. In his state of mind, if she fought him off, he'd no doubt pursue her and inflict some bodily harm, if only to relieve the pain, anguish, and hatred stored up in his searing heart.

586

His voice broke through her thoughts. "I have cursed your name and your memory a hundred times a day, over and over, until the hatred and anger I felt all those days after I left Las Marismas burned indelibly in my brain. Just when I felt sure I had rid myself of your memory, you have to turn up and display your body shamelessly and in such a place. I have suffered enough trying to do the right thing as befits a man of my class!" he snarled with a sudden brute force.

He brought both his hands down over her shoulders, held her roughly in his arms, and began to kiss her with vengeance until her lips felt crushed and parched. In a brief moment of ruthless despair, he thrust her from him and he turned his back to her. "I said undress, *puta*! Or shall I do it for you?"

"Very well, Manuelito, as long as you've decided that we must couple, I shall oblige you." She rose from the bed and began to remove her clothing. She lay her jacket carefully across the chair near the bed. She removed her blouse and skirt next, then her petticoat and lingerie until she stood as naked as he, quite next to him.

"Without protest?" he demanded airily.

"Without protest," she replied softly. It was the only way she could reach him.

He strolled in closer to her and stared at her fragile body as much as he'd stared at her the night before when he caught her act as *La Bomba*.

"I won't lie, Madelaina. You are as desirable to me now as you were when we were children, as you were to me last night when I saw you parading your nakedness before all those impertinent men. It was then I decided that, since you sold yourself so cheaply, I could afford you. First, I wanted you to come begging."

Madelaina felt the heat of his body as he moved in toward her, like the radiation of fire. She quivered inwardly as his arms reached for her. There was no haste in his movements, no urgency—no awkward fumbling of a man who didn't know women. He leaned over and kissed her. She was afraid he'd awaken the fires that

587

she'd kept smoldering for so long. She struggled slightly, and Manuelito misunderstood her movement to be a rejection of him.

"So, I'm still not good enough for the daughter of the illustrious General Obregon," he snarled. "For one moment—for one small moment, I told myself that maybe—maybe we could find those lost moments of our life and come alive. I see now it was folly. But I tell you, *La Bomba,* I shall have you like all the countless other men who've lusted for you!" He pulled her savagely to the bed and began to ravish her with the ferocity of an animal in heat.

"No—o," she began. She wanted to tell him that rape was unnecessary, but filled with uncontrollable violence and anger, Manuelito gave her no opportunity to talk with him.

Talk was not what he desired. It was revenge and the feel of Madelaina's body under his that he wanted. Only this would appease the torment the years had multiplied. To preserve his sanity, he needed this more than life itself.

His manhood stabbed at her body and finally entered her without preparation. Madelaina tried to hold back the scream that tore from her throat. His organ was like a bull's. She felt as if her body would split apart.

After the first few moments passed and her body had lubricated itself for him, she began to feel the pleasurable sensations that she hadn't experienced since Tolomeo. Slowly her body moved to his rhythm. The initial pain had passed. As she responded to him, she felt him grow more gentle, more considerate. She let herself slip into a euphoria of forgetfulness.

"This is what you've missed all these years," he whispered with a tinge of sarcasm. "This, the love of the most devoted man you will ever find."

"Yes," she whispered back. "I know, Manuelito. I've always known the love you held for me. It was written in every gesture—in everything you taught me even as you tried to avoid teaching me about the bulls."

"Silence, wench," he hissed, his body growing more

588

eager, more fervent. The heat of his body set her on fire. She stared into his dark eyes and clutched his black gypsy hair with her fingers as her body arched to meet his.

But Manuelito, burning and consumed with pent-up passion, couldn't wait. He was unable to control the boiling furnace threatening to explode in his loins. He couldn't. And when it erupted, it shook them both, even the bed vibrated from the enormous convulsions that tore at him as he experienced the raptures he'd dreamed of for so long. A loud, animalistic cry escaped his throat. "Madelaina! Madelaina," he cried with a noticeable tremor.

Madelaina, against her will, embraced him tighter. Unfulfilled, she gave no thought to her satisfaction, only that she could hear a low whimper escape him. She felt the warmth of his tears on her face, tasted their saltiness.

"What have I done? *Dios mios,* I couldn't even be a man for you—even after all these years that I've dreamed of making passionate love. I wanted you to know what pleasures you had missed. And what am I but a failure with you? I must ask your forgiveness. I find no whore in you. I am much ashamed."

"There is no need for you to feel ashamed, *querido mío.*" She reached up and silenced his lips with a fingertip. Instantly Manuelito caught it and kissed it.

"Do you have any wine, *chico*? I am thirsty." She smoothed the hair off his forehead. "Please?"

He sat up and turned on the bedside lamp. His dark eyes searched hers. "You are not angry? You aren't incensed by my unspeakable actions?"

She shook her head. "No."

Manuelito continued to search her eyes, hoping to find some answer to his dilemma. "You won't even slap my face?"

Again she shook her head, not sure of his mood. She learned soon enough.

"You are a cold, lifeless fish. Too elegant for the likes of Manuelito Perez, is that it? I could have taken

your wrath! Your anger and desire for retaliation for
so brutish an act. But not this detachment. This forgiving, sanctimonious endurance of yours. Why? Why are
you doing this, Madelaina? Am I so revolting to you
that you just put up with me?"

"Oh, Manuelito," retorted Madelaina with obvious
exasperation. "Why do you persist in this self-pity?
You torture yourself with self-doubts. You are your
own worst enemy!" she exclaimed, moving away from
him. She sat up and swung her legs over the bed. It
was then he saw the scars on her back.

He reached for her and pulled her back to him with
his strong brown arms.

"Who did this to you?" he asked huskily. His fingers
lightly traced the scars on her lower back as he
searched her eyes once more.

"Oh, those," she replied blandly. "You don't really
want to know."

"I do not ask questions for the pleasure of hearing
no answers."

"Very well, matador. Bring the wine and we'll fill
the gaps between us."

Reluctantly, he let her go and slipped off the bed.
He brought the wine and two crystal goblets, placing
them on the table next to the bed. He poured the ruby
wine in both glasses and handed one to her. "These
gringos live well, no?"

"To the rekindling of an affectionate and loving relationship," she toasted.

"It is not necessary to insult me. I know my place,"
he said drily.

They both drank, nevertheless. "Do you have a cigarette, Manuelito?" she asked lightly.

"A cigarette?" he asked, raising an eyebrow. "What
else does the *señorita* indulge in?" He spoke in a scath-
ing voice and she replied with maddening composure.

"We're even. Insult for insult. Although I can't see
that I insulted you."

She watched him pour more wine for them both and
replace the bottle on the table. "There are far more
590

devastating things that can happen to a young, impressionable woman than simply being *La Bomba,* Manuelito. I am not the sweet, innocent schoolgirl who once captured your heart," she began. For the next few hours, they sat close to each other like long-lost friends, bridging the gaps of time in their lives.

When Maneulito heard what had happened to Madelaina, he felt a remorse so powerful that it brought tears of shame to his eyes. "Why didn't you stop me? Why didn't you explain? Oh, Madelaina, I'm so ashamed to have put you through such torment. No wonder you couldn't respond to me as a woman should. I am an animal—a poor, demented animal without consideration."

"I didn't respond because you gave me no time," she chided. "How could you have known?" Then, on a gayer note, she prompted him to tell her about his life after he left Las Marismas. He began slowly, then as the wine warmed him and loosened his tongue, he began his story.

"Manuelito has lived and loved hard and swift, *querida.* I have buried my loins in the bodies of thousands of willing women, only to be haunted each time by the dark, dancing eyes and gay spirit of the woman for whose body I've longed and who now lies at my side. I am ashamed to say that I've lived and directed all my energies for a time such as this. No, no, let me continue," he said when she began to protest.

"I spent the years since we last saw each other perfecting my craft. I climbed to the top as king of the *corrida,* fighting any bull in any broken-down plaza in the fringe areas of Spain until I made the big time. Ah, *si,* I've starved and slept in the streets—in the gutters, dreaming of my success. And for what, *querida?* Shall I tell you? Waiting, biding my time for this moment when I would meet you face to face and with vengeance make you ashamed, repentant, and regretful that you wouldn't return the powerful ache of love I held for you in my heart. This love transformed itself over the years into a violent hatred and anger at you.

591

An all-consuming hatred which has driven me to take reckless and needless chances in the bullring." He inhaled deeply, bracing himself, then relaxed.

"You know why I have such a following of *aficionados, querida*? Shall I tell you the truth? It is because whenever Manuelito stars in a *corrida,* he will oppose the fiercest and bravest bulls. Because they know one day I'll not disappoint them. They know that my death in the bullring promises to be the bloodiest, goriest battle between man and beast they will be privileged to see."

"Manuelito—" protested Madelaina, finding the opening for which she had waited.

"No, *querida,* let me finish. It is the fashion in some circles in Spain to make wagers on this inevitability because it is a just and deserving retribution for a reckless man who courts death with arrogance. When Manuelito swaggers into the bullring to challenge his enemies for the afternoon, the crowds cheer and *olé,* knowing the end can come at any time for such a *muy loco* matador who defies every rule in the *corrida* against these killer bulls."

What Manuelito didn't tell Madelaina was the full extent of his recklessness. Such stupidity posing as talent was most apparent to his manager and his *banderillos*, the men who belonged to his *cuadrilla*—his team. These well-meaning men prayed to the Virgin de Guadelupe ten times each day, hoping the blessed saint would find a way to pour sense into this true champion, who could fight a few more years and retire a millionaire if he only ceased this foolhardy recklessness. They had all pleaded with their matador, begged him to use more caution until they could say no more without being fired.

Only recently, Manuelito had given them all a tongue-lashing with enough vitriol to intimidate a herd of charging bull elephants. He had seen how they wore their fear on their faces each time he entered the bullring. Their expressions, tense, taut, and fearful, had disturbed him more than their verbal reproach. His own endurance had its limitations. At his last appearance in Madrid, he had exploded. He cursed his *cuadrilla* up and down, accused them of acting like *viejas*—old women—and told him that if they didn't erase those apprehensive looks from their faces, he'd replace them immediately, before the scheduled tour to the Americas.

Their reaction was a natural one. Very well, they thought. If Manuelito is stupid and bent on suicide, why should they care? His rude, hostile attitude had transformed their concern for his welfare into apathy and detached indifference. Not permitted to show their concern, they began to secretly hope their fears would come to pass, that he'd meet his match one day. Only this way would his arrogance and ego be brought down a notch or two until he might be persuaded to take more precaution.

When she visited him at the hacienda on this night before the scheduled *corrida,* Madelaina knew about none of this emotional interplay within Manuelito's coterie of men. She only knew that she had to somehow deter him from appearing in the bullfights. Her dreams and visions had become more pronounced since she saw bills of advertisement announcing that Manuelito Perez would star in the *corrida.*

Manuelito had done precisely as Antonetta predicted when he received her invitation to be his guest at *La Bomba*'s performance. He hadn't recognized the scantily dressed woman in the photograph, the woman billed as *La Bomba,* dancer *extraordinario.* A special front table was prepared for Manuelito and his party, which included a bevy of stunning woman who fell all over the matador. It was placed at the edge of the stage and filled with elegant viands and choice foods fit for a king. Antonetta, shrewd business woman that she was, had let it be known that Manuelito Perez would be honored that night.

When the Perez party arrived, the countless hordes of *aficionados* who filled the Diamond Slipper to capacity arose en masse and gave the matador a standing ovation. Tonetta thought the rafters would cave in at the loud *olés* and cries of "Matador! Matador!" Manuelito accepted the fanfare and welcome as part of a normal routine. He strutted inside with the imperious attitude of *a gachupín,* with the pomp and panache of a matador. He bowed, waved his flat-crowned black sombrero to the crowds, and took the attention in his stride. Dressed in elegant black silk trousers, white silk shirt, and thin black tie, with a short bolero jacket trimmed in velvet, Manuelito Perez was perhaps the most handsome Spanish celebrity ever to grace the city of El Paso. Even the gringos turned out en masse to catch a glimpse of this romantic figure. The gringas especially fell all over him and he had difficulty brushing them off.

Antonetta had sashayed through the crowd to introduce herself and was politely requested to take the seat next to him.

"*Gracias,* matador," she replied with a dazzling smile. "The seat next to you is reserved for a very important friend of yours. With your permission, I request that it be given to no one else." She excused herself, eager to return to her overflowing cash registers.

Manuelito had given her remark no further thought. Such things happened frequently in his travels. Those eager to stand in the spotlight with celebrities always claimed they were important friends of his. Meanwhile, as he feasted and drank the choice wines, he paid scrupulous attention to one of the gringas in his party who flirted outrageously with him and made promises of the intimacies awaiting him when the festivities ended.

A fanfare of drums preceded the dimming of lights and persisted to beat out a soul-stirring rhythm as the colored lights outlined the scintillating body of *La Bomba.* So wrapped up in the gringa was Manuelito that he failed to be inspired by *La Bomba* for a few moments.

No performer, and least of all *La Bomba,* could stand not being appreciated by the guest of honor. Noting his attention on the gringa, *La Bomba,* it seemed, commanded the energy necessary for turning a mere performance into a spectacular, once-in-a-lifetime show which spectators would remember as the most magical stage moment they'd ever witnessed.

La Bomba concentrated her attention on Manuelito, commanding him, compelling him to notice her. Once he glanced her way, it was as if no one else existed for him. He was loath to turn his eyes from her. Her swaying hips, suggestive eyes, and the exquisite union of body, mind, and spirit concentrated into one effort reminded him of the discipline necessary in his own art. Even then, he didn't recognize Madelaina. Something about her, he thought, something stirred his excitement. An intangible. Perhaps the joy and pride an artist feels for another artist. It was her eyes, dark and penetrating, that seemed to magnetize him. Then suddenly, at the sound of muted trumpets she took the stance of a bullfighter. With the grace of a ballerina, she made passes—*verónicas* and half-*verónicas*—that caused Manuelito to give a start. How could this dancer—this *La Bomba*—have perfected what he had taught himself? How, he wondered. As quickly as one artist can detect a fraud or cheap imitator, so could Manuelito see that these were his own techniques. She was too good to be simply a dancer. He exchanged glances with his manager and a few members of his *cuadrilla*. They had also seen it. Manuelito wasn't just seeing things. Nor had he drunk too much wine. He stared intently at *La Bomba* as she climaxed her performance to a rousing stand-up ovation by the crowds who clamored for more.

She took six curtain calls and then permitted the next act to follow.

Manuelito became engrossed with thoughts of the dancer. How could *La Bomba* have so successfully demonstrated the very passes for which he'd become famous? Such expert imitation was the highest form of flattery.

Manuelito was still discussing *La Bomba* when Madelaina, in more sedate formal attire, was escorted to his table. Instantly the men sprang to their feet.

"*Señorita*," said Manuelito. "*Usted muy encantador*. You are most enchanting, *señorita*. Please, will you be seated?" His excitement was catching.

Madelaina knew that he didn't recognize her. Why would he? She was a mere child when they last saw each other. She had lived a hundred years in the past five. It was no wonder.

"*Gracias*, matador. With your permission."

He pulled out the empty chair until she sat down, then seated, he became most attentive and gracious. "What a superb dancer! What an artist! Truly you are extraordinary! Your billing does you little justice, if you permit me to be so bold." He poured champagne for her. "Tell me," he asked confidentially. "Where is it that you learned to master those techniques of the *verónica*? Especially that half-*verónica* interests me," he added.

"It was taught to me by a most important personality, years ago in a small village near Las Marismas in Spain," she began, half-taunting, her dark flashing eyes fixed on his. "His name was Manuelito Perez. Do you know him, matador?" She took delight in watching the changes on his face as he gave a start, then searched her face until he knew the truth.

Madelaina hadn't been prepared for his reaction. It was the hard and cold look he gave her, the stony expression that etched itself into his features that left her distraught and feeling she had trespassed on hallowed grounds.

"Don't you know me, Manuelito?" she asked when he had regained his composure. "It is not possible you've forgotten Madelaina Obregon?" She was unable to dismiss the terrible sinking sensation she experienced under his hostile glance.

"I know you. I have never forgotten you, Señorita Obregon. Now, if you'll excuse me." He called to his party. "*Ondolay, vamenos muchachos*."

He pulled himself up to his full, imposing height.

Nodding curtly to her, he and his party immediately filed out in a body, leaving Madelaina red-faced, confused, and humiliated by his iceberg reaction to her.

Not one to be deterred, Madelaina soon learned that Manuelito was staying in the hacienda—rather the mansion—of a gringo named William Benson, an American who had sponsored Manuelito's tour to the Americas. Benson was also breeder of the bulls Maneulito would fight on Saturday afternoon. Specially bred Chihuahuan bulls.

Aware of the fact that she might be insulted and turned away from the Benson mansion, Madelaina nevertheless chanced it. As she anticipated, when she presented herself at the door and gave the servant her name with instructions to tell Matador Perez, he returned with a polite and firm reply: Matador Perez knew no one named Obregon and didn't wish to be disturbed.

Madelaina, more humiliated than the night before and perplexed by this hostility, had left the premises terribly saddened by such a rude reception. Even if Madelaina Obregon deserved his arrogant dismissal, *La Bomba* didn't. Not even a jaded prostitute would be treated with such hauteur. What she had done to displease him and fall into such disfavor, she didn't know. But she had more avenues to pursue. She wasn't finished with him yet. She wouldn't give up that easily.

She returned to her apartment and called Antonetta. She discussed with her friend what it was she needed. A half-hour later, Doroteo Arango appeared at her door. "*Señorita.* Are you ready?"

"*Si, Jefe.* Is it all arranged? I hope that I don't put you in jeopardy, but it is a matter of life and death to the matador. And for some foolish reason he refuses to see me."

"It is arranged. I will take my chances."

Twenty minutes later, the carriage pulled up before the mansion of William Benson. Pancho was impressed. "This is how they live here across a river from us?"

"Not everyone lives like this. This Señor Benson, I

am told, is a wealthy *hacendado* who has much influence in Washington—and with Diaz," she added, unsure whether she should have mentioned *hacendados* to the very man who had good reason to loathe such political tigers.

Villa crossed himself. "*Dios mios.* If it is ever learned that Pancho Villa has stepped across the threshold belonging to such a man, he will be skinned alive, his *culjiones* fed to the coyotes."

"My lips are sealed, *Jefe.*"

He made an expression that was indescribable and Madelaina laughed the heartiest she'd laughed in years.

The door swung open. The servant, recognizing Madelaina, was hesitant to admit them. "Ah beg yer pahdon, suh. Are y'all expected?"

Madelaina translated in Spanish.

Pancho instantly spoke out in his pigeon yankee. "Please to tell jur boss, *el matador,* his guest has arrived."

"Very well, suh. Ah—step this way."

Pancho grimaced at the intolerable airs and winked broadly at Madelaina.

"Señor Villa," called Manuelito from the salon as he stepped forward to greet them. "I cannot express the thrill I feel that the *premier jefe* of all Mexico should honor Perez by his presence—" He stopped abruptly when he saw Madelaina. It wasn't proper that he should ignore her now. To do so would be an insult to Villa.

"It is my privilege, matador," said Villa in Spanish. "May I present Señorita Madelaina Obregon, a woman responsible for my many victories." He spoke with aplomb and the respect due a person of high social stature.

Manuelito bowed. As Madelaina surmised, he wouldn't dare ignore her in the presence of such a powerful figure as Pancho Villa, who was revered by the *peóns* in both Spain and Mexico.

They were both treated with the utmost courtesy and respect. Manuelito, the congenial host, ordered refresh-

ments and after the amenities were out of the way—
Pancho lauding the matador's bravery and skill in the
arena, and Manuelito, just as complimentary, lauding
Villa's feats—the *jefe* rose to take his leave.

"*Buenos suerte* at the Plaza on Saturday, matador,"
he said. "The *señorita* has informed me that you are
great friends, so I leave you both to your fond memories. Ah, one thing more, matador. It would please
me if you speak nothing of our encounter. You see,
I am on a—shall we say—sabbatical? I am traveling
incognito, you understand?"

Manuelito nodded. "I understand perfectly. God
bless you, *jefe*. I understand you are attempting to do
the impossible."

Villa glanced up at him with those twinkling eyes
that gave him the appearance of a benevolent grand-
papa. "It is you who attempt the impossible. You think
I'd face such machine of power like a bull? Ayeiii,
matador. You think Pancho is crazy?" He tipped his
hat and left them.

Instantly the atmosphere changed. It was zero degrees between them.

"Please, Manuelito, tell me why you are so displeased with me that you'd force me to put the life of
Pancho Villa in jeopardy just to see you?"

The matador had turned on her with anger, venting
his wrath.

That was two hours ago. Now they had filled in the
gaps of time, and they sat back quietly in bed in the
silence that engulfed them.

"So, tell me, why it was that you were forced to enlist the assistance of Pancho Villa to see me?"

"*Why?* You already know. What it is that I must tell
you is what I intend doing. Manuelito, please do not
ridicule me for what I am about to tell you. You must
not fight in the *corrida* on Saturday. You mustn't, understand?"

His silent questioning reached out at her across the
bed and she felt herself falter, but only for a moment.

599

"There is grave danger if you persist in making an appearance. Manuelito, for some strange reason I've been mysteriously given the powers of a *bruja*. I can see the future. And in my mind I've seen you fighting a Chihuahuan bull, in a place exactly like the Plaza de Toros, and the result is disastrous. *Por favor, chico*. I beg of you, do not fight on Saturday."

"For this nonsense, you called upon Pancho Villa and risked my doing you bodily harm?" Manuelito wanted to laugh in ridicule. Why couldn't he?

"I have seen this catastrophe for the past six months, *chico*. Don't dismiss it so lightly."

"Do you usually see pictures of this nature?" he chided.

"Oh, Manuelito. Don't make fun of me. I am new to all this. I have never been so concerned in my life. There is no way you can escape this destiny if you insist on fighting the bulls on Saturday."

"*Basta!* Enough, Madelaina! I have heard enough!" He sprang to his feet, opened a mahogany chest nearby, and slipped into a rich damask robe. His face had darkened in annoyance. "I cannot permit such thoughts of fear to enter my mind. You hear? I must perform on Saturday. I am bound by a contract. Besides, this debut in America will pave my way to triumph in Brazil and Argentina, where I go next to be granted the highest honor ever bestowed upon a matador." He tied the sash around him with angry punctuating movements.

"If you persist in performing on Saturday, you will never reach South America," she said dully.

"Madelaina! Stop! I command you! You say you saw—in these crazy pictures—the Plaza de Toros? What makes you so positive it is the one in Juarez? Why not the one in Mexico City or in Buenos Aires or even Madrid? They are quite similar, no?"

Madelaina arose from the bed, dejected and spent. "I tried, my dear friend, to make you see. But you will not see. Therefore, I can do no more. I will leave and permit you to dwell upon my words, matador. Try to bear in mind that a wise man is one who acts out of wisdom, not fear."

"So, now you say I am afraid? Is that it? Manuelito is nothing but a *niño* who is frightened of his own shadow?"

"Never that, Manuelito," she said, slipping into her clothing.

"Very well, Madelaina, you know me too well. I will speak the truth. I *am* afraid. I *am* scared. Every time I see the announcement of the *corrida* with my name on the bill, I shake in my boots. It begins at the start of the season and the trembling doesn't end until the season is over. You see? I am a fraud."

"You insist on being hard with yourself. It was you who taught me that to fight a bull when you are not scared is nothing. And not to fight a bull when you are scared is nothing. But, *amigo,* to fight a bull when you are scared is something. That is why Manuelito Perez is premier matador of all Spain."

Perez shrugged. "It isn't every matador who gets a preview of his own funeral, *querida,*" he said with a faraway look in his eyes.

Madelaina was dressed now. She walked toward him. "Will you at least say *adios* in good spirits? I'm not certain I understand any of this. Why, out of this entire world, was I chosen to bring you this message? I, too, am confused by such a mission. Since you will not heed my premonitions, I can only say *vaya con Dios,* Manuelito. I wish it could have been different between us. Different for you. You should have claimed your heritage, returned to Las Marismas as Manuelito Cortez. And I perhaps should never have left Spain." She moved to the door. "*Buenos suerte—good luck,* my dear friend."

"Madelaina?"

"*Si, chico.*"

"I thank you for all your effort. Before you leave, tell me one thing. Are you the woman of Pancho Villa?"

She was arrested by the question and tensed for a

moment. She shook her head. "Not I. It is the redhead who belongs to him." As soon as she spoke the words, she regretted them. It was a foolish move on her part and she spoke only to ease the pain in Manuelito who already thought her to be quite wicked. All his Spanish morality condemned a woman who displayed herself as *La Bomba*. But she was too fatigued to spar further with him.

"A los toros!" came the cries. "To the bullfights!"

For an hour, the Avenida Juarez had been jammed by a steady stream of carriages and throngs of people on foot, all hurrying to the edge of town, to the Plaza de Toros. Cowboys on horses maneuvered their animals through the crowds and tethered them in the stables nearby, paying a fee to guarantee no one would run off with them. Fancy horses, gaily decorated with feathers, drew carriages filled with men and woman dressed in their finest, with dusters over their traveling costumes.

Hawkers with sweets and tortillas and tamales milled through the throngs, selling their tidbits, and the crowds poured into the seats of the plaza. In the shade, where the seats sold for the dearest prices, the gringos, the Spanish, and the Mexicans of means sat regally in the boxes. In the sun, the broiling, melting sun, sat the commoners, the *peóns,* the *aficionadas* of the *corrida,* who cared not where they sat as long as they enjoyed themselves.

Madelaina, dressed in a pale yellow and white cotton dress with a whalebone corset pushing up her breasts and nipping in her waist until it seemed she had none at all, moved along with Antonetta in the shade and sat down behind five tall, wide-shouldered men who nearly obstructed their view. Chewing tobacco and constantly spitting out the juices, the men annoyed them, but they refrained from venting their feelings.

Antonetta, dressed in emerald green moire with her red hair piled high, wore a straw bonnet trimmed with bird feathers and ribbons. She was a knockout, thought

Madelaina, the epitome of femininity. She tried to recall how she'd looked as a *campesina,* but the image wouldn't form in her mind.

"What a man, that Arango!" exclaimed Tonetta. "What discipline. He refused to come today, however much he loves the *corrida. Pues,* he has so much business, this general with no army, no?" She laughed at the inside joke until she caught Madelaina's stern look.

"Hush, woman! You never know whose eager ears may be listening."

"Ayeiii," said Tonetta, dismayed. "Who can remember all this intrigue without a war or even a revolution around them?" she whispered in their native tongue.

From time to time the five rough and ready cowhands seated before them turned to gaze at the unescorted women. They gestured suggestively to each other. As men of their calibre were wont to do on occasion, they spoke inaudibly amongst themselves and continued to make exaggerated eye gestures over the presence of such women.

The women ignored their ridiculous antics. Their eyes were everywhere, watching the crowds, listening to the brass band, picking up on a conversation here and there. Madelaina glanced at the golden watch fob pinned to her dress. It was nearly four o'clock. Time for the colorful pageantry to commence, she thought with dismay as the stars were announced over the public address system. Manuelito Perez still intended to contest the bulls. Pray, dear Lord, that her premonitions were false, she said silently.

The blaring blasts of brass trumpets marked the beginning of the *corrida.* Familiar refrains of *"La Virgen de la Macarena,"* the *paso doble,* began. The crowd cheered and cheered; their cries reached a crescendo as the matadors entered the plaza followed by their *banderillos* and the picadors on horseback. Bringing up the rear were the drag mules. Leading this spectacular extravaganza were the constables, dressed in sixteenth-century costumes with gold-embroidered jack-

603

ets and wide beaver sombreros with pompoms on one side. Thick yellow padding protected their legs.

The *cuadrilla* dressed a shade less flamboyantly than the matadors, who wore costumes of thickly encrusted gold embroidery, so dazzling in the sunshine that the crowds often averted their eyes from the glare. It was a magnificent spectacle of ceremony, pomp, and grand tradition. Each phase of the dramatic *corrida* was cheered on by the wild and passionate cries of the people: mantilla-draped *señoritas,* elegant *dons* with broad-brimmed sombreros cocked jauntily over one eye, and of course the gringos.

"You know how long it's been since I've seen the *corrida*?" asked Madelaina, enjoying every second of the pageant. She tried not to show the nervousness and fear she felt over Manuelito's scheduled appearance. He had drawn the third bull. Two Mexican matadors would have an opportunity to show up this Spanish import first. The rivalry between Perez of Spain and the Mexican matador created an added note to the excitement already permeating the arena.

"I hope the bulls are brave, *chiquita,*" said Madelaina to her friend. "Some I've seen here in Mexico leave much to be desired. These Chihuahuan bulls cannot compare to the Concha or Miura bulls. Ayeiii, those are some bulls, Tonetta. Strong forelegs, alert, sharp-witted. But these Chihuahuan *toros* are much like the Salamancas—no strength either in force or character."

"How is it you know so much about bulls?" asked the redhead politely; she understood very little about bullfighting, except for its tradition.

Madelaina had no time to reply. The first matador was ready and the first bull entered the ring. She watched the contest between Mexican and bull and declared it had been a waste to see such an abominable showing. "The bulls are worthless. They respond poorly to all elements of the fight. See, Tonetta, they hardly charged the first capes, wandered away from the horses, and ignored the picadors. *Dios míos!*" she continued. "Look, they even have difficulty following the red *muleta* at the finish. It is cruel to kill such oxen! Bah!"

She began to think all her premonitions were false. Truly, she had no reason to fear for Manuelito if he was going to oppose such docile cows. If anything, it might be his pride which would suffer.

The next matador butchered the beast with three bad thrusts of his sword. Madelaina grew as indignant as the booing crowds. She snorted contemptuously, thoroughly caught up in the slovenly show of burlesque between man and beast.

"This is butchery—not a bullfight!" she exclaimed scathingly.

During the first two bouts, Madelaina noticed that one of the men seated in the box ahead of them turned in her direction whenever she remarked about the bulls. His aloof reaction to her statements turned into curiosity, then into a recalcitrant determination to put her in her place. The more he listened to her criticism, the more he realized that she had some knowledge of bulls. His outward attitude of censure gave way to piqued interest.

William Benson turned three-quarters of the way around in his seat to address her. "Pahdun me, ma'am. Ah jus' couldn't help ovahheahing youah comments." Because he spoke in the same west Texas drawl that had sent shivers up and down her spine for so long, she looked at the man more closely than she would normally have.

"Ah'd like to know mahself wheah such a lovely *señorita* gets ta know so much about bulls." He had removed his Stetson hat, revealing salt and pepper hair clipped close to his head and bushy eyebrows over piercing blue eyes.

Madelaina lowered her eyes and nudged her companion. She turned her nose up in the air at him. How dare he speak to her without benefit of a chaperone? Did he take her for some common whore? Tonetta had explained the ways of the gringo women, whose rules concerning such encounters were as stringent as the Spanish custom. She wasn't about to give this stranger the time of day. Why was the intermission so long, she wondered.

"Sorry, m'am. Ah meant no disrespect. Y'all wait heah for a moment. Ah'll be back in two shakes of a bull's tale." He lifted his huge frame from the seat and moved into the crowd.

"*Es un muy loco,*" said Tonetta. "He ees some crazy man, no?"

"No ma'am. Youah shuah wrong theah," retorted one of the men seated alongside William Benson. He turned in his seat to take a good look at Antonetta.

"Hot damn!" he exclaimed recognizing her. "It's *La Gatitta*! Damn, it's shuah good to see ya again, little *La Gatitta*."

Her eyes lit up in recognition. "Gringo? Ees ju, Waco? Ees long time no see ju. Where ju keep jurself, eh? Leesten, ju meet *La Bomba*? Ees new star attraction at Diamond Slipper."

Madelaina nodded curtly to him and gazed over his head, wondering at the delay in the ring below them. The three men now turned to gaze at her, then laughing at some inside joke, they nudged each other and howled uproariously.

"Something tickles your funny bone?" Antonetta asked icily.

Waco, obviously the spokesman for the trio, took off his hat and smoothed back this thinning hair. "That theah man is ouah boss, little *gatitta*. Name's William Benson. He's a big noise heah in El Paso. Foah that mattah, he's a big noise in the whole state of Texas. What weah laughing at—and no offense intended, m'am—is that Mistuh Benson usually has no truck with gambling house queens." He laughed again and the others joined in finding the situation quite humorous.

Even Antonetta found their confidence amusing. She laughed along with them. Madelaina, however, found nothing humorous in their roughhousing. She also felt

606

they were in some way ridiculing the man for showing an interest in what they called gambling house queens. Not wishing to embarrass either Tonetta or herself or cause her to lose business, she ignored them and kept her eyes on the bullring. So this was Manuelito's host, William Benson, she thought. She hadn't spoken too kindly of his bulls. Well, what of it? She spoke the truth. If he couldn't accept the truth, it was no affair of hers.

"*Chiquita,* what has theese gringo done?" asked Tonetta, nudging her.

William Benson returned to his box, dragging the mayor of Juarez with him. The official resembled Francesco Madero to such an extent that at first she was startled.

"*Señorita?*" The mayor pulled off his top hat with a forced flourish. He spoke in Spanish. "Permit me, with your permission, to present to you Señor William Benson. He wishes me to impart to your lovely ears that he means no disrespect. So enchanted is he with your knowledge of the *toros,* he wishes you to join him this evening at a dinner given in honor of Matador Manuelito Perez, so you can exchange with him such valuable knowledge of the bulls. You are most welcome to bring a chaperone, is Señor Benson's wish."

The nervous official had in the course of his speech recognized Antonetta. Torn by a burning impulse to advise Benson of exactly who she was, he was silently urged not to make such a mistake by Antonetta's articulate green eyes. He faltered and lowered his small bird eyes to stare at the tips of his patent leather shoes. Madelaina saved the moment.

"You may tell, Mr. Benson," she stated in English, "it is not necessary that I bring a chaperone because I decline his offer." Speaking directly to the mayor, she was able to avoid eye contact with Benson. "You will also inform Mr. Benson that the reason I decline his invitation, even if it is to honor a dear friend, Manuelito Perez, is because I am a working girl." She leveled

607

her dark fiery eyes on the three cowboys who flushed uncomfortably at her disclosure.

"I am a dancer at the Diamond Slipper. If he still desires to speak with me on the subject which interests him, the quality of his bulls, he can bring his party to the Diamond Slipper for dinner. I shall, when my time is free, sit with him to answer his questions." She rose to her feet. From the corner of her eye, she noticed his flushed face and rising anger at the rebuff. "Come, Tonetta," she said with polite reserve. "This bullfight is not worth our time. It is best we leave."

"Ah wouldn't do that, m'am," interrupted William Benson. "If ya do, ya might have to stuff youah words. The bull Perez has been puhsuadud ta fight isn't like the bulls y'all have seen tuhday."

The roar of the crowd at this moment drew her attention to the ring. Manuelito Perez had entered the arena. The third bull was his. When it came charging into the ring, she recognized instantly that it was dangerous and unpredictable. But Perez, out to cut an ear, made the animal charge back and forth in front of him so closely and gracefully that even his detractors were up out of their seats, yelling.

When it came time to kill the bull, he missed with the first thrust. The second dropped the animal cleanly. The crowd applauded, but they didn't wave their handkerchiefs. Perez had lost the ear; the crowd demanded perfection from this Spanish matador.

At least the bout hadn't ended in tragedy, thought Madelaina as she watched Manuelito leave the arena. But there was more. The trumpet blew and the next matador, a Mexican, took his turn with a bull. His art was applauded and cheered until the president of the arena granted the Mexican an ear.

Madelaina had lost sight of Manuelito, but now she saw him enter the arena, as the blare of the trumpet announced the final and most challenging bout. He strutted with the majesty of a king. He stopped before Madelaina's box and paused to bow. He removed his *montera*—hat—and waved it in a circle over his head.

608

With a quick, sudden move, he tossed his hat to Madelaina. She caught it and tossed him a lace handkerchief. In this small ritual, Perez had dedicated the bull to her.

All eyes were on her and she basked in the limelight. But suddenly Madelaina saw him. Terror struck at her. She sat down quickly, trying to slink behind the four Texans. She grabbed Tonetta's hand. "Quick, we must leave. Don't ask questions," she urged, her face drained of color. "When I say move, we both move, *pronto, querida.*"

Antonetta was fit to be tied. "Now, at the most interesting moment—just when everyone sees it's *La Bomba* to whom the bull was dedicated?" Her dismay was apparent, but the frantic silent appeal on Madelaina's face brought agreement to her lips. "*Muy bueno*—we go."

Before the crowd had resumed their seats, Madelaina and Antonetta were nearly outside the bullring, well on their way to Antonetta's carriage.

Safe inside the cabriolet, Tonetta, busting wide open for an explanation, heard only these words. "General Huerta saw me. I'm sure he recognized me."

Antonetta turned from her friend. She leaned forward in her seat. "One dollar extra for ju, *chico*," she told the driver, "if ju get us to the club in less than five minutes."

"All right, m'am!" called the liveried black man. "Weah already theah, m'am!" He touched his hat, grinned, and sent the whip sailing over the heads of the matched bays.

"Ju know who ees theese Meester Benson, *querida*?" she asked Madelaina. "Hee ees Meester Texas. Ees also one beeg man in Mexico, a man much respected by Diaz. Waco tells me thees."

"Diaz is no longer president," muttered the general's daughter, still clutching Manuelito's black *montera* tightly in her hands.

"*Chiquita,* ju know what Tonetta means. The gringo *hacendados* are beeg men here as well as in Mexico.

Thees wan has *mucho dolares*. Eef he theenks enough for ju, maybe he could help ju." In her next breath Tonetta proceeded to negate her words. "Waco teels me he ees some terrible man. Ees best ju ignore heem." She laughed aloud over the rumble of the carriage wheels on the stone street. "Ju got some guts to tell heem the truth, straight out. 'I am dancer at Diamond *Sleepar*!' " She repeated Madelaina's words, just as arrogantly as she'd heard them earlier.

"Ayeiii, *chiquita. Un guapa muy tempestuosa* ees what ju are! A real gutsy woman."

But Madelaina heard none of these words. Still shaken from seeing her mortal enemy in the crowd with a few other uniformed *Federales,* her mind whirled in confusion, wondering what he was doing in El Paso. There were other things annoying the daughter of General Obregon—visions of Manuelito just as she'd seen him earlier, falling to his death in the bullring at the mercy of the bull. She hadn't even stayed to observe the animal he drew.

Damn you, Huerta! She cursed inwardly. Will I never be rid of you?

"We must make certain Doroteo Arango hears of his presence in El Paso," she said *sotto voce*. "It is important the *jefe* learns, understand?"

"*Si,* Little Fox, I understand. It is not necessary to explain whose presence it is that must be brought to the attention of Señor Arango." She lapsed back into Spanish.

"*Muy bueno, chiquita*. We are in accord," replied Madelaina. She reached in toward Tonetta in a gesture of apprehension. "I am so afraid for Manuelito," she confessed. She told Antonetta of her fears and visions. "And after all my cautions I didn't even get to see my own foolishness. Pray God I was wrong."

Chapter 23

Manuelito Perez glanced up into the box seat section in time to see Madelaina exit with Antonetta following at her heels. She was lost in the crowd for a time. Even then the matador gave no thought to the possibility that Madelaina had actually left the Plaza de Toros. In truth he had no time to be concerned with her at the moment. Manuelito was determined to give the best performance of his life. As the gate swung open, the last bull of his entire life came charging and skidding out of the tunnel.

The instant he saw the beast hooking around the ring, he sucked in his breath. One of his men cursed aloud, "This one is bad, bad, *muy mal*. See how it hooks to the left? Stay away from this one, matador," he warned.

"Why?" asked Manuelito, arching his back stiffly. "Because I must go over the right horn to kill?" he retorted with scorn. "I have fought such bulls before. And for what they are paying, these gringos expect a master, not those Mexican *vaqueros* who make tricks and fancy cape twirls instead of art. They are clowns, not masters! Perez will show this crowd the real thing if it kills him!" Never had Manuelito Perez referred to the words, "death" or "kill" in the ring or at anytime during a *corrida*.

His teammate hesitated, struck dumb by his choice of words. Because the timing was not proper, he made no reference to such bad judgment. Later, he would recall with vivid clarity this telltale sign which should have told him tragedy was about to strike.

Manuelito placed the cape securely in his hands, slid through the fence opening and called to the bull.

"*Toro*, hah, *toroooo*," he called, shaking the cape before him.

The animal wheeled at the voice, its tail shot up, and he charged across the dusty ring. When the bull reached him, not once did Manuelito spin about or swirl the cape or dance around the way his Mexican competitors had done earlier. He merely planted his feet firmly and executed those skilled passes he'd taught Madelaina. He swung the cape slowly before the bull's nose, guiding the ferocious head with the tantalizing red cloth, so that the left horn sailed past ten inches away from his leg.

Without moving his feet, he took the bull back in another charge and the right horn stabbed at him a few inches from his thigh. Six more perfect classic *verónicas* followed, each closer than the other, finishing with a half-*verónica* so close that the bull's neck hit him, nearly knocking him off balance.

The crowd, delirious with excitement, cheered with abandon. Manuelito, in a classic pose, turned his back on the beast and accepted the roaring accolades from the crowd. "*Viva* Perez! *Olé* Perez!" came the hysterical cries. Here indeed was a master—the fearless king of all matadors.

Now, with the *muleta*, cape, his specialty, he worked closer to the thundering charge of dynamite, wondering as he did why he hadn't seen Madelaina's face in the crowd. He saw the face of the gringo Benson, who had dared him to contest this special bull, one he had bred and crossbred from a strain of killer bulls. What was their wager? Five thousand gringo dollars. *Muy bueno,* thought Manuelito. It is not so much the dollars, it was his pride that was at stake and his determination to prove Madelaina wrong. He wanted to win this extra purse, then beg the love of his childhood to marry him and leave this accursed land in which she had suffered so greatly. He could take care of her. He was a wealthy and highly respected man in Spain. He could give her the things to which she'd been born. These were the thoughts occupying Manuelito's mind as he

612

began the Pass of Death and his own perfected and highly dangerous *Perezinas*.

What followed was the most memorable day bull-fighting had ever known in that era. He paid no attention to his *cuadrilla* who were shouting, "No, No!" Nor did he give any importance to the crowds crying, "No, Perez! No!"

He performed over a dozen suicidal natural passes, those in which the sword is taken from the cape and only a small ineffective bit of cloth is used to divert the bull away from the body. And then, feeling secure, overflowing with ebullience and a marked cocksuredness, he did his famous and most death-defying fear—a fantastic pass where he looked disdainfully away from the bull up into the stands as the animal thundered by. He wanted to see the look of adoration in Madelaina's eyes. It seemed to the crowd as though the bull couldn't miss—but he did. By now the crowd was hoarse from cheering. What perfection! How superb! This indeed is a master! What domination he has over this beast!

It was time for the kill. He began final preparations, lining up the bull so its feet would be together, shoulder blades open. In the far distance, beyond the roar of the crowds and the smell of baked earth and animal stench, Manuelito heard his *banderillos* shout warnings to him. "Stay away from him! Off to the side and quick!"

Oh no. This wasn't for Perez! Earlier they had refused to grant him an ear. No further humiliation for the King of Matadors. This one—this final and magnificent ecstasy—was to be a gift to Madelaina, his bride, he told himself.

No running offside and stabbing it in the lungs to spoil so magnificent a performance. He'd head in straight, slip in the blade, give the bull a fair shot, and hope to the Virgin it wouldn't hook to the right.

There stood Perez the Magnificent in front of the deadly killer bull, sighting down the sword, rising on the toes of one foot. As the bull lunged forward, Manuelito hurled himself straight over the lowered right horn. The sword was sinking in, the horn cutting right by him. But suddenly the bull jerked its massive head to the right and sank its horn deep into the matador's groin.

Manuelito, trying to fight the horn from his body, was flung high into the air and slammed hard into the sand. The bull in a passion of fury gored him twice on the ground, then staggered, choked on his own blood, and flopped over dead, the sword, perfectly thrust up to its glittering hilt, between its shoulder blades. Pandemonium struck, the hordes screaming loud cries of horror and dismay. Quickly the crowd was stunned into silence. The crimson lake of blood in the sands was enough to inform his *cuadrilla* that Manuelito Perez was mortally wounded.

En route to the ring infirmary, he kept muttering. "The ears and tail go to Madelaina, *querida,* the love of my life."

William Benson and his men arrived at the infirmary. Only he was permitted admittance. Manuelito, laid out on a makeshift table while examined by a physician, raised his blood-shot eyes and fixed them frantically on the wealthy cattleman.

"I win, *señor gringo*?" He gripped Benson's arm, half-lifting himself from the table against the doctor's protest. "Promise me you will give the purse to Señorita Madelaina Obre—" He stopped in time. On his death bed, as he took his last breath of life, he remembered his promise not to give away her true identity. "To *La Bomba,* the star at the Diamond Slipper. Tell her I will love her for all time. I should have listened to her, *señor*. She predicted my demise on this day—"

Manuelito shuddered desperately as death's icy fingers reached out, extracting his soul from his body.

Two hours later, as Madelaina prepared for the evening's performances, she was still listening to the same tune from Antonetta as she exclaimed of the advantages and financial security open to a woman who married a man like William Benson. Finally in exasperation Madelaina demanded that she refrain from mentioning Benson again. "He means nothing to me. I will not occupy my thoughts with such a man who is openly known for his cruelty!"

"Very well, *chiquita*. I will not speak again of this most important *hacendado*."

"Tonetta!" warned *La Bomba*.

"Oh, jur crazy! I go now!" She retorted. "I 'ave enough of my business not to be busy with jurs," she said, slamming the door to Madelaina's dressing room.

Antonetta shrugged her shoulders back and patted the folds of her exquisite turquoise French original, a beaded, form-fitting sheath that flounced out at the knees. It makes no difference to speak of necessity to Madelaina, she thought. The woman still has a will of her own. So forget her. Attend to business. Her eyes lit up as she walked through the gambling palace to see it growing crowded, even at this early hour. The clatter of silver dollars drowned out the music, a sound welcome to her ears. Faro was the house specialty and the latest was a new game of poker, with several varieties called stud and draw that some of the newly rich oilmen seemed so excited about. These gaming tables were jammed packed with men eager to try their luck.

She continued to saunter through the large and brightly lit salon, nodding to some, waving to others, a fixed smile broadening into a grin at the sight of such business. All the while her attention was trained subtly on two exceedingly tall foreign-looking men dressed in civilian clothing, standing in an unmistakable military brace at the end of the bar. Coming toward her was a trusted employee, Jesus Morales, a young Mexican lad who spoke in Spanish.

"Madame," he addressed her respectfully, "two gentlemen wish to speak with the proprietress on a matter they will not divulge to me."

Antonetta glanced past him at these men, who were not exactly strangers to her. She'd seen them once or twice before here in her establishment and then in the vicinity of her boardinghouse. "Very well, Jesus," she nodded curtly. "I shall be there in a moment."

Since the revolution had commenced, these foreign-looking men had overrun Juarez and El Paso both. She approached them with the utmost courtesy and pleasantness, flashing a dazzling smile.

"*Si, señores,* what can I do for ju?" She spoke her pigeon yankee.

It turned out they desired to rent one of her small salons where businessmen frequently met to converse in the intimacy of a private room. The salon, to be provided with drinks and food and other refreshments, was booked and paid for in advance under the name Eric Von Klause.

The news of the tragedy at the Plaza de Toros hadn't yet begun to trickle in. It would take nearly two hours before her informers would run in with such news. Meanwhile she attended to business and busied herself throughout the establishment, wherever her services were needed. No question, she thought, the *corrida* will encourage thirsty men to drink, then gamble. Was this not why Antonetta was in business? To cater to the desires of free-spending men with unusual appetites.

How many times she had wistfully confided to Madelaina she wanted to operate a brothel, a whorehouse *extraordinario* like many of other establishments were running of late. Doroteo Arango, with his convoluted sense of Indian morality, wouldn't permit it. Since the majority of women would be Mexicans, he would not bring such shameful degradation upon the Mexican woman who was already regarded at a substandard level by the gringos.

"Ju don' see gringos operating such places with the gringas! No! So why permit them to satisfy their lust on our women?"

So negative and indignant had Pancho been over this, Antonetta pushed it from her mind. She didn't dare justify her desire by alluding to the immorality so prevalent among his camp followers. Nor did she dare suggest that it would be better for those *campesinas* to be paid whores than unpaid *putas* who struggled against

616

disease and death each moment of their existence.

Periodically she'd mention this secret desire and ultimate plan of hers to Madelaina. "Ju know how much gringo dollars we could make owning such an establishment, *chiquita?* Ayeiii! Eet makes me seeck jus' to theenk about eet. Bot, what can I say, eh? Pancho ees my man and while he ees my man, I do as he desires."

Antonetta moved behind the bar, swishing to one side as she kept her icy green eyes trained on the bartenders whose itchy fingers rang a melodious tune on her cash boxes. Her eyes would signal messages to Jesus, truly the most honest man she'd encountered, who was hired to watch the sticky-fingered men behind the plank. Whenever she spotted foul play, Jesus was an instant deterrent.

Her emerald eyes gazed about the smoke-filled room, alive with voices. For an instant, she froze. She thought she saw several uniformed Mexican officers enter the place. This in itself wasn't so surprising, the Diamond Slipper often entertained *Federales* who stopped in for a bit of fun while in Juarez on official business. Usually these men were of lesser rank than those men who flashed by her. By the time curiosity moved her through the congested room, they had disappeared. Had she dreamed them up, she wondered.

She craned her neck above the crowd and looked in all directions. She saw nothing of them. She shrugged and moved back through the room. She took a moment to glance at the small gold watch pinned to her breast. Half-hour to show time. The dining room was full, with more people arriving each moment. The first two shows had been sold out. She filled her thoughts with how she could keep the patrons happy and encourage them to remain for the last show as she moved regally about in her business establishment.

Elsewhere in the Diamond Slipper, upstairs in the private room booked by Herr Von Klause, a conversation was underway, which might one day change the course of history. Antonetta had seen no illusions earlier when she thought she'd seen *Federales* of high rank in her establishment. They had been slickly diverted to the upstairs salon by two foreign agents who prepared the clandestine meetings in their usual cloak-and-dagger manner.

General Vitoriano Huerta and Major Salomon had met their host Herr Von Klause and a clandestine meeting was underway. They spoke in German and often drifted into Spanish. General Huerta had been trained in Germany so language was no barrier. Most high-ranking *Federale* officers were trilingual; French, German, and Spanish, and sometimes English, came readily to them.

Downstairs, totally unaware of the drama taking place in her establishment, Antonetta received another surprise. Shock is more like the emotion she experienced when she saw Doroteo Arango, dressed in a black dinner suit, arrive and approach her quite matter-of-factly. How many times had she encouraged him to experience the excitement of watching *La Bomba*? Many more times, he had resisted. "I don't drink. I don't gamble. *Pues,* I don't even smoke. Why should I occupy the space of a paying customer?" he'd protest. "Besides, I might be recognized."

"But, *amoroso*," she had protested. "You must come to see the sensation of El Paso. You would never believe *La Bomba* is the Little Fox who followed you as *campesina, Jefe.*"

But he continuously declined. In all this time, her business had picked up. Each night's receipts exceeded those of the previous night. Crowds stood in long lines to see the Latin bombshell each night. Antonetta had even considered adding more tables, opening another section to handle the overflow. The uptown swells, the stuck-up gringos had started coming to the Diamond Slipper, and she had wanted to make the place a bit fancier to attract more of the monied crowd. Whenever she'd speak of these plans to Villa and voice her exuberance over such marvelous business, he'd stroke her face gently and tell her to be patient, to wait a little

618

longer. Each time her enthusiasm would diminish, and as she gazed upon him, she would see in his eyes the gathering of storm clouds.

And now, as he stood before her, dressed like a wealthy *hacendado,* she felt a deep pang of dismay, a suffocation that shook her composure. In these past several months of their renewed vows of love, Antonetta knew she'd follow Pancho to hell and back. She had listened to his quiet words with love-filled calf eyes and had taken no initiative to enlarge the club. His presence at the Diamond Slipper seemed to blast out loud and clear to her, the time was at hand. He would soon be leaving.

"A secluded table for me, *querida,*" he requested, "away from the sight of other partygoers."

Antonetta filled with dismay. The only available place was in a niche at the foot of the back stairs, close to the dressing rooms, at the edge of the stage, well hidden in shadows. Despite her protestations that it wasn't a suitable location for a man of his stature, Doroteo Arango assured his mistress that it would suit him fine. "All I wish is a glass of strawberry pop," he added, patting her hands affectionately.

Madelaina, dressed scantily in a revealing fandango costume, approached them as she left her dressing room en route to perform her number on stage. Doroteo Arango glanced up casually and fixed intent eyes upon her with an expression of mild astonishment. If he came to any conclusions about her, he said nothing. Not a glimmer of recognition passed his eyes or hers.

The house lights dimmed. The nattily dressed mariachi band, in their white satin ruffled shirts, dark trousers, and scarlet cummerbunds, presented a loud musical fanfare. The room was dark as pitch. Then the spotlight exploded into a circle of intense light. *La Bomba* stood at center stage. There came a loud clap of cymbals and the dance began. Two overhead spotlights, operated by men nestled in the rafters, trained on her and followed her every move.

La Bomba began gyrating to the beat of primitive

drums. She clapped her hands high above her head and beat a tattoo on the floor with her slipper. Each twist and turn tossed her hip-length coal hair about in satiny cartwheels like circles of black fire. The fandango began slowly, sensuously, growing livelier each moment. Increasing her momentum, Madelaina pulsated in rhythmic cadence as it rose to a crescendo, until the spectators were left breathless.

Upstairs in the private room, General Huerta, tiring of the negotiations, pulled the curtains apart and glanced at the stunning movement on stage to see what the *"olés"* and wild bursts of applause were about. For a few moments they all watched the performance, their interest absorbed by both the star performer and the uncontainable audience.

When the audience, unable to handle the sensuous stirring of their own emotions, reached the pinnacle of their endurance, the dance and dancer ended abruptly, leaving them stuck in outer limbo. For this reason, there followed several moments of stunned silence before the applause began. And when it commenced, it swelled to deafening proportions followed by the uninhibited cheering, whistling, and yahooing usually associated with a rowdier crowd.

When General Huerta and Major Salomon had finished their business, they took the rear stairs to a back exit, followed by their host, to avoid being noticed. Von Klause and his assistant, however, remained inside, pausing to watch the last moments of the show. Their attention was caught by the presence of Doroteo Arango, who hadn't noticed them. Slowly they moved in closer to him.

On stage the spotlights blinked on and off as *La Bomba* basked in the profuse attention showered on her. She bowed and graciously accepted the accolades as would a victorious matador. Finally she waved the spotlights off and stepped from the stage, as another, less vigorous, act followed. Madelaina passed Doroteo Arango's table and was about to pause when she noted the silent warning in his eyes as he turned from her to gaze upon the faces of the two strangers who approached him. She continued on to her dressing room, her face lined with shadows of concern. In the middle of her dance, Madelaina had felt certain she'd seen the face of General Huerta, with the drooping moustache she'd grown to despise and those black burning eyes of terror. She had felt a pang of fright for an instant, but when she whirled back into position from which she thought she'd seen him, there was emptiness. She convinced herself she was creating these images. She continued along the narrow corridor when she felt the tug of hands pulling her into the shadows. Tonetta had yanked at her and wrapped her in a silk shawl, a finger at her lips cautioning her to be silent.

"What is it?" whispered Madelaina hoarsely. "What's happening? Who are those men with Doroteo Arango?"

Again, she was cautioned to be silent. Tonetta whispered, "I am not certain. Come." She pulled her along the narrow corridor. "We can listen from here."

They had circled behind Villa, and in a small enclosure, Antonetta revealed a peephole through which they could both observe and listen to the goings on.

"General?" queried the man Eric Von Klause in German-accented Spanish. "May we intrude upon your privacy?"

"I am no general," replied Mr. Arango. "I am waiting for a friend who is also no general."

"Ahhh, how clever of you to be so cautious," replied Von Klause.

Arango stretched his politeness a hair longer. "My friend might be upset finding me with men I don't know and have no desire to talk with."

"What makes you so sure I am not that friend, General?"

"It's simple. My friend is a fiery-tempered redhead, prettier than you and equipped with more gadgets than you can invent."

"Ahhh, General. You're a man's man after all. I've heard rumors—by God, I'm glad they are true."

Arango grew sullen as his patience diminished.

621

"Look, who the hell are you and what do you want? I'm in no mood for games."

"Very good. My people have had you under surveillance since your arrival. We've attempted to speak to you in private before. You always evade us. Earlier I reserved a room here. I thought my business had ended until we descended these stairs and spotted you. If you desire, we can retire to the room where we won't be overheard. I presume this will meet with your approval."

"You presume too much," said Arango, growing very quiet. His instinct stirred him to disquiet. "I sit here comfortably."

Herr Von Klause glanced in every direction, then nodded to his companion who retreated into the shadows. He spoke in hushed tones. "I represent a foreign government who watches your every move. Believe me, General, you have a staunch friend and supporter in us."

"A government which has nothing to do but watch the comings and goings of a nobody like Doroteo Arango? Hah!"

"Heh, heh, heh, my friend. You have a sense of humor. Actually, you are greatly admired in my country. May I sit down?" He moved his enormous frame into a nearby chair without Villa's approval. "We wish to help your cause."

"My cause? What cause is it you speak of?" needled Arango.

Von Klause forced a tight-lipped smile. "Heh, heh, heh." He shook his head amiably, as if he found tremendous humor in the clean-shaven man.

"We wish to finance your revolution, *mein Generale*," he said conspiratorially.

"And?"

Again Von Klause looked about him cautiously. He leaned in closer. "We will help you crush your opposition, decimate them, grind them up for dust."

"And?"

"You see, *mein Generale*, we are not too pleased to

622

do business with General Huerta. His government leaves us somewhat disappointed."

"Forgive me," interrupted Arango, feigning temporary confusion. "Huerta's government? Did—uh—President Madero's government suddenly dissolve? Disappear?"

"Heh, heh, heh," laughed Von Klause, studying the Mexican inscrutably with black smoldering eyes as fierce as Villa's had been on occasion. "You are very amusing, General. I like that. A man with a sense of humor is a man to be trusted. Perhaps, when circumstances prove more favorable and we can boast of mutual success, we can indulge in such patter. At this time, I am suggesting to you that my government, a formidable one, *señor*, is interested in signing a peace treaty with your nation."

"Peace treaty? Ahhh, *si*. That's what all this is about?" replied Arango knowingly as his eyes twinkled in merriment. "Imagine—a peace treaty, eh? So, tell me, *amigo*, what else does your—uh—formidable government desire?"

"Why—uh—I—uh—nothing. Simply a peace treaty marking your nation and you, *Señor Generale*, as a staunch ally."

"Ahhh, I see." Arango kept bobbing his head up and down in agreement. "And what else?" he asked in a disarming manner.

"Well, we are fully prepared to back your struggle for the presidency with troops, solid financial backing, arms, and ammunition—the latest in military strategy and the proper propaganda, you see."

"Ahhh, and in return you'll want oil—land—precious minerals—what?"

"Oh, nothing much. A few submarine bases, a place for our battleships to refuel and tie in for repairs. You know, friendly ports." It was a throwaway statement.

"Ahhh, I see." Arango nodded his head as he observed both men. "You have no Castilian lisp, no *gachupín* manner, so you are so Spaniard. You are not stuck up and I can understand your words, so you are not British. You are all business—so you are not Italian—" he said, pushing a bit.

"We are Germans! Sent by the Kaiser, General!" retorted Von Klause, disdainfully tilting his nose into the air. He inserted a monocle into the crease around his eye and studied the man opposite him with apparent dislike.

"Ahhh," sighed Arango as he leaned in with apparent desire to intrigue with him. "Tell me," he asked confidentially, "what will the Kaiser do with the submarine bases? Attack the gringos?"

"Certainly not!" exploded Von Klause, his nostrils flaring. "Our aim is directed only toward a peaceful coexistence in the field of commerce."

"Hah!" retorted Arango. "What do you take me for? A chocolate-drinking *Federale* regular? Your Kaiser is not unfamiliar to me. I *read* about him every day," he boasted pointedly. "First, a war in Europe. He itches for it this very moment. Then he'll puncture the gringos' lifeline from below the border, eh? Pretty soon, we all speak Spanish with a German accent. And the eagle and the snake turn into black, red, and gold bars, eh? Is that it? All this with the help of that illiterate *peón,* Pancho Villa!"

Madelaina and Antonetta held on to each other tightly. They froze. "They know who he is," lamented Madelaina.

"You wait here, out of sight. Don't even go to your dressing room," ordered Antonetta. She moved out of sight, into the next room. Madelaina listened more intently as she observed the duo speak.

"That's absurd," protested Von Klause, stammering in full outrage.

"What if I permit this alliance and the gringos turn on me?"

Von Klause took hope. "Have no fear, General. We will protect you with full force, of course."

"How?"

"Our navy will be at your disposal, in your harbors—"

"Listen, you lunkhead, the gringos can swat flies across the Rio Grande, reach over and bury them before your navy has time to fart in midocean."

"Have you truly seen German power, General?" Von Klause tensed.

"Have you seen Pancho Villa's power?" countered the Mexican puma. "Peaceful coexistence in the field of commerce! Hah!" he roared thunderously. "Listen, *Señor Alemán,* negotiator at large, I am here as a guest of the gringos here, and good neighbors do not promote treachery." Arango rose to his feet, pulled the German up by his lapels, and with a swift right to the jaw, he flattened Herr General Eric Von Klause of the Kaiser's Imperial Army on his dignified rump.

Before another moment passed, two of Antonetta's burly bouncers moved in swiftly and tossed the foreigners out of the Diamond Slipper on their sorely abused behinds. If Doroteo Arango had anticipated the burning hatred in Von Klause's humiliated eyes and the promise of retaliation registered in them, he might have employed more diplomacy in handling the Chief of German Intelligence. However, Doroteo Arango, knew little of the cunning and skilled diplomacy employed by such treacherous jackals. He knew only the ways of oppressed Mexican hillsmen, straight talk—and if that didn't suffice, the remedy lay in the gun, the swiftest justice in man's unpredictable world.

Madelaina came out of the enclosure and seated herself next to Doroteo Arango, whose cover had surely been blown by now.

"That, Little Fox," remarked Villa knowingly, "was the beginning of an ugly sign. Who will this international negotiator seduce now that Villa won't whore for him, eh?"

"Who else?" hissed the fandango dancer, her eyes staring inwardly as if she'd clearly seen the picture—the sudden coincidences in their lives. "General Huerta. They are alike, those two. Speaking of that snake," she confided, "I saw him and and that devil Salomon at the *corrida* this afternoon."

625

"Huerta is here? In El Paso?" His eyes lost their twinkle. "You saw them?"

"What's more," interrupted Antonetta, swishing into the secluded alcove, "I, too, saw them, here in my own establishment earlier. It's true, I thought my eyes deceptive when they were swallowed up in the crowd, but all the time they must have been upstairs with these German negotiators."

Arango opened a small bag he removed from his pocket and passed it to the women. "Peanut brittle?" They refused. He took out a piece, broke it, and stuffed some into his mouth. He turned his attention to the remains of his strawberry pop, beguiled by the air bubbles fizzing to the surface each time he swished the contents of his glass. "Imagine—how do they create these?"

La Bomba retired to her dressing room, her thoughts wandering. How had they learned of Villa's identity? How had they recognized him? He looked nothing like the terrible Yaqui Indian hillsman, the savior of Mexico. Knowing that Huerta and Salomon were in the same city as she shook her. She began to perspire with alternate chills of heat and cold and relive in her mind the torture of Madrigal.

"I don't care what I promised you, Tolomeo!" she cried aloud. "One day Huerta and Salomon will pay for what they did to me. I had no business promising you I'd forgive them. I can't! I can't! I'm not divine! I'm human!" she sobbed.

The thoughts, comforting and confusing both, pacified her enough to apply the finishing touches to her makeup and slip into her new flamingo-red, beaded costume which covered less of her than the previous ensemble. She sipped the last of the brandy she'd taken to drinking of late to reenforce her courage each time she stepped onto the stage. With all her agility and talent and ability to mesmerize an audience, Madelaina Obregon was still embarrassed and self-conscious about flaunting her physical charms before strange men. She found brandy gave her the courage it took to transform her into an uninhibited bundle of dynamite that excited the senses of her audience and left them with a breathlessness that made her to them, the greatest of all entertainers.

Once again she was on stage. Here, with the brandy churning hot through her upper chest and body, she felt free and alive. What power she felt, whirling, twisting, gyrating, knowing every eye in the house was upon her. For these eight to ten minutes, she had perfect control over them and could bend them to her will.

No one, but no one possessed the magic of *La Bomba*. She was filling out in the right places again and no longer reflected the horror of her past life in those dark, sunken eyes that were so much a part of her. She moved to the side of the stage, dancing from table to table, twirling with such swiftness she only saw blurred faces. Around and around she went, again and again until she felt dizzy. Moreover, for an instant, she thought she saw the face of her husband, Peter Duprez. Again and again she moved, the room beginning to spin. Again she saw Peter's face. *I'll make it stop,* she told herself. *I won't let myself be deluded.* The dance finally ended. She stood quite still; only her breasts heaved and bounced as she tried to catch her breath from the strenuous act.

A fixed smile on her lips, her arms upraised, she accepted the applause. The image of Peter Duprez wouldn't dissolve. She blinked her eyes hard, trying to pierce the blinding spotlights and the smoke-filled room. A waft of blue-white smoke circled ceilingward and in its wake she saw him, plain as day.

He was seated at the number one table with others in a large party. Next to him was a stunning blonde, dressed exquisitely in a white satin beaded gown, cut low in front with a portrait neckline. A white fox fur cape was draped over one shoulder and her blue gringa eyes were fixed on Peter with the look of a spoiled vixen and the impatience of a schoolgirl unable to get her way. Peter's eyes were glued to Madelaina as if by a powerful adhesive, and hers on him. It would be an impossibility for anyone not to notice the vibrations between them.

It was this look between the dancer on stage and the man seated next to her that produced a sudden unexpected recklessness in Peter Duprez' impetuous companion, Valerie Townsend, daughter of the Texas governor, Hampton P. Townsend. The young woman picked up her cape with arrogant determination, stood up with a pause that cried for attention, and without glancing back at her companions, stalked haughtily out of the gambling palace. Her entire entourage, ten people in all, muttering protests and mild expletives, nevertheless arose and grabbing Duprez's arm, piloted him out the door in pursuit of the hot-tempered social butterfly.

Madelaina wasn't certain how she got to her dressing room. With trembling hands she quickly reached for the brandy, poured a stiff bracer, and downed it in a gulp. She stood before her mirror, staring at her pale reflection.

"It was Peter. It was," she told the image in the glass.

"What's wrong, *chiquita*?" Antonetta had followed her into the room and closed the door behind her. "What is it? What happened? What was that all about?"

Madelaina, unable to articulate, paced the floor a moment.

"You knew them? They recognized you? What? In God's name, stop this walking and tell me."

"It was my husband. Peter Duprez."

"That man was Duprez?" Tonetta frowned in reflection. "That man with the gringa?" Her eyes narrowed to slits. Earlier Antonetta had greeted the stuck-up El Pasoans, those high-society snobs. The man she knew as Tom Mix winked at her in secret understanding, and noting his uptown tuxedo and swanky accessories, she had discreetly refrained from greeting him as she might have if he had appeared alone. Her mind raced back to the time prior to the Battle of Juarez, after Little Fox had been abducted by her father's spies, when she and Tom Mix had engaged in conversation. He had certainly filled the description burned into her brain by

Little Fox, but when Peter had introduced himself to her as Tom Mix, Antonetta had let it pass.

"Oh, Madelaina," she cried out in dismay. "To think if he hadn't fooled me by telling me his name was Tom Mix, I would have told him about you and how you had searched for him."

"You know Peter? But how? When? Where—"

"Even that gringo *bastardo,* Captain Richards, called him Tom Mix. How was I to know, *querida*? How?"

"Who was the woman with him?" asked Madelaina. "Not his wife, I hope."

"*Querida,* if only I had known," she punished herself. "Not yet. But soon. It is in all the papers." She broke into pigeon Yankee. Che is de daughter of the Texas governor. Che is not so beeg a package, bot de father, ah, he ees beeg noise een Texas. They are how you say—*novios.*"

"Betrothed," said Madelaina. She couldn't have felt worse. She poured herself another drink.

"Too much of this stuff will make for ju worse troubles," said Antonetta, recapping the bottle. She was conscious of a twinge of irritation in *La Bomba.*

"Listen, *chiquita,* if the house wasn't so filled with people, I would send ju home, ju hear? In fact, *chiquita,* eef ju desire, *La Gatitta* will perform for ju. After seeing *La Bomba,* they will throw tomatoes at me, for sure. Bot at least there will be some show."

"No!" protested Madelaina. "I wouldn't do that to you on such a night. After the kindness you and Doroteo have showered upon me? I even have my own little *casita,* thanks to you. Now, leave me, *por favor.* I wish to think alone."

Tonetta sadly left the dressing room.

Madelaina lit up a marijuana cigarette and lay back on the red velvet chaise longue smoking, although with none of the usual feelings of relaxation, either from the booze or the grass. She thought she heard a knock at the door. No matter, she was drifting into a euphoric state and didn't care who might be wanting to see her. Her eyes fluttered heavily and closed for a moment or two.

Suddenly, she felt something heavy on her lap, something that fell with a heavy thud. Her eyes fluttered open and she sat up with a start. On her lap lay a thick canvas sack, the size of a man's traveling case. Her heavy-lidded eyes were forced open by sheer will, and she saw a pair of boots on the floor alongside of her. Her eyes traveled farther up. Black pants, solid gold belt buckle with an indiscernible brand encrusted upon it, shirt, jacket, string tie, large overpowering shoulders, sun-bronzed skin on a cold, marblelike face, black and gray hair, cut short with a crease from a spiffy Stetson.

William Benson stood there staring down at her. He was alone. She glanced from him to the heavy sack on her lap in bewilderment.

"*Señor*, what is this?"

"The money. Five thousand dollars. He wanted y'all ta have it."

"Who? What money? What are you speaking of? I assure you I have no idea what you are talking about," she said irritably, noting the cold arrogance and borderline disgust in his face.

"That there is Manuelito Perez' blood money. Ya told him he was gonna die and he did. Why he wanted ya ta have the money aftah y'all put a hex on him is beyond all mah comprehension, woman."

Madelaina tried to clear her head, to remove the sudden fuzziness that engulfed her like a thick curtain separating reality from fantasy. "Manuelito—blood money—dead?" His words came to her in disjointed bits and pieces which she had difficulty sewing together in any set pattern.

"Suppose you start at the beginning. You make no sense to me, *señor*."

"Hah! Youah'd like me ta think that, wouldn't ya? What exactly did ya mean to ole Manuelito?"

"Manuelito—dead?" Now it came together. She pulled her legs over the side of the chaise longue, removed the canvas money bag from her lap, and touched her head as if this gesture would magically clear it and bring things into better focus. She could feel his hostility as it permeated the room like a cold draft. She saw him wrinkle his nose and sniff the air suspiciously.

"Youah ain't smokin one o' them dopers, are ya? Those reefers that drive a man plumb loco? No wonder Perez was doomed, with such a harlot as you!"

"As a matter of fact, Mr. Benson, I am doing just that. Will you join me in one?"

"Ya can't shock me, woman. Ah've known women like ya before. Ah came ta keep a death bed promise ta a gentleman. He wanted ya ta have the money he won in a wageuh made with me. He bargained ta fight mah champion bull, a real killah ah imported from them Miura ranches in Spain ta intuhbreed with mah Chihuahuans."

Madelaina wasn't listening to him. All she knew was that Manuelito was dead. "If only he had listened. What more could I have done to convince him? Apparently not enough," she sighed wistfully. She wanted to cry, but no tears would come, something which William Benson picked up on immediately.

"Not even a teah for the dead?" he snorted with inborn cynicism. "That's the leahst y'all could do is ta show some concern foah a man who spoke youah name with his final breath. Y'all are some iron woman. No teahs!"

"Mr. Benson, I don't give a fig for either your thoughts concerning my relationship to Manuelito or what you think of me. As for this money Manuelito chose to leave me, I'm not sure I understand his gesture. But, if you'd be so kind as to learn from his managers the source of his personal charity, I'll be happy to turn the amount over to them."

William Benson leveled his surly blue eyes on the woman and saw the faintest quivering of her sensuous lips, giving her a strangely alluring quality. Her arms and shoulders reflected the subdued lighting of the ostentatious dressing room built to her specifications by Antonetta. Her black hair, falling loose over her shoulders, framed her small but defiant face. And those

631

eyes—those dark, jewellike eyes—reflected a way of life imposed against a strenuous code of morality that didn't add up in his mind. Standing there she looked like a young virgin fresh out of a convent. Yet, he knew all too well what she was. Her profession, as sordid and disgusting as it appeared to him, the kind that his contemporaries took in their stride, spelled it out for him. Still, her astute observations on the bulls weren't the patter that spilled from the mouths of whores or unrefined gambling hall queens.

She was an enigma, especially to William Benson. Her kind of women didn't return the purses left to them by their paramours. "Y'all would do that—return the money?" he asked hesitantly.

"To repeat myself is a waste of time," she snapped with an air of detachment. "Now, if you'll excuse me, I must prepare for the final show."

"William Benson is no fool, *señorita*. Will ya tell me why youah've been trying ta shock me and push me outa youah life, like I was some tainted devil from out the dark ages?" He smiled with a private amusement in his eyes. "Ah wasn't born yestahday, little filly. Ah know women. What is it—do ah frighten ya in some way?"

Madelaina paused a moment, surprised by the new tack he'd taken.

"*You* frighten *me*? The man rumored to be the most powerful man in the state of Texas? A man who, it's been said, chews bullets for breakfast and can outshoot, outfight, and outsmart every man around? I've no reason to fear you, sir. You've nothing I desire. Least of all a sour disposition and foul mouth and a propensity to exercise power over helpless people."

"So that's what they say about William Benson?"

"Worse."

"Worse?"

"Much worse."

"Ah admit ah'm ruthless, m'am. A man hasta be all the things ya said. A weakuh man just hasn't the sense ta stay outa mah way an' when he gets hurt, he cries lika baby. What else have ya heard about me?" he

632

asked as if it gave him a measure of importance to be spoken of in awe.

"What does it matter? I make it a practice never to believe what I hear."

"That so?" He brightened. "A woman after mah own heart."

"You've said what you came to say, Mr. Benson. I thought I'd replied as best I could. What my relationship was to Manuelito Perez is between us. I owe no man any explanation. Since Manuelito has left us, it's useless to resurrect the dead past. Now, if you'll excuse me, I must prepare for the next show," she repeated herself with more finality.

The more Benson listened to her words, her voice, and her subtle airs, the more the aristocratic background he sensed in her came through the tough pose. No whore he'd ever known spoke as she did or held herself with such poise, even if she was clad scantily in such revealing threads. No, thought William Benson, in this woman was something rather special. He sensed it earlier at the Plaza. He could have sent one of his men to deliver the money and message, but instead he chose to attend to the mission personally, to prove to himself this was some special filly.

"As a matter of fact, Mr. Benson, I felt certain that after you learned of my occupation in such a place, you'd make it a point never to cross my path." She flung her head back and eyed him defiantly.

"Look heah, little filly, y'all didn't have me fooled a bit. Ah knew all the time you was jus' puttin' on an act ta scare me off." He laughed good-naturedly, easing up a bit. "Ah didn't mean ta be so hard on ya earlier, ya heah? Men like me have gotta make shuah of any filly who intuhrests 'em. Ya see, ah jus' might be all the things youah've heard tell of me. But, then again, maybe ah'm not. Ah came ta tell ya, ah'm intuhrested in ya, see. It don't make no mattuh ta me what y'all had ta do with the matador. Ah'm fixin' ta get ta know ya better, so youah'd bettah fix it in youah mind what mah intentions will be."

Madelaina remained silent. She could say nothing else. Her thoughts were centered on Manuelito and why she hadn't communicated with him. Why hadn't she been able to convince him of the impending doom so that he might have been able to circumvent his fate? Benson's voice cut into her thoughts.

"Look heah, little filly. Ah've gotta leave. Ah can't even stay heah long enough ta see ya dance. Ah've already heard from mah men that you'ah a hot torpedo—dancing, that is," he added hastily when he saw her dark eyes flare angrily. "Ah jus' wanta ask ya ta have lunch with me in three days. Ah've gotta get me into Juarez and do some business south of the boahdah. This is Saturday. Ah'll be back on Tuesday. So ah'll warn ya, ah intend tuh pick youah pretty little brains apaht on them bulls y'all know so much about, heah? Will ya jus' tell me this much—wheah did ya learn so much about them *toros*?"

"In Spain at the hacienda of my uncle, Don Diego—" She stopped in time. "Well, I lived in Las Marismas, where the Concha bulls are raised. I am well acquainted with the *ranchos* where the Miura are bred. And the Salamanca as well. Manuelito taught me all I know about fighting the bulls. I was an apt pupil. Believe me, I learned the difference in the breeding of bulls, and I must say it is vast." She fairly glowed at the conversation and Benson noticed the change in her.

"You—a filly, fight bulls?" His eyes widened in disbelief. "Well ah'll be dang-blasted! The hell ya say, woman!" Benson slapped his thigh with his Stetson. "What's that ya said—Las Marismas? By the holy beard of Satan—Las Marismas! Mah dear child. Didja jus' happen to know of an *hombre* named Don Felipe Cortez? Well, it was this heah Don Cortez, mah good friend, who turned me onta breeding bulls. And it was him who allowed me ta meet up with Matador Perez. That's how weah arranged the American tour foah Manuelito. What a small world, eh? Ah tell ya, *señorita*, it will grieve me evah so much ta inform Don Cortez of the matador's fate."

Madelaina listened attentively. Her head was clear and free of any fuzziness she experienced earlier from the marijuana. She tensed incredibly at his words. Indeed, it was a small world. She would have to be very discreet not to mention her uncle or allow any tie in to her past to be aired.

"Then y'all will come ta lunch with me? Ah'll send a carriage foah ya. Wheah do ya live, m'am?"

She gave him the address. "I've a small house on Elm Street."

"Mah man will be by foah ya at 1 P.M. sharp. *Hasta luego,* little filly. Ya jus' done mah heart real good." He stood for a time, staring at her with the exuberance of a schoolboy on his first date. "Don'cha let any harsh words spoken about me allow ya ta change youah mind, heah?"

He placed his Stetson on his head, squaring it properly, shook her hand like a clumsy, self-conscious juvenile, and left. The incongruities in his behavior had disarmed her. She wasn't sure why she'd even agreed to have lunch.

The full extent of William Benson's wealth was not known in its entirety. This Texas millionaire, who owned one of the largest spreads in the Panhandle near Amarillo, Texas, presently owned several haciendas and rich cattle lands and bull-breeding farms in Mexico. Under the old Diaz laws, now perpetuated by Presidente Madero, Benson was a *hacendado* of enormous stature in both countries. As one of the most affluent cattlemen in the state, this man, whose political tentacles reached to Washington and the house of the American president, was often conducting business in El Paso and Juarez.

Benson, a tall, heavy-set man in his fifties, with blunt features and eyes that X-rayed when they stared, had a temper rumored to be the worst of any gringo. This brute of a man, reported as a tough, hard-hitting SOB, short on temper and quick on action, was a wrangler never without his six-guns.

When Benson roared orders to his ranch hands, they jumped through hoops like trained animals. He paid them fair wages, but made no bones about telling them he intended to extract twice as much work as he paid for. This self-made man with the bold swagger and impudence of a man of inestimable wealth and power, hired no man who professed to have brains. All he required from his help was physical endurance and the needed stamina to perform results without bitching like bleating sheep.

His own reserve brain power, enough for ten men, succeeded in making him one of the cleverest politicians in the state of Texas. He needed to be on top of things to outsmart the new breed of politician surfacing in the land where manipulation became the byword. It was rumored about that his only wife died quite young, bitterly disillusioned and heartsick over a loveless marriage and the impossibility of living with so ambitious a man. His greatest disappointment was the fact that he hadn't sired at least a half-dozen sons to take over when he died. His oldest son had left the fold at an early age, unable to bear the degradation to which his father subjected him in his efforts to make a man in his own mold out of him. Because he could no longer take the old man's despotic tryanny, Peter Duprez Benson left and hadn't seen his father in at least two decades.

Six months of the year, William Benson lived on his ranch near Amarillo. The remaining six months were spent between the haciendas in Mexico and his mansion in El Paso where he entertained high government officials, oil tycoons, and prominent government officials on both sides of the Rio Grande.

Recently, however, due to the extent of all his holdings and the nature of the political upheavals south of the border, William Benson had been forced to immerse himself more fully in the politics of both nations. Such a man of influence and wealth, who still enjoyed the profits and marvelous fringe benefits afforded a gringo *hacendado,* was bound to be approached by the

636

warring factions to use his monetary powers of persuasion to keep the status quo.

Stepping out into brightly lit *avenida,* reflecting all the electric signs of the countless night clubs, William Benson lit a fat stogie, proud that he'd achieved a pact of sorts with the girl named *La Bomba.* Why, he hadn't even asked her her true Christian name, he thought, chastising himself. Never mind, he'd know it soon enough, and when he presented this Latin bombshell with a string of perfectly matched pearls, she'd not resist him.

Puffing on the cigar, Benson nodded to his driver and stepped inside the enclosed carriage where his two very important guests had patiently waited while he conducted his personal business. The door closed behind him.

"General Huerta? Major Salomon? Ah thank y'all for youah patience in allowing me to conduct the death bed request of a dear friend. Now then, suhs, shall we proceed ta my little spread wheah we can discuss just what it is you need from mah President Wilson?"

"*Muy bien,* Señor Benson. It will be our pleasure to explain precisely what is needed by the government of Huerta and what Huerta will do in return for the American government."

"Ah see, General. By the sound of youah talk, ah take it that youah've got this heah Madero whupped pretty good."

"Señor Benson. Madero is finished. Believe me," said General Huerta with confidence. "At any moment, upon my bidding, Madero's government will dissolve as if it never existed."

"Well, suh, ya'll talk pretty big. S'pose we mosey on tah mah place and get down ta the nitty gritty?" Benson opened the cabbie overhead door. "Waco, get the drivuh crackin'."

"Yes, sir!" replied the burly cowboy, nodding to the driver alongside him. He felt for the six-guns he carried and patted his holster securely. "Move, Charlie."

Inside, General Huerta gave William Benson a pleasant enough look. "Your generosity to this—uh—professional dancer is to be commended, *señor*."

William Benson glanced sharply at his guest. "Mah, mah, news shuah has a habit of movin' befoah the deed's done. Now, tell me, how in the name of the bloody blue blazes, General, didja fasten youah choppers on ta such a morsel?"

General Huerta shrugged noncommittally. "When the death of so reknown a matador occurs on foreign soil, the people who are at his deathbed have a tendency to swell their superstitions beyond all proportions." He used his hands with a flourish in expressing himself. "It was rumored your wager with the deadman was in excess of fifty thousand dollars."

"It was five."

"That he made you abide by a deathbed oath."

"That's the truth."

"That you," Huerta temporized, "that you might not have fulfilled such an irresponsible wish and entertained thoughts of setting aside the last request."

"Nevah, suh! Nevah would William Benson do such a thing. Death ta me is as sacred as life. The responsibilities of both are too deah to fool with."

"That this *La Bomba* and the matador were lovers."

"Untrue! Why, they were raised in the same country, grew up together as children. They could have been brothuh and sistuh. Why, General, my deah friend Don Felipe Cortez loved Manuelito Perez as if he was his own son."

"This Don Cortez, a *hacendado* also?"

"One of the finest bull-breeding ranches in all of Spain. The Concha bulls. Why, General, that little filly, *La Bomba,* knows so much about the animals, ah've invited her to lunch with me. Ah heard her talkin' about 'em at the *corrida* earlier tuhday—" Benson stopped. Usually a quiet man of utter discretion, he wondered why he was suddenly bent on venting his feelings. He wasn't a man taken to boasting. He flushed beet red.

Huerta picked up on it. "Why, Señor Benson, it appears that you have grown fond of this—uh—dancer. It is a shame that Major Salomon and I, so involved in conducting out business, took no time to watch her perform. From the deafening bursts of applause, however, we have decided to make the Diamond Slipper our last stop before we depart for Mexico."

Benson remained sullenly quiet. Whatever possessed him to discuss the woman? Why, if the time ever came that he might ask her to wear his name, he'd have to bury her past. Now these two greasers know about it. Best to let the matter pass. But General Huerta, always anxious to know the foibles and peccadillos of the men he dealt with, and more anxious to acquaint himself with the skeletons such men kept hidden in closets, pressed the subject.

"What kind of a woman would be born in Spain on a hacienda, you say, and grow up close to a man like Manuelito Perez? Even a man like Don Cortez? How does it happen that a woman of such background ends up in El Paso as an exotic fandango dancer in a gambling palace. It bends the imagination, doesn't it, Señor Benson?" Huerta smoked through his solid gold cigarette holder with maddening manner of a highborn aristocrat with insufferable airs.

Benson frowned. "Ah really don't know a thing, suh. Frankly ah'm not sure ah want ta continue such a worthless beating of gums. All ah know is what the matador told me and what came from her lips. Perez apparently taught the girl how ta fight bulls and their friendship sprang up."

If Benson saw the the quick, sharp looks that passed between the general and the major in the dim light of the carriage, he gave it no importance. His manner indicated they had far more important things to discuss than the relationship between two comparative strangers. And he said so in so many words, just as the carriage rode into circular brick courtyard. The men entered the Benson mansion prepared to negotiate their worlds.

639

Chapter 24

Madelaina Obregon's only thought as William Benson left her dressing room was to finish the last show and go home where she could relax and think about the numerous events that plagued her life on this day.

Her last performance, as erotic and scintillating as her earlier performances, was finally over. She returned to her dressing room to change into street apparel and go home. Only now, as she shed her costume, would she permit her mind to dwell on Peter Duprez. She sniffed the air about her, puzzled.

All the old longing, the desperate need, the ache and need for him began to surface, and she found herself in a terrible state of disquiet. Thoughts so negative in nature kept her floundering as she removed her makeup with a thick white creamy emulsion mixed for her at the apothecary's shop. She hadn't bothered to turn up the lights in her anxiety to leave the Slipper. She completed her dressing in partial shadow. As she piled her hair up off her shoulders and speared it through with a tortoise shell pin, she heard a familiar voice call to her.

"Is it really y'all, Little Fox? Ah thought foah shuah ah had dreamed ya up earlier tonight."

She spun around and saw him seated in the shadows of the dressing room, nearly hidden from view. Quickly she pulled the chain on the lamp nearby. In the flood of light, she saw him. "Peter!" she began anxiously.

Then, collecting her strength and wits, she managed to remain cool.

"Oh, it's you." She sniffed the air, allowing the fragrant aroma of his aftershave cologne to descend on all her senses at once. No wonder she'd smelled something familiar earlier, she thought. She wanted to run into his arms, to tell him how desperately she needed him, to tell him she was all his, that there'd never be anyone else for her but him. It was the hesitation she sensed in him which prevented her from flinging herself into his arms.

Peter rose to his feet, all six feet of him. In his dinner clothing, he looked more gorgeous than she'd ever seen him. He walked toward her, slowly taking her all in, as if he couldn't believe the transformation he saw.

"They told me y'all were dead, Little Fox," he said halfheartedly.

"Whoever told you this was right. Little Fox is dead. Only I have survived her foolish stupidity and impressionable mind with all that idealistic talk of revolution and hope for a lost people."

"Whatcha doing heah in El Paso? Ah mean aside from ya being *La Bomba*? Don'cha know the city is full o' spies? Why, baby, ah've been told by Tracy Richards that General Huerta is in town negotiating a deal ta dethrone Madero—that the revolution is about ta bust wide open. Is that whatcha heah foah?"

"No. Only to begin a new life, Peter. I'm alone now, and I must consider the future. I, too, assumed you were dead. I asked about you wherever we traveled. I was told you were injured in Villa's last skirmish and died on the battlefield."

"Jus' goes ta show ya, ya can't believe all ya heah, sweetness. Can we go someplace, sweet thing, so we can talk and catch up on ouah pasts? We seem ta be strangers ta each other, honey. What's wrong?"

He crossed the room to her in long strides and put his arms around her. He brought his face in closer to hers, and Madelaina felt herself slipping into submission. Oh God, how she loved him. And he was betrothed to another. Her eyes closed instinctively as they always did at his nearness. She felt his moist cool lips cover hers tenderly, then with increased passion and a rising fevor, his arms tightened their hold. "Aftuh all weah've been through tugethuh, Madelaina, ya

641

can't tell me ya don't still love me," he whispered urgently.

"Oh, Peter, Peter," she began, struggling to summon the strength to push away from him. "Aren't you forgetting something important?"

His eyes opened, hurt buried in them at the rebuff. "Forgetting something? What?"

"Your future wife?"

"Oh, her," he said flatly. "Y'all know about her?"

"I learned only tonight from Antonetta. You needn't worry. I'll do nothing to stand in your way," she said in a manner that didn't reveal her inner torment.

"This isn't mah Little Fox talkin' ta me like a cold westerly gale. Why, ah thought ya'd be happy to see me."

"I told you Little Fox is dead—gone and buried. A lot has happened to both of us, Peter."

Madelaina couldn't reconcile this Peter with her *marido* of the past two years. And Peter found himself concerned that Madelaina didn't view him with the same passion she had when they last parted. They both wondered if their romance and feelings for the other had cooled due to the nature of their hectic lives. No, it wasn't that, thought Peter. Something has drastically changed her. Even when Rosalia Quintera had unhexed her, she never acted as distant and cool. Her ardor had always been there to stir his passion to the heat of a volcano. No, something else was stirring her innards, egging her on. Was there someone else? It was then that Peter caught sight of the canvas bag of money, bearing the WB brand on its leather bindings. He tensed.

"What's this?" he asked, suddenly turning frigid.

"What's what?" she asked.

"Don'cha play so cool and innocent with me, *chiquita*. Ah'm speakin' of this heah canvas bag." He picked it up and jingled the heavy contents. "Silvah bearing the William Benson brand?" He studied the circle within a circle brand with a five-pronged crown over it, and his heart hardened in reflection. How politely and calmly he spoke, when all the while he was raging inside, his anger barely controlled. She'd seen him like this before—not too often, but often enough to know what it meant when his eyes turned to blue dull stones and his lips pulled back tightly.

For an instant he reminded her of someone she knew—who was it? She couldn't think.

"That was left to me by a friend who died in an unfortunate tragedy today. It was delivered by a friend of his. I believe his name was the same you just spoke," she replied casually. "Surely you've heard me speak of him, Peter. Manuelito Perez, the matador who taught me all I know about bulls."

He turned to her, sorely ashamed of his thoughts. Still the canvas bore the William Benson brand. "Yes," he said, waving his hand about the air in an abstract gesture, "Ah heard about his death in the ring taday. It's a sad, sad, thing. Ah recall jus' how much ya thought of him. Ah'm sorry, sugah. It's sad ta lose good friends." His eyes lingered suspiciously on the brand and canvas bag.

"It was a wager he made with the gringo, Benson," she told him and explained what had happened afterward. "It is difficult to believe such a gesture," she added.

"Ya'll don't know just how hard it is ta believe, sugah," he added enigmatically. His mind was more concerned with that skinflint land baron, William Benson, his father. That she even knew him turned his stomach. He refrained from further conversation. Knowing Madelaina as he had in the past, and recalling her naïveté about matters of the flesh, she would have told him if there were any strings attached to her sudden inheritance. "Ya better put that in a safe place, little one," he suggested. "People have killed for a lot less. Listen, ah'll carry it safely ta youah house, heah. Are ya ready?" he asked firmly, not about to take no from her. He stood at the door waiting for her.

"Peter—" Her lips began to form a protest. The longing for him, having ached so long, with such intensity, destroyed all her earlier resolve. "Very well, then. Come along. Let's slip out the back way. Antonetta keeps a horse and carriage waiting for me each night to insure my safety home."

"Ya see? Didn't ah tell ya it was dangerous at night? Especially foah *La Bomba*. Such exquisite charms and talent must certainly attract a variety of stage doah johnnies. Am ah right?" he asked, leaning languidly against the door.

She didn't reply, but pushed him instead out the door and turned off the light behind him.

"Oh, mah little sweet darlin', how much ah've missed ya," he whispered later in bed. "Mah God, sugah, why have ouah lives been subjected ta such turmoil and stress and tragedy? What is it with us? Why can't we live like uthuh people? Can ya tell me, sugah? Why?"

Madelaina didn't want to talk. She wanted only to feel and remember the good things between them. She wanted to love him and be loved in return with wild abandon, the same way they'd made love in the past. He had possessed her as no one had possessed her and she only wanted this to continue.

His arms held hers in a viselike grip and together they soared up the mountain to ecstasy, one plateau after another, pausing to savor and enjoy the intoxication of new delights en route. His body, muscular and firm and hard, delighted her senses beyond belief. No one, no man in the world made love like Peter, she thought. For her, he was the only one. Why was it that for him there could be a thousand like her? For an instant, Madelaina tensed. Flashes of Tolomeo crashed through her consciousness, and his words burned in her mind. *"What if I cut off my sexual organ—would you still love me as you profess?"*

Madelaina shook her head wildly in denial. "No, Tolomeo, not now! Not at this minute. Don't do this to me!" she cried out hoarsely. "I don't want to hear your words. You aren't human—and I am!"

"What is it, *chiquita*," asked Peter, alarmed by her

644

wild-eyed frenzy and her animal thrashing on the bed, as if she were being dominated by some mysterious force. He watched her sit up in bed, hands clasped over her ears and eyes shut tightly to shut out the inner pictures. "Y'all ain't hexed up again, are ya, baby?"

She opened her eyes, startled to see him and at the same time grateful. "Oh, Peter, my love, don't let them change us. Don't let him make us into people we aren't!" She clutched at him tightly and ran her slender fingers over his warm skin, secure in the feeling of heat oozing from his body. This in itself always excited her, the feeling that she could generate such heat from his body. It radiated from his to hers, setting them both on fire, sending them both into raptures of love of so exquisite a nature, it fairly made her head spin.

And Peter, deriving from Madelaina what he had never got from another woman, filled with unendurable passion. Only his strong will and concentration allowed him to hold back the driving need he had to satisfy his desires until he had first satisfied her. Time and again, she let him carry her over that familiar and ecstatic road to bliss until she felt as if she could no longer endure the agony and ecstasy again.

Peter, unable to further articulate his feelings with words, did so with his body. As they reached the pinnacle of the mountain and exploded, Peter cried out hoarsely, "Ah'll nevah let ya go, mah sweet Little Fox, ya heah? Nevah!"

The explosion burst again into smaller fragments of cloudlike formations that cradled them and sent their souls into the unknown, until a mystifying force greater than either of them pulled them apart and sent them tumbling down into a misty darkness. . . .

After a few moments, Peter reached for her, and held her tightly. "*Querida*, I have something for you—something that belonged to my mother." He slipped off the bed, pulled a small velvet box from his jacket, and returned to her side.

Madelaina's eyes lit up at the solid-gold earrings shaped like a crescent moon. Dangling at the edge of the curve were seven separate crescents with diamond embedded in the tips of each moon. "Peter, they are exquisite. I can't take them—especially since they were your mothers."

"Because they were hers, I want you to have them," he insisted. "Please put them on."

She removed the full circlets from her pierced ears and slipped the new ones into place. She fluffed out her hair and lifted it away from her face and, turning from side to side, she asked, "You like?"

Peter studied her somberly, then, uttering a small gasp, he drew her in closer to him. "I like—I love—I adore you, *querida*."

They clung to one another, their passion rekindled and once again they made love. Afterward, his face buried in the curve of her shoulders and neck, inhaling the fragrant mass of her silken, raven hair, Peter sensed the change in her even before Madelaina did. Her mind had wandered back to Tolomeo, his face flashing before her mind.

Madelaina recalled now, with vivid clarity, every exquisite moment she'd spent with Tolomeo, and she wondered why, of all times, her mind should choose to bring it all into perfect focus now, together with his teachings and warnings. She gazed at her husband and lover with an air of detachment.

"Peter, do you intend to marry the governor's daughter now, after our reunion?" she asked him quietly in a voice that didn't disguise her feelings.

"Ya hafta ask me now? At this time? While mah body still drips with youah love potion? Can't ya wait until this feelin' between us has abated?" He reached for a cigarette on the night table. "Mah, mah, sweet thing, youah not like the bundle of love ah made love ta on the *Mozambique*. Remembah when ya'll wanted ta jus' exchange love with me?" He grinned rakishly, lit the cigarette, and inhaled deeply.

"I remember everything, Peter. Please answer my question. Do you still intend to marry Valerie Townsend?"

"Please, Madelaina, I don't wish to discuss it." He enjoined her to refrain from discussing the matter. "Can't you just let us enjoy each other while there's time?" He spoke with such urgency that she felt instantly there was something drastically wrong.

The woman in her wanted to lash out at him, fill with anger and hurt him as he hurt her with this—this— governor's daughter. "Is it because she represents much money? Is that it? You no longer run guns or fight with the Gringo Brigade, so you must make your money wherever you can find an opportunity. That's it, isn't it?" she pressed.

"Shut up, woman! Ya don't know whatcher talkin' about!" He puffed furiously on his cigarette. "Ah'm shuah ya didn't let any grass grow under yer feet since we last saw each other in Parral. Y'all had that theah Paco ta take care o' ya. Ya shuah was concerned ovah him, eh? An' jus' who is this Tolomeo, y'all rant ovah? Ya been callin' his name while my love wahms yer heart!" he snapped caustically.

He might just as well have slapped her viciously as to say such contemptible things to her. Peter avoided her eyes in the semidarkness, choosing instead to stare intently at some spot on the ceiling as his thoughts, sparked with live coals, were held in check.

"You dare say such things to me?" Her acrimonious voice climbed higher despite her attempt to subdue it. She swung her bare legs over the side of the bed and felt his hands holding her back. "Get out! Leave me alone! Leave my house!"

"No. We'll talk it out!" He pulled harder, drawing her closer to him.

"There's nothing to say! And don't you—don't you dare tell me you love me when I'm angry!" she charged at him. She caught a deep breath and exhaled it evenly, lowering her temper simultaneously. "You never wanted to be married to me—admit it. It was purely a business arrangement for which we both paid dearly. I convinced myself earlier that once we made love again, your obsession to marry this gringa would

647

pass. You can't couple with me as you did tonight and not feel something for me, Peter. Now you give me no satisfaction. You say nothing except you are bound by some mysterious force to marry her. Did you stop to think we are still married? That if I so desire I could stop this farce between you and this blonde emptiness you paraded before me as a woman?"

"Ya wouldn't do that! Ya mustn't. Ya jus' can't expose youahself or me to any such publicity, ya heah?" Peter stopped abruptly, frowning thoughtfully. He had already said more than he should.

Madelaina picked up on his frantic appeal. His words struck at her like a two-edged blade. "What are you involved in, Peter? Let me understand. Don't do this to me, Peter. Don't keep me in the dark."

Peter wasn't listening. He filled with self-recrimination. He never intended for her to learn his activities. Dangerous as his mission was presently, it could be even more devastating to her if she should in any way be linked to him. Here, in El Paso, where government agents and counterspies were thicker than gutter rats, life was as cheap as ten pesos to a willing assassin.

"Ah don't know wheah ya get such crazy ideahs, woman. Ah guess weah've been apart so long that the magic between us is gone. Well, ah'd bettah be movin' along, Little Fox," he said, gathering all his will power and inner fortitude.

Peter dressed in the dim light. He avoided looking into her hurt, bewildered eyes for fear she'd see the truth. What kind of a beast would put her in jeopardy after the travail she'd endured in her young life?

"Ah had half-hoped ya'd let me continue ta see ya, even after mah wedding. Ah mus' admit, Little Fox, the gringa isn't like youah in bed. Ah find mahself havin' ta pretend with her. Somethin' ah nevah had ta do with y'all."

"*Bastardo*!" she cursed in Spanish as rage boiled over in her. Even as she hurled curses at him, something inside her tried to break through the outer picture to whisper the truth to her. Only moments ago,

648

he'd told her he'd never let her go. Just as he had in the past. Their love had been more sublime, more complete than ever before. No, she told herself, no. He is up to something and he doesn't want to involve me. He's protecting me for some reason. Very well, I'll play his little game.

"It's best you leave my house, gringo. I have no respect for a man who marries a woman and wants to sleep with another."

"Really, sugah?" he quipped airily. "Why, ah was certain youah people thrived on such arrangements. All youah *gachupín* whoremasters have wives and a goddamn string of *putas* on the side."

"It isn't necessary to insult me. If you find this gringa more satisfying than Madelaina, then go to her. Sleep with her and dream of me! I curse you for this, gringo! You hear?" She screamed hoarsely at him, hoping he'd believe her performance.

"So, when it comes right down ta it, youah a bitch, like all the rest, eh?" He shoved his shirt into his trousers, slipped into his boots, and slung his jacket over one shoulder.

"Go, Peter, for God's sake, before we say things to each other we'll regret for all our days," she said. "At least we can part friends. You know I could never wish you ill or misfortune."

Peter stared at her in the dim light as she struggled into a thin wrapper.

She knows, he told himself. She knows what I'm up to. He tossed his jacket on a nearby chair and walked across the carpeted room to her. He gathered her in his arms. "Ah should've known bettah than to try foolin' y'all, sugah," his voice grew husky and filled with emotion. He reigned kisses on her, unable to stop. "Ah know that y'all know and unduhstand what it is ah can't tell ya. Ah don't know how ah know and I don't know how ya know. But it's as clear ta me as the nose on youah pretty little face. Jus' trust me. Ah know its askin' a lot. An' if ya heah of my marriage, don'cha believe it. Don'cha let it shake ya, sugah. Ah'm tellin' ya,

649

the minute ah can, ah'll come back ta ya. Ah'll find ya if it takes all mah born days. Heah?"

They made love until dawn. While Madelaina slept, Peter left to return to his hotel. He had to relax in a hot tub and do some thinking. He grabbed a bottle of whiskey from the top of a chest and began to guzzle it down as he waited for the tub to fill. He undressed and gazed at his reflection in the mirror, feeling a terrible emptiness. It had always been this way after making love to Little Fox. He could still feel her hot body next to his, smell the soft sweet fragrance of roses that unmistakably reminded him of her, and taste the nectar of her body. His senses were possessed with the intoxication of his wife, and he knew he could never be done with loving her.

He had to be strong in the coming days, if he hoped to pull off what he intended to achieve. He'd pow-wowed with Villa and Captain Richards for the past two months. With the governor's help he'd managed to gain audience with President Woodrow Wilson in hopes of securing his aid in the inevitable revolution that fermented and threatened to explode at any time.

Peter dispensed with the glass he'd been using and swung the bottle to his lips, guzzling half of it in a few long swallows.

It was necessary that his closeness with the governor be looked upon as a relationship between a father and prospective son-in-law, no more, no less. To carry out his plans, he would marry Governor Townsend's daughter Valerie if he had to. Love had nothing to do with it. As a matter of fact, he detested the empty-headed, spoiled darling of society. There'd been times when he had all he could do to refrain from putting her over a knee and spanking the tar out of her.

One night, she finally seduced him, an act for which he'd never forgiven himself, because it could have meant blowing the entire cause. Peter, with the control of a superman, had permitted the seduction to appease the headstrong, sex-driven harlot who was determined to give the performance of a high-paid courtesan. Long before, Peter had deduced that Valerie Townsend was possessed by a highly inflated estimation of her need for sex. He guessed she had hypnotized herself into thinking she was insatiable. Hell, Peter knew the difference between real emotion and that which was manufactured and phony.

Valerie was a spoiled adolescent at the age of twenty-eight and should have long since matured into womanhood. He had discovered she was incapable of any real emotional depth, and to boot, she was a lousy actress. His own performance that night, which fell way below par, drew phony raves from the woman who had even faked orgasm. If he had really cared for the wench or needed some reason to inflate his masculine ego, he'd have taken her in hand and taught her how it was to journey into the unknown realms of infinite passion, just as he'd schooled Madelaina so carefully.

He didn't even like Valerie and died a thousand deaths when he had to pretend to be in love with her. How many times had he cursed under his breath and began to truly realize how a prostitute must feel when she had to manufacture false reactions to the countless men who pay for her favors. He shuddered.

Soaking in the tub, he dismissed her from his mind. He concentrated on more pertinent things. Why hadn't Villa told him his wife was in El Paso? Why? Was it possible that Tracy Richards knew also and had withheld the information? He'd just returned from Washington yesterday afternoon, where for several days he had met clandestinely with President Wilson.

It had been a difficult chore convincing that professorial man in the White House just what the situation really was in Mexico. It was apparent to Peter, however, that the Commander-in-Chief regarded with undisguised contempt what his predecessor, President Taft, had caused to ferment south of the border. President Wilson himself disclosed to Peter that incalculable graft was running rampant; that the incredibly

651

callous speculation on Wall Street continued without regard or respect for the honor of America. Why, between President Taft and his Latin America ambassador, every effort at internal reform had been confused and abused until Washington had earned the bloody stigma attached to a bestial landlord—*hacendado*.

Peter recollected the encounter he'd had with President Wilson, Governor Townsend, Don Abraham Gonzalez, governor of Chihuahua, and Don Martino Espinoza, temporary governor of Coahuila. They had all met in the oval office to discuss the Mexican situation and Pancho Villa's aims for his nation.

Armed with dossiers on both Villa and General Huerta, documenting their lives and achievements, up to and including the latest obscenities performed under Huerta rule, he'd presented it to the stiffly dressed Commander-in-Chief.

The meeting had been underway for nearly an hour, and in that time Peter had been attempting, with the aid of the other men, to point out Huerta's double-dealing, and crafty, underhanded politics. "He's a dangerous man attempting ta overthrow the Madero regime," continued Peter. "This man's clearly a psychopath, a drunkard with a penchant foah political assassinations. Why, at this moment, suh, he an' political aides, moah butchers, are in El Paso dealing with the Germans."

"Are you trying to tell me, Mr. Duprez, that at a time when the crisis in Europe is at its worst, this ambitious tyrant is dealing with the Kaiser? Our southern neighbors are attempting to ally themselves with foreigners the calibre of the Kaiser?" President Wilson's apparent disgust concealed his wrath. That son of a bitch Huerta had already attempted through his emissaries to demand outrageous concessions from the U.S.A.! He said nothing of this to his guests, although he did a continuous burn during this conference in more ways than one. "If anything, that maniac should attempt to tighten the bonds between us! Hah! Not even in power and he's making ovations like a big gun."

"Isn't that the way deals are made, Mr. President?" asked Peter subtly.

Wilson shrugged. He glanced at Governor Townsend. "What do you have to contribute to all this, Hampton? Are you in agreement with Mr. Duprez' assessment?"

"I fully concur with him, Mr. President," replied the Texan. "I've read the extensive report and find him to be quite accurate."

"And you, Don Espinoza? What have you to say of this report?"

The Mexican governor of Coahuila shrugged slightly and puffed on his Havana. "I know the timbre of my people," he said officiously. "Their pride—their very deep pride. I am fearful of Pancho Villa's motives. Personally, I could never counsel the people of America to take any action which would cause any break in the friendship with the Mexican people themselves. Thousands of miles separate our thinking, although only the Rio Grande marks our boundaries. *Señor Presidente*, we have not sufficient proof that General Huerta has become everything they say he has. In my opinion, you should proceed with things as they are for the moment. But with care—and caution."

"*Señor Presidente*," objected Don Gonzalez heatedly. "Everyone knows that Don Espinoza is a *Huertista*."

"Just as you are pro-Villa and Madero?" President Wilson smiled tolerantly. "Don Gonzalez, if I am to be fair and impartial, I must listen to both sides of any controversy. All sides, as a matter of fact. It's only fair."

"That's true," replied Don Gonzalez, a true promoter of democratic ideals. "I agree with you. But I think you should pay particular attention to what Mr. Duprez tells you. His information is first hand, from a man who has fought in the thick of things."

President Wilson nodded and turned to Peter expectantly.

"Ah'm not prepared to say anything moah than

what ah've already stated. Mah report should give ya a pretty accurate account of what Huerta is up to."

"I wish I had your confidence, Mr. Duprez," replied President Wilson as he glanced at the younger man over his pince-nez glasses. "By the way, aren't you a Mexican citizen? Have I not been told you are married to a *gachupín*?"

"That's right. Ah married her, but then ah considered calling her an American citizen. Ya see, it works both ways. We held decided interests on both sides of the border. Ya see, we both believed in repelling injustice wherever it arises. We fought alongside of Pancho Villa and the revolutionists because we believe in what the man stands for. Mah wife and ah've been too busy ta concern ourselves with the future when the present is in such dubious straits. But now theah's no longuh a future fer her."

The president's eyes flickered with momentary compassion. "You have my personal sympathies. Then you intend carrying the standard for her, is that it?" Wilson mused a moment. "And what does your illustrious father have to say about all this—about your opposition to the precepts in which he believes?" He leaned in on one elbow to hear Peter's reply.

Governor Townsend also leaned forward, his eyes bright with interest.

"The politics of William Benson, suh, are in no way ta be confused with the politics of Peter Duprez. Just as ah've chosen sides and prefer ta speak foah mahself, so ah reckon will William Benson." Peter steeled himself. He'd protested often enough that politically as in every way he was apart from his father. "Ah thought ah made it clear, suh, by mah intervention in this matter that ah am a Villa sympathizer—as are the many hundreds of other freedom fighters fighting the *jefe*'s cause."

"Yes, yes," snapped President Wilson, pushing his glasses up on the bridge of his nose. "I've been made painfully aware of those freedom fighters. Now then, what does your father-in-law think of your political

654

persuasions and his daughter's rebellious attitude? He is General Alvaro Obregon, isn't he?" ventured the president, peering inscrutably over his glasses at the soldier of fortune.

"I've no idea what he thinks. I've never met the man."

"Yet you also oppose him. Are you such a rebel, my man?"

"I oppose injustice to any human being."

"And this *guerrillo* Pancho Villa, a rebel and a fugitive, has become your savior?"

Peter flinched at his acerbic words. "Pancho Villa fights for *his* people and *his* country, for a belief in freedom and equality and justice for all men. I'm only a warrior who supports his theory. How can I, an American who lives across the river from his land and believes what I do, be blinded to what goes on south of that river?"

The president was silent. He studied all the men in his office. All were respectable men with excellent backgrounds, known for their democratic leanings and pro-American politics. He also had communiqués from several men who weren't present, stating their views on this decision he had to make.

"It seems to me that the men with the most to lose in the event of trouble—with the most to gain from Pancho Villa's friendship—those with the largest holdings in Texas and Mexico are the men who urge caution. Why?" asked Wilson, still stinging from the reputation left by his predecessor, Taft.

"Ah urge caution against American intervention to support Huerta—*not Pancho Villa*," retorted Peter, burning at the implication. "Only because of what he stands for and what's he's initiated in order for him to carry the Mexican sceptre. Ah'm shuah youah espionage agents have informed ya of the countless political assassinations paving Huerta's bloody path to the top. Why, suh, supporting such a man indicates ya support his tactics!"

655

"Peter!" Governor Townsend's stern disapproving voice deterred him from saying any more.

"That's all right, Hampton," replied the president tolerantly. "He speaks with the zealous fervor of youth." He turned to Peter. "When you've lived a little longer, you'll be more tolerant of those men with graying hair at their temples who learned to temper their feelings with age. Experience comes with age, young man, and with it comes understanding."

"With all due respect, Mr. President, in the interest of both ouah nations, Mexico and America, ah've submitted mah findings. Ah feel ah've been impartial in mah reports. Ah also submit that if theah weren't some merit ta the man Pancho Villa, these distinguished men heah with me today wouldn't be in youah presence ta defend him—excludin', of course, Don Espinoza who after all is only an interim governor."

"Ummmhum," replied the president. "An' you feel deeply, Peter, that my deals should be made with Pancho Villa."

"Indeed ah do, suh. Why don'cha ask yer own generals, Hugh Scott and John Pershing? Ah unduhstand they admire the *jefe* somethin' fierce. Why, suh, ah've fought alongside the *jefe* in the Gringo Brigade an' ah've seen the stuff the man's made of. Ah mean he's revered by the people. They'll lay down their lives foah him, suh."

"You're speaking of—so that we both understand—that illiterate animal from Sonora whose maniacal temper has killed off half the population and caused rivers of blood to irrigate the land of Mexico? Why, Peter, he's nothing but a rag-bag bandit, hardly reformed, whose only pardon came about when he enlisted to fight Diaz. He has displayed no political inclination or talent."

"But, don't ya see, suh, that's what makes him so special. He has no political vices, no ambition to sit on the throne. And, suh, he's the first ta admit he was illiterate—"

"*Was* illiterate. Just what does that mean?"

656

"Well, suh, Mr. President. Recently he was jailed. While in jail he learned to read an' write."

"Jailed—whatever for?"

"Ah'm not certain, suh," Peter was trying to avoid the question.

"Come, come, Peter. You can't allow me to believe you'd let information as vital as this slip by you."

"Well, Mr. President. It was foah a mere infraction of the rules. As ya know, he's an army irregular, and well, suh, the charges were filed against him by General Huerta. That should ansuh youah inquiry. Insubordination and dereliction of duty."

President Wilson, an incurable busybody in foreign affairs, opened a folder and, adjusting his pince-nez glasses, scanned the report.

"Failure to follow orders from his Commander-in-Chief, Francesco Madero. Pancho Villa attacked Juarez against direct orders to the contrary. . . ."

"But, suh, that's just it. Villa had ta countermand Madero's orduhs because Madero, no military man, had no idea of what was involved. By attacking Juarez, Villa ended the revolution. It was a master stroke of genius, Mr. President."

"But the revolution has begun again. Where does that put Villa?"

Peter Duprez had avoided this question and he'd hoped the president would. But now he had to speak up. "He's still loyal to Madero, suh."

"You've gotta be kidding, Peter!" Wilson's pince-nez glasses fell to his lap.

"No suh, Mr. President. Ah wished ah was kidding. But it does say something about Villa, don'cha think?"

The president picked up his glasses and reset them on his nose. "Yes, it does say something. Only I'm not about to tell you what my mind is whispering. He's a neophyte, a political embryo, who one day might deserve American aid, my boy. But I'm afraid I can't wholeheartedly endorse such a man. Now then," he said, sweeping aside the Pancho Villa issue in a clear,

657

clean-cut sentence, "tell me what you know about a Señor Venustano Carranza,"

Peter had grown hesitant. "One-time governor of Coahuila State. Former member of Francesco Madero's first cabinet. An active political and revolutionary figure. Ah s'pose y'all could say he is stately, well-bred, and politically persuasive."

"I know. I know. Just wanted to see if you were on your toes, Peter. I know about Señor Carranza. And while I haven't made up my mind, I do believe he'd be the best man to place on the throne of the presidential palace in Mexico."

Peter's face darkened, but he kept his thoughts to himself.

"Well, what is it? You looked as if the bottom of the world had just caved in."

"Carranza an' Huerta are one and the same."

"Nonsense, they differ drastically in their political views," replied President Wilson in his all-knowing manner.

"At least Pancho Villa is a man of principle. He won't sell out to the highest bidder."

"You feel strongly in this matter, don't you, my boy?"

"Ah wouldn't be heah, tryin' ta make ya see what's goin' on, suh, if ah didn't know the kind o' man this Pancho Villa is in his heart."

"Very well, then. These things aren't solved in a moment. I'll dispatch a special committee to meet with your Señor Villa. If your man meets with our specifications and can promise us he can keep peace south of our borders, I promise I'll see that he gets an opportunity to prove his worth."

"Thank ya, suh, Mr. President. Ah couldn't ask foah moah."

The president then politely indicated that the meeting had come to an end. He bid good day to Townsend, Gonzalez, and Espinoza, but asked Peter stay behind.

"Peter?"

"Yes, Mr. President."

"Is the date set for your wedding to Valerie Townsend?"

"No, Mr. President. It's been mighty difficult convincing Valerie ta give up her freedom to become mah missus. But one o' these days, ah hope ta break down her resistance."

"Good, my boy. She'd make you a mighty fine wife. Knows all the right things to do. Been to the best of schools. Why, she'd be a great asset to any man on his way to becoming a state senator."

"State senator?"

"Oh, don't play the innocent with me. It's all been arranged. The governor insists on something formidable for his son-in-law. And if we can keep our heads and do the right thing for our Mexican neighbors, well, you are certainly entitled to a worthwhile prize. It's only fitting, wouldn't you say?"

"Well, suh, ah'm flabbergasted. Ah can't think of a thing ta say."

"Then don't. You just leave it to the old-timers who know their way around this political jungle. Good day to you. Peter. God bless you."

Peter had nodded and backed out of the office as one did with royalty.

"Good day ta y'all, Mr. President. And thank ya, suh. Thank ya."

Peter had left the White House wondering what he'd accomplished. Nothing! Absolutely nothing. He felt as if he'd been used. He also felt that his opinion of Pancho Villa held no special importance with President Wilson. It all seemed like such a farce. Even after being back in El Paso a day, he hadn't been able to confront Villa with the disheartening news. If Wilson had intended to help Villa, he'd have given Peter his reply instantly, since time was of the essence.

In spite of the rage and disgust he felt, the self-disgust at his inability to make his own efforts count, Peter found himself grinning over the fight he'd had with Valerie earlier over Madelaina. If he knew Valerie, and

659

by this time he knew her well, she'd probably have him followed by Pinkerton men to make certain he didn't frequent the Diamond Slipper.

She'd had screaming hysterics when he and her entourage caught up with her outside the gambling palace earlier that evening, but Peter wouldn't put up with her unreasonable jealousies and childish tirades. He had dumped her at the governor's mansion and bid her a curt good night. She had screamed at him, threatened to break their engagement, and cussing him out in the foulest and most obscene way, she'd threatened to kill herself if he didn't return that very instant and set a wedding date.

He'd hoped that President Wilson would have expedited matters with Villa, so he could have ended it with Valerie. This delay in Washington not only slowed Villa up, but it put him in an untenable position, especially now that he had to be concerned over Madelaina. He just wouldn't put anything past Valerie. She was a vicious, double-dealing little vixen, who had done a real snow job on her father. Why, she had the old goat wrapped around her little finger. He never guessed what a whore he'd sired. She was one of the most mixed-up little wenches he'd ever met. He found himself growing bored with her demands and her tantrums, and unable to face the prospect of a dinner engagement with her.

Inevitably she'd insist on winding up in bed with him, and Peter, who'd never worn a condom in his life, kept a supply on hand. The little bitch couldn't be trusted. She was the kind ta get herself knocked up, just to drag him down the aisle in a shotgun procession.

One night, he wasn't certain what had made him examine the thin rubber sheath before placing it on his penis, but he did. Damned if he didn't find tiny pin pricks in all of them. He could have confronted her—scolded her and brought her down a peg or two—but he chose not to bring it up. He let her think he was a dummy that could be fooled. He duplicated his supply and kept it well secreted. He used the safe rubbers each time. After months passed, he recognized her old surliness return. One day, he'd returned to find his apartment ransacked. It took a moment before he went to his secreted condoms to examine them. When he found them sliced in half, he burst out into roaring laughter. He never mentioned the incident, nor did she. Now he was bored—bored—bored with her.

Peter slid back in the tub, his head on the headrest. The cigar he had been smoking had died out. The whiskey bottle empty, he dozed in a stupor.

He was vaguely aware that the door opened, that he wasn't alone. Earlier, when he had placed the bottle and ash tray beside the enameled tub, he'd made it a point to place his six-shooters on the stool next to him, a habit that he hadn't parted from. Now, as he stirred from his drunken euphoria, he thought, if he tried, he could make a grab for them. He was limp, without a working muscle or nerve in his body. For one split second, in an instinctive reaction for survival, his eyes flared wide open and, like the lens of a camera, snapped a picture of his assailant. His eyes closed tightly and the impression of a lithe figure, dressed in a riding habit, her hair concealed under a velvet helmet, kept flashing in his mind.

Peter heard a loud explosion first. Then he felt a dull thud hit his chest. The sensation was like the bursting of a ball. The whiskey had so anesthetized him he felt little pain. He heard a loud sob, a scuffle of feet, and the door slamming.

He recalled nothing after that, except the fluttering of heavy eyelids as he tried to open them. In the split second of vision, he remembered thinking how colorful the water around him was, crimson, the color of blood.

For the next two weeks, Peter Duprez lay in a private sanitarium on the outskirts of El Paso, hovering between life and death. None of his friends knew his whereabouts.

Two days after this tragic incident took place, an article appeared in the El Paso *Times* announcing the surprise marriage of Peter Duprez to Valerie Townsend. The happy couple, the article went on to say, had left for an extended three-month honeymoon in Europe. This article is what started Peter's friends worrying.

"You believe this, *chiquita*?" asked Pancho Villa thoughtfully, entering Madelaina's dressing room at the Diamond Slipper.

"Do newspapers lie?" she asked solemnly.

"Who can tell? I know only that your *marido* would not leave without first telling Pancho."

"My *marido*! Hah! That's a laugh! Apparently my *marido* doesn't take his marriage vows seriously."

"Little Fox! Silence your tongue. I was unable to speak up before, but now I must. The gringo was working for me. Now I fear double-dealing. Take heart. I go now to find Captain Richards. He will know what such a thing in the paper means."

Villa left the gambling palace, only to return ten minutes later. The look on his swollen face was enough to alert the women. He sat down heavily in an overstuffed chair, newspaper in hand, his shirt soaked to the skin.

"What is happening, *chiquita*?" he asked the woman in a dead voice. "Has the world gone mad? First, Peter's disappearance, now this!"

Antonetta removed the crumpled paper from his tightly clenched hand. She spread it open and gasped audibly. The headline in the Juarez paper read: PRESIDENT FRANCESCO MADERO RESIGNS POST!

The article went on to say that, due to the events of a ten-day siege on the capital, Francesco Madero and his vice-president respectfully tendered their resignations to the honorable Chamber of Deputies. It was brief, terse, and to the point.

After the initial shock wore off, Pancho and Antonetta returned to the boardinghouse. In the seclusion of his room, while he was kept busy taking calls from aides trying to learn what was happening, plans were forming in Pancho's mind, plans which were immediately scrapped when Madelaina Obregon ran into the room, breathless and pale and obviously upset.

It was three o'clock, Pancho recalled it well. The clock on the mantle chimed just as he opened the latest edition of the Juarez paper, a hastily printed special put out on the streets less than an hour after the news was wired to them.

PRESIDENT FRANCESCO MADERO ASSASSINATED BY RIOTING MOB.

Pancho Villa's world and the world of those he loved had just crumbled to pieces. In a sudden burst of anger, Pancho Villa crumpled the newspaper and hurled it at the floor. His eyes were bloodshot, his face purple with rage.

"Goddamn them! Goddamn them all! They will pay for this disgraceful act! They will pay!" He picked up the phone and gave the operator a number. "Gringo!" he shouted loudly to Captain Richards. "Have you heard?"

"All of it, *Jefe*. All the goddamned black-hearted whole of it."

"Ju hear from Tom Mix?"

"No, *Jefe*." Captain Tracy's voice dropped sadly.

"Ju come with Pancho. We must talk. We must find Tom Mix—is understood? What of the story of the marriage?"

"The governor's mansion sticks with the same ole story, *Jefe*."

As they conversed, Madelaina excused herself. She was explaining to Antonetta that she'd be at her own house until show time. Her heart was heavy enough at not hearing from Peter all this time. Now, learning of his marriage from the newspaper instead of from his own lips, she felt terrible, low in spirits. "If you need me, you know where you can find me."

"Little Fox!" called the *jefe*. "Zorrita!"

Madelaina turned, startled by the tone of his voice. "*Si, Jefe*."

"Is better ju stay here with us. Ees more safe."

"I'll be all right. No one knows where I live besides you and Tonetta. That is, only Peter knew."

He shook his head stubbornly. "Is more better ju stay here."

She shrugged. "*Muy bien, Jefe.* First, I go home and pack a bag. I need some things."

Pancho glanced at Antonetta. She nodded. "It's all right. Madelaina can take care of herself. Take my driver, *chiquita*," she insisted.

"And what do I do with mine?" queried Madelaina.

"Let him go. I trust mine more. Ju come back before five o'clock?"

Madelaina glanced at her watch. "I'll do my best, *chica*."

Madelaina hardly noticed the day had been cool and crisp, rare for El Paso. A wind had arisen and swept in from the surrounding deserts. She tied her straw sailor hat under her chin and dismissed the driver. "Take the rest of the day off," she told him. Waving her hand overhead, she summoned Antonetta's black man. "Take me home, *chico*," she said, giving him a dazzling smile.

It wasn't until she opened the carriage door that she realized that the black man hadn't returned her greeting. But by then it was too late. Her abductors had seized her, pulled her into the carriage, and placed a blindfold around her eyes. They stuffed a gag into her mouth and bound her struggling arms and legs.

The clatter of horses' hooves slapped against the brick streets; the carriage creaked and swayed as it gathered momentum; the stench of the men, animal odors, and the nauseous smell of dirty clothing gagged her. All the old terrors of previous abductions returned, and Madelaina tensed with vivid visions of what might happen to her. She tried desperately to remain calm and detached, knowing that if she did, she might hear something that would give her a clue to the route they took. It wasn't easy, as she strained at her bindings, hoping not to gag. The constant swaying of the coach brought on waves of nausea. She felt as if she would vomit and might strangle if the gag weren't removed from her mouth.

None of this phases me, she told herself. *It isn't really happening to me. It will all pass and I will remain unaffected,* she continued to repeat to herself, wondering at the same time from where came this strength.

The nausea passed. Her mind was clearer and the heightened fear dissipated. She could even think without the earlier terror. *Where could they be taking me? Who is responsible for this?* When she pondered on these questions, she realized her assailants could be any of a number of persons, beginning with her father, and ending with General Huerta or Major Salomon. She understood that it was useless to struggle, so she sat primly in the corner of the coach where she'd been thrown and waited.

"Ah think weah heah, man," said one of the assailants to the other. His west Texas accent was even more pronounced than Peter's, she thought.

Madelaina had lost all sense of time. She felt the coach gradually slow down as the driver pulled back on the reins and braked the vehicle. Then she was lifted bodily from the carriage and carried by a burly man whose stench offended her. She was toted for a short distance and placed on her own feet.

"Now, ya just walk in a bit, m'am. No—no—straight ahead," said the sweaty-faced bounty hunter, Gus Madigan, as he led her to a chair inside a dimly lit, dank, and shuttered room. "Ah'm gonna hafta leave ya fer a while, heah? Now, don'cha try no funny stuff, or mah partnuhs ain't gonna take ta such liberty, ya heah?"

Madelaina nodded dutifully as they removed the gag from her mouth and took the scarf from her eyes. "Jus' don't try no foolish moves, woman, or these two, your escorts, will know jus' what to do. An' ah tells ya it ain't pleasant."

Madelaina's eyes blinked hard until they grew accustomed to the shadowy interior of the stuffy room. Her eyes fell on the face of the gringo, a foul-mouthed, grizzled cowboy with dirty trousers, boots and spurs, and a six-gun at either hip. He had a surly look on his face, but it wasn't the face of a man who'd do her harm. A bounty hunter, no doubt, who had abducted her for the right price. When she gazed at the other two, however, she gave a start.

Two Mexican *peóns*, dressed more scruffily than the gringo, wearing double *bandoleras* over their chests, with more ammunition and hardware at either hip, were eyeing her with narrow, suspicious eyes. It became apparent that she recognized them. They might have had an inkling that they knew her, but her lady-like appearance had them baffled.

Madelaina had committed these madmen to her memory. Jorge Molina and Feliz Galina were the men who'd abducted her from Villa's camp on her father's instructions. *Dios mios*! Jorge Molina especially! The man whose penis and testicles she'd shot off, the man she'd left for dead after his violent assault on her was alive! If he recognized her, it would be the end. She kept her eyes averted from his. Perhaps in this light he'd not recognize her. What folly do I entertain, she asked herself. They would certainly know her identity by name, wouldn't they? Her one consolation was that Jorge Molina could never again humiliate her with his body.

"So, ees *La Bomba* ju are, eh, *señorita*?" asked Jorge Molina as soon as Gus Madigan left them alone.

"Jorge!" hissed Feliz Galina in their native tongue. "What is the matter with you, man? You never learn, eh? Castrated as you were once for this very same thing, you still continue with such foolishness?"

Jorge turned around to face his companion, who at the moment seemed more like an enemy. "Shut up! Keep your woman's tongue locked tight in your head before I slit it for you! For why you think I live, eh?" His red-flamed eyes burned like torches as he stared at Galina. "You think *Dios mios* let me live in my condition if I were not to be avenged? *Demonio!* I will find that tough-livered daughter of a *gachupín* whoremaster to even the score if it takes all my life."

"*Si, si,*" Galina waved him off. "Is better we stick to business and make our money, *comprender*? And is best you forget what that little female tiger did to you. You had it coming, so stop lamenting."

Jorge turned on Galina, snarling like a vicious animal. He pulled his six-shooter, quick as lightning, and squeezed off a shot at his opponent, slicing a finger from the man's left hand. Galina screamed, fell to the floor, and rolled over, taking cover behind a chair and pealing two shots at the other. They were both cursing loudly and Madelaina, caught in the middle, sat stiffly, unable to move, just as the door burst open and Gus Madigan, followed by two gringo cowhands, stormed into the room.

"Goddamn greasers! Ah leave ya alone for two minutes and ah find ya fightin' over the woman! What the hell's wrong with ya? Too much fuckin' has fried yer brains."

"Fuckin'?" shouted an incensed Feliz Galina scornfully. "That motherless son of a *bastardo*'s *bastardo* hasn't got the equipment to do a manly thing." He wrapped his kerchief around the stump where only moments before a finger had protruded. An evil glint in his pain-filled, menacing eyes promised future retribution to Jorge. His gun had fallen to the floor close to Madelaina's feet, unnoticed.

"Issatso?" Madigan's eyes twinkled in merriment. "Now ain't that a pity? Well, at least ah can say ah feel a mite better, knowing ya can't damage the merchandise for Mr. Benson."

Madelaina's mind stopped at that remark. "Mr. Benson?" she asked. "*He's* responsible for this—for my abduction? But why?"

"Ah only follows orduhs, Miss *La Bomba*. Ah learned me long ago nevah ta ask questions of my boss. It's healthier thata way, ya heah?" He turned back to the two Mexicans. "Ya calmed down yet? Look, heah,

Galina, ya better get ovuh ta the kitchen and let cook fix yer finger—or ya might loose the fuckin' arm." He turned to Molina and grinned wickedly. "An' since ah knows ya cain't do the little missy heah no harm, ah guess it'll be all right ta leave ya with her."

"No!" screamed Madelaina hoarsely. "Don't leave me with this madman! He'll kill me! Believe me." Her voice climbed in hysteria. "He'll kill me!"

Jorge Molina turned to her with a look of innocence on his face and searched her features with a kindly, overexaggerated shrug. "Molina does a gringo woman no harm. For why do ju be so scared, eh?" He holstered his gun without menace. "Jorge's anger ees with that chicken Galina, not ju."

Madelaina turned her head, appealing to Madigan. "Please, you mustn't leave me here with this sex-crazed animal. I beg you. Señor Benson will punish you dearly if harm comes to me!"

"Ain't nothing ah don't already know. Now ya jus' sit heah quietly. Ain't nuttin' gonna happen ta ya, ah promise. Or ah'll have Jorge's head." He turned to the Mexican pointedly. "Ya heah, Molina?"

"Si, hombre. My word. No harm shall come to the gringa."

They were alone. For a time Molina studied her, then he began to roll a cigarette from a small bag of tobacco. Finished, he wet one end and curled it against moist lips under a thick handlebar moustache and finally lit it.

"Why ju are afraid of me?" he asked her in afterthought.

Madelaina didn't reply. She didn't have the courage to glance at him, not at this point, knowing he possessed so itchy a trigger finger. She'd heard with her own ears how he planned revenge on the woman who castrated him, hadn't she? God, how in hell he had lived after the gunshot wounds, when she and Feliz and the third man, Jose, left him in the desert to die, was a miracle.

Molina stood up and came toward her, eyeing her as

668

he tilted his head from one side to another. When he grinned as he did at this moment, he reminded her of Villa's sidekick, Urbina. It was an evil, lascivious grin that sent icicles through her blood. "Gringa, eh? Ju are *patrón* Benson's woman?"

Madelaina averted her head.

Molina moved in closer, his eyes narrowing. He reached in and with a grubby hand lifted her face so he could see her better. "Listen, gringa, how ju know Molina ees crazy, sexy man, eh?" Before she could reply, he leaned in and planted a wet, foul-breathed kiss on her lips. She struggled and with a free hand struck him hard across the face.

"Animal!" she screamed with burning hatred as memories of his vile abuse sprang into her mind.

Molina sprang back, startled by her reaction. He touched the side of his face lightly where he still felt the smarting of the blow. He laughed raucously, finding her actions humorous. "Ah, *si*, ju know Molina likes a tigress?" His eyes assessed her physical charms. "Because Molina is castrated doesn't mean he can't satisfy a woman such as you." He leered suggestively. "Molina still appreciates what a woman has and to look upon ju—ees something *muy bien!*"

Madelaina spat at him with all the vengeance she could muster. "An animal who knows only to rape a woman cannot appreciate a thing," she countered, wondering why she bothered. She knew she was playing with dynamite if she continued to goad him. *Let it pass, Madelaina. Do not speak to him and he'll not recognize you. You are defenseless without a weapon. Are you crazy to contest this animal?*

The small voices inside her kept nagging at her to keep her tongue. No matter how she tried to abide by their whisperings, something inside her demanded that she take her chances. She had to confront this animal with his own base and foul behavior and the hatred she bore for him and what he'd done to her when she was so defenseless.

"Ju are some brave woman," he said, staring at her

with revulsion for her high-toned manner. "Eef ju were no gringa, ju remind me of stuck-up *gachupíns* in my country." He kept tilting a bottle of tequila to his mouth, guzzling it noisily.

Madelaina breathed easier. She hoped they were still in America. She had gazed about the crudely constructed room and had no inkling as to where she was. But her wary eyes never left the face of this repulsive bear of a man for long. Having tasted his special brand of cruelty, she wasn't about to let it happen again. At one point her eyes came to rest on the gun that Feliz Galina had dropped on the floor not far from her feet. It still lay unnoticed by Molina, who apparently had other things on his evil mind.

Molina walked to the window and opened one of the shutters. His dark thoughtful eyes scanned the empty courtyard behind the large mansion of William Benson. It was deserted, he assured himself, as thoughts raced blindly through his mind. He wasn't making enough money on this job Galina had sucked him into. He turned back and glanced at the woman, thinking how much money he could make by selling her to the Mexicans as he made his way to Sinaloa. That is to say nothing of what he could get if he set her up in a house in Culiacan, eh? With her spirit and such a body, a gringa would bring him enough to retire like a *hacendado* himself. This Gus Madigan had called her *La Bomba*, some dancer, so what could she be—a whore, no?

His mind sped up like a turbine as he thought on the matter. Not even to that mealy-mouthed chicken, Feliz, would he tell his plans. His face broke into a more wicked grin than Madelaina had ever seen. It was enough to alert her—he was up to no good. His instructions had been to safely escort her to the Panhandle near Amarillo in a few days. Señor Benson had promised to pay them well for her safe journey to his hacienda. Who was to say what could happen en route to their destination? The more he pondered this, the better he liked it.

For an instant, he walked to the door, opened it, and peered outside. No one moved about in the dusky shadows of night. They were probably at supper, eating themselves sick. He glanced past the stables to the carriage house. If he worked fast, he could be off the estate at the edge of the city and onto southern roads before anyone missed them. For sure, that chicken, Galina, wouldn't return for a while.

In those few seconds Molina took to scan the exterior of the building, Madelaina reached down and slipped the gun into the folds of her suit. And not a moment too soon. He returned to her side, his eyes leveled on her.

"Gringa, listen to Molina. Ju want to escape? I will help ju to leave thees place. Is A-O.K.? Ju follow me and we go to the stable, find horses, and ride to safety. Ju believe Molina wants to help ju?" Craft and guile dripped from his voice.

Not for a second did she believe his turncoat tactics, although she couldn't help but wonder what he was up to, what his crazed mind was telling him. Knowing him, it could only mean more terror for her.

"Believe a castrated *Federale*, a bounty hunter?" She spat at him as her finger tightened on the gun. She let loose a string of curses in her native tongue that left no doubt in Molina's mind who she was.

He'd heard those same curses before, in the same voice, but where?

Madelaina reached up with her free hand and pulled out a few hairpins, allowing her raven hair to fall about her shoulders. "I thought I killed you once, *bastardo*, you obscene son of a fatherless whore, you putrified mass of decomposed humanity! You don't recognize me, eh? Take a good look at the daughter of General Obregon, swine."

For an instant Madelaina filled with a terror she'd never known before. The madman's eyes burned with volcanic fires of hatred. He came at her with death scrawled in his eyes, with a bitterness and a violence that was new to her. His blood-shot eyes fixed on her,

671

his mouth curled back over his yellowed teeth with animal hatred. "I vowed I'd kill you, *puta!*" he shouted in their native tongue. "Only Satan knows the plans I've in store for you." Before she could fire at him, he whipped out his gun and covered her. "No easy death for you, you castrating daughter of a ball-less *gachupín!* Before Molina is through with you, you'll wish you were dead."

He moved in toward her and pulled open the blouse of her suit, ripping the fabric and popping the buttons. As she moved to avoid his attack, Madelaina jerked back in the chair and the gun was revealed.

"Ahhh, what have we here, *chiquita?* A gun? My, my, what things we learn if we're smart." He viciously yanked the gun from her hand, holstering one and tucking the other in his waistband under his *camisa*. With a free hand he reached for one of her breasts and squeezed it so hard she whimpered painfully. Again and again he squeezed, leaving welts in and around her nipples. "You think I'm finished with you, *puta?* Never!" He dropped his trousers and forced Madelaina to look upon his mutilated testicles and penis.

She averted her head and he grabbed a handful of her hair, twisted it, and forced her head back into position. "Now, *puta*—suck! I said suck it! You were responsible for my condition. Now you make it feel better, before I do things to you that will burn in your memory until I kill you, hear?"

Madelaina's head was twisted in such a position, she couldn't free herself. One of Molina's knees was buried in her lap, pinning her into the chair. The other was straddled over the arm of the chair, his foot planted firmly on the floor as he forced what was left of his mutilated manhood to her lips.

So, she thought, *he has little memory of what I did. He dares put the remains so close to my teeth?* In her eyes was a loathing and violence so deadly that if Molina had noticed, he might have been intimidated enough to back away. But he didn't notice, and he wanted his sweet revenge, so he forced himself on her.

Madelaina, repelled by this foul animal, felt the adrenaline shoot through her. She wasn't about to succumb to the beast. She heard the groaning gasp first, looked up, and saw Molina grasp his chest, a look of startled anguish coupled with pain on his face. Low animal noises gurgled in his throat, his black eyes bulged enormously, and his body jackknifed forward and fell heavily on top of her. Only then did she see a knife buried to the hilt into his shoulders. Her dark wary eyes lifted to the figure standing in the doorway not far from them. The man walked forward, followed by William Benson and two of his hands.

It was Feliz Galina who had expertly sunk the knife into Jorge Molina's back. "When I learned who you were from Señor Benson," said Galina. "I knew you were in danger—"

William Benson strode quickly to her chair, and removing his jacket, he wrapped her up in it. "Forgive me, mah deah. Ah'd no idea of the danger youah'd face with this brute. But I'm heah on more vital missions. We must make haste. Come with me inside the main *casa*. All is in readiness."

Confused and dazed by the rapid turn of events, Madelaina's head whirled. She was unable to grasp the import of her abduction or understand William Benson's part in all this.

"What's in readiness?" she muttered. "I don't understand."

"Trust me, mah deah. Ah'll let no harm befall ya. Ya must put yoah faith in me. It's the only way ya can be saved." A note of urgency crept into his deep voice.

Madelaina struggled in his arms as they walked the pathway through the outer portico, lined with fragrant flowers, to the main house. She remembered the hacienda, all right. It was the same one she'd gone to to visit Manuelito Perez, the place where she had allowed him to seduce her. Her face flushed for an instant as she recalled the incident. However, more concerned with pertinent facts of her abduction, she protested. "What are you telling me? What missions?"

Her head turned sharply as she saw several people in the dimly lit salon, among them a man dressed in black, holding a black book in his hands. The sanctimonious expression on his face was so obvious that Madelaina frowned.

"What's the meaning of this, Señor Benson? I thought I had made it perfectly clear that I wasn't interested in such arrangements with you."

"Theah, theah, *señorita*. Ah promise ya—it's the only way." He turned to the preacher. "Now do youah stuff, parson—theah's little time to waste."

He nodded to the other men in the room. Instantly they drew their guns and took positions at the door and windows, standing guard.

About to protest that she couldn't marry him because she was already married, Madelaina looked at Benson long and hard, then kept silent. Something in his eyes signaled her to protest no further.

She hardly heard the words spoken. She found herself answering the questions and mouthing the words— love, honor, and obey, as if she was in a wild, distorted dream. Everything had happened so swiftly that she was unable to cope with the disjointed scenes of which she didn't feel a part.

The makeshift ceremony, a sheer mockery of the nuptial vows, had ended. A golden wedding band had been slipped onto her finger. Madelaina, still numb and bewildered by the whirlwind activity about her, studied the heavy-belted cowboys. Most were chewing tobacco, their eyes peeled outside in the darkness. She saw them tense. Waco, one of Benson's most trusted men, turned to his boss, and with burning eyes, he hissed across the room. "Heah it comes, boss. Be prepared." The others tensed, their postures indicating they were prepared to do battle.

She heard the sounds of horses' hooves first. Then the shouting of orders, the sound of marching feet beating a staccato on the brick courtyard outside.

There came a loud rapping on the door. She saw Benson nod to the butler. The liveried man bowed politely and crossed the main salon to the tiled foyer. She heard loud voices, demanding yet tinged with respect. Madelaina gave a start at the familiar sound of the voices. She glanced sharply at William Benson. His eyes silently reassured her that she had nothing to be concerned about. Then six Mexican *Federales* entered.

"Well, suh, to what do ah owe such an unexpected pleasure?" said the wealthy *hacendado*, catching sight of Major Salomon. "Do come in, Major. Ah'd like ya to meet mah new wife, Mrs. William Benson."

Madelaina tensed rigidly under the burning glare of Salomon's eyes. She felt her stomach cramp and knot as hot and cold chills swept through her. Why couldn't she have given Tolomeo's philosophy a chance, she wondered. Salomon's foul, satanic expression, as fearful as she'd once been of this man, didn't revolt her as it once did. For some unknown reason, she felt possessed of an inner strength she hadn't experienced before in his presence.

"Your wife, Señor Benson," Major Salomon stated flatly, as if he knew the daughter of General Obregon would suddenly elude him again. "And how long has this *fugitive* from my nation been *your* wife?"

"Fugitive? Mah deah major, y'all must be mistaken, aren't ya?" William Benson spoke words packed in ice, leaving no mistake as to his annoyance. "It jus' isn't possible that the wife of William Benson, friend to the American President Wilson, could possibly be married to a fugitive, heah? Ah suggest you bring that important information ta yer President Huerta."

For a moment, Major Salomon hesitated. Oh, he got the picture all right. He glanced at the parson, the witnesses, and the cowhands with drawn guns. If Salomon had misunderstood William Benson's words, there was one language that he as a soldier couldn't misinterpret—drawn and ready guns.

"I see. Yes, I see, Señor Benson. I shall relate this vital information to my *presidente* instantly. I am certain when the situation is fully explained to Presidente Huerta, he'll understand."

675

Madelaina paled excessively. *Huerta? President?* So! *He* was responsible for Madero's assassination! *Dios mios!* She could never return to her country—never! Not as long as Huerta was president. She missed the subtle silent interplay between William Benson and Major Salomon, but not the expression he gave her which promised future retribution as he nodded dutifully and withdrew with his escorts from the premises.

"Quickly, Waco," ordered Benson gruffly, shrugging his six-guns into place over each hip. "Y'all bring the carriage around. Is everything ready ta go?"

"Yes, suh. Shore is." He tipped his western hat back on his head and gave a signal to his men to follow him.

Benson walked over to her. He told her she mustn't worry, that as long as she was in his company as his wife, Mexican law wouldn't dare harm a hair on her head. He patted her hand in an unexpectedly paternal manner. "It'll all work out, mah deah. Weah going to mah spread, Seven Moons, up neah Amarillo, wheah y'all can rest up a bit, git a little beef on ya, and try ta foahget any o' this happened."

If Madelaina's lips formed any protest, she was shushed and wrapped into a long sable cloak he removed from a beribboned box. "A weddin' present fer the missus. Not really good enough fer ya, mah deah, but it'll hafta do until ah get ta know ya better."

They left El Paso, heavily cloaked and guarded by Benson's well-armed bodyguards and expert cowhands. Without the fortification of dinner or a snack, Madelaina's hunger pangs grew to the point where she could no longer endure the empty feeling in her stomach. She wasn't certain which was worse, the continuous creaking and swaying of the carriage, the hunger, or the apprehension of what was to come.

She saw very little of the countryside in the black of midnight with no moon lighting up the way. Less than an hour out she began to feel the effects of this hard journey. She kept quiet for as long as she could, and finally, just at the point where Madelaina could take no more, Benson ordered his driver to stop. From the carriage floor he produced a hamper prepared by his El Paso cook, containing cold chicken and wine. She tore ravenously into the chicken, bread, and cheese until she could eat no more. Accepting a glass of wine eagerly to wash down the dry food, she hardly gave it a second thought when wine spilled on her expensive sable coat.

William Benson leaned forward and with a linen napkin blotted the wet drops that clung to the luxurious fur. "Ya must learn ta take good care of youah apparel, mah deah," he said with patient, paternal tones. "Furs are exquisite and should be treated with moah care," he continued as they took a short walk to stretch their bones. He helped her back into the carriage.

"With my stomach fighting for its life, I can give no thoughts to my outer appearance," she said flatly, arranging her skirts. She uttered a sigh of temporary contentment. "When do we arrive at Seven Moons, Señor Benson?"

"Señor Benson? Mah deah, ya bettuh get used to calling me youah husband."

"Listen, Señor Benson," she began with annoyance. "I keep trying to tell you we can't possibly be married—" She stopped. "Seven Moons? Did you say Seven Moons?" On her face was a quizzical look. She opened her tapestried bag and unsnapped the middle compartment of her reticule. There, in the fold of satin, were the seven moon earrings given her by Peter. Coincidence?

"Now, now, let's not spoil ouah trip, mah deah. Theah'll be plenty o' time fer us ta be talkin' about such things when we get home. Yes, ah said Seven Moons. Youah'll love it, mah deah. You'ah just the kind o' woman that belongs theah." He reached across the swaying carriage to pat her hands. His voice raised to a level that allowed her to hear him over the squeaking wagon sounds.

Madelaina shut the bag quickly.

"Wait till we get ta Seven Moons—ah sweah, youah'll nevuh want ta leave."

Madelaina stared at him in the dimly lit setting. Burning candles, encased in glass holders the shape of miniature lanterns at either side of the carriage doors, reflected deeply etched sadness on his stony features, despite his bold attempts to conceal his feelings. He was a strange man, this one with many contradictory sides to his nature. Madelaina was still taken by the co-incidence of seven moons on the earrings. She shrugged off the strange feeling she got sitting next to this man and changed the conversation. "You might have at least permitted me to pack a bag. There are certain things a woman needs—"

"Ah've already seen ta ut, mah deah. One o' mah men has gone on ta yer place and will bring some of yer necessities. We'll stop off in Lubbock foah a change of horses. What evuh else ya need can be pur-chased theah."

Madelaina remained silent. The trip took nearly four days. They'd stopped only to change horses, dine, rest at wayside inns, and stretch their muscles. She still didn't understand why William Benson chose to ride in a carriage, when train travel or automobile was quicker. There was so much of Texas, she thought, ob-serving the unending landscape of desert and the emp-tiness filled with more cattle than people.

Throughout the journey William Benson had maintained an amiable flow of conversation, detailing the vastness of his own lands and of his cattle- and bull-breeding operation. Admittedly, he told her, the sturdier bulls were bred in Mexico—something about the land and climate. As if she didn't already know what made certain strains of bulls more precious than others. He told her he'd have given anything to have taken her to his hacienda near Chihuahua City first, so that in her own land, among her own people, she'd have had a chance to really acquaint herself with him. However, in light of Major Salomon's urgent desire to detain her, he felt it safer to shelter her in his country where no harm could come to her.

"Then, when that President Huerta has had time ta

678

cool down a bit, an' when he comes to realize wheah the real power lies, he won't dare ta bite the hand that feeds him, heah?"

Madelaina stared at him with sudden hostility. "You're telling me that you're behind Huerta's sudden rise to power, Señor Benson? You financed his presidency?" This was all incredible to her. "A gringo knowingly supports such a man?"

"Let's jus' say, ah'm protectin' mah interests. Ah've plenty o' contacts in Washington. Ya might say ah'm a mighty powerful man," he said expansively, as he lit a cigar and filled the carriage with smoke. "It's only natural ah'd be protecting my properties, now wouldn'tcha say?"

Madelaina waved the smoke from her face impatiently. "But Huerta?" Her face screwed up with distaste, leaving very little to his imagination. "You must realize the kind of man you turned loose on the Mexican nation?"

"Now don'cha worry yer little head ovah matters that don't concern ya, mah deah. Politics don't belong in the head of a lady." He dismissed the subject from their talk and for the remainder of the trip described Seven Moons. "It's simply the most marvelous land in the whole world, mah deah. Can ya jus' imagine seven lakes all shaped like crescent moons on mah spread? Well, that's wheah the name comes from—Seven Moons. Imagine on a Texas ranch?"

It wasn't until they had arrived at Seven Moons and Madelaina had rested for a time that she was asked by a servant to join *señor el patrón* in the south portico for refreshments. It was more of an order than a request. Nevertheless, Madelaina walked down the steps of the sumptuous ranch, built in the style of a Spanish villa, and stepped briskly along the immaculate tiled floor to the portico beyond the French doors. It was a splendid, well-constructed house with huge polished oak beams, stone fireplaces, and highly waxed wooden floors. Hunting trophies covered the walls, including the heads of some of Benson's prize bull studs with

679

bronzed name tags mounted on wooden plaques denoting the prize strains.

"Well, mah deah, will ya join me in a few refreshments? A glass of sarsaparilla—wine—iced lemonade? What's youah pleasure?"

Ignoring him, Madelaina pressed onto a subject which ate at her. "Why Huerta?" she insisted on knowing. "He's a butcher! A chocolate-drinking butcher, a stuffed shirt who lives by treachery, murder, and revenge. There's no love in his heart for Mexico or its people. He is one of a few corrupt *Científicos* who sprang from the loins of the Diaz dictatorship which can't be trusted. Did you know Huerta was the head of the Secret Service? He wormed his way into Madero's trust only to assassinate him! And you help such a man to the highest office of the land? Hah! Señor Benson, you are as stupid as you are foolhardy."

Benson's square jaw flexed and his temples pulsed as he clenched his teeth, trying to contain his indignation. "Ah'll jus' pretend ah didn't heah those words spring from the lips of mah wife," he said with tight-lipped tolerance.

"How many times must I tell you? I can never be your wife!" she stormed angrily. "I keep telling you time and again and you just won't listen!"

Benson turned his back on her, poured a stiff tumbler of whiskey from a glass decanter on a sideboard, downed it in two gulps, and patted his stomach contentedly. "An' how many times must ah convince ya that politics is a man's subject. Don't evuh let me heah mention of Huerta or mah business again," he said with pointed calm. "Nothing like a good whiskey ta cleah the Texas dust from a man's throat." He sat down and indicated that she sit on a love seat placed in a luscious garden setting of trailing vines, blooming roses, and various cacti and succulents. She'd have enjoyed wandering in the garden anytime, but on this day she was too angry and upset by his dictatorial manner to do anything but fume inwardly as she forced herself to listen to him. He reminded her of her father so much, she forced her lips tight lest she say something she might regret. After all, she was miles and miles away from any land or people familiar to her. To think of running away would be as foolish as committing suicide at this point. Although she'd considered it several times over the past week after hearing about Peter's wedding and honeymoon, she had reconsidered. No. She'd be patient. She'd be detached. Wasn't that what Tolomeo insisted would give her inner strength? Very well, detachment would be her key to the future. Detachment and objectivity.

For the next few moments, William Benson attempted to display his charm. He asked her only what good manners forced her to reply—questions about her father and of the people she knew in El Paso. Many times she wanted to protest that their marriage could never be consummated because she was already married. Yet, when she pursued the thought, the knowledge that Peter had remarried weakened her position. Still, she persisted in bringing it to his attention, and each time she was cut off.

"Youah protests aren't all that important, mah deah, foah whatever reasons ya might conjur up. Ya see, one night while at mah villa neah Chihuahua City, while ah entertained that General Huerta and his man—what was his name?—Major Salomon? Yes, that's the one. Well, mah deah, you can imagine how interestin' ah found it when ah overheard Huerta and Salomon discussing how they'd finally located the famed spy of the revolution, Little Fox—Zorrita."

Madelaina tensed, hoping he wouldn't notice her sudden paleness.

"Theah didn't know ah was eavesdropping. An' ah might tell ya ah wasn't about ta listen fer much longer, especially when ah heard talk about this heah Zorrita, a Mexican spy that had half the *Federales* and *Rurales* lookin' fer her. An' when it turns out that she was none othuh than *La Bomba*, dancer at the Diamond Slipper, well, ah tell ya ah was about ta fall flat on mah face." Benson moved his large frame about the courtyard, pausing here and there to examine some of the exotic blooms.

The hot sun shining directly overhead was diffused by the branches of trees and vines shading off the inner courtyard. A dry wind off the prairie moved the air beyond the ranch house, rustling the sparse vegetation close to the estate and creating wheels of tumbleweed, which danced crazily on the surrounding lands.

Benson removed his jacket with a look of apology on his face. He wiped the perspiration from his face and neck. "Youah'll get used to the heat. Soon ya won't mind it a bit. Now wheah was ah? Ah, yes. Well, ya see, ah wasn't about ta let happen ta a friend what those two political snakes were dreaming up. Ah mean, we are friends, aren't we, mah deah?" He moved away from the flowers, one special sprig in hand and returned to the empty love seat. "What ah mean is, youah a friend of a friend, Manuelito Perez. Ah couldn't allow anything ta happen ta ya, could ah?" He placed the unusual flower into her lap. "Ah call it the Seven Moon plant. It's really a *Calceolaria Darwini* and barely resembles a crescent moon, but ah needed a flower to pay homage to my lands and ah chose this species to take the name."

Madelaina glanced in fascination at the curiously shaped bloom with leopardlike stripes on a crescent-shaped, elongated bubble. "They're quite unusual," she replied politely, unable to take her eyes from them. "I can see why you've called them Seven Moons."

"Well, well," he said somewhat pleased. "Ah knew ah'd picked the right woman. You an' me is gonna be soul mates, mah deah." He took her hand.

Madelaina withdrew her slender hands from between his and stood up.

"For all your efforts in helping me escape the clutches of my enemies, Huerta and Salomon, I thank you, Señor Benson."

"Señor Benson?" He laughed amiably and rose to his feet. "Mah name's Bill ta ya, little *chiquita*. Yer mah missus now! Now don't go getting yer dander up," he said quickly, seeing the anger rise in her. "Ah intend ta give ya a little time ta get used ta wearing mah name before we consummate our marriage. Ah promise, ah won't force mahself on ya. Ah tell ya, ah've waited a long time ta find me a filly like ya, and ah shuah don't intend ta spook her up."

Madelaina held back her tongue. What was the sense of protesting? How many times had she tried to make him understand? *Dios mios!* What a stubborn burro. Her anger flared earlier when he called her "little *chiquita*," much like the way Peter addressed her. She resented those words from the lips of any but her husband. Perhaps after a good night's rest, she could draw more courage and tell him about her marriage to Peter Duprez.

Before he permitted her to leave, he took time to introduce to her all the servants and ranch hands serving the hacienda. Nodding numbly throughout the ritual, she acted very much like the new mistress of the house, a fact which pleased William Benson immensely. She'll do, all right, he told himself. Yessiree, suh, he'd picked a champion. He'd let her rest sufficiently and in time he'd demand to know her background. Class always came to the fore, and this woman had to be a champion—a real prize-winning champion, he admitted.

"Just one moah thing, mah deah." He took her hand and led her to another room off the patio. The stench of the animals struck her first, but the foul odor of excrement, urine, and pure animal odor was dismissed from mind the moment she saw the cage along one wall filled with busy, chattering, and indolent monkeys, swinging from vine to vine in what had been rigged to resemble a miniature jungle habitat.

Her love of any of nature's creatures superseded the offensive odors, and in moments she stood in total enchantment. William Benson removed a packet of food from a wall chest and busied himself feeding the animals at random. They flocked to him.

"Watch'em, mah deah. They are quite instructive. Monkeys, ah feel, are somewhat superior ta man. They

683

can only mimic, so theah stay out of trouble. Man has it much harduh. He has ta be someone special. He has ta outshine his fellamen and work hard to get to the top of the heap. An' when he gets theah, he's a target foah all the unkind remarks and sharp spurs put ta him."

Madelaina sensed he wasn't really talking about monkeys, so she let him ramble.

"Theah smart, really smart, these heah monkeys. They nevuh talk back, they know theah place. Theah mind theah own business and stay outa trouble. Ya see, they just don't go about tryin' ta invent ways ta outsmart theah fellamen. Ya know, a person can learn a lot from just watchin' em."

An instinctive dislike for this man came upon her. Still she was intrigued by his line of patter and wondered where it would lead.

"Ya evuh fed a monkey, mah deah? Heah—take some food. Watch 'em flock ta ya. See what it feels like ta be depended on foah someone's life. Why, if I wasn't heah ta feed these monkeys, give 'em watuh and care foah 'em when they are sick, they'd die."

"If you left them in their own world, among other things in nature, they wouldn't be dependent on you. They could fend for themselves. Survival is instinctual among the lower animals," she said matter-of-factly as she tossed a few morsels to the chittering, highly agitated animals.

"But many monkeys leave their natural habitat and roam onto other territories wheah they can't take care of themselves. What are we ta do? Abandon them? Turn ouah backs on them? That would be inhuman. So we care foah them, feed them, and as long as they mind their own business, they can adjust."

"Just what are you trying to say, Señor Benson?" asked Madelaina, brushing her hands together to rid herself of the remaining crumbs.

"Ah'm trying ta explain a part o' me so y'all will get ta know me bettuh. I guess what ah'm attemptin' ta say is that y'all should try ta be like these heah monkeys."

Madelaina's fiery indignation set off sparks of mercurial emotion in her which Benson misinterpreted as belligerence. It was understandable that she'd be furious—she had a head on her shoulders and knew exactly what he intimated. He always preferred to domesticate his own animals. Tame, they were too set in the ways of their tamer and this offered no challenge to him.

"What ah'm tryin' ta say and farin' badly at it is that it's easy to do as youah told, mind yer own business, that way ya stay outa trouble."

"I know what you're trying to say. I only question why you need monkeys to tell me not to cause trouble among your people. I know my place, and believe me, it isn't here at Seven Moons as your wife!" she snapped contemptuously.

"Well, theah, little *chiquita*, it does mah heart good ta see ya get yerself rattled. Ah suppose ah wasn't being too clevuh with ya. It was just mah way of saying, this hcah's mah spread—mah lands—mah Seven Moons. Heah, I am the lord of mah manor. Heah, youah'll do only what ah tell ya ta do. It makes things so much simpler."

"Lord of the manor," she retorted harshly. "Insidious, uncompromising dictator is more like it. Listen, Mr. Benson, no man tells me what I do or don't do. The sooner you understand me, the better we'll get along. I had no hand in this flimsy scheme of yours to kidnap me and marry me against my will. Perhaps I should feel obliged to thank you for saving me from the clutches of Huerta and Salomon. Very well. I thank you. Now, you will please make arrangements to return me to El Paso." Her tone and mood reflected her *gachupín* heritage. She made no attempt to cover this streak of aristocratic impertinence.

Benson smiled tightly. "Ah think youah simply tired," he said in patronizing tones that rankled her and added fuel to the fires blazing inside her. "It's best y'all retire foah a while. Ah've got a lot of work ta catch up with." He turned from her and walked away, leaving her to find her own way back to the house.

Madelaina's tranquility had transcended the storm clouds and she tried pulling herself back to her usual composure. She watched the monkeys for a time, then left to go to her quarters, too tired to give them more thought.

Madelaina stirred restlessly on the bed with the covers flung off her. She felt nauseous and feverish. How long had she lain in bed with thoughts of the past few days' events roiling her brain? She wondered what Antonetta would say and how Pancho Villa would take to her sudden disappearance. How would they even begin to find her so many miles to the north? As much as she needed sleep, she'd been unable to close her eyes the entire night. Affected by strange and alien sounds of servants puttering around the villa, of cattle lowing in the nearby lands, of horses neighing, and of the vast empty silence of the night, she had walked the floors before dawn, unable to sleep.

Standing before a large wall-length wardrobe, Madelaina pulled open the doors. Her astonishment at the contents of the closet, filled with negligees, velvet robes, traveling costumes, and riding clothes, knew no bounds. When, for the love of God, had William Benson thought to stock all these items? Why, he'd thought of everything. She reached in and pulled at random a pair of men's trousers and a shirt and boots. She held up the items before her, reflecting on her image in the oval-shaped looking glass, and decided they'd do.

She tossed them onto a nearby chair, crossed the tiled floor of the large bedroom which had a magnificent view of the gardens, and opened a door to the right of the large four-poster bed. The bathroom was a splendid combination of old war and new Texas charm. The white enamel tub stood on languid mermaid-shaped bases of bright shiny brass—or was it gold? The long marble commode with running water in the wash basin had matching mermaid handles. For several moments, she delighted in this.

It wasn't as if Madelaina had never reveled in such luxury before. She'd lived with it all her life, except for those long months spent as a *campesina* and at Madrigal de Los Altos where she lived in the worst squalor of her lifetime. She was actually born to such living and was grateful she could handle both levels of life. What actually surprised her was to find such luxury in the middle of such desolate wasteland. Only a very wealthy man could afford to house such luxuries under one roof, so far from civilization.

Over the next few hours, she found herself thinking more about this man William Benson. Alternately, as she dwelled upon him, she forced herself to eliminate thoughts of him, as if in so doing, her mind would be free to concentrate on more pertinent things.

She turned the bronze mermaid spigots and filled the tub with warm water. Sniffing several scents from an array of colored jars on the marble-topped commode, she poured the contents of one into the tub and inhaled the rose-scented aroma intermingled with steam emmanating from the tub. Just as the sun came up in the east and peered over the horizon, Madelaina disrobed and settled herself in the luxury of the tub. She tried to keep her mind blank, to refrain from thinking, but as she lay back soaking in the aromatic waters, she was unable to keep from wondering what would happen to her here at the hacienda of William Benson. What did he really intend for her? No man as lusty as he could keep away from a woman, of this she was certain.

All she knew of him was what Antonetta had told her. She had described his affluence as a Texas cattleman and his success in whatever else he immersed himself in businesswise.

As the early rays of light slanting through the stained-glass windows lit up the room, Madelaina's attention was focused on the unusual décor of the bathroom. At one end of the marble bath tub stood a glass chest, almost like an island, separating water closet from dressing room. Her eyes traveled to the wooden box high on the wall over the water closet and assessed the hand-painted cupids, cleverly designed to hide the function of such a convenience.

Then again as she marveled at the artistry that had gone into such a contrivance, her eyes traveled back to the contents in the glassed-in wall cabinet. A collection of perfume flacons, conchas, tintypes, turquoise stones, and small silver snuff boxes were painstakingly arranged and appeared as if they'd been untouched for years. Someone had gone to much trouble to set this up, and Madelaina was certain no man had conceived so feminine a bathroom. It was only natural her thoughts would drift back to the type of woman William Benson had once married. She wondered many things about her and why their marriage had broken up. No, Antonetta had told her Benson was a widower. Ah, that was it. The wife had died. Too bad, thought Madelaina. It appeared the woman might have had some softening effect on her man, and his losing her might have caused him considerable grief. Strange he hadn't remarried. With such crazy philosophies, those incredibly unfortunate monkeys, and his feelings about people, it was no wonder. What woman in her right mind would have him?

Madelaina sat up with effort and reached for the towel she'd tossed on a small bench near the tub. She'd soaked long enough. With her heart beating so rapidly, she wasn't sure she could take a nap before the entire household awakened. Wrapped in the thick toweling, she rubbed her body energetically until it tingled. Slowly, she walked to the glass chest to examine its contents. She gazed into the oval-framed tintypes, the oil painting of a stunning brunette with the face of a Mona Lisa, the same enigmatic smile on her face. Or was it sadness she'd detected on the woman's face?

She gazed at the others, photos of children. All at once Madelaina's memory sharpened and she began to roll the name William Benson over and over in her mind. Where had she heard the name before—much before Antonetta had spoken the name? An unexpected vision of the face of Lazaro flashed before her.

Lazaro of Madrigal de Los Altos. His name was Benson! What had she done with those files? She'd carted them from place to place long enough and for what reason she wasn't sure, except to one day confront her father with the fact that he'd been paying for the lodging of a son who'd died long ago. In her wildest moments, she never imagined she'd be in the presence of Lazaro's father.

William Benson, Amarillo, Texas. That was what she knew of Lazaro's father. Was it possible he was the same William Benson? She wrapped the towel tightly around her and tucked it in over her breasts, moving in to peer at the other tintypes. There were photos of the stunning brunette with a young man at her side, some with an infant in her lap, but none reminded her of the hydrocephalic Lazaro. She shrugged, thinking her imagination was working overtime. Madelaina unpinned her hair and let it hang loosely around her shoulders. She glanced about for a hairbrush. There was none on the commode or in the drawers. She opened a cupboard next to the glass chest and searched for either a comb or brush. On the second shelf she found a portrait of a young man.

She lifted it and studied the image in the photo. She got the distinct impression she knew this man. He was in his late teens or early twenties, clean shaven, tall, lanky, thin, and dressed in western garb. Something about his features convinced her she knew him. She had another unexpected vision of a face she knew well, of hard blue eyes that could soften and melt all her resistance, of a face that had grown fuller and more mature over the years, one she'd never forget. It couldn't be! It just couldn't be—Peter?

She thought herself imagining too hard, wanting it to be Peter, so he'd be close to her. No doubt it was William Benson as a younger man. But why of all places would the photo be in a woman's boudoir gathering dust? Why not downstairs in the study among the other memorabilia? She replaced the photo and forced herself to dismiss thoughts of Peter from mind. How could he have married Valerie Townsend after that last night they spent together? How could he have been so deceitful and not told her how soon his plans were to be consummated?

She walked back into the bedroom and slipped into the trousers and shirt and boots. The clothing was snugger than she usually wore and the boots a trifle too tight, but they'd have to do until her own things arrived. Every curve—every outline of her trim figure was readily noticeable, and she felt a sudden flush permeate her body and face as she studied her revealing body in the mirror. Why, the shirt barely buttoned over her full, round breasts!

A soft knock at the door brought her head up sharply from her reflection in the mirror, and she focused her attention on the door.

"Señora, con su permiso. . . ."

The Mexican servant, carrying a tray of steaming black coffee, scrambled eggs with peppers and tomatoes, and fresh bread, walked into the room. With averted eyes, she set down the tray on the table next to the bed. *"Bienvenida,* Señora Benson—" The older woman stopped and stared at Madelaina in shocked surprise. She shook her head vehemently. "No, *señora.* No! No!"

Madelaina spoke to her in her native tongue. "What's wrong, woman? What are you trying to tell me?"

"You must not wear those clothes. They belonged to Señora Duprez Benson. *Señor el patrón* will be violently angry. Never touch those things. Only from this chest can you select the proper clothing." Trying to be helpful, she began to remove the shirt from Madelaina's back.

But Madelaina had stopped at the name Duprez Benson. "Who are you speaking of? Who's Señora Duprez Benson?"

The old serving woman shook her head and with great reluctance avoided the subject. She shuffled across the room to the proper chest, flung it open, and told

Madelaina to take her pick. "But never, never must you touch those other articles of apparel. Understand?"

"*Como te llamos*? What are you called?" asked Madelaina.

"Pilar, *señora*. I am called Pilar."

Madelaina, flushed with annoyance, nevertheless complied with Pilar's instructions. She shed the articles and watched as the older woman with pendulous breasts and a wrinkled walnut skin picked up the discarded articles, smoothed them out, and reverently rehung them in place. She picked up the boots and wiped imaginary dust off them with the hem of her white apron before replacing them neatly in the wardrobe. Madelaina selected a pair of trousers at random, a shirt from the chest, and hurriedly donned them.

The aroma of coffee invigorated and stimulated her appetite. She hungrily moved toward the table on which Pilar had placed the tray of food and munched on a hot biscuit as Pilar, pouring coffee for her into a china cup, nodded in approval. Madelaina devoured the coffee and held out her empty cup for more.

"You mentioned Señora Duprez Benson, Pilar. Any relation to a certain Peter Duprez?"

Pilar nearly spilled the coffee. "*Con su permiso, patrón*. Please to repeat jur question," she asked in pigeon yankee.

The marked hesitation in her manner as Pilar glanced curiously at Madelaina caused the new bride of William Benson to dismiss the entire subject. "Never mind, Pilar. It was just an attempt on my part to be frivolous. There could be no possible connection between Peter Duprez and Señor Benson." She began to devour the Spanish-style eggs.

"*Los jovenes*, Pedro Duprez? *Ah, si, señora*. He is the son of the *patrón*."

It was something Madelaina hadn't expected. She glanced up from the fork she held in midair ready to taste the omelette and was held spellbound by the frightened look in Pilar's eyes. "*Por favor, señora*, do not tell the *patrón* it was Pilar who tells you such

691

things. There is *muy mal*—very bad—feelings between these two *hombres*. Such a shame, father and son who do not speak, do not see each other for so long."

Madelaina placed her fork across her plate, her eyes glittering with interest. "Are you telling me that the man called Peter Duprez is the son of William Benson?" she asked in disbelief. "Tell me, Pilar, do you have a likeness of this Peter Duprez—a photograph—something which I can look at?"

Pilar's dark eyes widened. She crossed herself religiously and shook her head furiously. "*Por favor, señora*, do not ask Pilar such a thing. She has said too much already." She pulled off the bed covers and shook the blankets vigorously.

The clock on the mantle across the bedroom chimed 6 A.M. It was early. She took the older woman's hands and led her to the sofa before the fireplace. Her voice was soft, tender, and understanding. "Please, Pilar. I must know. I am one of your people, one of you. I am the daughter of General Alvaro Obregon of Mexico City. I promise you no harm shall befall you. I give you my word I shall not betray you. It is important that I know if the man I know as Peter Duprez is that very one you say is the son of your *patrón*."

She looked deeply into the eyes of the servant for several moments, and in a silent understanding which comes from a knowledge of one's people, Pilar turned on her small feet and padded out of the room. She returned in moments with something hidden under her apron. Glancing about the room in a cautious manner, she closed the door behind her and removed a faded, somewhat worn photograph in a cardboard frame from beneath the apron.

Madelaina moved forward on leaden feet, wondering why all the hush-hush and fear in the woman's eyes. She took the photo from the older woman's work-worn hands, reluctant to gaze upon it. Her eyes left Pilar's face and lowered to the fading photograph of a young man in western attire. She studied the casual stance, the twinkling eyes, the lean, young face of a man ten years younger than the man she knew. It was unmistakably Peter Duprez.

"*Dios mios,*" she uttered huskily and fell heavily into the chair behind her.

"What is it, *señora*? You know this man? He is the same one you know?"

"He's the same one, Pilar." She took another look at the photo and instructed the woman to replace the photo to its proper place and return to her instantly.

When Pilar returned, Madelaina swore her to secrecy. "If I confide in you, Pilar, you must confide in me. I will say nothing of this to the *patrón*. You must promise the same. Now, tell me," she began. "Did *señor el patrón* and his wife have another son—one who possessed an infirmary?"

Pilar blanched. "You ask too much, *señora*. We have not spoken of such things for many years. I cannot answer you." She was visibly disturbed. On her feet, she avoided Madelaina's eyes. "I go now. I will be missed from the kitchens. *Señor el patrón* was up at an early hour. He asked that I bring the *señora* her breakfast and show you the rest of the *casa*. You eat now. When you finish, I shall be honored to show you the duties of the mistress of this house."

"Very well then, go, Pilar. You have my word, this conversation has ended in this room. Please do not fear anything from me."

Madelaina reached for her reticule from a drawer in a chest. "Pilar," she called to the woman. "Before you go, tell me if have you seen these before?" She held out the golden earrings Peter had given to her. The seven crescents glittering with diamonds dangled rakishly.

"*Dios mios!*" The older woman's eyes widened into circles. She crossed herself. "*Por favor, señora,* why do you plague Pilar?" she pleaded.

"Have you seen these before, Pilar?" asked Madelaina again.

"*Si, señora.* They are the property of the *señor's*
693

dead wife." Then Pilar rolled up her sleeve to show Madelaina a terrible scar above her wrist.

"For those golden earrings, *señor el patrón* almost cut Pilar's hand off." They were missing shortly after *los jovenes, Pedro*, leave Siete Luna. *Señor, el patrón* think that Pilar take them. I tell him, no, *señor el patrón*. I never see him so *furioso*. Ayeiiieee. *Por favor, señora*, do not show them to *el patrón*.

Madelaina put them back into her bag. Her mind churned rapidly. "You may go, Pilar. Say nothing to anyone about this, *comprender*?"

"*Si, señora. Si.*" The old woman, thick braids over each shoulder, lowered her eyes and exited softly.

Madelaina fell heavily into the chaise longue, unable to think, unable to clearly assess the situation. The facts were clear enough, but what to do? She needed time. Time. Time and more time to know how to handle the situation. A thousand and one thoughts plagued her. Of all the preposterous situations to fall on her. Her mind wandered back to those monkeys in the cage. No wonder Peter had run off at an early age. All Benson wanted around him were human monkeys with no minds of their own to think things out. He wanted automatons to do his bidding without question.

Madelaina fought a burning desire to run swiftly to the cages, open them, and release the poor creatures, she reasoned that most would probably die, unable to forage for themselves. She conceded they were probably better off here where they were fed and cared for. After all, they were animals—not humans. *Dios mios!* For a time she had categorized people as Benson had done!

Chapter 25

For several days, Madelaina had more leisure than she knew what to do with. No longer ruled by haste or forced to conform to a schedule, she took to riding through the surrounding countryside. She kept silent about her findings and continued to study William Benson with intense curiosity, trying with some determination to find the key to his thinking. He ran the hacienda and his men like a captain on the high seas ran a tight ship. Everything ran efficiently at the pace he'd set long ago.

Her presence in no way interfered with the routine of the servants. The library was stocked with many volumes on nearly every subject she could imagine, primarily the breeding of cattle and his second interest—oil. An unusual chess set, sitting on a special table near the large bay windows, remained untouched, as if interrupted in midgame. Whenever she asked Pilar about it, the older woman simply said, "Don't touch it; *señor el patrón* would be furious."

There had been days when she rode alongside William Benson on the bountiful lands of Seven Moons. Admittedly, it was some of the most unusual land she'd seen, with *arroyos grandes* and *arroyos secos*, rounded green hills shaped like the breasts of a woman, prairies, a belt of rolling countryside called the Black Prairie, areas of eroded regions, and isolated tablelands and canyons. The most marvelous of nature's offspring being, of course, those seven crescent-shaped lakes or ponds for which the ranch was named. Shaped like half-moons, these seven bodies of water could be seen in their entirety from the top of Black Mountain, clustered together like a thick chain winding its way through the rolling hills. Graceful willows bordered the crystal ponds. Farther in toward a more wooded area stood oaks and elms, cedar and mesquite trees in great abundance. Thinking the setting looked more like an artist's painting than real life, Madelaina watched as cattle lowed and quenched their thirst in the waters.

The north pastures were thickly dotted with Black Angus, the south stocked with Shorthorns, Herefords, and Aberdeen Angus steer raised for beef. In the east and west pastures Benson kept a breed of cattle called Charbray—white Charolias crossed with Indian Brahman bulls to produce a fleshier stock for beef.

Benson painstakingly explained each of the breeds and told her of the exhausting efforts he'd undergone to produce these prize-winning cattle.

"Why so many various breeds?" asked Madeliana, caught up in the excitement of his experience. "Why not perfect only one or two strains?"

"Well, ah tell ya. Maybe one day when ah've really perfected a strain, ah'll quit. But lookee ovuh yonder, down on the desert land. See them iron towuhs? We call 'em derricks. Oil derricks. One day, this whole land may be covered with them iron ladies, refusin' ta bend in the wind. An' then, little *chiquita*, and then—" He rolled his eyes skyward with vast expectation registered in them. "Then fer shuah, ah'll be the wealthiest man on both sides of the Rio Grande."

Madelaina had listened politely and patiently, hardly responding unless her own curiosity was piqued. Aware one day that her interest might be waning, he promised that the bulls in Chihuahua would be more to her liking since they'd recently imported more Concha bulls from Las Marismas. He seemed highly inspired by her presence, and there were times when Madelaina felt he might attempt to consummate their marriage vows regardless of their validity.

It happened one night at dinner. It was like any usual night, except that William Benson had been away for several days. He returned shortly after noon and secreted himself with his ranch foreman and other trusted cowhands.

Madelaina should have known by the attitude of Pilar and the servant girls, Lupe and Alicia, that something was underfoot. She'd never seen the women so industrious, attending their duties as if bedeviled by demons, then disappearing from sight. Madelaina was left to putter about the kitchen on her own, preparing something special for dinner. This in itself was frequently frowned on by Pilar and the cook. She'd been actually shooed out of the kitchen at times. On this day, they gave her free reign and when they disappeared at about 4 P.M. and didn't answer her summons, she shrugged, annoyed by their apparent petulance, and prepared the table in the dining salon herself, complete with champagne.

Outside, the *vaqueros* had struck up some music, and she thought the Mexicans had joined in what began to appear a festive time. She glanced outside at the cowhands and recognized the fact that they'd been drinking heavily. They shouted and cheered a few daredevil bronco busters in a nearby corral with their unrestrained yippies and yahoos, as the spooked horses attempted to throw their riders.

When William Benson entered the dining room, it became obvious to her that he'd been drinking heavily. His attitude was surly and withdrawn. In an effort to bring him out of the mood, she asked pleasantly, "What's going on out there? Seems like a fiesta of sorts." She wasn't prepared for gruff response.

"Ya hadda tell 'em. Ya couldn't have kept yer mouth shut like the lady of the house is supposed ta do? Ya hadda tell 'em yer one o' 'em."

Perhaps if Madelaina had persisted in asking Pilar about her unusual silence earlier in the day, she might have learned just what kind of a night this would be.

"What is it? What's wrong? I don't understand. Whom did I tell I was one of them?"

"The greasers, that's who. Now the whole crew

697

knows. Ah'll hafta take special measures ta protect ya. That means bloodshed. Just what ah don't need."

"From what, Señor Benson?" pleaded Madelaina. "Protect me from what?" She threw her hands up in the air. "I don't understand a thing you say."

"Don'cha know what day this is?" He poured another glass of champagne and guzzled it down like an animal. His manner was surly, his tone sullen.

He didn't remove his six-guns, and before he took his place at the head of the table, he strode through the room to the living room and bolted the front door. He shouted orders to two of his men, both armed and carrying shotguns, to make sure the back door and windows were bolted. His loud voice echoed through the rooms and sounded loud and clear to Madelaina. "Jus' ya tell those red-blooded, gun-totin' sidewinders if they dare come near mah missus, ah'll hang their carcasses out ta dry, heah?" The artillery at his fingertips threatened.

Madelaina shivered inside. Why would they come at her? For what? She moved to the French windows and looked outside at the setting sun. The men were still drinking, occupied with the unbroken broncs. They talked louder than usual, laughed with less restraint, but she saw no other reason to fear them.

William Benson ambled back to the dining room, fingered his six-guns and shrugged the holsters into position over each hip, then sat down. He poured himself another glass of champagne and avoided Madelaina's eyes when she served him from the silver chafing dish and placed his plate before him. She took only a small portion for herself, even though she'd labored long on the stuffed braised veal with mushrooms.

Seated, she glanced at him over the centerpiece of Seven Moon blooms. "Now will you tell me why your people celebrate—and why you are so angry with me?"

"It's a Texas tradition. Theah celebratin' the Texas War of Independence. The Alamo—remember the Alamo?"

"No, I don't. Should I?"

"Surely ya remember what that theah General Santa Anna of youahs did ta the people of San Antonio?" Benson chewed his food loudly and smacked his lips together, sipping more champagne. He glanced at Madelaina's sober expression and continued. "Colonel William Travis and his men had withdrawn ta the Alamo and were massacred in the massive assault leveled against them by yer General Santa Anna. Mah people haven't forgotten or forgiven the sound of the *degüello*."

"And for this terrible infamy, your people *celebrate?*" Madelaina's eyes widened in disbelief. "*Dios mios*, you gringos are strange people."

"Ya might call it a celebration of sorts. The men get themselves drunk an' then, they go crazy." He hesitated to elaborate any further and resumed eating. "Ah was thinking earlier ya might've enjoyed seeing the fireworks in Amarillo. Ah had even thought we might have ridden to Black Mountain. From theah we could have seen what the city folk do ta light up the skies."

"No thank you, William," she said tightly. "I've seen enough fireworks and drunken binges in my lifetime to suffice forever." She pushed her plate from her.

"It's outa the question, now, since ya told the help you were Mexican," he retorted as if she hadn't spoken her mind.

"Mexican?" Madelaina puzzled over this. Suddenly her eyes widened ostensibly. "You don't mean——? Is that why Pilar and Lupe and Alicia absented themselves earlier? You permit this brutal savagery? You, William Benson, a man who should know better?"

The fine hairs on Benson's neck bristled. His eyes narrowed. "Ah'll pretend ah didn't heah those words, mah deah." He forced a lighter mood and patted his stomach contentedly. "The food was delicious. Ah know ah have y'all ta thank foah it. Otherwise, I'd have been gnashing mah teeth on cold mutton and beans."

He had simmered down and he seemed to be attempting to assuage her anger. But Madelaina wasn't about to be humored.

Earlier she had sensed that William Benson intended to make ovations to her on this night. She'd seen the look in his eyes for the past two days, that unmistakable look of a man ready to conquest. So she had in a sense attempted to prepare for this encounter. Fill his stomach with good food, ply him with special viands, and perhaps he'd fall asleep early. Good thinking, she had told herself earlier, never counting on this state holiday to thwart her best efforts.

It was as if William Benson was blind and deaf to her manner and mood. He continued as if she hadn't spoken a derogatory word. "Again, ah thank ya fer preparing an elegant supper, mah deah." He lit up a cigar and puffed on it expansively. At intervals he'd cock his ear and listen as if he were monitoring the volume of the raucous hilarity outside.

"Ya see, mah deah, right aftuh 5 P.M. on this day, the decent Mexican women lock themselves up tight in their *casitas*—away from the Texans. Some of the ranch hands get a mite rambunctious when Old John Barleycorn's been pumped into 'em all day long. The greasers keep theah doors locked tight until tomorrow aftuhnoon when it's safe ta come out. It's bettuh that way. Ah wouldn't like nothin' ta happen ta any o' mah people. Ah need both kinds—ya see?"

Madelaina fumed inwardly. Her slender fingers tapped the linen-covered table top in a steady staccato. His bigotry and prejudices protruded like a sharp knife into her heart, inciting her to anger. "Señor Benson, need I remind you I'm a person of Mexican birth? I find your words in atrocious bad taste and a dishonorable gesture to a person of my class." Her personal fears seem to evaporate as she stared fiercely into his steely blue eyes.

"Well, shucks, now. Ain't no sense gettin' yer dander up. Ah didn't mean ta rankle yer bones. Ah ain't talkin about yer kind o' people. Ah'm referin' ta them

700

low-class *peóns* who don't know from nothin' how ta do fer themselves."

Madelaina's attention was caught up in the noises marking preamble to this nightmare of festivities. Loud shouts, continued wahoos and a long wail of yippies permeated the air. Gunshots peeled off time after time like fireworks.

Madelaina had seen the *Villistas* after victory. She'd seen their animalistic behavior, their lust, their drunkedness, even their bloodthirsty ways. It wasn't that she justified such behavior in her mind by telling herself they were entitled to their playtime after the rigors of revolution and war, of previous oppression and savage treatment by the *Rurales* and other government-inspired butchers. But here she was in what was considered a civilized country, seated opposite a wealthy, powerful, and politically inspired man with connections to the White House, watching him do nothing about such barbarism, as if it didn't exist. His refusal to put a stop to this inhuman custom appalled her.

In a voice dripping with sarcasm, Madelaina demanded, "Why do you permit such savage behavior, *señor el patrón*? Why do you permit your men to act like undisciplined, inhuman animals? You of all people should feel shame for this degradation."

Benson laughed aloud to cover his indignation. "A man's gotta keep his help happy—or he ain't gonna have any help ta keep."

Ignoring him, Madelaina rose to her feet, and swishing the skirts of her pink cotton dress, she moved across the room and flung open the doors to the portico.

"What in hell do you think youah doing?" shouted Benson hoarsely. He jumped to his feet and came in behind her to close and bolt the doors once again. "Get back, woman! Goddamnit!" he cursed. "What the hell's wrong with ya?"

He peered through the blinds. Outside, a large Texas moon, orange as a jack o' lantern and a thousand times larger than any normal moon, lit up the sky and gave the earth a hue of flamingo fire. A few shadows moved about, staggering in drunkenness. The men held jugs of whiskey to their lips in a perpetual pose, hardly pausing for a moment's rest. William Benson felt uneasy for the first time in his life.

Watching him, Madelaina wondered what in the name of God she was doing here. Why hadn't she forced the issue with Peter, fought for him, tooth and nail, instead of letting him return to Valerie Townsend? She was furious at him, at herself, at Pancho Villa for involving Peter in his cloak-and-dagger fiascos. Moreover, she was sick with humiliation for not having the courage to escape Seven Moons. After all she'd been through in her young life, why she was so reluctant to leave this temporary sanctuary didn't make sense.

Women's screams pierced the night air and penetrated the walls of the *casa*. Her eyes darted to William Benson's bloodshot, red-rimmed eyes as he ambled back to the table to guzzle more champagne. In these few moments Benson had changed visibly. He'd grown more sullen, his mood more hostile. *Dios mios*, why didn't he do something about such bestiality?

Never had Madelaina felt so lost and forlorn, so completely isolated from everything and all she knew, so alien in a world more alien and frightening to her than Madrigal de Los Altos had been. At least there she had hope of escaping. Here, what could she do? She didn't even know where she was. She could have been a million miles from civilization for all she knew. Riding horseback with Benson, she'd seen no other life for miles. Other than cattle and a few cowhands, there wasn't another family or sign of human life in more than eight hours of riding. Escape from such a place inevitably meant death—thirst, starvation, or falling prey to the lusty men of· the range who detested the Mexicans. *Dios mios*.

There was no way she could hide her frustration. Shrill screams pierced the air outside and she gave a start. "What's that?" she cried. "Women screaming!"

"Oh, that," Benson said flatly, sipping champagne directly from the bottle. "Probably one o' mah men catching up with a *señorita*, ah reckon."

"And you do nothing about it?" she asked indignantly.

"Well, well, coming from miss goody two shoes, ah reckon ah should consider the source. Ya don't mean ta tell me y'all ain't heard the likes of a woman screaming befoah, *Little Fox*? Ah mean among those filthy camps y'all tracked about in foah so long? Ah reckon them eyes and ears o' yers have seen and heard a mite moah screamin' than youah'll evuh hear at Seven Moons. What's moah, *chiquita*, ah'm not about ta let ya put me off no moah."

He reached for her, pulled her close to him, and roughly, without restraint, he kissed her savagely. After a moment he held her away from him and stared at her through embarrassed and disbelieving eyes. "Ah don't believe ya don't feel nothing fer me. Yer play actin' with me and ah don't cotton ta such temperament."

He struck out at her in anger, leaving vivid fingermarks across her face. Madelaina's detachment, her utter lack of concern and refusal to cooperate irked him intensely. She glanced at him without emotional reaction, with no attempt to shield herself. And this served only to annoy him further.

"Ah've been patient with ya, wench. More than with any other woman. But mah patience has thinned. Tonight's the night ah demand full payment. Ah saved yer worthless life from them two money-grubbin' murderers and this is the thanks ah get? Don'cha have no appreciation? Ah reckon ah've treated ya like a lady fer too long. Maybe if ah treated ya like the whore ya are, ah'd have gotten moah fer mah money. Now, make it easy on yerself, girl, you an' me is gonna have us a fine time." He grabbed her lustily, swung her over one powerful shoulder, and with a free hand grabbed a bottle of champagne and stalked out the room.

In moments he'd dragged the docile woman up the stairs and tossed her onto the four-poster bed in her

703

quarters. "Now, get yerself undressed, woman. Ah intend ta see what I paid fer." His eyes were bloodshot, his voice harsh and angry. He drank from the bottle he toted and reeled unsteadily on his feet as he began to peel off his jacket and shirt. His narrowing eyes seemed to pierce her like daggers.

"Ah said, undress, bitch! Ah found ya dancing in that whorehouse and ah heard from Huerta and Salomon that you were nothing but a lousy *campesina*, so don't think ya can pull the wool down over William Benson's sharp eyes, *señorita puta*. Ah'm William Benson and no one puts anything over on him, heah?"

"What is it you wish, *señor el patrón*? For me to submit to your greedy sexual excesses? You are a petty man with enormous ambition, *señor el patrón*, but I daresay not as ambitious as I. Perhaps I should introduce myself to you, *señor el patrón*." She spoke the words with dripping sarcasm each time they were uttered, while simultaneously keeping an unemotional posture. "I am Madelaina Obregon, daughter of General Alvaro Obregon of Mexico. I am niece of Don Diego Obregon of Las Marismas, and I do not care what that pig Huerta or that butcher Salomon have told you."

For only a moment Benson faltered under the weight of her words. Too much champagne had fuzzed his brain, and determined to have his way with her, nothing would stop him. He stood before her naked. Madelaina now saw where Peter got his physical stature and strength. Benson had the body of a man twenty years younger, lean, hard, and firm. "Ah don't give a damn whose daughter ya are! Ah told ya ta take yer clothes off, woman," he said sullenly, moving toward her. He reached in and tore off her blouse. "Ah see, ya prefer it with yer clothes on? Is that it? Then spread yer legs and ah'll show ya how a real man takes yer kind o' woman."

But Benson, a man used to having his orders obeyed, instantly grew impatient. He reached in toward her and with both hands picked up the torn shreds of her blouse and began to tear it. This being too slow for his pulsating manhood to take, he reached over on the floor for his discarded belt and from a sheath removed a Bowie knife. With a few expert strokes, he slashed through the rest of her garments and peeled the fabric from her trembling flesh. Finished, he cast aside the knife while his hungry eyes devoured the exquisite contours of her body. Spreading her legs apart, he mounted her and said drunkenly, "Now we'll see just how much of a bargain ah got fer mah money."

Madelaina thought quickly. She could take one of many postures. Remain passive and let it be a severe blow to his ego; fight him and chance that his sexual arousal would increase to the point he'd develop the strength of ten men; or kill him at the right moment. What to do? What to do? *Remain detached to understand life's riddles*, had been Tolomeo's teaching. And this was certainly one of life's riddles.

As it was, she didn't have to make an immediate decision. She heard snoring alongside her, and for an instant she sighed in relief. She was suddenly seized with a mad thought. Slowly, silently prodded by the devil, she slipped off the bed and padded toward the forbidden wardrobe. She selected a very sheer pale blue peignoir, slipped into it, and caught her hair high atop her head, speared through with a few hairpins. She paused long enough to loop the seven moon earrings through the holes in her pierced ears. Returning to the bed, she slipped in alongside him. Her movement caused him to stir and awaken. Through his drunken stupor, his bleary eyes stared at her unblinking for a moment and he began stroking her. Drunk and irrational, only God knew what he saw through his disbelieving eyes. It appeared to Madelaina that he was going through the erotic motions with another woman—not her. Someone he saw in the drunken haze of his mind—someone she didn't know and never would.

"Mah God, honey, how ah've missed ya," he repeated tenderly. "Jenny, mah love, how many times ah've come near ta killin' mahself since ya left me.

705

Theah's nevuh been anyone foah me, sweet baby, 'ceptin' foah youah. Now, aftuh so many years, y'all came back ta me, jus' like ah knew ya would, Jenny baby."

The sound of his melancholy touched Madelaina and she stirred, ready to announce she wasn't the woman he thought she was. It had been a dreadful thing for her to do—dress and pretend to be another. How could she apologize enough? It was an insane, unthinking, and blundering act on her part.

Her movements, as she strained against him, increased his desire for her, and Madelaina found herself raising her body to meet his in an effort to make amends. His voice grew as urgent as his powerful body thrusts and he cooed lovingly to her, whispering sweet nothings. Madelaina's juices, having been worked up for the first time in weeks, seemed propelled by Satan as she responded to him. She had hypnotized herself in these moments into thinking it was Peter.

For several moments, Benson stared at the glittering golden moons on her ears and said nothing. They served only it increase his ardor and make him moan with more anguish.

William Benson, more aroused with each passing moment, was both pleased and excited by her sultry and provocative responses. God, he thought, what passion she displayed. "Jenny, youah drivin' me ta the brink of madness! It was nevuh like this, ya gotta admit. Lord knows how many times ah wanted it ta be such sweet heaven. Why couldn't we have recaptured ouah love like this—why?"

The desire he felt for this woman, whom in his drunken delirium he mistook for his former wife, overrode his sanity. Even as he tried to be gentle, to caress her and give her time to be aroused, he couldn't hide his excitement. Jennifer had come back—returned to him from the grave—and he wasn't going to lose her again. He persisted against her protests, as one in fever and out of control, until he climaxed with a thunderous roar of animal grunts, moans, and primitive screams.

Wafting in and out of her own self-imposed purgatory, Madelaina awakened to the reality of the moment and panicked. She began to beat her fists against him. "Stop! Stop!" she screamed. "I'm not who you think I am! You don't know what you're doing!" She tugged at the hairpins to loosen her hair. She struggled under his weight to remove the pale blue sheer peignoir but was pinned down too tightly. She clawed at the fabric, tearing at it, trying desperately to remove it.

But William Benson wasn't attuned to her misery. He'd suddenly drifted into another world, another dimension of ugliness and bad memories.

He swore at her, cursed her in both English and Spanish, tossing in a few French words that brought a blush to Madelaina's cheeks. Then he held her by her long hair, pulled back savagely on it, thrusting back her head at an angle that nearly cut off her breath. He kissed her so violently, pressing his hard lips against hers until his teeth cut fiercely into her lips. She could no longer scream. She could no longer fight him off. She could hardly breathe. Unable to catch her breath, she moved in a sudden struggle for survival, and concentrating all her strength into a final effort, jackknifed with her knees in a jerking movement so unexpected it threw him off guard. He rolled uncontrollably, nearly falling off the bed.

The movement jarred his befuddled brain and brought him back to reality. He scratched his head and gazed around through bleary eyes, trying to orient himself as he pulled himself up, staggering to his feet. Meanwhile Madelaina hastily shed the sheer peignoir and pulled the sheets up around her. Benson appeared to have no recollection that he'd already taken his pleasure. Swaying drunkenly, he clung to the bedpost for support as he focused bleary eyes on her.

"Why are ya bent on bedeviling me, woman?" He reached over and grabbed her wrist and twisting it forced her to bend toward him. "Damn ya! You're the coolest animal ah've evuh seen." He pushed her back against the bed and fell on top of her, his hands touching her breasts as if he was wrestling a steer.

The blood rushed to Madelaina's head, causing dizziness to blur her eyes. She felt helplessly enmeshed in a situation too grotesque to contemplate and prayed to heaven in those moments she didn't conceive a child of her husband's father. Oh, God, that would be the most despicable thing that could happen to her.

"Damn ya, woman! Makin' love ta ya is like trying ta fuck a stone statue!" he fairly screamed at her in his rage. "Now show some life or ah'll make ya live ta regret tryin' ta make a fool of William Benson!"

"No," she replied flatly with more courage than she ever realized she had. "I don't want a son like Lazaro!"

For an instant, Madelaina was certain he would kill her. He stiffened like a crouched animal ready to lunge at an enemy. Her words sliced through his alcoholic stupor like a clean swipe of a two-edged knife, and when they replayed in his mind, he pushed away from her, his face hard as granite, his eyes like pulsating branding irons. He viewed her with dark suspicious eyes.

"What's that ya said? Speak up, whore, or ah'll tan yer hide!"

"Like you tanned Peter's hide as a child? You heard me, I said Peter. I can't show you the exciting response you desire because I am Peter's wife. Yes, that's right. Peter's wife. The wife of your first-born son. As for your second son, Lazaro, I'm the woman whose life was saved by the son you rejected long ago."

Benson jumped off the bed as if he'd been struck by a bolt of lightning. He stared at her as if she was some malevolent apparition, intimidated by what he saw and heard. "Who in damnation are ya? Who told ya such a pack of lies? Ya better come straight with me, whore, or y'all live ta wish ya were nevuh born, ta wish youah'd never talked such filth ta me! *Pilar! It was Pilar who told ya!*"

In those next few moments, Madelaina saw what it was that Benson's enemies feared. Never, not if she lived for all eternity, would she forget the violent and burning hatred in those black agate eyes that only moments earlier had appeared a bloodshot, bleary blue haze of staggering uncertainty. His face, filled with loathing, had swollen like a bull frog's. In his blind fury, Benson turned from her, staggered toward a chest, and removed a bull whip. He cracked it overhead several times, menace scrawled on his face.

"Tell me ya lied! Tell me or ah'll skin yer lying body alive!" Benson paused a moment. The golden earrings, catching a prism of light, shone brightly. "Where'd ja get them earrings?" he bellowed. "So now yer a thief as well?" He cracked the whip threateningly close.

"I'm no thief. My husband, Peter Duprez Benson, gave them to me. I am the wife of Peter Benson. It's no lie. Go ahead and skin me alive—kill me—do what you will. Nothing matters to me anymore." Her control disconcerted him.

"Do what you will with my body, but you'll never possess my mind. Not Huerta, Salomon, not even my father could bend me to their will. I belong only to your son, Peter," she said defiantly. "You'll never tame this monkey!"

Benson raised the whip overhead and sent it whistling toward her. It cracked across her breasts, splitting the skin open over both mounds. An angry, searing trail of blood seeped through the aperture. Again he struck her, and again, waiting for her to beg for mercy.

Madelaina bit back the screams strangling her throat.

"Lying bitch!" he screamed incoherently. "Why are ya doin' this ta me? After all ah did fer ya—saving youah lying hide from the *Federales*—this is the thanks ah get?" He raised the bull whip overhead, gathering strength for another singing strike to lash out at her in his blind and furious rage. But William Benson never made it. There came a loud swishing sound as something streaked across the room. A Bolo knife was sunk into Benson's shoulder. He staggered back, dizzy, his equilibrium shattered, and fell against an upholstered

709

chair, knocking it backward. Benson fell into a loose heap and blacked out.

Madelaina saw a blur of faces. Wrapped in a coverlet taken from the bed, she was slung across the brawny shoulders of a man she recognized. Captain Tracy Richards cooed to her. "Don't fret, Little Fox, you're in safe company now." He swiftly transported her out the door and down the steps into the foyer. Madelaina remained as still as possible, wincing at the open rivers of blood flowing from her breasts. Each movement was like a step in hell, but still she wouldn't scream.

Outside, drunken ranch hands, taken by surprise, had been herded against the tack room wall by Pancho Villa's handful of men. How they'd gotten past Benson's sober, well-trained guards stationed at the entrance to Seven Moons was one of those marvelous *guerrillo* tactics which had helped carved Villa's phenomenal reputation. Not a single shot had been fired!

Antonetta, dressed as a *campesina*, sprang from her saddle to receive Madelaina into her arms. "Come, *querida*, you must dress. There's no time to waste. Thanks to God Pancho knew where to find you." She glanced horrified at the rivers of blood oozing from Madelaina's breasts. "*Dios mios!* Put on these things, *pronto!*" She handed the girl a peasant skirt and blouse of coarse cotton.

"*Momentito*," whispered Madelaina as soon as she donned the clothing. "Give me your gun, Tonetta, and make sure it's loaded." Her glazed eyes burned like ebony. She was growing weaker from the loss of blood.

"Don't do nothing foolish, woman," cautioned Antonetta. "Ees best we go and *pronto* like I said." She glanced at Tracy Richards, reluctant to give the gun to her friend. "Ju got some bad injury, *chica*. Let's go. Forget what happened."

The daughter of General Obregon turned from her and grabbed the rifle from Capitán Richard's saddle holster. She addressed the gringo freedom fighter.

"Is it loaded, *Capitán*?" she asked without regard to her blood-soaked blouse.

"It's loaded."

"Bueno." Gun in hand, Madelaina ran toward the small, shabby shacks opposite the tack room which housed the Mexican colony working for William Benson. She ran the length of the shacks and stopped only when she saw a door ajar. Cautiously, she crept forward and kicked the door in loudly, shaking the structure on its flimsy foundation. Sprawled on top of the young girl Lupe, brutally ravaging the protesting child, was one of Benson's burly men. Lupe's obvious struggle against the drunken cowboy had earned for her bloody bruises and abrasions.

"Get up, pig!" shouted the arrogant daughter of a *gachupín*. "Up on your feet, beast!"

The drunken, boisterous, abrasive cowhand, reeling and stumbling in a stupor, managed to raise up on one knee to protest the intrusion. Before he actually saw the figure of a woman with a shotgun aimed at him, before he could plead for mercy, Madelaina squeezed off two shots with the Springfield and watched the rolling eyeballs of the drunken cowhand bulge in pain and shock before he fell back against the wall. Lupe, a dark-eyed waif of a girl, no more than fourteen, sprang to her feet and hugged Madelaina. "Save me, *señora*. Save me from thees pig!"

Captain Richards, who'd followed Madelaina at Tonetta's insistence, released the rifle from her frozen grip. *"Ondolay, chiquita.* Pancho can't tarry much longer, ya heah?" His Texas drawl seemed thicker than ever.

"Reload the rifle, gringo," ordered Madelaina brittlely. "There is one more job to do."

"Youah shuah it's important, Little Fox? We'd best get moving."

"It's important, gringo."

"Then maybe ya bettuh take this heah new gun ah jus' got inta my hands, *chiquita.* It's called the .45 caliber *Obregon* pistol."

Madelaina turned her head sharply and pushed Lupe gently from her as her eyes searched Tracy Richard's eyes. Her glance came to rest on the pistol in his hand extended to her butt first. She gazed at the weapon wondrously.

The perspiration rolled off her face and her hair clung to her head in long snakelike ribbons. "*Es veridad?* It's the truth? It's named after my father?"

"The truth. Seven shots in the magazine. Go ta it and move like hell. We've gotta make it the hell outa Texas, heah me, *chiquita?*"

But Madelaina had already left the shack and made her way toward the next one, where she'd seen Alicia retire after her day's chores. Cautiously, she moved on the balls of her sandaled feet, grimacing at the pain across her breasts. Her blouse was soaked with blood and the moisture seeping through was weakening her. One moment more, she prayed, and it will be over. Perhaps then, the gringos won't "Remember The Alamo" with such bloodthirsty vengeance.

She found Alicia in a worse condition than she'd found Lupe. Alicia was unconscious, unaware that she was being ravaged and raped by a man too delirious in alcoholic stupor to realize she couldn't cooperate.

"Waco!" she called to Benson's foreman, astounded that a man of his calibre would stoop to rape a mere child of twelve. "Waco!"

The older man half-turned his grizzled face in the dim lantern glow of the shabby hovel and peered blindly at the figure standing in the doorway.

"It's Mrs. Benson, Waco." She hesitated at the sound of the name, then quickly continued. "I understand you wish to continue in the tradition of your people and do what should be done to the filthy greasers that did your ancestors in. Well, c'mon, Waco. I decided it should be you who takes the *patrón*'s wife."

She could almost see the diabolical look of glee and disbelief, intermingled with desire and lust, register in his bleary, bloodshot eyes as he struggled to his feet, not bothering to pull up his trousers. The sight and smell of him nearly knocked her over. But she held her own, seducing him with a come-on look in her eyes.

For an instant, a flicker of hesitation in Waco's eyes alerted her that he might not agree to her proposition, but when his face contorted into an almost sheepish grin, she relaxed.

"Ya mean it, Mrs. Benson?" Again he hesitated, unsure of himself. "Does the boss know whatcher up ta?" He drew nearer to her shadowy form, still unable to focus clearly and never once seeing the Obregon automatic in her hand.

"Come, Waco, get it over with. My husband knows everything."

"Yahooo!" he shouted. "Yippeeee!" He fairly lunged at her, only to be stopped by seven consecutive bullets shot into his belly. His body bounced back from the impact of the bullets. "Ahhhhieeeeee," he shouted, clutching at his belly which was ripped apart from the missiles. He fell to the floor, writhing and twisting like a yelping dog until he was dead.

In a corner of the room, tied hand and foot to a standing floor pillar, Pilar watched through horror-struck eyes as Madelaina moved in to cut her bindings. "Listen, *chica*," she told the old woman. "Go inside and tend to *señor el patrón*. When he heals, you tell him the *mujer* of his son Peter Duprez Benson has done this to Waco and to the other man who dishonored Lupe."

Pilar's black eyes bugged from under her thick brows. "The *mujer* of Pedro Duprez, *los jovenes*?" She crossed herself, fell to her knees, and kissed Madelaina's hands. "He's alive? My *niño* ees alive?" she asked wondrously.

"Tell *señor el patrón*, only I am responsible for this. If any of my people are punished, tell him I will return to give him another taste of my vengeance."

She turned to Captain Tracy Richards, who stared spellbound at this supercharged *soldadera* before him. "*Vamenos, amigo*. Pancho Villa awaits us."

713

They exited the shack as the astounded Pilar mouthed the words—*Pancho Villa. "Pancho Villa? Dios mios!"* She ran from the shack to spread the news to the other Mexicans, so they might catch a glimpse of the legendary Pancho Villa.

Villa and his handful of men awaited the arrival of Madelaina and Captain Richards. She and Tracy mounted the saddled and waiting horses and joined the circle behind Villa, while he attempted to soothe the ruffled feathers of the slowly sobering Benson cowhands who seemed more baffled than frightened by this unusual-looking Mexican holding them at bay with his words.

He had introduced himself to them in his pigeon yankee, but it was plain to see not one man believed that the kindly, patronizing man with a benevolent smile was indeed the fierce and murderous *guerrillo*, Pancho Villa.

Apologetically, Villa relieved them of their weapons, and marched them into the tack room. Before bolting the doors, he asked them with servility not to make any attempts to follow them for at least an hour. "Unless, my gringo friends," he added, "ju do not care what happens to ju."

Villa mounted his horse and reared it on its heels. He waved his sombrero overhead and called to his miniscule army. *"Vamenos, muchachos!* We go to conquer!"

Book Seven

Viva La Revolucion:

Chapter 26

The entourage of six men, two women, eight horses, and eight guns followed him into the night. They rode with the wind at their heels, through back roads, stopping only to water their horses and freshen themselves at friendly bases established by Villa sympathizers.

Madelaina had time to think of the many ways Villa might have tracked her to the Seven Moons Ranch of William Benson. Most distressing of all was the possibility that Major Salomon himself had leaked the information to Villa's aides. It was the only way, he might have decided, Madelaina would return to Mexico and fall prey to his trap. It was the first thought she had in the matter and the one which persisted above all others. Even as she belabored this idea, she began to develop more insight in her involvement. She viewed the ways and means of resolving her future with more maturity. At the time, however, she had no realization that the words of Tolomeo had begun to work their way into her consciousness and that soon she'd be a changed woman in more ways than she could estimate. Having begun, the metamorphosis wouldn't stop.

By the time Villa and his followers crossed the Rio Grande and made camp along one of its tributaries, the River Conchos, Villa had gathered his trusted lieutenants to reconnoiter. Urbina, Soto, and Captain Richards relaxed after the long hard ride and sat by the fire with their *jefe*, drinking coffee laced with tequila and talking of future plans and strategy.

Nearby, as always, seated before another glowing campfire, Madelaina and Antonetta warmed themselves after taking a bath in the waters of the Conchos. Both women had changed into fresh clothing and dried their long hair with cotton toweling. Both had become true *soldaderas* in the past several days, and it would soon fall upon Madelaina to teach the *campesinas* how to shoot and care for their weapons.

The *jefe* had told them in no uncertain terms that the women would no longer be relegated to doing only cooking and female chores. In this all-out revolution to avenge the murders of President Madero, his key cabinet members, and all those other *Maderistas* who'd been massacred in the seige on the capital by Huerta, Pancho Villa would spare the life of no *Huertista*. That meant the entire army of *Federales*.

Madelaina poured coffee for both herself and Antonetta and handed the redhead a steaming mug. She sat down on a felled tree trunk at the edge of the river and sighed wistfully.

"Ju are thinking of jur husband, Little Fox?" asked Tonetta.

Madelaina traced figures in the sand with a stick. "Can you see so clearly into the center of my heart, redhead?"

"Ayeiii. Ees easy, *chica*. Ees written in jur face what I see."

"Why do I bother? Why can't I forget him? He made his choice. He married the governor's daughter. After all this time, I should understand he never loved me at all. I've been chasing a dream, *chica*. A dream that has no beginning and no ending. A foolishness which must cease for me."

"Listen, *chica*, listen to me," began Antonetta. "Pancho will kill me if he knew what I am about to say." She rolled her eyes skyward. "Don' ju believe what ju read in the papers. Jur husband ees doing business for Pancho. I can tell ju no more. But ees not like eet ees in paper."

If Madelaina heard her friend, she gave no sign, her attention was taken by the setting of the desert sun near the western horizon, at the sight of a fast-moving rider galloping swiftly toward the encampment. *"Jefe!"* she called to Villa, her hands cupped over her mouth.

Villa and his men stood up, shaded their eyes, and peered in the direction of the rider.

"*Bueno,*" said Villa. "It's our man Ochoa. I've been expecting him with good news."

Before the rider pulled up on his reins, kicking up mounds of sand behind him, he'd already slid off the horse with the expertise of a man born on horseflesh. He whipped off his sombrero and dusted his leggings. With his free hand, he slicked down his sweaty hair, leaving streaks in the dust on his face. Someone handed him a bottle of tequila. He guzzled nearly half the bottle, grunted, and now able to speak through a throat rid of dust, he saluted the *jefe.*

"Well, my friend. What did you learn?" asked Villa, watching him closely.

"Carranza has denounced Huerta and the Anti-Orozco volunteers have sided with him. It's been rumored that General Alvaro Obregon has responded with his Fourth Sonora Battalion."

Madelaina gave a start. Had she heard correctly? Her father was against Huerta? For the first time in weeks, her heart burst with hope and joy. She wasn't prepared for Villa's words as he announced he'd personally go into Chihuahua City to secretly meet with Don Abraham Gonzalez, the man who had initially enlisted his aid for Madero, the man who Madero made governor of Chihuahua.

"But, that, my *jefe,* isn't possible," insisted Ochoa, one of Villa's most loyal followers, the man who had related to Villa just how Huerta had killed Madero. "Governor Gonzalez has been arrested for treason. All of Chihuahua is under the military governorship of an old enemy, a *Huertista* to the teeth, *Jefe.* General Rabago."

Villa's dark eyes burned fiercely at this news.

"Is better you wait, *Jefe,*" cautioned Ochoa, growing more uncomfortable.

"What do you mean—wait?" countered Villa. "Wait? For what and how long?"

Ochoa, more subdued now, wiped the corners of his

mouth with his shirtsleeve. He glanced cautiously about the small circle. "Maybe is better you wait a long time," he began lowering his eyes, unable to look straight at the *jefe*.

"What are trying to tell me? It's not like you to falter—to stammer like a lovesick calf stammers to his woman." Pancho suddenly picked up on the man's thoughts. "Ah, what you're saying is I'm not wanted in the revolution—not needed? Perhaps they think Pancho Villa is finished, eh?"

"Not that, *jefe*," Ochoa said too quickly. He drew a sharp sustained look from Villa.

"Then what? You know, so tell me."

"I've heard that this Obregon is some military man. He's some strategist. He's a regular, all right, *Jefe*, but I hear he employs all the irregularities possible in his combat plans. Is true, *Jefe*, he is some military officer. Is better you know this. He studied the warring styles of the French and Germans, *Jefe*. He ees no fool. *Pues*, *amigo*. General Obregon is the only hope for Carranza."

Madelaina heard all this. She felt a tinge of pride, yet what was making Villa so angry? She watched him pace back and forth before his men, flailing his arms in the air. It had to be Carranza that he didn't like or trust. Another split in the revolution? What next?

She concentrated her gaze on Pancho Villa as he paced before his small consortium of loyalists. He was simply marvelous to watch, thought Madelaina. If you looked hard, you could almost see the wheels move in his mind as he gathered his thoughts and without silver-tongued oratory delivered his words with impact.

"So! You think Villa cares for the Germans or the French? This is Mexico! And Mexico is Pancho Villa. What the hell does Obregon or Carranza or any of those quarrelsome sons of whores know what is in my guts? I want to give Mexico a chance. I fought for Madero because he believed in me—me, Pancho Villa. He didn't forget about me," said Villa pointedly, looking directly at Madelaina. "He had to choose between his country and me, and I thank God he chose Mexico

because that showed me the kind of man he was."
Villa continued to rant and rave, more to himself than
to the body of men who'd gathered as he spoke, each
anxious to hear the *jefe*'s words.

"All those fake excuses for men, what do they know
of Madero's feelings for Pancho Villa? They gather
storm clouds of war with an outward show of vengeance, and they mean to exclude Pancho Villa, eh?
There's no room in Mexico for that lowly *peón* hillsman? Hah! Well, I tell you, my friends, those stinking
betrayers in the capital, those Judas goats have never
seen rivers of blood flowing, not like the ones Pancho
Villa will cause to flow to flush them and their kinds
out of our Mexico. Not if these pandering peacocks
should invent a second Trojan horse—not if they
should resurrect Napoleon to lead them, will they see
the battles Pancho Villa will inflict upon them. All the
military geniuses in the whole world—in *todo mundo*—
in a lifetime of battle have never seen the holocaust
that Pancho Villa prepares for them in his war of
revenge."

This small handful of men remained silent. In the
great silence of the desert, every man present felt the
enormous power of the puma who stood before them,
his fists upraised to the heavens and the supernatural
glow of a descending twilight at his back. Here stood a
giant of a man, powerful, determined, and possessed of
remarkable zeal and loyalty to a leader who was dead.
Fired by this fierce loyalty, spurred on by his promise
to the ghost of Madero, this Mexican, this Indian, who
had grown into a man stoked by the injustice and ineq-
uities meted his people, had transformed himself into a
tempestuous soldier, a leader of men, General
Francesco Villa.

In the awe-filled silence, Pancho Villa dropped his
arms to his side and said quietly, "Your *jefe* knows
what must be done. He is not *loco*. He is not possessed
with fever. I cry aloud, I sing, and, *amigos*, I dream
passionately of a better Mexico for all of us. I may be
a soldier without an army, but this soldier is not with-

721

out hope. Trust in me. I will leave you for seventy-two hours. You will meet me in San Andres." He turned to Captain Richards and Urbina. "You will be in charge until I return. Avoid any hostile encounter and let no one know of our plans. Understand?"

The gringo and the Mexican nodded solemnly. "What will you do, *Jefe?*" asked Urbina without the usual grin on his face.

"What will I do?" said Villa, staring at some inner scene in his head to which he alone was privileged to see. "What will I do? I will summon up the ghosts of our ancestors to lead us. From the mountains of Durango, the deserts of Chihuahua, from the villages of Zacatecas, and the farms of San Luis Potosi, I will sound the cry of war once again. The people will not deny me the army that is needed."

And Pancho Villa, true to his word, did just that.

In the hills of Sonora he found his sister, Concepción Montoya, and with her aid, he scattered her precious pigeons to the various sections of Mexico. In the north, east, west, and south, those people who received the white birds studied the messages intently:

Mexico needs us once again. Be ready when I come. Arm yourselves well.—Francesco Villa.

And so it was that the great whirlwind of Mexico gathered unto itself the people of the land. From the north, where poverty was extreme, the people dug up their rifles, guns, and bayonets, and saddled their horses. They collected their belongings and told their compatriots that the voice of Pancho Villa had called to them. In the south, where the drought had ruined crops and the Rurales *had wrought more devastation than the fierce elements, the peasants tilling their lands laid down their plows and vowed amongst themselves to complete what had been started long ago. Pancho was coming for them. They must be ready. From the east and the west, from the deserts and mesas and arroyos, they came galloping wildly in a northwesterly direction, looking for the spirit of Pancho Villa.*

Galloping wildly from the north country, heading in a southwesterly direction, a lone horseman broke cover and plunged across the shoulder-high Rio Bravo toward the Mexican shore. Once in Mexican territory, he waved across the river, holding a white silk scarf in the twilight to be seen. Four more riders joined him, and together they spurred their horses beyond the trees out into the open fields. Two men broke from the others, galloped ahead across the width of the field, and turned in opposite arcs, half-circles which brought them back to where the other horsemen waited silently, expectantly. The two riders brought their horses to a full stop, cupped their hands to their lips, and hooted softly. They stood up in their stirrups, waved their sombreros overhead, and hooted again.

Only the splashing of water against the horseflesh of hundreds and their riders could be heard as they left the protection of the Yankee shoreline to join their brave companions.

"Viva Villa!" came the cries of men and women once again imbued with the spirit of freedom—the spirit of the revolution—the spirit of Pancho Villa.

Listen, cried the people of the land. Listen to the rumble of the earth. Hear the music written in the wind. Feel and be inspired by the call to freedom. We, those pitiful people who sprang from the bowels of Mexico, we unfortunate people who mean nothing to people in high government, are the land-tilling *peóns* who mean the world to Pancho Villa. We who sit huddled on mountaintops, baking in mud huts, dying in the sweltering desert misery, and falling prostrate in the lost world of the cities, are waiting for the sounds of Pancho Villa. We are waiting for you, Panchito.

In that mysterious way Indians of the desert have of picking up vibrations without use of a wireless, the people waited and knew Pancho was on his way.

Deep in the heart of Mexico, Pancho Villa moved with the speed of a winged meteor, leaving behind him in the state of Durango, where his family were all buried beneath the earth, his childhood, his innocence,

723

and all dreams of an immediate peace. In a ritual to his ancestors, he'd prayed for the strength and wisdom needed to help elevate his people to a better world; for the stamina and intelligence to oppose his enemy on the field of battle, and the ability to become victorious. His supplications to God were to wear the laurel wreath of victory, not the thorns of defeat, so that he could help his people and make them human beings entitled to share in the glory of all men.

And so began General Francesco Villa's personal invasion of Mexico.

The war party grew by ones and twos and fours. By morning, after he'd left Durango, over one hundred had fallen in behind him. They commandeered horses, arms, and ammunition wherever they found them. By noon of the first day, they had whistled up volunteers from every tiny settlement in their path with their cry of revolution. Their war cries penetrated remote mountain pueblos, desert outposts, thickly wooded areas of the hillsmen. Men on horseback with their *viejas* waited, ready to fly, waving their weapons overhead, shouting, *"Viva Villa! Viva La Revolucion!"* As the swelling hordes cantered by, more revolutionaries fell into line alongside them, heading northward singing the Marching Song of the Bandits, "La Cucaracha."

"La Cucaracha, La Cucaracha, ya no puedo caminar. . . ."

From the northern deserts and the southern hills came the hordes of men and women. From all parts came the waves of chanting, singing, supplicating Mexicans.

"Porque no tiene, porque la falta, marijuana che fumar. . . ."

In droves they began to arrive at the appointed rendezvous, on horses, on burros, in wagons, on bare feet, braving the hot winds of the desert, exhausted yet filled with the hope and promise of a bright new tomorrow for themselves and their children.

"Una vieja y un vietito, se cayron en un pozo. . . ."

Their hopes and dreams were bound up with Pancho

Villa's hopes and dreams. It had been Pancho who aided them in the past. Only he gave them money, food, and shelter when all was lost. Had the government done as much? Hah! He'd beaten off the terrifying *Rurales* and outwitted the *Federales*. Why, that grand and glorious sonofabitch had won the revolution for Madero, hadn't he? Now, Madero was dead. "*Viva Villa!* Long live Villa!"

By the time the pregnant forces reached San Andres, they had exploded into a prolific 800 able-bodied men, not including the women. Villa had returned with hordes of hillsmen, some former *Federales* who'd escaped Huerta's clutches when they defected and crossed over into Texas to avoid the *Rurales*. Others had deserted the famed crack cavalry unit of *Colorados*. Now they had united to become *Villistas* to the end.

Daily, Madelaina searched the faces of all newcomers in Villa's growing army for the face she wanted to see the most—that of Peter Duprez. She wasn't aware that she wore her feelings on her face for all the world to see or that anyone near her could read her innermost thoughts, until one day Captain Richards pulled her aside and, searching her dark troubled eyes, he said compassionately, "Don'cha worry none, Little Fox, he'll find us when the time's right."

But his words had little effect on her. Madelaina had taken to having troubled dreams again. Dreams of Peter always calling to her. She continued to see him in a pool of blood and this in itself became so alarming to her, she couldn't concentrate on her work. She could only remember the ghastly pictures she had seen before Manuelito Perez fell to his death in the Plaza de Toros. Now, she worried constantly, fearing her own sanity.

It became incumbent upon Madelaina to teach the new women recruits how to use and care for their guns, a job she welcomed gratefully. To preserve her own well-being, she threw herself completely into the job of being a *soldadera*. It was a tough job, but one which brought rewards when those she taught responded by becoming dedicated crack shots.

One night shortly after Villa returned with the beginnings of his army, Madelaina was field-stripping her Obregon pistol, which she'd grown fond of as one might a trusty friend. Seated across from her friend, Antonetta, near a campfire in the dusky twilight, Madelaina studied the former sex kitten and admitted she'd never seen her as nervous and high-strung. Of late she had smoked much marijuana. As a matter of fact, it began shortly after Pancho left them on the shores of the River Concho. Since then, the redhead had become a different person, moody, silent, aloof, and given to periods in which she refused to speak, even with Madelaina. It was so unlike Tonetta that Little Fox began to think she lived with a stranger.

Even after they had settled into a confiscated hacienda, which housed many of the warring renegades, Antonetta had remained uncommunicative. Madelaina considered that all the former sex kitten needed was a few hours with her lover. *Muy bien,* she told herself, reaching in to light a piece of twig from the fires. She lit up a reefer and sat back, deliberately concentrating on Pancho Villa, attempting to conjure up his image in the fires. Once his face was fixed in her mind, Madelaina concentrated strongly on him. She sent out mental thoughts to him, attempting to allow her thoughts to filter in and mix with his.

Listen, you fool, Panchito. Listen to me! Here sits one of the most desirable women in the world, waiting for you, and you haven't time for her. What's the matter? Are you for certain some loco burro? If you were smart, you'd leave what you're doing and find Antonetta before she forsakes you for another of these muy macho hombres who throw themselves at her, just for a mere smile. Fool! One day she will not be here, then you'll regret it. Make hay, Panchito, while the sun still shines for you both!

Antonetta's eyes wandered to Madelaina for some inexplicable reason, and she watched her in fascination

726

as she stared into the bright flames of the fire. Of late Madelaina had been strange, she told herself. She would never forget the severity of the wounds inflicted on her by the bull whip of William Benson. *Muy mal.* She had guessed that Madelaina would forever bear the scars of that terrible night. Not long ago, before they left the River Conchos, she had watched Little Fox sprinkle a fine mist of dust from that leather pouch she wore around her neck. *Dios mios*, when on the next morning those scars had nearly disappeared, Tonetta had been unable to believe what her eyes told her. She had questioned Madelaina about her miraculous curative powers. "Have you turned into a *curandera*, my pet? Tell me. Tell me quickly how you do such things?"

Madelaina had admonished her to please say nothing to anyone of the miracle she had seen. "I myself don't understand it, therefore, I'd be unable to explain it to another," she had told Antonetta.

Since that time, Antonetta was bitten with curiosity, and she stared at the leather pouch each time she caught sight of it, mesmerized by the thought of its contents. As she watched Madelaina in fascination, wondering at her thoughts, some ten minutes had elapsed, Tonetta felt a gentle squeeze on her shoulder. She glanced up into the twinkling, mischievous eyes of Pancho Villa.

"Come, woman," he told her in a warm, seductive voice. "It's been too long since we've been together. Something told me, as I sat down going over reports and listening to my men, that I was wasting too much time for nothing, that I'd best get to you before some other *hombre* claims you and that would be a pity, because Pancho would have to teach him a lesson, eh, *gattita*?"

Antonetta, trying with difficulty to still her heartbeats, pretended to be coy and indifferent. She shrugged. "Who is this stranger speaking to me?" After first glancing at him, she turned her head with a soft toss of her fiery red hair. "This voice sounds familiar,

727

but the face—that face is the face of a stranger. Go away, man. I have no use for strangers."

Watching the scene from her position at the fire, Madelaina sighed. No one could have been more astonished than she when Pancho Villa showed up in reply to her mental summons. She hadn't even thought such a thing would work. Coincidence, she told herself. Merely coincidence! Why, if I had such powers, I'd summon Peter to my side! Instead of dealing with her own thoughts, she was furious with Antonetta's obvious game playing. That fool! Why doesn't she accept Pancho instantly? It's he she's been mooning over long enough!

Exasperated with the whole thing, Madelaina arose and shuffled down the dirt path toward the coral. What she would give for Don Quixote! Peter had told her he'd left the black stallion at his ranch near San Antonio, to be used as stud for the mares. Madelaina slipped a saddle on one of the horses, strapping it securely and mounted it. Just as she was leaving the corral, she saw Pancho and Antonetta, arm in arm, disappear into the hacienda. *Bueno*, she thought, as she signaled the sentries before she galloped out onto the desert.

"*Cuidado*, Little Fox," called one of the men. "Be careful. Enemy spies have been spotted not far away."

"*Gracias, muchacho*. I am well armed. I am not afraid. But, to keep your feelings easy, I promise not to go far. I need fresh air and time to think."

She waved to him and spurred her stallion into the dark of night. Behind her, she left lit camp fires and erotic, animal sounds that carried into the night as men and women found each other as lovers.

She rode swiftly in the balmy night air, trying to think of nothing in particular. A short distance from camp, she climbed a slight rise in the terrain and dismounted. Seated on a dark boulder, she could see the camp in the distance. Her thoughts concentrated on the military problems that might beset Pancho Villa in this attempt to implement a revolution that would count for

Mexico. How would he do it? Without money or weapons, the chances were slim. For several mad moments, she considered what she'd heard about her father's apparent opposition to Vitoriano Huerta. Was it possible, really possible that she might be able to help unite her father, General Obregon, with General Villa for the glory of Mexico?

It was a mad, totally insane thought. Wasn't it? Could her father ever come to terms with himself concerning a revolution? Such a union wouldn't be as farfetched as it might have been when she first moved to El Paso. Daily changes brought about strange bed partners in politics, she'd been told. Madelaina had lived enough to know you could never outguess fate. Just when you're certain of a particular destiny, the old sorceress conjures up another bend in the road and heads you in a totally unexpected direction.

Well, it was something to think about. Something she'd have to take considerable pains to work out in her mind before daring to broach the subject to General Villa. One never tells the singer to sing. It must be his own inspiration. Perhaps a little prodding? What would it hurt?

Chapter 27

The flamboyantly beautiful Antonetta had coupled with her lover and both had felt the familiar quickening of blood in their veins. He explained to Antonetta that he was growing less indolent than he'd been in El Paso, that in the past week, he'd grown to enjoy the weight of his guns over each hip and the clanking sound of his spurs as he walked. "Tonight, *chiquita,* I will be united again with Seven Leagues, my stallion," he said happily.

"And?" asked Antonetta quietly.

"And, little *gatitta,* you know who else."

"I thought so, *Jefe,*" replied Tonetta, moving away from Pancho on the four-poster bed that had belonged to some wealthy *hacendado* before Villa appropriated it for his cause. Pancho glanced at her with dismay.

"*Gatitta,* you and me, we've known each other a long time. *Pues,* I hate to think how long," said Pancho huskily.

"*Es veridad*, it's true," she said testily.

"In that time, between us has been honesty."

"*Es veridad*. That's also true."

"You have always known about *mi mujer,* Lucita."

"*Si. Es muy veridad.* That is very much the truth."

"Then why do you fret? Why do you look so sad? You know I will see her tonight." He reached for her, put a strong, well-tanned arm about her, and drew her to him. They had known each other a long time, had been most intimate, and Tonetta, never one to be shy, let her hands wander all over Pancho's naked body. His body provided an immediate reaction to her erotic touch, a response that gave Antonetta a secure feeling, one that in the past filled her with the knowledge that she hadn't lost her touch.

But Pancho felt a tinge of annoyance. He was a man. It was up to him who he desired to see, and tonight his strength must be saved for Lucita—his wife, his only real wife whom he loved and missed with a passion. He couldn't just up and quarrel with Antonetta as many men in his predicament often did when they needed an excuse to go whoring. So many men would deliberately pick a fight with their spouse or lovers, so they could justify a night away from the marital bed. But this was not the way of Pancho Villa, a red-blooded man who was also an honorable man. No. He would speak the truth with this woman, this green-eyed wench who'd stood beside him through thick and thin.

Antonetta was doing things to him that prevented his concentrating on the duty which faced him that evening. What a seductress she was, his little sex kitten. Even when he wasn't conscious of what she was doing, Villa had fallen into carnal traps time and again. She was always teasing him, tempting him, and growing sullen if in their little games he pretended to be indifferent to her. She was insatiable, this little tigress, and she made him feel the same. There are two of me to satisfy, he had told her so many times and she seemed to understand. One is Pancho Villa the desperate renegade, the *guerrillo* who lives by his wits and must of necessity take what he can in his travels from any lovely *señorita* willing to please him. And then there is Doroteo Arango, the man, the husband, father, and hillsman, who wants nothing more than to till the land and be a loving father, husband, and provider for his family.

Antonetta always assured him she understood. She was the fortunate one. It was she, Pancho made love to more often than his wife. Why should she deny Lucita a few nights a year when Antonetta had him the other three hundred and sixty nights? They had both discussed this, hadn't they?

His thoughts interrupted, Pancho Villa could

concentrate no longer. Antonetta had flown him to the moon with her and after a while they were both physically spent.

The room was silent. Only their breathing was apparent. Outside, the camp fires were cooking up dinners for the followers of Villa. He glanced at his wristwatch. He should have left for his house before this. He sat in bed and gazed at the stirring Antonetta, who opened her eyes.

"*Querido*, where are you going?" she asked.

"I told you where. Weren't you listening?"

"I was listening. I thought I had made you forget."

"So that's what I owe that trip to the moon, eh?"

"That and the expertise of Antonetta."

Villa laughed. He glanced at her. "Don't feel badly. Try not to think of me while I'm gone. It will abuse your soul and Pancho doesn't wish for the soul of Antonetta to be abused. It is too beautiful."

Antonetta, feeling terribly vulnerable, reached over and hugged Pancho's waist. "Oh, *querido*, your words are like the kisses of the stars at the deepest hour of midnight." Her long red hair fanned out like ribbons of fire across his naked thighs, and he looked down on her, gently caressing its silkiness.

"If you don't let Pancho get up, you know what will happen," he said huskily as his reaction to her touch and nearness became apparent.

Antonetta giggled with childish delight, and she stroked his manhood with expert manipulations. She was a real woman, this Antonetta. The kind of a woman a part of him needed desperately. Yet, there was Lucita. She would need satisfaction on this night, and if he permitted this green-eyed vixen to have her way, there'd be nothing left for his wife.

"Never did Pancho Villa ever think he'd have the strength to push you away, *querida*," he said firmly, removing her hands. "Now see what you've done. How will I prevent him from intruding upon my presence until I get home to my house?"

Giggling with pleasure, she forced a pout. "See if I

732

care. When you are making love to Lucita, I shall send my little *diableros* to haunt you. You'll see. Just when you are ready to climax, Panchito, it will be Antonetta's face you'll see, Antonetta's perfume you'll smell, Antonetta's body you'll feel!"

"Listen, you insatiable cat. Stop it!" he said abruptly. "Do not even say such a thing in jest." He twisted her red, silky hair in his fingers and pulled her head back. "I do not need such complications to confuse me."

Antonetta playfully shoved her tongue out at him.

"And stop that, too." Pancho let her go, and she rubbed her head and laughed at him as she watched him step into his leggings and shirt. Dressed, he strapped on his double, low-slung gun holsters, checked the barrels of the guns, and holstered them easily. Next came the double *bandoleras,* ammunition crisscrossed over his formidable chest. She felt sudden pangs of dismay.

"I shall always remember you best as you were in El Paso, dressed in your dinner tuxedo, *Jefe,*" she sighed in reflection. "When we were both safe from the uncertain horrors of war. You've changed considerably, *querido,*" she said softly.

A sharp knock on the door brought a quick response from Villa. He moved over to the side of the bed and planted a lusty kiss on Antonetta's lips.

"Vaya con Dios, querido," she whispered. "Return soon to me."

Villa stood over her for an instant. He placed his sombrero on his head and shoved it back. He slipped a bullet from his ammo belt and handed it to her. "If Panchito is so foolish to ever lose you—for whatever the reason—you have my permission to use this silver bullet to kill him."

Antonetta's face paled in the darkness. She was about to protest, but Villa had already left her to the memories of their togetherness.

Villa's night with Lucita, the wife he also loved passionately, was forced to an abrupt, unexpected halt. Fortunately, he'd finished coupling with her when the information reached him, vital news necessitating his immediate departure.

Madelaina Obregon, while out riding, had encountered an old friend of Villa's, a compatriot who recognized her from Parral. While riding back to camp, the former member of Urbina's brigade imparted information which caused Madelaina's brain to roil with interest. Another old compatriot of Villa's from his spectacular Juarez victory now *commanded* the garrison at Santa Isabella!

Madelaina immediately saw a chance for Pancho Villa to gain a real army as he'd done in Parral. She escorted the old artillery specialist to camp, then broke out in a wild gallop to find Villa in San Andres, but only after she gathered to her side as escorts Captain Tracy Richards and Tomàs Urbina.

Urbina, reluctant to disturb the loving couple, rejoiced when he learned that Pancho had at least enjoyed the first act with Lucita. He hurriedly requested Villa's presence at Madelaina's side.

Before the sun crept up over the eastern horizon, Pancho Villa found himself in possession of a Federal garrison, seven dozen expertly trained soldiers, machine guns, and desperately needed medical and military supplies. The conquest, thanks to Madelaina's fast thinking, was as important as finding his old friend Fidel Avila.

While Captain Richards and Little Fox inspected the garrison, the two old friends exchanged back-slapping hugs and disappeared into a private room. Madelaina and the gringo walked along the ramparts, watching the sun rise over the broiling garrison. "You think you could train Pancho's men to fight like the regulars, *Capitán*?" asked Madelaina.

Tracy Richards glanced at her in a half-amused manner, tilting his head tolerantly. "You *gachupíns* always ask the impossible, don'cha? And damned if'n y'all don't get yer way. All's ah can say is ya woulda made a handsome general at warfare yerself."

Madelaina returned his smile in that same half-amused manner.

"*Vamenos, muchaco.* Let's find Villa and tell him our idea."

"*Your* idea, Little Fox," he corrected her. "An' ah've gotta admit it's a brilliant one. As a matter of fact, while ah've the opportunity, ah've gotta tell ya how much ah've admired ya since ouah acquaintance."

"*Gracias,* gringo. Tell me, where is your woman, Rosalia Quintera?"

Tracy held up a restraining hand. "All right. All right. Ya done went and emasculated me. Ah meant nothin' fresh. Pete's too good a friend, heah? And foah you information, Rosalia will be joining us pretty soon."

"Good," she said. Suddenly Madelaina felt dizzy. She weaved on her feet and held on to the concrete abutmcnt on the walkway.

"What's wrong? What can ah do fer ya? Ya just turned the color of ash." Tracy was solicitous of her. He held on to her in a more than friendly way.

Madelaina felt waves of nausea engulf her. Her stomach felt queasy and she felt like heaving. She hadn't had breakfast yet. Perhaps that was it, she told herself.

"I'll be all right, *Capitán.* Just dizzy. Perhaps a cup of coffee might help." She sniffed the air. Below them in the courtyard, *Federales* were taking breakfast. In her state, she failed to notice the soft look in Tracy's eyes.

"Y'all wait here, *chiquita.* Ah'll go getcha some-thing. Ah suppose ya ain't eaten since sundown." He moved away swiftly, scaling the wooden steps alongside the garrison to the courtyard, glancing back at her with concern from time to time.

Madelaina, unable to stop the rolling heaves, felt miserable. Had she caught a germ or an infection from the others in camp? She was sure she had long since become immune to all camp ailments.

Tracy returned with the coffee and a few tacos. "Chew this first, *chiquita*, then the coffee," he instructed her tenderly.

"No, coffee first," she insisted.

"Ah'm suggesting it the othuh way around," he said ominously.

But Madelaina stubbornly persisted in taking the coffee first. Instantly she regretted her choice. No sooner had the steaming fluid settled in her stomach, than it came up.

"Chew the taco, *chiquita*," insisted the freedom fighter with a light trace of a smile on his face.

Madelaina hastily did his bidding and found, much to her amazement, that she was able to keep it down. She glanced at him in amazement. "But how do you know such a thing, gringo? And why do you smile at me in so smug a manner?"

"Well, ah reckon a smart little fox like y'all can figger it out." He tipped his sombrero to her. "If ya feel better, we'd best get along to see what Pancho's up to." He paused. "Ya can count on me anytime for anything, heah?"

"No!" she said in dismay as it came together in her mind. "It can't be! Not now. Not here. Not at such a time." She put down the coffee and taco and turned from him, gazing out at the blinding light of the sun, already causing radiations of heat to rise from the desert. *Dios mios!* Was it possible she was with child? It was too soon for the seed of William Benson to be germinating in her belly. It has to be Peter's child. It has to be! And he's married to another. She refused to believe it. Even if she did, she wasn't about to let the gringo know. She tried to find possible excuses. "It's the water I drank near the River Conchos. I've felt terrible for several days."

"Whatever ya say, Little Fox," he replied, quietly, noting her consternation.

They found Villa and Avila in the office, comparing

notes. In moments she was to learn that her mind and Villas' ran together like twin rivers.

"So, *muchacho*," continued Villa gleefully, "Huerta made you a colonel?"

"What can I say, Panchito? Madero was very generous to me and Huerta has yet to see the color of my loyalties."

"And you learned all this military stuff—marching, saluting, firing cannon?"

"It was either that or till the soil."

"*Muy bien.* Shall I tell you what your part will be in the revolution?"

"I am listening, *Jefe.*"

"*Bueno.* We exchange men, you and me. You teach my men how to be soldiers. March them. Drill them. Make them use bayonets. You'll start a military school for Pancho Villa's soldiers, understand? My friend, when Pancho finishes whistling up his countrymen, they will flock like bees to the honey pot. And they must learn what our enemies already know."

"*Bueno, Jefe,*" exclaimed Madelaina in full accord with his plan.

"Now yer talking, *Jefe,*" marveled Captain Richards over the obvious change in Pancho Villa's mental outlook. "Ya ain't the same man who took Juarez for Madero, *Jefe;* y'all are something else, all together." His eyes lit up in wonderment.

Even Avila couldn't contain his astonishment. "Is this to be believed, *amigo?* Pancho Villa, the *guerrillo,* turning coat into a regular? *Que va?*"

"You think I didn't learn something in the *calabozo?* You think Pancho doesn't profit from his errors? I learned I had to know more about this military business. I give him little credit, but Huerta taught me plenty. He was a fool. A stubborn, ambitious fool who kneels before the altar of whiskey. But that man wore some magic dark glasses through which he performed some miracles. It's true he runs his army with the power of ten generals. Now, then, *amigo.*" he addressed himself to Avila. "I've taught my men to be the best goddamned *guerrillos* in the world. You take over, finish the job, and we'll have an invincible army, one that will wipe the smile from that sleek, well-fed cat, General Rabago in Chihuahua. We'll reinstate Governor Gonzalez—"

Avila interrupted. "Panchito! Is it possible you don't know—?"

"Know what?" asked the *jefe*. "From the tone of Avila's voice he knew the answer.

"Your old friend, Don Abraham Gonzalez has been murdered."

Every nerve and muscle in Villa's body locked. His eyes narrowed. "Huerta?"

"Who else?"

Villa's black, red-veined eyes burned with vengeance. He glanced briefly at Madelaina and the gringo freedom fighter, then averted his fiery eyes. He rose to his feet, shrugged his holsters into place, then braced himself.

"Muy bien, chico. Where is your telegraph? Villa has something to say to an old *compadre.*"

Moments later, Villa sent the following wire to the military governor of Chihuahua City:

Señor General Rabago: The government you represent has sought my extradition from America. Bueno. To save us both time and trouble, I am already here in Mexico. With my army, I will combat the oppression of that traitorous jackal Huerta. Whenever you are ready—General Francesco Villa.

While the storm clouds of war gathered might, Madelaina grew more accustomed to the physical changes taking place in her body. Once the morning sickness passed, she tended her duties with her usual vigor. She walked tall and proud, her straight back outlined firmly under her clean blue cotton *rebozo*. Instinctive serenity had softened her dark, well-hardened eyes. Her gait had the natural guarded ease of a primitive woman carrying an unborn child. The shape of her body changed, filling her breasts to more than ample fullness, but the rest wasn't extensively distorted. In the

738

sixth month now, she only looked pleasingly rounded.

She had taken to walking rather than riding horses, for fear she might abort the fetus. She'd had one close call in her fourth month and nearly lost the child. But for the help of Antonetta and some of the other women, she might have miscarried. And Madelaina was determined to have this child of her husband's. She wasn't far from the encampment, and approaching a small village of San Martine near the Rio Grande, she paused under a clump of pepper trees, along a wall of organ cactus. Glancing around, she saw a bridge of loose stones at the edge of town where a hut, bearing the sign *farmacia* crudely scrawled on it, stood in near shambles.

She had come to buy a few simple herbal teas for the headaches and stomach cramps she had experienced of late. She paused at the bridge to dab her feet into the cool water. Her eyes, resting from the hot sun, fixed on the far-off mountain, a smoky blue under a hanging drift of clouds. This was the first time she'd come this far without an escort. True, she had her gun slung behind her and her Obregon automatic in its holster at her waist. But entering this serene little village of people who might have never seen a *soldadera,* she wanted to do nothing to frighten them. Besides, she was hungry, and although she believed none of the superstitions concerning pregnancy, too many of the women had whispered to her the terrors of marking her baby if she didn't gratify even the smallest in food desires.

She peered beyond the thick hedge of cactus which sheered up nakedly like knife blades set about a protected clearing. She reached for her knife and hacked away at a prickly pear cactus. She managed to cut off four, which she quickly plunged into the cool water and dammed by stones to cool off. By the time she headed back to Villa's camp, they would be cool and tasty enough to eat.

Just as Madelaina began to think it was unusually

quiet, she was alerted to the fact she wasn't alone. She felt certain she heard noises. She stopped short, moved off the main pathway, her hand swiftly unholstering her automatic. Shifting the burden of her weight slightly, she bent forward, shading her eyes to see more clearly through the hedge.

Antonetta, red hair shining like fiery embers in the sun, ran between jasmine bushes, lifting her knees in swift leaps, glancing over her shoulder, laughing in a quivering, excited way. Madelaina, about to call to her, realized she must be with someone. Probably Pancho. She had no desire to interrupt them. About to turn away and proceed on her own mission, she saw Rudolfo Fierro, running after Tonetta, nearly catching her. He also laughed in that strange breathless way. His white teeth set, both rows gleaming under his drooping moustache. She'd never seen Fierro smile, like a man blushing with love, and it startled her for a moment, taking her by surprise. Once she gained her composure, she saw Fierro catch up to Tonetta. He was a new man recently joined with the *Villistas*.

He seized her, clenching her so hard that her chemise gave way and ripped from her shoulder. Tonetta, whose turquoise-green eyes glittered in the sun as she stood next to this enormous man whom she'd labeled a vicious killer, melted in his arms. Fierro kissed her savagely; she didn't protest. She kissed him back with equal desire and ferocity.

Madelaina did not stir. She did not breathe. Hot and cold chills ran through her, and she felt a sudden weakness in her knees as if she were a traitor to spy on them. She was afraid the amorous couple would sense her presence, feel her eyes on them, and find her there in so untenable a position. But they didn't pass beyond that small enclosure made by nature to resemble a true lover's hideaway; tall saplings thrust into the earth, roofed with yellowed maguey leaves, flattened and overlapping like shingles, hunched drowsy and fragrant in the warmth of noonday.

Fierro lifted one of Antonetta's breasts and caressed

740

it gently. Antonetta smiled consentingly and yielded to his passion. Fierro, walking proudly as a game cock, flourished a grandly manner and spread out his jacket on the mossy ground at their feet. They both fell to the ground eager to sate their passion before it consumed them.

Fierro and Antonetta! Madelaina burned all over as if a layer of tiny fig cactus bristles as cruel as spun glass had crawled under her skin. She forced herself to move forward silently, telling herself this was not her affair. Not to involve herself. Her loyalty was to both Antonetta and Pancho Villa. She wouldn't think about them. Not at all. But an empty feeling had filled her. She moved on to the *farmacia* where an old woman, grumbling over being awakened during siesta, greeted her and sold her the needed items for the required amount of pesos.

She took some of the headache powder and drank it down with a ladle of water from the spring well not far from the *farmacia*. She glanced about the village and realized that siesta was the reason for the abnormal silence. She decided to return to camp. How would she go past that love nest without them hearing her, she wondered. Feeling the hot flush of embarrassment over her recently acquired knowledge, Madelaina scolded herself.

Damnit! It's not your business. Forget it. You must pretend that you know nothing! You can't be annoyed, shocked, or moved to any action by this. After all, Antonetta has needs, just as Pancho does, she told herself. None of this touches you. Forget it. She moved back along the path, careful not to be heard, and moving stealthily past the stone bridge, she found herself out on the desert again, the blue of her *rebozo* becoming a dancing spot in the radiating heat waves that rose from the gray-red soil. She had forgotten the prickly pears completely.

Madelaina never mentioned to Antonetta what she'd seen on this day, and she forgot—or tried to obliterate from her mind—the thought that Antonetta hadn't resisted Fierro at all.

It was simply amazing how these two kept their secret from being discovered. Fierro and Villa continued to be as close as cockleshells. Antonetta kept her distance admirably. If they continued their love affair, it never became apparent to Madelaina again. She caught herself watching them to see if they'd slip or give any hint of their intimacy. Nothing. Absolutely nothing. The only change in Antonetta was that she didn't call Fierro a bloody murderous villain as she had from the moment Fierro appeared in Villa's camps.

Madelaina as Little Fox continued with her duties, never shirking, never complaining. She and the other expertly trained *soldaderas* were always in the thick of the war, fighting alongside the military detachments in the field, and with Little Fox always in the lead, the battalion of experienced women of war swarmed the fields like locusts, gathering provisions for the *Villista* army. She cooked with the *campesinas* and ate with them what was left over after the men had finished. After the battles she went with the women to salvage clothing, ammunition, and guns from the slain before their bodies began to swell in the heat. How many times had they encountered women as tough as they from the opposing sides and entered into a second battle even grimer than the first?

Although it became more difficult for Madelaina to keep up, she didn't complain. Antonetta grew alarmed for her friend and tried desperately to encourage her to return to El Paso to have her baby. But Madelaina refused. She grew gaunt, as if something inside gnawed at her; her eyes were sunken and she spoke less and less with each passing day. She worked harder than ever with no complaint passing her lips.

They had traveled to the north and were camped near the Yaqui River when Madelaina bent over suddenly and, clutching a nearby blanket to her mouth to keep from screaming, glanced up at the faces of the women nearby. She couldn't utter a sound. It was as if she were strangling on her own parched and swollen tongue. Her ankles had swollen these past few days and the knowledge that something was drastically wrong hadn't struck her until this very morning. Still she refused to talk to the midwives about the condition.

Now she was helpless. One of the women saw her fall forward, dangerously near the fires. She screamed. Suddenly there was pandemonium as the women fluttered about her and summoned the men to help lift her.

She was carried inside one of the thatched huts nearby and laid out on a blanket, unconscious. Antonetta was summoned, and she huddled with two midwives who tried reviving Little Fox with tequila, potions, and chicory. They used charred owl bones and other concoctions the Indians used to conjure up spirits of healing, including singed rabbit fur, lizards, and the entrails of cats. These were strewn about the hut at random by the women, who paid more heed to this ritual than to the needs of the mother in premature labor.

Four hours later, when the setting orange sun no longer seared the eyes and a spectacular tropical twilight spread plum-colored comfort upon the earth, the premature son of Madelaina and Peter Duprez was born. The midwife spread a concoction of oils on the infant, wrapped him in swaddling clothes, and placed the child in his mother's weary arms.

The news reached General Villa and he stalked into the hut to celebrate the birth of the boy child as if it were his own flesh and blood. He brought force and turbulence into the hut with him and his dark eyes sparkled brilliantly in the candle glow. He looked at the infant, gathered him in his arms, and with a primitive shout raised the child high in his arms, grinning with the pride of a godfather. He shouted an Indian cry of joy, and lifting the child higher toward the roof of the hut as one might do in making an offering to God, he asked for the Lord's blessing.

"He is some handsome *niño*, Little Fox," he exclaimed with amazed delight. "Now, for the name.

743

What have you decided?" He displayed the baby to Rudolfo Fierro and Tomás Urbina with much elation, as if it were the most amazing miracle ever performed in his camp. His expression was a blend of masculine triumph, pride, and sentimental melancholy.

"With your permission, *Jefe*, I've decided to call him Alejandro Doroteo Duprez Benson." She smiled faintly at Villa's antics.

"Bueno," he said, handing the infant to Antonetta's outstretched arms. "Tonight we celebrate the birth of Alejandro Doroteo Duprez Benson!" he announced to his men. "Fierro, pass out the cigars. Since the gringo papa is not here, his godfather shall officiate at the baptism." He left the hut, excitedly calling to Captain Tracy Richards. "Hey, gringo! Gringo! We celebrate, eh? We got us another damned good yankee to join the Gringo Brigade!"

Hearing his words, Madelaina shuddered inwardly. *Dios mios, pray you close your ears to the words of Pancho Villa. For my son, I do not wish more revolution.*

And then as most women do after the birth of a child, Madelaina cried and cried, without knowing for what she cried. She missed her husband too much. She needed the comforting touch of his arms around her, the feel of his lips upon hers, reassuring her of his love. But there was no one to comfort her—no one except for a replica of Peter, however small. He would have to occupy first place in her life now. Her own exaltation over the birth of a fine son, so small and helpless, was burned out by the pain she had endured. There wasn't an ember of excitement left in her. She was tired, weak, and terribly depressed. For her, it seemed the perilous adventure had ended when Peter deserted her to marry Valerie Townsend. Peter had vanished as if he no longer existed. Their days of marching, eating, and making love between battles had been so few that the memory of them began to fade of late. Now she had another life to think of and to plan for.

She felt her veins overflow with unendurable melancholy. If only she could stop crying. Perhaps then she could think more clearly about what she'd do now that the responsibility of another life was in her hands. She was so tired, so drowsy she could hardly keep her eyes open. Worse, she had no milk for the baby. What kind of mother was she—no milk!

Outside, Antonetta, holding a clay jar in her hand, approached a gentle mother goat tethered to a sapling which yielded when she pulled at the rope's end at the farthest reaches of grass. The kid, tied up a few feet away, rose, bleating, its feathery fleece shivering in the fresh wind. From behind her came Rudolfo Fierro. Scooping up the baby goat in his hands, he brought it to the mother goat and allowed him to suckle a few moments.

"Now," he said gently to the red-haired beauty. "Now reach in and take the milk you need." Their eyes met for an instant in silent understanding. Then Tonetta quickly and with very deliberate movements drew enough milk for Madelaina's son, while Fierro's dark eyes lusted for her hungrily.

"Mucho gracias, mi coronel," she whispered. For an instant their hands met, then she reluctantly withdrew and returned to the hut to help feed the newborn infant.

"Por nada," said Fierro, watching her long after she'd vanished. The expression of desire on his face abated. But inside him, the proddings of lust and need burst into bright embers. For now, he had to be satisfied with stolen moments. Although used to taking what he wanted when he wanted it, this man felt an immense loyalty to Pancho Villa. And it was for this reason, that he hadn't already named Antonetta his property. He could wait. Meanwhile he'd do all he could to make sure Villa got to his precious Lucita, whenever the urge arose in him, thus leaving the red-haired vixen more free time for him.

Chapter 28

Peter Duprez wafted in and out of consciousness for
many weeks following the near fatal attempt on his life.
He knew without being told that he'd courted death,
that he was alive only due to his instinct for survival.
Moments before the near-lethal bullets tore into his
body, he'd lifted himself slightly from the tub, causing
the bullets to miss their intended mark—the heart. Instead, the bullets lodged in his stomach and groin.

When consciousness returned to him it came in
sprints of recollections, never in its entirety; hazy and
vague at moments, other times painfully clear. His
memory of the actual shooting itself was fleeting. What
stood out clearly in his mind was the nightmarish,
jolting ride in the back seat of a Hayes-Apperson auto,
wrapped in blankets, more dead than alive. Moments
of lucidity brought with it the perplexity of wondering
if he were still alive before blacking out into a delirium
of intense pain and feverish darkness.

Thoughts waxed and waned, always accompanied by
the feeling of being disembowled, causing him to experience a nightmare of agony, panic, frustration, and
a helplessness which manifested itself into a total annihilation of self. Pain dissolved his ego and consumed
him without abating. His awareness of the passing of
time alternated with periods of blinding sunlight, para-
lysing darkness, and a radiation of pulsating heat en-
gulfing his body.

Peter wavered precariously between the agony
echoing in his eardrums and a silent blackness swallow-
ing him periodically, yet there finally came an
awareness—slow as it was—prodding and pushing him
into reality.

Voices hovered over him, but he recognized none of them. He was unable to open his eyes, despite the warnings made by these alien voices that he must. If it remained incumbent upon Peter to choose, he'd have gladly remained in that euphoric state of outer limbo which followed the administration of medication to ease the intense pain and discomfort he lived with.

When he finally came to and recognized what was reality for him, he was in small sterile-looking room—a hospital? He was restrained in a bed, covered with snowy linens as white as the glaring enamel-painted walls in which a reflection could be seen. His body, from the chest down to the upper thighs, was wrapped tightly in bandages. In what appeared to him to be a senseless precaution, his legs were also strapped to the bed. He couldn't have moved if he tried.

His eyes blinked hard in an effort to orient himself. Yes, it was a hospital all right. He could smell the antiseptic odors indigenous to hospitals, hear the muffled and hushed sounds. All he could see was white— white—and more white. Over the door opposite him was a large white clock with black numbers, the hands pointing to eleven o'clock. A white cloth folding screen on rollers stood to one side of the door. To the left of this was a window overlooking a scene he couldn't see from the bed. Next to the bed stood a white enamel table covered with a collection of hospital and sick room supplies. A white, metal, straight-backed chair sat at the foot of the bed. His eyes fell on a large bouquet of yellow roses. He wondered who'd sent them.

He felt an uneasy queasiness knotting in the pit of his stomach before sleep overcame him. When he awakened, the hands of the clock pointed to seven o'clock. It had to be evening because very little light came in through the window. His awareness came alive as the sound of hushed voices stirred him. One voice in particular seemed apprehensive and concerned. For a moment he felt as though he were looking into the face of Theodore Roosevelt until he recalled how much

747

Governor Hampton Townsend resembled the former head of the Rough Riders.

"Can you hear me, Peter?" asked the older man. "They told me you regained consciousness this morning." The portly man, dressed in a dark serge suit with a stiffly starched collar and black tie, was duly concerned over him. "It's a miracle you're alive. Valerie is beside herself. I packed her off to Europe while you convalesced here under an alias. What a perfectly idiotic thing for her to do. I must admit when she announced your marriage and a subsequent honeymoon in Europe to the press, I was outraged. But it's certainly provided you with rest—without those sniffing bloodhounds of the press converging on you." Hampton Townsend spoke in subdued tones, careful not to be overheard by the other men standing near the door.

Peter tried to move. "What happened, suh? Ah'm a bit vague. How long have ah been heah?"

"Haven't they told you? How incompetent of the hospital staff. Nearly two months. For a month and a half we were unsure if you'd live. It's a miracle. A real miracle. It's over now, and thank God you're on the mend."

"What happened?" persisted Peter. "How did ah get heah?"

"Dear me, don't you know what happened? Have you no recollection at all?" The governor glanced over his shoulders at the others, then leaned in closer to Peter. "Have you no idea who your assailant was? You were shot at close range—in the belly and groin. I'm afraid, my boy, the injuries are quite serious." He avoided Peter's eyes. "Well, all that's behind us now. What counts is you're alive."

Peter shrugged. "Yeah, ah suppose ah should be grateful foah that, suh."

"When you feel up to it, my boy," said the governor, seemingly relieved, "I'd best fill you in on what's happening south of the border."

Peter had been looking at the three men who huddled close to the door. He felt below par and his instincts weren't performing efficiently. Still, something about the trio unnerved him. He cautioned the governor with his eyes to be aware of their presence. "Who are theah?" he asked confidentially.

"I was told, Peter, they are guarding your life. My boy, I presumed they were hired by you," he whispered.

"No, suh. Nevuh saw them befoah. It's best we say nothing, suh. Ya understand?"

"Just be thankful you're American—on American soil!" said the Governor Townsend, wiping the sweat dripping from his face. "Word's been out that President Huerta is seeking extradition of all war criminals. He especially wants the freedom fighters—namely you, Peter."

Peter's eyes searched his critically. He glanced at the trio at the door who were absorbed in their own conversation. "Namely me? Why me?"

"Seems you were married to a Mexican spy."

"She's an American through marriage, suh. And don't tell me President Wilson intends ta cooperate with that foul sidewinder, Huerta?"

"Up to now, he's stalled the Mexican president. But it seems they've had the cooperation of another very important American—a Texan at that."

Peter's eyes widened with interest. He could see readily that Governor Townsend felt awkward, ill at ease, and obviously reluctant to speak out.

"Dare ah ask who, suh?"

The governor cleared his throat, blinked his gray eyes hard behind those rimless glasses, and stroked his brush moustache. His brown hair was nearly white now, and he resembled Valerie more at this time than at any other, thought Peter. Here the resemblance ended. This man was a true gentleman and a scholar, who operated within a sphere of ethics that made him admirable. Valerie had to have been a bad seed. She had none of her father's laudable traits. As a matter of fact, Peter, having never seen him at a loss for words, grew concerned.

"It's William Benson, Peter. Your father" He spoke the words solemnly as if he had just imposed a death sentence on the young man.

"Governor," began Peter. "Is theah any way y'all might rid us both of those three men? Ah feel uneasy in theah presence, especially since youah words have just hit me with the impact of hurricane." Peter was shaking. He had no reason to doubt the words of the Texas governor.

The portly man moved with the grace of a bull moose. His manner, however, contained the efficacy of a diplomat. "Gentlemen, I wonder if you'd mind moving outside in the hall. The patient has grown weary and would like to rest. You may continue your conversation out there. I'll only be a few moments longer."

One man, an apparent secret service agent in the employ of the Mexican government shook his head. "I regret, Excellency, I must remain in the same room with Señor Duprez. This gentlemen is with your State Department." He pointed to the slim, dark-haired American wearing a plaid suit, stiffly starched collar, spats, and a derby, who instantly prepared to produce papers giving him authority by the state's attorney general to cooperate with the Mexican agent.

"Apparently you aren't aware I'm the governor of this state," said Townsend, drawing himself up to his full stature of six feet. His head arched imperiously, and the manner in which he glanced at the others through his bifocals gave him a more formidable appearance than usual. "Do I take this reluctance on your part to comply with my request as downright insubordination? What's your name, sir?"

"Fenwick, sir," retorted the man in plaid, instantly flushed with embarrassment. "I had no idea the involvement was at the executive level, Governor," he apologized. "My orders from the state attorney general are explicit." He turned over his portfolio for the governor's perusal.

Townsend glanced at them superficially, folded them, and handed them back. "They appear in order,

Fenwick. I have no desire to interfere with the commitment made by the attorney general with our friends south of the border. All I ask is that you permit me a few quiet minutes with an old and dear friend of the family. As a matter of fact, my son-in-law."

Before Fenwick or the Mexican agent could protest further or become aware they'd been politely put in their place, they were escorted out the door by the expansive governor who made light of the situation. Once closed, the door was quietly bolted and the Townsend tilted a chair beneath the handle.

"What is it, suh?" asked Peter, attempting to rise to a sitting position. He watched the distinguished man's antics with mounting curiosity.

Governor Townsend didn't speak for a few moments as he paced the floor thoughtfully. Soon Peter began to recognize those qualities of which President Wilson mentioned in the man who governed one of the most prosperous states in the union. His face grew taut, his eyes more secret. The planes of his face, sharp and angular, contrasted the deep hollows under his cheekbones. He began to speak as if to himself. Yet, added to the delivery of his words was a peculiar quality of strength and power formerly absent from his manner.

"So, Peter. It's worse than I imagined. They went over my head—didn't give a hint of their intrigue and shenanigans. Not even my spies reported what was underfoot." He stroked the outline of his moustache with the tip of his finger. "He's gone too far this time."

Peter's brows drew together in a puzzled frown. "Who, suh?"

The governor's gray eyes lifted to meet Peter's. His color was gone. For an instant Peter detected a marked hesitation before the words spilled from the official's mouth. "William Benson. Your father—that's who!" Then he gathered momentum. "Lucifer only knows how many acres of Mexican land were exchanged for his betrayal! Blasted fool! Doesn't he even guess

751

that one day his lands—even his life—will be worthless if a revolutionary becomes president? And it jolly well seems a likely prospect from where I stand!" His heavy shoulders shook visibly.

Peter couldn't reply quickly. It wasn't that he was surprised at anything his father did. He hadn't put the pieces together with what Townsend had told him.

"He's always been a maverick, suh," said Peter, then added hastily, "Ah'm not saying this in his defense. Ah'm just not clear on what he's done."

"A maverick's one thing, my boy," replied the governor, still moving about the room abstractly. He paused to glance out the window for a moment, then turned to the man in bed. "You're not clear on what he's done, eh? Well, I'll tell you, Peter. I'll tell you exactly what he's done. That son of a bitch just sold his son for thirty pieces of silver! That's what he's done. That legal document I glanced at so carelessly moments ago gave the Mexican *Federales* the legal right to transport you to Mexico City to be tried for treason against the Mexican Constitutional government, during the period of time you were evidently married to some Mexican baggage who, it turns out, is and has been a spy for the revolutionaries—namely Pancho Villa."

Peter grew alert. "But, how did he—how did my father know? I took every precaution to keep my life and my activities hidden from the public eye." As soon as he'd spoken, he realized the futility of the words. William Benson had access to and could uncover any man's secret life if he had a mind. That's what made him so feared among the circles of his peers.

At a loss to explain his father's participation, Peter wanted to set the record straight about Madelaina. "Foah youah edification, suh," he began. "She's not baggage, suh. She's the daughtuh of a highborn *gachupín*, a blueblood. As a matter of fact, suh," he said almost reluctantly, "she's the daughtuh of General Alvaro Obregon who presently commands the formidable Fourth Sonora Battalion, one of Mexico's most important redoubts."

Hampton Townsend's chin dropped in astonishment. He sat at the foot of the bed, one foot dangling free over the edge Suddenly he slammed a fist into the palm of his other hand. "The hell you say, boy! The hell you say!" He compressed his lips tightly, then bit his underlip in thought. For several moments the room was silent The only sounds came from an open window—a sudden fluttering of pigeons roosting on the hospital eaves when frightened by the loud sounds of horns coming from the new horseless carriages slowly replacing the equestrian mode of travel. Stanley Steamers and Haynes-Appersons were two of the most prestigious automobiles in Texas and could be found any place in El Paso with rambunctious drivers blowing their horns, frightening people half to death. *Why am I thinking about such mechanical conveyances,* wondered Peter, *when history is about to be made in one form or another by the steamroller of power standing a few feet away.*

Peter turned his attention to Hampton Townsend who continued to pummel his palm with a balled fist. Here, thought Peter, is a man used to all the political ploys at every level of government. Here was an inscrutable wheeler-dealer, who as a young man had fought the Indians for land, a man who'd worked his way through Harvard and fought side by side with Teddy Roosevelt as they charged up San Juan Hill in Santiago de Cuba. Here was a man who knew how to live by his wits and could exercise the diplomacy and cunning of a king. The strength of his personality was such that he projected his mental climate without a word or glance. And Peter knew he was presently preparing to do battle with another formidable Texan, his father, William Benson.

Hampton Townsend rose to his feet, rearranging the starched cuffs under his coat sleeves. One hand slickly caressed his tie into place. He was a tall man and in the next few moments, Peter thought, as deadly as William Benson.

"I've never revealed this to a soul, Peter, but it's

753

something I must tell you, before I set my plans into motion I've avoided—literally avoided—confrontation with Bill Benson ever since he lured Jennifer Duprez from my nuptial bed. Oh, don't look so surprised. Your mother and I were lovers long before Bill Benson entered the picture. You didn't know this? But, then, how could you? Jenny died when you were still a young man." Townsend reached into his back pocket and produced a silver flask. He poured himself a jigger of whiskey, offered some to Peter, and when he refused, he replaced it into his pocket. He smacked his lips heartily after he downed it, then continued.

"There's been bad blood between us long before you were born, my boy. We never took time to resolve our differences, mainly at the urging of your beloved mother—rest her soul. I made it a point to keep out of Bill's way, although I'm sure he didn't exercise the same prudence. Later, when I began to hear of the shabby treatment he gave the woman I loved, I had to keep my peace. After all, Jenny did pick Bill over me to marry. He was her husband under God and law. There's not much a disappointed suitor can do when spurned

"Then one day I received a letter from your mother, telling me all about you, what a fine lad you were, and the aspirations she had for you. Medicine, she said. You intended to study medicine and be a doctor. Was that it?"

Peter nodded. His curiosity piqued by this revelation, he lit a cigarette and sat with rapt attention as he listened to the distinguished man.

"We were close, your mother and I. Went to school together—childhood sweethearts. We should have married," he reflected sadly. "We were meant for each other, but I guess I somehow didn't spark the fires that burned deeply in her at the time. The depth of her emotions was lost to me because I was pursuing a political career at the time which took most of my attention. It wasn't until she wrote to me that I recognized her despondency over the unrequited love that drove

754

her after you were born. You see, my boy, Bill Benson always believed you were my son—not his. But it wasn't true. I wished it was the truth—that you were the seed of my loins, but he was wrong. You're his son all right, but it's easy to see you inherited your mother's compassion." Townsend lit up a cigar and puffed on it as he sat in the white metal chair opposite Peter. He leaned back, tilting the chair against the wall.

"I was proud of you when I heard you left home rather than cowing to Bill Benson. If you were my flesh and blood, I couldn't have been prouder and more pleased that you refused to buckle under his dictatorship. I followed your career from the moment you left Seven Moons to become a soldier of fortune. I hoped many times that we'd be drawn together. I hoped you might even pursue a political career. And then one day—one day while speaking with my friend Doroteo Arango, whom you know as Francesco Pancho Villa—I learned you'd become a trusted friend of his. Oh, I was aware you'd joined his Gringo Brigade in the early days before Madero took the reins of government, but I had assumed you'd gone away, guided by other interests.

"Through your knowledge—firsthand, I might add—I assumed that between us we could help settle this terrible infamy—this butchery taking place in the land of our southern neighbors. You realize, Peter, only the Rio Grande separates America from Mexico, and the differences in our standards of living keep those poor people in virtual slavery? They haven't ever been able to shake the shackles of foreign oppressors. How could they when their own kind sells out to the highest bidder?"

"Why is it that men forget their own roots when tempted with power and wealth?" asked Peter quietly. "Diaz—that freedom fighter who expelled Maximilian—was no better once in office. Graft and corruption ran rampant. Madero fell into the trap—not as much because he was less corrupt—and was killed for his efforts. Now, Huerta—oh, this man, Huerta—" Peter stopped, recalling all the things Madelaina had told him about the man who sat on the presidential throne in Mexico City. "Well, sir, he just can't be permitted to remain in power. Villa is right in fighting for Mexico's life."

Governor Townsend nodded silently. "We were speaking of William Benson. It's something I must get off my chest, boy. I was only a state senator at the time—before I became governor—when I began to smell the brand of William Benson's burning opposition to every bit of legislation I promoted. Hell, I was beginning to become the joke of the capital. 'If Townsend backs a bill, you could bet sure money and win that Benson will oppose it.' Those were the words that permeated the senate. An' if Townsend blocks a bill, five would get you ten that Benson would support it regardless of the issues. If I hadn't been so obstinate and bull-headed in my effort to save face, I'd have used reverse psychology on your father and publically supported those issues I didn't believe in just to make certain they'd get Benson's backing and victory. I didn't have those kind of guts then. A senator's political future depends on the calibre of issues he backs, regardless of their success." He smiled tightly at the irony.

Hampton Townsend paused abruptly. "What in blue blazes am I doing diggin' up the buried past and beating my gums about such things when we've got to resolve the business of your life?" Once again he reached for the silver flask, uncorked it, and tilted it to his lips, gulping freely. "Ahhh." He smacked his lips again. "Now then, we've gotta concentrate on you. Can you walk yet? Have they tried moving you about? What's your prognosis, my boy?" Suddenly the governor stopped. He leaned in and grabbed Peter's wrist, his face blanched whiter than the sheets on the bed. "The daughter of General Alvaro Obregon, you said?" His mind turned inward, struggling for total recall. *"Madelaina Obregon?"*

Peter nodded, regarding the governor with gravity.

"By the roaring blue balls of thunder," he exclaimed. "She's the very woman William Benson recently married in El Paso!" Townsend sank back into the chair, dumbfounded and aghast at the revolting situation looming before him.

Peter's troubled eyes swept over the governor's swollen features. It was pointless to ask him to repeat his words. He'd heard him loud and clear. There was no point in contesting his words, in insisting that Madelaina would have never succumbed to a William Benson if he, Peter Duprez, hadn't treated her so shabbily at their last encounter. The next few moments were filled with wild despair as the words struck at him deeper and deeper. No, he told himself, Madelaina wouldn't do such a thing. Never! Never in a million years! *She loves me! She loves me! She had to.* But his memories dug up moments that struck terror in his heart. The money bag bearing the William Benson brand in Madelaina's dressing room swam past his eyes. She said it had been a gift from Manuelito Perez. He believed her. He had seen no reason to reveal to her that he was Benson's son. Now, in hindsight, he realized he should have, so she wouldn't have been deluded by his father.

Why had she done this? Had she believed the story planted by Valerie Townsend? Had she intended to teach him a lesson? How could he have told her straight out he was acting as liaison among Pancho Villa, Governor Townsend, and President Wilson? Espionage for the revolutionary forces! To have told her would only make her situation more perilous. Peter forced himself to sit up in bed. His eyes were glazed in disbelief. He tremblingly lit another cigarette, took two puffs, and nervously snuffed them out. He felt like a wild animal in those moments. He wanted to spring from the bed, run outside and find his father, and finish this thing between them once and for all. Instead, he gave in to a feeling of absolute weakness that engulfed him, a feeling of hopelessness and helplessness and fell back weakly on the pillows.

Watching him, Hampton Townsend felt a flush of anger, both at William Benson and at himself for having been so outspoken. He could have waited a few days until Peter gained his strength. The crimson flush on his face deepened. He rose to his feet, and pointing a finger at Peter, he said in a voice as thorny as barbed wire, "I'll fight him, this time. This time I'll fight him with the same weapons, Peter! Bill's gone too far. Did he know of your marriage to this *gachupín*?" he asked, trying to make sense of Benson's last obscenity. "He must have! No one can tell me he didn't. Bill Benson knows everything he involves himself with, and no one can tell me different." He shuddered with rage. "Bastard! He's made his own rules for so long, he has no respect for the rights of others. I'll be damned if I'll let him win this time, my boy." The governor had chewed his cigar to shreds. He moved in closer to the bed and studied the pale, drawn face of the younger, more muscular man. His voice grew stronger, more compelling, his manner more decisive. "His own son! Imagine! His own son! Listen, Peter. You'll have to stay out of it for a while. Complain to the doctors, contrive a few more ailments. Let 'em think you aren't responding to treatment. I'll need time to reconnoiter. Some way I've gotta get you outa here and I'll need the governor's office to do it. I'm not about to let them extradite you. Damnit to hell, you're an American citizen! If I have to induce President Wilson to intervene with his army, I won't let 'em take you!"

"Do that, Governor, and all youah plans with Pancho Villa will go down a sewer," said Peter quietly, watching the smoke from his cigarette spiral to the ceiling. "If ah know mah politickin', suh, Huerta might just make a quick pact with the Kaiser's men, and German-made barbed wire will be strung up across ouah borduhs, and we'll be sucked into a worse war than the one already brewing in Europe."

"I can't and won't let them take you. Not if I have to enlist the militia to protect you!" The inexorable

758

note in Governor Townsend's voice reached Peter's ears.

"Hasn't the governor and his family already demanded too much of you," he asked wryly. "First, I ask your cooperation in this clandestine affair, then you're felled by the bullets shot by my hot-headed, spoiled brat of a daughter—nearly killed, and now this!"

Peter's eyes snapped open. "Then it wasn't some dream? Some figment of my imagination that I saw Valerie before the shots were fired?"

"You saw her and never mentioned a word to me?" asked Townsend, fully overwhelmed by the lad's loyalty.

Before Peter could reply, a sharp rap at the door, a loud pounding, and an attempt to force the door open brought the governor hastily toward the exit. He removed the obstruction under the handle and the door burst open with four men flying into the room in a rage. The Mexican agent, Leopoldo, and Fenwick from the State Department, accompanied by a nurse and a doctor, composed themselves when they saw everything in order.

"What exactly is the meaning of this?" demanded Governor Townsend, affecting to grow more indignant by the moment. "How dare you break into this chamber? Aren't I entitled to a few moments of privacy with my son-in-law?"

Apologies were in order, and while the men spoke their humblest regrets at the intrusion, the nurse moved in to take Peter's temperature. The doctor took his blood pressure and shook his head regretfully.

"I'll have to ask that you all leave. The patient is in stress and must be sedated."

Two of governor's aides appeared at the door, wondering what the ruckus was about.

"It's all right," the governor reassured them, reaching for his hat. "I was just leaving." He walked to Peter's side. "Now you rest comfortably. Don't you be

759

in any hurry to leave. You've had a serious operation and the important thing is that you recuperate. How long do you suppose it will be, Doctor, before the patient is ready to leave?"

"I have no idea," replied the physician, readying a needle to sedate Peter. "His pressure's up—too high, Excellency."

"Then, you think he shouldn't be moved?" The words were loud and clear enough for both Fenwick and Señor Leopoldo to hear.

"Decidedly not, Mr. Governor. This patient shouldn't be moved for at least two more weeks—perhaps four. Any movement might cause the wounds to open up and bleed again."

"Thank you, Doctor." Townsend winked at Peter, who remained unmoving on the bed as the shot was administered. He nodded to the others and left the premises with his aides, stopping briefly at the door to wave to Peter.

Peter Duprez lay on the bed, fatigued and weakened from the conversation. The emotional shock done to him had sapped his energy as well as his hope. Too many things swam about in his befuddled brain. Madelaina—Valerie—his father, William Benson—and his mother's faded picture superimposed above them all.

The narcotic began taking effect and the pain in his lower extremities, as acute as it was earlier when the governor had been there, began to abate. He felt lightheaded. A myriad of scenes formed in his mind, none as heavy as the earlier ones. He felt a sense of movement, saw a flash of strange faces crowd around him. Still more movement. He alternated between lucidity and a murky consciousness in which time had no meaning and thoughts were nonexistent. If there was confusion in his mind, if there was total disorientation to his senses, Peter had no real way of knowing it.

He awakened weeks later in strange surroundings. That he'd been drugged was a foregone conclusion. The identity of the drugs were not known to him.

Their effects—the cold, clammy feelings of withdrawal, stuffed nasal passages, chills and weakness as each ache in his body was magnified intensely each time he moved—remained with him for the next few days. He had no idea where he was, only that the tropical atmosphere and the balmy breezes indicated he was somewhere near a body of water. The room had a tiled floor, heavy oak beams across the ceiling, and a fireplace of polished stones. He wore a robe, and when he first awakened, he managed to get to his feet and tremblingly hang on to bedpost, chair, and wall as he made his way to the open-air balcony. He was in a villa at the top of a mountain overlooking a magnificent spread of blue sea. He inhaled the sea air and held tightly to the balcony as a wave of dizziness engulfed him, causing his head to spin and nearly making him lose his balance. His blue eyes, still dull from the heavy sedation, blurred for several moments until they grew accustomed to the intensity of the glaring overhead sun.

Immediately below him was a beautiful tiled terrace with furniture and a great abundance of greenery. Below that was a sheer drop to the sea. Slightly north of him on the ground floor was an enormous gate with four armed guards. Beyond the locked gate, halfway down the steep incline was a small structure resembling a gazebo. He couldn't make it out, but men, the size of ants viewed from this distance, wore uniforms and were armed equally as well as those closer to him. A few rare and exotic birds flew about in an aviary next to the terraced patio. Never had he seen the likes of such colorful flamingoes and cockatoos and parrots. Some tropical paradise, surmised Peter—*or else I'm dreaming.*

Walking slowly back into the room, he caught his reflection in a mirror. He was thickly bearded, his hair longer than usual. He'd lost several pounds, judging from the hollows on his face and the flatness of his stomach. If only he didn't feel so weak, so fatigued and depressed. He attempted to reconstruct parts of his life, and was frightened when his memory wouldn't respond. It seemed he had no recollection of anything except for this moment.

He knew nothing for certain—not even that he was alive—until he pinched himself. It wasn't until later, when a young man entered his room and introduced himself as Dr. Gonsalvez, that it was confirmed he was a guest of a high-ranking Federal officer in the Mexican government. He was told he was in the hacienda of this mysterious host, near the seacoast village of Santa Rosalia in the state of Sonora. Dr. Gonsalvez reluctantly refused to name the Federal officer's name. "In due time, you'll meet your host, Señor Duprez. Meanwhile, it is my responsibility to make certain your health vastly improves. Perhaps you'll be kind enough to explain what exactly happened to you? Since I have no medical or hospital records on which to base my prescription of medication and therapy, it would greatly assist me in my efforts. I'm overwhelmed by the major surgical techniques performed on your body."

"Ah was stung by a pea-shooter," said Peter snidely.

The high-toned doctor smiled with the unmistakable aroma of aristocracy. "That's some pea-shooter. More like cannon, eh?" He moved away from the bed. "We've taken into account everything to make your stay comfortable. I had hoped for better cooperation from you, but perhaps in a day or two when you grow less comfortable, you'll confide what was done to help heal you. If you need or desire anything—anything at all—don't hesitate to ring." He gestured to a pull cord close to the bed.

"A bottle of tequila, newspapers, cigars, and a roomful of cooperatin' little *chiquitas* might not be bad for a start," said Peter beginning to feel the necessity and urge to couple.

"I'll provide the newspaper and cigarettes, but I can't promise the tequila or obliging women," the doctor said discreetly.

Peter forced a light laugh. The atmosphere was relaxing, and the sun on the balcony would be a splendid way for him to regain the sun-bronzed look that faded into a near-death pallor when Valerie pumped him with lead. Hell's bells! Damned little vixen, he thought. She could've killed me!

The newspapers didn't arrive until the next day, but the accumulation of them for the past six months provided plenty of reading—the kind he relished. News of Pancho Villa's countless victories!

He read and reread them so many times, he could recite the headlines by rote: *VILLA CAPTURES SANTA ROSALIA! VILLA FORCES CAPTURE FORT IN ZACATECAS! DURANGO FALLS TO VILLISTAS! SAN ANDREAS—CHIHUAHUA CITY —JUAREZ—ALL SURRENDERED TO PANCHO VILLA*. Victory followed in Tierra Blanca, Santa Isabella, Conejos, Mapimi, Bermejillo, San Pedro de Las Colimas, Saltillo. There were a few defeats: Zacatecas fell back into Federal hands, but shortly thereafter Villa masterminded a grand military coup, swept out the *Federales*, and recaptured the stronghold.

The solidarity and growing might of General Villa's army had fairly shattered the resolve of Huerta's *Federales* who found themselves retreating more than advancing these days. The futility of resistance to the hordes of well-armed, militarily trained men was well taken by each garrison commander whenever the awesome army of conical sombreros and Winchesters sprang as if from nowhere to launch savage flanking movements to wild, hectic cries of *"Viva Villa! Viva La Revolucion!"*

Peter Duprez smiled when he read the rave reviews of the zephyr Villa, who moved with incredible swiftness and seemed to be in all places at one time. Even in El Dorado, a place remote to the machinations of Pancho Villa, the whispers of the people came in the form of a song, "La Cucaracha." It was on the lips of the lowly land *peóns*, the fishermen, and the hillsmen. Peter heard it morning, noon, and night until he felt he could no longer stand to hear it without taking up arms and following wherever Pancho's trail led.

On one of his visits with Peter, Dr. Gonsalvez had made it perfectly clear that any attempt to escape would inevitably result in death to him. He explained further that the estate was guarded by armed guards—all crack shots. That in kennels at the rear of the villa, a pack of ferocious Dobermans, trained to kill, were housed. He suggested tactfully that as long as Peter remained cooperative and made no attempt to reject the hospitality of so generous a host, he would be afforded the best luxuries at hand.

And until Peter regained his strength and his former vigor, he entertained no ideas of departing from such hospitality.

Shortly after his arrival at the Villa El Dorado, Peter sat on the balcony soaking up the sun as the servants entered to clean his suite. It was the usual routine that had taken place in the past except there was a new girl, dressed in the typical Indian skirt and blouse. She shyly kept her head averted from him as she skirted by the French doors about her business.

Something about her, thought Peter, seemed familiar. No, it's just the sun's heat making me tipsy, he answered himself. She passed him again, and this time her dark eyes stared at him seductively. Just as quickly she darted out of sight. Peter smiled. She's asking for it, he thought. He felt a little excitement stirring in him—not as in the past, but it was there and Peter sighed in relief. The bullet wound had done much damage, and for a time, with little feeling in his manhood, he worried that he might not be the man he'd been in the past. The doctors in El Paso advised that it would take time and he mustn't panic if he was unable to satisfy himself sexually.

Matter of fact, he hadn't the strength nor the desire to participate in any sexual caper for a while, and he felt certain the drugs administered to him to reduce the pain were responsible. He simply hadn't given it much thought until this moment, when the sight of the bronze-skinned mestizo with her fiery dark eyes that oozed seduction stimulated his appetite.

He could hear the women talk as they changed the bed linens and dusted. A guard, armed and ready for anything, always stood guard inside the door as they dutifully went about their chores. When they were finished, Peter remained in the sun, thinking he'd tell Dr. Gonsalvez to return the dark-skinned charmer to him later. He picked up the paper and read of Pancho Villa's recent assault on a Federal garrison, a story by a crack journalist, Miguel Guerra. Monterrey had been taken by Villa in an astounding manner. "But in and around the desert plains and foothills between Bermejillo and Torreon," wrote the reporter, "one of the most dramatic and critical events of the Mexican Revolution took place." The reporter went on to say, "By the sheer magic of one man's name—Francesco Villa— came the hordes of soldiers that composed the entire army of irregulars of all Mexico in one enormous force for a conference of the *jefes*.

"Pancho Villa arrived with a thousand strong. Tiburco with 200, Urbina with 800. Herrera with 400 first-class cavalry fighters, Contreras with 300. Then came the heads of lesser *guerrillo* bands and one man in particular, who instantly made his strength known to Villa. Coronel Rudolfo Fierro succeeded in obtaining a promotion for his unique and indispensable talents in their first confrontation."

Guerra went on to say, "Pancho Villa addressed the conference of chiefs with the suggestion that, 'We the most powerful single army in all Mexico should without a moment's hesitation advance on the vital city of Torreon and crush it!' And that's exactly what they did. Weapons fired overhead, cracking smartly, *vaqueros* shouting their *yiiipees*, and cheers of '*olé*' and '*Viva Villa*' filled the desert air. And as the remarkable force of military strength faced southward toward the Federal redoubt, the air filled with Villa's marching song—'La Cucaracha!' It was the most exciting sight of my life," commented Miguel Guerra. "The thrill of seeing such colorful pageantry within a well-disciplined army, to hear the clatter of horses and rattle of cannon wheels combined with the song of the people. Sombreroed, gun-belted soldiers and their *soldaderas* sung from the tops of trains, from their horses, and on foot. The Gringo Brigade, possibly the most colorful division in Villa's entourage, those Yankees who've been loyal to his cause, sang the loudest. They even drowned out the Indian drums and the guitars played by tequila-drinking soldiers. The song seemed to lift them right out of the depths of despair to which they were born and elevate them to a plateau where hopes, dreams, and aspirations for better life would come true.

"And then," continued Guerra, "It began. With the deadly intuition which has made Pancho Villa, General-in-Chief of the Northern Division, the most powerful military force in all Mexico, the *premier jefe* hurled General Urbina's brigade along the course of the river of Torreon to wipe out the defenses of the *Federales*. Herrera's magnificent Juarez Brigade moved against defenses of the western flank. *Federale* General Campa, entrenched with artillery and men repairing fortifications, put up an aggressive battle against Villa, but it was all to no avail. Even when Villa's artillery hit them, tearing apart massive defenses with shrapnel and explosives; even as Villa's cavalry smashed their flanks and his infantry ripped through the gaps in perfect order, the *Federales* wouldn't—couldn't—believe that it was General Francesco Villa defeating them by peerless strategy and top-notch soldiering. Two days later General Francesco Villa entered Torreon behind fleeing *Rurales* and Federal soldiers. Arms, supplies, trains, and prisoners all went to Pancho Villa. Correction, please. All *Orozquista* loyalists among the prisoners were instantly executed according to a promise made once by General Villa, a man true to his word."

Miguel Guerra ended his column by adding something of note. "General Villa has embarked on his first attempt to govern a city by establishing a garrison. He borrowed money from the money lenders to pay his war debts and finance future campaigns. The destitute families of the city were provided with food and clothing. Most important, General Villa built hospitals. Using railroad cars, he ordered them scrubbed and re-painted and equipped with requisitioned army cots, tables, stoves, and ice containers. And everything covered in clean white sheets. He hired the best doctors and established a medical corps. He enlisted the aid of every sub-chief to locate and return with all the medical supplies they could lay their hands on, including morphine."

Miguel further embellished his column by lauding the efforts of General Francesco Villa and openly declaring that this remarkable and dedicated man had become civilized. "His consuming passion for the welfare of the wounded, dying, and maimed supersedes that of the government's highest office. Presidente Huerta has never seen fit to establish the much-needed hospitals for those poor unfortunates who were willing to sacrifice their lives for their country. Neither Diaz before him nor Madero concerned themselves thusly."

Peter felt pangs of nostalgia as he read the vivid, clear-sighted report. What he wouldn't give to be with and share the glory with his old friends. His mind churned, wondering how this paper could be dispatched to Washington to President Wilson. He had to learn how Villa had truly reformed and become a leader of his people.

"*Señor,*" came the whisper.

Peter's head turned to the armed guard who walked in toward him. He removed his cap and bowed. "Dr. Gonsalvez wishes to inform you, the women are finished. He has left one of them for your pleasure." He bowed and left the balcony and disappeared into the room. Peter followed him inside, abounding with curiosity. Inside, the guard stood at the door, pointing to the voluptuous creature stretched out on the bed, lying naked in a seductive and languid pose.

Peter's eyes shot up in delight. He gazed upon her face and was about to exclaim aloud. He was stopped

767

short by the warning look in her eyes. Turning to the guard, he pointed to the door. "You don't intend to watch us, *muchacho*?"

The red-faced guard instantly left the room, locking the door behind him.

Peter turned to the girl on the bed. "Lucia! Lucia San Miguel! What in the name of Satan are you doing here?"

She held a finger to her lips and spoke aloud for the benefit of the guard in case he eavesdropped. "*Si, señor*. I am sent by the *patrón* to make your visit enjoyable. Your wish is my command." She led Peter in closer to the bed.

There was tequila and glasses and wine and a tray of cheese and fresh fruits on the table nearby. "First, gringo, we make love, then we talk," she suggested in complete compliance with his own feelings.

A shiver ran through Lucia as his lips pressed hers and the old expertise of Peter Duprez came into play. His lips caressed her temples and ears, and her own excitement grew insatiably. Her fingers, strong and sensuous, began to massage his shoulders, the back of his neck, smoothing away the tension as she'd done in the past. Her body rose to meet his, filling out the curves of his lean hard and sun-bronzed physique. Peter kept his eyes closed just to feel the warmth of a woman's body and the urgent need rising in her which used to excite him.

Lucia reached for him and with a teasing laugh kissed his eyelids. Her hands slid down slowly along his arms under his waist and over his hips and thighs. In a slow circular movement, and with the touch of a *mariposa*—a butterfly—her fingertips touched the surface hair. She felt him shudder uncontrollably and laughed with glee. "Lucia hasn't lost her touch, eh, *gringo*?"

"Not that ah can tell, *chiquita*." In a quick movement, Peter turned his body and picked her up, hoisting her over him. She straddled him now, bent over him, her firm young breasts dangling dangerously close

768

to his mouth, teasing him. They played for a time; he reaching for her nipples, she eluding him.

Lucia glanced at his chest, at the twisted railroad track of scars reaching into his groin. *"Gringo!"* she expressed alarm. "What happened to ju? *Demonio!* Ees like a cannon exploded on ju, no?"

"It's nothing," he murmured.

Lucia slipped off his body, reached for the glasses of tequila she poured earlier, and handed him one. *"Dios mios,"* she muttered. "Ees one lucky theeng ju are alive, *chico."* They touched glasses and downed the firewater.

Her hands busily traced the scar and found their way to his most vital part. For an instant Peter felt terrible that it was limp and unresponsive. Usually he was a step ahead in the physical part of any sexual act. All he had to do was think about it and his body would grow hard with overt desire. He'd been in bed with Lucia for the better part of a half-hour and none of the old responses came to life.

"Gringo, what's the matter? Ju don't like Lucia no more?" She pouted, filled with dismay.

He drew her close to him. "Ah don't know, *chiquita.* Ah just don't know. The doctors told me not to force anything. Ah guess ah was pretty badly shot up. It'll take time."

"Dios mios, gringo. Ju don't think they cut something from ju?"

Her fright, overexaggerated, caused him to laugh. "No, *chiquita.* Ah've just been pretty sick. It'll just take time."

"How much time eet takes, eh?" she asked again in that overly serious manner. This time Peter didn't laugh. He grew annoyed.

Caressing her breasts had formerly given him such an erotic response, but now, nothing. Absolutely nothing. He closed his eyes, hoping to concentrate on her and the erotic past they shared together. Again nothing. He forced himself to think of Madelaina—the true love of his life. He sighed deeply and pictured her as

769

they first met, how they loved on the *Mozambique,* and the lingering memories of their countless lovemaking moments. Again nothing.

Impotence was something frightening to Peter Duprez. He never dreamed he might be forced to deal with its frightening ramifications. He tried to tell himself to stop this ridiculous speculation. That it merely took time like anything else in need of repair. After all, a broken arm took time to heal. A leg—anything broken had to be repaired, didn't it?

Covering his temporary embarrassment and his own frustration caused by a willing mind, duelling with an uncooperative body, he turned Lucia over and held her in his arms. "Nevuh mind foah now, *chiquita.* Let's put the time ta good use. Tell me what youah doing heah. How did ya find me?"

Lucia snuggled in closer to him, her lips close to his ear.

"Ju know where ju are, *gringo?*"

Peter shook his head. "Santa Rosalia?"

"Ju are in the hacienda of General Alvaro Obregon, the father of your *mujer,* Little Fox."

Peter held her at arm's length and studied her intently.

"Ees true. Word reached us ten days ago. *Jefe* Villa say to me, 'Lucia, ju go find Tom Meex and bring heem to me,' *Pues, amigo.* Eees a beeg job for Lucia."

"You've seen Little Fox, my *mujer?* Where is she, Lucia? Tell me."

"*Que va,* tell me, be patient and Lucia will explain." She sipped more tequila. "Ju want more?"

"Ah want ya ta talk a bit faster, *chiquita.* Any time we may be interrupted."

"*Bueno. Bueno, gringo.* Ju must give Lucia time to prepare her words." She set the glass on the nearby table. "Ju got a smoke for Lucia—marijuana?"

"No. Cigarettes are on the table." He waited patiently while she lit up two cigarettes. She handed him one and smoked the other greedily, inhaling deeply. "Ees not like marijuana, but ees not bad. Leesten,

770

amigo," she continued in her pigeon yankee. "Ees better I talk so—they weel not understand my words. Is A-O.K.?"

Peter felt like strangling her for the obvious way she was stalling. Meanwhile, one of her hands was busy on his limp sex organ, trying to instill life into its lifeless shape. She was working her little heart out—to no avail.

"Huerta's men kidnapped ju in El Paso. Word came to the *jefe*, and Little Fox has been worried to death over you. Not far from us is Cuidad Obregon, a village taken by General Obregon. Soon Pancho and the father of Little Fox will contest each other in a battle to end all battles. Before all theese happens, Obregon will come here for a holiday to prepare for the beeg explosions."

"Y'all mean ah'm heah under the auspices of President Huerta?" asked Peter, trying to tie in her words to something plausible.

"No, Capitán Duprez," said a voice standing in the doorway. "You are here under the auspices of General Alvaro Obregon."

Lucia jumped from the bed and, gathering her clothing instantly, began dressing with lowered, shame-filled eyes. She glanced at Major General Felipe de Cordoba, waiting to be severely chastised for her feeble attempts at performing an act of liaison between Villa and Peter Duprez.

"Ah'm not certain what all ya heard," said Peter, pulling on his trousers, "but ah'd appreciate it if no harm comes ta the girl."

"Sorry. She'll receive the same treatment all spies receive," he snapped curtly. "Corporal," he called to the guard outside the door. "Take the girl away and lock her in the servants' quarters under guard. I'll attend to her later." He spoke in clipped, precise tones. He remained silent until Lucia left the room with her escort.

"Look," began Peter. "She said nothing. Nothing at all. Ah don't want any harm to come ta her, heah?"

771

"I admire your chivalry, Capitán Duprez of the Gringo Brigade, but the matter is out of my hands. I don't handle matters for the Secret Service anymore. I am attached to the Fourth Sonora Battalion under the leadership of General Alvaro Obregon. I report directly to him."

"Then you'll promise nothing will happen to the girl?"

"I promise you nothing. Now let's get down to business. We learned through our sources of Huerta's proposed treachery to entrap you in an effort to obstruct Madelaina Obregon, whom I'm sure you understand is the daughter of my commanding general. Despite their political differences, she is, after all, his one and only kin. He wants no harm to befall her at Huerta's hands," said Felipe, unbuttoning his tunic. He removed his snap-brimmed hat and flung it on a table. "Mind if I smoke?"

Peter extended his arm nonchalantly. "Ah'm youah guest, suh. Y'all do just what ya wish, heah?" Peter grew more aware with each passing moment that he was being scrutinized closely by his host. He began to feel a little ill at ease, being stared at by this handsome Mexican officer.

"You understand, *señor*, that if we hadn't intervened, your destiny might have been far more gruesome than this country club atmosphere so generously provided for you."

"Why is it, suh, that the moah you keep talking, the moah ah keep thinking the more gruesome fate might have been less involved?"

"Hardly," replied Felipe, pouring himself a tumbler of tequila. He downed it in two gulps. "Uuuuggghhh," he shuddered. "Why I ever drink this uncivilized fire is beyond me. Mind if I ring for wine?" He pulled the cord at the side of the bed.

Peter remained silent, as he lit a cigarette and puffed on it thoughtfully.

"You are well aware that Pancho Villa's victories

772

have been numerous of late. Have you also been aware that General Obregon has, for a specific purpose, refused to contest Villa? He has to date not sided with Huerta—although he's obligated dutifully to his country with a zealous fervor. He is also *not* committed to Carranza who appears to be the favorite for presidential material. At present, U.S. Generals Hugh Scott and John Pershing are making a report to your American President Wilson on the merits of General Villa. Before General Obregon commits his loyalty to any future president, he wants to make certain his efforts will put the right man in the presidential palace. I'm certain you can understand his concern for both his country and his people."

Peter laughed lightly. He uncrossed his legs and glanced at Felipe through amused eyes. "Ah understand, all right. Ah see that General Obregon has political aspirations that go beyond being general of the Mexican Army."

"Very clever of you to be so discerning. You're right. One day General Obregon will be president of Mexico. No one deserves it more. He has many fine friends across the Yankee border. He's a temperate man with a deep compassion for his fellow man. He's not an incompetent weakling as was Madero whose enemies found him out and made short order of him. His veins don't run rampant with graft and corruption as did his former countryman, Profirio Diaz. Nor does he maintain or support the alcoholic excesses of Huerta or entertain the delusions of grandeur running rampant in his drug-crazed mind. Damnit, Duprez, Huerta's propensity for political assassinations grows more obscene each day and his policies toward your country are nothing short of antagonistic."

"Felipe de Cordoba!" exclaimed Peter in sudden recollection. "Youah Madelaina's friend. Her deah, trusted, and devoted friend. She's spoken about ya often." His face lit up brightly, as he studied the handsome, clean-cut features.

"And you are the gringo husband of Madelaina Obregon," replied Felipe. "The man she sacrificed a royal life to be with. I have long wondered about you, *señor*. I must add, my feelings are not as generous as yours. I have loved Madelaina all my life and probably always will. I find it horrifying that you influenced her to abandon her way of life for one so foul and oppressive. My blood turns cold when I recall how I first saw her after a year as a *campesina* in the camps of Pancho Villa. For this alone, I loathe you."

Peter shrank internally and maintained his outer calm. "If it hadn't been me who opened her mind to the world around her, it might have been someone less concerned foah her welfare, someone who might have loved her less," he said soberly.

A servant brought a tray with wine and crystal glasses. Felipe nodded to her, dismissing her. He poured the wine himself. One for him and one for Peter. He handed the goblet to his guest. They toasted silently and sipped the ruby liquid.

"Ah, much better. A civilized drink, fit for a god," said Felipe, smacking his lips. He sat down in a comfortable chair. "Suppose we get down to business."

"Ah'd like that," replied Peter. Despite Felipe's cold assessment of Peter, the Texan found himself liking the officer in some odd indefinable way.

"My general wishes you to arrange a rendezvous with General Pancho Villa. He wishes to speak with the former *guerrillo* to see where his intentions lie."

Peter's ears perked up instantly. "Y'all realize what youah asking?"

"Believe me, it surprises me as much as it does you."

"Phew." Peter whistled low. He could just picture this confrontation, and the scene he saw wasn't one that might settle any case of indigestion easily.

"There must, of course, be no treachery, no traps, no subversive machinations to do the other in."

"On both sides," added Peter.

"Naturally."

"And that's all?"

"Not quite."

"What then?"

"Your promise to return Madelaina to her father, in exchange for your life and freedom."

Peter's blue eyes grew murky, the color of a stormy sea. "She's mah wife. Y'all ask too much."

"You work it out. Those are the terms and conditions."

"If ah refuse ta comply?"

"We turn you over to Huerta's man, Major General Simon Salomon. You'll spend your days at Madrigal in their den of hell."

"Mah life and freedom are worthless without Madelaina," he told Felipe.

Felipe studied Duprez. "I'm glad you made that apparent. At least I can see why she picked you."

"Besides, ah don't reckon Madelaina would go fer that at all. We've been through too much ta have it all end like the devastation done by one of Villa's tacos."

"Are you aware, *señor*, that during the past year that you've been absent from your *mujer*, she's become Pancho's *numero uno soldadera*? You might say she's become an astute adviser to the *premier jefe*. Is that the kind of life you wish for her?"

"None of us wish foah a life of strife, suh. We are born ta do what we must do ta help ease the pain of others less fortunate. We can't turn from the suffering and weah blinkuhs foah the rest o' ouah born days."

"I haven't the time to exchange philosophies, Señor Duprez. My duty has been completed. Now ah await your reply."

"How can ya be shuah ah'll comply with youah request, General? Once ah get outside these heah walls and join up with Villa, ah just might take my woman and cut for the borduh."

"Ah have no doubt you'll be a man of your word, *señor*," he said calmly. "You see, we have in our pos-

775

session the insurance needed to make certain you'll return."

"And that is—"

"*Your son.*"

776

Chapter 29

Madelaina had hardly slept since the abduction of her son. What meager sleep she did get had been a series of nightmares and obsessions which drove her to near hysteria and caused her to awaken, screaming in the night. Who could have been so cruel as to pluck a helpless three-month-old child from the comfort and security of his mother's breasts? In her son's case, born prematurely and in need of tender loving care, his sudden departure compounded her feelings of insecurity and fright.

Antonetta had offered her solace as best she could and in a way helped to subdue the rising hysterics to which Madelaina was prone to give vent in those few weeks following the infant's disappearance. Even General Villa took time from his countless warring strategies to comfort Little Fox. But there were no words, no expressions of sympathy or consolation to assuage the apprehensive fears for her sanity.

Madelaina had endured too many hardships during those early months of pregnancy: hard, fast riding on horseback, long, tedious journeys, battles and skirmishes where she suffered wounds and bruises. She shot her rifles at the enemy as her growing fetus kicked in her womb protestingly. The morning sickness, the near abortion when she hemorrhaged for a time, it had all been enough tribulation for the dedicated militant. Prior to the height of her pregnancy, she mixed in battle with the other *soldaderas*, expecting no favors, demanding no quarters or special privileges, and finally she delivered the child prematurely, a love child whom she doted on each moment up until she found him missing at her side.

For days following her son's disappearance she searched everywhere, asked everyone she met about the child. She wouldn't eat, wouldn't rest, barely handled her duties. Even after General Villa ordered her to rest, to remove herself from the front lines of battle, she resisted, insisting she had to keep busy to preserve her sanity. When it appeared her child was lost to her forever, it was a different Madelaina who plunged into her duties with a dedicated fervor. She grew silent, more introverted, performed her duties with the movements of an automaton without complaint or comment.

She walked barefoot when necessary, rode when horses became available, stole boots of dead *Federales* encountered in battle, gathered the much-needed weapons and clothing from the corpses of the dead, and continued to train the new *soldaderas* who multiplied in droves after each battle. On orders from General Villa himself, and out of respect for Madelaina's position of trust as an advisor—although Villa hardly let it be known that any woman advised him—the men from various brigades kept their distance.

It was General Villa's orders that Madelaina and Antonetta be heavily chaperoned at all times. However, so as not to incite the girls or add to their frustrations, the fact was known to neither of them. Colonel Rudolfo Fierro, who'd arrived a few military skirmishes back and made himself invaluable to Pancho Villa, had long since attached himself to the *jefe* with a fierce, dedicated loyalty not often seen among the stoic hillsmen. It was only natural that Fierro, always close at hand, would be appointed the honor of keeping his eyes on the women when he wasn't occupied in warring duties.

Even before Madelaina had discovered the affair blooming between Fierro and her alluring red-haired friend, the colonel had demonstrated an unusual fascination for both women. Madelaina had felt his probing, animal eyes on her from the day of his arrival at camp, and after that day she saw him with Antonetta in San Martine, she wondered if he knew she was aware of the affair.

On this day, Madelaina scuffled through the raw lights of an early pink sunset toward the adobe *casa* housing Antonetta. Weighted down by crisscrossed *bandoleros* of ammunition, hip holsters, and guns, she carried a rifle in her hand. Her orange and yellow cotton skirt and blouse were soiled. She was covered from head to toe with the eternal red dust of the desert. Sweat rolled off her face and streaks of dirt diffused any beauty that might be lurking under the mask of dust. The dust she raised scuttling among the *campesinas* turned the color of red clay and followed her like a cloud.

She felt dirty, tired, and exhausted when she entered the adobe dwelling.

Antonetta looked up, pausing as she spread out the remains of her tattered clothing. "Ju know how many times I ask Pancho to buy me some suitable clothing, *chica*? Time and time again. But there ees never time for Antonetta!" She sniffed the air distastefully. "*Dios mios*! What happened to ju? Ju know ju stink, *chica*?" She held her nose repugnantly.

"I know. I know. Ride with me to the River Yaqui, *chica*, to bathe and wash out some clothes. It's early. The sun will dry our clothing before we finish bathing." She shook her head at the redhead playfully. "Why don't you wear pants and a shirt, *chica*? I'm finished wearing skirts! It's too much trouble!"

"And be made laughingstock by the men?" Tonetta wasn't up to hearing cat calls each moment of the day, nor was she able to endure the wrath of Pancho himself who detested pants on a woman. "I will wear what I always wear. But in truth, I grow more disenchanted with everything rapidly," she confided to Little Fox.

"*Vamenos*," replied Madelaina. "We can talk as we bathe in the water. You know for how long I've been dreaming of a bath?"

"From the stink of you, plenty long," retorted the redhead, grabbing her clean clothing and the soiled garments she planned to wash in the river. She rolled them up and strapped the pack to her back. She buckled on a hip holster and gun and followed her friend back along the dusty path toward the corral.

Colonel Rudolfo Fierro, leaning languidly against a wooden support beam in the portico listening to a few of his comrades make jokes, tipped his sombrero forward. Under the shade of the large brim, his dark, beady eyes followed the two women until they mounted their horses and rode off in a northwesterly direction. Desire, craftily concealed behind his cold eyes, was instantly checked so as not to give away his feelings to the other men.

The women found the water delightful. After scrubbing out their soiled garments with bars of soap, they rinsed them out and spread them to dry on a sunbaked boulder at the bend in the Yaqui River, which was hidden by thickets and shrubbery from the passing eye. For a time they swam nude, and then they each took turns soaping their long hair and washing it squeaky clean. They frolicked for a time, like uncaring children, then, when they were spent, they relaxed naked and lazed in the hot sun, close to the jacaranda trees.

Antonette picked up on the conversation they'd begun earlier as if there'd been no break in the continuity. She reflected on her disenchantment at the substantial change in Pancho Villa's comportment and attitude. More than the noticeable change in the *jefe*, she protested the burning presence of Rudolfo Fierro.

"*Dios mios, chiquita*, how in the name of God did Pancho take up with such a barbarian?" she asked in a voice that seemed testy and guileful to Little Fox.

"Ask Pancho," retorted Madelaina, glancing sharply at the other woman.

"*Que va*, ask Pancho? Ju think I'm crazy? Since Fierro arrives in Pancho's domain, he tells me nothing." The redhead lifted herself up on one elbow off the grassy knoll on the riverbank and shook out her damp hair. She glanced at Madelaina's frail body and

780

shook her head negatively. "Ju better put some meat on those flanks, *chica*, or no man will look at ju when this hell of revolution ends."

Madelaina laughed gently, shaded her eyes with her hand, and turned to glance at the stunning redhead with turquoise eyes reflecting a thousand suns.

"Tell me, Tonetta, why do you stay? Why subject yourself to these gross inconveniences when you could be back in El Paso living like a grand lady? You have no stomach for revolution—for fighting, shooting, none of this."

"Listen, why ju think I grow disenchanted? Of late, Tonetta thinks more and more of the life she left behind. Why do I stay? Ah, *chica*. Why for sure? I stay because I love Panchito. But I begin to question such dedication. Each day I ask myself more and more why I stay. Shall I tell you something? Each day I cannot answer myself, so you see?" She shook out her hair to dry. "It's crazy, no? I do not see Pancho. He is too busy to make love with me as in the past. Oh, *querida*," she sighed despondently. "I admit I am not born to such a life. Even ju—why ju stay? From where comes such dedication? Ju don't love Pancho like Tonetta loves Pancho?"

"You think the love of a man could keep me here?" she asked.

"The love of a man drew you to such a life."

"That was long ago."

"Then why ju stay?"

"Because—because—" Madelaina faltered. "Because I have no place to go."

"*Que va*, no place to go? Ju married William Benson, no? Ju can go to the hacienda of Benson and remain his wife. Listen, you recall that hacienda a few kilometers outside of Juarez, where Pancho camped before the battle?"

Madelaina reached over and took a few rolled marijuana cigarettes from the saddle bag, where she placed her leather pouch, given her by Tolomeo. She struck a red devil against the rock and lit one. She took a few hits from it and handed it to Tonetta. The redhead puffed and inhaled deeply, then falling against the rock, she said cryptically. "Like jur earrings, it's called Seven Moons, just like the *rancho* from where Pancho and me and the others took you, near Amarillo."

Madelaina glanced sharply again at her friend. Did she know in some way that Peter and Benson were father and son? She hadn't mentioned it—ever. Had she?

"You know I can never return to him. It's useless to even discuss the subject." Breathing deeply, she allowed a relaxation to overtake her. She needed this rest off by herself. For so long she'd been wound up like a spring, tense enough to snap. She'd been cold, hard, and unemotional for so long, she was afraid she'd lost all her feelings. Since her baby had been kidnapped, she had closed everyone from her.

"Only the other day, I tell Panchito this man Fierro frightens me. Pancho laughed. He told me Fierro is valuable to him, that he was a first-class brakeman who works on trains—that he can even send messages through the air—"

"You mean telegrams?" She puzzled at Antonetta's line of talk.

"*Si*, whatever." Antonetta spoke in Spanish, so she could ramble without stumbling over her pigeon yankee. "That desert weasel Tomás Urbino found Fierro when Pancho was in the *calabozo*. It seems that Fierro is an A-number one combat leader in whom Pancho finds no fault. I protested that he was too bloodthirsty and shall I tell you what Pancho replied?"

Before Madelaina could answer, Antonetta's outrage accelerated. "Pancho said, 'True, my little kitten, the man is a bastard. But when it comes to war, he's the kind I want—not saints.'"

Madelaina managed a slight smile. "Pancho makes sense, no?"

"Oh, ju are terrible!" she exploded in pigeon yankee. "What can I expect to hear from a woman who has become a man—hard like a rock, eh? You and Pancho are alike! Ju know what else Pancho tells me? He swore Fierro killed more than 100 artillerymen by himself—at one time!"

Madelaina's eyes widened. "Without exaggeration—100 at one time?" Her eyes tilted playfully in mild tolerance.

"Urbina saw it with his own eyes. Fierro told the Redflaggers to get off the train. He lined them up along the tracks and told them he was going to kill them. With a .45 in each hand and two aides walking alongside him to hand him loaded pistols when the bullets in each gun ran out, he shot them all."

"Every last one?" She subdued her mirth as she listened to Tonetta's exaggeration.

"Ayeiii, Little Fox. Every last one. That story is what made Pancho take notice of such a man—no, such an animal! And now, I tell you, Madelaina, they are two of a kind—Villa and Fierro. Fierce, bloodthirsty, irresistible, and of late, *muy* frightening to me. Pancho is not like *my* Pancho of the early revolution. He means business this time and it is this business which frightens me."

Madelaina, still naked, sat up on the rock and drew her knees up to her and rested her chin on them. She took a last puff from the rolled grass and flipped it into the water and watched it disappear in the ripple.

"We are none of us the way we were in the early days of the revolution." She turned to face the redhead. "Tonetta, if you feel so strongly against Fierro, why do you let him make love to you?" she asked impatiently.

Antonetta's face grew redder than her hair. She stammered, stuttered, and her lips quivered as she searched for the proper response. She knew that somehow Madelaina had guessed her secret. It was of no use to pretend or to continue to play the silly game.

"How long have you known?"

"Almost from the beginning, I suppose."

"From the beginning?"

"One day at San Martine . . . before the birth of my son."

783

"Ahhh," she said knowingly, recalling that wonderful summer day. "That was the first time." Her eyes filled with mysterious lights she alone was privy to.

"Why do you humiliate yourself by calling him a beast, an animal?"

"So no one guesses what I feel for him."

"And what of Pancho?"

Antonetta shrugged. "He has his Lucita."

"You know what it would mean if he discovers your treachery?"

"I know. I know. I cannot help myself. If he didn't leave me alone so much—"

"What if someone like Urbina had seen you—or any of those other *campesinas* who would gladly pull out your hair, just for a chance to taste Pancho's passions?"

Antonetta shrugged as if she had no control over destiny.

"Think it over, *chiquita*. Think it over very carefully what you and Fierro do at this critical time. Earlier you said they are two of a kind, both Villa and Fierro. That Pancho is not like *your* Pancho of the early revolution. That his business frightens you. *Bueno*. You are far too smart, *gatitta*, to not know how all of us—you, me, Pancho, Fierro, Urbina, Richards—all of us have changed. What is it that makes you disloyal to both men, now? Are you afraid you'll lose Fierro to the same cause as that which Villa has committed himself?"

"I don't know what I think," Antonetta pouted. "I know only that it's Pancho I truly love, but I need a man, too. Sometimes I get so mad—so mad I see fire. Then I go find Fierro. I know I am playing a dangerous game of passions, but sometimes I don't care what happens." Antonetta was breathless.

"It's not enough the *jefe* has to think of all Mexico, but you make for him so many more complications? The small games you play can only end in a passionate manner—bloody and deadly with the sacrifice of one or all three. And for what? Pray tell me for what?" persisted Madelaina. "Listen, *querida*, you above all should know that it's time for survival and victory, not for death and defeat. Thank God we're on the side of the victors. *Dios mios,* Antonetta, you've seen what's happened to those who've been defeated—the wastelands of death left behind us."

"Exactly. For what do you think I've been talking?"

"You expect perfection. It can't be that way. All we've seen—all we've done must affect us. Only one side can win. God, let it be us!"

"Can it not be done another way? Can it not be discussed and negotiated, this hard business of war?"

"If we were dealing with men of honor—men who kept their words—men who believe in humanity instead of its destruction—perhaps. But there are no such men in Mexico, *chica.* The *Federales* are trained to kill, not to barter or negotiate. The *Rurales* are murderers who have no use for the spoken word. Only those who provide them with food, clothing, and shelter are they loyal to. And the *Colorados*—well, they do what they must, just as the others do. They remain loyal to the men they believe in."

"Then we are hopeless as well as helpless to the butchery that pervades our land?" Antonetta paused a moment. "If that is true, how can I believe in what Pancho is doing? How can you be loyal to such a butcher?"

"Antonetta!" Madelaina glanced up sharply at her friend. She glanced about the thicket, frantically worried. "Be careful of your words. You never know who is listening."

"Why? I speak only the truth. Pancho knows how I feel—that I grow more disenchanted each day Fierro is in our company. Villa and Fierro are destined for each other. I know it. Pancho is certain of it. Listen, *chica,* you don't think I know that Pancho Villa—Don Francesco Villa—has become bigger than the revolution itself? You know the adulation Pancho had for Madero? Well, it is now the same. It is Fierro who adores Villa. He is ready to die for the *jefe*! And each

785

day Pancho grows more determined to crush Huerta, as if fuel has been put into his hands by Fierro. Even if it means joining Carranza to oust Huerta! Such complications!"

"If Fierro adores Villa, why does he seduce his woman? You are frightened of losing both, is that it? You intend to play one against the other?" Madelaina was aghast. "Is that the game you play? It isn't worthy of you, *chica*."

"Then it's time for Tonetta to leave Pancho—and Fierro."

Madelaina's eyes widened in fearful speculation. "Pancho will be crushed, *chica*. Listen, I'd hate to venture a guess on Fierro's response after seeing you two together."

"It's not true. Pancho won't notice I am gone. He has not come to me in many weeks. If he doesn't make haste, Tonetta will throw discretion to the winds. She will make her affair with Fierro no longer a secret. Then see the sparks fly,' she said with devilish lights in her eyes.

"Tonetta! You wouldn't dare! You realize what will happen? Chihuahua! A minor revolution! Oh, *chiquita*, you expect too much from Pancho. *Dios mios*, look at the advances made by the Revolutionary Army, at the gains we've made. Without Pancho we are lost!"

"And what of me? Does it no longer matter that without him Tonetta would be lost?"

"The revolution is bigger than any of us. Look how many have died that Pancho Villa might lead Mexico to freedom. You can't even think of breaking up Villa and Fierro."

"Why wouldn't I dare break up the Villa-Fierro alliance? Fierro broke up the Villa-Antonetta alliance, didn't he? Besides, what do I care for advances if no advances are made to Tonetta. Maybe I do this before I go, eh? Stir up the kettle good."

"Go? Where will you go? Why are you acting so crazy, *chica*?" insisted Madelaina with overwhelming emotion. "You can't do this to Pancho and you can't leave him either, not now. We can't both leave at the same time."

"Ju, too?" asked the flabbergasted redhead.

"I must find my baby," she said with sudden desperation.

Tonetta's compassion was superseded by an instant intelligence in such matters. "In this land, ju think you can find one little *niño*?" She reverted to her pigeon yankee. Tonetta's instinct made her pause and glance curiously about the immediate area.

"I must. Don't you see, I must."

"Jur crazy. Ees best ju stay under protection of the *jefe*. I will go to El Paso. Ees easy to find me when this mess is finished."

"If you go, I go." Madelaina studied her friend's uneasy comportment. "What's the matter, *chica*—"

Before either of them could move or speak, a loud voice assaulted them from behind.

"Ees more better if you both remain here."

Madelaina and Antonetta made a quick scramble for their guns and were instantly subdued and restrained by two uniformed *Rurales*, military police who stepped on their weapons, preventing their use. With powerful blows struck at them, the women were sent reeling off their feet. Felled by the unexpected clouting done in whirlwind fashion, the women were too stunned and stricken to make a break.

Crouching on all fours, Madelaina tried springing to her feet. She was coldly struck across the face by one of the *Rurales*, a heavily moustached man with a thin-lipped, vicious smile, and sent reeling back off her feet again. Tonetta fought like a cat, clawing, scratching, kicking, and struggling fiercely to free herself of the other man's clutches.

Madelaina called to her in English, hoping these cruel, Cossack-trained beasts didn't understand. "Play coy," she pleaded in silky, sugary tones. "Pretend to cooperate. Don't fight or it will go worse for both of us. Let them have their fill, then, at the right moment,

787

we'll surprise them, *chica*." She could feel the welts and weals rise on her face and swell.

Instantly both girls became docile, seductively batting their eyelids like the lowliest of whores in Villa's camp.

"It's not necessary to rape us, *Capitán*," said Madelaina in her most seductive, whorish manner. "Not when we are both willing."

The *capitán*, called Gerardo, smiled wickedly. "Very well then, woman, let's see you cooperate." He unbuttoned his trousers and removed his swollen penis, brandishing it about like a valor badge, his black eyes glittering evilly.

"Like that—like an animal in heat? Take off your jacket, remove all your clothing so I can feel the strength of your body flowing through mine," cooed Madelaina.

Gerardo grabbed Madelaina's hair, twisted it hard, and pulled her into him. "You will fuck me the way I am, you hear, woman! If I desire to perform the act with my clothing on, it is my business. But you try one funny thing and I'll slit your lying throat. Now, lay down and spread your legs."

Madelaina complied.

Antonetta was dealt with more severely when she snuggled against a corporal named Hugo. Her hands trailed behind him toward the holster at his hips. In a quick, sudden blow, he smacked her hard against the ground. Hugo dropped his trousers and fell upon the redhead, panting. The smell of uncleanliness made Antonetta want to retch, yet she tried to encourage Hugo. With both arms pinned back, it was difficult for her to function. Her eyes darted to the grassy mound where Madelaina's saddle bag lay open. If she could maneuver him two feet over, she could grasp Madelaina's knife laying partially hidden from view. She began to coo, protesting that she couldn't make him feel the real enjoyment he would if he only permitted her to cooperate. "Just let me put my arms around your neck—let me move my hips the way a woman is taught to do by the very nature of her body," she whispered to him, "and I'll make this a time you'll remember for the rest of your days."

Madelaina wasn't faring as well. The *capitán*, a suspicious, hard-line military policeman, wasn't the kind to want more than to relieve the need in his groin. He didn't care for the artful ways of love. He wanted instant relief for the load he carried. When she asked him to smoke a marijuana cigarette, to make him feel more mellow, he laughed at her.

"You think I am a wet-nosed *niño*, still suckling my mother's breast, whore."

"But even tequila would serve us better. You are so tense, so tight, and so hard, *amigo*," she said in her sultriest drawl. "I am used to being used by men, but I tell you, *hombre*, you need more pleasuring than you take." She forced a light laugh and threw her head back teasingly so he had a chance to appraise her more fully. "I am a little too thin perhaps for your tastes, *mi capitán*, but others have found my treasures more enjoyable."

"You have tequila, whore?"

"On my horse is a bottle in a leather pouch. I'll get it."

"No You come with me. Any funny business and I promise to slit your throat. No one will miss you, *comprender?*"

"*Si, mi Capitán*," she whispered meekly. *Haughty, proud-faced bastards, All you Cossack-trained sons of whoring pigs,* she told herself as she permitted herself to be dragged to the horse. *I'll fix your unworthy souls.* The taste of rage was bitter as bile in her throat. She glanced cautiously at Antonetta to see how she fared and noticed the girl was edging toward the open saddle bag. *Mry bien, the sex kitten has a head on her shoulders.*

The *capitán* found the bottle, and holding it in one hand, he dragged Madelaina back to the grassy knoll. He shoved her to the ground, kneeled over her, and remcved the cork from the bottle with his teeth. "Now, drink, girl. You want the tequila."

Madelaina took the bottle from his hand and, raising the bottle to her lips, locked eyes with his in a teasing, taunting, seductive roll of her eyes. So fascinated was he with the promise buried in those dark, wicked eyes, he failed to see her movements. Faster than he could see, she threw the contents of the bottle into his eyes, blinding him with the gasoline. Gerardo bounced back, screaming in alarm and pain. In the space of those split seconds, Madelaina rolled over and picked up the rifle from the ground and opened fire. Thunder exploded all around her.

Hugo, faster than lightning, rolled over on top of Antonetta, grabbed the knife she'd reached for, and plunged it into her neck. By the time Madelaina aimed the weapon at him and pulled the trigger, the rifle was empty. She panicked as she scanned the area looking for a weapon—anything to use against him. Hugo lifted his gun and pulled the trigger, aiming it at Madelaina. Simultaneously two more shots were fired, then two more. It all happened so quickly, she didn't know what happened. The scene was a madhouse of powerful explosions, sights, and sounds.

She saw the *capitán* rise from where he'd fallen in the momentary confusion and pain of blindness. He reached for his holstered gun and fired blindly at anyone and everything in his immediate range. No question that his eyesight, impaired by the fiery liquid, incurred a vengeful anger and he'd gone berserk in an attempt to retaliate in some equal measure to the whore responsible.

Madelaina saw him spin around from the impact of bullets fired at him from some distant point. He whirled like a drunken man unsure of his footing and moved out along the riverbank where he was felled by a round of shots. Madelaina fell to the ground, glancing about, trying to locate the source of the shots. She crept, half-crawled to her clothing, shimmied into her skirt and blouse, her heart beating so fast she felt it would burst.

It was at that moment she looked for Antonetta. When she saw the ribbon of blood banding her friend's neck, her own knife buried to the hilt in it, she screamed and ran to her side without care or concern for the sniper shooting at them.

She kneeled over the girl, her troubled eyes sweeping the redhead's frightening wounds. She reached in and pulled the abominable and obscene weapon from Tonetta's body and dropped it as if it had suddenly turned to live coals in her hands. Swiftly she tore at her petticoat and wrapped the wounds about the girl's neck. Then, as no life emerged from the girl, she cradled her in her arms, rocking her gently to and fro.

"Tonetta," she whimpered. "No, *querida*, not you, my dearest, sweetest friend." Tears streamed down her face. "*Querida*, what will I do without your friendship? What will Pancho do without you? Fierro?"

Faint gurgling sounds came from Antonetta as her eyes fluttered open. Those sparkling, emerald eyes of jewels and blue seas grew duller and duller.

"Go, *querida*," she could barely whisper. "Go while you can. Tell Pancho I will wait for him in the land of our ancestors." Her eyes lit up once more before fading to a murky blue. Sobbing, Madelaina pressed her fingertips over the girl's eyes, closing them for the last time. She crossed herself. "*Dios mios*, take care of this woman. She was the best woman who walked the earth," she said in supplication.

The sound of a twig snapping startled her. Now, only survival counted. She tensed, slipped her arms from around the dead girl's body, and crept back into the bushes, alerted like an animal. She reached for her Obregon automatic, gripped it tightly in her hands, and pulled her saddle bag close to her. Instantly she slipped the leather chamois pouch around her neck. Her hand instinctively felt for her lower abdomen, for the area of the solar plexus, and she silently prayed for strength. Whoever it was stalking about was as clever as she, she told herself, when after several moments with her ear to the ground, she heard only the wild beating of her own heart.

Like the silent whisper of the wind after a storm, she felt the presence of another being. She felt the slight pressure of a hand on her shoulder before she reacted and with a gasp sprang to her feet, ready to do combat.

"Consider yourself fortunate, Senóra Little Fox," said the unsmiling, sober-eyed, and cautious Rudolfo Fierro. "If I hadn't been so fascinated by the charms of Antonetta and followed you two women, you'd have fallen heir to a worse fate." He paused, his eyes sweeping the ground where Antonetta lay dead.

The terrible Fierro—the man whom Antonetta found most threatening in her recent world—moved to her side and knelt on one knee to stare at the sight of the broken woman. He shook his head in disbelief, picked up strands of her red hair, the fascinating red hair with which he'd been mesmerized since he first joined with Pancho Villa, and let it lay like a satin ribbon of fire across his rough, callused hands. He pulled it in close to his face and lay his cheek on it, feeling its softness, delighting hedonistically in the color of fire and the smell of cleanliness. It was a baffling ritual, totally unexpected from a Rudolfo Fierro. Watching him in rapt absorption, Madelaina found the scene incredible. Here, the man Antonetta labeled a barbarian was as gentle with her as she'd seen him the first time with the redhead. No question, Fierro on the battlefield was every bit as hard-hitting, brutal, and bloodthirsty as Tonetta had described. Now, watching him, so vulnerable as tears spilled from those ferocious black eyes, the evil of the man was erased.

He leaned over and tenderly picked up the dead girl's nude body in his arms as if she were the most precious thing on earth to him. He accepted the blanket Madelaina handed him from her bedroll and wrapped it around Tonetta. Slowly, he walked to his horse and draped his saddle with the inert body. He turned to

792

Little Fox as he removed a Bowie knife from his thigh sheath.

"It's important we go quickly to inform the *jefe* of this atrocity. You wait, only a moment," he told her. He walked over to where Hugo the *Rurale* lay dead, his blood spilled in the dirt. "This is the pig who killed her?"

Madelaina nodded, wondering what he was up to. Fierro leaned over and hacked off the man's bloodied hand. He wrapped it in the *Rurale*'s kerchief and tied it to his belt without a flicker or trace of emotion on his features.

Madelaina felt sick. She wanted to vomit. Controlling herself, she followed him back to the horses and both mounted their steeds. She noticed that Fierro gently picked up the body of Antonetta and cradled her in his arms, as he urged the black stallion into position. They galloped off swiftly, the fading sun at their backs, and returned to Villa's encampment. *Dios mios,* he was in love with Antonetta. Only love could exact such a performance, she thought.

It was a strange sight to see Rudolfo Fierro, credited with being the fiercest of Villa's men, sitting tall in his saddle, like a king returning from a conquest, holding in his arms a queen for sacrifice. Information reached Pancho Villa's ears even before the unusual riders rode into the draw. It was a funereal procession fit for royalty. And Madelaina promised herself to remember it for all eternity. There was a lesson to be learned here—but what it was she had yet to know. They continued in a slow canter as if to some funeral dirge heard only in Fierro's mind. He stopped his horse before Pancho Villa, who had stepped out of the run-down, confiscated hacienda, and stood at attention.

Fierro raised his left leg, turned his body, and slid off the sadde of his stallion, still holding Antonetta. His eyes, without expression, looked glazed as he stared at Pancho Villa. So intent was the message in his eyes that Pancho himself was unable to remove his own eyes from those so compelling as Fierro's. Only when Fierro stood before him and extended the blanketed body to Villa, did the *premier jefe* remove his eyes from the other's and look down at the body in his arms. Fierro snapped off the blanket as a magician might do in a famous table trick when he miraculously separates a cloth from the table keeping the china intact. Then he draped her nudity with it, baring only the incredible red hair.

Villa stared down at the body of his beloved Antonetta in a state of disbelief and shock. He glanced up at the circle of faces moved by curiosity to witness this strange happening. The Indians removed their sombreros, reverently stunned by what they saw. Their brown-skinned fingers formed the sign of the cross.

A hush fell over the courtyard as hundreds began to gather. Word traveled swiftly. When something touched the heart of Pancho Villa, it touched his people. General Villa turned, the body in his arms, and he entered the adobe hacienda as a silent storm of unanswered questions assaulted his senses.

The women hurried inside, preparing for the angels of death to descend upon the house of Pancho Villa. Upstairs, taking the steps one at a time, Villa moved like a phantom toward the bedroom, where he hadn't spent enough time with Antonetta. Inside the bedroom, he moved toward the bed and gently placed his beloved sex kitten on it. In the pulsating silence, he turned to the others, and they knew without words that he wished to be alone with the corpse of his beloved Antonetta. They shuffled out, compassion overflowing their hearts, and closed the door behind them.

Inside Pancho knelt by the side of the bed. He lifted her slender white hands and placed them over her breasts. He pulled a coverlet from the end of the bed as if she were sleeping and he wanted to ward off any possible chill. Suddenly a huge sob wracked his body. He leaned over, his face on her breasts and sobbed like a child.

"*Dios mios*, why did you have to take her? She was a good woman. As good as they came. Forgive me for being so busy with the business of this goddamned war. Oh, my little *gatitta*. Pancho loved you as he loved life itself." He stroked her hair off her fragile white face, which grew more waxen as the lines of fatigue faded.

Sometime in the next few hours, while Pancho Villa grieved his beloved in the custom and manners of his ancestors, the women entered the room unnoticed by their *jefe*. They had brought candles and lit them at either side of the bed. They brought flowers and commenced to silently arrange them as best they could.

Outside the door, Rudolfo Fierro stood guard, his face a stoic mask. He seemed unmoving, like a giant force of power protecting his *jefe* from any outside interference during his private grief. No one, not even Tomàs Urbina dared to violate that inner sanctum. He talked with the others outside, and they all wondered how it happened and who was responsible. Not even Madelaina could be approached in this blackest hour of Villa's life. She was as silent and uncommunicative as Fierro. Until Pancho Villa learned what happened, none other would know.

Madelaina sat in the downstairs salon of the delapidated hacienda. She was hunched over at the end of the leather sofa, smoking endless cigarettes, her eyes swollen with tears.

She saw Rosalia Quintera and Lucia San Miguel from a distance as they walked with Captain Tracy Richards toward the open front doors of the *casa*. She blinked hard. The sun was setting and the shadows playing funny tricks on her caused her to avert her eyes, then glance back at the foursome. Three, she had recognized. But the fourth, a man, she hadn't been able to see as well, since the hot sun glittered on something bright and metallic, possibly a belt buckle?

The Gringo Brigade in their dusty beige trousers and shirts moved in and surrounded the foursome obstructing them from view. Then came members of the other various brigades as they hailed the newcomers with subdued voices. The sun, it seemed, disappeared behind a mountain in the distance. There was no mistaking the free-swinging hips of Rosalia Quintera nor the carefree attitude in which she swung her naturally curly hip-length auburn hair. Even Lucia was the same, thought Madelaina. Then she saw him. There was no mistaking him. She'd know that tall, swaggering walk any place. His face was shielded by a dusty sombrero, shrugged forward on his head, but not enough to disguise his handsome features from her. He seemed taller than ever. Because he'd lost weight, she wondered.

She saw him pause, shake hands, and embrace several men, backslapping the others affectionately. Madelaina trembled, hardly able to form his name on her quivering lips. His brown hair was longer than she remembered, and the shadow over his upper lip turned out to be a drooping Mexican-styled moustache. It emphasized his lean, reckless face with those azure blue eyes so startling against his coppery skin. As he moved forward, climbing the steps to the main *casa*, her heart pounded as if it would never cease.

Peter Duprez stood in the doorway of the open entrance several moments before his eyes grew accustomed to the dimly lit interior. Then he saw her. Their eyes locked fiercely. Madelaina faltered, stalling for time, unsure if she should be thrilled beyond all belief to see him or angry over the last year of agony he'd inflicted upon her. She watched the expression in his eyes turn to one she didn't recognize. Was it possible they could be like strangers to each other?

Remain detached and aloof, she told herself. Don't let him see how much you really care, how much you ache for him and need him. Hadn't his marriage worked out? Had his wanderlust caused an itch in him to get back into the thick of battle. Hadn't his *wife* objected? These and a thousand other questions filled her with confusion. When the silence between them grew too unnerving, she finally spoke his name, "Peter. How good to see you."

Peter strode toward her, the others respectfully remained outside, permitting them to share their reunion without onlookers. Captain Tracy Richards closed the two front-entry doors and took the women toward his encampment.

The air filled with instant hostility and a venom Madelaina hadn't expected. His voice when he spoke was harsh, sarcastic, and contemptuous.

"I finally found you," he said, adding with scorn, "*Mother*."

If he'd slapped her, she couldn't have been more astonished. "You have no right," she countered, "no right at all to speak to me in that manner. You married another woman first! Even when you had no legal right to do so!"

"And you did, I suppose? You, a married woman, committed bigamy with your husband's father, adding incest to your already depraved life!"

"Stop it! Stop it at once. I don't care what you think of me. All your words and evil thoughts will have to wait. The angels of death hover over this house tonight, and you can at least hold your vile, vicious thoughts until the mourning is over." She averted her face so he wouldn't study her facial bruises so intently.

Peter's features softened. "Death? Who?"

"Antonetta—the woman of Pancho Villa."

"The sex kitten from the Diamond Slipper?"

Tears brimmed her eyes. She nodded. She was feeling worse now that Peter arrived. It was all wrong, terribly wrong, and she was unable to do anything to set it straight between them.

"Ah'm sorry. Truly sorry," he said, moving toward her. "Y'all must ache inside like a thousand bullet wounds." He reached out to her and embraced her. They melted into each other's arms as if there'd never been any distance between them. When he asked about the welts on her face, she couldn't reply.

It was Peter who pulled back first, a strange and peculiar sensation shooting through him. He felt nothing in his body, just as he'd felt nothing in the arms of Lucia. This, added to the pressing reasons for his arrival here, confused and frustrated him. If he could feel

23   797

nothing with Madelaina after all this time, then the injury done him by Valerie Townsend had to be permanent.

He shoved her from him almost roughly, his troubled thoughts turned inward. At first he experienced a sensation of hostility and anger toward Valerie, toward the whole goddamn revolution that had gotten him into this mess, toward his own inadequacies and stubborn drives and toward his father who shared prominently in the blame for his fate. He flung open the doors, searched for Tracy Richards, and asked where he could find an adequate supply of whiskey.

Before anyone could reply, Madelaina, with the fleetness of a gazelle, was at his side. "If it's whiskey you want, Peter, there's plenty inside." She closed the door behind them again and led him into the smaller salon, Villa's private office. She opened a locked cabinet and removed a bottle of wine and two glasses. "We might as well celebrate our reunion, eh, gringo?"

"Gringo? Not my husband, lover, long-departed sweetheart? So, it's back to gringo, eh?" His narrowing eyes sent shivers through her.

"What brings you here, Peter?" she asked, trying to remain cool and detached.

"I've been sent on a mission to locate the daughter of General Alvaro Obregon, the wife of William Benson," he said snidely, before drinking the wine.

"Don't you have anything stronger than this?" He glanced behind her in the wall cabinet. "Ah, holding out on me, eh? I'll take the Napoleon brandy," he muttered, taking the decanter from the shelf. He poured an ample amount into a glass.

Madelaina watched him with a concerned expression on her face. She'd never seen him deliberately imbibe alcohol like this. When he gulped down the brandy with hardly a pause, she knew something of a black-hearted nature ate at him. He wiped his lips and his moustache with the back of his hand, and Madelaina, watching him even more inscrutably, felt she had to know what lurked inside his heart and mind, eating at him like a sickness.

She pulled his hands and led him to a leather sofa near the window and sat down next to him. Because her holster annoyed her, she removed it, rolled up the gun belt, and set it on the table before them.

Here they were, two people who loved each other desperately and needed each other more than at any other time in life, unable to speak or communicate in any meaningful way. Perhaps, thought Madelaina, it's because the angels of death hover over the house that they couldn't express their true feelings.

Peter wondered if all hope was lost for them. Drinking to excess, keeping busy, and indulging in therapeutic sex no longer could sustain what they once shared. And now, the loss of his manhood, devastating enough, loosened a sulking madness in his brain. How could he tell her? Perhaps it was all meant to be. This way, if he sustained his anger and intimidation, he could convince her to return to her father and son.

He'd begged Felipe de Cordoba to allow him to see the child, but the major general had been adamant. Only at the very last, after Peter had agreed to his conditions, did Felipe relent and against orders permitted him a moment with the infant.

Peter had only to look upon the infant to know he was the boy's father. His eyes, the color of blue sapphires, the physical traits—even at that age—Peter recognized as his own. He'd held the infant in his arms, felt the soft, tender smoothness of the child's skin, the tight, firm grip of tiny fingers around his own and his heart surrendered to him. Peter knew then, as he knew now, that his own life would be utter devastation if he couldn't be allowed to see the son of his loins again. He also knew, by Madelaina's physical appearance, that she'd suffered greatly at the separation between mother and child.

Madelaina thought, has he forgotten how it was when we parted—following the conception of our son? He had married another woman. Madelaina be damned! He's forgotten we slept naked together, that we generated much heat and our kisses were the sweetest of all honeys, the most intoxicating of all elixirs. In his eyes I see nothing of the love we once shared. Her sadness overwhelmed her and she remained silent. No words would form on her lips or in her heart.

"Well, what is it? What did ya wanta ta say ta me?"

"Perhaps it's better if you tell me why you've come."

Peter frowned. The brandy warmed his insides and on an empty stomach he felt queasy after the exhausting ride in the hot desert sun. The combination of all three factors, plus his close proximity to Madelaina, made him feel awkward at first. Then he coughed to clear his throat and removed his buckskin jacket. "Like ah said, ah've been sent on a mission. Youah father, General Obregon, wishes ya ta return ta his side, Madelaina. They made me a proposition, one ah felt to be a fair one. Youah life foah mine."

"*My* life for *yours*?" she exclaimed. "*My* life for *yours*? What exactly does that mean?"

"I've been the general's prisoner for the past few months. Major General de Cordoba came to me and put it to me, rightfully so, that y'all belong in the house of youah father."

"And I suppose you concur?" she asked icily.

"Ah do."

"And what right do you have to think I'd entertain such a proposal? You think I care what happens to the life of a man who deserted me for another woman?" she snorted contemptuously. "You left me at the mercy of the fates without care, without concern for my life, Peter Duprez *Benson*! And you have the nerve to address me as *mother*! Why didn't you tell me William Benson was your father? You had plenty of time to tell me!" she snapped.

"Why did ya marry him?"

"You think I had any power over the circumstances which made me wear his name for a time?" And then, Madelaina told him the full story and she capped it off with, "I don't give a damn, Peter Duprez Benson, if you believe it or not! It wasn't until I was at Seven Moons and saw pictures faintly resembling you, and I coerced Pilar to tell me the truth, that I knew you were related. Don't you think I died a thousand deaths after he molested me and I learned I was pregnant? I prayed to God it was your child—not his. And when it was born—*when it was born*, I knew it was yours, yet you both look so much alike, who can prove it? Time was the only reward I felt. I counted each day, each night to the moment we made love. Only then, could I be certain." She was shaking, tears brimmed her eyes, yet she continued, her voice barely above a whisper. "He's gone, that son of ours, that love child. Stolen from my bosom. He was all I had left of you. Now, here you are, bold as you please, looking rested after your long honeymoon with a woman you aren't legally married to, and you tell me I should return to the house of my father with whom I have nothing in common, because you've made some agreement with him!" Madelaina was out of breath, her temper was close to the breaking point, and she bit her lip to try to keep from spilling more tears. "How dare you tell me what to do with my life? How dare you!" she retorted. "Haven't you done enough to me already?"

"Ah didn't marry Valerie," he said quietly, his blue eyes boring into hers.

"How can I believe this ridiculous story you tell me about my father? If your story was true, he wouldn't have permitted you to leave. He'd have sent a messenger," she continued not hearing him. She built her anger in waves.

"Ah nevuh went away on any honeymoon," he added in softer tones.

"My father's pride is at stake. Any day now he will encounter Pancho Villa, general to general, and he only wants me at his side, so that history will document it as such. What a blow to his ego! His *gachupín* pride would be shattered if history recorded that the daughter of General Obregon sided with the revolutionaries—that when he fought Villa in the contest to determine total victory or total annihilation, his daughter remained at Villa's side." Her anger precluded hearing a word he spoke.

"Valerie knew we spent time togethuh and in a fit of rage came at me with a gun. Her marksmanship put me in a hospital foah several months until mah father sold me out ta the *Huertistas*, so they could get ta ya through me, heah? Youah father's people intervened and kept me secreted at El Dorado."

"Why—why—I—uh, what are you talking about?" She stopped abruptly as Peter's words replayed in her mind. "*You never married her*? But the papers—the papers all wrote about it." Amazement seeped into her face. "You were at El Dorado?"

"Ya know better than ta believe the printed word, Little Fox. Didn't ah teach ya nothin'?"

"William Benson turned you over to Huerta?" Madelaina was aghast. "Oh, *querido*, whatever for? Your own father? *Dios mios*!"

"The way ah heard it, it was so he'd secure himself and his monetary interests in Mexico with the present administration."

"You never married her? Oh, *querido*! I've died a thousand deaths!" She fell into his arms and for several precious moments, they kissed and hugged dearly.

Then, Madelaina wiped the tears from her eyes and spoke with candor.

"So, it's all power and wealth? That's all that ever really counts, isn't it?"

"Reckon so," Peter replied dully.

Their mood was interrupted by a loud wailing, moaning sound echoing through the main *casa*. It was more than a piercing scream that reverberated and bounced off the walls. Madelaina's face blanched; she cocked her head to listen. Peter, instantly alert, turned to her questioningly. Never had they heard such lament, such soulful cries of agonized longing and wailing over the departure of a loved one. "It's Pancho Villa!" she exclaimed, turning and heading out of the room, across the main salon, and climbing the stairs swiftly with Peter behind her.

They were obstructed by Rudolfo Fierro, who stood motionless as a stone statue, guarding the door to the bedroom. Immovable, unflinching, his head bowed over his rifle, he looked like some fierce god guarding his beloved's temple.

"Fierro, let us pass. This is my *marido*, Peter Duprez," she said softly.

It seemed intolerably long before Fierro raised his head and, revealing red-rimmed eyes swollen from crying, nodded mutely to them. He allowed them to pass.

Inside, Pancho Villa sat in a high-backed throne chair, his hands hanging limply over the cushioned arms. His face, turbulent and drained of color, didn't acknowledge the presence of either Madelaina or her husband. On the four-poster bed lay Antonetta, smiling palely and serenely in her final sleep. A silken scarf of silver threads and pale blue silk wound around her neck concealed the horrid pattern of her death. Her hands were folded over her breasts, and her red, silken hair streamed over her shoulders and milk white limbs. A sheer silk cloth covered her nude body. She seemed strangely alive, as if an unearthly glow hovered over her, illuminating her in this shuttered room of shadows and candlelight that smelled of paraffin and dying flowers.

Outside, the Yaqui drums beat a soft tattoo of steady and arousing sounds as the strange ritual of death began. And outside, the people, all of them, the soldiers and *soldaderas* and *campesinas* whispered and wondered. Their *jefe* hadn't come to them to tell them anything. Fierro had said nothing. Little Fox even less. Soon their *jefe* would come to them to tell them. And then would come the retribution. How had his woman died? In the eyes of those women who hated Antonetta because she was first in the *jefe*'s eyes, there was talk of whom he'd pick next to grace his bed. Their eyes gleamed excitedly with no feelings of remorse for the red-haired beauty whose gringo appearance always made them feel unworthy.

Madelaina felt a terrible urge to comfort Pancho Villa, and she flung herself at his feet and lay her head on his lap, as Peter watched her.

"If there is a God, Pancho, rest assured she is cradled at his bosom."

Pancho's coarse hand reached out and stroked Madelaina's black hair, his face an expressionless mask of gray concrete. His eyes reflected dead black stones. He didn't respond to Madelaina's words. Pancho Villa had mourned in his own way. He was a realistic man now, a man changed by the many adversities in life. He was a man who would keep his emotions to a minimum. He had enjoyed Antonetta every moment of their life together and now she was gone, forever plucked from his bosom. He would never, from this day, speak the name Antonetta again. But until his dying day, he would hunt down those responsible for taking her life and show them no mercy. After her burial at sundown, in the manner of his ancestors, by a fire strong enough to transport her to the heavens of eternal rest, she would vanish forever, escorted by the black angels of death to her next abode. There was one thing more left for him to do. He rose to his feet, pulling Little Fox to her feet with him. He turned to Peter and signaled for him to take her from him.

Slowly he moved in toward the bed, and with his knife, he whacked off a thick strand of that strange and alluring red hair, the color of pink fire. Folding it in two, he quickly slipped a leather tine from his holster and bound the bent end. He laced it through his belt and tied it securely. Once again his black eyes swept over the still, pale face, then he turned and left the room.

At the door he spoke to Fierro and the man fell into step behind him, following him down the stairs and into an anteroom where they closed the door after them. Madelaina and Peter paid their last respects to

804

the dead woman and left the room as others began the pilgrimage.

Downstairs, seated quietly in one corner of the room, Madelaina stared at all the passing faces. The drums outside had stopped beating, and a small group of musicians began to play mournful musical dirges. Madelaina watched in fascination the combination of pagan and Christian funeral rites. She'd never forget the manner in which Pancho whacked off Antonetta's hair. Later Rosalia Quintera explained the ancient rite of the Yaqui Indian in which fetishes were made of the hair of their beloved. With the red hair of Antonetta strapped to his victory belt, Villa would have no trouble recognizing the face of his beloved when he passed on to the next life, where after their earthly separation they'd be united again for all eternity. If he didn't wear the fetish he'd have no way of recognizing her, for often the souls changed appearance. Later, Fierro would also wear such a fetish and amaze Madelaina by his profound devotion to her memory.

In his office, Villa's black mood permeated the room as he listened to Fierro's story. Then he summoned Madelaina to listen to her account of the tragedy.

Madelaina and Peter hadn't had time to resolve their own differences, but in light of the *jefe*'s needs, they postponed their business and hoped to comfort Pancho Villa in his darkest hours of personal grief.

Villa's face lit up when he saw Peter Duprez. Then he glanced swiftly to the face of Little Fox, who stood quietly beside Peter, weighted with sadness.

"We shall be avenged, Zorrita," said Pancho walking toward her. "You and I have suffered the most, felt the deepest, and have little to show for our efforts. Tell me your story. What happened out there?" He inspected the bruises on her face grimly.

Madelaina substantiated most of Fierro's story and more. Two *Rurales*, acting seemingly on their own. No, she didn't know if there were more in the vicinity. Had either Fierro or Madelaina stopped to search the dead policemen for orders? *Dios mios*, no! The shock had

805

been too great. Pancho immediately dispatched Fierro and Urbina to ride back and find the bodies and relieve them of all clothing, weapons, and identification.

"Now, Little Fox, ju please leave me with your *marido*? Ees much we must talk on." Pancho Villa was returning to his former self.

Madelaina nodded and left them together. She hadn't had much time to reflect on Peter's words. He *hadn't* married the gringa daughter of the governor after all. She went outside to be by herself, to think and mull things over in her mind.

Her father wanted her to return to his house. Did he mean all was forgiven? Or did he mean he wanted her to turn on Pancho Villa? Why would Peter's life be sacrificed for her—why? Why would Peter even make such a proposal, knowing how deeply she felt about her father's politics? None of it made sense. Not even Peter's position in the matter. He was out of General Obregon's clutches, why would he concern himself with keeping his word? They were together. Why not just run away? Head for the border and once across the Rio Grande, they were American citizens. They couldn't be touched—could they?

No matter how she thought things out, nothing could convince her to return to the house of her father. Nothing would ever make her do this short of death! How could Peter have made such a pact? How did he ever hope to persuade her to comply with the wishes of her father?

These and many more questions arose in her mind. By the time she walked around the perimeter of the hacienda and returned to the *casa*, she saw a considerable scurrying of activity. She glanced around in the moon-filled night, wondering what the *Villistas* were up to. *Dios mios*! They were packing, preparing to move out!

Her steps quickened. What had happened? In less than an hour—that's all she'd been gone—new orders had been issued. She had to fight her way through the throngng people making haste, rolling up their possessions.

She searched everywhere for someone who could make sense. Captain Tracy Richards called to her. "*Chiquita*, youah husband is looking foah ya. Weah leaving foah Chihuahua City!" He wheeled his horse in close to her.

"Why? What for? Why so sudden? Why are we to suddenly pick up and pull out?" She held the horse's bridle, calming him.

"The *jefe*'s orders. Peter was with him a long time. The decision's been made. So get a move on, *muy pronto*, ya heah?" He cantered back over the path.

Madelaina made her way toward the *casa*, elbowing her way, trying desperately to find Peter. All around her, horses, wagons, and trundling cannon kicked up blinding dust so thick she couldn't see through the congestion. She raced to her quarters, gathered her belongings, and took her place with the *soldaderas*, prepared for battle. There was no time for emotions, no time for regrets. Only the call to duty was important, the cry of the revolution: "*La Cucaracha, La Cucaracha, yo no puede caminar*," came the song of war. "*Viva Villa! Viva La Revolucion!*"

There was no time for tears. The best of Villa's fighting forces, loaded onto trains, headed for Chihuahua City in a sudden move calculated to capture and control the capital of that state. Villa was determined to control the state, eastern Durango, and southwestern Coahuila, all of vital strategic importance, for it meant controlling all the railroads from Juarez to Zacatecas, the commercial lifeline of all Mexico.

Chapter 30

General Pancho Villa, dressed in his uniformed khakis, with the bright glaring sun overhead catching the fiery red-haired fetish of Antonetta attached to his uniform jacket, sat on Seven Leagues and gave the signal for his men to surge forward into battle.

Three separate attempts were made to rush the garrison. Each time the *Villistas* were bloodily repulsed. Two more attempts resulted in failure, for the fort was heavily armed and manned. Then Villa did something to baffle his enemies. He ordered a total withdrawal of his fighting forces.

Federales, hot in pursuit of Villa's rear guard, returned to the garrison to report their victory. "Villa was in full flight," they rejoiced, convincing the defending General Orozco of the Redflaggers and General Mercado of Villa's bitter and devastating defeat. "I tell you they are gone—all the rebels have disappeared. The deserts around Chihuahua are clear! Not even the ghost of Villa remains," persisted the young officers who drank toasts to their monumental victory over the crafty puma, that Centaur of the North.

While the *Federales* reveled in their smashing triumph over Villa, only General Pasquel Orozco remained uneasy. His Indian instincts told him that it wasn't over. He knew his old compatriot too well.

What Orozco didn't know and had no way of discerning was that General Villa had Fierro and the telegraphers of the Northern Division busy tapping wires, listening and intercepting the Juarez-Chihuahua communications. Orozco also had no way of knowing that Pancho Villa, alerted to the arrival of an ammunition train from Juarez, had sent two of his brigadier generals to intercept the train and had already helped themselves to the ammunition and succeeded in loading the empty freight cars with their men and horses.

At a particular substation a few kilometers from Chihuahua, ironically named Madero, Colonel Fierro, looking like a satisfied Cheshire cat, had relieved the startled telegrapher of his post and called to his *jefe* for further orders.

"Take this message to the commandant of the Juarez garrison. Please say: *Villa in full retreat to the south. Am sending you reenforcements of 1,000 men with ammunition and supplies by returning train.* Sign it Orozco."

In a matter of moments Fierro deciphered the return message. "They've acknowledged."

"Tell me," asked Villa. "Any confusion?"

"None. We also learned the code to identify the returning train through all stops and highball us in without problems." Fierro's lips curved into a smile.

"Bueno," said Villa. "Now my friend." He winked at Fierro. "Cut the wires, both ways." He touched the brim of his Stetson and left to command the other brigades, leaving a well-pleased and diabolical gleam in the other's eyes.

At one o'clock, the city of Juarez, except for the casinos and night clubs, was sleeping. In the section known as Old Chihuahua, where the night life was coming alive, the sounds of music and loud, raucous shouting and wild behavior echoed through the streets. Countless people swarmed the *avenidas* and crowds from saloons, restaurants, cantinas, whorehouses, and gambling palaces spilled onto the sidewalks clear to the American border. The gaudy lights of the entertainment center never seemed brighter, as the unending clamor of music and singing and laughter filled the air.

Close by, not far from all this activity, a freight train from Chihuahua City lumbered into the railroad yards at Juarez and was sided while "Federal reenforcements," unloaded in full combat gear, were formed and marched toward the barracks in the heart of town unnoticed.

Troop movements in this frontier city were no novelty. Under cover of this activity, Colonel Fierro, pistols in hand, quietly entered the office of the stationmaster and announced politely that the communication center was now in the hands of General Francesco Villa. He nudged the four men over against the wall while his aides tied them securely and shoved them into an adjoining stockroom with gags stuffed firmly in their mouths.

There wasn't the slightest hint of suspicion that the revolution was about to burst wide open at any moment. Not until the outbreak of revolutionary cries pierced the night air, arresting people on the spot.

"Viva Villa! Viva La Revolución!" came the cries.

Mexicans, *Federales*, tourists, and everyone in that section of town were jolted and terrified by the sudden outbreak of artillery fire. Turning around at every conceivable spot, they saw, as if in a dream, *Villistas* in broad-brimmed sombreros and heavily rawled spurs, chests crisscrossed decoratively with ammo belts, rush into the night clubs, rounding up all Federal officers, while outside machine guns swept away all resistance by their troops.

Madelaina, Rosalia Quintera, and Lucia San Miguel, followed by other *soldaderas*, rushed into Antonetta's Diamond Slipper and did to the people what their male counterparts had done in the other establishments. They herded nearly two-dozen Mexican *Federales* into a corner of the room, amid stinging and snide remarks that Pancho Villa was hiding behind the skirts of women. One officer, showing his contempt for the women, reached for his gun. He never made it. Madelaina cut him in two with her Winchester rifle, oblivious to the screams and terrified wailing of the women and other civilians lined up against another wall.

The *soldaderas* moved in and began to remove jewelry and watches and other valuables. From the tables they took the money strewn about. Madelaina, about to protest that Villa's women were not *bandidas* and force the girls to abandon their thieving tactics, was arrested at the sight of one face in particular.

Through the smoky haze filling the large gambling casino, she saw him. He wore the uniform and markings of a major general, but there was no mistaking Simon Salomon, the enemy of her lifetime. Raising her rifle slowly, her forefinger curling tightly around the trigger of the weapon, she hesitated a split second just as a bullet caught her in the shoulder. Two more blasts were fired, whizzing right past her ear, and she saw a sniper fall from the overhead beams. Rosalia had killed her assailant. The place was sudden pandemonium as Urbina's men swept into the casino like ants and took over before she could protest.

It would have been so easy—just a matter of moments—to have pulled the trigger and ended all dreams for the man who'd so savagely scarred her life. Goddamnit! He lived a charmed life for sure! She looked for him, but in the crowd, he was lost to her. Everything happened so quickly, she thought she'd dreamed him. Only when she felt a hot sticky substance trail down her arm and over her breasts, did she realize she was bleeding profusely.

Madelaina gazed about the room as a misty, somewhat hazy apparition whirled about her head in confusion. For several moments she saw herself dancing on the stage as *La Bomba*. She even heard the sensuous, rhythmic music in the caverns of her mind, saw Antonetta moving about the old haunt. She closed her eyes and felt herself being hustled out the door by Rosalia and Lucia. She tried to shut out the painful pictures. Recollections of Tolomeo came at her and she faltered, swaying in the street, falling against the building walls. She was sweating fiercely, her dark hair clung to her like wiry coils. Her eyes fluttered open and shut as the lights around her began to whirl overhead.

Rosalia Quintera called to her. "*Chica! Vamenos!* Quick, we go to the customs house. *Ondolay, pronto!*"

Seeing the condition of her friend, she rushed back to Madelaina's side. *Que pasa?* What's wrong, *chica?*" She studied Madelaina's pale face under the lamplight, recalling all too vividly the staggering Indian rites she'd undergone to unhex the *mujer* of Tom Mix and Paco Jimenez and exorcise all those *diableros* and *brujas*. Now again she appears obsessed? "*Dios mios!*" It can't be, not again.

"Tolomeo!" cried Madelaina over and again. "What do you want of me? What am I doing that disturbs you so?" Flashes of their precious moments together whirled about her head in a brilliant fog of memories. Pictures of Peter's accident at Valerie Townsend's jealous hands mixed in with hers. She actually saw the gunshot wounds as they exploded while Peter was in the tub. She lost consciousness after that.

For three days after the infectious bullet was removed from her upper arm, Madelaina lay in bed in the house Pancho Villa had commandeered, totally unaware that the victory of the *Villistas* had been total, with General Villa in absolute command of Juarez.

News of his amazing and stupifying victory, reported by American newspapers, flashed the name of General Francesco Villa to the four corners of the globe. The landless Indian peasant from Durango, this man whose soul cried for the injustices of the poor to be righted, became the man of the hour! He'd tricked a garrison of 3,000 well-trained soldiers and captured the most vital and important city in northern Mexico without suffering a single casualty. But this of itself wasn't enough for General Villa. His mind dwelled on that irresistible seat of power, Chihuahua City!

News from his spies reached the *jefe*'s office that Generals Orozco and Mercado were mobilizing 5,000 soldiers to attack Juarez and decimate all Villa's forces. Eleven trains had been assigned by his enemies for their counterattacks on Juarez.

"My, my," said Villa, smiling at the information. "Imagine that. Eleven trains."

Four days later, scouts reported to Villa that the

Federales had departed from Chihuahua City and were en route to Juarez for an all-out war.

Madelaina, recuperating from her wound and still bedridden from fatigue and lack of nourishment, had to satisfy herself learning secondhand of the *jefe*'s spectacular accomplishments. She'd never been so annoyed at herself for stopping that bullet. Now, through the eyes of Miguel Guerra, she was forced to read of the heated and marvelous accomplishments of General Villa instead of being right in the thick of the action.

"When news reached General Villa that the *Federale*'s reenforced columns of soldiers were taking the offensive in attacking Juarez, he gathered his 800 men and marched right out to meet them. Unknown to his enemies, General Villa rendezvoused with the other brigades of his Northern Division precisely at a destination his enemies least expected him to be: Colonel Fierro's mission was to handpick a detachment of railroad men and dynamiters to circle in behind the Federal troop trains and cut the track, preventing retreat. Within twenty-four hours the entire Northern Division stood at attention, resupplied with Villa's vast Juarez stones, prepared for battle.

"Even I," wrote Miguel Guerra, "received a shock when I saw the entire rebel army sprawled across the tracks. You can imagine what went through the minds of the *Federales* when their trains came around the bend to reveal the spectacular and magnificent strength of the entire *División del Norte* already there and waiting for them. Forced to attack prematurely, only half-prepared, the *Villistas* promptly counterattacked, and for the next three days the battle raged. The *Federales* finally attempted to withdraw to Chihuahua City.

"It was then that Colonel Fierro, struck with inspiration, ignored General Villa's orders to destroy the railroad tracks. Instead, he concentrated on the last of the Federal troop trains. Blocking the rails, he and his men charged the train, and surprising the troop escort, he disarmed them and shot the officers. Then, in another mad but workable scheme, he uncoupled the engine and packed the train's cowcatcher with enormous loads of dynamite, woven through the grating with explosive caps. The colonel opened the throttle and leaped off the engine, leaving it to charge ahead, racing northward around a bend in the road, where the ten Federal trains lay stalled, end to end, by Villa's attack.

"As the dynamited cowcatcher collided with the last caboose, an earth-shattering explosion ended all hopes the *Federales* might have entertained for retreat. The explosions burst into flames and triggered off further explosions. Only after a thick cloud of black smoke lifted and the fire died down did this reporter see the remains of troop trains as they lay scattered over a half-mile. A broad stretch of track had been twisted into blackened junk and the *Federales* ran into a hasty retreat.

"Ten valuable engines loaded with war materials sat waiting for General Pancho Villa to take them over. Meanwhile General Urbina of the Juarez Brigade fell into savage pursuit of the panic-stricken *Federales*, cutting them to pieces.

"It was learned that Generals Orozco and Mercado and the entire Chihuahua garrison subsequently gathered the remnants of a once-powerful army and retreated from the capital, leaving it to the *Villistas*. For General Villa, this wasn't enough. He split his Northern Division once more and personally led the attack on Chihuahua on all the remaining *Federale* troops. The last government troops north of Chihuahua have ceased to exist. Those *Huertistas* who could escaped across the American border and have been interned. Those who didn't escape were executed by General Villa's firing squads."

Madelaina laid down the paper, recalling the friendship of Miguel Guerra in the early days of the revolution and how he protected her for a time from her father's spies. She moved to the window overlooking a portion of Juarez beyond the planted terrace of her roof garden. Each morning for the past three days since she regained consciousness, she searched the streets, desperately hoping to see Peter. She knew he'd joined with Tracy Richards and the Gringo Brigade, but Tracy had returned two days ago and made no mention of Peter. She slipped into a bath, prepared for her by Rosalia Quintera, who'd looked in on her and taken care of her with the tenderness of a loving relative. When Rosalia learned Madelaina's baby had been abducted from her side, she expressed her compassion, one mother to another. Still no words could console her friend.

Madelaina lay back and closed her eyes after she'd soaped and scrubbed herself, but finding herself unable to fully relax, she lifted her body from the wooden tub, dried herself and, wrapped in heavy toweling, moved toward the bed. She slipped the leather chamois around her neck. She recalled Tolomeo's words: if she felt poorly, without energy, she should sprinkle some mushroom powder in the area of her solar plexus and meditate on strength. Nothing else had sufficed and she continued to feel sapped of energy.

Why not do as he'd suggested? She felt a pang of guilt for not having tried harder to live by his philosophy. Her life had been just as difficult after she left the land of Tolomeo, hadn't it? Perhaps not as tumultuous and earth-shaking as before she'd encountered him, but none the less quite hard and rocky. She sprinkled a minute amount of the powder on her flat, hard stomach and rubbed in a circular direction, commanding as she did that the second brain of her body give her the needed energy.

No sooner had she closed her eyes to rest a bit than pictures instantly formed in her mind. She blinked hard and opened her eyes with a feeling of dismay. Was she forever to be cursed with these confounding pictures? She tried to keep her eyes open wide, but they grew too heavy and the desire to close them overpowered her. There they were again, a series of pictures like photographs in motion of a place, a location she'd never seen, high above the sea, surrounded by tall graceful trees and a thick vegetation. She was walking through rooms of an unfamiliar hacienda, passing through them as one might on a guided tour, glancing at the wall hangings and art objects with interest until she stopped in her tracks at the sight of a familiar face. She drew closer and closer and there he was. Felipe de Cordoba! She was certain. And there behind him in a brass cradle was an infant. Moving in closer to the cradle, Madelaina was able to look down at the moving child. Her heart filled with joy at the sight of her child. It was her son, Alejandro! Of this she was certain

Her eyes snapped open and the pictures faded. Madelaina sat up in bed with a start. She glanced around the room as her heart accelerated rapidly. What did it mean? *Dios mios.* These pictures were like the pictures she'd seen of Manuelito Perez and those of Peter when he was injured. For so long she hadn't seen these pictures, she almost forgot they happened. She reached for another cigarette, lit it, and frowned at the pile of butts in a mound in the ash tray. She smoked for a time, inhaling deep breaths, hoping against hope that her heartbeats would subside. She detested this breathless feeling that left her edgy, nervous, and shaken.

She closed her eyes again. In moments the pictures returned. They were different. These pictures were of Peter Duprez in a hospital. Of the comings and goings of doctors and other specialists. She watched them examine Peter and she saw the enormous scar tracks from his stomach to his groin.

"Who are you?" she asked. "And why do you persist in forming pictures in my mind?" She heard herself ask the people in the pictures. She heard a doctor's voice telling Peter that for a while he might be impotent, that he shouldn't concern himself, that in time the situation would resolve itself.

Madelaina's eyes snapped open again. This time she pulled herself up off the bed, just as Rosalia Quintera walked in with a pot of hot coffee. Lucia came in behind her and remained in the background, avoiding Madelaina's eyes.

"*Chica*, where is my husband?" she asked Rosalia.

"He has crossed the border on business with Pancho Villa. He will return with Pancho and we are to progress to Chihuahua City, *muy pronto*."

"Travel again?"

"*Si*. We travel once more. This time in style, not as *campesinas*. Urbina and Fierro will escort us to the capital city." She handed Madelaina a packet. "This is for ju, *chiquita*. Lucia and I will be back with our belongings." The two mestizos left Madelaina to her privacy.

Madelaina hastily opened the envelope when she recognized the handwriting as Peter's. She began to read: "Madelaina, my love, my sweet: Knowing that we, neither of us, resolved our differences, I, in all good conscience had to write you before I left on business for Villa. It's necessary that you know the most important person in your life awaits you at the hacienda of your father in El Dorado—*our* son.

"Yes, my beloved, *our* son. He is safe and has been from the moment your father took him from your bosom. I knew none of this—not even that you'd borne us a son. I wanted no part in this, but, due to circumstances over which I had no control, I am forced to become an unwilling pawn.

"I've thought about Felipe de Cordoba's words. I also sense the deep love he's always felt for you. As things grow more hectic and dangerous in this revolution to which we've both committed ourselves, I grow increasingly alarmed over your safety. It is for this that I insist that you return to the sanctuary of your father where both you and our son will be safe from harm. You've dedicated yourself long enough to the cause of Pancho Villa. Now, with the responsibility of another life, our son, I plead with you—return to him and stay safe.

"It's my hope that you will try to carve a future for yourself and our son. Madelaina, you must know, my darling, that I've loved you from the moment I was approached by that slim-hipped, boyish woman I met in

817

Sanlucar four years ago. In the past I've learned to memorize all of you until you remain indelibly etched in my mind. Somewhere a clock keeps ticking away for us, taking more precious time from us. My sweet, sweet *querida*, the whole of the love I feel for you has never found time to be consummated except for the god-given replica of us come alive in our son. Take care of him. Take care of yourself.

"There is something I must confess, so that you understand. I am not the same man you married. I never will be. Therefore, it is God's will that you return to your son and prepare for his and your future. There can be none for us. If you do not understand what I am trying to tell you, I can only say—forget me. Our life can never be. May God bless the both of you Peter."

Madelaina's heart was so full, she felt it would burst. Tears sprang from her eyes and spilled onto the paper. She understood very little of this letter. Her swimming eyes scanned the third paragraph. What did he mean—*I am not the same man you married? I never will be?*

It wasn't fair! He should have told her before he left. She might have been able to convince him they belonged together. God! What hell she'd been through to keep this marriage of hers together! God wouldn't have paved the road with such perilous twists and turns and tumultuous emotional upheavals only to make her give up when the end was near. No! No! She was sobbing now.

She'd flung herself across the bed; the letter had fallen to the floor near her. Sheer desperation and the fear of not knowing what to do in these next few moments was so overwhelming that she couldn't think straight. Even as she gave vent to this rising hysteria, this mixture of joy at learning of her son's safety, coupled with a feeling of haunting at losing Peter forever, something deep within her attempted to stabilize her distraught emotions.

Rosalia and Lucia returned, their bedrolls strapped

to their backs, to find Madelaina still crying. Rosalia's eyes fell to the letter. She picked it up and slipped out of her backpack. Her eyes darted over the letter. She spoke to Lucia in her mestiza dialect. "Her man has left her. Then it's true what you told me about the gringo?"

Lucia nodded halfheartedly. "*Si*, it's true. But it's like I say to him and like Dr. Gonsalvez say to the young major general, that it will take time for him to be a man again. It isn't all lost. But the gringo, *pues*, you think he listens? That stubborn ass. He tries three, four, mebbe five times with Lucia—and nothing. Now he volunteers for the most dangerous job—the most foolish. He looks to be killed, that Tom Mix!"

Hearing their voices, Madelaina sat up and dried her eyes with the hem of her skirt. She glanced at Rosalia hotly when she saw the letter in her outstretched hand. "How dare you read my letter?" she shouted venemously, reaching for it.

"Read jur letter? Shooo, Little Fox, ju theenk Rosalia knows to read? *Dios mios*! Eef only eet was true, *querida*," she lied. "It was on the floor. Rosalia removed it from the floor, that ees all. Are you ready to move with the company of escorts?"

"*Si*. I'm ready." She hastily gathered what few belongings she had and rolled them up as the other women had done. She slipped out of her blouse and skirt and reached for her dark trousers and shirt. She slipped the bandoleros of ammunition over each arm, crisscrossed across her chest, and hooked on her hip holster in which her Obregon automatic was slung. "*Vamenos, muchachas*," she said abruptly in an authoritative manner. Her previous vulnerability was gone.

In coming to terms with herself, Madelaina thought of many things en route to General Villa's headquarters. First, she decided that her baby son was perhaps in the best place possible, at the home of her father. Neither he or Felipe de Cordoba would wish harm to the small *niño*, so her decision to remain with Villa until her own father's position in this revolution was made clear seemed the right one. She was convinced that her father was riding the fence, since he seemed reluctant to declare his loyalty to Carranza and had definitely split with Huerta at some time in the past.

Whatever the reason, he was reluctant to declare himself for Carranza, it appeared that Don Venustano was the heavy contender for the presidential throne. Obregon had to make his decision because the time was drawing closer and closer for the contest between himself and Pancho Villa.

Only destiny, it seemed, would know the outcome of this confrontation, thought Madelaina, and it was certain the fickle whore wasn't talking—not even to the four winds.

The way Madelaina saw it, and it was confusing at times, President Huerta, as the keeper of Mexican power, controlled the *Federales* and the *Rurales*. Determined to dethrone him was Venustano Carranza, self-declared First Chief of the Revolution, who'd gathered unto himself all the former *Maderistas* with the exception of General Pancho Villa, who was just as determined not to seat Carranza in the presidential palace. General Villa, by the very strength and force of the army he'd built, was considered General-in-Chief of the Northern Division of the revolutionists. He wanted a liberated Mexico, free of all oppressors—and that included Carranza. Her father, General Obregon, was the man whose position perplexed her. In truth, he was a *Federale* who'd split from the *Huertistas* and inclined himself toward Carranza, but not quite.

It was clear to her that Carranza needed both Obregon and Villa, but it wasn't until President Wilson showed favoritism toward Carranza that Obregon even threw his Fourth Sonora Battalion in to support Carranza. True, he'd taken a few minor garrisons in Carranza's name, but not wholeheartedly. His determination to stall was what concerned everyone, including Pancho Villa, who'd once declared Obregon his fiercest enemy.

Who can keep up with these political intrigues, she asked herself on many occasions. It's enough to drive a person crazy, with changing loyalties from day to day. Who knew one's real enemies—or friends—in such turbulent times?

Madelaina had been in Chihuahua City for nearly two weeks, working in the office of General Villa, immersing herself in necessary clerical work before she actually saw the general. He had just returned from El Paso after having met in secret with U.S. General Hugh L. Scott and other political supporters in the United States.

For days he remained uncommunicative. If he appeared astonished to see Madelaina busy at work in the building he'd appropriated for his administrative offices, he said very little, except to tell her that her husband was in Washington on vital business for the revolution.

She had said very little to him. Trying desperately to reorganize the office so that the filing system wasn't too complicated for a child to handle, she had enough work to keep her mind off the urgent longings she felt for Peter.

Several times in the coming weeks, as she busied herself across the hall from General Villa's private office, she'd hear him rage to Rudolfo Fierro, who'd become a general since his spectacular, quick thinking in the Juarez siege, that he couldn't in all honesty and decency comply with the recent suggestions made by General Scott that he amalgamate with Don Carranza, contender for the presidency of Mexico, the moment Huerta was ousted. The breach between Villa and Carranza had become too great to be spanned for the common good, he'd told Fierro.

"But what if President Wilson fully endorses Carranza?" asked Fierro.

There was silence for several moments, then Villa roared. "Damnit, Fierro, don't confuse me. How can an honorable man like Wilson endorse so dishonorable a coyote like Carranza? You think he can't see a skunk's stripes under his coat?"

"You think President Wilson can see through a coat?" asked Fierro.

"Listen, that American has much education, see. He can see through anything, *amigo*. Especially since he wears those fancy glasses. He must see twice as much as this uneducated *peón*."

Madelaina hadn't seen the expression on Fierro's face, but she had smiled at Villa's naïveté. He placed so much importance on education and literacy. Why, with no education at all and a thirst to read countless books, General Villa had done more in the short span of months than cum laude graduates did in years. She concentrated on how she could convince him of his own worth.

In Washington, President Wilson was still debating over the most logical man to support in Mexico, and although still at a loss to decide, he finally outlawed Huerta. The man was a psychotic drunk, too dangerous to be allowed to occupy the highest office in our southern neighbor's government. Still he was undecided between Carranza and Pancho Villa. Word got to him that Carranza was encountering difficulties with his Chief of the Northwest Army, General Obregon, who either wouldn't or couldn't carry out Don Venustano's directives. Having met General Obregon in the past, President Wilson found him to be a reasonable man, well educated, and dedicated to his career. He could understand Obregon's position. After all, Huerta was still president. His cooperation with Carranza could very well be considered treason in certain circles.

Other leaders had risen and fallen these past many months of the revolution, yet there was always Villa. The man President Wilson had first labeled a ruthless butcher, an illiterate *peón*, was suddenly emerging a brilliant, outgoing man displaying an astonishing native intelligence that his well-educated counterparts had difficulty understanding. Why, the former *guerrillo* who once had difficulty expressing himself had begun to

822

show an astounding and spectacular administrative ability.

Peter Duprez had been meeting in chambers for the past three weeks with President Wilson and General John Pershing who, along with General Scott, had nothing but praise for manner in which Pancho Villa, using the democratic guidelines of his northern neighbors, grasped the reins of government. Daily they attempted to convince the president of the vast changes taking place south of the border. And it began to appear, after lengthy conversation, that Peter was winning points for Villa. Right after lunch one day, Peter picked up where the conversation had ended before the break. He'd grown bolder in recent days and took considerable effort to point up the plus side of Villa's activities.

"It's clear ta see, Mr. President, that once the firing squads fade away, General Villa's concern centers around his people. He's freed political prisoners, restoring their full rights. He's established schools, making education mandatory. Ya must admit, it's moah than Diaz or Huerta have attempted. Why, suh, he's lowered railroad rates to benefit the poor who wish ta migrate elsewheah foah work. He's permitted Mexicans returning ta Mexico ta bring in furniture and automobiles duty free. Suh, he's employed qualified help ta supervise schools, hospitals, and other government agencies. He's taxed industries and put ceilings on prices to protect the poor from profiteering. Already he's entered into business relations with American industry. He plans ta import better engines, passenger and freight cars. Mr. President, in mah humble opinion, there's no one better than General Francesco Villa to help cement better and stronger ties between ouah two nations."

Woodrow Wilson, that myopic and sanctimonious president, regarded all Peter had told him with an air of sobriety. Even Generals Scott and Pershing had lauded Villa highly after the few encounters they'd had with the former *guerrillo*.

"What you say coincides with the other reports I've had on the man and his reforms. It's been brought to my attention that liquor laws have been enforced rigidly for the first time and that U.S. Customs authorities have been given powerful aid to deter the smuggling of drugs across the border."

"Yes, suh. All of that and moah," replied Peter with rising hope.

"Very well, gentlemen," replied the president. "I'm all but totally convinced. Again I must ask your indulgence to give me until the end of this month to make my decision. While I view with appreciation all you've done to bring me a clear picture of the activities of this barely reformed bandit, from other sources I hear that he represents no cause other than his own."

Seeing the flickerings of discontent in the eyes of his guests, the president hastened to add, "Yet, he does hold all the meaningful territory, including vital border crossings which must be kept open to American commerce."

"Yes, suh," said Peter a bit too quickly. "That he does, Mr. President. That he does."

The meeting was dismissed on a high note. After all, thought Peter, winking at General Pershing, the end of the month was less than two weeks away. He could be patient, all right. They all could if it meant victory for Villa's cause.

Unfortunately, none of the men present could begin to imagine what the fates had in store for Pancho Villa. Least of all, Peter Duprez Benson, who was bound to be most affected by the storm gathering in Chihuahua in the office of General Villa.

Deeply engrossed in the filing that had accumulated over the past several weeks, Madelaina and Rosalia Quintera hardly saw the tall stranger charge boldly through the hall, bellowing aloud, demanding to see Pancho Villa. She'd been attempting to teach Rosalia the simple system of filing she'd devised when she heard General Villa's secretary sparring in a conversation with a gringo *hacendado*, protesting the gringo's presence without an appointment.

Their words grew heated and tempestuous, and as they disappeared behind closed doors, the women could hear very little.

"*Dios mios, chica,*" exclaimed Rosalia, pausing in her work to swing her hip-length auburn hair off her shoulders. "Even the rafters shake at the booming of such angry voices." She studied Madelaina for a time. "Perhaps it would be more better if I wear my hair as ju do?"

Madelaina's slick, trim look, with her hair pulled back tightly and wound into coils above her neckline, seemed far cooler than her own appearance. Besides, it was hot and stuffy inside these offices. She liked the shirtwaist dress, boots, and belt worn by the *gachupín*, which appeared demure and well suited for the sedate office work. Even her gun belt looked less intimidating.

Madelaina smiled. "It makes things less complicated when you are dressed to suit the work, *chica*. Soon, now, you'll know my work well enough so I can leave for a rest." She spoke half to herself and bent over the work on her desk. Her mumbled words were hardly heard by the auburn-haired, seductive-looking Rosalia, who complained she had no head for business. "Only for making love, *querida*." She laughed easily. "And why not? For what else ees woman put on earth, eh?"

For a time, there was silence as the girls concentrated on the work at hand. They had no idea that what was happening a few feet away from them would turn the revolution upside down.

Inside General Villa's private office, the *jefe* stared over the gleaming walnut desk at the tall, over-powering gringo who dared shove his way into his office.

"What exactly is it ju want from me, Señor Benson?" he asked evenly.

"That tax ya imposed upon unconfiscated haciendas! S'posin' we begin right theah?" William Benson bellowed loudly.

"*Bueno*, Señor Benson. Ju just pay 1,000 head of

cattle and that's that." Villa summoned his secretary. "My man here will attend to details, gringo."

"Just who in hell do ya think ya are talkin' ta me like that, man? We've got unfinished business ta attend ta, Villa," roared William Benson. "Have ya got any idea who ah am?"

"I know who. What the hell do ju mean bustin' in like this? Tell me what ju want."

"If ya think ah'm about ta pay youah bloody thieving tax man, you'ah plum loco. What's moah ah'm sick an' tired of seeing your goddamn thieving brigade marching up and down along mah lands! Theah makin' mah bulls jitterier than hell. And last but not least, we've got unfinished business. Y'all kidnapped mah bride from my Texas ranch, Seven Moons. Foah that, suh, I can have ya jailed!"

Villa stood up behind the desk. Still he had to look up at the big Texan. His eyes blackened and his temper had shoved into first gear. "Ju listen, gringo. Pancho Villa is short on nerves because he's tired, ju understand? First, since the Mexican *hacendados* pay my tax, why should I make exception of ju? Second, consider jurself fortunate that I didn't confiscate jur hacienda. Third, my blood boils when ju call my soldiers thieves. And last, the woman who escaped Seven Moons was not jur bride. She was the legal wife of one of my officers. Now, where the hell do you get off bustin' into my office, mouthing off like some foolish *borrachón* who stinks of bad whiskey?" Villa fanned the repulsive liquor breath from his nose with obvious disdain.

General Villa, in his shirtsleeves, up to his ears in paper, had given no thought to the fact that he was unarmed. Who would dare threaten his life in his own stronghold? His secretary, Carlos Ramierez, a quiet, studious-looking man with rimless glasses, seated at Villa's side at another desk, glanced nervously at Benson, whose temper, fired with rage, hurled insults and threats at Villa over the desk.

Under Benson's greatcoat, the outline of a large gun

formed a visible impression. Villa had no gun at his immediate disposal, nor did he seem to think he needed one.

To Benson's right, slightly behind him, totally ignored by the room's occupants, stood the dark, thick-set figure of a uniformed man with black, narrowed eyes. He wore a white campaign hat. Over his shoulders, a long black cape covered a trim uniform caught at the waist with a heavy gun belt. Rudolfo Fierro, tensed and alert, trained his lethal eyes on the American.

"Don'cha think foah a moment ya can scare me, ya whoring son of Satan," yelled Benson. "Ah've got me plenty o' pull in Washington, ya lousy fuckin' peasant—"

"Jur under arrest!" shouted Villa wrathfully. "Jur in the territory of General Francesco Villa. I'll teach ju to speak with such disrespect, *cabrón*—cuckold!"

"Youah'll teach me nothing, ya stinking swine—" Benson went for his gun. In that same instant, Fierro's gun roared. William Benson fell dead at Villa's feet, a bullet through the head. Everything happened in an instant.

The door swung open and Madelaina dashed inside, her face drained of color. Her eyes darted about the room, and seeing the *jefe* unharmed, she sighed in relief. Her eyes fell on the collapsed heap of the gringo. She walked in closer and looked down just as Fierro turned the body over, allowing her to see his face. Her hands flew to her face in shock. She glanced at Villa and at the smoking gun in Fierro's hands. Her body grew slack, her head shook in disbelief. "You know who this man is, *Jefe*?" The consequences of the act shook her.

"I know," said Villa ruefully. "The father of your *marido*. By his own words, a man with much political pull. His death can do much to jeopardize the work of your *jefe*."

"Oh, what a luckless *peón* I am on this day!" he lamented. "Tell me, Little Fox, what would the Americans have done if some half-drunken Mexican had broken into the El Paso City Hall and attempted to shoot their mayor? Are we in Mexico supposed to be fair game for the abuses and caprices of any whoring mother's son of a foreigner?"

"What will this do to Peter's mission in Washington with the gringo *presidente*? she asked without expression.

"You know about that?"

"I know, *Jefe*."

"I care more what Peter will do to avenge the death of his father," he told her.

Madelaina blinked hard. She had no answers. "It's more important to what your enemies will do, *Jefe*. Carranza, for instance. If the American president removes his support from you, rest assured it will be Carranza he supports. Then what?"

"Then what? Then what? *Pues, querida*, then comes more complications. For instance, that fence-riding father of yours will be forced to declare his position. What do you suppose his position will be?"

"Perhaps we'd better think on such a matter, *Jefe*. And pretty damned quick," she retorted.

They didn't have to wait for long to learn how Washington viewed this atrocity done to an American citizen. The government began an immediate investigation. As for the president, in his cool, complacent, aristocratic manner, he told himself and others that he knew all along that Villa was a savage barbarian not fit to rule his country. He informed Peter Duprez of this when the tight-lipped, somber-faced Texan responded to the presidential summons. "Will you continue to apologize for General Villa now? Honestly, Peter, how can you think to defend a man who shot your own father?" His words, spoken emotionally before a mask of political reserve set in, brought color to his lined cheeks. "I'll wait for the investigation to submit the findings before I can reexamine my earlier willingness to support this—uh—er—man, Villa," added Wilson hastily as he endured Peter's long cold stare.

By then, Peter knew Villa's cause to be lost. Just as he booked train accommodations back to El Paso, without waiting for the reports to be resolved, lawyers for his father's estate contacted him in Washington to suggest he return to Amarillo at once. Peter felt obligated to do their bidding, especially since he was urged to cooperate with them by Governor Hampton Townsend.

On the long ride back to Texas, Peter pondered the situation. He wondered what had happened to bring about the fatal encounter between his father and General Villa. Why exactly had Benson been shot? Knowing his father, he readily assumed the worst. Still Benson was his father. He owed him that much at least. Governor Townsend had put it quite succinctly: it was time for Peter to leave the house of Pancho Villa and concern himself with the affairs at the house of Benson.

They had spoken long distance when Peter was in Washington. He'd insisted to the governor that without hearing the facts, he didn't hold Villa responsible and that he felt sure that Villa was justified in defending himself.

Governor Townsend had coughed with embarrassment and sputtered, "It's commendable of you, my boy, to be so generous in your appraisal of the affair in light of the fact that you don't know the circumstances which led up to it. Just you remember, boy, blood's thicker than water. By the way, it might serve ya well, my boy, to head up the investigation against Villa."

Peter went numb. "Governor, did I hear you correctly?" asked Peter testily. "Your shifting loyalties serve only to confuse me."

There was dead silence at the other end of the phone, followed by a rash of embarrassed coughing and the clearing of Hampton Townsend's throat. "You just have to understand, Peter—"

Peter Duprez Benson hung up on the high state official. He stood for a long time in the long distance phone booth staring into the mouthpiece. His problem was that of late he'd been thinking too deeply, more profoundly than usual. Impotence had done this to him. His thoughts of late had been clearer and in sharper focus than ever before. He'd begun to assess his own life and that of Madelaina. Many questions previously unanswered in his mind began sifting, sorting, and clearing.

Well, first things first. He'd go home at last and see why the lawyers were sending up smoke signals. Yes, that was as good a place as any to begin to come to terms with himself. He almost looked forward to seeing Seven Moons again, especially now that he would not have to tolerate the presence of William Benson.

In Chihuahua City, in the lair of that Centaur of the North, General Pancho Villa, the man who'd succeeded in racking up astonishing victories for the revolution had just adjourned a meeting with his chiefs and subchiefs. For several hours Villa had been attempting to find some direct route through the maze of countless complications that had besieged him ever since the shot that killed the gringo William Benson had echoed around the world. Unable to resolve many things, he dismissed his men, just as Madelaina Obregon entered the study of the confiscated hacienda.

"Come in, come in, Little Fox," he called to her as the officers filed out of the room, somber-faced and without their usual jocularity.

The men, Urbina, Richards, and the others she'd grown to know so well throughout all the campaigns, nodded perfunctorily in passing. Rudolfo Fierro touched the brim of his white Stetson and moved past her without expression.

Madelaina in turn nodded easily, hardly glancing at them, and sat opposite the *jefe*. He poured her a glass of wine, offered her a cigarette, and sat back in his chair, selecting a piece of peanut brittle from a silver dish on the desk for himself.

"It's good of you to come, Little Fox," he said, biting into the candy. "Recently my spies tell me that even my friends, my so-called friends, plot against me. So, you see, it is refreshing to know I can trust you. Shall I tell you how much I miss Antonetta?" Tears sprang to his eyes "Besides being my lover, my *gatitta*, she was my best friend." He crunched on the candy with relish.

"I'd like to think I fall into that category, *Jefe*," she said.

"You? You, Little Fox? What the hell's wrong with you that you don't already know such a thing? You are more than a friend. You are like my right arm. You don't know that? I called for you today, because we must talk."

He finished with the candy and wiped the corners of his lips with his fingertips, his merry eyes twinkling with self-consciousness. "Me—a grown man—liking candy so much," he scoffed with mild embarrassment. Then he began. "Recently, *querida*, I've given much thought to what might happen if I should fall in battle. Who would there be to carry on the standard first lifted by Francesco Madero, eh? Can you help me to name one man?" He sighed heavily when Madelaina, after a slight hesitation, shook her head. "You see? Precisely my feelings. Among my men, there is no one—not even me—fit to occupy the presidential throne in the palace in Mexico City. So why do I fight?

"Freedom for Mexico is my dream, *chica*, my dream for existence. Without it, I'd be lost, whipped back into an ignorance and slavery which dehumanizes, warps, and eventually destroys man's soul. For this I fight. Yet, as I grow closer to my goal, I look for a man to carry on my work. Shall I tell you who I see? Like you—no one. I say to myself, I could make peace with Carranza, back him, and elevate him to lead our beloved Mexico. But he is no better than Huerta—worse than Diaz. He's a German lover prepared to make deals with the Kaiser. You think the American president believes this? Hah! The gringo who sits in the White House believes only that Pancho Villa is a

831

crazy bandit, killer, a man with no education, a *guer-rillo*, who has much empty space under his sombrero."

"How can he believe such foolishness after the victories you've amassed?"

"You think I can answer you? Hah! Sometimes I wish I could drink like my men, Urbina and Fierro. I promise I'd get stinking drunk, then perhaps I wouldn't care as much as I do."

"Why do you punish yourself, *Jefe*? What's been done has been done and nothing can alter the facts. Perhaps if you set your thoughts down on paper in a letter to the American president, speak to him through your heart, as you speak to me, he might reconsider. You must tell him that Benson shot first and Fierro shot in your defense. You can't allow this unfortunate incident to deter you, *Jefe*. You mustn't," insisted Madelaina.

"But for who? For who do I fight. Even if the American president assists me by sending arms and reenforcements to oust Huerta—for whom do I sacrifice the lives of thousands? In good conscience, there is no one I can place on the presidential throne."

Madelaina was aghast. "You can't just give up and turn Mexico over to the political predators who would eat it up and suck it dry." Their eyes met long and hard.

"Listen, Little Fox, I've been preparing to attack Zacatecas, so I control all of the north to that southern point. Is plenty, no? Word comes from Carranza. 'Unite our forces,' he tells me. 'Take Saltillo, first. Forget Zacatecas.' "

Madelaina's forehead screwed up in thought. "If you do that, you'd be sacrificing your campaign for his benefit and glory. Saltillo is the capital of Coahuila—Carranza's home state, no?"

"You see how clever you are, Little Fox. If you were a man, it would be you I would place in the presidential palace—*como*, no?"

"*Jefe*," she said, flushed with embarrassment and

832

enough sobriety to make Villa think. "Such an honor could never be accorded a woman. That golden throne isn't for the likes of a woman with my past."

Villa agreed with her first statement, shrugged at the second. Then they both laughed at the utter absurdity of his statement. A woman—indeed.

"You know, perhaps it's not so bad an idea." He entertained the thought with a merry twinkle in his eyes. Then he grew serious.

"The question is, *chica*, if I take Saltillo for Don Carranza, am I giving prominence to a worthy man? Or will the sacrifice of sufficient red blood be done to dignify an ignoble lout? I must be certain of what I do, that it is for the good of Mexico, because, you see, the price I will pay is the lives of many good men."

His words struck at her emotions. "What a good man you are, *Jefe*. I saw such nobility in you when first I skulked around your campfires waiting to serve you. For this I sacrificed my former life, to serve you in the revolution for a better Mexico. If those gringos in Washington knew this side of you, if they could see the tenderness in your eyes when you speak of Mexico, they'd whistle up a brilliant madrigal for Pancho Villa and allow their troops to march to its tune."

Watching him, Madelaina saw this wasn't the reply Villa wanted. Compliments, although welcome, bounced off his back when more pertinent issues were to be examined. "What is it, *Jefe*? Are you asking me to tell you the kind of man Carranza is? What do I know of him?"

He nodded slowly, allowing a piece of peanut brittle to melt in his mouth. "Ayeiii, perhaps that is what Pancho is doing. Listen, *chica*, if I throw 20,000 men into a fight, one of every twenty will die—perhaps more. What will I say to their *soldaderas* when their babies suffer and they themselves weep with sorrow and loneliness? You think that a few pesos, a little food and shelter will erase the fact that I, Pancho Villa, ordered them to their deaths, if I support a man who turns out to be a *bastardo*—a second Diaz? You understand I must justify this to myself as well as their women."

Madelaina, visibly moved, rose from her chair She walked across the room, opened the shutters, and glanced out at the courtyard filled with moving figures: *campesinas, soldaderas*, with their men and children, milling about the fires making preparations for supper. She knew Villa awaited her words as a hungry man might be ready to pounce upon a meal denied him for a week.

"What I know of Carranza, even from childhood, is perhaps an old story to you. My observations of Don Carranza and his stuffy family are colored by my own emotions." She gazed out the window, seeing nothing in particular.

"Naturally. Why else would I ask, if not to know Little Fox's opinion of such a man? The eyes of children always speak in truth and record their thoughts in truth. It is only after they grow up that they shade the bad things to conform to all things around them."

Madelaina turned to him. "Carranza's a four-tongued viper. He is crafty, full of guile, and has the duplicity and cunning of a four-sided man. He pretends patriarchal concern for the nation like Diaz. And like Diaz, he's a stuffed shirt, an opportunist whose real desire is to reestablish the old Diaz regime with himself in the seat of power. He is not a militarist like you or my father, even though he's conferred upon himself title of *el premier jefe*, since President Wilson shows an inclination to favor him as possible presidential material. Yes, First Chief of the Revolutionary Army is what he calls himself. But whose army, *Jefe*? Yours? Obregon's? Mercado's. *Aye*, Carranza is a fox. He's a snake. He's a badger. All three rolled into one. It is for this that my father, General Obregon, refuses to lay down his sword for this chocolate-drinking pansy."

"All this leads me to the question I intend putting to you, Little Fox. The question of General Alvaro Obregon."

She knew what was coming. It's just that she didn't expect it so soon.

"I hear that General Obregon has found the exploits of my colorful *Dorados*—" Villa's hands rolled in a circle in the air before him, groping for a word,—"exciting?" he finally said for lack of a more descriptive word.

"Why wouldn't he? The best-trained crack cavalry troops in all of Mexico. Any military man worth his salt would find them a glorious group—especially since they are the brainchild of Pancho Villa."

"Bueno. You think it's time to arrange between us—a meeting—under the white flag of truce?"

The fact that this was precisely the thought she'd entertained for the past few weeks gave her a jolt of satisfaction. But she was wise enough to know it would have to be Villa's decision. Even so, thought Madelaina, there was always the question of her father's reaction. The animosity between these two warring tigers was vast. Could Obregon set aside his personal feelings toward the man who'd won his daughter's loyalty in the revolution? Could he? Would he? Her silence was misunderstood by the *jefe*, who began to drum his fingers on the table in a slow, almost calculating manner.

"I know what you must be thinking. Politics. Stinking politics again. Perhaps you think I'm a traitor to our cause to even consider dealing with an enemy—a formidable one at that. But I've come to learn that anger in a debate causes the argument to be forgotten. And the argument here is the glory of Mexico, not any one man. Truth of the matter is, *chica,* these past many weeks since the death of the gringo *hacendado* I've given much thought to victory and defeat. In my campaigns, I've wounded and wounded deeply, knowing full well that after such a battle, nothing is sweeter than the peace which follows. For these severe tactics, I've been chastized, criticized unjustly by our gringo neighbors."

"What do they know of the suffering here? They remain deaf and dumb and blind to our pleas. They won't listen to the cries of the people whispering in the wind," said Madelaina in his defense. "It remains for a man like you, *Jefe*, a man with heart, soul, and conscience for his people to take up the standard and carry it through to perch atop the highest steeple at Zocalo."

Villa tried hard to blink back the tears that watered his eyes at her touching words. He shook his head slowly. "What will happen if I *cannot*—or *will not*—rule our liberated Mexico? That is the question. Who will rule Mexico once Villa has won the revolution? You see, nothing is easy. Even victory presents more complications than I've bargained for. Since the light was turned on in my mind, all I do is worry, worry, worry. Such is the fruit of a thinking man."

"What good will it do to prepare a parley with my father?"

"It is useless to shoot arrows into an iron statue, *chica*. Obregon grows in strength daily. Make no mistake, Little Fox, General Obregon is better trained in the military than is Pancho Villa."

"He's been in the military all his life. It's only natural that he thinks like a *Científico*. But do you deny that your conquests are greater than his?"

"Obregon's campaigns are far less complicated than the bloodbaths we've left in our wake. Where I hit heavily fortified garrisons, your father is more clever to conserve his forces and he continues to win territory and a reputation."

Madelaina retorted hotly. "Why wouldn't he, *Jefe*? Whenever you attack, you attract all the *Huertistas* from the coast, giving Obregon the opportunity to take over the weakened garrisons, and so doing, he comes out smelling like a rose." To emphasize her point, Madelaina pointed to several areas on the map tacked to the wall along one side of the room. "Not only that, after you've captured a town and moved on, leaving a flimsy crew in charge, he assaults the village and takes it back, weakened and in desperate straights, without booty."

"Precisely," said Villa smiling. "Perhaps working hand in hand, we can march into Mexico City side by side. It is not for naught that my people have a saying—'Two that are of the same opinion can conquer a city.'"

Madelaina got the picture, but she shuddered inwardly at the complications this scene posed in her mind. "*Jefe*, my father is an ambitious man. It would bear well to remember that among my people there is another saying—'The fox favored by fortune conquers the lion favored by strength.'"

"Ayeiii, *chica*, but remember, all those sayings work both ways."

"My father lacks political polish—"

"*Muy bien*. What you are saying is that Obregon needs Carranza to gain this—uh—political polish, eh? Perhaps as much as Carranza needs Obregon's strength—"

"And both of them need you, General Villa, to grind the *Federales* of Huerta into cattle feed!" retorted Madelaina, pouring herself another glass of wine. "With your permission, *Jefe*?" She held the glass up toward him.

"That's true, what you say. Very true."

"Recently, in an interview with Miguel Guerra, you publically labeled my father a chocolate-drinking, pig-headed, mad goat."

"That's true, too," said Villa, suppressing a wicked smile.

"That means my father must be out of his head to beat you at every turn."

"That's also true. You think you can arrange such a meeting between us before I meet with Don Carranza?"

She gave him the shadow of a smile. "Insults stir his *gachupin* blood to boiling. You have a parley planned with Carranza?"

"Of course. The spider is from birth a weaver. It's important to see the sort of web this spider Carranza weaves. Now, what you say, Little Fox?"

"It's been said, *Jefe*, that we *gachupíns* always demand the impossible and somehow get it accomplished."

"Then you'll act as emissary to General Obregon?"

"First, I must tell you what it entails."

Madelaina proceeded to explain that her son was in the hands of her father, and of the purported deal made with Peter Duprez for her return. "I don't know how the general will take to such a proposal. If I go, it may mean I will be detained longer than I intend to be detained."

"Then it's out of the question, Little Fox." Villa paused and looked at her intently. "Unless, of course, you desire to go of your own free will."

"He has my son. I have longed to see his face, *Jefe*."

"I will send an escort with you. Obregon will not dare to detain you as long as you're an emissary of mine. In war, father or not, he's a military man."

Before any decision was made, General Villa and his guest were interrupted by an announcement that Don Venustano Carranza had arrived to speak with General Pancho Villa under a white flag of truce.

"Speaking of Lucifer—" began Villa with amused eyes. "He's ahead of time."

"I will go and think on your proposal, *Jefe*," said Madelaina. "I leave you men to your politics. It's best that Carranza doesn't see me if I'm to confer with Obregon on your behalf. Who knows what treachery lies beneath that white-haired, aristocratic benevolence dressed in a German coat?"

"*Bueno*. Go this way." He indicated to a side door.

Madelaina pulled a black scarf over her head, partially shielding her face, and left the premises. Outside, she trudged along the parched, cracked earth, kicking up little puffs of smoke in her wake. She had much to think about concerning Villa's request. She thrashed a

838

small riding crop alongside her boots as she walked, absorbed in her thoughts.

Approaching her from another direction, his back to the sun, came the imposing figure of the man recently labeled "Villa's Butcher." Rudolfo Fierro's steps were slow and languid, in the rhythm of a great cat. He called to her.

"Espera, señora. Wait for me.'

Madelaina stopped, shaded her eyes against the hot, glaring sun, and recognizing him, waited as his steps quickened to catch up to her. Fierro removed his hat with a sweeping gesture of courtesy.

"You have a guest, *señora,* who insists upon seeing you immediately." Fierro's stone face indicated neither pleasure or displeasure over this. He did add apprehensively, "Be careful of this one. She appeared like a bird in flight from nowhere. How she got past our sentries is what I intend to learn as soon as I escort you to her. She is in your quarters at the hacienda."

Madelaina nodded and fell into step alongside him, filled with curiosity. A woman? Clever enough to get past the cadre of officers guarding the military compound? Most interesting. She continued to strike her boots absently with the riding crop as they made their way to the rambling building and entered the villa proper.

Inside, Madelaina discarded the *rebozo* covering her head and shoulders and jerked her head back, swinging her long dark hair off her shoulders. Her eyes, adjusting to the cool, dimly lit interior, scanned the room for the uninvited guest.

The young woman, dressed in a full-skirted, Indian peasant's dress with a low-cut blouse, was seated primly in a highbacked chair, a backpack at her sandaled feet. She was thinner than Madelaina recalled, but it wasn't difficult to recognize the one-time *puta* of General Obregon and Paco Jimenez.

"Dolores Chavez," she said in a moderate tone. "What brings you to the camp of Pancho Villa?"

"*Señora Obregon! Dios mios!* I am happy to have found you after all this time." She rose to her feet and ran to Madelaina's side, expecting a warmer greeting than the frosty reserve shown by the daughter of her one time paramour. She recoiled instantly and immediately fell into a subservient role. She glanced at Rudolfo Fierro, and sensing the cold brutality in the man, she lowered her eyes and stared at her open-toed sandals.

"Please, *señora*, it is in private that I must speak to you."

"You may speak before General Fierro," said Madelaina.

The girl shrugged. "It is your *niño*, your baby He is *muy mal*. Has much fever. Generale de Cordoba, he say you come, *pronto*."

Madelaina's dark eyes were leveled on the girl She stepped in toward her, fingering her knife with menace. "Hear me, woman. If you are not speaking the truth, I shall finish the job *La Condesa* apparently forgot to finish." For added emphasis, Madelaina struck the palm of her hand with the leather crop.

Dolores Chavez fairly cringed. "*La Condesa? Dios mios*, no! *Por favor*, not that evil one, Golden Dawn. I have not seen her long since I leave Zacatecas"

Madelaina relaxed somewhat, but not entirely She didn't trust the girl. "What is the matter with my baby? Where is he?"

"In Zacatecas. He is with a strange fever. *Muy mal*—much fever, *senora*."

"Not at El Dorado? What exactly did General de Cordoba say to you?"

"Only to find you and return with the wind, *muy pronto*. Only a mother knows how to care for her *niño*."

"Why didn't they think of that before they snatched him from my breast? Oh, never mind. Why didn't he think to return the child with you? It would have been better and saved us all time."

"Why so many questions, *señora*? Is it not enough that I risk my life to find you?"

"Perhaps, Dolores," she temporized, leveling her dark, cold eyes on the girl.

"Besides," added Dolores, a bit hastily. "The major general was concerned that the child should fall into the wrong hands—for instance, Major General Salomon." Her eyes secretly challenged Madelaina, then the fire died out.

Madelaina's dark eyes smoldered at the sound of Salomon's name. She forced herself to keep in check "Now then, be kind enough to explain to General Fierro and myself just how you got past our sentries."

Fierro's appreciation of Madelaina Obregon increased considerably. *What a cool one, this Little Fox. She asks the right questions*, he thought. *Now, let's see where it gets her.* He fingered the red-haired fetish at his belt.

"You forget I am a *campesina* of the *Federales*? For years, I, too, know how to gain access to forbidden places. I am a Mexican *peón, señora.* I know the land. I may be a common whore to you, used by your father whenever he had the need, but I am of the people, a Mexican."

"How did you get past the sentries?" Madelaina repeated patiently.

"You think it was difficult? I hid in one of the wagons filled with supplies coming from Chihuahua. No one stopped to inspect the contents. They just waved the driver, Pepe Rodrigues, on into the compound. I made my escape while he unhitched the burros. It was easy." Glancing at Fierro and the fetish, Dolores shuddered involuntarily.

Madelaina's eyes lifted to Fierro's and carried a silent message, which he'd already picked up. He'd make certain a man named Pepe Rodrigues had actually hauled supplies from Chihuahua, that all supply wagons were to be stopped for inspection, even if Pancho Villa himself should drive one onto the compound.

"You may leave us, General," she told Fierro.

"With your permission, I'll remain until your decision is made."

"Then, it's done. I must see to the safety of my child." She pulled Fierro toward the door and spoke confidentially to him, so Dolores would not hear. "I leave on a mission for the *jefe*. Tell him I'll do his bidding. I shall return when I've obtained the proper reply." Then she spoke aloud. "General, have the men prepare a wagon for me with enough supplies for two to last until we get to Zacatecas."

"You don't intend to make such a journey by wagon, *señora*?" called Dolores aloud with obvious dismay.

"And why not?" countered Little Fox, turning abruptly to the girl.

"Time. Too much time! By train we can be in Zacatecas in a day—not five. Unless you wish to accept the responsibility of your baby's life!"

Madelaina's eyes narrowed. She stared at the girl, studying her brazen, outspoken manner. She turned to Fierro. "The girl makes sense." She rang a bell summoning a servant woman. "Feed the woman, she's traveled far," she instructed the older woman. Madelaina led Fierro out the door and told him Dolores was the *puta* of her father, that she'd known her for some time, and although she didn't understand why she'd be given such a sensitive mission, she could understand that a *campesina* would fare far better than an officer of the *Federale* army in an attempt to pierce enemy lines.

Fierro hardly flickered an eyebrow at this. He touched his hat and left to attend to his work. She watched him head toward the front gates of the compound, then joined the former mistress of her father inside.

"While you fill your belly, I'll pack a small bag of necessities. Tell me, did they summon a doctor for my child?"

"I'm certain everything that can be done has been

842

done. They tell Dolores nothing. Only to summon you."

Madelaina, uneasy about the whole thing, still persisted in her questions.

"Why didn't they send a Federal courier—or a military attaché—even a military escort under a white truce, if they knew my whereabouts? Even a wire?"

"Perhaps because your father's memory serves him well. You might have run away or resisted as you've done in the past."

Dolores' momentary naïveté sprang from an effort to pretend to a lack of worldliness and was weakly enacted. Madelaina saw that the girl was indeed a poor actress. Why, for *dos* pesos, she'd have tossed the girl out. Not for a moment did Madelaina trust her. She excused herself when the older serving woman brought food and Dolores pounced hungrily upon it.

Outside, once again, Madelaina's steps quickened as she headed toward the telegraph station. She hastily scribbled a message and handed it to the clerk with orders to send it immediately. The bespectacled clerk, a thin, young man with a thick crop of black hair, scratched his head wondrously. "But this is incredible, *señora!* To receive an answer before a message is sent is not how this machine works! *Dios mios!* Miracles of miracles!"

"Stop your jibberish," she said sternly. "What are you talking about?"

"Perhaps, he means this, *señora*," came the voice of Rudolfo Fierro behind her. He was holding a message in his hand, outstretched to her.

Madelaina was given to surprises, but never had she been so amazed and at the same time grateful for the astute thinking of General Fierro. No wonder he was so invaluable to Pancho Villa. She read the message:

To Federal Garrison Commander, Chihuahua City. Be advised that the mission of which you inquire, by one Dolores Chavez, is legitimate. The child is critically ill. The mother's presence is needed. Code F ac-

knowledged. Major General Felipe de Cordoba, Fort Zacatecas.

"You had your doubts as I did?" Madelaina folded the message and tucked it into her camisole. "Perhaps you'd better send another wire, General Fierro. Announce that Madelaina Obregon is en route as emissary from General Villa and seeks audience with General Alvaro Obregon."

"Are you crazy?" he spoke in faultless English. "The message might be intercepted by *Huertistas*, and thinking you might be an excellent prize, kidnap you for ransom. I'm sure both General Villa and General Obregon might be encouraged to make many concessions to secure your release."

"Damn!" she cursed softly. "Of course, I wasn't thinking! How stupid of me." She paced before him in the small, wooden structure serving as a wireless room: "*Bueno*, General. Let's walk back to the hacienda. I have a plan," she told him.

An hour later, Madelaina was dressed in the smart gray travel suit and matching hat, her hair piled atop her head, looking every bit like a gringo tourist, with the proper papers identifying her as Mrs. Peter D. Benson, giving her resident address as Seven Moons, Amarillo, Texas. She was accompanied by Dolores Chavez, traveling as her maid, with papers to indicate she, too, was from Amarillo, Texas.

If Madelaina saw two well-dressed businessmen enter the car and sit to the rear, never taking their eyes from the women, she paid them no mind. Two additional men, boarding the car ahead of them, and two more in the car behind them brought no suspicions to her mind. They had all taken specific seats, each with their eyes fixed on the panes of glass separating the cars, through which they could see the women.

The train ride, dull and boring, was considerably faster than a wagon. She noted it was far more comfortable than the jostling one was subjected to in a carriage. With the advent of progress, things were vastly improving, she admitted. The train made several stops en route to their destination. At lunch time, Dolores opened a food hamper and handed Madelaina a package containing dainty American-style sandwiches, a small bottle of wine, and figs. Madelaina munched heartily on her food as did the other train passengers, and for a long while the unusual aroma of food was difficult to ignore.

Before midnight the train stopped in Torreon, the midway point. They got off the train, stretched their legs, purchased newspapers and a few sweets, and after making use of the public convenience facilities provided for travelers in the train depot, boarded the train once again.

Marveling at the progress made since the revolution first commenced, she had hope that Mexico might one day become as progressive as their American neighbors.

Once the train pulled out of Torreon, Madelaina began to squirm uncomfortably. She wanted to smoke a cigarette, but for women in the first-class section, this was forbidden. She was growing increasingly uneasy, attributing it to the need to smoke. Finally, she forced her eyes closed, as the overhead lights dimmed, allowing those passengers who wished to sleep to do so without annoyances like lights to disturb them.

Madelaina's thoughts began to shift and change as pictures formed in her mind. For several moments she saw what appeared to be ghouls in purple shrouds with empty black holes for eyes. Then this shifted and the pictures appeared. She saw herself running frantically, pursued through a strange, thickly wooded place. Blood dripped from her hands and she seemed unable to catch her breath. She couldn't breathe; she felt a terrible struggle inside her as if her heart would burst if she didn't get some air. She stirred frantically, struggled, fought with all her strength as the face of Simon Salomon flashed before her. God, how she grappled and exerted herself, thrashing about. She attempted to blink her eyes, but they refused to open as

845

if a powerful adhesive had been applied to glue them shut. A peculiar odor filled her with nausea, and she felt herself falling, catapulting into black abyss. Then it was total darkness and complete immobility.

Chapter 31

As consciousness returned to her, Madelaina became fully aware that she was no longer on a train. An aromatic odor clung to her, and she tried desperately to orient herself. She couldn't move. Her body, she felt certain, was spread-eagled on a bed, judging from the feel of a mattress. Her arms, spread back and tied to the posts, were as rigid as her feet and as firmly secured. Unable to see due to the blindfold tied over her eyes and unable to cry out with the gag stuffed into her mouth, she was helpless.

She was sweating profusely, the drops rolling off her face and neck like raindrops. The room was sultry, and she was aware that her clothing had been removed. The knowledge of this left her feeling more despondent. She had no weapons to defend herself with. What had happened?

The last thing she recalled was lying back in her train seat, the lights dimming overhead—then nothing after that. Absolutely nothing.

Madelaina cocked her head and listened. She tried to familiarize herself with natural noises. Was that water falling? Rain? The ocean? A river? What? She couldn't tell. She heard voices speaking in hushed tones, nothing loud or clear enough to discern. At least she had her senses, and outside of the discomfort she felt, she didn't feel wounded or harmed. How long she lay there, trying to piece together parts of a puzzle, she didn't know.

Someone had entered the room. She tensed and strained against her bindings. The panic she experienced reminded her of the diabolical exposure to the sadism of Heurta and Salomon. If only she could speak or cry out. If only she could see. *Dios mios*, this was worse than anything. Without eyes to see or a mouth to speak, of what good were the other senses except to instill a morbid fear in a person? She attempted to tilt her head back to see under the blindfold, but the room was in total darkness. She wanted to cry out, to ask who it was in her room, to plead with someone for mercy, to remove the gag choking her lips, but, of course, she couldn't.

Whoever it was in the same room with her had seated himself alongside her on the bed. She knew it was a man by the heavy way in which he fell onto the mattress. She heard an unfamiliar rustling sound, labored breathing, the faint flopping sound of boots being removed. Then she felt her flesh shrink and quiver as the touch of human hands lightly caressed her body. She felt her body recoil from the touch, yet simultaneously she found the feeling pleasurable.

A voice whispered huskily. "You and I, Madelaina Obregon, have unfinished business to attend to."

A sudden feeling of terror made her gasp and choke on the gag.

"If you promise to cooperate, I'll remove the gag," whispered the man seated on the bed with her. "No one will hear you if you scream, so you might as well understand that. And if you do scream out, I can easily allow you to inhale more of the floral scents you inhaled last evening. Do you wish that?"

She shook her head furiously.

She felt the gag being untied and the strips of cloth removed from her parched lips. The blindfold was still intact.

"Would you like some water?" he asked, tilting her head up to receive some of the desperately needed liquid.

Madelaina swallowed, fairly gulped the water as it streamed down the corners of her lips onto her face, neck, and shoulders. But she didn't care. Anything to relieve the dire thirst that pervaded her for the past hours of consciousness.

"I'd remove the blindfold, too, if I didn't think you'd cause harm to yourself when you see me. For the time being, I'll leave it on. Then, after we've enjoyed ourselves and I've succeeded in taming you, I'll remove it."

"Please," she begged. "Who are you? Why are you doing this? I'll pay you money. You have mistaken me for someone else. I am Mrs. Peter Benson from Texas. I don't know any Madelaina Obregon."

"Lies, dear Little Fox, will get you no place," came the hushed voice of Major General Salomon. "You didn't think I'd let you get away with all the minor victories you've lorded over me, did you?"

Madelaina recognized the voice. As hard as she prayed it wasn't the man she knew it was, she visualized him clearly as the man in her visions pursuing her through the forests. She fought against her restraints, all to no avail.

He pinned her down to the bed with his strong hands. "Tonight we make up for all the injuries meted to me at your hands, you understand me, *chiquita*? From the first time I saw you, I knew what you were, a whore at heart, and I decided to make you mine. I was patient, wasn't I? I watched you at Madrigal and I lusted for you. I've lusted for you from the first time I set eyes on you at President Diaz' birthday party. Do you know the extent of my desire? I've won you. Yes, I've honestly won you. President Huerta wanted you—your neck hanging from a noose on his most cherished tree inside the palace courtyard, but I won you from your fate. And now you are mine to do with what I please."

Salomon continued: "I don't intend removing the blindfold from your eyes, not yet. I want you to feel the body you've tried to kill with such vengeance that you almost succeeded. I want you to feel first what you've been missing."

Madelaina blinked several times under the blindfold. No question about it, she'd know that voice, the scent of his overpowering colognes anyplace. She fought the urge to lash out at him and found herself relaxing her lips from a loathsome sneer into an inviting smile.

"So! Simon Salomon, it's you. We meet again." She spoke with a calm that momentarily unnerved him.

His laughter filled the room. "What a woman! What an incredible woman you are. Just the right sort for me. I always knew it. Pity you've remained blinded to the fact that we are suited to one another, madam." He delighted in her unusual powers of emotional recuperation whether feigned or real. "Even when your life is on the line—and this time there is absolutely no one to come to your rescue—you still have the monumental audacity and courage to speak so imperiously." He chuckled again. "You *are* something special. Not that I haven't always known it," he said, softly caressing her breasts with his fingertips in a circular brushing motion causing her nipples to stand erect.

"Feel how your body responds and is eagerly awaiting my artistry? Now, my pet, when your mind also bends to my will—and touch—I shall truly perform for you in a manner you shall be unable to resist."

How she loathed this man. Words couldn't describe the anguish, pain, and violent disgust this man had inflicted on her and now this! How was she to cope? If she could see him, she could command her senses to obey her—not his touch. Through the blindfold she could discern nothing, for the room itself must have been thrust in semidarkness. She could only feel him, and this in itself was maddening because her body responded to his touch. What to do? What to do?

She tried to writhe and recoil from his fingers, but she was helpless. She decided to change tack. "So the mighty Salomon imagines himself to be a descendant of Eros, is that it? A man who thinks he's been given a godlike power over women, to make me swoon helplessly in your arms? Very well, go ahead. Take your fill. Do what you will with my body, but know in advance that my mind will never bend to your will—never!" she told the man who'd once devised countless sexual tortures and forced on her various drugs which

850

prevented the mind from exercising any power over the pleasure of the flesh.

"My pet, I have the power within me to make you succumb to anything."

And now, Madelaina heard more clearly what she earlier thought was a river or water of sorts. It was raining outside. A crashing peal of thunder split open the skies and rain gushed forth in a tropical storm. Lightning streaks illuminated the room for split seconds and the sound of rain startled her.

Simon Salomon was evoking the proper sexual responses he wanted from his captive, even though she tried with all the will power she could muster to keep herself frigid and unresponsive. God, how much longer could she resist this man she loathed with her body and soul?

Involuntary moans and sighs escaped her lips as his manipulations aroused her erotically. She sensed him leaning in close to her face, holding himself inches from her lips. Repeatedly she jerked her head from side to side to avoid his lips on hers. He patiently held her head between his hands until she no longer squirmed.

"Might as well enjoy it," he said huskily. "It's going to happen whether or not you want me." He moved in closer and closer, barely touching her and with the tip of his tongue traced the outline of her full lips. A quiver shot through her and she tried not to enjoy it, to hate each moment of it, but God wasn't going to let her off easily. She found herself responding to his touch with a pent-up passion new to her. Blindfolded, even the sound of rain excited her as never before.

Salomon took a sip of wine from the bottle on the nearby table and moved toward her and kissed her, letting a little of the wine seep inside her lips. In her prone position she was forced to swallow the drops and found the warmth of the wine invigorating. He permitted some of the wine to spill over each breast, then with loud sucking sounds, he lapped it up with his tongue, watching her breasts grow firmer and harder as if they might explode at any moment.

He was too well practiced, too well schooled in his art to be a bumbler. He knew every erotic zone in her body; and in a matter of moments had her responding far too willingly to his machinations. *Demonio*! He was right. Her will was bending to his and to make matters worse for Madelaina a powerful desire swelled in her loins and throughout her entire body for him. *Dios mios*! What was wrong with her? Why couldn't she force her body to reject him—to remain cold, frigid, and hateful?

Salomon watched his captive respond to his touch with an expression of calculated strategy, the look of a man awaiting a specific reaction from an experiment he conducted. There was a certain degree of lust registered on his face, but there was more, something more than Simon himself could fathom.

She continued to writhe and squirm and quiver under his intimate, exploring touch, and when for a moment he stopped to cross the room to open a case and remove a few articles, Madelaina found herself straining to listen. What's more, she found herself anxious for his return to finish what it was he began.

"You miss me already, my pet?" he asked, watching her head move toward him. "I'll only be a moment. Would you like more wine?" Finished with what he was doing, Salomon returned to her side. He poured a glass of wine and held it to her lips. "That's it, it will relax you." He set the glass down and continued with his artful strokes. "Ahhh, my pet, I see the honey begins to drip between your thighs. You see—you've wanted me all the time. All these years of wasted time and emotion between us. Why, we could have been the toast of all Mexico, you and I. Our bodies together will warm this bed and many other beds where lovers might lie." He raised himself over her body and lowered himself into position. His lips devoured hers hungrily.

At the same moment, Madelaina felt a stabbing shaft of agony between her thighs that tore all the way into her belly, causing her body to arch up against his in a shock of pain. She felt as if she was about to be ripped to pieces. She heard whimpering, moaning sounds like an animal agonizing pain and realized those sounds escaped her own throat. He's killing me, she thought. He's finally killing me and I can't resist him. She tried to drag her legs up, to jackknife and expel his body from hers, but it was no use. She couldn't move. And she'd not give him the satisfaction of knowing how badly he'd hurt her. Whatever her movements they only increased his apparent lust. He drove himself deeper and deeper inside her body, forcing his tongue inside her mouth, probing and stroking until she needed air to breathe.

It was no use. She was as helpless as a child in the grip of a satanic monster bent on violating her, a demon for sure.

All at once, Madelaina tensed. She felt a hot sensation searing her insides, more shocking than the earlier pain, like a flooding warmth of liquid spilling out from her body, between her legs. "What's that?" she asked, half-reluctant to speak out. "Am I bleeding? Have you torn me apart?" she whimpered, unsure of the sensations shooting through her. "I'm burning up. What have you done to me?"

"I knew you'd enjoy it. You do like it, don't you?" he asked suggestively.

"No. I don't know," she stammered. She desperately tried to isolate the countless sensations shooting through her. The mixture of pain and pleasure, agony and ecstasy was driving her wild. Her head reeled and the room, despite the blindfold, was swirling round her head. Colors flashed in her mind and she felt a sudden elevation, a floating sensation, one of suspended animation where feelings blended into a tremendous wave of erotic delights far superior to anything felt on a carnal level. Tiny explosions of light burst in her mind. Sensations of floating, of transcending the terrestrial limits of earthly beings transported her higher and higher until she was lost in infinity.

A soft, self-satisfied chuckle brought her back to reality. "My, my, what a little tigress you are," he told her. "What would happen if I untied your legs?"

Her throat was parched, but she managed to whisper hoarsely. "Untie them and see for yourself."

"And if I untie your arms?"

"See for yourself."

"You'd like that, wouldn't you? You want to claw at me, scratch at me, and bite into my flesh, don't you?"

"Yes! Yes! Yes!" she hissed between clenched teeth. "All that and more."

"Tell me how you've wanted me. Tell me!" he commanded her.

"Yes," she growled low in her throat. "Yes, I've wanted you. I've always wanted you."

Simon Salomon laughed softly, pleased with himself, as he watched her react to his commands with no will or volition of her own. "And now, tell me what you feel when I perform my next speciality."

She felt him unloosen her legs. She moved her ankles in a circular motion, trying to get the circulation back into them. Instantly she drew them up to her chest.

"Don't be so greedy yet," he told her. "In a moment you'll feel a sensation you've never felt. Then I'll know you'll be my slave for all eternity, Little Fox." He spread her legs apart and slipped his body down over hers and positioned himself between her slender limbs. "From the French came the art I'm about to perform on you," he told her.

Madelaina felt the warmth of his heated breath, first, then a velvety softness, as a thousand little shocks burst all around her. Suddenly she knew what he was doing and she didn't care. All she wanted to do is experience the sensations—every one of them. Madelaina had no control—not over her words or her body. And when she spoke the next few words, it was as if someone else uttered them. "Had I know how it would be with you, I'd have succumbed sooner, my dear, sweet, Simon."

Her legs straddled his back and she pressed him in closer to her, harder and harder. If she had any recollections of this man and what he'd caused to happen to her in the past, they were dimmed by the powerful intoxicant of uninhibited sexual desire. Madelaina wasn't certain of how long she remained with Simon Salomon or he with her. She remembered only the pleasurable sensations and immediate gratification of a deeply rooted physical need which hadn't been fulfilled since the night she and Peter conceived their only child.

Madelaina had been kept forcibly drugged for nearly two weeks before she gained insight into her true predicament. Permitted to wear her own clothing now, she dressed simply, even though Salomon had placed several lovely gowns at her disposal. On this day, as she eagerly awaited Simon's arrival, she selected the seven moon earrings to wear as the only jewelry adornment. She stared at her reflection in the mirror for a long time, watching them move fragilely, then forgot them.

She'd been unaware of the passing of time and had forgotten the reason for her mission to Zacatecas. She hardly gave thought to Dolores, gave no mind to Pancho Villa, the revolution, her husband, not even her father or son. She lived only for the moments she could spend with Salomon. She no longer entertained the pain and longing she'd once endured. It was as if no memory existed of her life before these past few days of sexual fulfillment with Salomon. She thought only of him and the satisfaction of her physical needs and desires.

Simon Salomon was by normal standards a handsome man in his thirties. After seeing the sheer bestiality in the man and his many brutalities in Madrigal, his features had brought loathing and disgust to Madelaina. By the manner in which she greeted him on this day, you'd never imagine that she once detested him with uncontrollable emotion.

Madelaina heard his soft whistle and ran to fling open the shuttered doors, her heart all aflutter like a young schoolgirl. He smiled with unusual tenderness,

855

and looking well pleased with himself, he brandished a bouquet of bloodred roses, which he'd concealed behind his back. Dressed in his immaculate khaki uniform, with the brass buttons and braid and decorations of a major general, he cut a dashing figure for any woman who glanced at him.

She thanked him profusely for the flowers and waited for him to take her into his arms as he'd customarily done each day since they had coupled.

She took his hands and pulled him into her room, one of many in an old convent situated close to Ojocaliente near Zacatecas. Madelaina, of course, had no knowledge of her whereabouts, nor did she care. She eyed Simon with the eyes of love and pouted when he sat down alongside her on the long sofa, refraining from making his usual ovations to her. She placed the flowers on the table nearby.

"My dear," he began. "I must leave you for a while. It's unfortunate that we must be parted, but until these savage and despicable rebels can be halted, our time must of necessity be postponed."

"Rebels? What rebels?" she asked in all innocence.

"You aren't aware of the revolution in our country that tries desperately to oppose our love and all the things it stands for?"

Madelaina glanced at him with the petulance of a spurned lover. "You mean, Simon, that you'll be leaving me? But why? Can't you tell the world to get along without us for a time? It's not fair. We've only just met and already you're called back to duty."

"Don't you worry. I'll try to return as soon as I can. If only I knew a way to put that bloody *guerrillo* in his place. We've sent out spies to try to pierce his network of activity, but they can't penetrate the tight cordon of loyalty that surrounds him. His people pretend to stupidity. His soldiers, when caught, prefer torture at its worst, rather than betray him, and he seems inclined to recruit our own soldiers who defect to him by the dozens daily." Salomon sighed. "What a pity. I will miss you." He eyed her testily as if he were baiting her.

"Oh, Simon," she cried with a burst of disappointment. "What will I do without you? I'll be so lonely, I'll die. Is that what you wish for me to do—die?"

"Of course not, my dear. If only we knew what Pancho Villa was up to—what he intended doing—then it would make my job so much easier. I'd be finished and back to your bed before the week is ended." He watched her craftily, as her reactions, confused and irrational, mounted. She perspired a bit and couldn't seem to breathe, but none of this phased her at the moment.

A servant appeared with hot chocolate, a beverage Madelaina in the past had learned to detest. Now she looked forward to drinking it two and three times a day. Usually after drinking the chocolate, Madelaina perspired freely from the hot liquid. On this day, after her first cup, she shivered noticeably as if she'd suddenly come down with a chill.

"What is it, my dear?" he asked, forcing himself to exercise more patience.

"N—nothing. It's nothing. I suppose the news of your leaving has left me somewhat nervous and upset." Again a chill ran through her and she shivered. "Isn't that strange," she told him. "It must be 100 degrees outside and I'm shivering."

"Oh, my dear. What can I do for you?" Instantly he became solicitous of her. He placed an arm around her and held her protectively. "Does your head ache again? You've complained several times this past week. Perhaps I should summon a doctor for you?"

"I've complained before? Oh, dear, I don't even remember. Nothing seems to matter to me except for our time together. I swear, at times I feel intoxicated by you, Simon. I can't recall anyone having such an impact on me. My love for you grows deeper each day."

"I can't believe that," he said, "when you continue to wear those foolish gypsy earrings. I've bought you several beautiful things, including those fine negligees—the latest from Paris, I was told—and you still

857

cling to that absurd wrap and those—those peasant earrings."

Madelaina's hands flew instinctively to her ear lobes and felt for the small bangles of crescent moons. "Oh, these? Does it matter so much to you, Simon? I shall remove them at once. I shall put on the maize negligee if you promise to remain with me and not go off to that silly war. I don't want you to leave me. You must stay with me, you hear? You must stay!"

"I would if only you'd cooperate, my dear. You, as Little Fox, would know exactly what Pancho Villa has in store for us, and if you wanted, you could keep me at your side forever." He slowly removed her arms from around his neck, where she'd clung to him in an almost maudlin manner. His face close to hers was wiped clear of any emotion. His dark, concentrated eyes bore into hers.

"Little Fox? Me? I know of Pancho Villa?" she asked, a puzzled look swimming across her face. She changed expressions. "You must be confused. I know of no one by that name."

"Oh, but you do, my dear. Think. Think carefully, difficult as it might seem. You do know him. You are called Little Fox, his most trusted confidante," he said in a suggestive manner.

"Simon, why are you bent on deviling me like this? If you are trying to frighten me, you've succeeded. Now stop it and don't make me feel so despicable. I have nothing whatever to do with your going off to war." She poured another cup of chocolate, trying to sift through the crazy thoughts suddenly illuminated in her brain. She fairly gulped the hot liquid in a desperate attempt to warm up.

"I'll leave you to think on my words. I'll return in an hour," he said finally, glancing at his watch. In an hour she'd be feeling worse. Withdrawal would be setting in, and her memory, as painful as it might be, would return to her. Then he was sure to secure her cooperation.

An hour later, as Salomon predicted, Madelaina was

in a worse state of mind. Alternating chills and hot flashes, a state of anxiety and marked agitation possessed her. Memory returned in spurts. Thoughts that she'd been a willing participant in love trysts with a man she'd vowed once to kill filled her with insurmountable guilt. Memories of her life before the abduction compounded the increasing waves of guilt. She grew more anxious, more depressed, and decidedly phobic. She paced the floor in a flurry of agitation and at one point tried to open the door to walk on the terrace, only to learn it had been bolted from the outside. She ran to the shuttered windows, tried to open them, and noticed they too had been secured from the outside. She grew claustrophobic.

Her hands flew to her face. Desperately she tried to subdue a rising hysteria gnawing at her stomach. She felt as if she'd been put through a wringer. Pausing before a mirror, she caught sight of her reflection. Earlier she'd admired herself. She hadn't eaten much these past two weeks and the loss of weight had begun to be noticeable. Now, as she stared in the mirror at her skeletal appearance with dark circles under her eyes, she no longer recognized herself.

Her body shuddered with chills, and she grabbed a shawl to cover herself. Sweat rolled off her face even as ice flowed through her veins. She felt a heaviness in her hands, and her arms sagged, pulling her shoulders down. Her nose began to run and she wiped at it with the back of her hand. Madelaina grew alarmed. One moment she felt as if the flesh were melting off her bones, the very next, she felt as if she'd turned into an icicle.

She scurried across the room and quickly set about building a fire in the fireplace. In moments a fire blazed on the hearth and she grew so hot, she felt as if once again she was on fire. She felt suffocated. Her hands flew to her throat as she glanced wild-eyed and frantic about the room. Spying a pitcher of water, she dashed it on the fire. It sputtered, crackled, and popped, then flamed again as the fire caught hold. "No!" she screamed. "Damnit, no!" She ripped at her clothing, tearing it to shreds, trying to cool off. She grabbed a blanket and began to smother the fire with it, as her eyes flared frantically and her breath came in spasms. Finally subduing the fire, Madelaina gave a thankful sigh and picked herself up from the floor where she'd flung herself to obliterate the fire. She was exhausted.

A shudder of chills tore at her, and she grabbed for anything in sight to drape around her to keep warm and to prevent her teeth from chattering. She pulled at the scarf from the top of the dresser and in so doing scattered her few belongings. For an instant she didn't care what had been disrupted, then her eyes came to rest on the chamois bag of dried, powdery mushrooms.

She glanced at it feverishly, then glanced away, giving it no importance. Once again her eyes traveled back to the bag lying on the floor not far from her. She reached for it instinctively, not certain she knew what it was or what to do with it. She held it in her hands for several moments and continued to shiver.

She fell onto the sofa, drew the covers around her, and sat huddled in a heap, staring down at the leather pouch in her hand. Slowly, as if led by some force unknown to her, she pulled the bag open and peered inside. There was very little left, but whatever it was, she grew curious. She wet her fingertip with her tongue, reached in, and when a few particles clung, she raised her fingertip to her lips and tasted it. She repeated the ritual, and as the bitter powder mingled with her saliva and was swallowed, she began to feel an easier, more relaxed glow permeate her being. In her desperate search for a rational explanation to what was happening, Madelaina concluded that she didn't know anything except for the distortion of depth and sensation, which cleared as quickly as it appeared.

As the haze in her mind cleared, a sudden and instant recall of everything up to her abduction from the train came to her. What remained unclear was how she'd gotten here, to wherever it was she was being detained. Moreover, the recollections of her intimacy with

Simon Salomon became so clear, the pangs of guilt she experienced made her want to retch.

How could she? How could she have willingly permitted that beast to make love to her? Worse, the memory that she'd enjoyed it gave her the feeling that she'd been submerged in dirt with the foulest, most revolting creature on God's earth, and her shame was intensified tenfold by the increasing disgust at her weakness. Why hadn't she killed him as she'd threatened to do so many times in the past? Twice before she had him in her gun sights and hadn't pulled the trigger! Why? Had she really wanted him to make love to her all along just as he'd intimated so many times? Her horror-stricken feelings of despair and disgust began to dissolve as the mushroom powder took more effect.

And she began to recall more—and more. Tolomeo! *Rub the powder on you if you need strength and power*. Yes, yes, she told herself frantically as she rubbed the powder on her lower abdomen. You need strength, Madelaina. You need power. You must never reveal the secrets of Pancho Villa to this odious General Salomon.

Love your enemy and you rob him of his power! "Oh, Tolomeo!" she cried dispassionately. "Whatever do you mean—*love your enemy*? Even that didn't work. It only made me more vulnerable! What is the mystery behind those words? What?" she agonized. "What? Show me and release me from this purgatory!"

Madelaina grew quiet and subdued. She began to think methodically over her predicament. It occurred to her that despite the answer she received from Zacatecas to her inquiry about Dolores Chavez, nothing ruled out the girl being a double spy. After all, no one had more good reason to despise the Obregon family than Dolores. They'd robbed her of her paramour, Paco Jimenez, and after the Golden Dawn affair, her relationship with General Obregon had certainly deteriorated. She had lost everything meaningful to her, so she'd be a ripe target for Huerta and Salomon's admonitions to retaliate against the Obregons.

Very well, thought Madelaina, *where does that leave me? So Dolores is a spy. Now what?* She threw off the blankets and coverings as her temperature returned to normal and began pacing the floor, chain smoking in the process. Tolomeo's words preyed on her mind: *Love your enemy and you rob him of his power.* The words spoken over and over burned in her memory, but still they formed a riddle in her mind.

She gave thought to Pancho Villa's encounter with Carranza. What had been resolved? She hadn't even seen her father to discuss Villa's proposition. What could they be thinking? Before she left, she told General Fierro she'd send him a wire, somehow, even it was only to advise him of her safe arrival. Surely they missed her, didn't they? How on earth would they find her?

While Madelaina struggled hard for answers to her dilemma, a loud rumble from the north was beginning to grow into an outrageous roar.

Pancho Villa's encounter with Carranza hadn't resolved a thing. What it had served to do was to define each man's position in the revolution more clearly than before. Villa had tried to cooperate with Carranza. He'd even decided to set aside his planned attack on Zacatecas. Abandoning his plan, he captured Saltillo instead. Just as Little Fox had suggested, the victory merely advanced Carranza's image. And Villa, in a rage when Carranza announced he'd sent another general to attack Zacatecas, greeted the white-whiskered, self-declared First Chief of the Revolution, cowed by the announcement that President Wilson sanctioned the tricky old bastard, despite the growing rumors of his German leanings. Now, to cap it off, Carranza had the audacity to visit Villa again and ask him to cooperate with the general he'd sent to attack Zacatecas.

"No," countered Villa. "I refuse to send my good

862

men to get your man out of difficulties. Goddamnit! You knew I wanted Zacatecas! You send another man to take it and you ask me to keep my tail between my legs and cooperate? Hah!"

"I do what's necessary for the revolution," replied Carranza in that slow, deliberate, nerve-wracking speech designed to enflame Villa's heart.

Villa stormily paced the confines of his study, staring daggers at the man who continuously rocked his boat. He'd been a fool to fall for his sweet talk. Yet, until Little Fox returned with word from Obregon, he had felt it necessary to cooperate with this lout. But Carranza asked too much! Too much, by damn! He saw readily that Carranza was out to get his goat, to shame and humiliate him by goading him into an animal-like reaction. *Very well*, thought Villa, determined not to be used or outwitted, *I'll play his little game*. Suddenly, he saw the way for Carranza's defeat. He bowed graciously, suddenly quite submissive.

"Very well, First Chief of the Revolution," said Villa mockingly. "You tell me General Natera needs help in Zacatecas? *Bueno*. He gets help."

Carranza eased forward, eyes filled with suspicion. "What sort of help?"

"Everything! Isn't that what you desire? Full cooperation from Villa."

"What you mean—everything? Explain."

"Everything is—everything. All of it. Have no fear. Zacatecas will fall."

"What you mean—everything?" Carranza persisted.

"I will send Natera the whole Northern Division."

"Ridiculous," scoffed Carranza, puffing on his Havana cigar.

"With me alongside."

"Preposterous! I won't permit it."

"Permit it? You won't permit it? You forbid me to move my own army?"

"General Villa, I am doing exactly that. You will send 6,000 men as I've directed, not one more or less.

Unless you wish to branded insubordinate to your commanding officer!"

"Ah," said Villa. "*Muy bien*. Then please consider my resignation tendered."

Carranza, unable to fathom this move, assured Villa that his joke was not amusing.

"What joke?" He sat down at his desk and wrote, "I resign" and signed it Pancho Villa. "There is my resignation. I assure you, it's no joke."

"If you think you are being clever, I'll be a step ahead of you. Before Mexico wonders why you've resigned and asks why you lost your army, I'll announce my reward for the hero of Torreon and Saltillo. I'll make you governor of Chihuahua."

It was Villa's turn to be stupified. "*Que va*, me a governor? Me—a governor?" he repeated wondrously as if Carranza was truly one crazy man.

"Why not? Already you've done an excellent job of running things, but I may have to rescind your order giving the lands to the *peóns*."

Villa saw red. Like Zapata, whose intent it was for the peasants to own their own lands, Villa stood adamant. "You touch one inch of those lands, and I swear by the sainted hair of my mother's head, I'll kill you! Yes, I, Villa the barbarian, the bloodthirsty *guerrillo*, will do such a thing, civilized or not."

With that he moved toward the door, his uniform jacket slung over his shoulder.

"You step through that door, General Villa, and I'll immediately summon all the leaders of the Northern Division, instruct them to elect a new *jefe*, then I shall order 6,000 men to Zacatecas. Do I make myself understood?"

"Summon whoever you please, take my army, my rank, the whole fucking state of Coahuila, and stick them up your ass. Do I make myself understood?"

He stalked out of the door, motioning to his two aides in the outer office to follow him. "You hear it?" he asked as the trio moved out of the building.

"We heard."

"Well, there you are. He's your new boss."

"Not mine," said Urbina.

"Nor mine," said Fierro.

"Nor mine, either," said Tracy Richards joining them.

"We go where you go," Urbina insisted, grinning incorrigibly.

"Es veridad. That's the truth," offered Fierro.

"Me, too," echoed Captain Richards.

Pancho Villa stopped and turned to his friends, a smile radiating his features. *"Amigos,* I don't know about you or the entire Northern Division, but Pancho Villa goes to Zacatecas. And he will take it as planned at one big party."

"Who else is invited to your party?" asked Urbina.

"Whoever wishes to come," Villa retorted.

"Departure time?" queried Urbina, tilting his sombrero rakishly over an eye.

"Departure time? Departure time?" Villa mused. "It depends on how much luggage we carry. What you say to that?"

Fierro smiled. "May I have the first dance at your party?"

Don Carranza heard the staggering news while seated in the office of the governor's mansion. Villa had left during the night, but he didn't depart alone.

Every man, gun, cannon, war wagon, war bonnet, cartridge, and train belonging to the Northern Division had pulled out for Zacatecas. Villa had not ordered them out. He merely loaded his 300 *Dorados* and his new woman on his personal train, and the whole of the remaining division followed him.

Madelaina Obregon thought at first an earthquake had struck. The earth itself rumbled and shook under her. The walls of the old adobe convent shook, plaster ripped off the wall as cracks split the severed structure in more places, leaving a maze of fine lines like cracked porcelain. Running to the windows, she struck at the louvered shutters with her bare hands, breaking slats at random. Outside, she saw nothing in the ebony darkness. Muffled sounds of familiar artillery fire came from the distance. "What is it?" she cried aloud. "What's happening? Let me out someone, please!" She banged on the door until her fists were swollen red.

Outside, she heard the sounds of marching feet shuffling about the courtyard. She ran to the window, picked up a chair, and smashed the shutters into pieces. Barred windows obstructed any chance of escaping, but at least she saw a contingent of *Federales* forming in the yards below, rifles at the ready, preparing to board a few motorized vehicles, while others mounted their horses and headed out the gates. Madelaina strained to see in the distance, and she realized she was approximately ten miles from Zacatecas as the crow flies. Zacatecas! If only she could escape, she could make her way there easily.

What was happening? She tried the door again—no chance to escape. She was stuck, stuck in this stupid place, until someone came to her rescue. What a revolting situation!

She had no idea that history was being made in Zacatecas by Pancho Villa and the entire *División del Norte*. That at the signal given by Villa, wave after wave of horsemen surged forward at a brisk gallop as the roar of cannon echoed through the nearby mountains. Over 20,000 men transported by Villa's trains faced 15,000 *Huertistas*. The entire Federal garrison was surrounded by artillery, cavalry, machine gun snipers, and every last man in Villa's army.

Buglers sounded calls echoed by other buglers from each brigade.

All were in readiness as Villa shouted: "Brigade Juarez . . . Advance!"

"Bri—gade Fierro . . . Ad—vance!"

"Bri—gade—"

The earth exploded in flames. The mighty Northern Division moved forward like a loud, flame-throwing, prehistoric monster determined to pulverize its enemy into mounds of broken bones that would crumble to dust. Within three hours, the Federal garrison was in shreds, their trenches broken, their cannon overrun. By nightfall, General Francesco Villa was master of Zacatecas.

General Fierro, having captured several officers, put the questions to them that brought instant results. Without informing his *jefe* of his mission, he rode off in a southwesterly direction in the company of two other men.

They stopped at an appointed tavern. After the exchange of a few pesos with the innkeeper, Fierro took the steps two at a time and followed the dark hallway along the centuries-old building, falling prey to time, and knocked softly at the door three times in the signal given him. The door opened a wedge, Fierro's huge shoulders shoved it open, and he stood face to face with a terrified Dolores Chavez.

"Now, *puta*, you and I are going to have us a nice talk," he said in the most syrupy voice he could muster, one that sent chills of terror through the traitorous soul of the whore. He slammed the door behind him and bolted it without the faintest trace of menace either in his voice or his face.

Chapter 32

At the end of this day, June 23, 1914, Madelaina, unsure of what was happening not far from her, walked the floors of her prison at the convent, chainsmoking one cigarette after another. Her supper, brought on a tray hours before, remained untouched. She knew something had happened militarily, but what? She had no idea of the time. She guessed it might be about eight or nine o'clock in the evening. Outside, she heard the cooing of doves, the rustling of a mild wind.

She picked up a few magazines and periodicals brought to her by one of the servants, thumbed through them for the dozenth time, and finally tossed them all aside in annoyance. Perhaps, she thought, it was best that she tried to rest. Lord only knows what was in the offing for her.

Her thoughts traveled to Peter. She wondered why he hadn't contacted the *jefe* from Washington. Why he hadn't sent her a message by courier or wire? Where was he? Had he returned to Seven Moons to attend to the funeral of his father? A thousand and one questions about her infant son plagued her. Was he really in Zacatecas? If so, was he free from harm during the apparent attack on the fort? She had assumed whatever artillery fire she'd heard earlier that day had to have been directed at Zacatecas. *Dios mios*, pray take care of my son.

Dios mios. Villa had told her he wanted to take Zacatecas. He'd also told her he'd wait for the reply from her father. What had happened to accelerate his plans, that is, if it was Villa who attacked the fort? She was unable to stop the constant barrage of questions forming in her mind or halt the fears over her son.

Madelaina paused in her hysteria to make some common sense assessments. Villa wouldn't have attacked the fort knowing Madelaina was there. Apparently General Obregon wasn't there, either—not if Villa really wanted to come to terms with him. Of course not, she told herself. Then it followed, if General Obregon were not at Zacatecas, her son wouldn't be there either! Neither would Felipe de Cordoba. She took heart. Then it all was some plan of treachery. Even the wires must have been intercepted as Fierro hinted they might be.

Madelaina's wretchedness began to dissolve. Her thinking came into better focus. Taking all that had happened to her into account, she realized that by the time Simon Salomon returned to her—if he returned—he'd expect to find a highly irrational, extremely nervous, and high-strung woman, one who might be overly dependent on him and acquiesce to any thing he suggested. *Yes*, she thought, *I'll have to be far more clever than Simon Salomon could ever guess.*

With this in mind, she began to plot and plan and calculate her next move. It wouldn't be easy, but she'd have to be the most consummate actress in the world. Madelaina washed and perfumed herself and did her hair up atop her head. She donned the most fetching of fur-trimmed negligees furnished by her paramour of the past weeks. Disgusted as she was with herself over their intimacy, she had to force herself to drain all the maudlin self-guilt. She hadn't been responsible for her acts while under the influence of whatever potion had been administered to her, so with strength of mind, she used suggestive means to absolve herself of any guilt feelings. *Listen*, she told herself, *while you sit back and wallow in guilt, you'll not have a clear head to think, nor the courage to follow your plan. So forget everything, except the need for survival.*

Madelaina was prepared for many things, but certainly not the news brought to her by Major General Salomon a half-hour later.

"Simon!" She gushed at him and fell into his arms, when he entered her boudoir. "Oh, my dearest, I've missed you so." She was superb.

Simon Salomon himself wasn't prepared for this demonstrative gesture on her part. He held her at arm's length, studied her face, imbued with adoration, and tried to assert himself as best he could, even as disbelief struck at the very heart of his emotions.

"Madam, I've come to transport you to Mexico City. A change in our plans necessitates an immediate departure," he said, clearing his throat self-consciously. He gestured abstractly and eyed her askance, unsure of what to make of her.

"Simon, beloved, must we? My dear, you've been so good to me these past days that in your absence I've designed a most special night for you, full of all the delights that will titillate your senses. Pray, say you'll abandon your other plans at least until this night is over."

Salomon, totally disarmed by her manner, stared at her wondrously.

"May we please have some hot chocolate, my dear?" She fluttered about him like a jittery *mariposa*. "I'm not certain what that hot toddy contains, dear, dear Simon, but I've been so nervous and cantankerous all day without it. How naughty of you not to have left orders with Josefa to serve me some while you were away. But now that you're back, I can have some, my sweet, sweet lover. Can't I?"

The *Huertista* stood stiff, almost in a military brace, as he watched her in utter fascination. Recalling all he knew about Madelaina Obregon, he grew testy at this new personality emerging. Could the drugs have had such an effect on her? Goddamn, she was too downright amorous. She must have had time to come off the drug—certainly she'd be showing signs of withdrawal. What had happened?

In any event, he had a duty to perform. Huerta

wanted to talk with her. Since Villa had captured their most important stronghold—Zacatecas—*El Presidente* was a mighty worried official. He wanted to use her as a weapon to keep Obregon in his stable. Already the General-in-Chief of the Fourth Sonora Battalion was gaining too much popularity and strength. Added to that, word had reached *El Presidente* that Villa and Carranza had merged. Now, if Obregon defected to their side, all would be lost.

So it had been decided: Madelaina would be the pawn to keep either Villa or Obregon out of the capital. Whether or not it would work, it was something Huerta had to try. Simon Salomon knew all this and he had to prevent Madelaina from learning she was headed for the presidential palace. Moreover, he intended to say nothing of Pancho Villa's victory for the time being. He'd humor her. It was the only way. Then, when she wasn't expecting it, he'd use chloroform as his men had used it on the train when they abducted her. It was best that she remain docile during their travels. This little tigress was too clever, too wise in the ways of escape, and he could take no chances.

"It's chocolate you desire, my pet?" He spoke softly, falling into her mood. "But, of course. And while we're at it," he added, unbuttoning his tunic, "there's no reason not to take advantage of our solitude. As you say, Mexico can wait."

Salomon pulled the cord, summoning an aide. He ordered chocolate. "The usual for the *señora*," he said, winking his eye to the aide behind Madelaina's back. He turned to her. "Now, then, my pet, you were saying earlier, you'd planned something rather special for me. I can hardly wait."

"And I, neither," she gushed, helping him out of his tunic. "Oh, let me help you with your boots, beloved." Once they were off, he removed his gun and holster, took out the gun, checked the clip, and shoved it into the waist of his trousers.

"Oh, Simon," she pouted like a spoiled courtesan, "I could hardly sleep this afternoon with all your men shooting outside. I thought we'd had an earthquake for certain with all that artillery fire. My dear, what was happening?"

"You heard from that distance?" he asked, watching her pour him a small glass of wine from the liquor cabinet.

"I tried to sleep, to rest up for your return. I was planning such erotica for you, and I daresay the noise interfered with my concentration." She handed him a glass, took one for herself, and linked arms with him, drinking a toast. "What will happen to us in Mexico City? Can we take an apartment and continue to be lovers?" she asked without shame.

Salomon, embraced totally by this sudden new personality, was on his guard, yet quite flattered to think he'd had this much influence on her. "You may not be interested in me when we arrive in Mexico City. You might have a change in heart, then where will that leave me?" he asked artfully in a beguiling manner.

"Bite your tongue, Simon. My dear, don't you know how much I love you? I never dreamed, when you first told me, you were capable of enchanting me, of loving me, and performing magic with your expertise. Well, I'm living proof. Dear, sweet, sweet Simon, can't you make them hurry with the chocolate? I have such a craving for it. I just can't explain it, sweet." She fluttered her hands.

"It will be here shortly. Now come give me a sample of what treasures are in store for me, my pet." He reached for her, embraced her in a passionate near-savage manner, and with clenched teeth, he tilted her head back and commanded, "Now, kiss me as you've dreamed of kissing me. This may well be our last night together for a while, so we might as well do it up right."

Madelaina gave a small gasp as his mouth closed over hers. She wanted to bite him, scratch his eyes out, reach for the gun between them and pull the trigger. Then what? How would she get past the small army camped outside her quarters and those in the courtyard? She shoved such thoughts from her mind, prepared to give the best act of her life. She forced her body to go limp against his, to become as yielding as a paid whore. She shivered noticeably, forcing her teeth to chatter.

"What's wrong?" he asked, pulling back to watch her face.

"I don't know." She hugged her arms about her and rubbed them with her hands, affecting an excellent pose of one going into withdrawal.

"You'll be all right as soon as the chocolate arrives. Now, my dear, you know the rules. Get the blindfold."

"Blindfold? Oh, not again, Simon. We've done it your way all this time, now can't we do it my way for once?" Her voice held a tremor or two, convincingly.

"You know better than to ask, pet. That's the excitement—the unusual thrills that spring from the fact that you can't see what it is that I'm doing. You don't want the thrill to pass?"

"Well, no," she pouted again. "But it would be nice for me to look into your hypnotizing eyes, which make me shudder and tremble under their power."

"It's enough that I untie your legs to give you more pleasure. Now, don't you wish to give me the same pleasure?" Simon was growing annoyed, playing the silly game with her. The things he did for *El Presidente*! He removed the perfumed, lace-edged handkerchief from the cuff of his shirt and held it under his nose, inhaling deeply. "Ahh, that's more like it," he rhapsodized for a few moments. "The only relief I get from inhaling this perennial dust of Mexico. Does everything here stink of cornmeal and stale chili peppers and *ceverza*? Please, my pet, put on the pale yellow chiffon negligee for me."

Madelaina nodded and opened the hand-painted wardrobe. She slipped out of the negligee she'd selected and donned the pale yellow one he'd requested. She moved about the room, circling around like a fashion model. "Does this suit your imperial highness?" she asked making light of the situation and not certain which road she would embark upon shortly.

"Much better, my dear. Much better." He walked into the adjoining bathroom and looked around the room containing a bathtub, commode, toilet basin, and overhead chain pull. He inserted a key into the wall cabinet and removed a small box of tablets. He returned to the bedroom, poured water from the jug on the dresser into a glass.

"Here's a tablet for your headache, my pet. I don't want anything to spoil our last night here. I'm going to take a bath. By the time I return you will be more relaxed and totally free of any headaches." He watched her slip the tablet into her mouth and sip the water.

Madelaina had thrust the tablet under her tongue and sipped the water, pretending to swallow. "Ugh," she said. "Why is it so bitter?"

"Aspirin is always bitter. Is it not?" He returned to the bathroom.

"What do I do if the chocolate comes?" she asked, lighting a few more candles and a few sticks of incense. She spit the headache powder in a spittoon.

"Tell the corporal to use his own key, leave the chocolate, and lock up again as usual," he called back to her.

Madelaina, finished with the candles and incense, lit a cigarette and paced the floor in agitation. Salomon acted as if nothing had happened. And it had. She knew it. The sound of artillery fire for most of the afternoon told her something was underfoot. She hadn't been a *soldadera* for nothing. She could smell the odor of gunpowder in the air. She gazed into the courtyard below. Except for a few sentries, the usual hustle and bustle were missing. Earlier she heard sounds of wagons lumbering out of the courtyard as if the army contingent housed in this facility was on the move.

Yet Salomon himself remained cool and complacent. What did he have in mind? She had to know. Was that really a headache powder—or something else? To keep up the pretense, she assumed it to be a sedative of sorts. So, she had to fake being drowsy for a time.

By the time Salomon emerged from the bath, more relaxed and refreshed than he'd been earlier, Madelaina lay prone on the bed in an affected state of drowsiness. Clothed in a royal blue damask robe with velvet shawl collar and cuffs, he walked to her side, lay a cool perfumed hand on her forehead, and studied her face. He leaned over her, forced open a thickly lashed eyelid, and then let it flutter heavily back into place.

He poured himself a glass of wine from a decanter on the dresser, then from a drawer he removed a few pieces of silken rope. Returning to the bed, he proceeded to tie her feet to the bedposts. "Are you asleep, my pet," he asked softly.

"Uhhh," she replied lazily as her eyes fluttered open. "I'll wake up in a few moments. Whatever made me so drowsy?" she asked.

"Your hands, pet," he ordered, waiting to tie them to the bedposts above her head. Before she extended them to him, a knock at the door interrupted them.

He placed the rope on the nearby table, picked up his automatic, and crossed the room to the door. The room in partial illumination from the glow of candlelight, with flickering shadows playing tricks along the walls and ceiling, made it difficult to see clearly. Salomon opened the door. "Set the tray down on the table," he instructed the aide. "Leave us. I'll knock when I wish you to unlock the door."

He turned from the aide, allowing him to pass without glancing at him.

The heavy-set man moved silently across the room and placed the tray containing the hot chocolate on the table. Madelaina glanced casually at him and felt a sudden jolt of excitement which she instantly attempted to subdue. She quickly averted her eyes at the silent signal telegraphed to her from the glittering eyes of Rudolfo Fierro. Her heart, beating wildly, thundered so loudly in her ears, she was certain Salomon could hear it. She tried with superhuman effort not to give either herself or Fierro away.

Sweet, sweet Jesus! They hadn't abandoned her. They'd found her!

Salomon waved Fierro out of the room with his gun tip and locked the door behind him. He waited to hear the double lock from the outside. Satisfied, he shoved the gun into his robe pocket and walked toward her.

The radiant glow on her face was due to Fierro's presence, but in gazing upon her, Simon Salomon misinterpreted this radiance as a genuine affection bestowed upon him by this woman he'd succeeded in taming. Puffed up with importance, he sat down next to her on the bed and opened her negligee to lift out her firm, full breasts. He took one wrist and tied it to the bedpost.

"Why won't you let me be free so I can reciprocate your love?"

She feigned a few amorous gestures, knowing they stimulated him sexually.

"Let's not discuss it further," he retorted, tugging firmly on the ties. "I've already told you how important this is to me." He secured her other hand, then arose to pour some chocolate for her. He returned to her side and allowed her to sip the contents of one cup. He refilled the cup and brought it back to the bedside, placing it on the nightstand.

"And now, my dear," he said, his face glowing with super macho ego, "we begin out night of a thousand delights." He placed the blindfold around her, tied it securely, and planted a brutally hard kiss on her lips, as Madelaina struggled for air. Apparently this time, Salomon didn't secure the blindfold tightly enough and Madelaina could see under it. She'd been besieged with an overwhelming desire to see what it was that he was so secretive about, but knowing that Rudolfo Fierro wasn't far away lessened her desire and increased her edginess.

She saw Salomon rise to his feet and remove the robe. Madelaina gave a start and gasped aloud.

Strapped around his middle, just above the genitals, were the largest penis and testicles she'd ever seen. No wonder she felt as if she'd been ripped wide open. The apparatus was harnessed around his hips with a series of smaller straps. It was difficult to make it out, and she wouldn't have if it hadn't been for the fact that Salomon seemed to be trying the apparatus out. From the sac of the testicles there extended a small bulb that released a fluid from the tip of the penis.

She wanted to speak, tried to find the adequate words to say, but didn't dare because he'd know she'd seen. But the utter farcical quality of this entire scene as everything came together in her mind stimulated her to scornful laughter.

His head jerked around to her. "Why are you laughing?" he demanded scorchingly. "Can you see? Has your spying, sneaky mind compelled you to force this humiliation upon me?"

Madelaina's laughter froze. She was helpless again, unable to move. Why didn't Fierro come for her? Now, before anything terrible happened.

Salomon savagely tore the blindfold from her eyes. "Very well, you tainted whore, take a good look. See what it is that's made you bend like a reed in the wind. Yes, that's right! Not even flesh and blood!" He paraded before her, one hand on the inflated false appendage as if it were the standard of a proud flag. He began to gallop around the room as if he were astride a wild stallion, pumping the dildo as if he were ejaculating. His eyes turned fiery and swollen as he moved in toward her. Holding the hollow rubber penis in one hand, he pressed the bulb and squirted fluid all over her breasts.

"It's better than flesh and blood! Has more endurance. How well you know that, my pet, don't you?" he asked, his voice growing hoarser. "I hadn't meant for you to learn of this yet, not until I had won you over totally."

Madelaina fairly shrank from him. She tried to turn away from him. The whole episode was sickening, and she felt like vomiting from the sight of him. She was right the first time, when she labeled him a sexual pervert, a psychotic who needed institutionalizing. She wasn't prepared for the next move on his part. He jumped on the bed and forced the repulsive thing to her lips.

"Open your mouth and taste the elixir," he commanded.

She shook her head, clenched her teeth, and pressed her lips firmly together. She was in a state of frenzy.

"Open your mouth," he commanded again, his face hardening.

She shook her head fiercely. Salomon pinched her breasts with such force, she screamed out. He took that moment to shove the rubber dildo into her mouth. His hand squeezed the bulb and her mouth filled with a fluid she readily recognized by its offensive odor. She shook her head from side to side, dislodging the apparatus, and spat the fluid into his face. "Filth! Pig! You bastard!" she screamed. "Fucking low life, the worst obscenity of a pig!"

Her words were drowned out by his raucous laughter. "You were better at Madrigal, my pet, when I let all those creatures have a go at you. I should have remembered to use more Spanish fly, as I did last week, then you'd have been more amenable to this."

One of Madelaina's hands had tugged free of its restraints. So surprised was she at this, she didn't allow him to see it for a moment. When the time was right, however, she'd fix his tail. Earlier, she taken her seven moon earrings apart and had slipped a few pointed crescents under the mattress. At the right time she'd planned to pierce his eyes with those sharp points. Once again, he'd chosen to tie her down. She had hoped he'd have left her free when she suggested she wished to reciprocate. Now, realizing why he hadn't, she had to think of a different plan.

It all happened so swiftly that later, when she tried to reconstruct the continuity of events, she wasn't certain which came first. She saw Simon Salomon stiffen, his head shot up and arched backward. At that moment, Madelaina's free hand reached out from behind her and she tugged at the crazy contraption he wore, breaking it free from his body. Her eyes widened in amazement as she stared in the area of his loins. Simon Salomon had the sac and penis of an infant boy! Why, her son Alejandro had more than this man had, she later recalled thinking. She looked up into his eyes, glittering maniacally like an animal's in the night. Simon Salomon was pulled off her bodily, and she shrank back away from him as Rudolfo Fierro's large frame loomed from out of nowhere, enveloping the *Huertista*, his elbow caught around Salomon's throat, pressing, pressing, pressing until Salomon's struggles ceased and his body went limp. Only then did Fierro release the former secret service captain who'd risen from the ranks to enjoy the title of major general in the *Federale* army, and now departed earth to meet his maker. Fierro dropped the dead body to the floor and removed his knife from Salomon's back. He wiped the bloodied knife on his trousers and called imperatively to Little Fox as he slashed at her bindings.

"Quick, we have no time to lose. Get dressed." He glanced at his watch as she hurriedly donned a pair of trousers and a shirt. "Follow me, *señora*. Do only as I do and once you've mounted your horse, ride with the wind. In less than ten minutes, this place will explode. Understand?"

"*Si, mi Generale*. I understand. Fierro?"

"*Si?*"

"Thank you for saving me."

"We've no time to give thanks. *Vamenos!*"

"One moment, please." Madelaina rinsed out her mouth with wine and shuddered as she recollected the earlier events. She reached under the mattress and collected the golden earrings. "*Bueno, muchacho. Vamenos!*"

It was Rudolfo Fierro's turn to stare down at the childlike genitals on the overgrown man, almost reluctant to tear his eyes from the spellbinding malformation. "So this was Huerta's *vieja*, eh? He spat at the man, silently hating the pot-bellied, hairless man with rounded hips proportioned as a woman. It was almost as if his own manhood was threatened by the sight of him.

He shuddered and shoved Madelaina out the door. They made their way down the steps, past the courtyard, stumbling over a few dead bodies Fierro had disposed of en route to free Little Fox. Crouching down in the shadows, hugging the building, they moved swiftly like silent Indians, until they reached the stashed horses. Instantly they mounted and rode off into the night, making their way out onto the desert and nearby hills like riders born to this earth.

From the top of the hill, both Fierro and Little Fox, panting and out of breath, relaxed their lathered horses briefly to watch the old convent at Ojocaliente be reduced to rubble. One explosion, two explosions, three—one after another—shot debris into the air, as the very earth beneath them roared and rumbled in angry protest. Flames shot into the air, as fire spread rapidly in every direction.

The sound of fast riding came at them and Fierro tossed her a rifle. "Those crazy dynamiters," he grinned in a rare moment. "They did it again." He waved to Captain Tracy Richards and two more men from the Gringo Brigade, and the foursome rode swiftly to the fort at Zacatecas.

Central Mexico was in a state of confusion, with *Huertistas* attempting to recuperate their losses, and *Villistas* enjoying the fruits of their labor, and the men of Carranza unsure of who would reach the capital first.

On July 8, General Obregon patiently and methodically threw his 20,000 men against Guadalajara and won his greatest victory to date. The *Federale* garrison lost 2,000 dead and 5,000 prisoners. Obregon's booty was twenty cannon, twenty-nine locomotives, and an enormous warehouse of small arms and ammunition.

On July 15, *El Presidente* Huerta, seated on that throne in the presidential palace, reassessed his position. With western ports cut off, main railroads and cities blocked by Pancho Villa in central Mexico, and an army of Mongol-like hordes led by Emiliano Zapata coming from the south, Vitoriano Huerta took his best shot. He pilfered two million pesos from the national treasury and beat it the hell out of Mexico City and for a time was exiled in Cuba. Huerta's iron rule of terror and conspiracy, deception and disgrace was over at last, and the man responsible for his downfall was the man he'd once set before a firing squad and on whom the fates had shined.

Huerta's flight brought about another defection. Orozco, abandoning his Redflaggers, fled to the American border asking for asylum.

The news reaching Zacatecas was cause for celebration and the entire fort was in fiesta. Only General Villa, happy as he was about the departure of his two worst enemies, couldn't drink or get drunk enough to forget the revolution, not with the same abandon his men employed to relax and celebrate.

Madelaina had wandered about her old haunts at the fort in Zacatecas, reliving old memories when as a child all she had to concern herself with was playing soldiers with Felipe de Cordoba. In the past few years, she'd grown up to know a world entirely different than the one on which she'd been weaned.

Every nook and cranny of her old home stoked up powerful memories; some good, some bad, and many others which no longer had meaning for her now that her life had come around to a complete circle. She had much time to think over her recent circumstances and wonder over her strange involvement with Simon Salomon. Somehow she began to justify his satanic behavior. She recalled all the vile and contemptible insults she'd hurled at him at Madrigal de Los Altos. She'd called him a half-crazed psychopathic killer, a boozed-up *borrachón*. She had also called him a poor excuse of a man—a castrated eunuch! Little did she know the pain and anguish he must have carried all his life to have been born. She understood now why he chose to be a voyeur instead of a participant in those sadistic parlor games he inflicted upon her at Madrigal.

Preposterous! Am I suddenly going soft in the head, she asked herself. *What the hell's wrong with me? Justifying his malevolent behavior*! She shuddered and recalled all that had happened at Madrigal. She found her fists clenching and unclenching as waves of guilt fell upon her once more when she remembered the intimacies shared with Salomon and that giant false phallus! *Dios mios*! Would she ever forget it?

Oh God, Peter! Where are you? Why didn't you take me away from all these bad memories? Why did you ever open my eyes to the suffering and pain in the world? Better that I'd been born blind—with no feeling—without the capacity for compassion! By the time it all ends, I'll be an empty shell, without feelings, without shame or conscience. She moved into the rear courtyard of their old villa, next to the gates where she and Felipe had witnessed their first execution before a firing squad order by Diaz. She could almost hear the crunching of pebbles as boots marched to the point of execution, the clicks of bolts as they were pulled back before the bullets exploded to fell the old man. What was his name? El Lobo? Something like that. Seated under the jacaranda tree, Madelaina couldn't stop the flow of memories or thoughts.

She must have been there at least two hours. *Finally,* she thought, *here I am again, only a different man, not my father, sits in command on the fort.* What had really changed over the past few years? Nothing. The same petty thoughts, restricting ideas, and the greed for political power was ever present. The people were still hungry, living in near-destitute conditions, with disease and death hovering close to them. Only the faces of the people changed around her, replacing the dead and gone.

General Villa was right. Yesterday he had addressed his chiefs of staff after the revelry had died down. He

882

had told them of his plans and ended by admitting, "There is still so much more to do!" Madelaina agreed with the *jefe*. There was so much more to be done. The question was, could it all be done?

Madelaina's hopes and aspirations weren't as optimistic as Pancho Villa's. Especially not on that August 15 when news reached Zacatecas that General Alvaro Obregon had marched on Mexico City to claim the capital for the Constitutionalist government of Don Venustano Carranza. Nor were her hopes raised further when five days later on August 20, Carranza made his triumphant entry into Mexico City. Word reached the fort that Emiliano Zapata and his swollen hordes, some 20,000 strong, waited in Cuernavaca for word from General Villa. Meanwhile, the Centaur of the North had left 30,000 *Villistas* along the northern garrisons outside the capital and returned to Chihuahua City to continue his important work in agrarian reforms.

It was from reading the newspaper columns of Miguel Guerra that Madelaina gained insight into what was happening in that den of political lions, tigers, jaguars, and snakes in Mexico City. The nonconformist reporter, who rode herd with *Villistas*, told it like it was:

"Carranza made his position clear to new Revolutionary Chamber of Deputies," stated Guerra. "But reception to this man was polite and remote. It appears that three distinct political groups have formed. Pro-Carranza, Pro-Villa, and pro-conventionists who feel that the Chamber of Deputies should rule Mexico through a neutral president. Carranza sought to win over these factions by delivering a character assassination speech against General Villa. After a long, drawn-out, and windy speech, he concluded by labeling Villa a power-crazed despot who seeks to become an omnipotent militarist and wishes to dominate all powers of the union by maintaining a formidable army, which could overwhelm the power of the Republic. He also stated that he viewed General Zapata in the same vein.

"Carranza's statements, aimed at frightening members of the convention into naming him president, fell flat when General Villa's immediate reply was read to the deputies. It was terse, to the point, and devastating: *Carranza contends that Pancho Villa constitutes a danger to Mexico. I contend Carranza is the one to fear. Since we are at an impasse, I propose for the good of our nation, we both meet before this delegation, or at some appointed place, where we both commit suicide and thereby remove all threats to our nation.*"

The message, greeted by thunderous applause and cheers, deadlocked the convention and the conventionists chose General Eulalio Guiterrez as interim president. Guiterrez' first act was to confirm Villa as General-in-Chief of the Northern Division and select that division as protector of the convention's rights. Furious at this gross disregard of his virtues, Don Carranza disavowed the convention and left for Veracruz where he established his "government" in exile.

The talk had ended. Hordes of gun-heavy men who fought together to defeat Huerta stood looking at each other with friendship for the last time. They turned and left Mexico City as enemies. Pancho Villa and Venustano Carranza were openly at war.

The morning of December 6, a year since he'd escaped Mexico as a Federal prisoner, General Francesco Villa, magnificently garbed in a field commander's uniform and gold braid, seated regally on Seven Leagues, his stallion, shared the spotlight with General Emiliano Zapata, dressed in a splendid *charro* uniform. They rode together at the head of the combined forces of the northern and southern armies. On either side of them rode Villa's Generals Urbina and Fierro and Zapata's Rafael Buelna. Behind them came the stellar and colorful *Dorados*. These were followed by Villa's crack shot *soldaderas* headed by Madelaina Obregon. Then came the artillery and what the newspapers affectionately came to call the Terrifying Horsemen of the Northern Division. These were followed by countless more brigades and regiments of the two formidable forces. Zapata's quaint peasants in pantaloons and sandals provided music from the south. Villa's khaki-clad bands played music of the north.

The 50,000 first-class fighting men marched down the Paseo de la Reforma, Avenida Juarez and Plateros Avenues into the Royal Plaza—Zocalo. Villa and Zapata, side by side, flushed with victory and power, marched toward the National Palace, not fighting over the spoils like mad dogs, but doing what two sane men could do with victory, with freedom—give it to the people.

It was a day to remember, thought Madelaina, as swarms of people moved like gigantic ocean swells all around them. How much more wonderful it would have been to have Peter by her side instead of the six bodyguards surrounding her. On orders from General Villa, every precaution was taken to protect Little Fox. Concerned with what had happened to her recently, he was doubly squeamish over the fact that if General Obregon caught sight of his daughter, a kidnap plot might be effected.

The victorious generals, swamped by reporters and cameramen, dismounted before the palace and walked inside, accompanied by their staff members. They stood in the balcony receiving the accolades, then, accompanied by President Guiterrez, they walked back into the main reception chambers where the enormous, golden presidential chair sat.

General Villa stood staring at the chair for which he'd fought for years, never intending to sit in it, but certainly intending to see someone seated on it.

Not far from him, yet unable to see what transpired, Madelaina stood on the balls of her feet to see what was causing the commotion. The newsmen jokingly wanted to take Villa's picture seated in the ostentatious presidential chair.

"Just one picture, General Villa. Just one. It won't take a moment," they cried.

Villa's half-embarrassed, half-joking smile couldn't deter them. He was led toward the chair. Villa coaxed Zapata. "Let's go, Emiliano. You take the big one. I'll sit next to you and Urbina."

"No," said Zapata. "The gold one's more your style."

"Not mine, damnit."

Madelaina tugged at her escorts to push up front. She wanted to see this comedy. By the time she got in the front line, Villa was seated in the gold chair Zapata, in the chair alongside; and General Urbina to Villa's right.

The photographers got their photo and cried for another. Villa resisted. "That's enough," he told them, waving his hand in a self-conscious manner. He spotted Madelaina in the front lines and called to her.

"You know what, Little Fox?" he confided. "That damned chair's too big for me. I'd get lost, you hear? *Vamenos*. Let's get out of this crazy place of gringos and *políticos* who connive to rob man of his eyeballs. *Dios mios*, when a man is up to his ass in alligators, its pretty damned hard to remember his intention was to clean out the swamp."

Madelaina and all the *Villistas* returned to Xochimilco. The campfires blazed brilliantly and the air filled with the aroma of spicy, tantalizing foods. Listening to the soldiers singing and dancing with their *soldaderas* and *viejas*, Madelaina felt overwhelmed by nostalgia and sorrow. She had to be by herself. By the time she reached the water's edge and sat on a mossy tree bough swinging low over the magnificent array of exquisite floating gardens, she began to sow the seeds of discontent in her mind. The fragrance of the sweet-smelling tropical flowers intoxicated her, creating a hungry yearning for Peter and their son.

She was tired, very tired of this life. She missed Antonetta like life itself. She hadn't taken to Villa's new woman and had no desire to extend herself in any more useless relationships. She hardly saw Rosalia Quintera or Lucia San Miguel. They were always with their gringo men. And Madelaina was always alone. She was lonely enough to give thoughts to sneaking off to Cuernavaca to gaze up upon the house of her childhood, but sensible enough to take no more unnecessary chances. She wanted her son desperately—and her husband. She was obsessed by this desire.

Madelaina remained camped here with the other *Villistas* and watched General Villa go back and forth to Mexico City on business, pleasure, or whatever the agenda provided. She watched General Villa unwind and relax to the point that his posture in the capital grew more scandalous each day.

Newspapers carried red-hot stories of his affairs with one young whore or another. And Madelaina, in reading all the accounts, felt a burning anger at this civilized society—and at Pancho for not recognizing the pit he was falling into.

His crude, unpolished behavior, his provincial manners and quaint peasant eccentricities, however charming, practical, and formidable they might have been in the deserts and hills, became the laughingstock of snobbish Mexican society. The women who teased him, flirted, played coy and hard to get confused him, puzzled him, and incited him to anger. Thoroughly rankled when called to task over his macho attitude toward these same women who openly made ovations to him and declined to accept his genuine masculine responses, Villa shouted to the reporters eager to pen his unguarded remarks. "To hell with protocol. To hell with propriety. Where I come from a woman's invitation means action! The only action I know in this instance is to tumble the skirt in the hay, what else? Is it any different here in Mexico City than in our deserts, plains, and mountains? Fornication is the same here as the world over, no? Perhaps not in China," he temporized much to the reporters' delight. For some reason Villa was never partial to Chinamen because they were the money lenders, the men who charged interest, something he could never understand. You borrow—you pay back. *Que va*, this business charging for the service? Wasn't it enough to get your money back?

Having tasted the bitterness of ridicule and a growing distrust among the disdaining *políticos* in Mexico City, General Villa, perplexed and homesick, informed Presidente Guiterrez he was leaving. "Let those *políticos* sink or swim. Pancho Villa has work to do."

Shortly after the Christmas holidays, General Villa reassigned his units, shipped his *Dorados* and their horses by train back to Juarez. He gathered his men and Madelaina, and with what appeared as a secretive glimmer in his eyes, he informed her they had much work to do.

For the first time since she'd willingly dedicated her life to him, Madelaina bridled under the strain. "Perhaps it's best, *Jefe*, that I search for my son. I've procrastinated long enough. Besides, you don't need me any longer."

"You've come with me so far toward victory," insisted Villa. "Do you not wish to join me in our total victory at the final outcome?"

"From where I observe the goings on, it will be a long time before those *políticos* in the capital make up their minds—as usual," she added ironically. "No, *Jefe*. I'm tired. I think it's time for Little Fox to retire."

Pancho Villa had never learned how to wrestle with the mental gymnastics of a woman as complicated as Madelaina Obregon. It was perhaps this, plus an inborn set of ethics and behavior toward such women, that never allowed him to make ovations to her of a romantic nature. She had viewed him from the first in a paternalistic light and he was satisfied to remain so. However, now he had to insist on her making this trip, for more reasons than one.

He had planned this surprise for a long time. If it meant abducting her, he'd find a way to keep her close to his side. In the name of good conscience and good sense, he knew he wouldn't force her against her will. Knowing Little Fox well enough, he knew she'd find a way to do as she pleased. No. He'd have to resort to trickery and guile with her. God forgive him.

"Where will you go, if not with us? You can't return to the house of your father, not now, while things remain unsolved between you. Believe me, it's best you come with Pancho. It's not far where we'll be from the northern hacienda of your father in El Dorado. I will send my spies to locate your *niño*. When we locate him and are sure of no trouble, I shall instruct my men to abduct him back for you. Is A-O.K.?"

Madelaina had no other way to go. Villa was right. Then, with her son, she'd return to El Paso and raise him there away from revolution. "Very well, *Jefe*. I understand and believe you. My trust is in you."

Chapter 33

Two days before the *Villistas* finally departed Mexico City, Madelaina felt the need to go shopping. She was in dire need of undergarments, soaps and perfumes, and those small things which make life more endurable for women.

She took Rosalia Quintera with her, and in her appreciation for what the girl had done for her in the past and the nice courtesies extended her by the mestizo, she showed her the glories of Mexico City.

First, they hired a carriage for the day. Accompanied by a lone *Villista* bodyguard, who waited on them patiently, their first stop was at the baths. The steam baths featured in the beauty salons along the Avenida Juarez. They giggled like schoolgirls and luxuriated in the soothing, relaxing waters and even had their hair dressed and toes and fingernails manicured. They put on airs like those displayed by the haughty *modistas*. Nothing was too elegant for them: lingerie, camisoles, the latest in fashions were brought out for their approval. They purchased sailor-type suits, with middy jackets, large white collars and cuffs, belted at the waist with a contrasting ankle-length skirt.

"Bustles are gone?" Madelaina asked the uppity shopgirl.

"Oui," she replied in a Spanish-accented French. "But of course, *señorita*."

The shopgirl put on such airs that Rosalia on impulse would have enjoyed pulling the girl's hair. Madelaina cautioned her not to make a scene, and instead she took over. Did the clerk carry other, more elegant creations? Something perhaps by Doucet, Worth, or even Amelie?"

890

"You know of such fashions, *señorita*?" asked the bug-eyed clerk.

Employing all the aristocratic airs of a *gachupín*, Madelaina stared scorchingly at the girl. "Bring what you have at once. And don't tarry. We haven't all day."

The clerk stared at them, their peasant dresses strewn on the floor, and shrugged her shoulders in a disdaining manner. "Very well, at once," she said with overpoliteness as she exited the dressing room. *One can't ever tell who has the money in these days of hectic political upheavals*, she told herself. Why, only two days ago, one of the rebel soldiers came in, put down several thousand pesos, and gathered all the garments, regardless of size and color, his arms could carry. He left them speechless, but a lot richer.

Ten minutes later, Madelaina was garbed in the most spectacular and elegant gown she'd ever seen. A pale mauve shade, graduating into darker tones from the bustline to the hem, the evening gown was low cut, off the shoulder and caught under the bustline in empire lines. The hobble skirt was asymetrically draped with embroidered beads, colored to match the shading of the filmy English net at the hemline where it formed a train at the rear. The shimmering bugle beads and glittery stones caught the spotlights trained on her from overhead, and Rosalia Quintera gasped and sucked in her breath .

"*Dios mios, chiquita*. You look like a star in the heavens, shining from the sky," she rhapsodized with peasant candor. "You must have thees dress."

Madelaina stared at her image for a long while. She didn't recognize herself. Her hair, piled atop her head, was caught with a brilliant tiara. She shook her head at the reflection. "What would I do with such a gown? Where would I wear it? Can you just see me stumbling through the camps, holding up my train, trying to look like an elegant lady?" Her wistful voice wasn't convincing, even to herself, but she had spoken these words only in the clerk's absence.

"Listen, ju take it, hear me?" Rosalia was enraptured with such a dress. When the clerk returned to the dressing room, carrying other creations, Rosalia turned to her. "How much it costs such a—such a—*como se llamos?* What you call such a dress, woman?"

"A ball gown," replied the snooty clerk. "It is 1200 pesos."

"Ayeiii! So much for so little?" Rosalia's face turned a berry red, more at the clerk's arrogant and unbearable manners.

"I'll take it," snapped Madelaina, watching the interplay between the two women. "And hurry it up. I'll take all the accessories and these other items also." She indicated the other garments stacked on a chair.

"Do you have an account with our house, *señorita?*" asked the offensive clerk.

For a moment Madelaina was tempted to answer in the affirmative and charge the items to the account of General Obregon—just to rankle the shopgirl. She changed her mind. "What's the matter, you don't take cash in this bourgeois establishment?" She slipped out of the shimmering creation of net and beads and let it lay on the floor for the clerk to pick up. From the canvas money belt she'd lain carelessly on the chair in the dressing room, she pulled out a thick stack of pesos and tossed them at the girl "If that isn't enough for everything, charge the balance to General Francesco Villa. Tell him Little Fox made the purchase!"

The name Little Fox had been publicized in all the Mexican newspapers from the very moment Villa's *soldaderas* marched into the Zocalo, the square outside the presidential palace over a month before. Newspaper reporters had interviewed many of the willing publicity seekers, the *soldaderas* who thrilled at having their pictures taken on their horses with rifles at the ready.

Headlines had captured the imagination of every young woman who yearned for the adventures of a *soldadera*, touting them to become one of the foxes trained by the best *soldadera* of them all—Little Fox.

They had never mentioned Madelaina's real name, probably because they didn't know her true identity. For this she was grateful. For some reason she wouldn't even admit to herself, she didn't want to hurt her father any more. Was this a sign of maturity—of growing up, she had asked herself on occasion.

It was difficult for both Madelaina and Rosalia to keep straight faces when they saw the expression of electrifying shock on the face of the shaken clerk as she rushed from the dressing rooms, purchases flung over both arms, to complete the transaction.

They were still laughing when they left the *modistas* and stopped to give their parcels to the driver of their carriage and their waiting bodyguard.

"We're going across the street, to the café across the square next," she told the solemn-faced, well-armed young man. "We'll return soon enough."

He tipped his Stetson and kept his steely black eyes on the two smartly attired women, unable to believe they were the same two he'd escorted into the city that morning. "Chihuahua!" he muttered. "What beauties!"

"And now, *chica*, I shall show you how the other half lives," she told Rosalia, admiring the figure cut by the woman of Tracy Richards in her new sailor suit. "My dear, you look like a fashion model. With your gorgeous auburn hair done up so fashionably and your make-up done so impeccably, you fairly take my breath away."

"Ju aren't so bad jurself, Little Fox," laughed Rosalia, pleased at the compliment. "I still see the face of that stuck-up girl when you mention Pancho Villa. You see what she did when she learned she was in the company of Little Fox? *Dios mios*. I'll wager her pantaloonies were not too dry, eh, *chica*?"

They both laughed heartily and with good humor. Looking the epitome of fashion and a bit daring since they were unescorted and without the company of a *dueña*, the two young women sat at a table outside among the other fashionably dressed people in the sparkling sunshine of a beautiful day. All around them it seemed the conversation on the lips of the people was about Pancho Villa and his utterly abhorrent behavior in society. For a time they listened to the snide remarks and obscene jokes made about their *jefe* without flinching.

"Imagine? That fool wants to marry every woman he seduces. Don't ask me why? Some primitive and savage rite among those barbarians, I suppose."

"Why, only the other night, he was bent on taking the daughter of the French ambassador to bed. All she'd said was the whole world knew the name Pancho Villa, and he turned to her and declared they were to be married on the spot."

Madelaina grew angrier by the minute. Rosalia leaned in to ask her friend why everyone was so disrespectful to the man who was liberating Mexico for them. Madelaina proceeded as best she could to outline the differences between the two societies, unaware that she was being inscrutably observed by a group of *Federale* officers seated a few tables away.

"For two pesos I'd give those lying sons and daughters of whores a lesson in respect," hissed Rosalia, her sparkling brown eyes leveled hotly on the people surrounding them.

"You mustn't let it upset you. People will talk no matter what a man does. One thing for sure, it would be an impossible task to defend the *jefe* to such people who have no knowledge of the life we live or what we do to win victories. Let it alone, Rosalia. Things over which we have no power shouldn't affect us, and the thoughts of others and their words shouldn't disturb us."

"*Bueno*," said Rosalia, catching a glimpse of the officers ogling her. Fighting to keep a straight face, she whispered to Madelaina. "Oh, *chica*, if these *hombres* knew we were *Villistas*, the desire on their *gachupín* faces would turn to shocked impotence, no?" She laughed brightly, enjoying the attention. "It would serve my gringo lover right if I were to flirt with them," she flipped with outrageous overtones. She sipped her lemon ice through a straw, making loud, slurping noises, prompting Madelaina to show her the proper way to drink through a straw.

"Why must I *sip* through a straw, for the love of God?" she said in frustration. "Is much easier to pick up the glass and drink."

"But, it's not ladylike, *chica*. Dressed in clothes as fine as yours, you must act the part of a woman of finesse and high refinement. Only *campesinas* and *soldaderas* act rough and tough like men. There is a saying, 'When in Rome do as the Romans do.' It means you should adapt yourself to the mood and manners of the place you're in."

"Why?" asked Rosalia naïvely. "Are you saying this dress makes me someone else—not Rosalia?"

Madelaina smiled at her own asinine attitude. "Why? Why, indeed? To be honest, I'm not sure why I bothered to explain. Don't listen to me. I've been trapped between two worlds for so long that I find it difficult to know to which I truly belong," she replied wistfully.

"Ees too complicated, too confusing to be civilized. No wonder the *jefe* is most unhappy here. We don't belong here, him and me. You, yes. But not the likes of Pancho Villa or Rosalia Quintera. Aye, is best we go, for sure." Rosalia removed her broad-brimmed sailor hat, unpinned her hip-length auburn hair and let it fall into shiny bright, coppery coils on her shoulders and down her back.

"*Chica*," cautioned Little Fox. "You mustn't do that. Not here. Not only isn't it ladylike, but it might be dangerous as well as unaccepted behavior."

"Not ladylike? Is true, Rosalia is no lady. So I do what makes Rosalia comfortable."

Madelaina's face burned with embarrassment when she glanced about and saw they were the center of attention. Their eyes on her made her uncomfortable. "It's just that the others will think we're common whores if we don't restrain ourselves in this section of the city."

"So? Is that not what we are? Whores?"

"Rosalia!" Madelaina was aghast at her crude manners and her outspoken candor. She quickly searched her reticule for a few pesos, placed them on the table, and suggested to her companion they'd best leave. Madelaina felt terrible. Ordinarily Rosalia's brutal candor wouldn't have phased her in the least. Suddenly, back in her old environment of social mores and staid protocol, she'd taken umbrage at the truth. What a hypocrite she'd turned into. How would she ever adjust to the old ways, she wondered. Burdened with the guilt of her conscience and of her double moral standard, she steered Rosalia away from the café.

Waiting for the traffic to pass before they crossed the street where their carriage awaited them, Madelaina failed to see a carriage gathering speed as it headed toward them.

It happened so fast, without forewarning. The carriage came to a stop before them, obstructing their path. A door opened and Madelaina alone was whisked off her feet and hustled into the carriage before a startled Rosalia Quintera, who jumped back out of the way to avoid being trampled by the frisky horses.

No one heard the warning from Villa's man who'd seen the four-horse carriage coming down the *avenida* at a fast clip. Catching her breath, Rosalia ran swiftly across the street, dodging on-coming sedans and hansoms, screaming at the driver and escort to hurry and pursue the carriage in which Madelaina had been abducted.

By the time the horses gathered speed, the first carriage had circled Chapultepec Square and disappeared on one of the several streets branching out from the circle. Dismayed and highly agitated after an hour's search, Rosalia suggested they hurry back to General Villa, who waited for them at the Reforma Hotel to report Madelaina's plight.

Inside the swiftly driven carriage carrying Madelaina and her abductor, Major General Felipe de Cordoba, the two old friends were renewing their acquaintance.

896

The horses had slowed down and cantered along the winding path in and about the wooded section of Chapultepec Park.

"What a dramatic and clever way to say hello," she told him when her astonishment at his daring feat died down. Glancing through the window of the carriage behind her, she saw no one was in pursuit.

"I had to see you, to speak with you, *quireda,*" Felipe told her. "Ever since I saw you riding in the parade at the head of the *soldaderas,* I tried to locate you." He took Madelaina's slender hands in his and stroked them affectionately. "We miss you. Your father is protrate over your absence and misses you more than he'll admit."

"I doubt he has time to miss anyone. He's still too in love with his work," she said caustically.

"Aren't you?" he countered.

His eyes turned the color of jade reflected against azure skies, she thought, gazing into them. "I think not, Felipe. I find myself growing disenchanted with the life of a *soldadera,* even if it does bring a certain prestige being a *Villista* these days."

They talked for over an hour, bridging the gap of time between them.

"Come home," begged Felipe. "You're needed there."

"I don't seem to know where home really is these days, *querido.* So how can I go home? Besides I have many things to do and searching for my son is one of them." She leveled intent eyes on him. "Felipe, do you have him? How could you have been a party to such a cruel ploy. When I heard, I refused to believe it."

"*Querida,* hold off a moment," he said, a look of bafflement on his face. "Surely you are jesting with me?" He looked intently at her, searching her face. "Are you telling me the child isn't with you?"

Madelaina paled. "If this is some kind of a joke, I don't appreciate it."

Felipe's face screwed up in thought. "The child was returned to you three months ago," he said in a voice barely above a whisper.

"You're saying you no longer have my son?"

He nodded reluctantly.

"How is that possible? I don't have him. I haven't seen him since he was stolen from me." She panicked. "Felipe! What have you done with my son?" Tears sprang into her eyes, her throat constricted, and she felt unable to breathe.

"There, there, *querida*. There has to be an explanation for all this. I left El Dorado to march with your father, the general. We were in Cuidad Obregon for two weeks before I returned to the hacienda. When I arrived, I was told you'd come after your son. My instructions to the servants before I left were to protect him from all dangers. I never thought you'd arrive with a court order from the capital of Hermosillo, or I might have warned them not to have turned the child over to anyone. They were positive it was you who claimed them. Matter of fact, the papers are still locked in my desk at El Dorado."

"Oh, Felipe," she wailed. "It wasn't me. Who then? Who has my child?" She grew hysterical, unwilling to be comforted. "How could you, how could you do this to me?"

Felipe felt terrible. "I had no business in this, *querida*. From the beginning, it was your father's plan to lure you away from the *Villistas*. When we heard you'd had a child, he was concerned that you should bear the child in the wilderness. His concern grew into a plan to kidnap the child and bait you to return. Your father misses you dearly."

Madelaina dried her eyes. "It was a horribly brutal thing to do—to take my child from me. If you only knew the anguish it caused, the fears and insecurities, the nightmares and endless frustration, you'd not have been a party to such a dastardly act."

"Yes, I can see it might be inhuman to take the child from you, but the intent was well meant. Try to see it in that light."

"Oh, Felipe, how can you say such a thing, especially now, since my son is missing and I haven't a clue in the world as to where to begin to search for him." She dabbed at her eyes and swallowed the lump in her throat.

"And it's all my fault," he said bitterly. "For once I should have refused to aid the general."

"You've never been able to refuse him, Felipe," she said flatly with a tinge of contempt in her voice.

Felipe pulled back the top hatch cover and instructed the driver to get back to Zocalo. "Your friends are probably looking for you. I'd better get you back as soon as possible. I'd prefer to keep you here with me forever, but now that I know your child isn't with you and hasn't been, I am incensed. Appalled that I should have been a party to influence you so unfairly to return. You'll come back some day, and when you do, it will have to be of your own accord—when you're ready—and not before."

"Thank you, Felipe," she said gratefully.

"Where can I reach you if I must, Madelaina? Surely we can trust each other, now that we've been candid," he said when she instinctively pulled away from him. "Incidentally, as difficult as it was to find a likable and admirable quality in your gringo husband, I confess I could see why you chased the country over to find him. I liked the man. Truly I did. I even told the general that I did."

Madelaina lifted her wet eyes to his and observed him for a moment. "Write me in care of general delivery, El Paso, Texas. Or the same in Chihuahua City. I'm not certain where I'll be. I'd give you our wireless code, but it can be too easily picked up by an enemy."

They had entered the square opposite the presidential palace at a canter. Glancing out the window, Madelaina suggested, "It's best you let me off here. I'll find my own way. I shouldn't want any of my companions to see me in the company of a *Federale*," she said tightly. "It might cause complications for both of us."

The carriage pulled over a slight distance from the front gates leading to the palace. Felipe shoved the carriage door open, alighted the cab, and helped Madelaina out. He gazed about the square, looking for a free carriage. "It would mean nothing, *querida*, for my driver to drop you off at the Reforma," he insisted.

"No. It would be too dangerous. There's a free carriage," she called, pointing to one dismissing his fare.

Felipe told his driver to hail the man and hold the vehicle for them. It was nearly dusk, a time when shadows played tricks on the eyes. He pulled her in close to him and kissed her ardently.

"*Vaya con Dios, querida*. I'll be in touch as soon as I can."

"Bless you, Felipe. Bless you," she told him and ran off toward the waiting carriage.

Three loud shots rang out, blasting her eardrums. Madelaina stopped in her tracks and took cover near the waiting carriage. Horses bolted into the air, spooked by the loud sounds, their forepaws clawing the air as a cursing driver tried to calm them. She turned to glance back at Felipe in time to see him clutch at his chest, wheel around as one hand clung to the carriage door before it slipped off, and fall to the ground, blood gushing from three holes in his body.

"No!" she shouted. "No, Felipe!" She ran toward him, just as a pair of strong arms swept her off her feet and tossed her into another waiting carriage. She pounded her fists against the man holding her tightly, beat on his chest protestingly. When, in the dim light of the carriage interior, she recognized Rudolfo Fierro, she collapsed in a dead faint.

Book Eight

Madelaina of the Seven Moons

Chapter 34

Less than three weeks later, Madelaina was in El Paso in the house she'd bought when she worked at the Diamond Slipper for Antonetta. Standing before a mirror in the exquisite gown she'd purchased in Mexico City, she was preparing for a private party given in honor of General Villa by the political dignitaries of Texas who had promoted the *jefe*'s revolution in the interests of freedom and justice for his people. Madelaina had agreed to attend the ball primarily to act as his interpreter; and she almost had misgivings over her promise.

She'd been a virtual recluse since Felipe's death, and in the security of her own little *casa*, she attempted to pick up the pieces even as turmoil erupted in Mexico City. She kept asking herself why any of it should matter to her any longer. She was a woman—not a man. She wanted only to be a woman, live like one, be loved and exist for the rest of her days in a quiet, serene atmosphere where she could forget those terrifying days of the revolution, those horrifying times when her life meant little or nothing and she'd survived for some mysterious reasons not fully known to her. She wanted nothing more than to erase all those bloody scenes of misery and hardship where death raged around the clock, memories burned so indelibly in her memory, that they prevented her from drawing an even breath.

God, what she'd do to relive her life with different values. What had driven her? Why had she been so stubborn, willful, and foolishly determined to show her father she had a will of her own? Why? If only she'd learned what had stimulated that stubborn streak of obstinance, that need for self-assertion and approval, all her experiences wouldn't have been for naught. Why did she have to be different than most women? Why couldn't she accept—without questioning—the things she read in the papers or what she read in books? Why did she feel she had to ask perpetually, why—why—why?

She'd cried enough over the lost years. In May she'd be twenty-two years old. Twenty-two! She felt 102. Somewhere she had a husband and a son. Had she been some sort of a demon to have lost the people she loved most in the world? Her father, Peter, the baby, Manuelito Perez, and now Felipe de Cordoba.

She stared at her reflection in the mirror, unable to determine or care that she posed a picture of grandeur and such magnificence it would generate excitement from any of the guests planning to attend the evening's gala.

She sprayed a fine mist of her favorite cologne from an atomizer shaped like a graceful swan, patted her up-styled hairdo into place, and allowed the wispy tendrils to fall around her face and neck. Her diamond tiara and earrings were set into place, and before the general arrived to pick her up, Madelaina draped her fox cape on the chair in the living room and poured herself a bracer of brandy. Madelaina gulped it down and stared at her reflection in the mirror over the mantle. The diamonds in her hair and ears glittered with silver and violet and yellow fire. *If only I could sparkle like diamonds*, she told herself, trying to elevate her spirits. She could at least be a suitable companion for General Villa on this night, perhaps one of the most important of his entire career.

"This is Little Fox?" asked Pancho Villa, staring at the apparition before him. "Fierro," he called to his constant companion. "Please to take a look. Is this the *soldadera* of Pancho Villa, or is it some majestic queen who honors us with her presence?" he asked, utterly enthralled by her appearance.

Fierro's face flushed with appreciation. "Incredible.

What a transformation. Such a woman bears no resemblance to a *soldadera* of Villa's camp!" He whistled low. Her appearance intimidated Fierro almost as much as it did Pancho Villa, for they remained silent all the way into the elegant residential district of El Paso.

"I am happy you honored me with your presence, Little Fox. *Que va,* Little Fox. I can't call you Little Fox in the presence of all these social butterflies, *señora*. What shall I call you?"

"Why not Señora Benson?"

"Ayeeiii, another name that is painful to me," lamented Villa. "Obregon is bad enough, but Benson? I shouldn't wish to remind these gringos of that name tonight. Señora Duprez? Does that name offend you, *chica*?"

"Let it be Señora Duprez," she replied, not really caring.

"I am happy ju came," he said, switching to pigeon yankee. "Ees best I talk gringo, out of respect for our northern friends, *si*?"

She nodded.

"Jur heart ees no longer een revolution, eh, *chica*?"

"I've tried to conceal it—" she began.

Fierro smoked a long black cigar opposite them in the carriage. As usual, he never opened his mouth to speak unless spoken to. Tonight even he looked more acceptable. He and the *jefe* wore formal dinner clothes. But not far from their reach were hair-triggered six-shooters. She wondered how they'd fare when asked to check their firearms before entering the party. The thought brought a smile to her lips.

It was a beautiful April night, with a full round moon shining overhead, lighting up the bricked streets. New street lamps had replaced the old with brighter electricity lighting up the shadowy paths formerly lit by gas jets. The graceful street leading to the governor's mansion was lined with tall eucalyptus trees and magnolias, filling the night air with a sweet fragrance pleasing to the senses. Up ahead the sprawling estate built

905

much like a Southern manor was ablaze with lights, and the sounds of laughter and music spilled out into the night.

The circular driveway was lined with both horseless and horse-drawn carriages. Liveried chauffeurs gathered together in a body, comparing notes as their masters and mistresses attended the festivities inside. The carriage carrying Villa and his guests pulled to a stop at the gates, where two uniformed rangers flashed a light inside the carriage inquisitively.

Instantly one of the rangers braced in a military salute. "Pleasure ta meet ya, General Villa. Hey, Jack, it's Pancho Villa himself," he called to his companion, waving the carriage on through. He tipped his hat and returned to inspect the next carriage. At the front entrance to the house, two liveried footmen sprang forward to open the doors. Madelaina, draped in a floor-length white fox cape, emerged first, followed by Villa and Fierro.

"Ju know what, *chica*? I like the way the gringos make a party. Ju watch me so Villa doesn't do something foolish like wanting to marry the first girl who flirts, eh?"

A rush of music greeted them. A small mariachi band hired for General Villa's pleasure wove its way through the large rooms, singing and making music. Everywhere people milled about in small groups, talking, sipping champagne.

From the moment they entered the splendid manor all lit up like a festival, Madelaina's stunning appearance drew the eyes of every awestruck man and envious woman in the main salon. She felt their eyes on her, wondering, staring, whispering, who's the woman with Pancho Villa? She wouldn't deny she enjoyed every moment spent basking in the limelight as much as Villa and Fierro did. How long had it been since she had entertained the feelings of being someone special? Too long ago. How marvelous for the ego, she thought, as the attention paid her rekindled a sense of worth she thought she'd lost somewhere in her journeys.

She heard their names announced by a major domo: "General Francesco Villa . . . General Rudolfo Fierro . . . Señora Peter Duprez."

The assembled guests fell silent. Whispers began slowly and swelled like a wave. "There's Pancho Villa and his butcher, Fierro. So that's the man who killed Bill Benson? Who is this Señora Duprez? Daughter-in-law to William Benson? In the company of the man who killed him? How shocking." No matter what their thoughts were concerning the Benson affair, these people had gathered under the governor's roof to pay homage to the legendary Pancho Villa and this is precisely what they would do. Awestruck by General Villa's imposing presence, they began to applaud him as the trio moved along the receiving line, caught up in the rush of introductions.

So many faces, so many names to remember, thought Madelaina. Governor and Mrs. Townsend, General Hugh L. Scott, General John Pershing, Major Mickie, and so many more, including prominent statesmen from both the military and State Department in Washington. They all clustered around the man of the hour, complimenting him, firing questions, badgering him, even joking with him over his spectacular achievements. Madelaina was relieved when General Fierro, who spoke impeccable English, stepped forward to interpret for Villa. She felt an instinctive resentment on the part of the gringos that a woman should translate their words. She was to learn later that Fierro had already been designated for the job and that her role in the evening's festivities were to be bound up in an altogether different mission.

When she found herself nodding mechanically, and the frozen smile on her face beginning to ache from the strain, she excused herself and walked out on the terrace, unable to endure the forced gaiety any longer. She wanted a cigarette so badly, she was shaking. She opened her beaded bag, uncertain that El Paso society would accept such a gesture and removed a cigarette. She didn't want to do anything to place the *jefe* in a bad light. The publicity in Mexico City had been devastating enough without adding to his discomfort here in El Paso. She lit it with a miniature red devil struck against the concrete balustrade and puffed on it. She took two more puffs, inhaled, and began to calm down.

She walked along the outer portico, inhaling the floral scents of the garden, enjoying the peace and tranquility among the well-kept lawns and shrubbery, listening to the music that drifted out the windows and open doors. Madelaina paused outside the French doors of a room filled with male guests who were engaged in talking with General Villa. She was unaware that from another terrace, some thirty feet from her, she was being observed through the Dresden blue eyes of Peter Benson, her husband. Coming toward her from another direction, she was hailed by a voice from her past. "Madelaina! Madelaina Obregon. Is it really you?"

She turned toward the owner of the voice and gazed upon the tall figure of a handsome, well-dressed man whose steps quickened until he reached her. Her dark, luminous eyes searched his face for some recognition. He looked familiar.

Behind them, Peter moved away from the lights, closer to the building, so he wouldn't be seen, his eyes intent on the scene a few feet from him.

"Do I know you, sir?" asked Madelaina, still uncertain as to the man's identity.

"You don't remember me? My dear, I am crushed. Absolutely crushed, that you'd forget me after only six years." His twinkling blue-green eyes seemed all the merrier for her awkwardness.

"Armando! Armando Cortez!" she exclaimed as his features became clearer. He picked her up in his strong arms and whirled her about, and for a few moments, they were like happy children.

"*Dios mios,* Madelaina, you are something to behold! Could I ever in my life believe that you would have blossomed out into such a ripe beauty? Look at you." He extended her at arm's length and twirled her about

908

as if she were on parade like a model. "My dear, you are positively ravishing. But I am very unhappy with you—running off without so much as a good-bye, after all we meant to each other."

Madelaina blushed in spite of herself, "We were children, Armando. Mere children. So much has happened since then."

"Well, we've got all our lives to reminisce, *querida*." He grinned irascibly. "Let me look at you again and drink you in with these eyes," he began eloquently.

Madelaina smiled. "You've not changed at all, Armando. Still the romantic, no?"

"And why not, *querida*?" He drew her closer to him. "We have many marvelous moments to remember."

"I'm a married woman, Armando," she said. "Tell me, what brings you here to Texas, *chico*?"

"Alas," he sighed. "I, too, am married. To a gringa. Imagine? My father was incensed when he heard the news. His *conquistadore* blood turned cold when I brought my bride to meet him. Not even the fact that she was the Texas governor's daughter would appease him."

Madelaina stiffened. "You married Valerie Townsend? I can see why Don Felipe was displeased," she replied acidly.

Armando's smile dissolved. "She's really a fine person in her own way."

"Armando, I'm sorry. I meant nothing by it. It was unfair of me to make any remark since I've never really met the woman. I can only hope that you both will be very happy." She reached to pat his hands reassuringly.

"She drives me insane, *querida*. I'm not certain what it is she does that drive me mad, but she married me and for a time it was all fine—romance and parties and the gay life—you know. Then suddenly there are more men in her life. It is something my Spanish blood will not tolerate, so when she left me in Madrid, I followed her to Paris, London, New York, and here to El Paso. But I got here only yesterday and already she managed to leave. Out of respect to her family, I promised to spend the week before I go looking for her. *Querida,* I swear, she's a cat!"

"Poor Armando," said Madelaina, drawing him close to her in a gesture of friendship, never knowing that this act would later be misunderstood by the man who was watching this interplay between old friends.

For a time, she led the conversation back over their youth and the passion she had for bulls. They had both grieved for the loss of their childhood friend, Manuelito Perez. "If it's any consolation, *chica,* in Spain, he had risen to the greatest of heights. He became *el grande matador* of all Spain."

They were interrupted by a servant who informed Armando his presence was requested in the library by his father-in-law.

"You will excuse me, *querida.* But you must tell me where you live, where I can reach you. I have so many questions to ask the *soldadero* of Pancho Villa." He bowed and kissed her hand, then clicking his heels together, he said suggestively, *"Mi querida,* until later then. We have so much to catch up on."

Madelaina nodded and remained on the terrace. Behind her, having observed the tête-a-tête, Peter Duprez put out his thin *cigarro* and went inside to confer with the men in the library. His eyes had turned to steely points.

Inside, the conversation turned to accolades for General Villa. Madelaina could hear every word spoken as if she were in the room with them. She sat down on a garden chaise and lit another cigarette.

General Scott had the floor and was explaining to the room's occupants the agenda of the afternoon. "Did you know, gentlemen, that General Villa owns four military airplanes? Yes, it's true. This afternoon, the *jefe* took me to one of his factories, a foundry, to demonstrate the prototype of an armored vehicle far in advance of anything owned by the United States Army."

"I'll vouch for that remark, gentlemen," said the

governor, nodding as Armando entered the room to join the others. He puffed on his Havana cigar in a grand imperious manner. "I told you the man's a genius. Far ahead of his time. He's already conceived the idea of air warfare. He's convinced that when things pop in Europe—war's inevitable—air warfare will decide the victor. My son-in-law, Armando Cortez from Madrid, has already informed me the Germans are working to perfect airplanes." Armando nodded his head in agreement with the governor's words.

Keeping General Villa informed of the remarks made by each of the speakers, Fierro translated into Spanish exactly what the others said. The pleasant smile and twinkling friendly eyes never changed, even at some of the acerbic remarks and candid opinions expressed by a few who related the personal opinion of President Wilson, which Fierro didn't bother to disguise.

"If ya gentlemen think those achievements to be rather unusual foah an unlettered man of dubious origin," began Peter Duprez Benson, moving to the center of the group, "youah are in foah a surprise."

Governor Townsend smiled and extended his arm. "There you are, my boy. Gentlemen, you all know Peter Duprez—uh—Benson, I'm sure." The men nodded to each other. "Peter should know firsthand. He rode with the General Villa in the much-publicized Gringo Brigade."

Outside, Madelaina gave a start. Had she heard correctly? Her heart began to beat rapidly. Peter was here? She sat up on the chaise, swung her legs over the end, and on tip toes, moved in closer to the French doors. Her eyes tried to pierce the smoke-filled room, sweeping past each face. She stopped.

There he was. It was her husband. Only when she saw those remarkably blue eyes, tanned handsome features, and powerful shoulders as he towered over the other men, did she allow herself to believe it. She slipped back away from the window as her pulse quickened and she heard Peter's voice continue.

"This man, General Francesco Villa, known ta his men as Pancho, has risen from virtual obscurity and transformed inta the role of a true leader. He deserves much moah recognition from ouah nation than he's received. Do ya know how many foreign nations have courted him, trying ta woo him inta selling the United States inta the sewer? But the *jefe* heah is loyal ta his northern neighbors. Ah jus' hope y'all can convey this ta Mr. Wilson." Peter lit up a thin *cigarro* and strutted about like a man born to affluence and influence.

"Did ya tell 'em, General Scott, about the *jefe*'s rollin' airdrome?"

"Haven't had a chance, Peter. Since you are more learned on the subject, suppose you go ahead."

"What those two words, 'rollin' airdrome' mean," continued Peter, "is that General Villa can transport his aircraft by train to the rendezvous of battle, service them, and launch them from any spot along the tracks, and drop bombs on his enemies."

"Incredible!" exclaimed General Pershing. "Not even the Europeans have made such progress." He turned to Peter. "You were a member of the much-lauded freedom fighters that went south to assist General Villa?"

"Yes suh, from the early days when Madero mobilized the revolutionary forces," replied Peter, knowing what was coming.

"And you are also the son of William Benson?"

Pancho Villa didn't move a muscle. Fierro's dark eyes scowled.

"Affirmative, suh."

"Yet you laud General Villa for all he's done—despite the unfortunate and tragic results of the altercation? Mighty commendable to have such charity, sir."

The men in the room tensed. Governor Townsend's face colored brightly. Armando Cortez stared at Peter Benson with arched brows. The other statesmen leaned forward in their chairs, not sure of the outcome of the moment's discomfort.

"That ah do, suh." He laughed. "Why, theah ain't a
912

man among ya that hasn't tasted the scorching temper of William Benson—including me. Knowing him like ah do, ah believe the *jefe*'s version of that confrontation. Why, the general heah was unarmed. General Fierro did what any other man might have done in the same circumstances, when a man draws first, ready ta kill."

Well, there it was, thought Governor Townsend. *They heard it first from Benson's son.* Now, by damn, he hoped the air was clear of this stigma. A murmur of mixed feelings and thoughts swept through the room, but Peter took hold again and led them in a body over Villa's talented achievements.

"Ah can't laud General Villa more than he deserves, gentlemen. With hundreds of my fellow Americans, who fought at his side, we all came to respect him in moah ways than one. Let me jus' dwell on his many achievements and accomplishments in what can be called modern warfare. He thought ta mount cannon in armored railcars ta aide us in warfare. Did ya know the *jefe* dreamed up the ideah of hitching explorer cars befoah the engines ta trigger off enemy mines along the tracks?" Peter paused a moment until he was certain every eye in that room, including Villa's, was on him. Then he continued. "So far all ah've told ya is what he can do and how good he does it in war. And like ah say, it's mighty damned good. But, mah friends, moah important is the fact that General Villa has given every spare centavo, every free moment ta the people of his land. In all my time with him, ah nevuh saw an ounce of graft or corruption flowing through the veins of this red-blooded man. Why, if any of ya have any influence on Mr. Wilson, ya must point out ta him that no man befoah Villa has done this. Not Diaz. Not Madero. Certainly not Huerta. Not even that unprincipled chocolate drinker Carranza has done a thing for his people." Peter paused, out of breath. He caught the appreciative twinkle in Villa's eyes as Fierro translated his words.

There were pros and cons and arguments offered to

substantiate the theory that Villa had promoted graft and done a few shady things during his career. They were too polite to refer to him as a bloody, murdering *guerrillo* in his presence. But Peter offered more arguments on behalf of Villa.

"Will you accept the word of an American citizen who knows firsthand what transpired—or will you believe the propoganda ground out by Huerta's malevolent and diabolical Secret Service, a carryover from the Diaz regime, which Carranza hopes to reinstate?"

"Well," said General John Pershing, rising to his feet. "I for one am highly impressed with everything I've seen and heard. Rest assured I'll do my darndest to convince President Wilson of this man's incredible loyalty and his phenomenal achievements." He turned to Villa. "Tell me, General, how long did it take you to build this magnificent army of yours?"

"All of it?"

"The whole military strength and organizations, including those stupendous and simply amazing *Dorados*."

"Tree jeers," said Villa, holding up three fingers. "I talk Eengleesh for ju, *mi amigo*. For to make frenship weeth United Estates always and too for Mexico. Ees hokay?"

"*Mucho bueno.* Is okay," said General Scott, moving in to shake hands with Villa. "You are some fine general. As far as I'm concerned, I'll stand behind your qualifications and your character, one hundred percent."

"How far will your president stand?" asked Fierro imperatively.

"Mr. Wilson?" General Scott drew himself up and pulled down on his tunic. "Well, sir, the most of us here are behind General Villa. And General Pershing and myself are advisers to the president. That's why he sent us together this time. It's likely he'll take our advice. Now, if we could only convince Señor Carranza that Americans desire peace in this hemisphere."

"You convince Wilson," said Fierro expansively. "We convince Carranza."

Madelaina had all she could to do sit still and listen. She'd been so thunderstruck by Peter's presence, that she found herself actually disbelieving it was truly him. Waves of dizziness engulfed her and that powerful feeling stirring her loins, sometimes referred to as butterflies, had been uncontrollable until she forced herself to calm down. She had entered a dialogue with herself, an internal dialogue that left her shaken but filled with resolve.

For the past many months, she told herself, since you last saw him, all you've done is mope, wishing for him. Now that he's here in the flesh, are you going to let him slip past your arms without putting up a fight for him? Now's your chance, woman. Plead. Beg. Do anything you can to resurrect your marriage. Only in God's name don't let him evaporate from your life again, for no one. Not for Pancho Villa—not for Mexico—for nothing. You hear?

Confronted with these absorbing, whirlwind thoughts, she scarcely knew the meeting had ended inside. She hadn't heard him approach her. Only when she felt a hand on her shoulder, did she spin around from instinct and see him.

"Madelaina," he said softly.

She sank against him, into his arms, unable to speak. They kissed for a long while, fierce, hot kisses alternating with sweet, tender, and incredibly passionate kisses. When they paused to stare into each other's eyes, the look of love glowed and came alive. Her throat burned and swelled, constricting words.

"Come, beloved. You're coming with me," he said gruffly, leading her by the hand.

"Wait. Where are you taking me?" she asked hoarsely.

"Does it matter?" he asked abruptly.

Her face burned. "No. I'll go wherever you want me to go," she replied submissively. She filled with unendurable excitement and an indescribable thirst and hunger for him as happiness engulfed her.

They skirted around the house, avoiding those rooms where crowds congregated, and made their way toward the front entrance. Not once did Madelaina give any thought to General Villa or Rudolfo Fierro until she heard his lusty laughter coming from one of the salons.

In the foyer to the mansion she paused once again. "Perhaps I'd best tell the *jefe* where I'll be," she began as he wrapped her fox fur around her.

"You'ah a big girl, now, sweet *chíquita*. Or haven't ya noticed? Ya think it's time foah ya to foahget all this revolution business?"

"It's time, Peter. Dear God, it is time!" she said, leading him out the door, past the liveried butlers.

At a quarter to midnight, Peter's open touring car drove into the Benson estate in El Paso. Madelaina felt a chill run through her as countless memories flooded her consciousness. She recalled Maneulito Perez and the night she spent with him. Her marriage to William Benson replayed in her mind. Why did Peter have to bring her here? Why? Why not her own house that filled with pleasant memories of their last night together, when they conceived their son. Her heart fell. She would have to tell Peter about their son. Dear God, if it wasn't one thing, it was a hundred that kept them pried apart.

He helped her out of the touring car and picked her up in his arms unexpectedly. In a few long strides he had her at the front door of the painfully familiar Spanish-styled villa. Inside, in the foyer, he let her slip from his arms, and clinging to her cohesively, he kissed her with increasing passion. For several wild, ecstatic moments, Peter felt a tingling in his groins that had been absent for too long. His feelings gave rise to hope as he removed her fur wrap and flung it on a nearby chair, and he grew ecstatic.

Holding her hand like a child's, he moved across the

large living room to the bar. For a moment he released her, long enough to pop the cork on a bottle of chilled champagne that stood in a bucket. She didn't remark on the prepared bottle or the glasses on a tray, although she wondered who he expected to entertain. She didn't care. She didn't want to know. He poured the sparkling amber-colored liquid into both glasses, handed her one and took the other.

"An' now mah sweet Little Fox, mah dearest, sweetest wife, ah toast ta ya and ta us." He clinked glasses with her and drained his entirely.

"What's the mattuh, darlin'? Don'cha like champagne? I prepared it especially foah you."

Madelaina placed the glass on the bar. She lifted her dark eyes to meet his. "Peter, we have to talk. There's something I must tell you—" she began.

He placed his fingers on her lips. "No, not now, sweet. Don' let's spoil it foah us. First, ya gotta trust in me, heah?"

She attempted to speak once again, to interrupt him.

"Ah said, not now." He looked lovingly into her eyes. Once again, he kissed her and held her tightly. Peter was ecstatic when again he felt the tingle in his manhood. He felt himself quiver with passion and his hopes were high, so high.

"Now, enough of this foolishness between two grown-up people. Ah've got a surprise fer ya, mah love."

"All right," she said submissively. He was so alive, so filled with ebullience, she hadn't the heart to bring him down to reality.

"Come with me, sugah," he said, leading her up the stairs, her hand in his. With the other wrapped around another glass of champagne, he led her up the circular stairs and paused before the same door to the room in which she made love to Manuelito. He felt her pull back and was prompted to say above a whisper.

"It's all right, honey. Youah'll see." He opened the door softly, peering into the dimly lit room. Then, turning to her, he nodded. "It's all right. Come in."

The room was in shadow, partially lit by a very small lamp on a chest. Her eyes, adjusting to the darkness, found nothing familiar. The room had been redecorated since Manulito occupied it. Suddenly, she saw it. Right before her eyes. Her heart raced madly and she turned to him with wide-eyed wonder. "Peter—it was you! You who rescued our son!" She sprinted from his side, reached the crib at the end of the room near the bay window, and her eyes widened with delight, happiness, and contentment. Tears of joy misted her eyes as she lifted the mosquito netting and stared down at the peaceful repose of her cherubic baby.

So strong was the inner desire to pick him up, squeeze him, smother him with kisses that she stood shaking nervously, not knowing what to do first.

"Well, is that all ya can do—stand about like a stone statue?"

She turned to Peter, tears streaming down her cheeks, and leaned over the crib to tenderly pick up the infant. She held him close to her, recalling everything sweet and loving about the child and between the joy and tears murmured sweet nonsensical things. "Thank God you're safe, *niñito*," she cooed. "How you've grown. Your mama has missed you more than you'll ever know."

She glanced at her husband who had moved in behind her and held the two of them silently, possessively, and for all eternity.

"Let him sleep, *chiquita*. You'll have the rest of your life for him. Tonight belongs to the both of us." He took the bundle from her arms and placed him back in the bassinette, brushing a tear from his misty eyes.

Madelaina took a small hand into hers and felt the tightening grip around hers with exquisite pleasure. "He's grown so, I hardly recognized him," she whispered, gazing down on the child. What happiness she felt. What joy!

"Let's hope you'll say the same thing about me," he whispered back with a devilish grin to his face.

Madelaina couldn't have asked for anything more when she left the nursery holding Peter's hand. She was consumed with happiness. Her baby son was safe, she was with the man she loved, and nothing else mattered—nothing.

They walked through the upper corridor to his bedroom where he paused to embrace her. "Madelaina," he whispered hoarsely with a new urgency to his voice. "Mah dearest, sweetest evuh lovin' *chiquita*."

Inside, they clung to each other tightly. Her hands felt the familiar muscular play rippling under his shirt. The warmth he generated when excited stimulated her intensely, as it always had in the past. She couldn't think. Time stood still for them both as he did all the exciting things that generally turned her into putty for him. His slightest touch, the lightest caress caused her to thrill and shudder with ecstasy. It was time only for feeling and love; music to which souls dance.

Dreamily she half-closed her eyes as she felt him undo the hooks and eyes of her beaded gown. "Mah sweet, sweet love, ya can't imagine how ah've longed foah ya, how much ah've missed ya," he said softly with a catch in his voice. Her gown slid to the floor unnoticed. She stood naked before him except for the garter belt and silk stockings she wore beneath the gown.

Astonished that she wore nothing under her gown, Peter gasped appreciatively. He leaned over and swept her up in his arms and carried her to the large, oversized bed, and with a free hand as she clung to him, arms around his neck, he pulled back the covers and laid her gently on the silk sheets.

"Hurry, beloved," she whispered dreamily. "The desire in me for you is overwhelming."

Peter paused to pour himself a stiff drink of whiskey from a crystal decanter on a nearby table. He commenced undressing in the shadowy room, his back to her. When he approached the bed, standing nude before her, and she saw the ghastly tracks and scarring from his stomach to his groins, she cried softly in compassion. Her hands tracing the scar brought a shiver of sensation to him.

"Oh, my dearest *querido*," she whimpered. "What pain you must have endured." She reached out for him and hugged him about the waist, lying her feverish face against his bare stomach. "Make the world go away, Peter. Make it go away. We've been too much a part of it. And I'm so tired of responsibility."

"Ah'll try, sweet suguh. Ah'll try. But first youah an' me is gotta have us a talk, heah?" He gulped down the whiskey bracer, avoiding her eyes.

"Can't we talk later?" she implored.

"No. Now."

The tone of his voice alarmed her. She backed away from him and looked up into his blue, blue eyes. He sat down on the bed alongside her and unhooked her garters. "Madelaina, a lot has happened to us, both of us." He slowly peeled off the wispy hose.

"It's the God's truth, *querido*. Too much, to both of us. There is so much you don't know about me." She began thinking this to be a moment of personal confession between them, and she was willing and eager to own up to every moment of all indiscretions, whether voluntary or done under duress. "It's best to talk, my husband, to erase all the bad that's happened so we can make a fresh beginning."

Peter studied her closely. "Ah'm not shuah ah understand ya, sugah. Look what ah've gotta tell ya may make the difference between ouah staying togethuh foah all eternity—or you gettin' a divorce."

"Divorce? *Dios mios*, are you crazy, Peter? Why would I desire a divorce? I have everything I've dreamed of having these past many months, all any woman could want." She reached for his hand, removed the silk stockings from them, and turned fully to him. Only Peter slipped out of her arms and moved toward the whiskey bottle again. He refilled the glass and gulped it down, letting the fiery liquid burn a trail in his chest.

"Mah fathuh thought of everything when he built this heah villa. Ah nevuh gave it much thought until now that ya might a spent youah honeymoon in this heah room."

"Peter!" she cried softly, hurt that he should even bring up the subject. "I told you all about that part of my life—all of it. The ceremony was performed downstairs, but it was at Seven Moons that he—that he—" she faltered, her face burning.

"Seduced you?" he laughed harshly. "Ah, then that explains it."

"Explains what?"

"Why he left Seven Moons to you. All of it."

Madelaina couldn't believe her ears. "To me? You mean to us?"

"To *you,* my dear. *Your* performance must have been superb!" As soon as the words were out, Peter felt terrible. He hadn't meant to say such things, but he couldn't help himself. He gulped the drink and poured another.

Madelaina recoiled and eyed him through curious, hurt, and wondering eyes. "Have you brought me here to humiliate me, to bring up the past over which I had no control, and lay it before me at its worst implications?"

Peter moaned softly, lay across the bed, and pulled her into her into his arms. "No," he whispered hoarsely. "Damnit, honey, ah've no intention of hurtin' ya. Ah'm not shuah what's gotten inta me."

"If you persist, I'll turn back into the iceberg I've been since our son was born," she said coolly, in a voice that hinted at detachment.

"Iceberg? You?" He laughed ironically. "Mah deah, sweet wife, that could nevuh happen ta ya. Maybe if it did, ouah problems would be settled."

"Problems, Peter? What problems?" she scoffed. "We are together. All else is in the past. All the bad dreams with those frightening pictures will evaporate now that we've found ourselves. Why are we using strange words to build walls between us?" She shook her head when he held a whiskey glass up to her. "Neither of us are to blame for what happened. Thank God that we're alive. So many died. So many—" her voice trailed off. "Give thanks that we found each other. Nothing else matters." She sat up and fell into his arms, and her hands began immediately to explore his body.

Catching her hands, Peter removed them gently from his body. Madelaina, hurt, confused, and shaken by this subtle rejection, sat back against the headboard and watched him pour another tumbler of whiskey. Confronted with an absorbing inconsistency of thoughts, she was unable to express her quandary at his behavior.

It never occurred to her until this precise moment that something was drastically wrong. In all the time she'd known him, including those first days aboard the *Mozambique* after the ice between them was broken, he'd never been an inhibited man. Whenever he'd wanted her, he'd taken her. Of course, she had always been willing, for only with him had she felt the overwhelming passion of love and fire of any duration. Only with Peter . . . and Tolomeo. *Damnit! Forget Tolomeo! You're with Peter now. He's the only one who counts. Don't let any other thoughts beguile you or influence you.*

"Heah, sugah, drink this up," insisted her husband, forcing a drink into her hands.

"If you want me to," she said reluctantly. She recalled vividly when Peter drank too much he was unable to make love as he desired. Why, now, does he pick this night to become a *borrachón*, a drunk? Gulping the drink down quickly, she turned the empty glass upside down on her nightstand. "You have a spare cigarette around?" she asked.

Peter lit two, gave her one, and smoked the other. "Want a refill?" he asked, gesturing to the glass.

922

"No, thank you," she replied, puffing on the cigarette, inhaling and expelling the smoke. "Too bad this isn't marijuana. It would relax you and me both."

Peter cautioned her about the use of reefers in Texas. "It's against the law, heah, so ya be careful who ya tell ya smoke it. Texas ain't Mexico, heah?"

Peter watched her as an enemy watches his prey. How could he tell her? Earlier, when they kissed so passionately he'd felt a hardness in his loins that silently gave rise to hope that his impotency had passed. The moment he faced her nakedness and his desire mounted, his manhood had deflated into a total lack of response.

God, how he tried! He had used a few of the Mexican girls from Old Chihuahua every night, sometimes twice a night and nothing! Absolutely nothing had happened. When General Villa wired him that he was bringing Little Fox to El Paso, Peter's hopes had soared and he put them all on the line. If anyone could stir his manhood into pulsating joy and stimulate him as a man should be stimulated, it was his wife. Madelaina could jolt him back to life again. He was certain of it. Love transcended sex anytime. He had every right to believe his wife was the only one who could restore his manhood. She wouldn't fail him, not his Little Fox. She'd lift the curse that had afflicted him for the past year. He'd confide in her. He felt deeply that he had no right to hold her to a marriage in his condition, but before he threw in the towel, he would ask her to help him.

He hated being so vulnerable. Goddamn it! Some of the whores he'd brought for a night had looked upon him as less than a man. They'd laughed contemptuously at him when he couldn't perform. Well, all that was over, now. Madelaina was with him. She'd put an end to those frightening feelings of desperation and hopelessness he'd experienced in the past.

With a light curse of despair, Peter rose from the bed and said, "We've gotta talk, Little Fox. We've gotta."

"So, talk, my husband," she replied patiently. "I'm listening." Then suddenly Madelaina was afraid to hear what it was he was trying to tell her. Her body tensed and she knew what he was trying to communicate to her. All those visions that came to her, primed to illuminate her mind, had been ignored. She gazed covertly at his limp sex organ, hoping he didn't see her for fear he might misinterpret her interest. And she knew. *Oh, Tolomeo! What wisdom you had stored inside of you. What do I do now? You tried to tell me. You made it quite clear, and I ignored and misunderstood your warnings. You tried to impress me with the right values, and what did I do? I ignored your wisdom.*

Clearly she recollected the time Tolomeo held a knife upthrust in his hands, prepared to cut off his precious manhood.

What will you say, Madelaina, if I severed my phallus? Would you still love me? Would you remain with me until death as you insisted? Will you love me if I can no longer couple with you? Ah, then you don't love me. You love my sexual organs. Good, then I shall cut them off and give them to you to take with you and love evermore.

Dios mios! Madelaina shuddered inwardly. Here it was, just as Tolomeo had tried telling her it might be. What to do? What to do? This was moment of truth. What she did and said in these next few moments would affect three human beings for the rest of their days. *Help me, Tolomeo. Help me, God. Help me, anyone. Have I become a seer? A psychic? Or am I going mad? What is happening to me that I have been gifted with vision? I don't want it! Take it away. It's best that I remain blind to such things,* she agonized desperately.

Tears spilled from her eyes. She turned her head from Peter so he wouldn't see. *This must be a terrible time for Peter, and here I am acting the fool. He expects more from Little Fox and he shall get it,* she told herself.

Peter handed her a robe. "Heah, put this on," he told her, slipping into another himself.

It was something he'd never done in the past, cover his nudity. He'd always been proud of his manly, well-proportioned body. Never one to mince words, Peter, as he'd always done in the past, faced her abruptly and spoke straight out. "Madelaina, ah'm impotent."

"Yes, I know," she said quietly, her dark wide eyes fixed on his in love.

"You know?" He was aghast. His eyes narrowed suspiciously. "How do you know? Who told you?"

"No one. I've known almost from the start," she said in truth.

"But how? Who?" He didn't believe her and told her so.

"Don't ask me how. I couldn't explain it so you'd understand." How could she tell him about Tolomeo? He'd think she'd turned into some crazy woman. And it would only add more fuel to the fire smoldering inside him.

"Ya say ya knew all the time? Yet ya were prepared to let me make a fool of mahself tonight?" Now Peter grew angry at her, resented her.

"Things aren't always what they appear to be—" she began.

"That's disgustin'. Youah were waitin' foah me ta make a jackass outa mahself. Why, that's a pretty low thing—"

"No! No," she interrupted. "That wasn't my intention. And calm down, Peter. It's not the end of the world!"

"Hah! That's easy foah youah ta say!"

"Why is it any easier for me than you?" she demanded fiercely. "If I remember correctly, I, too, was unable to function as a woman for a time. Who came to my aid? My husband. So, husband, here I am to help you, to love you and help ease your pain."

"Pity, ah don't need," he said scorchingly.

"Pity?" exclaimed Madelaina hotly. "Who speaks of pity?"

925

"And don't give me that wifely duty business, either!"

"Are you so hurt, so humiliated, so terribly ashamed of your condition that you won't give me a chance to help you, Peter?" she asked softly.

"The only way youah can help me is ta give me an erection! That's the tall and short o' it!"

"No!"

"No?" He stared at her dumbfounded and resentful.

"No! You heard me. Not when you demand it. You're trying too hard. It's not that important, at least not to me."

Peter laughed uproariously at the ugly joke this presented to his mind. "Not important? Why, Little Fox, without a piece o' tail, you'd be outa youah evuh loving mind! A hot little piece of baggage like youah has gotta have a stud bull in the barn or ya couldn't live. Poon tang is youah life, mah sweet," he said bitterly.

Madelaina stared at him contemptuously. "How little you know me, gringo," she said, standing, her hands on her hips, feet spread apart like a *campesina* from the early days. She undid a few hairpins from her upswept hairdo and let her raven hair fall to below her shoulders. "I tell you it is not important. You don't believe me. I tell you we hardly know each other, that we must first get acquainted. Will you listen to Little Fox?"

Peter, tense and wound up to the point of cracking, had wanted desperately for a miracle to happen this night, like in a story book when the prince walks off into the sunset with a princess to live happy ever after. He reached up for her and pulled her down on the bed, his head against her wildly beating heart.

"Ya think it might help, *querida*? Ya think ya can do it—make a man outa me?" His voice reflected his inner torment.

"What you ask is impossible. You already are a man—some wild, crazy man," she said lightly, hoping to raise his spirits. She stroked his forehead, quietly as-

926

suring him of her love for him. "We can do it, *mi marido,* together we can accomplish miracles." Inwardly she thought, *God, show me how to perform such a miracle.*

They fell asleep in each other's arms. Peter, first. Madelaina, when dawn erupted in the sky, fell exhausted from the countless thoughts burning in her mind.

Chapter 35

"It saddens me, Little Fox, that you and your *marido* will not join Pancho Villa in his most spectacular of battles," said the *jefe* over luncheon a few days before his departure for Mexico. "It will not be the same without you seated at the head of my *soldaderas*. They will feel your absence as much as I will, but I shall learn to get along without your expert counseling," he said, smiling brightly with a twinkle in his eyes. "Ain't that right, Fierro?" He addressed himself to the unsmiling, bearish man who sipped champagne and enjoyed the lavish spread at the buffet table by making short order of it.

Madelaina glanced at Fierro with a smile on her face. She would miss this adoring animal, even though at times his might and cold-blooded nature had frightened her. He still wore the red-haired fetish on his uniform, dangling from the Sam Browne belt he wore over his tunic. She wondered if Villa ever learned of his affair with Antonetta. Somehow she felt deeply that he knew and had accepted it as a human and natural everyday occurrence.

"Please know, *Jefe,* that I, too, will miss you and the others. But I must devote time to my husband and child. They both need me. And if you will pardon my candor, I am tired of revolution. We both are, aren't we, Peter?"

"Shall I tell you that I, too, am tired? *Chica,* this past trip to El Paso has given me hope—new hope. Our gringo friends in Washington have begun to hear my tunes, so perhaps now they'll help us waltz our way to the capital."

"Let's hope so, *Jefe*," she replied, wondering why Peter had remained silent.

"Not yet," said Captain Tracy Richards, entering the patio where the gathering took place. He removed his Stetson, gave it to a servant, and ran his fingers through his stringy brown hair. He wore a strange, taut expression on his face.

Peter walked toward him, hand outstretched to shake hands, a champagne glass in the other to thrust in Tracy's hands. The look in the man's eyes arrested his host. "What's the mattuh, pal? Ya look like ya lost yer last friend."

Tracy nodded and moved in toward General Villa. He saluted the *jefe* and removed a wire from inside his tunic. "Sorry, *Jefe*. I raced as fast as I could. This just came in from Chihuahua City." He handed Villa the paper.

Villa accepted the wire, his dark eyes, unsmiling, were fixed on the captain. He glanced at the message and read: *Obregon back in Mexico City. Carranza back from Veracruz. Presidente Guiterrez fled with 10 million pesos from treasury. Hell has erupted. Advise, Manuelo Isabel.*"

General Villa handed the wire to General Fierro. "Confirm this," he ordered. Fierro's eyes scanned the contents without expression.

"Ah already did, *Jefe*," replied Tracy Richards. "Ah took the liberty of checking with the Juarez wireless office. They just got the word from Mexico City."

General Villa turned to Madelaina. "Let Little Fox see the wire."

Madelaina glanced from her husband to Fierro to Villa, then read the message. Her eyes lifted to meet his.

"Ju know what theese means, *chiquita?*" asked Villa gently.

"I know. Your battle with Obregon—my father."

"I wished for a different result."

"I know. Time was our enemy. Then go. *Vaya con Dios* and may the best man win," she told him tearfully

929

as Peter put a strong arm around his wife. He read the wire and handed it to Villa. The *jefe* directed his words to them.

"Is best ju stay here for theese wan. There will never be a bigger, more forceful thrust than this war against Obregon," he said tersely. "For a long time it's been coming," he told her in Spanish, as he buttoned his tunic. "Come, Fierro, we go. You too, gringo?" he asked Tracy Richards.

"Try and keep me out of this one. Ah got me a feelin' this one will be the beginnin' o' the end of revolution for Mexico, eh, *Jefe?*"

"Perhaps, gringo. Perhaps," he said sadly, taking his leave.

Watching him and the entire entourage leave their home, Peter and Madelaina stood in the courtyard, waving to them with a feeling of great loss.

Peter turned to his wife and smiled tenderly at her. "Foah a while, sugah, ah felt shuah youah were going ta leave me. Ah know y' all wanta be right alongside of the *jefe*. Ah find mahself weakening every moment."

Madelaina turned to him and pressed her fingertip against his lips. "No! I want to be with my husband and child. We shall have to content ourselves with reading about the war from Miguel Guerra's columns, *querido*. Oh, *amado mío,* haven't we had enough? I thought we had made our decision."

"We did, sugah. We did," he said solemnly, embracing her tightly.

It was to be a considerably long while before Madelaina and her family would go to Seven Moons. Peter had immersed himself in pressing business matters. He'd changed so drastically in personality and temperament that Madelaina felt the need to consult with the physician who performed the surgery on her husband. Without Peter's knowledge, she paid a visit to Dr. Clancy Towbridge. The man in his late forties with salt and pepper hair, wearing a stiffly starched round collar with a narrow tie under his white coat, recalled the case intimately.

"Why, shucks, m'am, ah was shuah that Peter had become as frisky as a two-tailed burro by now. Theah's no medical reason why he shouldn't be performin' like a jack rabbit. If theah are problems in that department afuh so long, it's gotta be all in his head. An' youah jus' tell him ah said so, heah?"

"That may well be, Doctor," she said politely. "And if it is as you say, perhaps you can explain better to me what I must do to help him get back his manhood. I don't wish to compound the state of mind he's in by saying or doing anything that might cause him more anguish."

"That's a right sensible gal, ya are, Mrs. Benson. Ah admire such spunk. It isn't every day ah meet such a brave woman." He paused reflectively. "Ah jus' don't know wheah ta begin. It could be from many things— such as a very poor home life. What ah mean is not poverty, ya understand, but a wrongful relationship between parents. What ah'm attemptin' ta say ta ya, Mrs. Benson, is something that medical science tuhday doesn't understand. Sometimes childhood frustrations don't manifest themselves in a person until the late twenties, thirties, and sometimes in mid-life. Ya understand?"

"No, Doctor. I'm afraid I don't. Are you trying to tell me my husband has a sick mind?"

Dr. Towbridge laughed. "Not quite. But ya might say a little bit like that."

"I'm truly confused. He was shot, sustained severe injuries, and he was told impotency might result. It did. Now you tell me, impotency isn't a result of the surgery, that it's in his head. Couldn't you be more specific?"

"If ah could, ah would, m'am. There just isn't enough known about abnormal pyschological behavior."

"Abnormal psychological behavior? You are the most confounding doctor I've ever spoken with," she said, fully irritated. "Dr. Towbridge, my marriage is at stake. What can I do to help it stay together?"

"Be patient and understanding."

"Words, Doctor. Those are just words. How can I be patient when I'm not certain of what I must be patient? How can I be understanding when I don't know what I'm supposed to understand? For a doctor you are incredibly uninformed!" she quipped as her aristocratic *gachupín* blood boiled. "Can't you at least refer me to someone else? Someone who might be more knowledgeable on the subject? Forgive my impatience and somewhat boorish manners, but, Doctor, if I don't conjure up a miracle, my marriage will end."

Dr. Towbridge glanced at her over the top of his rimless glasses and nodded as if to himself. "Yer Mexican, aren't ya?"

Madelaina bridled angrily. "What has that to do with anything?"

His face flared with a pink flush. "Well, I—er—well, sometimes, Mrs. Benson, a man marries a woman in her country and when he brings her ta his land, she jus' don't fit no how. This can make a man regret—" He found words more difficult under Madelaina's hot, melting gaze. "Ya understand it's nothing personal. What ah'm trying ta say is that a man might feel he made a mistake and he feels strangled and he can't be a man."

"Thank you for your honesty. I assure you this isn't so in our case," she told him imperiously with controlled anger.

"Ah gotta say one thing in yer favuh. You'ah a persistent filly." He picked up a pen and scribbled several names on a script pad. "Y'all have ta mosey ovuh ta San Antonio foah the answers, ma'am." He handed her the information she needed and wished her the best of luck.

"Let me just say a word about the man youah gonna meet. Dr. Thaddeus Oemolot, pronounced *Amalot,* isn't what ya might refer ta as the average physician ya see about El Paso. Or anywheah else, foah that matter.

He's a little unorthodox. But most of them head shrinkers from Freud on down were a little tetched in the head, according ta theah contemporaries." Towbridge sighed. "Well, mebbe in the next fifty yeahs, theah'll be a few changes in ouah society and people will begin ta wake up the real values. Thaddeus Oemolot is unique among men, the only one of his kind, if ya ask me. He's bright, he's well informed, an it ain't all outa books that he comes by his uncanny perception and his phenomenal diagnostic abilities. But why do ah rant like this? Y'all meet him, decide foah youahself. Ah think the two of ya might hit it off fine. Ya see, he was married to one of youah people. He can tell ya plenty about the difficulties that face ya in Texas."

"I thought the Alamo incident took place over seventy-five years ago," she snapped caustically. "Texans probably have it all over the elephant! *Buenas tardes, senor el doctor. Muchas gracias.*" She spoke Spanish purposely.

She was shaking when she left the physician's office. Damned if she'd admit to this—this—doctor that of late she'd been entertaining similar thoughts. No question she'd encountered the racial prejudices, bigotry, and narrow-minded biases of her neighbors, who hadn't come to call on her since her arrival.

Thank God I have the blood of a high-born Spaniard, she said to herself a thousand times over. *If I'd been a peón with no education, I'd probably walk around like a wounded animal, ready to dig my own grave.* It wasn't fair, she told herself. In Mexico the gringos are treated like gods. Here in America we are treated like dogs. She hadn't brought the subject out in the open to discuss it with her husband, not yet, with all the problems besetting him presently.

But—one day—one day she'd settle this Alamo business so her people wouldn't have to suffer what strangers had done to each other nearly a century ago.

Enough for racial prejudices, she reasoned. Get back to Peter. He'd changed drastically from the reckless, easy-going, freedom-fighting libertine he was when they met. She hardly knew him anymore. He'd grown more introverted, hardly communicating with her. Something rankled him. Something ate away at his insides and the pity of it was she couldn't get close enough to him to find out what it was that was causing such alien behavior.

She'd observed him in silence, hoping to instill in him the old feelings of security and self-assurance she found so attractive in him. A few times she'd chided him about his personality change and he'd stare at her as if seeing her for the first time.

"Ah'm a property ownuh now, a man with responsibilities. Ah jus' can't run off inta the world lookin' ta save humanity. Ah've got mah own little world heah ta set straight first."

What frightened Madelaina more each day was the startling resemblance between his actions and those of his dead father. His impotence had changed him into a hardened, two-fisted, gun-toting *hacendado* who was skillfully manipulating himself into the political sphere of action that kept El Paso at the center of international intrigue. Worse, he refused to confide in her over the nature of his mysterious covert involvements which kept him absent from the villa for longer than she cared to dwell upon.

In a way she was grateful for the time to herself, because it allowed her to spend more time with her son. He'd grown into a fine, strapping two-year-old who kept the entire Benson household gravely concerned because he hadn't taken his first step yet. Peter remained the most anxious, and his concern that it might be something physical rather than the normal way of things kept Madelaina in borderline frustration, trying to reason with him that boys took more time to walk.

"Not to worry, Señora Benson," Pilar would tell her. Peter had brought her from Seven Moons to care for the child in Madelaina's absence, and she was perfect for him, playing with him, giving him the care and attention he needed. "Ees you, Pilar concerns herself weeth. Ju and your *marido*. Are theengs hokay?"

934

Madelaina would smile and nod her head. "As long as we're together, Pilar, nothing can be wrong." But the old woman knew better. Her Indian instinct told her it wasn't right for such newlyweds to be sleeping in separate bedrooms.

Even Madelaina found this unacceptable, but Peter, who had become nocturnal, stayed awake most of the night worrying, and in his desire not to disturb his wife, he insisted on their occupying separate quarters.

Peter had made no sexual overtures to her and Madelaina hadn't pushed. Instead, she attempted to build an emotional closeness with him, tried to share his interests, and did nothing to raise any suspicions in his mind. She exercised all the patience she could muster. She had tried to figure some way she could go to Dallas without raising questions in Peter's mind. His overt possessiveness was beginning to grate on her nerves. She was unable to go to market without his asking her incessant questions about who she'd seen or spoken to.

Then one day it happened. Peter came home in the early afternoon and announced he had to make a short trip to Washington. Unfinished business, he told her. He'd return in less than a week, he reassured her when she expressed her disappointment in not going with him. She'd said nothing when she entered his room and he quickly shut his travel case, so she wouldn't see its contents. But she'd seen his six-shooters and holster. How she wanted to ask him more about his secret comings and goings, his mysterious behavior, midnight callers, and the like. She felt if she pried, she'd disturb the rapport she'd hoped to build to inspire his trust and confidence.

They kissed warmly. "You'ah shuah y'all be fine?" he asked with concern.

"Yes, Peter. We'll be fine. I promise. Remember I managed to survive the revolution in your absence."

"Ya hafta bring that up all the time? Damn! Ah thought all that was in the past. Ah thought we agreed not to talk about it no moah." He stormed out the door, briefcase, travel bag, and coat in hand without saying goodbye.

It would have been easy for Madelaina to resort to tears and feelings of humiliation. Instead, she summoned all her strength and cool temperament and grew more determined to fulfill her mission. It was San Antonio for her. She was going to get her answers—or die in the attempt.

She told Pilar where she could be located in the event of an emergency and left stern instructions not to tell anyone of her whereabouts. She packed an overnight bag and booked passage on the train to San Antonio.

During the long train ride, her thoughts again turned to Peter and his unusual behavior of late. They were more like strangers these past five months. One night, in one of his foulest moods, he addressed her with a hardness she'd never recalled in him before.

"Why don't ya take on a lover, for God's sake? That—what's his name—that Armando fella—the one that took yer virginity!"

She had been astounded. "Why do you think of him now?"

"Listen, don't play the innocent with me. Ya shuah carried on with him at Townsend's villa the night of the gala for the *jefe*."

Madelaina could say nothing. She knew he spoke out of sheer frustration. And her words in defense of her own innocent actions could be easily twisted to suit his own depressive mania. Her silence only incited him to lash out at her, to hurt her by bringing up all she had tried so desperately to forget.

"How many lovers have possessed that body? Ah remember what y'all told me of Madrigal and that theah Simon Salomon—that ya hated him. Well, deah, sweet Little Fox, ah also learned that ya were shacked up with him foah ovuh two weeks. Now tell me that ya hated him?"

Madelaina had glanced sharply at him, totally astounded by his words. "How—where ever did you hear that?" she asked.

"Don't deny it. Ah hate liars!"

"I don't intend to deny the truth."

"Then ya admit ya were with him, close as turtle doves?"

"Why are you doing this?" she asked gently. "Why didn't you speak of this long ago? Why are you trying, like an angry child, to hurt the one you love most in the world?"

Peter had no defenses to fall back on. In a voice steeped in agony, he told her to leave him. "Get a divorce. Or we'll end up like my father and mother, hating each other, creating a living hell for us."

"I haven't given up yet, my husband," she told him. She was desperate and it showed. It also served to increase Peter's guilt feelings that he wasn't properly performing his role as husband to her.

This trip to San Antonio was Madelaina's last chance. She had to learn what was wrong with Peter, how to cope or go stark mad.

Chapter 36

Dr. Thaddeus Oemolot, an eccentric, was everything
and more the El Paso physician had described him to
be. He was a man in his late forties, with well-tanned,
unlined features and marvelously warm turquoise eyes
which reflected the dancing rays of the sun streaming
in through curtained windows in his cluttered office. He
had a high, wide forehead framed by a thick shock of
snowy white hair. His nose was straight with flaring
nostrils, somewhat Grecian in shape, his square jaw
with a cleft in it gave him a strong countenance, one
which inspired confidence.

He greeted her in a curt, professional manner in
thickly accented English, which she later learned was a
combination of Swiss, French, and German. Please, she
asked, could he speak in either Spanish, French, or
Italian to enable her to better understand him? He
nodded and then proceeded to speak in impeccable
Spanish, complete with a Castilian lisp.

As he began to outline the complexities involved in
cases of impotency and the ramifications surrounding
the onset of symptoms, Madelaina found herself totally
bewildered by the alien and incomprehensible words he
used. *Dios mios!* She should have brought with her a
dictionary, she told herself. As if she had to be told
that impotence was an impairment in the desire for
sexual gratification! For this she had traveled hundreds
of miles.

Madelaina complained of his semantical snobbery,
his use of words she didn't understand. The inveterate
chain-smoking, coffee-drinking addict who kept both
coffee and cigarettes within reach of his roll-top desk

smiled, begged her pardon, and spoke more in layman's language.

"Senõra Benson, I'll try to speak with less complications for you. As I was saying, fatigue, worry, and a long list of seemingly innocent ailments can temporarily impair sexual potency. In my opinion—and I do not make light of the situation—prolonged or permanent impotency before the age of 55 is generally the result of psychological conflicts. It's a study that we of the medical profession specializing in this field know little of at this time."

"Certainly you can give me more encouragement than that?" she asked, gazing at the white cockatoo perched in a corner of the messy office, contentedly eating sunflower seeds.

"Perhaps, if you persuade your husband to explain his own case history, I could make a swifter diagnosis. It isn't customary to work in this manner without first examining the patient or at least speaking with him. You see, whatever the mental block preventing him from performing with you, it must be dissolved—totally removed. Personally, I don't see how I can do anything for him without seeing him."

He glanced concentratedly at the medical report she brought from El Paso, containing the history of the gunshot wounds, subsequent surgery, and the superficial case history compiled of the psychological studies done by Dr. Towbridge.

"This Towbridge was thorough enough. He sewed your husband back together well enough, no?"

"Apparently not good enough or he wouldn't be in such a sad state."

"Señora," he said patiently. "Believe me when I tell you his problems are mental—not physical," he said, tapping his forehead. "How can I convince you?"

"Very well, where are we? We rule out physical impairment. *Bueno*. You can eliminate any feelings of shyness or inferiority with the opposite sex. My husband has been a lusty man from the moment I first met

939

him, and I'm sure he was even before our acquaintance some six years ago," she said candidly.

Dr. Oemolot nodded in approval. "You've been doing some reading, *como no? Muy bien*. Then if you will, tell me more about him, this freedom-fighting soldier-of-fortune business. His thirst for adventure, desire to champion the rights of the downtrodden. Tell me all you can of his background," he instructed.

She did the best she could for some two hours of constant narration.

"Can we rule out any guilt feelings he might harbor over an extramarital affair, *señora?* What I mean is, has he been unfaithful to your married vows?"

"Such a question! A man with his lusty macho qualities? But of course. He is only human, no? Perhaps you weren't listening when I described our roles in the revolution, Dr. Oemolot?" She dug a sharper spur into him than was intended, with more candor than she thought herself capable of. Then she flushed under his melting gaze. "Perhaps not since the accident, if I can believe my husband—and I do." Madelaina squirmed uncomfortably in her chair and lit a cigarette to cover her discomfort. The cockatoo ruffled its feathers and closed its eyes.

From the moment she'd entered his modest, efficient-looking office, surrounded by walls of books, dark leathers, and living plants, she had a strange feeling they weren't strangers. Logically she knew they'd never met before, but there was that intangible energy, that force of attraction stronger than a magnet which compelled their lives to cross. What was it, she asked herself countless times during this initial visit. Had she known him at some time in her life? Madelaina, whose memory was too acute at times, searched every open drawer in her mind for the connection to him. She found none. Still the feeling persisted.

He listened patiently and smiled from time to time at her eagerness, this determined effort on her part to find a solution to her present dilemma. Thaddeus Oemolot admired her spunk and wondered what sort of a man wouldn't have come himself to solve his own quandary and unmanly behavior. Didn't it mean enough to him? It apparently meant a great deal to his wife.

"You are married to a gringo, *señora*? And you are —French—Spanish—what?"

"It makes any difference?" she asked frostily. "I am a Mexican."

"Everything makes a difference and can be vital in such a case," he replied, giving it proper importance. "*Señora,* please tell me of any significant quarrels or arguments that have passed between you and your *marido*? Are there any hostilities between you?"

"Is it necessary to know such personal things, Doctor. Much of what you suggest sounds quite preposterous to me, if you must know my feelings."

His voice had an instant mesmerizing richness and a depth of understanding, but he seemed a bit impatient with her at times. "If you expect me to help restore your husband's potency, yes. It's necessary that I know, however personal or ridiculous my questions sound."

Madelaina glanced at her watch with an attitude of annoyance. "How much time do you have?" she asked in a challenging tone of voice.

"How much do I need?"

"However much time it takes to tell you our full story. It's long, involved, and at times highly incredible even for me, one who's lived it."

Dr. Oemolot impatiently pounded the small bell on his cluttered, oversized roll-top desk. Across the room, the white cockatoo started and ruffled his feathers.

"Be quiet, Pablo," commanded the physician as his nurse entered the room, dressed in a white starched uniform and cap. She stood in the doorway expectantly.

"Yes, Doctor?"

He instructed her to cancel all his appointments for the balance of the day, to set over his next day's patients for the following day and be certain to make his apologies to his evening guests, that he'd call them as soon as time permitted. Before the astonished stiff-lipped nurse could either object or dispute his orders, Dr. Oemolot had removed his white coat, slipped into his Oxford plaid jacket, belted at the waist, removed his bifocals, and slipped them into a case which he thrust into his inner breast jacket pocket. From another pocket, he removed a pair of dark glasses.

"The inexorable hot sun of Texas becomes man's worst enemy at this time of the year," he said, opening the outer door to his office. "*Ondolay, señora*. If you've a long story to tell me, it's best we get started." He nearly shoved her out the door, then stopped abruptly. "You like Mexican food? I sincerely hope so, because I'm taking you to a restaurant I enjoy. *Bueno?*"

"*Beuno, senor el doctor.*"

Five hours later, Madelaina was still telling him about her incredibly adventurous life with Peter, of her own experiences as a *soldadera* and revolutionist. They had left the Mexican eatery where she'd found the food atrocious and told him so. "You call this garbage *comida*—food?" She'd turned up her nose at it in typical *gachupín* fashion. "If I had the time, Doctor, I would cook for you authentic Spanish food that would make of you a true *aficionado* for life."

"That would be a total waste of time, *señora,* since I am already an *aficionado*. Besides, I didn't promise you Spanish food—it was Mexican food I offered. On that I am an expert." His words, however truthful, rankled her.

For a few moments she bridled hotly under his chafing remark, then as he drove maniacally through the streets of San Antonio in his Stutz Bearcat, she, dressed in the duster he insisted she wear, hung on for dear life, giving little thought to his impudence. With her life in the hands of this crazy maniac driving this crazier horseless carriage, she could think of nothing else. *Dios mios!* Even in the thickest of battles she hadn't experienced so many new feelings of fright and apprehension, and she later wondered at her own lack of inner fortitude.

"Perhaps I may keep you here in San Atonio long enough to sample your Spanish cooking. Señora Benson," he said, taking a sharp corner off a paved street onto a dirt road leading, it seemed, to nowhere on the vast desert.

"I live very close, another mile or so. I prefer living in the desert, close to nature."

"If you continue to navigate this horseless monster whith such fierce determination, you'll be dead before I leave San Antonio!" she exploded her fright with a frontal attack.

Dr. Oemolot found this terrible amusing. "*I* frighten *you, señora?*" He laughed with gusto. "A *soldadera* whose has seen front-line fighting? *Chiquita,* you are something very special. I would not think you are capable of being frightened. We both have faced death a thousand times. What can be worse than that?"

"Yes," she agreed. "What could be worse than death? Living—and its thousands of complications and uncertainties."

He turned to her for an instant, taking his eyes off the road, and in that moment, he swerved the car, forcing her to take a tighter grip on the handle bar. She swallowed hard, grimly determined not to register another complaint.

"Look, *señora!* Over there. It's the Alamo! Remember the Alamo? It's quite a landmark. It was close by, so I thought you might enjoy seeing a famous historical structure.

Madelaina's eyes reluctantly assessed the well-preserved building with rancor. "I prefer not remembering such an atrocity, regardless of how much a part of history it's become. I detest what it stands for in these days of racial prejudice. Why, the damned gringos worship it as they would a saint! How barbarous!" She shuddered at the unhappy memories it stoked in her mind.

Thaddeus Oemolot beeped his loud, clangorous horn and made an unexpected 180-degree hairpin turn in the dirt road, carefully avoiding the sand at the shoulder's edge and retraced his path toward town. He turned off the road onto a deserted trail, and in a few moments he pulled up before an isolated desert dwelling resembling an Indian pueblo, standing stark in the middle of nothing but desert and cactus.

"More historical places?" she asked, still catching her breath over the perilous turn he'd made in the road earlier.

"But of course, Señora Benson. It is the home of Thaddeus Oemolot." He turned off the motor and blew the horn with gusto. In moments a man servant appeared. "José, put a cover over her. I won't need it for the balance of the day. And mind you—don't get carried away with it."

He helped Madelaina down from the auto, took the duster from her and placed it in the seat of the car, as the dark-skinned, toothy servant nodded and replied, "*Muy bueno, señor el doctor.*"

Madelaina sighed with relief when she felt the firmness of earth under her feet. "You are a rugged individualist, doctor," she told him once she entered the unusually decorated house. It was truly a simple pueblo outside, but once inside, you got a vast feeling of space under the domed open-air ceiling of the atrium from which other rooms branched off. It contained the newest innovations, a forerunner of the pace-setting homes that would sweep the western desert states a half-century later.

With a feeling of glowing pride of ownership, he took her on a short tour of the five-room haven which he had designed and helped build in his spare time. It was deceptively large, spacious, and cooler inside by several degrees. The floors throughout were of hand-set terra cotta tiles, buffed to a high sheen. A huge fireplace stood at the center of the living room as a focal point, and the room itself rambled into a dining room and library at the other end. The kitchen and butter rooms were outside in another area adjoining the house, connected by the solarium, containing endless tropical flora and an aviary of exotic and tropical birds of magnificent plumage. The one large master bedroom was upstairs on what appeared to be a cantilevered area overlooking the entire lower level, including fireplace and the hanging gardens of the atrium. It seemed immense, yet Madelaina knew it was a smaller dwelling than Seven Moons. She instantly fell in love with the place. A warmth and loving feeling permeated the entire house, and she felt at home in it from the moment she stepped over the threshold.

"And what do you call this—paradise?" she asked, enthralled by what she saw. Madelaina gave a start at the feeling of something hot and velvety near her hand. She turned and gazed into the glassy black eyes of a sable-colored puma.

"*Dios mios*, you gave me a start," she told the animal, ruffling its neck and patting it affectionately as if seeing one were an everyday occurrence. "How beautiful you are, *gatto mas grande*."

"It has no name, *señora,* until now. I will call it Oemolot's Paradise." He studied her comportment with the puma until the puma moved away from Madelaina and sauntered slowly to his master, stretching its large jaws in a yawn.

"It is strange how Dionysis takes to you," he muttered. "I am delighted that you approve of my taste. I'm not certain why I brought you here, except that I felt certain you'd appreciate it." He petted the animal as he continued to watch his guest through calculating eyes. "Since the death of my wife, I've brought no one here, not even my friends."

"Don't they object? You must be obligated to do much entertaining in your circle of professional friends and acquaintances."

"My circle of friends?" He chuckled ironically. "You know what the friends and acquaintances think of Thaddeus Oemolot? They think he is one crazy man—*muy loco*. It tickles my fancy to observe them as they attempt to analyze me. Especially when I drive through the streets of San Antonio, honking my horn

945

out of the sheer joy of living. They assume that I am some crazy idiot."

Madelaina reflected a moment, wondering at her own sanity for putting her trust and faith in a man deemed ridiculous by his peers. *From this eccentric* viejo *I've come for help for my* marido? Perhaps it was because she too had felt the spur of rejection and ridicule by her peers that she found an affinity with this man. Or was it because of the nature of the man so predisposed to enjoying the real things in life—the flowers, plants, birds, and animals that most people had no feeling for. She wasn't certain. She knew something intangible kept her here in the company of Dr. Thaddeus Oemolot.

They sat on the flower-lined patio of the atrium with the ceaseless singing and chattering of the birds as background music. The puma curled up at his feet. Beyond the perimeter of his property lines, all she could see in the beginning of a golden, coral sunset was desert sand the color of the sky's reflection.

Dr. Oemolot had changed to more casual western attire, and Madelaina had removed the trim navy blue jacket and relaxed in her camisole and skirt, her long hair piled atop her head. He lazily packed his pipe with tobacco from a humidor on a rolling cart brought out by José's wife, Maria Inez, a plump woman with gray hair pulled back tightly into a bun at her neck, dressed in a gaily colored peasant dress. She left a large pitcher of iced tea and retreated quietly.

"Ahhh, this is the life," he said, patting his stomach contentedly. "I keep promising myself to take more time to live, but, alas, each day my patients swell to such proportions that I wonder where I'll find the time to counsel all of them. People who can't cope with their everyday existence in the changing pace of time. God save us if the next fifty years continue at the same rate of speed. We are a growing nation and with growth comes many responsibilities. May I call you Madelaina? You please call me Thaddeus or Tadeo whichever pleases you." He spoke in that same slowed-down, mellow voice which earlier gave her the soothing feeling of being bombarded by cotton puffs.

She nodded and sipped the refreshing iced tea.

"Doctor is so stuffy. It gives man an importance he doesn't deserve. Now then, *chica,* all those tales you related earlier? They were gospel? The truth?"

"I told you it was an incredible story."

"Does your husband know all this—all these experiences of yours?"

"Of course. Perhaps not every precise detail of every moment, but most of it."

"And you, Madelaina, have you ever been unfaithful to your *marido?*"

Madelaina faltered. "That depends on what you mean by unfaithful. In body? Spirit? Mind? What?"

"Oh, come, my dear. Unfaithful is unfaithful. To be more explicit, have you gone to bed with other men?"

Her face burned. "I told you what happened at Madrigal—"

"*Si, por Dios,* you did. What I am speaking of is—willingly."

"No." She paused, averting her eyes. "That is—" A tremor shot through her, a feeling of unsettling guilt. "Tadeo, it's not easy to explain. I will try." She described the seduction of Simon Salomon after he'd arranged to abduct her. Of the drugged condition to which she's been subjected and how she responded. "Do you consider that—willingly?" She had avoided telling him of the outcome, how Salomon had so artfully deceived her. "Do you consider that a willing arrangement?"

"No. Not if it's the truth."

"It's the truth," she retorted hotly. "Why would I lie? You don't know me. I know less of you. I am here only to help my husband. What good are lies?"

"All right, Madelaina. All right. Don't get your Irish up."

"I'm not Irish. I am Mexican—and proudly so. The daughter of a *gachupín.*"

947

He smiled gently. "I didn't mean to infer you were Irish. It's just an American expression—"

"Dr. Towbridge suggested because I was Mexican, Peter might have experienced considerable shame to be marrried to me here in his own land. He indicated it could be a probable cause for his impotency," she blurted out defensively.

He sighed. "In these days it's not an unheard-of situation—not the impotency, but the shame a Texan feels for consortin' with a Mexican. Now hold on, young woman. Don't direct your wrath at me," he said easily, noting her indignation. "Those are not the ideas of Thaddeus Oemolot. I try only to convey to you what might go on in the mind of proud and mighty Texans, especially a self-made man."

Madelaina's astonishment left her totally dazed momentarily. "You know who I am? The identity of my husband? But it was not my intent to reveal this. My husband would die if such information were to be maliciously spread about. You can understand, Tadeo. You must promise me not to speak of it—to no one!" She grew alarmed by the moment.

"I am no gossipmonger, Madelaina, simply a doctor. I received a call from Dr. Towbridge who told me to expect you and felt obligated to run down the case to me. He was only trying to help."

The incredible vast silence of the desert was upon them and it seemed an eternity before she replied. "If my husband were to learn I've betrayed him by even discussing his infirmary with you—*Dios mios!* It would make him more angry, more upset—more impotent. You understand?" Her eyes left his and came to rest on the puma Dionysis. She felt a strange, eerie feeling as she attempted to connect something out of her past. His voice arrested her.

"*Bueno,* Madelaina. *Bueno*. At least you are beginning to understand," he said, nonchalantly puffing his dead pipe. "It is the external things which make a man impotent. At the same time, the more the mind dwells upon those external happenings, the more they transform themselves into internal realities."

"Are you saying that a thought, if permitted to grow in the mind, no matter how foolish, transforms itself into that person's reality? It no longer remains a fleeting wisp of imagination?"

Dr. Oemolot had reached into his pocket for a few seeds which he held in his hands for the few birds that moved in nearer to them. A bright red parrot flew to the table and waddled over to him, cocking its head until Tadeo fed him the seeds. A frustrated mynah bird perched on his shoulder, demanding both attention and affection. Madelaina was fully entranced by it all. She felt as if she were back in Las Marismas, where countless species of birds migrated, and in their presence she felt an inner peace and tranquility.

"Once again I commend you for your quick perception," he said. "We can talk till the end of time, but if I could spend a few hours with your *marido,* it would hasten my work and speed up results."

She shook her head. "Impossible, Tadeo. He'd prefer being caught dead than to confide such a shameful thing to anyone. In truth," she confessed, "I am sure he resents me for knowing. That in a moment of weakness he poured out his heart and soul. He's a proud man. Why, only recently he's told me to go out and find a lover! Imagine? Find a lover!"

"If you'll pardon me for being outspoken, it would serve you well to point out to him, a man can't eat pride and it makes a pretty lousy bed partner, too."

Madelaina smiled, despite herself.

"Now then, let's get back on the track. Have you ever gone to bed with another man willingly?" Finished with the seeds, he stroked the puma's head.

"Back to that again, eh?" She lit a cigarette before he could strike a lucifer and do it for her. If he seemed surprised at her smoking, he said nothing.

Nothing about this unusual woman could shock or surprise Thaddeus Oemolot after the strange and unusual story she'd told him, yet he wondered at her reluctance. Her increased agitation as she mulled over his question earlier and the same hesitation now was answer enough for him. She was troubled by something. What?

If he only knew, she thought. If he only knew. She'd only told him part of the story. Nothing of Tolomeo. How could she speak of that unique experience when it still seemed more like a dream than reality? Yes, she had more than willingly entered into sexual relations with Tolomeo. Had she truly been bewitched? If it had been bewitchment, it wouldn't be construed as willingness on her part.

She toyed with the semantics involved and felt a strong inclination to deny she'd been extramaritally promiscuous with any man. Just as she was about to reply, she thought vividly of William Benson. Her heart sank. After a moment's struggle to collect her thoughts, she realized she had to tell this doctor the entire story. Humiliation and embarrassment flooded her face. What would he think of her?

This was no time for regrets, she told herself, as she gritted her teeth and plunged headlong into the story. She didn't have to wait long to witness the gradual changes reflected in Oemolot's face. Even before she finished the story, she knew the course of his next few questions.

"My dear Madelaina," he began gently. "This is a classic example of how impotence manifests itself in the body of a virile young man. From what you told me, and I assure you my statement isn't purely academic, such abnormal manifestions are common occurrence. You told me Peter left home at an early age, that he and his father, an awesome figure to him, were in constant conflict over his mother. Not only do you—the love of his life—end up marrying William Benson, but you also indulged in sexual relations with the man he loathed. How would you except him to feel?"

Her mortification was complete with the assault of his words. Tears sprang to her eyes. It wasn't enough that the entire episode with Bill Benson had been a degrading, disgraceful experience to her, but now she had to have it flung in her face like month-old garbage. She grew defensive. "It wasn't my fault. It wasn't a willing act. I was abducted, I told you. Forced into the marriage by a man who felt some protective, paternalistic emotion toward me. At the time I didn't know he was Peter's father. They didn't even wear the same names. I swear, Tadeo, he forced sexual relations on me the night the macho Texans celebrated 'Remember the Alamo!' She spat with contempt. "It was a nightmare I'll never forget till my dying day!" She was shaking with rage when she finished.

"*Por favor, señora*. It is not my wish to stir up these painful recollections for you. I am not trying to bully you or make you confess to anything and place the guilt upon you. My only point in discussing such an experience is to explain what it can do to a man when such complications twist his mind. It can fill him with doubt, hate, suspicion, anger, jealousy, and a countless number of destructive emotions. When insurmountable anxieties continue their wrath unchained and unchecked, the manifestation is always a physical one. Subconscious frustrations and negative forces of destruction must be resolved or more violent behavior and tryanny will manifest in your man. Such things can turn inward reaping havoc."

"Peter was impotent before his father married me!" she retorted defensively to cover the fact that she didn't understand his words.

"Physically, you mean? The accident prevented him from copulation. Yes, I understand all that. But tell me. The very next time you met, did he know about his father and you?"

Madelaina set her own frustration aside and stirred her memory. She'd seen Peter the day Antonetta had been killed by the *Rurales*. She nodded slowly. "Yes. He had learned it from—" she paused. "He never did tell me how he knew of the marriage—only that he knew." She explained that his bitterness extended over into his greeting when he bitingly addressed her as "Mother."

Tadeo struck a lucifer on the bricked patio and drew the flame toward his pipe to relight it. The air filled with the aroma of fresh tobacco.

"Don't punish yourself, Madelaina. We have a long, hard pull to go before we can help Peter. First, tell me, do you love him.?"

"*Que va,* do I love him? What question is this? Of course I love him. He has been the only driving force which has helped me keep my sanity all these terrifying years of revolution."

"You really love him? Totally? Unselfishly? Enough to be willing to put up with the pandemonium in hell to make him whole with you?"

"If necessary I'd fight Lucifer and all his *diableros* for him," she said with grim determination. She sat tall in her chair, her hair shoved high off her neck in the hot desert air, with resolve scrawled in her fiery eyes.

"That's just what you'll have to do, my dear woman. And may the Lord watch over you and console you when you find the road precarious and at times utterly hopeless to traverse."

For the next few hours, between wine, a few snacks of fresh fruit and cheese, Dr. Thaddeus Oemolot explained the normal rivalry between father and son over the love of a wife and mother. He called it the Oedipus complex, all of which sounded like some fairy tale of a Greek tragedy to her. She listened to his commentaries seemingly without interest, yet all the while absorbing every word he spoke. And when he explained its counterpart, the Electra complex, which exists between father and daughter, Madelaina's ears perked up even more. On this day, she not only learned much about Peter, but she acquired insight into her own problems with her father.

"Of course, my dear, we are still babes in the field of psychiatric research. Buried in our subconscious minds are untrue records which drive us into weird fields of behavior, and compulsions that cannot be explained.

My greatest wish is to be alive when some brilliant researcher uncovers the key to our emotional conflicts, so we could open the door and dust out the dusty chambers of horrors that some keep locked up for all eternity and never have a momen'ts peace." He rhapsodized eloquently over the possibilities of man's future without the hangups that keep him chained to an abnormal life. "If only man could fully know himself in a lifetime," he despaired. "Unfortunately, most of us remain unenlightened and uncaring until our death."

Madelaina liked him for including himself among the idiots of the world. She also knew that he didn't do this out of kindness, but as a didactic device.

"You're welcome to spend the night here in this paradise, Madelaina, if you wish. Or I shall be happy to drive you back into San Antonio."

"It's best that I return." She glanced at her watch. "Is it bedtime for you?"

"Not at all. I was thinking about you. I know your time is limited."

"It is but this is far more important. What precisely can I do about my husband's condition? If you will explain in detail, I will follow your instructions to the letter."

"If only there was some device by which I could open your husband's head, reprogram him, remove all the insidious thoughts that are rendering him impotent, it would solve your problem. Unfortunately there is no such device."

Madelaina grew reflective. "Tadeo, do you believe in psychic phenomenon?"

He shrugged indifferently.

"Would you believe me if I told you that I saw pictures in my mind telling me that Peter was impotent, long before he told me?"

Tadeo sat forward in his chair and set his pipe down. "What kind of pictures?"

"It's difficult to describe them. They come to me when I am totally relaxed, when my inner dialogue has been silenced and all thoughts are erased from mind."

953

"Do you realize what you're telling me?"

She shook her head. His interest grew more profound. Rising to his feet, he paced the bricked patio thoughtfully, his eyes reflecting unusual lights again.

Madelaina, watching him, felt more strongly that she'd met him before. She was unable to take her eyes from him. Worse, she was unable to explain her quandary to him. From the first there had been a magnetic pull between them, something undefinable. She had unburdened her soul to him as if she'd known him all her life.

They parted on this last note and he drove her back to her hotel.

The following afternoon, shortly after lunch, Madelaina returned to Dr. Oemolot's office. She wrote out a check for a thousand dollars which he protested was too much. She insisted and added that he was to put it to good use in helping her people. "One day, Tadeo, you must come to Seven Moons to visit us. I shall keep you informed of my progress. When I achieve success—"

"You mean when Peter achieves success," he interrupted.

She blushed pleasurably. "Yes, that. When it happens you shall be the first to know. I shall then send you a check for ten thousand dollars, for you to pursue your dream—the clinic you plan for my people in San Antonio. Are you amenable to this?"

Thaddeus Oemolot was astounded. "But how do you know what I've entertained in the back of my mind since my wife's death?"

"Let's just say that I learned you had marrried a Mexican woman and subjected yourself to all the social taboos imposed by the gringos here in Texas, *bueno*? It will be a step in the right direction." She didn't tell him that she'd seen his wedding pictures in the living room of his home and didn't have to be told that Mrs. Oemolot's dark features were those of a *latina*. Nor did she mention that she'd seen an artist's concept of a proposed clinic on the desk of his nurse in the waiting

954

room or that she'd heard the nurse speaking to one of his patients on the phone, concerning the lack of local interest and contributions to so noble a gesture as providing a medical facility to research children's mental diseases for the Mexican population.

He was so excited by her words that he gushed. "We'll name it the Madelaina Clinic!"

"No, Tadeo. Not Madelaina. It shall be called the Clinic of Tolomeo," she said cryptically." You realize that your name spelled backward reads: Tolomeo? In addition, I wish to have one ward named the Lazaro Benson Ward. I promise you, if my husband responds to the treatment you've prescribed, I shall personally assist you in raising far more money than you'll need. My husband has many business interests here in San Antonio. As a matter of fact, we also own land here. But first things first." She rose to her feet, extended her gloved hand to him, and grasped his between two gloved hands. Impulsively she leaned up to kiss him.

He turned to her abruptly. "I'll drive you back. I must ponder a few things by myself this evening. Keep your love for Peter burning brightly in her your heart like a beacon guiding you to the solution. This above all is the important thing. And try to keep yourself detached from the situation," he added.

"Detached? *Si.* How in the hell does a woman remain detached in such a case, Tadeo, when her heart is swollen, ready to burst, because her husband hasn't touched her in over a year? What does a woman do to ease her own needs? How does she command those heavy, pendulous devils poking around her stomach to disappear? How does the heaviness in her heart take flight?"

"How has this woman done it for over a year?" he asked tersely.

She stared into his clear jade eyes, into those mesmerizing, soothing, and tranquil eyes that calmed her and replied, "As you said earlier, we both have faced death a thousand times. What could be worse, eh? So, there's nothing to be lost. I'll try to remain as clear-headed, calm, filled with love and understanding, and by all means as detached as possible." Her lips trembled and her hands shook.

"Madelaina—" he began, moved by her words and her feeling.

"*Si*, Tadeo? At this moment, Madelaina wanted solace, sympathy, and the support of someone stronger than herself, something she needed above all else. What she got was silence, solemnity, and a soft condescending smile.

"It was nothing. For a moment you reminded me of someone I loved greatly." Then he added, "What I am attempting to say is, don't allow your emotions to ride roughshod with you, now that you approach the last legs of the longest journey of your life,"

For the next few hours he dealt in specifics, what she must do, how to approach it, and that in everything she must exercise the patience of a saint.

"It makes me nervous when you talk to me with such apprehension in your voice," she told him.

"I'm aware of it. I'm deliberately trying to alert you to the seriousness of the role you must play. It's important that you fulfill the role exactly right. If I stress the dramatic possibilites of the situation, it isn't for effect. I'm simply giving you time to prepare yourself for the necessary adjustments which must be made to your own nature."

"*Muchas gracias,* Tadeo. Thank you for everything. Please pray for us." She fled his office before the tears ran freely, leaving a bewildered, perplexed, and somewhat dazed physician still trying to figure the whole thing out.

"You forgot the books I gave you," he said to an empty room. He picked up the three volumes of Freudian psychology and shrugged. Very well, he'd mail them to her at Seven Moons.

Dr. Oemolot sat down behind the roll-top desk, scribbled a note of instructions to his nurse, and slipped it under the cover of the top book. With pen in hand, he printed his name backward: TOLOMEO.

It was the Spanish spelling of the name Ptolemy. Brother of Cleopatra. Also the name of fifteen Egyptian kings. Also the name of a general in the army of Alexander, King of Macedonia. Also the name of an astronomer, mathematician, and geographer who contributed much to the present-day knowledge of our solar system. What had the name Tolomeo to do with Madelaina Benson?

Why should he care if it meant that his dream of a clinic should be realized. He sat immobile for a long while, trying to sort and sift through the events of the past twenty-four hours. He had mentioned nothing to the *señora* about his wife, yet she seemed to know of her. He wondered what she might have said if she'd learned that his wife's name was also Madelaina?

He felt he was in a state of unusual reality, elicted by the euphoric state brought about by that refreshing, extraordinary, and quite unbelievable young woman, Madelaina Benson.

Outside, she asked herself for what was she crying. She didn't know. A feeling of intense relief shot through her, jolting her into plateau of expectancy where, with hope and faith and downright perserverance in the days to come, Peter would be his old self.

She returned to the Tampico Hotel in downtown San Antonio to find the lobby swarming with cattlemen, cowboys, and uniformed officers, as many as in El Paso and other border towns. She hardly paid them any attention, but instead walked up the circular staircase to the mezzanine floor to make certain she could take the evening train home. She waited fifteen minutes, then asked the clerk to call her room with the necessary information.

She removed her hat inside her room, took off her dove gray jacket, and took two headache powders. She hurriedly packed her bags, then when all was ready, she lay on the bed to rest. She frowned when she saw the time and picked up the phone on the table next to the bed. She called the train clerk. It seemed there was a delay, and she might have to wait until morning.

"What's the problem?" she asked.

"Government troops have requisitioned the train. All civilians are rerouted to morning passage. Would you consider taking a bus, Mrs. Benson?"

Mrs. Benson would not. "Please call me for the first available space out of Dallas," she insisted. "I'll be in my room waiting for your call."

The clerk agreed he'd do his best.

Madelaina hung up. *Government troops requisitioned all trains to El Paso?* What on earth for? She paced the floor, smoking for several moments. Next door to her, the occupants were involved in a heated discussion. If the conversation hadn't been so heated and in Spanish, Madelaina might not have paid attention to it. That, coupled with the fact that one or two voices sounded very familiar, caused her to cock an ear. The tempers abated and she could better understand their words.

"You will please thank President Wilson. Assure him that General Alvaro Obregon will not disappoint him. Our strategy has worked. Whereas I am not in full accord with Señor Carranza's philosophies, he is the lesser evil between the contenders."

Madelaina was glued to the door. Was it possible this was her father in the next room? It was his voice all right. But what on earth was he doing in San Antonio? Why not Corpus Christie or Matamoros, closer to the Mexican border? She leaned in closer to hear.

"You know, General Obregon, what our president really suggests? It's you he feels will be the proper man to govern Mexico. He's quite taken with your ideas and the cooperation you've shown your northern neighbors. Why delay the inevitable? I suggest you take advantage of the good will and cooperation extended to you by the United States. Move to take the helm of your nation and steer it properly."

"I thank you, General Pershing, and you other gentlemen who've been most helpful in assisting me. This will give me considerable experience—all this involvement. I return now to my country and victory.

958

Once the rebels are eradicated, and I've observed more accurately the needs of my people, I'll accept the role your president feels I should play. Meanwhile I'll throw my full support to Carranza and do my level best to cement good relations with America."

"There's one other thing, General Obregon. About Field Marshal Von Klause."

"Forgive me, I know no such man," replied Obregon.

"It is our understanding that Carranza has made a pact with the Germans."

"Not to my knowledge."

"Would he keep you abreast of any negotiations, Obregon? What we mean is, there's no chance Carranza can be double-dealing without your knowledge?"

There was silence.

Another man spoke up. "If the rumors prove to be true, we'll stop all shipment of arms into Mexico and give you no further assistance."

Madelaina sank back against the wall in utter anger. Less than three months ago, these same men had assured Pancho Villa they'd give him their cooperation. What had happened? She'd read the papers—what little they got of accurate reporting from the papers in El Paso—and knew only that Villa had waged several battles victoriously. On the other hand, she'd heard that her father had also been racking up countless victories in and about Mexico City with Zapata's forces. Now this! America's intervention to assist Carranza! No wonder American troops had requisitioned the train. Something was up. If her father was about to engage in the long-awaited battle with Pancho Villa, he couldn't lose—not with American arms and ammunition.

Stop this, she told herself. *Why are you involving yourself? Revolution is in the past. All that matters is your life with Peter and Alejandro. Forget this conversation.* Even as she tried to force a detachment from all she heard, she knew she was fooling herself. Her life was irrevocably bound up in Villa's and Mexico's.

As she mulled over Dr. Oemolot's words about this terrible rivalry between herself and her father, Madelaina became confused. She knew a little, but not enough to carry her through the inner torment of those few moments.

What could she do to help Villa? And if she did, would she bring death and destruction to her father? General Pershing had suggested her father might be president of Mexico! She recalled the Felipe de Cordoba had told her similar things—that her father was indeed someone special. Was she so conditioned to hating him that she couldn't see the merit in his leadership? The qualities others saw?

Dios mios! It was Madelaina who needed to heal her sickness in her head. Why had she turned from her father? Why? She knew deep down in her heart that as a child she had loved him. Why couldn't she love him now? Six years ago? Why did she always have to find the faults in the man and never see the achievements or positive qualities that the American president had seen in him?

She paced back and forth, eaten alive by tormenting thoughts. Only yesterday she'd talked with Thaddeus at length about her father and how she'd rebelled for so long, bringing destruction, agony, and considerable devastation to her own life. His reply turned out to be something quite profound. "Unless the Electra or Oedipus complex is resolved between parent and child early in life, the child's life will be forever affected." In what way? "She'd be seeking her father in every man she met, subconsciously motivated by either her love or hatred of him," had been his reply.

She had scoffed at Thaddeus's explanation until he elaborated. "If you hated him enough, you'd be looking for those qualities in your man quite the opposite to those of your father. If you loved him, you'd naturally try to find those same qualities in a man. If the relationship between father and daughter isn't resolved in its true perspective, you'll be bound up in the shallows of misery and malcontent, because you've

never given yourself a chance to attract and be attracted by the man you truly need. All this is predicated, of
course, on the facts presented to us by a master psy-
chologist, Sigmund Freud," he added. "It would be
best that you read it thoroughly, Madelaina, for yourself, so you understand the specifics involved."

One thing was certain, Madelaina Obregon's life had
been very much affected by the poison between father
and daughter. But, for the love of God, she lamented,
how does one remove this poison? How? It was too
complicated for her to understand, much less to resolve
such a question.

So, woman, she asked herself, *if it's come to a showdown between Pancho Villa and Alvaro Obregon,
which side do you choose? Who will you support? You
might as well face up to the situation, the alternatives
are measured. Help your papa and—you will inevitably destroy Pancho Villa, all he's worked hard for,
and what he stands for. Help Pancho Villa and you'll
destroy your father. Which will it be? Why does it have
to be either? Why one or the other? Why couldn't she
ignore them both?*

Madelaina had turned into a complete nervous and
physical wreck. She had smoked all her cigarettes, the
butts piled high in an ash tray. She'd give anything for
a drink. She needed something. She sat down at the
edge of the bed and picked up the phone. The voices
next door had quieted down and she could barely make
them out.

"Please send a bell man to my suite," she said into
the mouthpiece of the phone when a voice answered.
Amost as soon as she hung up the bell man appeared.
She gave him a fifty-dollar bill and ordered a bottle of
wine, cigarettes, and a sandwich, it didn't matter what
kind.

"For fifty bucks, lady, I can even bring you Mexicali
gold."

Thinking it was a new beverage, she asked, "What is
this Mexicali gold of which you speak?"

The thin, scrawny, weasel-faced bell man glanced

cautiously about the room and whispered confidentially. "Marijuana—you ever hear of reefers, lady?"

"*Bueno*. Bring some," she quipped and shut the door after him.

As soon as he returned, Madelaina lost no time in rolling a few reefers. Marijuana always had a calming effect on her. She needed something to calm her down as frustration shot through her, combined with nervous speculation and an all-consuming fear of not knowing what to do in the situation she found herself with Peter and now her father's presence next door. It seemed too much for her to cope with presently.

She lay back on the bed, smoking and inhaling until the calming effect took place. She was fingering the chamois bag she still wore around her neck. There was hardly any powder left, but she was never without it. Peter had asked about the small pouch and why she wore it. Her answers had been vague and ambiguous. She'd told him only it was an amulet to ward off evil spirits. Following the session in Parral when Rosalia Quintera and Lucia and Lola exorcised the evil spirit of Golden Dawn from Madelaina, Peter never suggested the amulet to be hogwash or some foolish nonsense. He simply accepted it. He'd seen too much that day to disbelieve the power of sorcerers.

As Madelaina lay back, she felt much improved, calmer, and able to sort things out in her mind. Even before the pictures began forming, before they gave her insight into what she must do, she knew what course to take. *Detachment and love* were the key words to solve this dilemma. Love and detachment.

Now, if she only had learned the lessons well enough. Madelaina rose from the bed. She stood before the mirror over the dresser and brushed out her long hair. She twisted and turned the long strands and piled them atop her head. She brushed on a small trace of lip rouge and slipped into her jacket.

Picking up the phone, she told the desk clerk she'd be gone for a few moments and to please continue to work on her reservations, She replaced the receiver and walked out the room.

Something mysterious forced her to do what she must.

Madelaina knocked on the door of the adjoining room. After a pause, the door opened a slit. A voice spoke through the crack. "Go away. No one sent fer ya."

"Please, I'm here to speak with General Alvaro Obregon."

"Ya got the wrong place, lady. Ain't no one here by that name.

"You will tell the general that his daughter wishes to speak with him and be fast about it!"

The door closed in her face. Madelaina was certain she had caused considerable commotion inside the room. When it opened again, the door was propelled by a force that nearly shook it on its hinges. General Alvaro Obregon stood face to face with his daughter, his face a mask of marble. His black, fierce eyes looked at her as if he could kill her. His features contorted into a scowl.

It was the look on Madelaina's face, a softness, almost glowing look of love, which arrested him and caught him off guard. Behind him she saw several uniformed men, but more shocking to her was the presence of Armando Cortez. He sat in profile and hadn't seen her yet, since he was engaged in an involved discussion with General Montalvo, another *Carranzista*. Why was he here?

"Can we speak, Father? If it's not convenient here, we can go to my suite. It's next door."

General Obregon closed the door behind him, telling the soldier at the door to lock it. "I'll be next door," he said softly.

In her room, Madelaina asked him to sit down.

"I can hear what you may have to say, standing, if you don't mind."

"May I offer you a glass of wine—cigarettes—marijuana?"

963

"I want nothing. Tell me what you wish—why you've chosen to speak with your father, after the long drought of emotional consideration between us?"

"Can't we end this thing between us? Does it always have to be this way?" she asked quietly. "Please sit. It's easier to talk." She took a chair and indicated the other nearby.

He finally acquiesced and seated himself stiffly on a corner of the chair, moving his gun and holster about so it wouldn't disturb him.

"What brings you to San Antonio?" he asked, filled with suspicion.

"I came to see a medical specialist. I hope to return on the evening's train, but I've been told American troops have requisitioned the entire train for three departures."

"Why are you really here?" he asked, disbelieving her reply.

"I told you. Why do you never believe me?"

"Hah! Coming from you that's got to be a joke. A *Villista* in San Antonio at so appropriate a time, eh, Little Fox?" His bitter laughter was laced with irony.

"I am no longer Little Fox. I've retired from the revolution. Long ago I realized there is nothing that I can do to prevent history from taking its course."

"I wish I could believe you, Madelaina. But I don't," he said harshly. He cocked his head, as if listening to the voices next door. "Is that how you knew I was here? Listening in at keyholes? Or did your spy system apprise you of our arrival and secret rendezvous with the Americans?"

"What's the use? I tell you the truth and you don't believe me. I came here to see a doctor, not as a spy for the revolution—not as a *Villista*—not as Little Fox. It's finished, Father. All behind me. Thank God. Do you have a spare cigarette?" After she accepted it and lit it, she continued.

"It's not important if you don't believe me. We can easily allow things to deteriorate between us if you like. I can return to my home and family and pretend as I have in the past that you no longer exist. But I've grown up these past few years. Yes, I have, Father," she insisted at his disbelieving glance. "I've lived a thousand years in these past few years in a life I never dreamed I'd live. In conditions far more revolting and offensive than most people could cope with." She sat back in the overstuffed chair in a posture of relaxation, one arm draped around the back of it.

General Obregon studied his daughter. She seemed older, more mature, and dressed quite stylishly. He'd lost track of her after Felipe de Cordoba's death in Mexico City, and for a time he didn't care if he ever saw her again. But now, seeing her in the flesh, in so subdued a mood, he had difficulty believing her sincerity. Her presence meant there had to be an angle of some sort, some devilish plot that had to be exacted. He just didn't trust her at all.

"I heard what General Pershing told you about being president of Mexico. Why are you so modest? You know your eyes have been on that choice plum a long time. Felipe mentioned it, a hundred years ago," she sighed wistfully. "Why don't you jump at the chance?"

"You heard that?"

"Yes."

"What else did you hear? Not that you'd tell me—"

"What I heard doesn't interest me any longer. What must I do to prove to you I am no longer a *Villista?*"

Obregon kept his stoic mask without expression. He watched his daughter pour two glasses of wine after breaking the seal. He noticed the rolled reefers on the table and the untouched sandwich.

"Wine, Father?"

He took the bottle from her hand, read the label, and made certain the bottle hadn't been opened or tampered with earlier. He nodded.

Madelaina smiled. "You think your own daughter would plot to annihilate you?" The words were out and she knew what he'd say. He didn't disappoint her.

"Yes. If there's anything under the sun that I can be

965

certain of, it is the treachery of Madelaina Obregon, especially where her father's concerned."

Her face flushed. "I deserve that. Or shall I say Little Fox deserved that a few months ago. I keep telling you it's all in the past. Please let's not waste our time arguing." She pressed the glass into his hand and took the other for herself. She raised it into the air in a mock toast. "Suppose we drink to Presidente Alvaro Obregon?"

"No. We drink to Presidente Venustano Carranza," he said firmly.

Madelaina put down her glass. "That I won't do."

"Then you're still a *Villista*."

"If you involve Carranza, then, yes, I agree entirely with General Villa."

Sparks flew in her father's eyes and his fists clenched tightly.

"Villa again! Goddamnit! I told you once I didn't want your lips to speak his name in my presence! You still shove his shit in my face and cram him down my throat whenever we meet!" In a burst of violent temper, he threw the filled wine glass across the room. It splattered in a grotesque pattern of bright crimson against the wall and dropped in a myriad of bloody streams.

"It's amazing how much alike you are—you two. You know, Father, you even have the same birth sign. You are Gemini—the twins. No two men that I've met have the same dual natures to their personalities. *Es veridad*. It's true. I must tell you this much, General Villa sent me on a mission to Zacatecas to meet with you under a flag of truce. His greatest desire was to join forces with the man he so admired and defeat Carranza, because he knows Carranza is not the man for the job. Beware, Father, the man is treacherous. Carranza will sell you down the river before the boat docks."

"When did Villa send you to Zacatecas?" he asked, somewhat surprised at this revelation. "He wanted to intrigue with me? Pancho Villa?"

"The week before Villa stormed the fort. Right after he broke with Carranza."

Obregon used his superb memory of recall. "I was nowhere near Zacatecas then. Why didn't Villa's spies inform him properly?"

She told him about Dolores Chavez and her subsequent abduction by Major General Simon Salomon. How the false ruse served to distort the picture—how the interception of the telegrams worked. "The *Huertistas* were after me to use me over your head as a wedge, so you wouldn't defect to Carranza. And now, Father, you insist on supporting a man like Carranza who can be worse than Huerta and Diaz? Why?"

Obregon was on his feet pacing the room, thinking on all his daughter told him. "Villa wanted us to join forces?" He pondered heavily.

"He told me, if he could come to terms with you, his entire Northern Division would have been behind you. You know how sad the *jefe* is because he's thwarted and unable to find the man who should sit on the presidential throne?"

"Sad? Hah! The man lusts for the power himself. Why, that stupid photograph of him seated in the gold chair at the palace made him laughingstock!"

'No one *is* more aware than Villa that he's not the man to occupy the presidency of Mexico," she told him, ignoring his foolish remark.

"I know that to be a gross exaggeration of the truth. Why the *animale* lusts for the power the presidency will bring."

"Is that the fertilizer fed you by your informants? Is that the bull dung Carranza feeds you, Papa? Well, it's always been one of your failings. Your head is buried so deeply in military strategy, you fail to see the fangs of the tigers waiting to devour you the moment you secure victories for them. I never believed it before, but it's all true, the stories I heard about you. You are no politician. But you best damn well learn and *muy pronto! Comprender?* Or you'll be ground down to hog feed the moment you hand Mexico over to Carranza.

Listen, there's a game of cards the gringos play called poker. It's best you learn to play such a game so you can practice keeping a poker face when you play politics with men of Carranza's calibre."

Obregon flushed at the display of contempt on his daughter's face. "How dare you? How dare you come into my life again and incite me to anger at a time like this when I am weighed down with heavier things— more important than the life of any one person? You made your choice long ago. Very well, I've conditioned myself to that choice. Nothing you can say, Madelaina, will permit me to believe you. You protest vehemently you're no longer a *Villista*. Bah! You are a *Villista* to the teeth! I know it. You know it. And nothing can convince me differently!"

He had to think as a militarist. He had to prevent her from leaving San Antonio for at least a week. The marijuana. That was it. He could inform the police that she had it in her possession. In the States the gringos strongly enforced the drug laws. He needed time to get the arms and ammunition across the border before she could get word to Pancho Villa. He couldn't trust her, could he?

"Where's your husband?" he asked cagily.

"In El Paso," she lied, not about to tell him Peter was in Washington.

"Liar!" he spat harshly. "You almost had me believing your story—this unplanned meeting of ours. A repentant daughter trying to make up for the lost time with her estranged father. So much for your lies. Your husband, the *gringo gun runner*, is right here in San Antonio, making deals to smuggle arms to Pancho Villa." His voice dripped with sarcasm and resentment.

Madelaina recoiled in bewilderment. "You lie!" she countered, assaulted by the implication of his words. "That was finished long ago. He's no longer involved with General Villa, nor am I. I swear to you, Father, it is the truth I speak to you. We have finished with the revolution—" She stopped suddenly as she thought back to the mysterious comings and goings—the mid-

968

night rendezvous with strangers, Peter had involved himself in of late. Her face blanched.

"You know I'll have to detain you, Madelaina. I have no recourse."

"Nothing I can say will ever convince you of my sincerity. I regret having made the attempt at reconciliation," she said in a crestfallen manner. "It's a pity we can't resolve our differences."

"The leopard can't remove his spots," he said pointedly.

"You dare say that to me? All the while Carranza hides his under that long coat he wears to deceive you?"

"Back to Carranza again. You won't stop trying, will you?"

"If I thought I could ever pry open your eyes to what Carranza is, I'd ride into battle at your side—even against Villa, if need be!" Her eyes sparked with brilliant lights and her voice, having risen a notch or two in volume, dropped down to a whisper.

For an instant Obregon faltered. Madelaina had always been brutally honest with him except for the time she'd conspired with Concepción for Pancho Villa. Even then, she'd attempted to tell him about Huerta. Hadn't it proven true? Even Felipe had sided with Madelaina in this. He hadn't believed her then. Now, it was as if history was repeating itself. What if she spoke the truth? How would he feel having her jailed? Now that America had agreed to sponsor Carranza as president, Obregon had little time to learn the answers to his questions. A loud, harried knock at the door brought his head up like an ostrich as he turned in the direction of the sound.

"Who is it?" asked Madelaina.

"Open the door, General Obregon," called his aide.

The general moved across the room and opened the door a slit.

"Your presence is immediately requested inside, *mi Generale*," said the aide.

Obregon turned to his daughter as he removed the

key from the lock. "You'll remain here until I've decided what must be done with you."

Before she could utter a protest, he disappeared out the door. She heard him instruct his aide, "Stand here and don't let a person in or out the room—or I'll have you cut and quartered!"

"*Si, mi Generale*," came the man's reply.

Madelaina was furious. It served her right. She knew better than to bare her soul, divulge her real thoughts, to a man like her father who wasn't complete.

She had never in the past been able to convince her father of the truth in any issue. Not about Huerta or Salomon, not about Villa and now not about Carranza. Why? Why was she so incapable of persuading him? She could never make her father realize the truth. Why, for the love of God, even if his scenting sac was removed, she'd never be done with the smell of that skunk Carranza. Why couldn't General Obregon detect the same stink? Could he be so deluded he is unable to see through the man's double-dealing?

As she paced the floor of her room concerned with her own dilemma, she felt a terrible sinking sensation. He'd told her Peter was here in San Antonio! Impossible. He was in Washington, wasn't he? Her eyes darted about the room to the window. She ran to it and glanced down two stories onto the street below.

Peter wouldn't have lied to her, would he? He would have had no reason to lie. He had a spread outside of San Antonio, but she never learned the exact whereabouts, nor had she asked. Damn! Damn! What a predicament! She opened the window and looked out at the fire escape. She could make it down those iron bar steps. She'd been in far worse predicaments, hadn't she?

Pulling her head back inside the room, she glanced hurriedly about for her bag. She had plenty of cash with her. She could take a bus back to El Paso. Her eyes fell on the phone. What foolishness? Why didn't she use the phone to call the hotel manager? Surely they'd come and rescue her. With a military guard outside her door and two imposing generals next door—who'd be-

970

lieve her in any contest? She could at least call home. Of course! Why hadn't it occurred to her?

In a few moments Madelaina had Pilar on the phone. Did she have *señor el patrón*'s telephone in Washington? "What's wrong, Pilar?" she asked when the hysterical woman made no sense.

Pilar tearfully explained that *señor el patrón* had called and was angry to learn she wasn't at home. She had given him the name of her hotel in San Antonio and asked her forgiveness.

Madelaina thanked her and told her not to worry. She was returning home as soon as possible. She hung up before the woman could respond.

Grabbing her small leather bag, jacket, and hat, Madelaina eased herself out the window and began to descend the ladder. Much to her chagrin, she found her weight insufficient to extend the bottom rungs of the fire ladder to the ground floor. She glanced inside an open window on the floor below her and decided she had to chance being discovered by another hotel guest. Crawling cautiously inside, she expelled a sigh of relief to find the suite empty. Scurrying across the room, she flung open the front door and stopped dead in her tracks.

"Madelaina!"

"Armando!" She'd nearly collided with him as he was about to enter the room.

"What in God's name are you doing here?" he asked, drawing her inside the room. He didn't bother to close the door.

"I might ask the same thing of you, if I were interested. Being a turncoat must be the accepted behavior of society these days," she quipped icily. "And don't bother to deny you've shifted loyalties. What would your father-in-law say to this if he knew you were intriguing with his enemies?"

"You don't know what you're talking about," he said lightly. "Perhaps you might be kind enough to explain—"

"Oh, Armando! Don't be a fool! I know. I know ev-

971

erything! I saw you with my father and the other gringos, upstairs!"

Armando moved in toward her. "I've always loved to see you when you're angry!" He reached for her and drew her close to him and kissed her lustily as she fought him off. She beat her fists against his shoulder and tried with all her strength to put him off.

"So—my beloved wife—this is where I find you?" came a voice behind them.

Instantly Armando released her. Madelaina looked up into the stormy eyes of her husband. Behind him was Tracy Richards. Both men, wearing western garb, carried six-shooters slung low at their hips. They came into the room and closed the door behind them, both studying her disheveled appearance through narrowed eyes.

Peter addressed her. "I'll attend to you later," he said provoked beyond reason. He turned to Armando. "All right, *conquistadore,* suppose ya tell us all about it, eh?"

"What exactly do you wish to know?" asked Armando with a bland expression of innocence on his face.

"We can do it whichevuh way y'all want," said Tracy, fingering his knife with a diabolical gleam in his eye. "When did ya sell out Villa?"

Armando turned to Madelaina. "Is this some form of a joke, *chica?* Who are these men? Are they friends of yours?" he asked with that irksome blue blood coursing through his veins.

Madelaina stiffened. "You have a short memory, Armando. Do you forget my husband, Peter Benson? And this is Captain Richards of General Villa's Gringo Brigade. It's better you do as they request. They are not playing games, *amigo.*"

"So this is the man tamed by Valerie Townsend?" he asked, leveling his icy eyes on Peter. His lips twisted into obvious loathing.

"And you'ah her new plaything. Ah see she's lost all her taste," said Peter nastily. "Now, get cracking. You

972

better tell us about the arms shipment due ta cross the borduh."

"I haven't the slightest idea what you're referring to, *señor*," he said in his heavily accented English. "If you choose to use force on me, believe me when I tell you I will not hesitate to inform the authorities. You see, I am here under diplomatic immunity as a fully authorized representative of the Mexican government. Would you care to see my papers?"

"He was with them, Peter," hissed Madelaina. "With my father, General Pershing, and more gringos from Washington. I saw them."

Peter gazed at his wife blackly. "Stay out of this. Ah can handle the likes of this Spanish *hacendado*," he snapped at her. "Look, Cortez, ya bettuh cooperate with Tracy, heah, and me. If ya don't, weah gonna turn ya other to Villa's butchers, and by God theah'll make a fancy fruit tree outa ya. Ah'm shuah ya heard of Villa's fruit trees. Them *Villistas* ain't nevuh heard o' diplomatic immunity, heah?"

Armando turned to Madelaina. "You'd do this to your own father? How low have you fallen, whore? I heard rumors of your treachery, but had to see for myself that the daughter of Alvaro Obregon is nothing but a common *puta,* a vile and contemptible, lowly pig of a woman who married a whoremaster to keep her enslaved. *Bruta bruja!*" he spat at her, as Tracy Richards moved in and with the butt of his gun caught him from behind and knocked him out.

Madelaina recoiled at the verbal assault. For an instant she was stunned until she understood how Armando would be driven to say such things.

"Take him to the ranch, Tracy. I'll get there as soon as ah can. The whole place is swarming with American troops and turncoats ready ta blow the whistle at us as spies!" He turned to Madelaina. "And y'all bettuh get on back ta El Paso. Ah'll settle with ya as soon as I can!"

She stood firm. "Peter, what are you doing in all

this? I thought we both agreed not to get involved in the revolution," she said when they were alone.

"Ah am involved, don't ya see? Ah can't leave the *jefe* dangling just as his former friends are fixin' ta hack off his balls!" His face reddened at the analogy.

"Supposin' ya tell me what the hell you'ah doing here in San Antone?" His voice blistered her eardrums.

"You wouldn't believe me if I told you," she said unhappily.

"Try me!" he challenged.

Her eyes caught his and held defiantly. "All right." She nodded her head. "All right, I'll tell you. I came here to see a doctor about you."

"Ya what?" His voice echoed through her head painfully.

She winced, then repeated herself.

Peter's anger, his humiliation and degradation was total. He slapped her across the face and sent her reeling backward against the wall.

"Ya hadda tell someone else about me? After ya promised it was ouah secret? Now the whole world will know Peter Benson's no longer a man!" In his raging fury, he struck at her time and again. Suddenly he stopped. His confusion was such that he became bitterly ashamed of his actions. Worse was the fact that Madelaina had hardly reacted to his momentary brutality. She had stood her ground without flinching under the blows, without a whimper.

"That's the truest statement ever to pass your lips! Peter Benson is no longer a man! He's a vile animal. Not because you're impotent, Peter, but because you've lost all sense of reason." She picked up her bag and hat that had flown under the blows. "If you ever come to your senses, I shall be at Seven Moons with our son. You better hear this, Peter Benson. I refuse to live the life William and Jennifer Benson lived with their son, Peter. I'll not permit to happen to Alejandro what happened to both you and your brother Lazaro. When you finish with this gun running and your desire to be a satellite to Pancho Villa, and resume instead command

974

of your own world, then come to me. Perhaps by then I shall have found the answers to this confounding life for both of us." She stormed out the door and left San Antonio more dejected than she'd been on her arrival two days before. Madelaina had finally grown up.

Chapter 37

The contentment Madelaina received as she rode through the vast lands of Seven Moons was inexplicable to her, when she considered the place brought recollections of many unhappy experiences. She rode to Black Mountain on Lorca, the black stallion, son of her own Don Quixote, a magnificent, well-coordinated mass of superb horseflesh.

Lorca scaled the mountain ridge with the fleet-footedness of a winged horse. Madelaina could feel the ripple of his strong muscular body and the skillful ease with which he performed the task of transporting her to the crest of the rugged incline. In these moments she felt as deep a sense of pride in the breeding of horses as she had in the breeding of bulls for which William Benson had made Seven Moons famous. She dismounted at the top of the mountain and allowed Lorca to graze lazily nearby.

It was one of the bright, crackling Texas mornings. No clouds marred the horizon to interrupt the flowing blue velvet sky. It was an inspiring day of breathless beauty in which she found communing with nature an inspiring feat. She sat down on the craggy boulder gazing down at Seven Moons—those crescent-shaped lakes lined by weeping willows and groves of eucalyptus trees.

This morning she was obsessed with thoughts. What a magnanimous gesture for William Benson to have deeded this property to her. Even now, with the reality of Seven Moons staring at her from all sides, she found it difficult to believe it was all hers. With the deed came a letter written in Benson's handwriting. In it he had expressed his most profound regrets and apologies

976

over the despicable behavior he'd forced on her the night Texas celebrated the Alamo. He also expressed personal disappointment in the fates which propel man's life. If he'd met a woman like Madelaina earlier in life, he had written, a woman with the same interests he shared in land, animals, and politics, his entire life might have been different. It was to Madelaina a sad commentary that a man purported to have everything in life should in truth have lived so empty a life.

Madelaina wondered if Peter had read this letter. She could see how intimidated he might have become to feel that the man he'd despised all his life and had gone to such lengths not to emulate had indeed seduced his own wife.

She'd come to know more about Peter's medical problems after she'd read the books sent to her by Dr. Oemolot and the follow-up correspondence in which she asked countless questions of him. The insight she'd acquired into the problems of impotency was well and good as far as theory was concerned. Now, the question arose in her mind, how she could help to resurrect his potency? Could she do it? Would she still have the needed strength and stamina to endure the countless obstacles that were bound to thwart her at every turn? How could she possibly obtain the cooperation of a man who hated her—and hadn't once tried to contact her since they last met in San Antonio?

Madelaina sighed and gazed out at the restful panorama, stirred by the breathless beauty of the place. Perhaps here at Seven Moons, in this somewhat magical land that held her in total fascination each day, she could work the miracle needed to draw them back together.

She was amazed, when she arrived at Seven Moons, at the length to which Peter had gone to make her arrival and stay a welcome one. Nothing astonished Madelaina more on her arrival with Pilar and her son Alejandro than to see the familiar faces of Paco and Lola Jimenez there to greet her. Peter had hired these two bright and cheery people as caretakers in his absence.

It had been a warm, happy reunion, one in which Paco bridged the gap of time since they'd last seen each other with his countless tales of adventure. He'd told Madelaina that on their arrival in Zacatecas, General Obregon was not to be found. Worse, Paco Jimenez, listed among the dead, would have been immediately jailed as a deserter if he made his identity known to certain officers.

So unappealing was the sound of jail to him and Lola, they both decided to travel north again and try to enter El Paso to make a new life for themselves in the U.S.A. They had applied one day for work at the El Paso residence of William Benson, where, to their astonishment, Peter had greeted them and hired them instantly. Later, he encouraged them to travel to Seven Moons to prepare the place for the day Madelaina might appear.

After a while Madelaina found herself speaking of Tolomeo to Paco and Lola. She learned they'd confided to Peter many of their strange and unusual experiences in that fascinating land of Tolomeo and Lago Diablo de Los Muertos.

Peter, naturally interested in what had transpired after witnessing the complications that had beset the man after the infliction of near-fatal wounds to Paco's shoulder, had been clearly baffled when Paco in a moment of boastfulness bared his shoulder to reveal no scars to hint at the diabolical and devastating injury that had kept them in fear for his life.

"One thing led to another, *señora*," Paco had explained. "So it was only the right thing to do, to tell your *marido* the truth about Tolomeo and all that happened. Of the magic performed, of the serenity we felt and most especially of the spectacular Tolomeo who was more of a god than a man to us. Did I do wrong?" he had asked when he saw the deep disturbance on Madelaina's face.

"No, Paco," she had reassured him. "You didn't do

978

wrong." Yet, Madelaina saw clearly why Peter might have felt even more threatened when he learned of the intimacy between his wife and Tolomeo. She reasoned that his fears of having to compete with such a man for his wife's affection might have been compounded by what Paco and his mestiza wife might have added to what he already had been told—which wasn't enough to allow a clear picture of the situation.

Strange, thought Madelaina, as she lit a cigarette, Peter had never mentioned any of this to her. He had upon occasion asked her the identity of the man whose name she spoke of in her sleep and the source of that special chamois pouch she wore around her neck, and she had answered as best she could.

As part of her legacy at Seven Moons, the private library of William Benson had proved tremendously helpful to her on her arrival. With a cursory glance at the books on her previous visit, she'd never really taken the time to sort and categorize them. She had sufficient time and opportunity to browse and found to her amazement many books delving into the human mind—what the layman might consider a home library on medicine. She was even more astonished to learn that many of these books belonged to Peter, that he'd studied medicine in college, a fact he'd never shared with her.

Now, as Madelaina sat on the boulder, smoking her cigarette, looking down at Seven Moons, she had a sudden and strange thought, similiar to those that come to a person just before they drift off to sleep. It was more than a mere thought, a complete image would be more like it. She saw a montage of pictures of activity taking place below her in the wind-swept fields adjacent to the clear crystal blue lakes. She focused her attention on the seven bodies of water as a plan formulated in her mind. It was as if some mystical power had opened her head and poured into it a set of elaborate blueprints, as if all she had to do was crank an imaginary mechanism and out would come the final result.

Madelaina was so excited by what she saw and felt,

so inspired that she was moved into action. There could be no doubt as to what she must do, no conjecture—no dawdling. She rekindled all of Tolomeo's teachings in her mind and came to the conclusion that his philosophies might be the key to all the answers she needed. In the past she had stubbornly clung to her old ways and refused to take the necessary time to prove his farfetched theories. Now Madelaina had all the time in the world.

She filled with such inspiration that she quickly mounted Lorca and rode swiftly, the wind at her heels, until she reached the ranch house. She knew the way now. She lost no time to begin preparations on what might be termed fanciful plans by most standards. To Madelaina they were real.

That night at dinner she told Paco and his wife, "One day when the revolution ends in our country I shall return to visit the land of Tolomeo."

They both looked at her quizzically, then averted their eyes as an uncomfortable sensation surged through them. Lola, the sensational beauty, nudged her husband. "Tell her, *chico*. Ees better ju tell her now."

Paco shook off her insistent urging and refused to look Madelaina in the eye.

"Tell me what, Paco?" asked Madelaina.

Ten minutes of prodding passed before he'd speak out. Finally, he had no more resistance against these determined females. He scratched his temples and drank from a bottle of *cerveza*. "Very well, *chica*," he said submissively. "Who can deny you anything? It's like this, *señora*. Lola and I, both of us were so affected by what we'd seen in the land of Tolomeo that when we decided to leave all that filth, poverty, and dirt in Zacatecas, we both agreed to return to Tolomeo and live with those wonderful people for the rest of our days. Truly, we gathered what few possessions we owned and headed back over those same roads we'd traveled before. We followed the same trails leading out of Parral, climbed those mountains in the Sierra Madre's belly. We passed the same landmarks, th same trees—even those same man-eating insects that had so viciously attacked us before. Shall I tell you that Lola and I could not find Tolomeo—or his people? *Dios mios!* Word spread from village to village that two *muy locos*, Lola and I, were looking to find some crazy place. 'Phooo!' they tell us. 'Such a place in the interior! You are some crazy burros.' "

"What are you trying to tell me?" demanded Madelaina thunderstruck.

Paco swallowed hard and made an agonized grimace. "Only that there is no such place as the land of Tolomeo. That Lago Diablo de Los Muertos doesn't exist. It never has."

"I know about the lake—" Madelaina stopped. She laughed as if she was the brunt of some silly joke. "Paco, for sure you are *muy loco*. I was there with you. Tolomeo saved your life. Look." She removed the chamois bag from around her neck. "Don't tell me you don't remember this?"

"Ayeiii. For sure *I* remember. It was *my* arm nearly off my body. See?" He opened his shirt to reveal his shoulder. "Even today ees no scar. I tell people I nearly lost an arm and they laugh when they see no scar." His eyes gazed off to view a remote scene in his mind. "All except your *marido*—he didn't laugh," he said solemnly. Then, resuming his earlier mood, he said, "All the other people call me *borrachón*, a crazy drunk who dreams up fanciful stories."

"You must have gotten lost," insisted Madelaina. "You must have made an error in judgment in your travels. It's easy to get lost in those intricate lands. We were there, all three of us. *Dios mios,* my life has never been the same. That's it, Paco, the only explanation. You were lost."

"Me get lost? A scout for the army of General Obregon? *Nunca!* Never! But let us suppose you are right. You forget Lola was with me. Lola, a true Indian, *caramba, chica*. Lola can find the trail of a caterpillar."

Madelaina walked away numb from the conversation. That night and for many long days following she felt as if the very life had been snuffed from her. Had she believed in a myth all this time? What exactly was this strong compelling force that had fed her mind ever since her experience with Tolomeo that had changed the course of her life—her destiny?

She was no longer the angry, resentful, and hostile child of her youth filled with an incomprehensible compulsion to compete with men. The change, however gradual it was, had occurred in her and became irrevocable. It had been an indomitable strength which seemed to rise from her toes and surge through her body like a magic potion of power that pulled her up from the doldrums, from out of the dark helplessness of despair which she had found totally unacceptable. How easy it would have been to adopt the malingering ways of a helpless, clinging female caught in a world threatening to leave her emotionally impotent. Already in the time spent at Seven Moons she had steadfastly refused to submit to the overwhelming feeling of disappointment and discouragement she had felt with regard to Peter.

She wasn't about to spend the rest of her life chasing after a pot of gold at the end of a rainbow, only to find it empty. Not Madelaina Obregon Benson. Not Little Fox. No self-pity for her. None of those negative feelings, which could imprison a soul for all eternity, would find shelter in her mind. She had no time to swoon or succumb to the vapors. She'd learned too much in living and in reading. Why, she'd learned so much about the human mind she hadn't known existed outside the realm of her own reality that she could no longer relate to the small world in which she'd once sought refuge. How much more she could do armed with the knowledge that overflowed in her mind?

The first thing Madelaina did when she came to terms with herself was to impose a rigid schedule upon herself. She rode to Amarillo, recruited an architect whom she paid handsomely and swore to secrecy. For hours she sat with him pouring out her plans. She intended to change everything at Seven Moons to conform to her newfound freedom of expression. Everything about her world would undergo a complete rebirth, with little or none of the past around to remind her or anyone else of the past years. The past was gone—dead and buried—and Madelaina wasn't about to resurrect it.

Back at the ranch she worked feverishly from sunup to sundown, as if there weren't enough hours in each day to meet the schedule she imposed upon herself. Late in the evenings she would retire to her room and study and practice her new way of life.

At first Paco and Lola thought her to be possessed with demons again. They watched her with great apprehension until they began to see the shape of things taking place. Soon, an all-knowing appreciation grew in their eyes and their entire demeanor changed. Then both Paco and his wife threw themselves into the work wholeheartedly. Their cooperation so accelerated their own excitement, Paco could be seen watching the workers with the critical eyes of a self-appointed foreman, making sure the work conformed with the plans.

Not once in the following three months of beaver-like activity at Seven Moons did Madelaina hear from Peter. She had no idea of his whereabouts. She had prayed daily for his safety and knew when the time was right, he would appear at Seven Moons. Meanwhile her responsibility was to prepare herself for the encounter. She no longer concerned herself with the revolution, Pancho Villa, or her father. Long ago, when she first understood things as they were, she'd mentally turned these men over to their own destinies, knowing full well that in the final analysis she would have no influence over the destinies of either of them.

And then one day, having completed her renovations at Seven Moons, she was ready for the final episode in her long-range plans. Her son, Alejandro, was nearly three years old. He not only walked, but he spoke many words. He'd been a precious addition to her life, and she kept him at her side daily for as long as she could before he grew sleepy and took his nap. He looked like

983

a Benson. He had Peter's blue eyes, her own raven hair. The winsome smile and alluring charms of his father were incorporated in every gesture and glance.

Seven Moons had undergone a complete tranformation. Now, finally, she was ready to put all her experiences and knowledge on the line for the man she loved.

Peter Benson had left El Paso on the early morning train hoping to be in Amarillo by evening. He'd called ahead and had his Hayes-Apperson waiting for him. For the past several weeks he'd been unable to concentrate on anything, not business, pleasure, nothing. An inner compulsion, one that wouldn't be assuaged by any will power, drew him to Seven Moons. He consciously argued with himself, citing all the reasons for not going, including the stirring of painful emotions for both Madelaina and himself. But he was helpless to counteract this intense magnetic power that compelled him to go to Seven Moons.

He'd already told himself he couldn't live without Madelaina despite the strength of his determination to do so. He had rationalized that it wasn't fair to her to live with a man who couldn't satisfy her sexually. She was the kind of a woman who needed a man to make her whole. Any red-blooded man could tell that by merely looking at her. Since he was no longer equipped to fulfill such a role, the only decent thing he could do was divorce her, let her go. Months ago he'd taken these measures. All the proper papers were complete, requiring only her signature. Yet he hadn't been able to send them to her. He wasn't prepared to release her and make a free woman of her. He glanced at his briefcase, next to him on the train. He'd packed the divorce papers in it earlier. Now he wondered how he'd open the subject. Straight out was the only way.

Peter hadn't known he could love and hate at the same time, nor was he aware that these same conflicting emotions were at the seat of his sexual problems. He hadn't had time to sort out these feelings because he'd seen to it that each spare moment was occupied, leaving him no time to think. The past year had succeeded only in making him more hostile, more of a driven man than he realized. For whatever reasons his brain had devised, he'd ceased being the easy-going, swashbuckling freedom fighter of the past few years. Of late he drank to excess, became cold and calculating in his business ventures, and entered all involvements with a fierce dedication of a man in perpetual motion.

It never occurred to him that he'd been making an unconscious effort to emulate his late father. Since he'd inherited the bulk of the Benson estate and the formidable political power of the Benson name, he was determined to use both against those double-dealing, political hypocrites in Washington.

Damnit ta hell! What in cotton' picking blue blazes was that idiot in the White House thinking of to back Carranza? It had been enough to make Peter lose confidence in his government. A man who permitted his own personal prejudices to override the recommendations of his own advisers was a fool. It sure in hell was a choice President Wilson would live ta regret, thought Peter. He had increased his efforts to send arms and ammunition to General Villa every chance he had. Recently he'd made a deal with a Belgian arms maker for the largest shipment ever to cross the border. As soon as he returned from Seven Moons, plans to smuggle the arms across the border would fall into place.

Things in that department had been going fairly smooth until he found Madelaina in San Antonio in the arms of her childhood sweetheart, Armando Cortez. He wasn't certain why he felt so betrayed or why it should even matter that Armando had been the rogue who deflowered his wife. All these things never mattered in the past—why should they loom important now, he wondered. He felt such a hatred toward Armando, not only regarding his past relationship to his wife, but also because he ironically had been the one to marry Valerie Townsend. It caused him to color his attitude toward Obregon's spy. Through Peter's and Governor Townsend's efforts, Cortez was still held incommunicado on a series of trumped-up charges and had been incarcerated in a remote Juarez prison cell until the governor was good and ready to release him.

He never forgot that day in San Antonio. The fact that Madelaina had seen her father had increased his suspicions of betrayal. After all, back in Vera Cruz she'd left him with such suspicions no matter how much she explained the situation when they were reunited. Even Pancho Villa concurred that blood was thicker than water. Would she have betrayed Pancho Villa? Had she? Damn! Why Peter continued to entertain thoughts of betrayal when he'd never questioned Madelaina's loyality in the past disturbed him and left him filled with disquiet.

On this train ride, he had time to think, a luxury he'd refused to indulge in before. If anything, Madelaina should be furious with him. He hadn't confided his continuous involvement with the *Villistas*. She had believed his assurance that he'd ceased all activities in this vein. Why had he felt the need to deceive her? Why? After all they'd been through together since their tempestuous marriage, why should he suddenly feel the need for deception and subterfuge? In Peter's distorted mind it began to look that between them, he and Madelaina, there was nothing worthwhile left to salvage. Without trust there was nothing. Damnit ta hell! Why ever did she go to San Antonio? It had served only to heighten the breach between them.

He never considered that she'd told him the truth, even though he'd lashed out at her in fury for giving him that convenient story about consulting a specialist over his condition. He wasn't about to listen to such rubbish and closed his mind to it. His insufferable pride and damaged ego led him into a back alley of self-torture, where shame and humiliation superseded all logic and reasoning, turning him into a wild-eyed, frenzied animal. Jealousy possessed him. Violent hatred and burning anger motivated him into shutting out all thoughts of Madelaina's true character. He saw only what he wanted to see regardless of the destruction done to his marriage by such self-inflicted myopia. He anesthetized the pain with indifference.

Peter had managed to keep himself busy these past few months. Immersed in dangerous missions, intriguing with desperados, never knowing if they'd kill you, rob you of your money, and bootleg the arms and ammunition, Peter had in a sense been forced to be alert and on guard. He had had little time to think of Madelaina or their ramshackle marriage.

However, this past month, Peter, in spite of himself, found every waking moment occupied with thoughts of Madelaina, more than he wanted to—when he should have been concentrating on something else. Visions of her sun-kissed face, dazzling smile, and dark, exotic eyes thrust themselves upon his consciousness too often for it to be coincidence. He could feel her soft sensuous body and almost smell the cool, sweet scent of her cologne. It interfered with his work so often that he found himself growing angrier that she should still have such power over him.

He felt certain he had managed to expunge her from his life from that moment in San Antonio when he decided it was the best thing for all concerned. Yet, the recurring thoughts of all those wonderful times they shared in the past, along with the countless times they fought side by side, facing unknown dangers together, possessed him to a point he could no longer voluntarily eject such thoughts from mind. Moved to action, he had to pursue this overwhelming compulsion to see her.

The train was approaching Amarillo when Peter realized most of his own actions had been predicated on the fact that his pride had been terribly injured. That plus the fact that he couldn't possess her as a man should possess a woman had caused him to build a wall of defenses around himself, so he couldn't be hurt any more. Now, as he considered all this, he wondered at the intelligence of his presence at Seven Moons. Why, damnit ta hell, Madelaina hadn't once tried to reach him since the San Antonio escapade. Damn that bitch! She was too damned independent. That's what rankled him and always had, he told himself. With nothing else to take Peter's attention from the situation at hand, he was forced to examine his thoughts more critically, in the manner he once assessed all things. And he came to the conclusion that he himself had contributed to Madelaina's independence. He had only himself to blame for what Madelaina had become. He'd taught her how to be a free thinker, a revolutionist, and hadn't he transformed her into his sex goddess?

Peter detrained in the bustling depot in Amarillo, overrun with cowboys and ranch hands and the overpowering stench of stockyards and dust. Passengers elbowed their way roughly, going and coming in the swarming station. His car was waiting. Tossing in his bags, he dismissed the driver, preferring to drive himself.

It was early twilight when Peter approached the entrance to the place of his birth. Countless old emotions surfaced and a feeling of uneasiness overwhelmed him, constricting his guts more each moment. Peter's growing curiosity at the sights that greeted him instantly neutralized those old feelings as new sensations replaced them. Perplexed, he glanced sharply about the area, wondering if he'd taken the wrong turn off the main road. What in tarnation is that, he asked himself at the sight of the high adobe wall encircling the area of the old ranch house? When he saw the two enormous and brightly lit torches at either side of two gigantic carved oaken doors, he got the distinct feeling he was either plunged forward or backward in time as a visitor in some mysterious land. He forced himself to reread the bronze plaque several times to make certain he was on the right property. *Seven Moons*—that's what the sign read.

What in tarnation had happened, he wondered as he yanked on the pull chain that promptly sounded a melodious series of chimes. The enormous doors opened and Paco Jimenez greeted him warmly.

"Señor Benson, what a pleasure to see you. Please to

988

come in." He took Peter's bags and gestured him ahead with overt politeness.

Peter was totally dazed by the splendor of the lush, tropical gardens that greeted him in the inner atrium. He turned in every direction, pivoting first on one foot, then the other, as he circled his way into the building proper. His open-mouthed amazement was total, his curiosity insatiable. The aviary of magnificently colored birds commanded his attention, and for several moments he paused to stare in fascinated absorption, unable to speak. When he could, he asked, "What happened? Whose idea was this?" As if he didn't know. The question was why? Just as Peter focused his attention on the interior of the house, he came to a sudden and abrupt halt. The adrenaline pumped furiously and his heart stood still. Two sable-colored mountain lions sauntered across his path. Peter remained absolutely still, his eyes alerted to possible danger. Across the room where for years the formidable gun collection of William Benson had occupied an entire wall, there was nothing—nothing for Peter to reach for self-protection.

"What in the name of Jesus is the meanin' of this?" he called cautiously to Paco, indicating the cats.

"It's nothing, *señor el patrón*. They are quite tame—like all the others."

"All the others? Theah's moah?"

"*Si*, ten in all. These two are the friendliest. They are called Tracy and Rosalia." Paco tried to suppress a grin.

Peter smiled despite himself. Once assured of his safety, he entered the enormous room off the atrium. Surprise after surprise exploded before his eyes as Madelaina's triumph, a replica of Dr. Oemolot's desert paradise, blended with some of the magic of Tolomeo's land, came alive before his eyes. He had to admit it wasn't a place he'd ever seen or lived in before, but it was enticing. All those birds! He couldn't be done gazing at the unique beauty all around him.

From the Mexican quarters, Peter heard the soft music of the people played on guitars and muted trumpets. He moved on about the room, noting the obvious painstaking plans that figured prominently in the creation of this spectacular structure.

"Wheah is the *señora?*" he asked Paco when he finally disguised his amazement long enough to speak. Indescribable feelings overwhelmed him.

Paco turned from him to gaze at the top of a cantilevered staircase. Peter's eyes darted in the same direction.

Madelaina stood on the top step, dressed in a simple, flowing, pale yellow caftan, her dark luxurious hair, parted in the center, fell freely to her waist. The only other adornment were the golden seven moon earrings dangling from her lobes. Her dark and vibrant eyes contained the unmistakable look of love.

Peter stared critically at her as an art critic might view a valuable and priceless painting for the first time, assessing every aspect of her. There was something rather special about her, far different than he'd remembered her. What elegant poise and self-containment she demonstrated, he thought, as she descended the steps that seemed to float toward him from out of nowhere.

Paco left the room at a nod from his mistress.

For a brief moment, Peter felt awkward. He couldn' greet her as they'd greeted each other in the past. Too much strife was between them, creating a formidable barrier.

"Hello, Peter," she said in a deeper, huskier voic than in the one she generally spoke. "How good to se you," she said politely.

"What have ya done ta Seven Moons?" were th only words he could find.

"You like it?" she asked pleasantly.

"Theah was nothing wrong with the old place," h said again for something to say.

For an instant Madelaina was prompted to say, " there hadn't been anything wrong with the old plac you might not be in the state you're in." Of course sh said nothing like that. She turned instead to address th old serving woman who had soundlessly entered the room.

"Pilar, please bring Alejandro to see his father." She turned to Peter. "You can see him and enjoy him until dinner." She withdrew from the main room as Pilar brought the child to be reunited with his father.

She paused at the threshold only to say, "Don't feel awkward. He knows you well even if he hasn't seen you much."

Peter turned his attention to the young child and his heart spilled over with love and endearment. "Hello theah, boy," he said gruffly to hide the moistness in his eyes. He knelt down on one knee and opened his arms to the child.

Alejandro paused a moment, then walked timidly toward him. "Are you my father?"

"Ah'm youah fathuh," said Peter, sweeping him into his arms. He held the child tightly and kissed him affectionately.

Outside in the solarium, Madelaina watched the reunion with joy. God give me the strength to fulfill the rest of my plans, she said, tingling with an excitement which threatened to jar her artful poise. She prepared the drinks for them, and as she did, she opened the chamois pouch on a chain at her neck and sprinkled a few specks of the powder into Peter's drink.

When he finished with Alejandro, Peter joined her in the solarium and accepted the drink from her. "Well, what all do we drink ta?" he asked tightly.

"Why not Seven Moons?"

He nodded. "Seven Moons it is," he replied, downing the drink in one gulp. He smacked his lips. "Mmmm good. Whadda ya call it?"

"Tequila, lime, and passion fruit," she said lightly. "The nectar of Seven Moons—just the thing to drink in this atmosphere of serenity. I hope you brought an excellent appetite. Do you wish to wash up before dinner?"

"Ah can remember when there were times we—" Peter stopped. He was about to recall those days on the deserts in Mexico when there was no food, no conveniences to wash—but sweet Jesus they were happy days. Instead he said, "If y'all will point me in the right direction ta find the proper accommodations. Ah'm lost in this—" he faltered at a loss for the proper word.

"Home." She supplied the word. "Right through that archway to your left."

She watched him loosen the collar of his shirt. His face was flushed as the effect of Tolomeo's dried mushroom powder was taking effect. At least she hoped it was.

When he returned, she promptly led him to the dinner table at the far end of the solarium. "Do you mind dining out of doors? It's so balmy. And look! The stars over Texas are bigger and brighter than I've seen in a long time," she remarked, pouring him another drink, as Peter's eyes searched the sky.

"That's a powerful potion ya fix," he told her. "Ah can't remember when ah've felt mah drinks moah," he said amiably, in a somewhat mellower mood than earlier. "As a mattuh of fact, Madelaina, ah'm not even hungry. Ah thought ah was earlier, but somehow mah appetite has disappeared."

She smiled. "We can always eat later," she said, leading him back to the deeply cushioned sofa before the fireplace. She made every effort at being a marvelous hostess. The fragrant scent of her special cologne drifted to his nostrils. She saw him inhale appreciatively and knew she'd stirred a powerful lot of desire in him.

"Now, then, tell me about yourself. What have you been doing in all this time?" she asked lightly, hoping he wouldn't detect the desperation in her voice. God, how she'd missed him. She'd wanted him from the moment she'd laid eyes on him. He seemed thinner, more tense than she'd ever seen him before. As the drink relaxed him, he seemed less knotted up than he'd been earlier. Her hopes soared. She wanted to fall into his arms and end the charade, but couldn't.

"I've missed you," he said quietly.

She glanced at him swiftly. "I've missed you, too," she said finally.

He caught the desire and urgency in her voice that she tried to conceal. Turning from her, he swallowed hard and muttered, "Don't make it anymoah difficult than it is." He reached into his jacket pocket and pulled out a letter. "This came jus' befoah ah left El Paso. It's from Tracy. Ah saved it so we could read it togethuh. That all right with y'all?"

"I thought we had agreed to forget the past," she said quietly.

"It's about the *jefe*'s campaign against youah father—"

Her eyes lit up for a moment. Just as quickly they dimmed.

"Listen, Madelaina, theah's no point in tryin' ta bury the past. It's still too much with us," he said stretching his neck above his collar. "It shuah is pretty warm up heah at Seven Moons."

"Please remove your jacket and tie. You don't have to stand on ceremony in your own home."

"Correction. Youah home. Now, more than ever," he said glancing about.

"Our home," she corrected him. "Our home for as long as you want."

Then she added, "If you want to read the letter, I would like to hear what Tracy has to say."

Peter removed his jacket and tie and sat back down again. He sipped his drink this time, instead of gulping it down as he had the first. He lit two cigarettes and handed her one. Then, his face flushing with color from the effect of the mushroom powder, he propped his feet up on a hassock and stretched contentedly. The change in him was already apparent to her.

It was marvelous to watch his inhibitions melt away as if by magic. Madelaina wished that he wouldn't take too long reading the letter. She had things to do with him, things that would determine their fate. She saw him pat the empty space on the sofa next to him as he used to do. Watching him as a hawk might watch a chicken before she moved in, she finally slipped into the spot he designated with his hand.

Peter opened the letter and began to read: "Mah deah Peter and Little Fox: Hell, it's been a long spell since we visited, ole buddy. Y'all know me. Ah ain't one fer writing. But since it's been a good while an' ah got me this chance ta send a letter off to ya, ah decided ta make up fer lost time. Ah jus' hope this heah lettuh gets ta ya and not inta the wrong hands.

"As ya might've guessed, none of us is as happy as we'd like ta report. But 'sposin' ah begin from the beginning? If we'd of won that first skirmish with Obregon, the whole picture might've been different.

"Y'all know the *jefe* wasn't about ta leave Mexico City to the likes of Carranza, after Obregon marched back inta the capital. As soon as ah left ya, *amigo*, back in El Paso, ah returned to the *Villista*. The *jefe* wired general mobilization orduhs ta all his northern garrisons and, man, ouah power turned southward. Carranza in the meanwhile ordered General Obregon ta vacate Mexico City and proceed to the center of Mexico ta confront General Villa.

"Ah guess the *jefe* approached the battle with Obregon as we Texans might look ta enter inta a personal gun fight. Everything was at stake. And ah suppose that Obregon, now in full command of a Constitutionalist Army equal to the *jefe*'s, grew just as cocky as they come, and decided it was a long overdue showdown between 'em. Obregon was as anxious as Villa to get this confrontation ovuh with. Trouble was, Pete, two of ouah most vital brigades were off on far-flung courses with large portions of the Northern Division at least a full three days' ride from our intended point of impact with Obregon.

"Man, ah tell ya we was all mighty concerned. Even Fierro grew as morbid as they come when Villa kep insistin' ta us he wasn't worried. He felt shuah the other brigades would arrive in the nick of time. They always had in the past, he assured Fierro and the rest of us.

"Well, by now y'all must have heard what happened in Celaya. But jus' ta set the record straight, Peter, ya can believe it when ah tell ya it was the bloodiest god-damned battle ah was evuh in. Wooooooeeeee.

"We finally got word from the Chihuahua Brigade and General Angeles to wait the three days for the delayed arrival. We heard nothing from Urbina's Juarez brigade. Still the *jefe* remained optimistic as hell. Despite his optimism, ah gotta tell ya ah never saw Villa as unreasonable. He wouldn't wait for Angeles. The only thing on his mind was ta meet Obregon, attack, and crush him instantly. That theah is some burning grudge he holds against the father of Little Fox. Well, since it don't do no good ta be cryin' over spilt milk, ah'll try ta be as sparin' as ah can and describe what all happened.

"Ah don't hafta tell ya that Obregon used every fuckin' military strategy he evuh learned against the *jefe*. God almighty, he dug trenches, strung barbed wire backed by machine guns, then placed his artillery behind high ground an' he waited. An' man, Villa fell right inta it. The *jefe*'s tactics, that overpowering blow that had shattered every enemy he ever had jus' didn't work in this instance.

"Ah tell ya, Pete, it was the meetin' of two distinct minds it was. Obregon, cool, calculating, willin' ta wait forever foah victory. Villa, as usual his impulsive, reckless self, willin' ta wager everything on his daring ability ta shock his enemy. These two opposing forces have some malignancy between em, an' we all feel it. Shoot, man, it's touched every last one of us.

"But heah's the shocker. We just got the word that behind Obregon, supportin' his defenses was a man named Von Klause. Bettuh known as Field Marshal Von Klause of the Imperial German Army. That's right. The fuckin' Germans are backing Carranza! Y'all just get that information back ta youah uppity Mr. Wilson in Washington. . . ."

Peter paused pointedly. He sipped the remains of his drink and stared into space. Madelaina, caught up in the letter, grew annoyed. "That's not so," she insisted. "My father wouldn't sell out to the Germans. He may be many things, but his loyalty to the Americans is well known. I heard General Pershing tell him—" Madelaina stopped, realizing how she'd fallen back into her former role.

"Why would Tracy say such a thing?" said Peter matter-of-factly.

Madelaina shrugged. This wasn't working out as she'd planned. Always the revolution! Always something between them! Damn! With fierce control she made light of it until she rolled the name Von Klause over in her memory. Of course! "Von Klause was the name of the German agent who attempted to coerce Pancho into making a pact with the Kaiser," she told Peter. "You remember?" She recalled her father's words clearly when General Pershing asked him if he knew the German Von Klause. Her father denied it. Had he known of President Carranza's double-dealing all the time? She just didn't want to believe it of her father. "Peter, do you think my father is capable of playing both sides against the middle?"

Peter turned to her. "Isn't that a naïve question to ask, when ya realize how many times youah father has switched sides? First, he was a *Porfirista* unduh *Diaz* then he served Madero until Huerta took power. Then he became a *Huertista* until Carranza courted him properly, with added incentives, ah might add. Sugah theah ain't enough paint in the world ta cover th stripes of so many skunks. Ah speculate that if the *jef* had played the proper tune for Obregon, he might have come bouncing down the road dancing to 'La Cu caracha.' "

"What you say is that my father still thinks like Cientifico—a true dyed-in-the-wool militarist?" Sh flushed with embarrassment. "He can only dance to th tune of another man—not his own?"

"That's about the long and the short of it," replied Peter. "Some men are natural born leaders, others a made. While still others will only be followers all the

996

lives. It ain't no real shame and that ain't ta say that he don't have a brilliant military mind. But there's only so far a *Científico* can go if they don't have a creativity to make themselves leaduhs." Peter reached over and pulled her legs closer to him the way they used to sit close in a posture of love.

Madelaina secretly thrilled to the manner in which he was responding, as if there'd been no breach in their relationship, as if none of the bad things had ever happened. Perhaps reading this letter was a stroke of luck. It drew them closer together. She lay her head on Peter's shoulder and he reached up to stroke her face gently.

He sighed with an inner contentment, fully relaxed, without tension, then commenced reading:

"At Celaya, Villa opened the battle with artillery, followed by a cavalry charge supported by more artillery. Obregon's counter battery fell ta Villa's rear while mines, barbed wire, and machine guns tore us apart. Over and again ouah charges went in and again Obregon's well dug-in infantry, artillery, and sputtering guns littered the hillsides with torn bodies, kicking and dying horses.

"If ya could have seen the *jefe* rage, *amigo,* ya would have thought Pancho Villa was no longer human, but a fiercely raging animal. Ah nevuh saw the fire in his eyes burn with such violent hatred. Then, he came through for a time. Just when it began ta look like the whole Northern Division was kaput, he and Fierro appeared on foaming horses, pistols in hand as Villa's voice, echoing in the desert wind, commanded his *Dorados* to charge.

"Pete, ah never saw anything so magnificent in all mah born days. Why, the whole goddamn lot o' em crazy men thundered up the hill, threw themselves at Obregon's forces, staggering the hell outa 'em. Obregon returned shot for shot an' still one entire squadron was shot out from behind 'em. Villa returned for another charge and another. Each time they staggered Obregon's forces with their spectacular and wild charges. Ah tell ya, Obregon's forces were as solid as the Rock of Gibraltar. Even so, he was on the verge of crumbling, when suddenly from out of nowhere he was saved by a fresh column of 2,000 men arriving at the peak of battle.

"God Almighty, man! Ya nevuh saw Pancho Villa in such a tempest. Ah could heah his voice echoing through the desert. 'Wheah's Tomàs Urbina and the fuckin' Juarez Brigade?' Word came that General Angeles had been intercepted by a *Carranzista* column in the north. But nothin' came from that sidewinder, Urbina. An, lemme tell ya, Peter, from that moment on nothing went right foah us. General Villa knew we done lost Celaya, but he wouldn't admit ta the bitterness of defeat—not by Obregon.

"As time went on, Fierro, wounded three times, was out of action. By the end of April Urbina's disappearance was explained. Damned little weasel! Ovuhcome with battle fatigue, he also came down with a case of itchy fingers. He deserted the brigade and took with him a million-peso payroll belonging ta his troops.

"All this weighed heavy on the *jefe*, still he had the goddamned balls ta disengage, reorganize, and make a thunderous comeback ta strike again at Obregon.

"Well, mah good buddy, then came the final meet. Villa and Obregon met again, their lines strung from Celaya to Leon. Villa's cavalry advanced. Obregon fell back. Villa charged once again. Men fell by the hundreds—then, thousands, littering the hills with bloodied bodies and ruined equipment. Ya should have seen that goddamned, sweet sight, Villa's *Dorados.* Man, if the whole Northern Division had been as sharp and as devastating as them *Dorados,* the government army would have been pulverized. They charged, covered by artillery fire, actually broke over barbed wire, past machine gun nests into the trenches, trampling and killing *Carranzistas,* at pistol range. And when Villa's airplanes flew over their trenches, you would have thought Obregon was finished. And for a time he nearly was.

"Then, Pete, came the mind-boggling mix-ups. Ya know that ammo we got from Juarez was the wrong kind? It was 25-35 calibre, useless for our 30-30 Winchesters and Mausers. Someone had sabotaged the shipments is all ah can say.

"Listen, tell Little Fox we just got word that on June 2, General Obregon, while out on personal reconnaissance of his front lines, got caught in an outburst of gun fire, was flung from his horse, and lost an arm in the skirmish."

There was a break in the letter, a passage of time.

Peter paused once more to glance at his wife. Madelaina flinched at the news, lowered her eyes and shook her head. "He's too proud a man to be able to withstand the shame. Not at the loss of an arm," she added. "For being caught off guard enough for it to have happened to him."

"Ah'm sorry," Peter said softly. "But in war anything can happen. Ya oughta know it moah than anyone."

"Yes, I suppose I do. Isn't it a pity words can offer no solace? Please continue, Peter," she said, fixing him another drink.

"Ah gotta say youah are some iron lady, Madelaina. In the past few yeahs, ya've taken a lot. Still ya take it like it all falls off youah shoulder like tiny rain drops."

"*Si,* I'm some iron lady," she muttered to herself, handing him the drink.

He took another sip to wet his lips and continued:

"Obregon was outa commission. In his place came a sharp-thinking general who made a brilliant decision when he quickly untied five army columns in one desperate attack against us. Foah Obregon's forces it was a stroke of luck. Foah us it proved devastatin'. If Obregon had been conscious, his strategy would have been ta wait, by then we'd have had plenty of time ta replace the faulty ammunition.

"As luck had it, it was the worst sight ah evuh saw from the camp of a *Villista*. We were unable ta defend ouahselves. All around us ah saw men throw away theah empty rifles, retreat into the hills, fully scattered befoah the enemy's cavalry and constant artillery barages.

"By nightfall as we climbed aboard the waiting trains in retreat, Lady Luck shifted foah the *jefe*. Ouah guess was that Obregon's sidekick didn't know how much devastation he'd really done—that further resistance was impossible merely for the lack of ammunition. So, in his hesitation to pursue, he waited too long.

"The *Villista* army had had it. Suddenly we all became *guerrillos* again. We made desperate demonstrations ta confuse ouah enemies by firing sporadically, but without ammunition ouah grand and glorious *Division del Norte* was in full retreat, northward. Listen, ah know y'all read of the broad advances made by Obregon when he regained consciousness a week later. During the month of July he made a complete sweep, recapturing many of Villa's garrisons.

"But all wasn't lost. Rudolfo Fierro pulled some mighty brilliant tactical maneuvers. His arm still in a sling, Fierro detached hisself from Villa's main force and swinging around ta Obregon's rear, that devil went ta town. He began by surprising outposts, sending false wires, tangling troops and supplies, destroying rails and communication lines and routes, and razin' Carranza garrisons to the ground. As Villa's main forces retreated into Chihuahua, Fierro's brigade had retaken Celaya, Leon, Queretaro, San Juan, Tula, and Pachuca. He finally rejoined us at the end of July.

"Now ah come ta the point I've been leading ta. Pete, unless we get help from the U.S. as promised to Villa in El Paso, it may all well be ovuh fer us. Ah'm not shuah what ya'll can do aftuh that San Antonic muddle up, but ah'm keeping mah fingers crossed. Yer good buddy, Tracy Richards. P.S. Ah forgot ta tell ya, me and Rosalia got hitched in May. With luck we may see ya one day."

Normally Peter would have discussed the contents of the letter, taking sides and analyzing both positions like a former soldier might in replaying the battle. Not this night. His mind refused to attribute any importance to the letter.

Peter let the letter fall to his lap. He lay his head back against the sofa and closed his eyes. There was so much he wanted to say, but his mind refused to concentrate. Nothing mattered it seemed, nothing except for this moment. So many thoughts about Tracy's letter stirred in his mind, but he could find no words to articulate them. Even more unusual was the fact that he didn't seem to care.

For several long moments they were both silent. Their hearts raced with that excitement of new, unexplored love, that made them both quiver internally.

The sounds of laughter and music wafted in through the open-air solarium, and Madelaina rose to her feet and walked to the edge of the floral boughs where the multi-colored birds in the aviary were cooing and chirping contentedly, soothed by the music. She flung open the screened doors and stepped out onto the flagstone patio under the bright illumination of a tangerine moon against a midnight blue sky of luminous, giant stars, the Texas variety. "Not even the stars of Mexico can compare to these in Texas" admitted Madelaina as he moved in quietly to join her.

"Ah gotta admit they don't grow 'em no place like they do in Texas." His attention was taken at a point past the patio where the Mexicans were celebrating a gala. Paco and Lola stood at the center of the activity, dancing their hearts out.

For a time they both watched the excitement. Peter's arm slipped around her shoulder and she leaned in closer to him, wordlessly.

Keeping time to the rousing music, the spectators clapped their hands in a wilder more pointed staccato. Paco with wild abandon whipped his sombrero from his head and with a flourish tossed it on the ground and began to dance in and around the brim, keeping time to the loud clapping of hands. As the tempo increased and the dancing became more frenetic, Lola, a vision

1001

in bright yellow, her dark hair whipping around her, whirled and swayed her body sensuously, like dancing serpents. Her turquoise eyes, like fire, flared seductively. The tempo rose to such a crescendo, the clapping so fast that the dance ended abruptly when hand and leg movements could no longer be distinguished.

Rousing waves of laughter and applause followed as the small mariachi band played a more romantic, less feverish rendition of a slowed down "La Cucaracha."

"That little girl is still somethin' special," he lit up in appreciation of Lola's performance. "Ah always had a hankerin' foah her, remembuh, Little Fox?"

Madclaina smiled. "I remember. You were highly susceptible to her."

"Seems like old times, doesn't it, sugah?" said Peter softly. He just couldn't reconcile these new feelings surging through him.

"The old times are gone," she said softly. "It's time to make new memories and plan for a future, *querido*."

"Hmmm." Peter mumbled, meaning nothing in particular because he wasn't thinking. He gave vent to all these mild sensations creeping inside him, pleasurable sensations that removed any feeling of disquiet. Something gave him a particular breathlessness; something provoked him into an effervescent-feeling ebullience that excited him more than the dance he'd just seen. He held on to his wife with more possessiveness than he ever felt the need for in the past.

Madelaina moved with feeling, filling the empty air between them. "You haven't kissed me yet, *querido.* Don't you find me desirable any more?"

For an instant Peter hesitated. In the next moment a soft cry of anguish escaped his lips. He gathered her into his arms and kissed her like a love-starved man. They clung together as waves of passion swept through them. He couldn't stop kissing her, and finally, when Madelaina led him inside and up the cantilevered steps to the open-walled bedroom, he followed like a child, his hand in hers.

Peter stood in open-mouthed amazement, letting his
1002

eyes drink in enchanting atmosphere of tropical splendor, like a dazed neophyte from a far-distant land. A large bed on a cantilevered base gave it the appearance of floating in space. Behind it, one wall was a screened-in hollow containing countless plants and fronds and date palms with love birds of every variety cooing and singing in pairs. Along another wall, an oversized portrait of Peter, done in oils from a photograph, hung in a special gold frame over what appeared to be a small altar in mahogany. Several large candles flickered, casting oblique shadows on the portrait. An emperor's chair stood before it.

Nearly everything in the room was done in white with gold accents. The sheets and silk coverlet were white, trimmed in gold. The furniture was gilded—sparingly. The sweet scent of roses permeated the room and Peter's sense memory was stirred to a spine-tingling, feverish excitation.

"That picture," he asked, when he found his voice. "Wheah did ya get it?" It showed Peter naked from the waist up, his thick drooping moustache and sideburns, longer than usual. His curly and tousled hair and sun-bronzed skin captured superbly by the artist was the perfect setting for those incredibly blue, blue eyes that reached across the room at her. It wasn't the sort of picture an artist would choose to paint, let alone hang in an intimate boudoir, unless one was possessed with the love of that man.

"I stole the picture from Lucia San Miguels. Remember when you were in Moreles with Zapata—before we were united in Parral? It was taken by Miguel Guerra when he interviewed you and Tracy."

"I never posed for such a picture—not without my clothes—without my hat," retorted Peter, recollecting the incident with the reporter very well.

"Of course you didn't, silly idiot. I simply paid the artist to undress you to please myself, so I could see you only as I know you," she temporized. "And perhaps the way a few thousand other *chiquitas* like Lucia have known you, eh?"

1003

Peter flushed with pleasure at the compliment until the memory of his recent travail clouded his sparkling azure eyes to a murky gray. "Why the candles?" he asked, gazing at them under the portrait. Were you sending out prayers for me?"

Madelaina smiled enigmatically. "You ask too many questions, *querido*. Come with me." As she led him into the next room, Madelaina said to herself, If you only knew, querido, how many prayers I sent out to you. Every day for the past two months, when he plans had been nearing completion, she had sat on that throne chair, her eyes fixed to the portrait for a period of an hour a day. She had pictured him in her mind as she knew him, sending mental suggestions to him wherever he was. This part of the procedure taught to her by Thàddeus Oemolot was a sort of mental telepathy. She didn't know the principles behind such an occult teaching only that it worked. Peter was proof of it. Her suggestions, once she was in a state of meditation, were to always speak to him as if he were present. She told him this was his home, where he belonged. That his wife loved him, needed him, and wanted him desperately. Together they could build on their love. She transmitted thoughts of love to him. And these daily procedures, which she at first thought to be quite humorous and ridiculous until she clearly recalled the incident of Golden Dawn in her life. How else could Golden Dawn have hexed her, if not through a negative form of telepathy? If it worked negatively—why not in a positive vein? *Bueno*, she had told herself. She would try it. And *Dios mios!* It had worked!

But this was to be Madelaina's secret, one she wouldn't share with Peter.

Madelaina pulled open the two sliding doors that recessed into the wall at either side, and led Peter into a mirror-walled bathroom far surpassing the one she had marveled at on her initial visit to Seven Moons. At the center of the room was a tiled platform leading to a sunken marble Roman bath, decorously set against a backdrop of green plants and exotic flowers. One entire wall contained a cage of monkeys who were chittering noisily as they swung from vine to vine, branch to branch, or engaged in lovemaking.

"What in the cotton pickin' blue blazes prompted ya ta cage up them theah monkeys?" he sputtered, aghast at such a spectacular innovation. "Ah jus' don't believe mah eyes. How in tarnation did ya manage all this? Wheah did ya find the workmen? Wheah did ya get all these birds and animals?" He bombarded her with a thousand and one questions, as his disbelieving eyes drank in all the remarkable changes done to the place he could no longer relate to as he had as a child.

Peter watched his wife open spigots of bull's horns over the tub and temper the water to the correct warmth. She tossed in perfumes and scented crystals and let the water rush into the tub. She still hadn't answered him.

"Tell me, jus' what do ya intend ta do with all these entrapments?" he asked in a husky, but testy voice.

"What a loving wife would do for her loving, long overdue husband when he decides to come home."

He studied her critically, preparing to barrage her with countless questions, but all he could say was, "Ya still love me aftuh the way ah've treated ya and hurt ya?" he agonized, trying to get his bearing in these new surroundings. His eyes were fixed on a few uninhibited monkeys in the cage as they began to copulate.

"Some of these monkeys were here, left over from your father's hobby. I integrated them with new animals and see how happy they are? It's simply amazing what you can learn from monkeys—"

"Madelaina! Y'all ain't gonna give me the same crap mah father handed ta me when ah was growing up?"

"They don't have to clutter up their minds with imaginary thoughts. They function normally, without inhibitions, without words to get themselves muddled up."

Reluctantly Peter shifted his attention back to the caged animals. He watched them in fascination. "Ya nevuh answered mah question," he said quietly.

"Do I still love you? I've never stopped loving you,

1005

querido. From the moment you taught me how to be a woman—*your* woman, I became yours for all eternity. You put your stamp on me—your brand. 'Do not touch,' it said. 'Property of Peter Duprez Benson.' Since then I've been yours. None other's. Only yours, do you understand?"

"I told you to forget me. I was sure you had after all this time."

"Forget you? Your face—name—kiss—and warm embrace? The love that we once knew, knowing for you there'd be no one else? *Querido,* I've remembered only you, your walk, talk, the sweet tender things you used to say. I've remembered even the cruel, honest things you told me to open my eyes to the world around me. Yes, all those harsh, unacceptable, yet steadfast truths which made me aware of myself and my world. Forget you, eh? Your laugh, your twinkling, yet fiery and seductive blue eyes, that turned on an eternal flame in my heart. I would never forget you, *amado mío,* not when all these things live in the son of our loins. In everything about me that is you."

Madelaina never took her eyes from Peter's. He was growing less and less inhibited, watching two monkeys, two particularly virile and frisky animals in the process of copulation.

"Y'all figure ah can learn from these heah little buggers, is that it?" he said amiably. "Well, mebbe ah can. Mebbe ah can."

Madelaina fixed him a drink from a cabinet of wines and other spirits. She handed it to him and poured another for herself. *Bueno,* she thought, he was beginning to relax to the point where she was ready for him.

He hardly resisted her when she began to remove his shirt and trousers, as if it were a normal ritual between them. When he stood nude before her, she helped him into the tub. He stepped into it and sat down, luxuriating in the relaxing warmth, his mind a complete blank. Only the process of feeling was important to him.

"Relax, my husband. Relax," she cooed softly. "Close your eyes and lay back and let yourself feel the comfort of the water against your skin. That's better, *querido, mi amore*. Listen and I'll whisper to you the secrets of Tolomeo."

His eyes fluttered open encumbered by invisible weights. "Tolomeo? Who is Tolomeo?"

"A man of great wisdom," she said, leaning over him. She kissed his lips lightly with her hot and moist eager mouth and then began to speak with a rhythmic pacing to her voice. "You remember Parral, Peter, when I couldn't respond to your passionate embraces?"

"Ummmhum," he muttered as the tenseness left his firm and muscular body, and relaxed him into a euphoria of pleasantness and tranquility.

"I put into your drink a calmative powder like the one the doctor in Parral administered to me. No, don't be alarmed. Trust me, beloved. Trust the woman who loves you more than life itself." She rubbed his forehead, the back of his neck and upper shoulders soothingly until he purred like a kitten. Her voice droned on in lulling, hypnotic effect. "You've become a victim of a false reality, Peter. Something you've painted in your own mind through your fears. With your help, we will unlock your mind, permit the untruth to take flight and leave you in peace. Only then will you realize you've been a slave to figments of your distorted imagination.

"We will implant new pictures in your mind, as you were when you were whole, more complete. There is nothing you can't do that you haven't always done except for this period of stagnation when you allowed a false picture in your mind to direct you." Madelaina's eyes watched him—his every reaction critically. His eyes had grown so heavy he could no longer keep them open. His arms hung limply at his sides in the water, his head sagged slightly, his muscles relaxed without tension.

With instant recall, Madelaina continued her ritual as it had been prescribed by Dr. Oemolot and from papers she'd read on the subject of suggestion and hypnosis. What she hoped to do was transfer her thoughts to his mind. What she had going for her, most important of all, was the strength of her love and a profound faith in what she was doing. It had to suffice.

"Soon you'll see the truth implanted in your mind. You'll only remember the truth—not the distorted counterfeit of truth. You will be whole again, Peter, and feel the power of my love—our love—the most vital bond between man and woman."

Pictures began to form in Peter's mind. He saw himself standing at the top of a mountain with arms upflung like a god, making a sacrifice to the heavens. He stood in this powerful pose, nude under the power of a full erection. The picture dissolved and he saw Madelaina as he first met her in Sanlucar de Barramedas. This picture dissolved into one of their countless intimacies aboard the *Mozambique*. As one picture dissolved, another instantly appeared in a montage of vignettes. Every picture, each scene was crystal clear to him, depicting all the sweet, tender, and savage love they'd shared. Some showed the anguish of their pain-filled separations, others, their joy-filled reunions.

All the time she guided him through their hectic and adventurous life, Madelaina made verbal suggestions bringing into focus in his mind only those positive suggestions that embellished his virility. Finally, her repetitious words and pictures had saturated Peter's consciousness to the point she felt was enough for this first session.

Her strong arms slipped around his waist. She helped him to his feet and wrapped a huge terry towel around him to dry him off. In this semi-dreamy state she led him to the waiting bed. He was like putty in her hands, not a shred of resistance thwarted her in her preparations, not a protest escaped his lips.

Once he was on the bed, Madelaina removed her caftan, and standing nude over him, she removed the chamois pouch from her neck and turned it inside out using every minute particle of the mushroom powder that was left, she allowed it to fall in the area of Peter' genitals.

Slowly she began to massage the powder into th

area of his groin and about his penis as she chanted in a whispering monotone, "Oh, Tolomeo, pray it's enough to make the magic work." She pressed the area of his solar plexus firmly in a circular motion. "Give him the strength he needs," she continued to chant.

"Focus your attention on nothing except my voice. Clear the pictures in your mind, Peter. Think of nothing. Erase every untrue and false picture in your subconscious mind. Only the truth shall set you free. The truth of my love for you—yours for me. You shall no longer be tricked by vain imaginings into believing falsehoods, even if you attempt to plant such seeds they will be uprooted. I come to you as a pure vestal virgin, my love. Only your love will blow the breath of life into me. There has never been anyone before you, nor shall there be anyone after."

Madelaina paused as she began to feel movement in his loins. Before her very eyes his manhood was throbbing, swelling, trying to come to life. Madelaina traced her fingers lightly over the thick scars of his stomach.

"Unleash the strength girded in his loins," she prayed, tears misting her eyes, and grateful for the miracle.

Peter's eyes snapped open as the most exciting feeling of his life was upon him. He could feel life creeping slowly through his body like a powerful unchained force of manhood growing—growing—swelling into a monolith. Too excited to move, all he wanted to do was feel—feel—feel. Desire mounted inside him to such an electrifying crescendo that Peter found himself at a loss as to what to do first. His hands moved to touch her with incredible disbelief in his eyes, to feel her and explore all those familiar places he'd staked his claim on long ago.

And Madelaina's dark, swimming eyes darted quickly to his face.

"Madelaina, Madelaina," he whispered hoarsely. "Is it for real?" He was afraid to look for fear it was all an illusion.

"It's always been for real. You've been blinded for a time, but now you've been gifted with sight."

He moaned softly and drew her close to him and clung tightly to her. Her arms wound about his strong neck and the sweet, burning pressure of his lips on hers fused them together, blotting out everything except for this moment, suspended in all eternity.

"You've returned to me, my love."

"I've never been away," she told him in truth.

In the next few moments, it took superhuman effort for Madelaina, the talented pupil of Thaddeus Oemolot, to do what she had to do. She slipped out of Peter's arms, turned up the lights, and yawned sleepliy. Peter, more in a daze of total confusion than he'd ever been, sat up and blinked his blue eyes hard several times.

"Wheah are ya going, *querida?*"

"Where else after such a fulfilling display of love, *querido?*" She drifted behind bathroom doors and closed them. She could hear his protestations, his quandary. She stood shaking from the exertion, from the force it took to subdue the desire in her own body. She gulped down a glass of water and quickly looked about for a cigarette. Finding one, she lit it and puffed eagerly until she calmed down a bit.

Madelaina panicked when she thought she had six more such sessions to endure before she would let Peter satisfy himself. Dr. Oemolot had warned her. It's possible that he'll get an erection and become so excited at the prospect of performing that he'll summon up the old fears and grow impotent again.

Dios mios! What of Madelaina? How could she endure the overexcitation of nonperforming, she asked herself, gulping more water to off-set the terrible thirst and scratchy dryness in her parched throat.

Madelaina endured. She managed to make Peter believe he had performed when he hadn't, just to bolster his damaged ego. And on the seventh night, Madelaina, after leading Peter back over the same rocky course, to which he responded without the use of mushrooms, marijuana, peyote, or the other hallucinogens she'd used to prepare Peter for the ordeal they'd both face, was ready for the final test.

Prior to this seventh night, Madelaina had taken the initiative, firmly telling Peter to lie back and feel the sensations. On this night, after a week of growing trust, love, and compassion, she was ready to be a woman. And Peter, unaware that he hadn't already been a man many times over, displayed some of his old control and libertine air. He was more like the soldier of fortune she'd met in Europe than at any other time they shared together. It was a good sign.

After a wonderful day spent together, they dined and had a few drinks and listened to a hand-cranked victrola play some unusual records of an opera sung by a star of the Metropolitan, Enrico Caruso.

All this was merely the prelude, and Madelaina began to feel an electrifying excitement as the expectations of what was to come inflamed her senses.

Peter took her hand at some time during that evening. She didn't remember when and didn't care. All that mattered was the overflowing pot at the end of the rainbow. They bathed together and frolicked like children. It was simply marvelous to see Peter, filled with confidence again, without one single doubt in his mind.

Lord, sweet Lord, she prayed. *Let him be whole tonight and forever.*

Only the glow of two large candles flickered in the Roman bath, their reflection multiplied to hundreds as they bounced off the mirrors on four sides and the ceiling. Madelaina was warm, her damp skin glowed in the candlelight. It was quiet, as if all the sound had been turned off. Moisture clung to the green leaves of the plants like a thousand dewdrops, swelling and glistening like diamond gems in the glimmering lights.

Peter lay next to Madelaina on the thick white bear rug next to the marbled tub on the floor. Their hot feverish bodies clung together cohesively as if they could never be pried apart. Peter kissed her lightly, at first, barely touching her lips, which felt like the fluttering touch of a hummingbird's wings. His

1011

strong hands traced lightly the contours of her body.

Madelaina ached for him as she'd never ached for him before. His lips nuzzled her neck in such a feathery touch she hardly felt him, but the shiver of excitement he sent through her body was sheer heaven. It was the anticipation of his touch that made her frenzied and feverish.

So much time had passed that she had almost forgotten just how his passion could arouse her. Madelaina's firm round breasts, no longer virginal, had matured and rounded gracefully and now as they grew unbearably swollen and tender to his touch, she felt as if they'd burst wide open. Every nerve in her body came alive and she felt her stomach doing somersaults. She felt as if she were tied on a whirling zephyr to the moon and couldn't stop. Her hands went out instinctively, reaching for him, but Peter placed them firmly at her side.

"It's gonna be like the first time we were together *querida*. Remain passive so the sensation will heighten ya heah?"

Madelaina nodded. If she wanted to speak, she couldn't have, her mouth was parched—her throat was without moisture. His seduction and lovemaking had surpassed anything she'd ever experienced. What was happening between them was incredible. His velvety touch between her legs as he traced the fire that surged through her caused involuntary shudders to course through her. She made little animal noises deep in her throat. He spoke honeyed words to her.

"Ah'll nevuh let youah dark brown eyes turn blue evuh again, mah sweet, sweet love," he purred. "The honey from youah treasure pot is dripping sweet, mah love. Ah've waited a long, long time ta taste its sweet nectars." He took one of her cool slender hands and placed it on his tumescence. "Ah've nevuh been so big in all mah born days, *chiquita*. Ah promise ta be gentle to mah little virgin. Trust me, mah darlin'."

"Yes, yes, I trust you, *amado mio*," she managed to whisper through parched and feverish lips. She felt Pe-

1012

ter's hands under her, lifting her. Madelaina raised her body to meet his.

"Not yet, mah love. Not yet," he said.

She felt her passion rising, wanting him as she'd never wanted him before. With an increased surge of madness, she wanted to possess every inch of him and never be done with him. She was ready to burst. It was agony. It was ecstasy. It was delirium as she'd never known it. Feeling, without touching, was a sensation she'd never imagined to be possible, but she was wrong. It served to heighten each of the senses separately.

An involuntary gasp shuddered through her. She opened her eyes and stared at their reflection in the overhead mirror, then at either side of them. As the mirrors converged at one point, she could see the reflections of countless Peters and Madelainas and it heightened everything between them.

"Ya little vixen," he whispered hoarsely. "Ah know what yourah tryin' ta do ta me. Youah've turned Seven Moons into a miniature Madama Tarragona's bordello," he purred with a smile in his voice.

He entered his wife slowly as if he were creating a special artwork, like an artist painting a canvas. Every stroke, every movement nearing perfection. He penetrated her deeper and deeper, making no sharp, hard thrusts. Only slow and sensuous movements, deliberate and perfectly controlled, orchestrated her to his will. They both soared higher and higher and just before that moment of climax, Peter took her moist face between his two hands.

"Look into mah eyes, Madelaina. Right inta mah soul. Ah'm about ta pour mah life and love inta ya foah all time." His fiery blue eyes burned into her mind, body, and soul, and Madelaina screamed like a wild animal. From the very balls of her feet to the top of her head, she felt a series of explosions, one after another. Her body convulsed wildly. She could hold back no longer.

"Look inta my eyes, mah sweet *chiquita*. Love me.

1013

Feel me. Open youah succulent lips ta receive me." He leaned in closer to her, lips over hers, eyes staring into hers until they both went soaring into infinity.

Hours later, as dawn broke over eastern skies, Madelaina's eyes opened. At some time during the night they had both moved to the bed. Now, as she lay back in full contentment with the weight of his body still pressing on her as he lay half-asleep, her hands stroked his body lightly just to get used to having him near her. Her thoughts ran rampant as she focused on those who'd made all this possible.

Thadeus Oemolot, you are a genius, I thank you. Thank you, Sigmund Freud. Thank you, Tolomeo, for all you taught me. I am the luckiest woman in the world to have been singled out for such worthwhile teachings. A shudder passed through her, so involuntary she couldn't control it. The movement awakened Peter.

He lifted himself on one elbow, blinked open his eyes, and straddled her body with one of his lean, powerful legs wrapped around her. His free hand traced the firm, erect nipples on her breasts and traveled upward to her lips and ears, where he paused to toy with her glittering golden earrings.

"Oh Madelaina, mah Madelaina of the Seven Moons, ah love ya so much. My life, mah love, mah heart an' soul," he said in his heavily accented and atrocious Spanish. "Ah'll nevuh leave ya again, heah? We'll nevuh leave each other—nevuh!"

"What about Pancho Villa? What if he sends for you?' she asked guilefully.

"Ah won't go," he said adamantly, then he gazed at her through tilted blue eyes the color of a clear morning. "Besides theah are other ways ta fight than on a battlefield."

"Peter?"

"Yes, *querida*."

"What exactly are you scheming now?"

"Me? Why not a thing, *querida*."

Madelaina sat up in bed, turned on the night light, and looked deeply into his merry, telltale eyes.

"Well, Little Fox, ya caught me redhanded. Ah was

1014

lying ta ya. Ah was scheming something. Truly, ah was. Ah can't lie ta ya."

Madelaina lay back, dismayed.

"What ah was scheming is that we both do something ta increase ouah family. Are we both in accord?"

"Perfectly." She sighed contentedly. Off went the light and she reached for him.

"Mah Little Fox," he purred as he felt her hands teasing his manhood.

"Yes, *querido*," she sighed, ecstatically happy.

"Would ya mind or object strenuously if we raise ouah family inside the governor's mansion in El Paso? Or perhaps in Washington, if I became a senator?"

"Governor's mansion? What are you saying?" She sat up in bed again and turned on the light. She stared at him, her hands on her waist, contemplatively.

"Only that ah've tossed mah hat inta the political ring. Ah'm running foah office in the next election," he said sheepishly. "Ah just can't make up mah mind as ta which ah should do, first."

"Oh, Peter," she sighed despondently. "Whatever for?"

"Someone has ta watch ovuh the *jefe,* wouldn't ya say?" he said softly. "Aftuh all, we owe him something. If it wasn't foah him we might never have seen each other again." He reached up behind him, turned off the lights, and embraced her in a tight passionate grip that fairly took her breath away. His lips crushed hers hungrily.

"Make the world go away, my love," she whispered. "Make it go away, *mi amor*."

"Ah will. Ah will, mah Little Fox," he replied hoarsely.

As he spoke those words, Madelaina knew their future was inextricably bound up in the strange destinies of Pancho Villa and Alvaro Obregon.

She had demanded perfection. It had fallen a little short. But she couldn't have been happier. As long as she and Peter could share the future together—she had everything she ever wanted.

Well, nearly everything. But there was still time—for everything.

1015

Epilogue

Chapter 38

Eight Years Later July 23, 1923

Just as Madelaina had promised, Dr. Thaddeus Oemolot received the ten-thousand-dollar grant. He had long
since begun the dream of his lifetime. Now it was his
turn to reciprocate.

On this day, he and several colleagues, well-known
specialists in the field of psychiatric research, stood in
the reception line at the dedication of *Clinica Siete
Lunas*. Next to this imposing consortium were a half-
dozen state dignitaries, the governor of Texas, congress-
men, and senators.

Senator Peter Benson had never been so magnificent—so eloquent and a sheer delight to the attending press. Reporters had come from all over the state
and Washington to interview him and his wife. It was a
well-known fact that Mrs. Benson had no taste for politics and was quite retiring, despite rumors that she'd
descended from a long line of conquerors dating from
the time of Queen Isabella of Spain. Curious rumors
circulated about this unique woman, most prevalent
being she had been a *soldadera* in the Mexican Revolution!

Studying her, standing so regal and dignified next to
her husband, the reporters knew these rumors to be
unfounded and cruel. Why, the very idea that such a
genteel and refined woman would demean herself to
trudge in the filth and squalor and live among those
desert desperados was idiotic. On this day, her day, a
the dedication ceremonies of so special a project as a
research center for the cure of children's mental dis

eases, those rumors were about to be ground to a halt.

You never saw a prouder man than Senator Benson as he stood next to his wife, before the imposing complex built on the spectacular site of seven cresent-shaped lakes in the middle of God's country in Amarillo. The senator, a man who had helped solidify relations with Mexico, had become one of the most dominant figures in present day politics. Why, the man could become governor—even president—if he wanted.

Word was he'd tossed his hat in the political ring for the governor's cap a few years back, but he had changed his mind. No one really knew why, but like those other vicious rumors that infiltrated certain pressure groups from time to time, they threatened to expose some dark sinister secrets concerning Mrs. Benson again. Why, you'd think they leave the poor little woman alone.

Look at the humanity in her. The love she contained in her bosom to even donate such a handsome piece of property to mankind. Half the cost of the building and equipment had been funded by her personal wealth, the other half had been raised through various social functions and charity balls, all of which were spearheaded by Mrs. Peter Benson.

After the dedication ceremony, the reporters and guests were taken on a private tour of the buildings at the *Clinica Siete Lunas*. If they were impressed at the outset, they were elated when many notable of the medical consortium spoke their personal views and praises of Mrs. Benson's dedication to the somewhat intimidating field of psychiatry. No one seemed to know why she was this devoted.

The ceremonies had ended, the ribbons were cut, the power was turned on, and the dream of a lifetime for many dedicated people was about to begin. Reporters were departing, their copy still hot in their hands, with a rash of photo negatives to be developed for press time.

Driving toward the cluster of people, Paco Jimenez gunned the motor of the open touring car, waving his arms wildly, causing the car to career back and forth off the road. Riding at his side, hanging on for dear life was the alluring mestiza, Lola, heavy with child for the fifth time. Once Paco stopped that crazy machine, he jumped from the driver's seat calling, "*Senador!* Señora Benson!"

He removed his western hat and swiped at the dust on his pants.

"Telegram, *Senador*." He handed Peter Benson the wire and wiped the perspiration from his somber face. His eyes avoided direct contact with both Peter and Madelaina, and he stared at the tips of his dusty boots.

Peter opened the envelope and stared at the contents for several moments. He handed it to his wife and stared off at the last of the crowd departing in their vehicles. Madelaina searched her husband's face for a telltale sign. Her eyes dropped to the printed paper and she read: *At eight o'clock on this day, Francesco Pancho Villa was brutally assassinated in a political plot by known parties. The Centaur is dead.*—*Lucita Arango*

Madelaina glanced at the somber face of her handsome husband. She folded the wire and tucked it into her handbag. Peter took her hand in his, placed it over his arm, and escorted her to the awaiting auto. "It's hard to imagine General Villa no longer with us. After three years of peace in which the *jefe* ended his role as protector of Mexico, he deserved better than assassination," he said.

"Yes, he deserved much better," she replied wistfully. She turned to him, pausing as she did. "Why, Peter? Why wouldn't they leave him alone? Are there still some who considered him a threat to Mexico?"

Peter slipped a hand inside his coat pocket and handed her another wire. "Ah didn't show this ta y earlier because ah wanted this day ta be youah triumph with *Clinica Siete Lunas*. Since you asked the question ah'll let ya be the judge, mah deah."

Madelaina hurriedly opened the second. Her eye fell to the printed words: *In a revolt against the Carranz*

1018

egime, United States fully supports the Obregon re-
ime. Alvaro Obregon is now president of Mexico.

Madalaina gasped. Their eyes met in knowing
ilence. They walked the few steps to their car and got
n the rear seat, their driver waited until Pilar and their
hree sons, Alejandro, William, and Peter Jr, got into
he next car with Paco and Lola Jimenez before start-
ng the motor. He wheeled the auto around in a full
ircle and drove off toward Seven Moons.

"How long will it be before Obregon is felled by an
ssassin's bullet?" she asked her husband softly, tearing
p the wire. She scattered the bits to the four winds.

"That, mah deah Little Fox, is a question only time
vill answer."

A SELECTED LIST OF CORGI BOOKS
FOR YOUR READING PLEASURE

WHILE EVERY EFFORT IS MADE TO KEEP PRICES LOW, IT IS SOMETIM
NECESSARY TO INCREASE PRICES AT SHORT NOTICE. CORGI BOO
RESERVE THE RIGHT TO SHOW AND CHARGE NEW RETAIL PRICES
COVERS WHICH MAY DIFFER FROM THOSE ADVERTISED IN THE TE
OR ELSEWHERE.

THE PRICES SHOWN BELOW WERE CORRECT AT THE TIME OF GOING
PRESS (APRIL 78)

☐ 09305 X	NOR THE MOON BY NIGHT	*Joy Packer*	
☐ 10442 6	VALLEY OF THE VINES	*Joy Packer*	
☐ 10375 6	CSARDAS	*Diane Pearson*	£1
☐ 10414 0	SARAH WHITMAN	*Diane Pearson*	
☐ 10271 7	THE MARIGOLD FIELD	*Diane Pearson*	
☐ 08849 8	THE GLASS VIRGIN	*Catherine Cookson*	
☐ 08251 1	KATE HANNIGAN	*Catherine Cookson*	
☐ 10321 7	MISS MARTHA MARY CRAWFORD	*Catherine Marchant*	
☐ 09796 9	HOUSE OF MEN	*Catherine Marchant*	
☐ 10074 9	THE FEN TIGER	*Catherine Marchant*	
☐ 10445 0	A KIND OF LOVING	*Stan Barstow*	
☐ 09475 7	A RAGING CALM	*Stan Barstow*	
☐ 10098 6	RED ROSES DYING	*Nan Maynard*	
☐ 09889 2	WALK INTO MY PARLOUR	*Norah Lofts*	
☐ 10347 0	BELINDA	*Mary Loos*	
☐ 10029 3	ONCE IS NOT ENOUGH	*Jacqueline Susann*	
☐ 08523 5	THE LOVE MACHINE	*Jacqueline Susann*	
☐ 07807 7	VALLEY OF THE DOLLS	*Jacqueline Susann*	

All these books are available at your bookshop or newsagent, or can be ordered direct
the publisher. Just tick the titles you want and fill in the form below.

CORGI BOOKS, Cash Sales Department, P.O. Box 11, Falmouth, Cornwall.

Please send cheque or postal order, no currency.

U.K. send 22p for first book plus 10p per copy for each additional book ordered
maximum charge of 82p to cover the cost of postage and packing.

B.F.P.O. and Eire allow 22p for first book plus 10p per copy for the next 6 books, t
after 4p per book.

Overseas Customers. Please allow 30p for the first book and 10p per copy for
additional book.

NAME (block letters)...

ADDRESS ....

(APRIL 78)..